Fiona McIntosh was born and raised in Sussex in the UK, but spent her early childhood commuting with her family between England and Ghana in West Africa where her father worked. She left a PR career in London to travel and found herself in Australia where she fell in love with the country, its people and one person in particular. She has since roamed the world working for her own travel publishing company, which she runs with her husband. Fiona lives with her young family in South Australia.

Read about Fiona or chat to her on the bulletin board via her web-site: www.fionamcintosh.com

Find out more about Fiona McIntosh and other Orbit authors by registering for the free monthly newsletter at www.orbitbooks.co.uk

By Fiona McIntosh

The Quickening Trilogy
Myrren's Gift
Blood and Memory
Bridge of Souls

BRIDGE OF SOULS

THE QUICKENING BOOK THREE

FIONA McINTOSH

www.orbitbooks.co.uk

ORBIT

First published in Great Britain in December 2005 by Orbit

Copyright © Fiona McIntosh 2004

The moral right of the author has been asserted.

A CIP catalogue record for this book
is available from the British Library.

ISBN 1 84149 375 9

Typeset in Garamond by
Palimpsest Book Production Limited, Polmont, Stirlingshire

Printed and bound in Great Britain by
Mackays of Chatham plc, Chatham, Kent

Orbit
An imprint of
Time Warner Book Group UK
Brettenham House
Lancaster Place
London WC2E 7EN

www.orbitbooks.co.uk

GH . . .
this one's for you.

Fx

Acknowledgments

It's a special feeling to bring a huge story to an end. A lot of people have travelled this long and traumatic journey with Wyl Thirsk and thank you to all the readers who've been so faithful to his cause. Here's hoping this final book brings satisfaction — I have truly enjoyed hearing your thoughts and ideas, your hopes and despair for the characters. Enjoy closure!

And each time I set out to thank people for their support I realise there are new names who must be added to the list. On this occasion let me offer my sincere gratitude to Gary Havelberg, Sonya Caddy, Pip Klimentou and newcomer, Judy Downs, for their draft reading efforts, research and enthusiasm for the tale. Thanks to the gang at the Heartwood Bulletin Board who offer ongoing support and welcome all newcomers warmly, especially our international readers.

Robin Hobb . . . quietly in the background, always full of encouragement, ever inspirational through her own work. Thank you for being so supportive and for choosing this story to accompany you on your signings around the world.

Thanks to all the booksellers in Britain for their enthusiasm for The Quickening and to my agent, Chris Lotts in New York and especially to the gang at Orbit for liking the story and giving it a chance to be read in the UK. As I'm orginally a Brighton gal it means so much to be published back home.

Special thanks to my Orbit editor, Darren Nash, for seeing the tale's potential when he read the books on the train, baffling fellow commuters with his sudden gasps as certain grisly events unfolded. I gather the Ylena moment in book 2 created the loudest exclamation.

Family and friends, my gratitude for the constant support – you are never taken for granted. And finally love and endless thanks to my patient husband Ian and our sons Will and Jack who make it so easy for me to have fun in worlds beyond our own, but always lure me back.

Fx

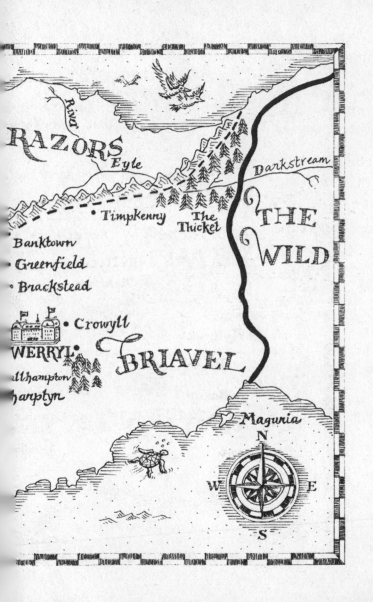

PROLOGUE

It felt like an eternity to Fynch.

There was brightness; unbearably sharp, and combined with a hammering pain. He squeezed his lids tightly shut but the dazzling gold light hurt his eyes all the same as he helplessly relinquished control of his small body to the vast agony exploding through it. He believed himself to be flopping around like a fish caught on a hook, but that was purely his imagination. In truth he was rigidly still; his teeth bared in a grimace as the force of magic gifted from Elysius radiated painfully into him.

At one point he thought he glimpsed the sorcerer passing through him to his death, like a distant memory he could not quite bring into focus. Elysius appeared whole again and he was smiling. The sense of him offering thanks was vaguely present but Fynch was unable to lock onto it as the pain claimed all of his attention.

The sickening throb of power began to pulse through his body in time with his escalating heartbeat; each push harder, each more breathless in its intensity until he lost all sense of himself. He no longer knew his name or where he lay. He was a flimsy craft being tossed about on a stormy sea of sensation, unable to navigate or steer. Fynch simply had to let go into the excruciating pain and ride the ocean of distress until, finally, he glimpsed its end. How long his journey had lasted he could not tell; could not even guess. The agony ebbed gradually but steadily, until he realised he was bearing it. He had survived. His pulse was fast but his heart no longer felt as though it might explode through his chest. The blinding light had dimmed to flashes of gold, as if he had been staring at the sun too long, and his breath was no longer panicked and shallow but came in deep, rhythmic draughts.

His wits returned. Fynch remembered who he was and what he was doing here.

Trembling from a chill which now gripped him, Fynch opened his eyes to slits. He registered a new layer of pain and closed them again; this time it was a headache which prompted instant nausea. He felt like crying. But where other youngsters might have the comfort of a mother's voice nearby and her love to cling to, there was no such consolation for Fynch. He had no family — nor even friends any longer. Wyl had gone. He hated the way they had parted. He knew Wyl had wanted him to leave the Wild immediately and had watched his friend battle his inclination to say as much. Poor Wyl had been forced to inhabit his sister's body, and Ylena's face was too expressive to mask what her brother was thinking. And yet Wyl had said nothing; had permitted Fynch to make his own decision, which was to remain a little longer. Fynch felt a profound sadness for his friend who had suffered so much loss already and would suffer more yet, he sensed. He wished he knew of a way to spare Wyl more pain, or at least to share some of it with him.

He sighed. The nausea had passed. His eyes were still closed and the pain had dimmed considerably he realised. But the loneliness remained. There would not even be Elysius to offer solace. No. The boy suspected he was alone in the Wild, save for the strange four-legged beast he considered his companion.

Full consciousness sifted through his shattered nerves and Fynch became aware of a pressing warmth at his side. The source moved, having sensed he was alert again. A low growl confirmed it was the dog.

'Knave?' Fynch croaked through a parched throat.

Never far, a voice replied in his head. It made him flinch.

The boy turned towards the great black dog. 'Did you speak to me?' he said, tears welling. 'Can I finally hear you?'

Depthless eyes regarded him and he heard Knave's reply in his mind. *I did. You can.*

So there was a friendly voice – one he had never thought to hear. Fynch managed to command his reluctant arms to obey him. Slowly, painfully, he wrapped them around the big animal's neck and wept deeply and without shame.

Elysius? Fynch asked after a long time, testing his newly acquired power. It was a startling sensation.

The dog's response was instant. *Dead. It was quick. And he was glad to go.*

Where is his body?

Everywhere. He became dust. The massive transfer of his power to you disintegrated his physical being and then dispersed him.

Did he say anything before . . . before he passed on?

*That you are the bravest of souls. He agonised that he might
be wrong to force this burden upon you*, the dog admitted. *He
regretted the pain you would experience and the journey ahead,
but he believes there is no one else who can walk this path but
you.* The dog leaned closer and spoke very gently. *In this
I know he is right.*

Fynch pulled away from his friend, eyes still wet. There
was so much yet to learn. *Knave, I don't know how to use
this power. I have no—*

Hush, the dog soothed. *That is why I am here.*

The boy took the beast's huge head between his tiny
hands. *Who are you?*

I am your guide. You must trust me.

I do.

The dog said no more but Fynch sensed that it was
glad. Perhaps there was even relief there, he thought.

But there is something I must know, he went on, his tone
almost begging.

Ask it. Knave's voice was so deep that Fynch suspected
that if the dog could speak aloud he would feel the sound
rumble through his own tiny chest.

Who is your true master? Where do you belong?

If a dog could smile, Fynch felt convinced Knave was
doing so now. *I have no master as such. But I do belong.*

Where? Please tell me.

I am of the Thicket.

Ah. Fynch's tensed muscles relaxed as understanding
flooded through him. The neatness of the dog's answer
pleased him. *Are there others like you?*

*I am unique. But there are other enchantments within the
Thicket*, Knave answered somewhat cryptically.

So Elysius didn't send you to Myrren?

Elysius did not know me until we both came here, although he knew of me. And Myrren was not the person I sought.

This was a revelation. Fynch pressed his hands against his eyes in an attempt to ease their soreness and to clear his swirling thoughts. *Then why didn't you just search out Wyl?*

Because Wyl is not the one I sought either.

Fynch looked up sharply. *Who then? Who must we now search for?*

The search is over. It was always you, Fynch.

What? The dog's unerring gaze told Fynch it would never lie. *But why?*

You are the Progeny and I am the guide.

I thought I was the Wielder, Fynch wondered, confused.

That, and so much more, Knave said reverently. *You are many things and it is you we seek.*

The Thicket sent you to find me?

Yes, but it did not know who would be the next Gate Wielder.

But it must have known Elysius was dying in order to send you in search of his replacement?

Yes.

So your role has never been about Wyl or Myrren . . . or protecting Valentyna? Fynch sent wonderingly.

Knave's response was measured. *My task is to protect you. When the magic of the Quickening entered Wyl, the Thicket believed he was the next Wielder. Elysius wondered the same.*

Are you saying that it was pure coincidence you came into Myrren's life? Fynch asked, desperately trying to piece the puzzle together.

Not exactly. She was Elysius's daughter. Magic was part of her even though it was not strong in her. It was she whom the Thicket decided to keep watch over, and it chose correctly. When

Myrren made such a strong connection with Wyl, we thought he might be the one. It was only when I met you that I realised it was you we searched for.

But how can you tell?

There is an aura about you, Fynch. Unmistakable, and invisible to all but those of the Thicket.

Fynch sighed as if he had suspected as much. *So I was born with this aura?*

Yes. Your destiny was set.

Elysius never mentioned it.

Elysius didn't know. The Thicket told him who you are.

It talks!

Communicates, the dog corrected.

Fynch held his head and groaned. These revelations were causing fresh gusts of pain through his already aching mind. *It hurts, Knave. Will it always be so?*

You must control the pain. Don't allow yourself to become its slave. Master it, Fynch.

Is this how it will kill me?

The dog held a difficult silence between them.

I would know the truth, Fynch insisted. *If you are my friend – my Guide, as you say – then tell me honestly.*

He sensed the dog's discomfort as it began to explain. *This is the beginning. You must use your powers sparingly. Talk to me aloud whenever you can. Hearing my response in your mind will cause you no distress or repercussions. The pain and other weakenings will only occur if you send the magic yourself.*

How long have I got, Knave?

The dog raised its head to look Fynch directly in the eye. *I don't know. It depends how strong you are; how sparingly you use this power.*

If Knave expected despair it did not come. Fynch wiped

his eyes and, using his companion as support, raised himself wearily on unsteady legs. *I must rest*, the little boy said gravely.

And then we must go to the Thicket, Knave said, equally sombre. *It awaits you.*

CHAPTER 1

The vineyard sprawled before them, the land suddenly sloping away in the distance down to a small shingle beach and the channel of sea. The tang of salt in the air was invigorating and the bright day with its cloudless sky and sharp light reminded Aremys of his love of the north and how much he had secretly missed it all these years. He inhaled the air now and smiled. It felt good to be alive despite the new and sudden complexities in his life.

With his memory now blessedly returned Aremys felt much better equipped to accept the King's invitation to 'walk the rows' of vines at Racklaryon. The mercenary learned that it was one of Cailech's great pleasures to see his vineyard bursting with new life in spring, showing the spectacular results of the savage pruning his vignerons insisted upon each year.

They looked out now across the neat rows and Aremys could almost taste the wine this field would produce at summer's end. Bright green leaves, like the protective wings of a mother hen, shaded their yet-to-mature babies: bunches of fruit that hung like tiny green jewels, fattening and ripening daily as the plants sent out fresh tendrils to weave and curl their way along the special lines that supported the vines. The Mountain People had pioneered this method of support. In the south, the vines were left to themselves, to grow tall at first before stooping over. It made for a ragged, untidy vineyard but, in truth, did not affect the quality of the fruit. In the north, however, the vine support lines had been developed to air the fruit, as some months were humid and damp. It also looked spectacular.

Cailech's people took pride in the ordered appearance of their vineyards. Not only were the rows straight but each vine was sung to as it was planted – a small prayer to Haldor for each new beginning that it might yield life of its own. At each row's end, the Mountain People planted a flower called a trineal. It was beautiful but fragile, very susceptible to lack of water or other natural attacks. Cailech's vignerons maintained that if the trineal foundered, then they would have a few weeks to find the solution to prevent the vines following suit. It was an ancient tradition but one still faithfully adhered to. The bright rainbow colours of the trineal bushes were an attractive feature in this, Cailech's favourite vineyard, and they stood proud, colourful and healthy at the heads of the rows. It would be a bountiful harvest, the men muttered.

The King was rarely alone; today he was flanked by Myrt and Byl. Aremys had come to know these particular fellows well since his curious arrival in the Razors. He felt comfortable in their presence and over the past days he had started to view them as companions as much as his captors. Nevertheless, he had chosen not to reveal that his memory was fully restored. It suited him that these Mountain Dwellers knew only as much as he was prepared to share, until he could learn more of their intentions for him.

The small company had ridden to the vineyard beyond the lake and Aremys was sorry to see that the King had not chosen to bring the intriguing black horse which had caused him such fright on their previous ride. He mentioned his disappointment to Cailech.

'Ah yes, Galapek,' the King replied softly, and Aremys felt the weight of that green gaze upon him. 'I had the impression that he disturbed you somehow the last time we rode together.'

It was said without accusation but still Aremys felt the scrutiny couched within. Wyl Thirsk's warning burned in his mind: that only a fool took any comment by Cailech at face value. *Everything he says has a purpose*, Wyl had impressed upon Aremys during their journey together from Felrawthy. *He misses nothing*.

The mercenary thought back to the moment of disturbance the King spoke of. It had occurred only a few days ago. Aremys had admired the King's mount but, on casually touching the horse, had felt a blast of magic rippling through his hands where they rested on its strong neck. It had been an intense shock for Aremys – not only that the creature was alive with magic, but that he could sense it. Far worse, it was a dark, tainted magic and its touch had caused him to stumble in distress. He had been unable to regain his composure and was forced to excuse himself from the party of riders. That action had been embarrassing, but no doubt had also appeared suspicious at a time when he was striving to convince his keepers that he was not a Morgravian spy or any other kind of threat to the Mountain Dwellers.

The only positive outcome was that the shock seemed to have caused his amnesia to dissipate and he was able to piece together what he was doing in the Razors. He remembered following Wyl Thirsk, who now walked in the guise of his sister, Ylena, courtesy of the powerful gift, the Quickening. Together they had entered the mysterious region in the far north-east known as the Thicket. Aremys recalled Wyl asking him to whistle so they would not lose one another amongst the tangle of this dense landmark. He had obliged, could even remember the tune he had chosen, but then all had gone black and he had woken, disoriented, on the frozen rocks of the northern mountain range and lacking a memory. Cailech's men had discovered him there and somehow he had managed to muddle his way through those early and dangerous stages, not helped by his own confusion. Living by his wits, he felt convinced now that he had carefully won not only their trust but that of their King too. Wyl had warned Aremys that the Mountain King was changeable, capricious even, and had recounted the terrible night of the feast when Cailech had threatened to roast alive the Morgravian prisoners his men had captured and feed them to his people. This was definitely not a man to second-guess and so Aremys had been as honest as he could with the Mountain King, even disclosing his identity when it finally returned to him.

His only major secret from Cailech right now was the fact that he was linked to Wyl Thirsk, the former General of Morgravia, and that Wyl was possessed by a magic which had already taken the life of three people – one of them Romen Koreldy, in whom Cailech had shown a keen interest. And if the Mountain Kingdom held its own secrets, then he would learn them and at least be useful in some small way to Wyl, who had promised to return to the Razors some day in search of his friends Gueryn and Lothryn, both of whom had offered their lives to save his.

It had taken Aremys hours of musing to accept that the Thicket must have somehow repelled him. It was a difficult notion for him to get his mind around. Until recently he had neither particularly believed nor disbelieved in magic, but growing up in the far north, on the Isles of Grenadyn, meant he held a loose acceptance that such a power might exist, and was not necessarily something to fear.

The discovery that magic certainly did exist, however – having met Wyl and shared the sorrow of his plight – was a whole new matter. Suddenly the legend of the Thicket was a real phenomenon and took on a sinister character. To acknowledge that this enchanted place had purposely separated him from the person he had sworn to protect was disturbing enough; but accepting that the Thicket had also affected him in such a way that he now possessed the ability to sense magic was terrifying.

The horse itself couched a darker mystery. Just touching the animal had made him feel ill. This was not a whole beast. It reeked of evil – and yet also of despair. He needed to see the horse again, reach towards it once more. Perhaps his captors had no idea of the darkness in Galapek? But how could Cailech know the horse had been the cause of Aremys's disturbance . . . unless, of course, he knew the creature was tainted.

Aremys realised that Cailech was still watching him carefully. The mercenary, practised at subterfuge, stretched a lazy smile across his generous mouth. 'It was nothing to do with the beast, my lord. I felt very off-colour that morning and I slept for many hours after that event.'

'Probably out of discomfort at almost spewing on the King's boots!' Myrt added, safe in the knowledge that Cailech encouraged a more casual atmosphere when he was away from the fortress and the formalities of being their ruler.

Myrt's jest gave Aremys the opportunity he needed to remove himself from the King's scrutiny. It suddenly occurred to him that Cailech knew more than he was giving away. His instincts had rarely yet let him down, so he listened to them now.

'It reminded me of the time,' he said, seizing the opening, 'when a very aged and strict aunt came to visit the family.' His companions, sensing a tale in the making, came closer. 'She was a cantankerous woman who despised social gatherings, yet insisted on everyone celebrating her nameday each spring. Oh, how we hated that day and her arrival with all of its pomp and ceremony. But our family was obliged to her, for this rich crone had gifted much money to the town and I would be lying if I said we too had not benefited from her gold.'

Aremys saw with relief the loose, expectant grin on the King's face as he bent to inspect the juvenile grapes on a vine. He continued with his tale: a dare by his brothers that went horribly wrong and culminated in him tossing the contents of a chamber pot over the head of the town's special guest.

The men roared with laughter. Aremys noted that

Cailech was less responsive but he was nonetheless amused; a wry smile crinkled the weathered face and sparkled in his eyes. 'I would never repeat such a tale if that had been me,' he said.

'Nor will I again,' Aremys admitted, rather impressed by his story which was wholly fabricated. His dear, sweet old Aunt Jassamy was much loved and her nameday cele-brations had been the town's idea, not hers, and well deserved for the money she had invested in its livelihood. 'But I am trying to impress upon you, my lord, the level of my dismay,' Aremys went on, grinning. 'This sorry tale has now been relegated to the second most embarrassing moment of my life. I hope you can guess the first.'

'You are forgiven, Farrow, and it's forgotten,' the King said, as the other two men moved off through the rows.

Aremys did not believe him. 'Thank you, sire.'

'Perhaps you would like to ride Galapek?'

Aremys had not expected this and his hesitation was telling, he felt. The King was testing him and both of them knew it. What *did* Cailech know? The mercenary quickly gathered his wits. 'It would be a privilege, my lord.'

'Good,' the King replied, his steady gaze unfathomable. 'I will arrange it.'

He looked beyond the mercenary. 'Ah, here comes Baryn. He is head of the vineyard.' The previous topic seemingly forgotten, he strode towards his man, calling back over his shoulder, 'Don't you love the Thaw, Aremys? Spring unfurling her fronds, pushing through her shoots, warming the ground and melting the ice?' Cailech pointed as Aremys caught up. 'Just look at these vines, fairly bursting with joy as tiny green buds and tendrils begin their life journey.'

'You should write poetry, sire.'

The King smiled at the compliment. 'I have a proposition to put to you, Farrow.'

Cailech's sudden twist took Aremys by surprise. He would have to be careful; Wyl had warned him of this. 'Sire?'

'I have been thinking on our conversation.'

'Oh?' Aremys was not sure which particular discussion the King referred to.

Cailech must have sensed this. 'Regarding Celimus.'

Aremys nodded. 'I recall suggesting a parley.'

'There is wisdom in what you advise and I have decided to act upon it.'

Aremys wished he was able to keep the surprise from his face and his voice. 'Really?'

Cailech nodded. 'Yes. I am going to Morgravia, and not under cover of disguise or stealth. Actually, let me correct that. *We* are going to Morgravia.'

'You and your chosen men, sire?'

'Me and *you*, Farrow.'

Aremys searched the King's face for any sign of guile, then realised he would not be able to tell if Cailech was bluffing, for the man was a master at hiding behind a granite expression. Although on this occasion Aremys thought he detected the barest hint of amusement.

'Then I am honoured, King Cailech.' Aremys took the chance that this was the response the Mountain King expected.

Cailech simply nodded. 'You will set up the meeting, as you know Celimus. You will be my emissary.'

The King strode away, leaving the newly appointed envoy for the Mountain Kingdom open-mouthed.

'Close it, friend,' Myrt said, returning to captor duty.

'He can't be serious,' Aremys murmured, watching as the King's broad figure joined the vineyard manager amongst an ocean of green leaves.

'He never jests about such things. Take it as a compliment, Farrow. He must trust you.'

'When do we leave?'

'As soon as the streams run with the Thaw, he told me.'

'But that's now!' Aremys said, turning to look at Myrt. The man grinned. 'True. Come on, we'd better head back – apparently you are to ride his prize stallion this afternoon.'

Aremys's stomach clenched when he caught sight of the magnificent horse being led out of its stall by Maegryn, the stablemaster. The stallion flicked its tail constantly, as though angry. A weak sensation of nausea rippled through the mercenary. He forced himself to relax, for he had been holding his breath as well and was ashamed at himself for allowing this animal to have such a dramatic effect on him. Perhaps he would be able to bear it this time.

It's only a horse, damn it! But he berated himself to no avail; the sinister feeling intensified.

'He's a beauty, this one,' Myrt commented by his side.

Aremys fought the swirling dizziness. Did no one else feel it? 'Is Cailech not joining us?' he asked through clenched teeth.

'No. Rashlyn will be riding out though.'

'Who is he?' Aremys asked as innocently as he could. He recalled Wyl's description of the man who seemed to have an unnatural influence over the Mountain King.

'The King's barshi — a detestable creature,' Myrt told him. 'But if you ever claim I said that, I'll deny it first and kill you later.'

Aremys grinned. 'A man of magic then?' he said, watching as Maegryn saddled Galapek.

His companion nodded and Aremys felt his stomach twist again. 'Can he sense other empowered people?' He hoped Myrt could not hear the anxiety in his voice.

'I have no idea. Why do you ask?'

Aremys forced a shrug. 'Oh, no reason. I've always been rather intrigued by those with the power, that's all.'

'To be honest I wish he'd leave the mountains. His influence upon our King is too strong. There are times . . .' Myrt did not finish.

Aremys glanced towards his captor. 'Go on.'

The Mountain man shook his head. 'No, I speak out of turn.'

Aremys could see it would not be wise to push Myrt further right now, although it pleased him that Myrt felt safe enough around him to be candid. It was a good sign.

It looked as though Maegryn was satisfied with Galapek. He was barking orders now for the other horses to be led out.

'Where did Cailech find this magnificent horse anyway?' Aremys asked brightly. He seemed to be growing more accustomed to the magic nearby.

'It's the strangest thing,' Myrt replied, clearly relieved to have been let off the hook on his previous comment. 'I really don't know.'

'What do you mean?'

'Well, the very best horses come from Grenadyn — as

you would know – but this animal just seemed to turn up one day. He certainly isn't from our stock.'

'You mean it just appeared from nowhere?' Aremys asked, astounded, wondering if the stallion might also have been cast here by the Thicket.

Myrt laughed. 'No, I didn't mean that. But Maegryn knows all the foals born here. And if we bring horses over from Grenadyn then it's quite a big event because they have to be shipped in. I don't recall this animal being brought across the channel – it would have surely caused a stir if he had.'

Aremys was intrigued. It was not his imagination then. There *was* something mysterious about the King's horse. 'What does his handler say?'

'Maegryn's very tight-lipped on the subject. I get the impression that Rashlyn might have gifted the horse to Cailech, though I couldn't guess at where he would find such a beast. Perhaps the King has asked both men to keep it quiet. Cailech can be quite unpredictable on occasion – in case you hadn't noticed.' Myrt grinned.

'I have,' Aremys said wryly.

'As much as he likes or trusts you, be wary. He is a great man but he can be contrary at times,' Myrt warned, before adding softly, 'I know that worried Lothryn.'

Aremys forced himself not to overreact at the name of Wyl's friend. 'Lothryn – who is he?' he commented absently.

'A friend. Formerly second in command to our King. A man I would follow without question into any situation. A man who broke our hearts with his betrayal.'

Maegryn was leading the stallion towards them now and Aremys felt the sickening pull of the magic again.

'So where is he now?'

'Gone,' Myrt said, ending the conversation. 'Your mount is ready – and here comes Rashlyn. Be warned – he is a strange man.'

The barshi was already mounted on a chestnut mare. He stopped just steps from the mercenary and gazed down upon the tall foreigner. 'You must be Aremys,' he said in his strangely hesitant manner. 'Cailech suggested we meet. I hope you don't mind if I join you?'

'Not at all,' Aremys lied, instantly taking a dislike to the wild-looking man with the dead eyes and unwilling smile. He raised his hand in salutation, having decided he should avoid all physical contact with the barshi. If Aremys himself sensed the horse's magic through touch, perhaps Rashlyn could do the same with him and then life would become even more dangerous. He was beginning to wonder whether Cailech had specifically asked Rashlyn to watch how he reacted to the horse today.

Which means they are definitely up to something – and worse, suspicious of me, he thought. The stench of Galapek's magic buffeted his senses as the handler halted the stallion alongside the mare.

'Master Aremys, you'll be riding Galapek this afternoon,' Maegryn said. 'Be firm with him, sir. But also give him his head on the flat. He likes to gallop. Could use a good run today.'

It was all Aremys could manage to nod agreeably and take the reins from Maegryn. He wished he had been more careful and not backed himself into this situation. Nausea threatened to overwhelm him, but he fought it and deliberately turned his back against Rashlyn as he mounted. He could not allow the barshi to read his fear.

Waves of revulsion pulsated through him as he took his seat in the saddle. It required all of his courage not to leap from the horse and flee. 'You lead,' he said tightly to Rashlyn, hoping to get the magic man ahead of him.

Unfortunately, Rashlyn had his measure. 'Myrt, you know the best paths,' he said. 'You lead.'

The party of three set off with Aremys now fully convinced that he was under observation by the King's sorcerer.

CHAPTER 2

Myrt suggested a path via the lowlands surrounding the lake. Aremys grunted his agreement, still struggling to dampen his revulsion for the horse beneath him. Myrt did not linger for a comment from the barshi and set the direction. Once the horses were moving at a steady canter Aremys felt better, and when they set them at a gallop with the wind in his face the exhilaration seemed to alleviate the sickening taint permeating his body from below.

For the first half of the ride the men said nothing and Aremys was happy about this, lost in his thoughts and the pure pleasure of being out in this breathtaking valley. The lake was mirror calm today and he marvelled at how it reflected the lower rises of the Razors. The cacophony of the waterbirds drowned any potential for conversation, which suited him perfectly. Although the sun was high overhead now, there was no real fire in it yet, but still the riders were glad to feel its gentle spring warmth upon their shoulders, loosening winter's firm grip on the land.

Aremys felt he was able to control his reaction to the stallion now that their bodies had been touching for some time. Whatever initially caused him to gag wretchedly in front of the King had diminished to a constant queasiness, which he was mastering. His revulsion had given way to an intense sorrow for this animal. He wondered what was provoking such empathy. The beast moved beneath him with superb grace, all muscle and power, eager to respond to his rider's urgings, but Aremys sensed something beyond the physical; something he would almost equate with human emotion.

'We can stop over there and rest the horses.' Myrt butted into his thoughts, pointing towards a cluster of rocky outcrops which formed a loose semi-circle and a natural suntrap.

Aremys nodded unhappily. He would have preferred to keep going but had no doubt this was all being carefully orchestrated.

They settled themselves against the boulders while the horses grazed contentedly on some tender grass shoots. They were far enough away that Aremys could converse without the magical stench threatening to upset him. Nevertheless, Galapek called to him. Not in words, not even a true sound as such, but an insatiable pull. The more confident Aremys became in his resistance against the revulsion, the more strongly the horse pleaded to his senses.

He looked away from Galapek to the stream gurgling nearby, bringing sweet, fresh water from the highlands. Aremys saw the silvery flash of a fish jumping courageously against the current and immediately likened the creature's struggle to his own as a prisoner of Cailech, but also to his odd relationship with Galapek. The horse's call to him was so intense and strong, a current constantly pounding against him as he bravely pushed against it to stop it dragging him down and under. *What did it want him to do? What was this creature that it could generate such loathing as well as sympathy?* A new thought struck Aremys: not *what* was this animal but *who?* The notion was so striking that it washed away his fear. *Who was this animal? Who was calling to him using the magic of the Thicket? Could the beast be under an enchantment, like Wyl – a man trapped in another guise?* The thought revolted him.

As he shook his head clear of such a shocking notion, the barshi embarked upon the expected interrogation.

'The King tells me you have lost your memory,' Rashlyn said, without any preamble.

'I have,' Aremys answered Rashlyn. 'It is a terrible feeling to not know anything about oneself.'

'I gather it is returning gradually?' the man replied, reaching to unwrap the hunk of cheese and hard biscuit which Myrt had packed.

Aremys noted the man's grubby fingers and looked away. The Mountain men were tough and capable of living rough, but he knew they bathed regularly. The King led by example: he was always scrupulously clean. As it had struck Elspyth not so long ago, Aremys had also realised that the people of the Razors were a sophisticated race with great artistic and creative skills as well as a love of the land and a deep respect for each other. Since Cailech had stopped the tribal fighting and had drawn their people together, that respect had extended beyond simple courtesies to living alongside one another in a manner that promoted cleanliness and protected them from disease. Aremys had noted with surprise the special ablution blocks built around the fortress, proof of how highly

Cailech rated the importance of proper sanitation. The King was convinced of a link between human waste and disease, and so it was rare to see any Mountain Dweller squatting in the fields or in a corner of the fortress to relieve themselves. Instead, carts rolled away daily from the many ablution blocks to deliver the waste into pits dug deep into the ground, far from the main living areas, where it would harmlessly break down and return to the earth. It was part of the modern thinking – along with regular bathing, education, and the maintenance of the old languages – which Cailech insisted upon amongst his people. But this man, Rashlyn, with his dirty hands, his unkempt appearance and offensive manner, did not fit the Mountain folks' mould. How did they tolerate him?

Rashlyn was staring at him. 'Yes, slowly,' Aremys answered, finally. 'I know my name, at least, and where I hail from.'

'Would you like me to check your skull for any damage? I am a healer,' Rashlyn offered, along with some of the cheese.

Aremys was not taking chances. He could not risk that this sorcerer, or whatever he was, might sense through his touch the Thicket's trace of magic. And Shar alone knew where those filthy fingers had last been. 'Thank you, no,' he replied. 'I am not hungry and my head is fine.'

The man frowned. 'It must have been a firm blow to knock your senses so. You really should let me examine you.'

'No need,' Aremys replied briskly, glancing towards his quiet companion and hoping to be rescued. 'Myrt here has already looked me over. There is no sign of any damage.'

Myrt did not deny Aremys's claim but did not support it either. It seemed to Aremys that he too was fighting a battle of loyalty. It was fairly obvious from his body language alone that Myrt despised Rashlyn.

'This business of your lost memory is odd then,' Rashlyn said. He spoke through his food and bits of the cheese crumbled and fell from his mouth into his tangle of beard. Again Aremys looked away, disgusted. 'How could you lose your wits if not from a blow?'

'I have no idea,' Aremys said, and then shrugged. 'I don't remember.' He found the barshi's probing stare most unsettling; there was madness lurking there, he was sure of it. He stood and said politely, 'Excuse me whilst I take a drink,' and glanced again at Myrt, this time for permission to sip from the stream.

Myrt nodded and Aremys walked as casually as he could to the stream's edge and bent down. He splashed freezing water over his face and swallowed some of it, enjoying the refreshing trickle of droplets that found a way into the front of his shirt and slid down his chest. As he straightened, flicking water in all directions, he sensed someone directly behind him. He turned abruptly, expecting to see Rashlyn reaching towards him. The thrill of fear that passed through him nearly unbalanced him into the stream. He felt stupid. He was definitely becoming paranoid, he berated himself silently and angrily.

Yes, Rashlyn was standing behind him, but instead of reaching out for the mercenary he was digging in his pocket to retrieve a tiny jar.

'Apologies, I didn't mean to startle you,' the man said, a little slyly, Aremys thought. 'Here – this will ease the headaches I believe you have been suffering.'

'What is it?'

'A soothing blend of herbs with a dash of laudanum. It won't harm you, or dull anything but the pain, I promise. Sip it every hour as you need it.'

Aremys was trapped. Rashlyn's filthy hand was extended with the small bottle in its palm. He had to take it, or risk throwing yet more doubt into the mind of Cailech. It was certain that Rashlyn would be required to report back to his monarch precisely how the afternoon had unfolded. If the King was waiting to hear that Aremys had vomited again or had refused to ride his stallion then he would be disappointed, but this moment might yet be his undoing. Aremys saw the healer's eyes narrow at his reluctance but still he hesitated.

'I can easily make up some more; you're not denying anyone by taking it,' Rashlyn assured, the softness in his voice almost threatening. Aremys was sure the man was daring him to refuse.

He took a moment to shake his head free of the water droplets, then paused to wipe a sleeve across his face. 'Thank you,' he replied, reaching out slowly, hoping Rashlyn would simply drop the phial into his hand.

Before that could happen, Galapek alarmed all three men by rearing up behind them, screaming loudly as though in pain. Myrt reacted first, running towards the horse. Aremys took his chance, moving swiftly away from the healer. 'Let me help!' he called.

The horse clearly wanted Myrt nowhere near him, rearing and screaming even more wildly as the warrior approached. To Myrt's surprise, however, the stallion calmed a little at the sound of the big mercenary's voice and allowed Aremys to sidle up to him.

Aremys reached for the reins and called again to the big horse. 'Galapek, there boy. There now. Settle, big fellow,' he whispered. The horse stood still now, trembling and angry.

'Poor Galapek, I shall save you. Whatever has happened to you, I shall rescue you, I promise,' he said, stroking the animal's broad, magnificent muzzle. 'Be calm now, boy.' He buried his face in Galapek's beautiful mane and, for the first time, the stench of the magic did not attack him. Whatever this curse upon the stallion was, it was somehow communicating with him, flowing through him and around him, begging him to keep his promise.

And then came a word in his head. It was faint and desperately called, but he was not imagining it. *Elspyth*, he heard, just once, and then it was gone, like a sigh given to the wind and borne away.

Aremys was so shocked he stood rigid against the horse's neck, trying to recapture the word, aching to reach for it, but it was lost. *Elspyth*. Surely that was the name he had heard? The urgent voice of Myrt broke through his haze of confusion.

'Farrow! For Haldor's sake, man!'

Aremys turned from the horse, surprised by the anger being levelled at him. Then he saw Myrt's expression – not angry as he'd thought, but distraught – and followed where his friend's hand pointed. By the water's edge, where he had left him, Rashlyn writhed on the ground, shouting gibberish as spittle foamed and flew from his mouth. His arms and legs flailed wildly.

'Check the horses are secure,' Aremys called over his shoulder as he ran to the prone figure which had suddenly fallen still. He wished Rashlyn might be dead but luck was not with him. He lifted the small man's chin to ensure a clear breathing passage, but stopped short of breathing any life-giving air into that mouth. 'He has a pulse, I'm sorry to say,' he risked to Myrt who had come up behind them.

Myrt did not smile but something akin to a twitch of amusement flitted across his face. 'What's happened, I wonder?' the Mountain man queried.

'Is he prone to fits?'

'I don't know. I've not heard of any occurring before.'

'Could it be the cheese?' Aremys wondered aloud.

'Fresh. Nothing wrong with it.'

'Something else then. It seemed to occur at the same time as Galapek took fright.'

'What are you saying?' Myrt squatted, saw the indecision in his companion's face. 'Speak freely — I have protected you before.'

Rashlyn lay rigidly still at their feet. Aremys lifted back the man's lids. The dark, madness-filled eyes had rolled back into his head. The man was unconscious; he was hearing nothing.

'I'm not sure I should air my views. You're a loyal Mountain warrior, after all.'

'Not to him!' Myrt spat disdainfully on the ground. 'Like you, I wish he was dead. He's a danger to all of us.'

'Because of his magic?'

Myrt nodded reluctantly. 'He uses it for evil, I'm sure of it.'

'I think it's his magic that has prompted this episode.'

'I don't understand. Be clear.'

'I can't. I don't understand it either.' Aremys sighed and decided to take a chance on Myrt. He hoped his instincts would serve him truly. 'Were you given any instructions about me and this afternoon's ride?'

Myrt frowned. 'Nothing special. I was briefed to give you a chance to enjoy Galapek because you had expressed such interest in the horse.'

'The King didn't tell you to keep a special eye on me?'

'My job is to keep an eye on you, Farrow. You're our . . .' he hesitated, 'our guest, after all.'

Aremys grinned ruefully. 'Myrt, you are more friend to me than most people I have met over the past decade. But let's be honest here: I'm a prisoner — I have to accept that. However,' he went on, scratching his head, 'your King is entrusting me with a very serious task, which means he has faith in me. Sadly, I can't be quite as honest with him as I can with you.'

'Why not?'

'Because he is in the thrall of this man. You've told me that much yourself, and spending just an afternoon with Rashlyn has convinced me he's not someone to trust.'

Myrt said nothing, merely frowned again.

Aremys pushed on. He glanced towards the horse. 'I could be aiming completely off target here, but I think there's something very odd about Galapek. No, not odd. Enchanted.'

Myrt rocked back on his heels as if slapped. 'Magic?'

Aremys nodded. 'Worked by Rashlyn, I'm guessing. And known of by your King.' There, it was said. He had admitted his fears.

Myrt stood and began pacing. He said nothing for a while and Aremys kept the silence, watching Rashlyn for any signs of consciousness.

'I don't believe this,' the warrior hissed eventually, pointing at Aremys.

'You don't have to,' he replied calmly, having anticipated the anger. 'I'm just offering my own thoughts. I'm not suggesting that your King — whom I like and respect — is in complete agreement with Rashlyn.'

'Then what *do* you mean, mercenary?' Myrt said brusquely.

Aremys felt sorry that he had pushed his friend so far. It was obvious from his anger that Myrt had suspected something not so far from what Aremys had suggested. But the truth sometimes hurt, and the blood between the Mountain People ran thick with loyalty. Wyl had warned him as much and he should not have toyed with the idea that friendship might override that loyalty — although, of course, it did in the case of the man Lothryn, who had chosen love and friendship over his monarch.

'I'm sorry if I've given insult, Myrt. It was not intended, especially not to you. What I meant is, I think Cailech — under the spell of Rashlyn, as you have pointed out — has permitted something to be wrought upon this horse. And no doubt other enchantments too.'

'And how for the love of Haldor's arse would you know, Grenadyne? Are you a practitioner now to know when magic is being wielded?'

The harsh words bit at Aremys, as intended, but how could he ignore the truth? Could he risk divulging it to Myrt and still keep his life?

'Myrt, do you trust me?'

The man passed a weary hand over his eyes. 'I'm not sure.'

'What does your gut tell you?'

'That you are reliable.'

'Good. We have to get Rashlyn back to the fortress. Come, help me lay him across his horse and I will tell you everything I know as we travel.'

They took the same route home but slowly. Aremys had tethered Rashlyn's horse on a lead some distance behind them, so if the healer regained consciousness he could not hear their conversation. He would have to alert them by calling out. 'An old mercenary trick,' Aremys had said and winked.

On the return journey, Aremys began to share with his friend all the information he was prepared to risk bringing into the open. He cast a silent prayer to Shar that he had this man's measure, that he could trust him not to betray him. He said nothing of Wyl, of course, simply explaining that he had been in the employ of the Morgravian sovereign. Myrt accepted that the mercenary would not explain what specific task he was employed to do for Celimus, merely nodding when Aremys assured him that it was nothing connected with the people of the Razors.

'Let me simply say that I was tracking someone of interest to the Crown,' Aremys offered.

'And that's what brought you so far north?'

'Yes. I've remembered that I came to a place called Timpkenny in the far north-east of Briavel,' the mercenary lied. 'I believed this person I was following had passed through there.'

'And these people who set upon you – just common bandits, you think?'

'Mmm,' Aremys nodded. 'Added a little something to my ale to make me feel sick so I would stagger outside the inn late at night. I'm guessing now — all of this is a little hazy, thanks to the drug — but they must have thrown me over a horse to remove me from prying eyes. They led me to the fringe of a region called the Thicket. Have you heard of this place?' Aremys held his breath.

Myrt was staring at him intently. He nodded. 'They say it has powerful magic.'

'It does, my friend, or at least I think it does. They left me there after robbing me. Something must have frightened them, because I expected to be beaten at the very least.' Aremys steered himself towards the truth. 'The last thing I remember is a strange noise coming from the Thicket itself.'

Myrt's eyes were huge. 'A creature?'

'No creature I know makes that sound. No, I can still hear it — it was a sort of humming sound — and then the air became thick and oppressive,' Aremys replied.

'Then what?'

Aremys made a gesture of apology. 'Then nothing. I woke up to the sound of your men's voices and no memory of what had occurred or even who I was. You know the rest. My memory came back gradually over the next couple of days, and it's still returning slowly.' He shrugged, then added for effect, 'I can even remember the faces of my family now.'

Myrt was stunned; he kept shaking his head. Finally he spoke. 'I believe you, Aremys. No one could make up such a tale, and we know of the Thicket's legend. I just find it difficult to hear its magical reputation confirmed.'

'Myrt, I don't know what happened, that's the truth. I can only presume that the Thicket, or something inside it, had something to do with me appearing in the Razors at a location that it would take days to reach by normal means. You checked the area: there were no signs of other people or animals, so I couldn't have been kept drugged and led in by horse – and why do that anyway? Why go to the bother of leading me anywhere if money was all they were after? I doubt I would have recognised any of them again – the drug was too powerful.'

'I believe you,' the big warrior impressed, his hands raised in defence.

'Well, I don't want to put any strange ideas in your head, but my only explanation is that this place called the Thicket is enchanted – I too have heard the old tales – and it did not like me being there, let me tell you. I felt its animosity. I think it got rid of me.'

'That's impossible, man!' Myrt said, desperate for something rational he could cling to.

'I agree, but there's no other explanation. Obviously I couldn't tell this tale to the King. He would have laughed and probably had my throat slit a moment later. You understand now why I had to keep this part of my story to myself? As to how the Thicket rid itself of me – it repelled me. I can't think of any other way to describe it. It would be great to believe a nice family of tinkers found me, picked me up and carried me with them on their journey through the Razors but I think we'd be making up an explanation to help ourselves feel better about a notion we don't want to accept or understand. Plus, there would be signs of the tinkers. No, Myrt, I am convinced that magic has been wielded upon me. I have other reasons to suspect as much.'

Here it was, the very core of his tale. Myrt would either give himself over entirely to Aremys now or brand him a madman and go running to Cailech. He took a deep breath and waited for Myrt's inevitable question. He risked a glance behind. Rashlyn lay draped over his horse, still unconscious.

'What do you mean by that?'

The fortress was all but upon them now. Aremys could see the people working the orchards, others driving carts and still more going about their chores. He shivered, noticing for the first time that a chill had descended into the valley and a slight breeze had picked up, causing ripples across the surface of the formerly mirror-like lake. The disturbance matched his own mood.

'Tell me,' his companion implored.

Aremys reined Galapek to a halt and the other horses followed suit. He knew Myrt could tell this was difficult for him and was giving him time to find the right words. There were no right words so he just told it how he saw it.

'I think I've been touched by the magic of the Thicket. It temporarily knocked out my memory with the force of its power, but it gave me something in return.'

Aremys could not imagine Myrt's eyes getting any rounder. He hurried on. 'It left me with the ability to sense magic.' He held up his hand. 'Before you jump in – no, I can't wield it, I just sense it. And magic is with us now.'

'Where?' his companion said in a whisper.

'Right here, beneath me.'

Myrt predictably looked towards the ground.

'Galapek,' Aremys said. 'The horse is not natural, Myrt. He is riddled with magic, bad magic. It's tainted – it smells evil and repulses me as effectively as the Thicket transported me all those leagues. This horse reeks of enchantment and I think Rashlyn is responsible for it. That's why he is so suspicious of me.'

'And why you were so keen to avoid his touch,' Myrt finished, tying together the threads of all he had noticed but had not been able to understand.

'That's right. That's why I disgraced myself on our first ride together when Cailech rode Galapek. The magic assaulted me and I had no control over my reaction to it. I didn't even know why I was behaving so strangely. It took me a while to work it out, but I know I'm right.'

'And now?'

'The magic still revolts me but I have it under control now. I have mastered my reaction to it.'

The warrior whistled through his teeth. 'So that's why you seemed nervous riding out this afternoon.'

Aremys nodded. 'I was terrified. I had no idea how I'd handle it, but I knew that Rashlyn had been sent to watch my reaction and so I had to be very careful.'

'So you're saying the King sent him?'

'Of course. Cailech's too smart to allow my episode on that first ride to go unnoticed. He's testing me.'

'He speaks well of you, Aremys, you should know that,' Myrt defended.

'Thank you. I've grasped as much, and yet I know I baffle him — understandably so, because if he's got something to hide with this enchantment then anything which threatens it is a danger.'

'You're risking much by telling me this.'

Aremys nodded gravely. 'My life is in your hands, Myrt. I trust you, and Shar knows, I had to tell someone or go mad.'

'What do you want me to do?'

'Nothing. Just keep my secret for now and I will not leave you in the dark regarding anything I discover.'

'I cannot be a party to anything disloyal to Cailech,' the man said carefully.

'I wouldn't ask it of you. I just want to learn more about the horse – and Rashlyn, whom I wouldn't trust if he was the last man alive in this land.'

'None of us would, except the King,' Myrt replied, disgust lacing his tone. 'And you think the horse's rearing and shrieking and Rashlyn's collapse are connected?'

'Yes. Something has tampered with their magic or disturbed the link between the two. I'll admit to something else . . .'

'Yes?'

'I felt it too, but only lightly. As Rashlyn was holding that medicine out to me, I came over light-headed, slightly dizzy. I thought it was the fear of him touching me, but I think I know better now. The magic of the Thicket was resonating within me again . . . perhaps warning me, or maybe something has happened – connected with the Thicket – which has disturbed the horse. I don't understand how. Who knows, it might be that the Thicket can disrupt the actual enchantment on Galapek, or why would Rashlyn also react? I know they're connected now.'

'But you don't know what?'

'No, it's frustrating!' Aremys frowned. 'But I intend to learn more. Will you keep my secret?'

Myrt nodded unhappily. 'I will.'

'Thank you. I won't betray you or your people – you have my word.' He banged his fist on his chest in an oath only another northerner would understand.

Myrt mirrored the movement and then the two men banged fists together. The bond was made and it was no small promise. If broken, the betrayer would forfeit his life.

After they had ridden on some time in silence, Aremys decided to push his luck with the Mountain man. 'Now that you know my secret, perhaps you would share with me whatever it was that you held back earlier about your great friend, Lothryn?'

Myrt looked taken aback. 'It was nothing of importance.' But his reaction said otherwise.

Aremys shrugged. 'It seemed to me that you were troubled by the mention of his name. I thought you might want to share your burden with someone who would not judge you for it – an outsider you can trust.'

Myrt glanced back at the barshi's unconscious figure, then looked around surreptitiously, his expression showing the new battle going on in his mind. *Come on, tell me*, Aremys urged silently. He knew if ever there was a moment to learn about Wyl's saviour it was now. Myrt would never again be in such a fragile state of mind or more obliged to him.

'Lothryn . . .' Myrt spoke the name as if in veneration. 'Brave Lothryn was brought back to the fortress after the Morgravians escaped – all but one, of course.'

Aremys desperately wanted to jump on that detail, but bit back the question that was in danger of exploding from his throat, intent on not disturbing the man's flow of speech now that he had begun to reveal what he needed to learn.

'Koreldy and the woman, Elspyth, managed to escape because of Lothryn's aid and the fact that we were facing several ekons at the same time. Lothryn and I fought back to back together on Haldor's Pass, a dangerous escarpment. We killed three ekons that day and lost several men. When the battle was over my great friend turned to me and held his wrists out to be bound. He didn't ask for mercy or even a quick death – both of which I had expected, and might even have given, for I loved him enough to give my own life for him. I knew Cailech would execute me if I showed such mercy. But Lothryn knew Cailech would have instructed me to bring him back to face his ruler. And he allowed me to keep my faith with my King.'

It was Aremys's turn to whisper. 'What happened?'

Myrt's expression became distraught. Aremys knew there was some nuance here he was not picking up, but now was not the time to pursue it. His voice shaking with tightly held-back tears, Myrt continued: 'I delivered him to Cailech. It was a private meeting and I was not permitted to be present. I have no idea what passed between them. Later, all the King would tell me was that Lothryn was undergoing a special punishment and we would not see him again. I asked whether he was to be killed; I'll never forget the King's reply. He said, "He probably wishes I would kill him", and then he looked at me strangely. I saw a mixture of pain and regret in his face, Aremys, for the King loved Lothryn like a brother. He could have saved him, but Lothryn's betrayal cut deeper than any other wound ever could.'

Aremys sighed. 'And there's been no sign of Lothryn since?'

Myrt shook his head, deeply upset. 'We've tried. Rashlyn knows something but he's as mad as a pit full of burning snakes. He makes little sense at the best of times.'

As if on cue, they heard a sound behind them, a weak cry from the man slung across the trailing horse.

'He's stirring. We've tarried long enough. We shall speak again when we next get a chance alone,' Aremys said, and he clicked Galapek on towards the great stone arch that would swallow them into the fortress.

CHAPTER 3

Wyl's progress along the Darkstream was slow as he travelled against the current back towards the Thicket. His
emotions were still in turmoil at the loss of his sister,
Ylena, whose body he now inhabited, but this sorrow was
deepened by the disappearance of Aremys. This was
someone he had called a friend and there were precious
few of those in his life now. To lose him so soon was devastating. Further, his mind felt burdened rather than light-
ened by his meeting with Elysius and his heart was
especially heavy at leaving Fynch.

Fynch, Wyl mused, was the only constant in his life
just at present. As he inched his way towards the Thicket,
he realised how important the youngster had become to
him. Whilst others such as Elspyth and even Aremys had
accepted the strangeness of his life, it was Fynch who had
always believed in him. Fynch who had guessed his secret
from the start and had protected him. Little Fynch, so
humble and yet so wise, who had saved not only Wyl's
life but that of a sovereign with his ingenuity. And it did
not stop there. Fynch, following his own path, had left

the safety of Werryl to track down Romen's killer, and then had felt the pull of the Wild. There was definitely more to Fynch than hero worship of Wyl Thirsk. It had occurred to Wyl that Fynch's involvement was not co-incidence; the boy was deeply enmeshed in this whole business of Myrren's gift, or at least in the curious life that Wyl was now leading. It was this realisation of Fynch's importance that caused Wyl's anger at himself for not insisting that Fynch should leave Elysius and travel with him.

The truth of it was, he suddenly felt he needed Fynch. Their lives, strange though they both were, were entwined. He loved Fynch too and would not forgive himself should anything happen to the little fellow.

Wyl's thoughts raged in so many confusing directions that his only firm plan at this minute was to return to Timpkenny. He would overnight there before making a decision on his next move. His journey up the Darkstream was curiously and happily uneventful, and Samm was nowhere to be seen when he alighted, relieved, from the small craft where he had moored it by the overhanging willows. His intention had been to avoid the boatman and so it suited him that his cottage appeared deserted.

Wyl did not relish the notion of again passing through the mysterious Thicket, but he knew he could not wait too long to find the courage. Evening seemed to fall heavily and fast in this place, and he did not want to risk Samm coming across him.

He walked more briskly towards the dark line of yews that marked the border of the Thicket. Wyl was convinced that he could hear a dim buzz emanating from the enchanted forest; it frightened him, but as he had been allowed to pass through once before, he was counting on similar generosity again.

Wyl took a deep breath, closed his eyes reflexively and pushed into the tangle. The Thicket's cool atmosphere chilled him instantly. The silence was disturbing. The forest knew he was here, and the thought that this place could sense, think and make decisions for itself was the most disconcerting notion of all.

Oddly, this time there were no snagging branches and no confusing pathways. The previous time Knave had led him through Wyl felt sure that alone he would have lost himself amongst the yews for good. This time paths seemed to open themselves up to him. He shook his head with wonder. The Thicket was guiding him swiftly through its depths. It wanted him gone. Was as glad to be rid of him as he was to have his back to it.

'Thank you,' he whispered in genuine relief, feeling compelled to communicate with this living phenomenon which both fascinated and terrified him. Whether or not the Thicket heard he could not know, but he felt better for offering his gratitude.

It was Wyl's continuing fear that Aremys might still be blundering around in the Thicket, trying to escape. If it could guide him out, Wyl reasoned, it was just as able to keep Aremys in and never relinquish him, if it so chose.

He overcame his intense fear, took the chance and began to call to his friend. The somewhat desperate edge to his voice carried loudly through the dense overgrowth but did little more than scatter small animals he could not see. Within this tension he had created for himself, Ylena's fear of enclosed spaces began to threaten again; he felt it first as a tightening in her chest. He recalled the identical tautness of emotion which had occurred just before he lost control of himself on his first journey on the Darkstream and nearly drowned.

The familiar shallowness of breath hit him and he stopped moving. Was the Thicket's magic acute enough to sense this change in him? Instinctively, he began breathing into his cupped hands. Wyl could not imagine how he remembered this trick but it was something his father had taught Ylena when she was an infant. Panic, he recalled, often overcame his young sister, prompted by the suggestion of the game hide-and-come-seek, or looking into the dark depths of the well, or playing under Wyl's bed. Anything connected with being enclosed or hidden seemed to provoke an irrational fear in her. To his knowledge, Ylena had not experienced this terror since she was a child, but obviously its ability to strike had travelled with her into adulthood. Wyl was grateful now for his memory of Fergys Thirsk's trick to calm his daughter; he quickly noticed a marked change in what had been steadily rising panic levels.

Whether or not the Thicket was aware of his discomfort, Wyl was fairly sure it deliberately steered him towards what might, at a stretch, be described as a clearing. His relief – or, more to the point, Ylena's – at the space was evident by the way he flopped to the ground and took deep breaths. It remained cool beneath the yews but the oppressive atmosphere was not so marked, and if he could only get his breathing under control he knew he would feel less anxious. He put Ylena's pretty head between her knees and forced her lungs to breathe slowly and deeply as foot soldiers, suddenly overcome by fear of battle, were taught to do before the command to charge. He held this position for several minutes and was relieved to feel the anxiety lessening.

A soft sound above prompted him to raise his head and he was confronted by the largest owl he had ever seen. Strikingly marked, the majestic tawny creature blinked slowly and deliberately, in the way owls do. Wyl watched it as intently as it was regarding him, wondering which of them would capitulate first, if that indeed was what was expected.

He lost the staring contest.

'And you are?' he said, feeling ridiculous but comforting himself that he had spoken to Knave without embarrassment. Why not this curious owl with such intelligence lurking in its large yellow eyes? This was a magical place after all. He was rewarded for his faith.

I am Rasmus, the owl said into his mind, startling him.

'I hear you,' Wyl replied, in awe of the splendid creature.

That was my intention, it said, somewhat disdainfully, then rotated its head in a disconcerting manner.

'How is it that we can communicate?' Wyl persisted. 'Is it because of Myrren's gift?'

The owl made a disgusted sound in his head. *It is because I allow it, and because you are here.*

'In the Thicket, you mean?'

Where else could I mean?

Wyl felt an apology springing to his lips but resisted it. This creature was either baiting him or simply did not like him. He decided to take charge of the conversation. 'What do you want with me?' he asked, his tone direct now.

Again the owl blinked. Wyl felt a temptation to laugh. How would he ever explain this to anyone else? *We want you to leave*, it said firmly.

'Well, can't you just rid yourself of me?' he replied, determined not to be cowed by this strange creature.

If we choose to.

Wyl sighed. 'Then choose it, owl, for leaving here is what I want too. Trust me.' He was irritated by the owl's superior manner. 'Who is "we" anyway?'

If you want to be gone from here, why do you linger? Rasmus asked, his tone suggesting he too was losing patience.

'I am not lingering,' Wyl snapped. 'I was guided to this spot and, if you're as magical as I suspect, then you can probably sense the sorcery that has touched me.'

I can.

'Then you know that this is not the body I was born with.'

And so?

'And so this particular body does not care for the density or fearsome atmosphere of your Thicket.'

It is not mine, the bird countered.

It was Wyl's turn to blink — with exasperation. He took a steadying breath; showing his fury would not help here. 'The person whose body I walk in is scared of this place and was having breathing difficulties.'

We gathered.

'Was this clearing deliberately created for my benefit?' Wyl was determined to find out whether the Thicket was able to think for itself.

Yes. Are you ready to leave?

'Not until you answer a question.'

I am not beholden to you.

Wyl took a gamble. 'If you trust Knave, then you should trust me, for he and I are friends. I mean you and the creatures of the Thicket – or indeed the Thicket itself – no harm. The secret of your magic is safe with me.'

There was a pause. Wyl wondered if the owl would communicate with him again. He stood up, frustrated by its stare and its silence. 'You have let me pass through previously. I know you have no intention of killing me.'

Ask your question, the owl finally said, irritably.

Wyl curbed his enthusiasm and took a moment to consider how best to phrase his question. He sensed the owl would, at worst, answer cryptically, or at best literally, so his question must be very clear in order to gain him a precise answer.

'Where is Aremys living?' he asked carefully.

There was no hesitation from the owl. *He lives in the Razors.*

Wyl's relief spilled over. 'Is he safe?'

I have answered your question, the owl replied, fractious now.

'Please,' Wyl beseeched.

Rasmus made a peevish clicking noise. *Aremys is safe.*

Wyl decided there was nothing more to lose other than the owl's patience, and that was already fast depleting. 'Rasmus,' Wyl began reasonably, 'you have shared your name. Mine is Wyl. But then I'm sure you know that. Can we not be friends?'

Yet another tiresome question?

Wyl defied the owl and sat. 'Yes, I have questions. I will not betray the Thicket. I owe it for keeping my friend Aremys safe and for helping me so far. I am your friend also.'

The Thicket has no friends of your kind, save one. You are not he.

Wyl had no idea what the owl was talking about. Perhaps the bird referred to Elysius. 'Then let me ask what I need to so I can help the others you do trust — Knave and . . . Fynch.'

He had intended to say Elysius but Fynch came to his mind and slipped out first. He saw the bird react as he spoke his young friend's name, and the shrubs around him seemed to shudder. Was it the boy who interested the Thicket?

'I will protect Fynch always,' he risked.

And was rewarded with a testy reply. *He does not require your protection. He has the protection of the Thicket.*

'I see,' Wyl said, not really seeing anything but harking back to his earlier suspicion that Fynch had some special purpose in this dangerous game they seemed to be playing. It was, no doubt, why Fynch was reluctant to leave the Wild, Wyl reasoned. Then a notion came to him suddenly, like a wasp sting and causing similar pain. 'He's not coming to Werryl, is he?'

The bird said nothing at first, then sighed. At that soft sound in his head, Wyl felt hollow. He had lost Fynch.

Fynch has his own path to follow now, Rasmus confirmed.

It shocked Wyl to hear his fear spoken aloud. It was one thing to suspect something and quite another to have it proven. Fynch was clearly on a new path, and a dangerous one, or the owl would not have mentioned protection or sound so sorrowful. Wyl also realised there was precious little he could do about it, as he imagined the Thicket would not permit him to return to find Fynch.

It obviously had its own reasons for helping the boy to follow this new road.

'Knave will be at his side, of course?' he ventured.

Always, Rasmus said.

'Thank you,' said Wyl, and meant it. 'I shall leave now. I am grateful to you, Rasmus, and the "we" you speak of for allowing me this time and for answering my questions.'

He stood and bowed to the huge bird with marked respect, then walked away, presuming the Thicket would now guide him quickly to its fringe and towards Timpkenny. He was surprised to hear Rasmus call after him.

He turned. 'Pardon?'

I said, where are you going? the owl repeated.

'I must make my way south to Werryl as quickly as I can.'

We will send you there.

Wyl looked at the large bird quizzically. 'Send me?'

Come back to the clearing, it said.

'I don't understand.' Wyl was feeling a little fearful.

You will. Stand before me and close your eyes. Do not open them.

'I won't.'

If you disobey us, we shall never allow you to leave, the owl warned.

Too much depended on his safe departure from this place. Wyl did as asked, wondering if this 'sending' business which Rasmus spoke of was a small show of friendship after all. He was glad now that he had bowed to the owl.

Be still, the owl cautioned. *It will feel strange but you must trust us. Do not resist. Just let your body float. Remember, do not open your eyes.*

Wyl understood none of it but obeyed as a man used to taking orders.

Farewell, Rasmus said and Wyl felt a vast, chest-crushing pressure against his body. He wanted to open his eyes but fought it, having given his word. Breathing was all but impossible but he refused to panic. He had to trust the owl.

If he had disobeyed the owl's strict instructions he would have seen Fynch shimmering before him. Wyl could not see the tears on Fynch's face nor how he mouthed a goodbye to his friend, but he felt the touch of the Gate Wielder as Ylena's trembling body was pushed through a thickened disc of air and disappeared.

It is done, Rasmus said. *Be at rest, Faith Fynch.*

'Why do they refer to me as Faith?' Fynch whispered to Knave, who sat tall and imposing beside him in a special sunlit divide. Unless he had seen it with his own eyes, Fynch would never have believed such a clearing existed in the Thicket. Curiously, the small light-drenched space added no particular cheer to the dense, dark and brooding atmosphere, but Fynch was nonetheless glad for the brief respite from the chill.

It is how we think of you.

'What do you mean?'

We have faith in you.

Fynch wanted to ask more but the words were stilled in his mouth as creatures — many known to him only from folklore — began to gather at the fringe of the clearing.

'These are your friends?' he asked, his voice filled with wonder.

They are the creatures of the Thicket.

Fynch's attention was caught by a magnificent lion that watched him from the shadows. The animal shook itself and Fynch gasped to see wings extending from the proud cat's shoulders.

'Knave, that's the winged lion of legend.'

No legend, as you can see. He exists.

'I only know of him from the old tales and the carvings at Stoneheart. He . . . he is Wyl's mythical animal, who protects him.'

And yours?

'Mine?' the boy said, awed as he caught sight of the equally legendary great bear. 'My animal is . . .' Fynch hesitated as another creature invaded his mind, demanding to be named. He felt treacherous and pushed the thought away. 'My animal is the unicorn.'

He comes to you now, Knave said.

The other creatures fell silent as the beautiful animal emerged into the light. Its coat had a hue of the palest of blues but the overall impression was of a pure, dazzling white; even its famed horn was a silvery white. It walked slowly and with such grace that Fynch held his breath, utterly captivated.

Tall and broad, the unicorn towered over the boy and his companion. *Child,* it said in a deep, musical voice. *It is my privilege to welcome you amongst us.*

Fynch was so overwhelmed by the fabled creature's magnificence and the notion that this animal was his protector that he began to weep. The unicorn bent its great head, careful not to touch the boy with its lethal horn, and nuzzled Fynch, who put his small arms around the creature's neck in worship. *My name is Roark,* it added, for his hearing alone.

'The privilege is mine, great Roark,' Fynch whispered.

Be bright, Faith Fynch, you are our hope, it returned into his mind.

Fynch gathered his composure and dried his eyes. He looked about him uncertainly, registering the expectancy which hung in the air, and tried not to gape at the amazing troupe of creatures gathered around him.

As one they bowed, including Knave and the graceful Roark.

You must acknowledge them, Knave whispered into Fynch's startled mind. *Put aside your awe, son. You are the one to whom we give our loyalty. Assume your birthright.*

Fynch understood none of this. He was a gong boy. A child of low birth and even lower rank. How could he acknowledge homage from these majestic creatures of legend? Who was he to assume such a role?

It was as if Roark could hear his thoughts. *Fynch, will you accept our loyalty?*

Elysius's words echoed in Fynch's memory. *Perhaps the Thicket needs you for more than simply watching over a Gate.* He could not escape his destiny, he knew this. His life was no longer his own, to direct or to decide. Choices had already been made and promises given.

Fynch steadied himself and found his voice. 'Creatures of the Thicket,' he called, 'I will make myself worthy of your faith.'

He bowed, low and long. When he stood upright again, he felt as if a new strength was pulsing through him, from his toes through to the tips of his fingers. He realised that it must be the Thicket communicating with him; sending him nourishing power. He felt charged with it and could not help the radiant smile that broke out across his face.

'Tell me what it is I must do,' he asked the creatures. 'I am your servant.'

It was Rasmus who spoke on behalf of the creatures and of the Thicket itself.

Be seated, Fynch, he offered from his perch.

Knave and Roark remained standing, flanking Fynch on either side.

Child, you already know what it is we ask of you, the owl said.

'I do?'

Elysius shared the same desire.

'Rashlyn,' Fynch murmured.

The creatures and trees all shuddered their shared hate for the man.

Yes, Rasmus concurred. *You must destroy him.*

'What is it that frightens you so about this man?'

He is tainted, and he wants to use his power to corrupt all that is natural about the world. His evil is born of his jealousy at being unable to manipulate Nature. More than anything he passionately desires the power to control all creatures. With this at his disposal he would rule all realms. Imagine him being able to call upon eagle or ekon alike? Imagine commanding them to do evil and the animals powerless to refuse him? You must destroy him!

'Am I capable?' Fynch wondered aloud.

The Thicket and its creatures will help you.

Strengthened by the thrum of power that bristled through him from the ground of the Thicket and emboldened by the love and loyalty that surrounded him, Fynch gave them his answer. 'Then I ask for nothing more than your faith in me.'

It was the right thing to say. Knave confirmed as much

with a gently uttered *Bravo, child* into his mind, whilst the creatures showed their trust and delight, some leaping into the air, others rearing to stand on two legs, still others squawking or braying.

Fynch laughed. He was filled with a joy he had never known before. He suddenly felt he belonged to all of them. He reached for Knave and touched the great dog's head.

I don't believe it, Knave said, his tone humble. Fynch thought he even heard a tremor in it. *The King comes.*

'The King?' Fynch repeated, puzzled. Since they had begun communicating via this special mindlink Fynch had found Knave's manner to be mostly serious, like himself. The dog was not one for jests or shallow thoughts. He spoke only when there was something to say and during most of their conversations it had been his role to counsel Fynch. The boy knew of Knave's graveness, and the dignity that emanated from his solid, dependable presence, but never had he seen the dog show humility. And this was no small humility: Knave sounded filled with reverence for whatever it was that was arriving. 'Knave—'

Hush, said the dog and a powerful beating sound made Fynch raise his head and squint into the light above. Something plunged towards them – a suggestion of a shadow at first, that darkened until it cut out the light entirely and Fynch no longer squinted but was wide-eyed with both fear and awe.

'The warrior dragon,' he breathed.

Our King, Roark said softly, veneration in his voice as the mighty creature alighted in the clearing.

The creatures bent low to exalt the hallowed creature that stood before them, its famed, darkly shimmering colours gloriously filling the silence.

Fynch needed no prompting. He fell to his knees immediately, then prostrated himself. He closed his eyes and cast a prayer to Shar in thanks for the blessing of this day and what it had brought him.

Fynch, said a voice as rich and mellow as treacle.

'Your majesty,' Fynch replied, not daring to raise his head.

Come stand before me, the voice commanded.

Fynch summoned his courage. With Knave and Roark's whispered firm encouragement, he opened his eyes and looked upon the King of all the beasts. There was no doubting that royalty stood before him; no wondering if this glorious creature was worthy of such exaltation. Fynch held his breath as every fibre of his being suddenly felt newly alive, restored somehow in the presence of such grandeur.

Fynch, like everyone else who looked upon the dragon pillar in Pearlis Cathedral with awe, had believed it was just legend. Associated with the Morgravian sovereign, it was the most impressive of all the mythical creatures but no more real than the winged lion. But now the King of Kings stood in all his glory before him, as real as Fynch himself.

Faith Fynch, the King said. *Be welcome*.

'Thank you, your majesty,' he stammered, bowing. 'I am proud to serve you.'

And we are indebted for that service, child, which is given so bravely by one so young.

Fynch said nothing. What could one say to such generous praise?

The warrior dragon continued: *And still we ask more of you.*

'I will give my life if it is so required.'

The King regarded him through dark, wise eyes. *We shall do everything in our power to prevent you relinquishing something so precious.*

'Please tell me, my King,' – *my true King*, Fynch thought to himself – 'what it is that you ask of me.'

The beast wasted no further time. *The King of Morgravia brings shame to his kind. He is of the warrior clan – of my blood, you could say – but he disgusts me.*

'Celimus is indeed shameful,' Fynch agreed quietly.

That said, there have been Kings before who have disappointed and we have ignored them. The Thicket and its creatures do not meddle in the affairs of men, child. We have watched you kill each other for centuries and we have not involved ourselves. But on this occasion we have been drawn into the struggles of Morgravia and Briavel because of the misuse of magic.

'You speak of Myrren's gift, your majesty?'

The King hesitated briefly. *That included, yes. It was wrong of Elysius to channel his power through his daughter to such a vengeful end. His power, once we granted him access to the Wild, was to be used only for the good of the natural world.*

Fynch felt compelled to defend Elysius. 'I don't think he fully realised what the repercussions could be, your majesty.'

Magic is always dangerous, Fynch, even when used with the best of intentions. There are always repercussions; sometimes we are unable to see what they are until it is too late. This is why the Thicket and its magic has been deliberately shielded from men. Myrren's gift has already claimed four lives. Wyl Thirsk should have died; instead he is abroad and carrying a deadly enchantment. None of us knows where it could end.

'Wyl didn't ask for it, your majesty,' Fynch mumbled, not meaning to sound petulant.

I know, my son, the King replied gently. *I feel great sorrow for Wyl, who is one of the best amongst men — as was his father. It is the magic itself that troubles me and how it will continue to reverberate through the world of men. I mean to end it here.*

'Destroy Wyl?' Fynch exclaimed.

In a way he is already dead, the creature answered.

Fynch did not like the resignation in the Dragon King's voice. He grasped for placation, desperate to prevent this powerful being from hurting Wyl. 'The Thicket and its creatures have asked me to kill Rashlyn, your majesty, and with their help I will endeavour to rid the land of the destroyer. Both brothers will be no more. The magic will end.'

Not really, child, for now you possess it. Rashlyn wishes to control the natural world. He is a corrupter of natural things. He wants power over the beasts. But Celimus is just as dangerous. He too wants power but of a different kind. I fear that if we do not destroy Rashlyn these two ambitious men might join together. I know how the minds of greedy men work, and should they claim the Razors and Briavel as their own, they will almost certainly turn their attention towards the Wild. With Celimus's help, Rashlyn will try to destroy the Thicket. The King sighed. *We do not wish to engage in such a confrontation.*

'What can I do to help, your majesty?' Fynch asked, desperation seeping into his voice.

I grant you permission to use the magic of the Thicket to aid Wyl Thirsk in his bid to rid Morgravia of its King, for without Celimus I do not believe Rashlyn's madness can be fully unleashed.

Fynch nodded thoughtfully, relief flooding his small body that the Warrior King did not mean to attack Wyl directly. He recognised that the dragon warrior had not offered his own mighty strength or powers, only that of the Thicket. Fynch also knew that the creatures of the Thicket would insist on keeping their secrets. He already felt a part of this mysterious community and was convinced he would do everything in his power to protect them and their magic.

'Celimus has no heir,' Fynch cautioned, even though he presumed the royal creature knew as much.

Morgravia will survive. Do what you must. Knave is your Guide – use his wisdom well, child, and your own powers sparingly. I presume Elysius explained the price you may be required to pay?

Fynch nodded. 'He did.'

The King waited, wondering whether the child would expand on his brief answer. A plea for mercy perhaps; a musing as to whether his life could somehow be spared despite the rule of the use of this magic. But no further words came. The King beat his wings in appreciation of the humility of this boy who was prepared to give everything of himself on behalf of those he loved and who asked for nothing in return.

The warrior dragon's gaze penetrated deep into Fynch's heart and he was surprised to see there a startling and precious secret regarding this boy. He had not expected it but the discovery warmed him. Should he share it? The child's life was already forfeit; what could be gained from adding more confusion? The King felt sorrow well up that they would use this boy so. But there was no other way. Fynch was the sacrifice, though it cut him deeply to send his own to die.

Then we remain in your debt, Fynch. The Thicket and its

creatures will always hold you in their hearts. We bless you and hold our faith in you with reverence.

There was too much emotion swirling through Fynch for him to risk another word to this mightiest of beasts. Instead he bowed to show his complete acceptance. The royal creature acknowledged it with another powerful flapping of its wings, driving Fynch to the ground as it lifted effortlessly into the air and disappeared.

Roark and Knave were at the boy's side again.

He has not appeared to us in an age, Knave said, the awe still evident in his voice. *He came to pay homage only to you, child.*

Fynch was unable to respond, overwhelmed by this fateful meeting with the King of the Beasts.

Knave understood and nuzzled his friend's small hand. *Come, Faith Fynch, we have a journey to begin.*

CHAPTER 4

Lost in bleak thoughts, Queen Valentyna leaned on her elbows against the cool whitestone of the walkway that linked two of the palace towers. It was her private place, one which she rarely shared. The last person she had permitted to spend time with her here was Koreldy, and before him, Fynch. She could not help but think of those two friends now; both lost to her, both so keenly missed it felt like an open wound. With her face cupped in her hands she stared out across the Briavellian moors she loved so much and marvelled at a hawk hovering far ahead in the distance, watching patiently as it waited for its prey. Suddenly it plunged, arrowlike, towards the ground, making the Queen feel breathless for the small creature about to lose its life.

That was how she felt. Vulnerable, and now suddenly exposed and helpless. Celimus of Morgravia was the hawk and she the creature giving up her life to him. Valentyna straightened, shook her head clear of her dark musings and tried to focus on happier times. During her childhood she had nicknamed this corridor the 'bridge' and had taunted her nursemaids by hiding from them on its narrow height. Her father had delighted in her fearlessness, even while admonishing her for disobeying her carers.

Despite her best attempts, the happy memories were no match for the present-day threat from Celimus. He re-entered her thoughts to quench the brightness like a stormcloud blocking out the sun. Rumblings of war were filtering back via Briavellian spies in Morgravia. By all reports, the Legion was preparing for battle and Valentyna did not have to ponder too hard to guess at their enemy. Was it a ruse? Just an empty threat? Her instincts told her so, but still she would need to tread with the greatest of care. Valentyna's good sense warned her that her relationship with Celimus teetered on a knife edge and all that stood between peace for her subjects and almost certain slaughter was her written consent to marriage with the Morgravian King.

For that tenuous security she owed thanks to Chancellor Krell who had forced her hand and made her send the letter. And yet Valentyna could only hold her head in despair at the damage done by Chancellor Krell's subsequent well-meaning but short-sighted interference in writing to his counterpart in Morgravia, Chancellor Jessom, to advise of recent developments in Briavel. Now Celimus was aware that Felrawthy not only still had a duke but one with sympathies for Briavel. Oh, she could scream just thinking on it. In fact, she was still so angry at the old man's actions it had taken all her willpower to maintain her composure at Krell's funeral. He had been quietly buried in the palace cemetery. No family had come for him; he went into the ground as lonely as he went to his god, believing he was despised.

Krell had diligently and tirelessly worked for the Briavellian royal family for nigh on two score years. He was like a piece of old furniture: comfy, reliable, always there in the same place. Valentyna had grown up knowing that her father relied on him, and had come to appreciate his loyalty and advice herself. Despite her anger that he had invited such ruin with an ill-considered move, Valentyna could not help but feel a keen sorrow that this good man would be remembered for that one poor decision amongst a host of wise ones during a solid and devoted career serving the Crown.

Right now, in a quiet moment of reflection and private recrimination, she regretted her harsh words to him. She had no doubt that she had prompted his suicide and it was something she knew she would have to live with. Valentyna had shed tears for him in private and she would be lying if she did not admit to herself that she missed his steadfast counsel. But she had also spoken the truth when she told him she could never forgive him for his terrible error. He had overstepped his authority and in doing so had risked the lives of all Briavellians.

Morgravia's King was vain, avaricious and cruel but he was not a dullard. Due to Krell's poor judgement, Celimus would now know about Alyd Donal's remains being smuggled into Briavel, and that the Queen he thought he had well and truly cornered had serious misgivings and was consorting with his enemies.

A man cleared his throat quietly at one end of the walkway to interrupt her musings. She looked towards him, knowing who it would be – one of the few she allowed to come to her here if duty called. All other servants were banned from tracking her down to the bridge.

'Liryk. Please join me,' she said. He bowed in respect and walked to the centre of the bridge.

'It's beautiful, isn't it?' Valentyna said wistfully, indicating the view before them.

'More than that, your highness,' her army's commander admitted. 'It feeds the soul.'

'Liryk,' she said, unable to help herself, 'you're a poet.'

It was good to hear her playful. That tone had all but disappeared these past weeks. 'No, your majesty. I just never get tired of these moors. Always happy to see them when I return to Werryl after being away.'

'And so how are you and I going to give this up?'

'My Queen?'

'This,' she said, moving her hand in a sweeping arc. 'We will be giving all this to Morgravia.' There was a note of anger in her voice now. 'It will no longer be ours.'

'Not giving, your highness,' Liryk proposed gently. 'I'd prefer to think of it as sharing.'

'Celimus is forcing us to give up Briavel to him,' she said coldly. 'He is blackmailing me, Commander, and there's not a thing I can do about it. If I want our young men to live, I have to give up the realm.'

'Pardon me, your highness, but I – and I think I can speak for all of your loyal subjects in this – do not view it that way. We applaud this move.'

The Queen sighed. 'And I am grateful for that,' she said. 'But will you thank me when King Celimus starts to stamp his own brutal form of authority across Briavel?'

Liryk had no answer for this and the Queen did not expect one.

'What news, anyway, Commander Liryk?'

'The Legion is certainly gearing for movement east now,

your highness. If we are going to placate our neighbouring King, we need to do it soon.'

Valentyna closed her eyes and took a deep breath. She cast one more fond glance towards the moors and then gave her orders briskly.

'Have Crys Donal summoned, please. I will meet with you both in my study. Elspyth too.'

'At once, your highness.'

Valentyna watched him leave, hating what she was about to do.

The Queen dismissed the servant and poured the two men a glass of wine herself.

'Where is Elspyth?' she enquired of Liryk as he took the goblet from her.

'Your highness, she is nowhere to be found,' he answered, silently happy for the woman's disappearance. He had agreed with Krell that Elspyth's influence on the Queen was dangerous. The Morgravian woman had fired their Queen's spirit; made her feel strong and capable of determining her own destiny by defying Celimus.

Valentyna glanced at Crys who shrugged. 'I haven't seen her for a couple of days if truth be known. I thought she was with you, your majesty.'

'Strange,' Valentyna murmured. 'Your search has been thorough?' she asked her commander.

'I've sent several runners to comb the palace, your highness. She's certainly not in any of the usual places.'

'Has anyone checked her chambers?' Crys asked. 'You lent her some garments, your highness,' he added. 'Are they still there?'

'You think she's fled?' the Queen exclaimed.

'Did she tell you about a man called Lothryn?' Crys replied, calmly sipping his wine. He suspected that they would not find Elspyth. She had mentioned several times to him that she was no longer needed here. He also suspected his own stay had worn thin, and who could blame the Briavellians with the Legion gathering in force across the border.

The Queen nodded slowly. 'Only vaguely.'

'There's a story attached to him,' he explained. 'It involves Koreldy.' Once again it pained him to see the Queen react to the man's name. Wyl had given firm instructions that Valentyna was not to learn the truth about Koreldy, but it seemed unkind to Crys not to enlighten her that the person she obviously loved was not dead as she suspected but roaming the land in a new guise. The thought disturbed him, but Crys had personally witnessed the transference of Wyl's soul from one body to the next. There was no escaping the truth: Wyl Thirsk lived. Through the curse upon him, he had claimed first Koreldy, then Faryl, and, more recently and chillingly, his own sister, Ylena. Crys felt a lurch of despair as he remembered that terrible night at Felrawthy. The next day had been worse, but he knew he must not think on that now. *Bury your hurts*, his mother used to say. *Bring them out only when you are alone and strong enough to look at them*. And so he had somehow buried the despair of losing his family so cruelly and tried not to dwell on their deaths.

'Crys?'

He was embarrassed to realise both the Queen and Liryk were watching him.

'I – I'm sorry. Lost myself there,' he said, not wanting to say more.

'You were telling us about Elspyth and Lothryn,' Valentyna prompted, deliberately avoiding mentioning her former lover's name.

'That's right,' Crys continued. 'The Mountain Dweller, Lothryn, saved the lives of Elspyth and Koreldy in the Razors. No one knows if he survived Cailech's wrath at helping the prisoners to escape. Elspyth is determined to learn his fate.'

Neither of them referred to the fact that they knew Elspyth was in love with Lothryn. 'And you think she's gone back?' Valentyna suggested.

'I think she's capable of doing something that bull-headed, yes,' he said and smiled gently to reassure the Queen that he admired Elspyth for her courage.

'Into the Razors?' Liryk queried. 'Alone?'

'I don't know, sir. She's a passionate girl. I don't think fear stops her doing anything. If not for Elspyth I would be dead with the rest of my family.'

The new Duke of Felrawthy could refer to his loved ones now without threat of anger or tears. His brief time in Werryl, offering a distance from all things familiar, and the new title by which everyone was determined to address him had made the difference between him collapsing into inconsolable anguish or rising to the challenge of what he was born and bred to do. It was what his fine parents would have expected of him.

A knock came at the door. Liryk put his glass down. 'Shall I see to it, your highness? It may be the messengers.'

'Please,' the Queen said, distracted as she pondered the business of Elspyth's disappearance. 'I miss Krell,' she muttered.

Crys held his tongue. No one had heard the exchange between the Queen and her Chancellor, which had preceded his death, but Valentyna had openly admitted that she had driven him to anguish with her harsh criticism. Crys had to admire the Queen for her forthright manner; she refused to shrink from blame but accepted and dealt with it as best she could. Krell's death had been a shock for everyone, most of all Liryk, but the doughty soldier had kept his feelings to himself and remained stoic throughout the funeral and the ensuing mourning that had gripped the palace.

Crys sipped his wine quietly, wondering why he had been summoned to what appeared to be a formal meeting and imagining how Morgravia could only benefit from having this woman sitting upon its throne, even though it meant she shared it with the hated Celimus. It would be better for her, he was sure, if he was to leave Briavel. Perhaps he should offer and save her the trial of asking him to do just that.

Liryk returned to disturb his thoughts. 'Your majesty, we found this note in Elspyth's chamber.'

'Anything else?' Valentyna asked, as she broke the wax seal. 'Clothes?'

'Nothing, your highness,' he replied, watching her frown as she quickly read the note's contents.

Valentyna looked up and sighed. 'Your hunch is correct, Crys. She believes she has done what she came here to do and has taken her leave.'

'Gone to the Razors?' Crys enquired.

'It doesn't say but I suspect you're right. I know how fond she was of this man Lothryn. If I were her, I too would want to know the truth of his fate.'

There was another knock at the door. Valentyna could not disguise her frustrated expression at being interrupted again. She stuffed the note into her pocket and stood. 'Gentlemen, I'm going for a ride. We shall continue this meeting this evening, please, when we can talk without disturbance. There are many things to discuss and I need to think. Liryk, would you see to that?' She nodded towards the door. 'I'll leave by the back way.'

The two men stood and watched her go.

The highest point of the moors was the furthest Valentyna could get from her subjects – or so she liked to believe – and the ideal place to vent her fears or frustrations. However, the ever-present soldiers, of course, were not far enough away, so the blood-curdling shriek she longed to let rip was not a good idea. She gave a deep groan instead. Too many of those she had loved or trusted had been taken from her or had left her of their own accord. She stared back towards the palace and counted them off softly to herself.

Her father: murdered. Wyl Thirsk: murdered. Romen Koreldy: murdered. Fynch, her little rock of strength: disappeared, and with him the strange yet somehow re-assuring presence of Knave. Now Elspyth, her new friend and confidante, had disappeared as well, almost certainly advancing towards her own death as she ventured into the Mountain Kingdom to discover the fate of her beloved Lothryn.

Valentyna paused in her account of her personal sorrows to think on those of Crys Donal. An entire family slaugh-tered in one evening. So much death. And now, in order to protect Briavel, she would have to banish her latest friend too. That was what she needed to discuss with the new Duke of Felrawthy, but this afternoon had proved impossible with all of its interruptions.

The Queen of Briavel shook her head with despair. Almost all of this destruction swirling about her was the work of one man. One cruel, scheming, greedy man. The man she would have to marry if she wanted to prevent further deaths.

She cast a disconsolate glance towards the soldiers shuffling in the shade of the copse in the distance. Three were now being sent to shadow her every move. She hated it, but put up with it. Liryk's caution was well-founded but she missed her freedom. She waved to them to ensure they understood that she was fine and was just taking some time alone. She inhaled the sweet air of the moors and felt even more despondent. Everyone seemed to be worrying about her at the moment. She sensed her advisers observing her; could feel their concern tightening around her like a bandage, constricting her free will. Valentyna knew what they feared – and they were right to fear it, for if she could find a way to avoid this marriage, she would renege in a blink. Except her good sense told her it was impossible. No one was going to save her. The nobles had told her to find Ylena Thirsk, but that was pointless. How could it make any difference? Ylena's word might convince them that Celimus was a cold-blooded murderer, but in all truth she knew it would not make them change their minds about the marriage.

She thought about Ylena Thirsk and the terrible things the young woman had experienced. Crys had explained to Valentyna what Ylena had been through just to get herself to Felrawthy. It had made the Queen shudder to imagine how Wyl's sister had coped with yet more terror after what she had already suffered at Stoneheart. Ylena was younger than her and had shown such courage. She would have to find similar courage now and face her destiny. Her father had fought to keep Briavel safe. She must do the same, just in a different manner. She would buy its peace with her body. Give herself over to this hateful man and let him parade her before his minions and use her for his pleasures. But he would not have her love – ever. That belonged to one man alone, and he was now dead. So she would give herself to Celimus in the hope that some bright, sparkling, untainted good might come of it. They might produce a child. And into that child she would pour all of her love; everything she denied Celimus and had hoped to give to Romen Koreldy. She would raise a proud sovereign to take the throne of Briavel one day.

Valentyna sighed as the soft breeze tousled her already messy hair. 'Give me a sign, Shar,' she said to the gentle wind, hoping it would carry her plea to the god. 'Show me that marrying Celimus is the right decision.'

She felt like weeping at her pathetic words. Instead she wiped away the single tear which had fallen, rubbed at her other eye just in case, and willed herself to be strong and live up to the woman her father believed she had become. She strode back towards the soldiers. They had already spotted her movement and busied themselves with preparing the horses ready to ride again.

Squinting into the sun, Valentyna did not see the bird at first. It was its gentle song that attracted her attention and she looked around for the music-maker. It was perched on a low branch of the great elm she was about to walk beneath. She recognised its family immediately; King Valor had been a keen bird-spotter and had gone to some pains to school his only child into recognising various species. It was a beautiful little chaffinch and its pretty music made her smile. She whistled back at it and it kept singing long after she had passed by, taken Bonny's reins and departed the copse.

It was only as Valentyna guided her horse onto Werryl Bridge some half hour later that she realised she had been humming a tune to herself on the journey back. The bird-song had reminded her of a well-known ballad created by Briavel's leading jongleur in honour of her nineteenth birthday: 'Wait For Me, My Love'. Valentyna had always loved the melody and its lyrics were beautiful. She began to sing them privately in her mind and they stayed with her as she ascended into the palace proper.

Ranald, a stableboy, bowed and reached for the Queen's reins.

'Thank you, Ranald,' Valentyna said and found a smile for the eager boy.

'Your highness,' he beamed, unable to mask his pleasure at serving the Queen so directly.

'It was a lovely ride,' she said to him, enjoying his enthusiasm; wishing she could be ten again, without a care in the world.

'I'm glad, your highness. Bonny's a beautiful girl. My favourite,' he chirped, ignoring the scowl from the stable-master who had come out to watch his young charge receive the horses correctly and no doubt thought him far too chatty.

'Mine too,' Valentyna said and winked at Ranald.

As she turned away from the boy the refrain of the

ballad filled her mind again — and its resonance struck
her.

> *Wait for me, my love*
> *I shall return one day*
> *Accept not another's words*
> *Be with me only, I pray.*

Valentyna stood rigid in the courtyard as the words played
over in her mind. Men walked around her and horses
neighed. Dogs growled over a bone and busy servants
criss-crossed the yard on various errands, calling to each
other. Amongst the activity, their Queen stood still and
silent, deep in her own thoughts. What had sounded so
poignant and charming on her nameday now sounded like
a message from the dead. A warning.

'Romen!' she whispered fearfully, her breath catching
in her throat.

'Your majesty, are you unwell?' someone enquired.

'I'm fine,' she stammered, coming back to the present
and almost running from the courtyard. She flew into the
palace and up the beautiful staircase, and up the next
flight and the next. Servants watched perplexed as their
sovereign ignored their salutations and curtsies, fleeing
past them towards her study on the topmost level, her
boots clicking loudly on the flagstones. Finally she came
to her father's former chamber and slammed the door
behind her.

Leaning against its solid wood panels, she held her head
as her breath came in great sad wrenches. *Wait for me, my
love.* Was this Shar's sign? Was this a message? What had
prompted the song and its lyrics to come into her head?

The bird. A chaffinch! Was this a warning from Fynch? Was he asking her to wait? For whom? Romen was dead! Cold, lifeless, bloodless . . . gone.

She realised she was sobbing and felt ashamed of herself for losing control. What was happening to her? Storming out of meetings, crying violently, listening to birds, believing in magic. She was going mad.

But she had asked for a sign. Perhaps this was it. She could be imagining it, of course, clutching at anything to save her from the touch of Celimus, but it felt so right to believe in it.

'But who am I waiting for?' she said into the quiet of her room.

She was startled by a knock at the door.

'A moment, please,' she called, instantly embarrassed at being found in this state. Let them wait, she thought more coldly, as she splashed water over her face from a basin in a tiny closet. She dried herself with a linen cloth and smoothed back her hair as best she could.

She touched her fingers to her father's desk and drew strength from his presence which she still felt in this room, then took a steadying breath. Her mind was racing in all directions but she had duties to perform and it would not do to become flighty and hysterical when she most needed to be steadfast. She reminded herself that Briavel still looked to her for leadership, even if it was collectively casting her to the wolves – or wolf, should she say.

Valentyna cleared her throat. 'Come.'

One of the older pages opened the door and bowed. 'Your majesty, forgive my disturbance.'

'That's all right, Justen, who has sent you?'

'Commander Liryk, your majesty. He asked me to find you the moment you returned from your ride. He says it is urgent.'

'Oh? A problem?'

'A visitor, your majesty.'

Valentyna frowned. 'Another one? Can't Liryk handle it?' she said irritably, even though she knew Justen could not answer. He was simply following instructions.

The page blinked, not sure what to say. She felt immediately sorry for showing her vexation.

'Did Commander Liryk give you the name of this visitor, Justen?' she said, more gently now.

'Yes, your majesty. It is a woman by the name of Ylena Thirsk.'

CHAPTER 5

Maegryn met the riders and was alarmed to see one man return in a worse state than when he had left.

'He'll be all right,' Aremys assured the anxious stablemaster as he handed him the reins of Galapek and Rashlyn's horse.

'I couldn't care less about him,' Maegryn said, and the vehemence in his voice surprised Aremys. 'The horses are my concern. No problems there?'

'Galapek got himself a little rattled over something but he calmed quickly. Just skittish,' Aremys answered, skirting the truth. The fewer lies he told the better. 'He's more incredible to ride than I could have imagined. Thank you, Maegryn.'

The man could not help himself: he enjoyed the praise and it showed. 'Yes, he's a beauty this one. A real find.'

'Where did he come from?' It was a casually put question.

'The barshi gave him as a present to the King. Had the horse sent secretly in from somewhere apparently. He won't tell anyone from where.'

'That's a little odd, isn't it? You'd think that if there were more like this one the King would be keen to know.'

Maegryn shrugged. 'We're not allowed to ask too much about Galapek, sir.' He looked embarrassed. 'I'll be off then, sir. I'm glad you enjoyed the ride.'

Aremys knew there would be little further information to be won from Maegryn today. The stablemaster had suddenly closed up.

'Thank you. I hope you won't mind if I look in on him again?'

'I'm sure he'll be glad to see you, sir. You're one of the very few he permits near him. I think he's taken a shine to you.' He smiled.

Aremys stroked Galapek's twitching withers as the horse was led past him. He was hoping for another sign from the animal but got nothing.

Myrt was barking orders for Rashlyn – who was lying on the ground still mumbling his strange nonsense – to be taken to his private quarters. Myrt called for a physic as well.

Then the Mountain man turned to Aremys. 'Come on,' he said. 'The worst is still before us.'

Aremys sighed, needing no confirmation. Cailech.

They tracked the King down to his wine cellar, catacomb-like chambers dug into the ground beneath a separate stone building. Descending the flagged stairs into the musty darkness Aremys smelled earth and spice; mixed with the aroma of yeast and the oak of the barrels it was a comforting blend. It was cool down here but not cold; the temperature would remain much the same year round, he guessed, and the vaulted ceilings combined with the peace and stillness to give the cellar a chapel-like quality. It felt safe here.

'We're sorry to interrupt you, your majesty,' Myrt began.

The King turned from his discussion with the cellarmaster and grinned at the newcomers. Obviously in a good mood, Aremys thought. What a pity we're about to ruin it.

'Farrow, you have to try this!' Cailech called over the barrels. 'It's to be our best vintage yet.' The King slapped his cellarmaster on the back in praise, then lifted the long-handled tasting cup to his lips and drained it. 'Ah, nectar,' he said, delighted.

'Sire,' Myrt bowed. When he straightened, his expression in the diffused light of the beeswax candles was sufficiently sombre to win Cailech's attention. The King's smile faded.

'You look like you've swallowed bad meat, Myrt. What's wrong?'

'It's the barshi, sire,' he began. Cailech handed the tasting cup back to the cellarmaster who stepped aside. 'He's unwell,' Myrt added.

'Oh?' Cailech looked towards Aremys. 'Farrow, what's this all about?'

Aremys was surprised to be brought into the conversation. He wanted to clear his throat but figured that might make him appear nervous so he just began talking, sticking as closely to the truth as he could. 'We were resting, my lord, or at least the horses were after a ride around the lake.'

'We were at the Ring, sire,' Myrt interjected.

Cailech nodded. 'Go on.' Again he looked to Aremys.

'I was drinking at the stream and Myrt and Rashlyn were leaning against the boulders. Rashlyn was eating, and was seemingly in good health. We had been discussing my headaches and he approached me at the water's edge to hand me a small bottle of a concoction he said would ease my discomfort – when the horses distracted us.' Aremys had decided that the plain truth, rather than a version of it, was the only course with Cailech.

'It was Galapek, sire,' Myrt said. 'Something startled him: we don't know what. We couldn't see anything near him.'

'And?' Cailech said, the hard green gaze impaling Aremys where he stood.

'Well, as I recall, I rushed over to help Myrt calm the stallion. His panic was over as quickly as it began – perhaps he was stung by a bee or something irritated him, we have no idea. When we turned back to Rashlyn he was lying on the ground, seemingly having some sort of attack.'

'Attack?'

'Like a fit, sire,' Myrt qualified.

'He lost control of his body for a few moments,' Aremys said, 'and then he became rigid. I checked immediately for a pulse – which was strong – but by then he was unconscious.'

The King's face showed nothing of what he was thinking. 'How long did this episode last?'

'It was over almost as soon as it began,' Myrt said. 'We laid him on his horse and got him back here as fast as we could.' He dared not look at Aremys as he said this. Hurrying back to the fortress had been the last thing on their minds.

'And where is Rashlyn now?'

'He seems to have regained his wits, sire, so I had him carried to his rooms and sent a physic along too,' Myrt reported.

'You have no idea what this is about?' The King looked between the two men.

Myrt shrugged and shook his head. Aremys figured the King needed more than sheepish shrugs. 'I thought it might have been the cheese that stuck in his throat but his passage was clear,' he fabricated. 'And Myrt tells me the food was fresh so we know he has not been poisoned by it. Does he suffer from fits, my lord?' he added innocently.

'It seems he does now,' Cailech growled, the breezy mood blown through and replaced with what felt like a gathering storm. 'I shall go and see him. How was Galapek, Farrow?'

The King switched subjects and disposition so adroitly, Aremys was sure he would never succeed in preparing himself for it.

'Even more magnificent than I'd hoped, thank you, sire. A truly beautiful creature. I hope you will let me ride him again some time.'

A glance passed between the King and his warrior. 'I'm glad to hear it. Myrt, you can accompany me to the barshi's chambers. Farrow—'

'Sire?'

'I'll see you later. You will be leaving in the early hours of tomorrow for Morgravia.'

Aremys, back in his chamber with the familiar guard outside, sighed in frustration. He was not going to attempt an escape and felt sure Cailech knew this. But it seemed the King was keen to remind him that he was a prisoner and under the control of the monarch, hence the armed guard.

'Not for long,' Aremys muttered under his breath as he flung his water flask into a corner. He would gladly leave for Morgravia in a few hours, and from there he would win his freedom. He liked the Mountain People. He did not even mind living here in the fortress amongst them, could almost see a pleasant life in the Razors stretching out before him, but he was beholden to no man, not even a King, and certainly not one who stopped just short of shackling him.

It irritated him that Cailech could be so friendly one moment and so domineering the next. Surely the King knew that Aremys would far rather give his help to him than Celimus? In truth, though, he could not blame Cailech entirely for remaining suspicious. One didn't stay a King if one trusted everyone, especially strangers who appeared out of the blue with no tangible explanation for how they had arrived.

That took him back to his musings about the Thicket and his realisation that the strange clump of nature was clearly able to make a decision for itself, and had decided to expel him. But the Thicket and its magic was a phenomenon to be pondered another time. His immediate interest now was Galapek and how to help the horse.

Aremys replayed the afternoon's events in his mind. Rashlyn's collapse had definitely coincided with the animal's shriek, he was sure of it, which meant something had disturbed them both. There was nothing in the vicinity to alarm them or it would have created a similar reaction in himself and Myrt. No, this was something else. More like a disturbance in the strange magic that riddled the horse. Could it be that the wild-looking healer was bound to the stallion in some way?

Aremys followed that line of thought. What if Rashlyn himself had cast some sort of spell upon the horse? That might account for a bond between them. Why though? It wasn't as though Rashlyn had shown a particular attachment to the beast, so the link was not a personal one. And if it was his magic that permeated the stallion, why had he interfered with the animal?

Because Cailech asked him to?

But why would the King ask something like that? Aremys thought it unlikely that Cailech possessed the cruelty that would prompt the idea of hurting an animal in this way.

But what if the idea had come from Rashlyn? 'Because Rashlyn could perform the enchantment and Cailech allowed him to,' Aremys said quietly into the stillness of his chamber.

The notion took a firm place among his thoughts. He nodded. Yes, that made more sense. Aremys thought back to Wyl's account of Cailech's horrific threat during the feast when he had presented the Morgravian prisoners as a dish to his people. Wyl had been sure Rashlyn was behind that hideous episode, but that suggested the barshi was capable of persuading the King to do things not of his own volition. How could Cailech, usually so dominant, be so weak in the company of Rashlyn?

Aremys had no answer for that. He returned to his original puzzle. Something had disturbed the magic linking the barshi and the horse. It couldn't have been the Thicket or he too would have felt the effects, but perhaps it had resonated through the Thicket for him to feel it at all. Had Wyl done something to disturb the balance? Unlikely, or the Thicket would probably have protested more strongly.

Aremys put his head in his hands, frustrated by his swirling thoughts that took him nowhere. *Think!* he commanded himself. Could it be something to do with Elysius? Had Wyl made it through and met the manwitch? Was that it? 'Possibly,' he muttered but that did not help him to get any closer to the riddle that was Galapek.

And then he remembered the most chilling moment of the whole sorry afternoon. How could he have forgotten it? The horse had somehow communicated a name to him: Elspyth. He began to pace now. It could be a coincidence, of course, but an unlikely one. Aremys felt positive that the horse had once belonged to Lothryn, or somehow held the secret of what had happened to Lothryn. He wanted to yell out his frustrations, but that would bring the guard running. He punched the wall instead.

If Cailech wanted to punish Lothryn, why hurt his horse? And how would a horse know of Elspyth, for Shar's sake!

'You're going mad, Farrow,' he told himself finally, when nothing made sense any more. 'Now you've contrived a magical talking horse.'

He decided to clean up and go in search of Myrt and more answers. Something else had begun to niggle at him and he wanted to find out if it had any basis in fact. Discovering he was right might not advance his cause but it might provide some leverage if and when required.

Aremys opened his chamber door and explained to the

guard, a nice young fellow with an unfortunate harelip, that he needed to find Myrt. The guard nodded and a shy smile emerged on his deformed mouth when Aremys said, 'After you.' It was a joke they shared from when the guard, Jos, was first assigned to Aremys and had made the wry comment that if he proceeded first, the mercenary might bash him on the head and escape.

This, of course, had made Aremys laugh. 'Look at you, lad,' he had replied, grinning. 'I'd need an axe just to dent you. You're built like an ox. You terrify me.' He could see that Jos had taken the remark as a rare compliment coming from a man akin to a bear. They had never spoken at length but Aremys had been sure to keep the words they had shared light-hearted and friendly and Jos had always responded, albeit cautiously. The guard was only just into manhood and still establishing a reserve of confidence to draw upon, a process probably made more difficult by taunts about his affliction, Aremys figured. When they walked shoulder to shoulder, as now, the mercenary was careful always to defer to his guard in the hope that the young man might take some self-assurance from it.

They found Myrt at the main stables. The Mountain man nodded when he saw them. 'Go get your meal, Jos. Leave him with me. I'm getting our stuff ready anyway. We leave soon.'

Aremys grinned at his young keeper. 'Don't forget what I said about that young lady,' he said, referring back to an earlier exchange. 'You should tell her,' and he winked.

Jos chuckled, a hand flying up to cover his crooked smile.

'What have you been filling that lad's head with?'

'Nothing that didn't fill yours when you were his age, Myrt,' Aremys replied, helping him to lift a heavy crate into a cart. 'Why aren't you with a woman, Myrt?'

'Who says I'm not?' the man countered, somewhat sharply.

Aremys shrugged. 'You haven't mentioned a wife—'

Myrt reached for another crate. 'I have no wife.'

'I see.'

'Oh? And what do you see?'

'Nothing, my friend. What's wrong with you?'

The warrior flicked away what sounded like an apology. 'Cailech's furious about what happened. Kept asking me what you were doing when Rashlyn passed out.'

'Mmm, I thought he might. I told you he suspects me of knowing something.'

'He's not so suspicous that he's not pressing ahead with the journey. In fact he's brought our departure forward — we leave at sundown. You, me, Byl and two others.'

'So what's all this stuff?'

'Gifts for the Morgravian King.'

'Ah, goodwill.'

Myrt grunted. 'Help me load the rest of it.'

They worked quietly and quickly for the next few minutes.

Maegryn appeared. 'I've picked out the horses you'll be taking, Myrt. I've given Farrow Cherub.'

'Sounds a bit effeminate for me,' Aremys said, joking.

'Does that worry you?' Myrt asked.

'No,' Aremys replied cheerfully. 'I'll just feel ridiculous calling out "Whoa, Cherub".'

'That's the joke, Farrow,' Maegryn said, grinning. 'He's anything but!'

The two Mountain men laughed and Aremys joined in, but he was sure of it now: Myrt had a secret of his own and the mercenary intended to exploit it.

'We're expected at the King's chamber,' said the warrior. 'He wants us to sup with him before we leave.'

Aremys nodded. 'Are we finished here?'

'Yes, I'd say so. Thanks, Maegryn. Back later then.'

'As it suits you, Myrt. I'll be waiting.' The stablemaster turned back to the stables.

'I need to talk to you first,' Aremys said as they made their way towards the fortress.

'I reckoned you might. Follow me.'

They walked in what Aremys hoped was a companionable silence through several courtyards towards a part of the fortress he had not been to before.

'Where are we going?' he said.

'My home,' came the brief reply.

Myrt stopped a few times to share swift words with various people. He asked one youngster to find Byl and have him call at Myrt's home after dusk. The big warrior introduced Aremys to all those he spoke with and the mercenary noted how they deferred to Myrt. He presumed the man had taken on a stronger leadership role since the demise of Lothryn. He mentioned as much.

'I suppose so,' Myrt replied. 'I don't really want it, but Cailech finds it easier to rely on me to pass on his orders. I'd prefer everything to be back how it was.'

'With Lothryn as the King's second, you mean?'

'Yes, he was worthy of it and good at it.'

'Why was he better than you?'

'Because he understood Cailech, and because he was not afraid of him. They grew up together; they were friends first and foremost. A bit like how it was between the old Morgravian King and his General, that Fergys Thirsk. They were great friends from childhood, I was told.'

'So I've heard,' Aremys said.

'Well, friendships made young like that have longevity and there's great affection there too. I'll never have that kind of relationship with the King. And when a relationship like that is broken, it hurts.'

'You sound like you're speaking from experience, Myrt.'

'In a way,' the man muttered, hurrying Aremys down a short flight of steps.

'Did you know Lothryn from childhood as well?'

Myrt glowered at Aremys and his persistent questions. 'Yes, as a matter of fact.'

They emerged into the open again, into what appeared to be a walled community. The place took Aremys by surprise. 'Shar! How amazing.'

His obvious delight broke the tension. Myrt grinned. 'More of Cailech's dreaming. This is his great social experiment.'

'Explain it to me,' Aremys said, gazing around at the hive of activity.

'Well, not everyone chooses to live in and around the fortress, as I'm sure you've gathered. Originally the Mountain Dwellers were different tribes, spread throughout the Razors. Cailech not only united us into one people but dreamed of forming a small city – he wants the fortress to become the true heart of the Razors and he is encouraging people to settle in amongst it. He dreams of his own Pearlis or Werryl, I suppose you could say. He has built homes for the settlers and has encouraged markets to be held regularly. He's even set up a school, which is very popular and getting bigger and bigger. Our King encourages education and at his urging, more people are bringing their children to the classroom, which, of course, leads them to see the benefit of settling close to the school. Cailech has organised special rewards for families who set up home here permanently. It's really quite a new experience and a lot of our folk are watching to see how it goes. I think it will work. I believe Cailech will have his city in years to come.'

'It looks like the community is thriving,' Aremys said, unable to keep the awe from his voice. 'I can see from the layout that it's been thought through very carefully.'

'It has.' Myrt smiled. 'The King didn't want it emerging too haphazardly. So he put together a group of people who could plan for a village, out of which could grow a town, and who had the vision to see how a city might emerge one day. I was one of the first to live here and that encouraged others to come too. Lothryn lived not far from here, amongst a smaller group of senior people – formerly tribe leaders and family members distantly related to Cailech.'

'Does Cailech have a family of his own?'

'Oddly, no. We Mountain folk tend to have large family groups but Cailech was an only child. His mother died by accident, in a fire. Cailech was about thirteen when it happened. He was away with his father at the time, settling a dispute between the tribes.'

'Does he blame himself?'

'No, I don't think so. He knew it was an accident. But Lothryn told me the King never really got over the loss. That's why he's so keen on keeping families together, and he loves the youngsters. Part of his belief is that children thrive when they have elders around them and big family groups to teach them the right ways. I agree with that creed.'

'I would have thought that he'd have a wife then, his own family.'

Myrt shook his head and Aremys thought he saw something painful flicker across his expression. The Mountain man fought down whatever demon was rising. 'He hasn't had time to take a wife yet, I suppose.'

'And you, Myrt, what of your family?'

'I have a sister. I live with her. Her husband was one of those killed in the Grenadyn disaster. He was seventeen; they'd only been married a few weeks. I suppose you've heard of that incident?'

Aremys nodded. He knew only too well the story of Grenadyn's unwarranted attack on the Mountain People and the slaughter that ensued.

Myrt sighed. 'Well, my sister never got over her loss. She all but raised me. Now, I suppose, I look after her.'

'No love of your own, Myrt?'

The Mountain man walked on. 'One. That person did not want me,' he answered in a thick tone, and prevented any further conversation by stopping to chat with a shop-keeper selling candles.

Aremys took a moment to marvel again at Cailech's embryonic city. The laneways had been cobbled with stone from the mountains and it looked to him that more building was already under way, with more streets leading off the main one. It certainly was not Pearlis but it was bigger than any village he had encountered. There was a sense of sprawl about it; the place seemed well on its way to developing into a bustling town. He could not help but be impressed by this still relatively young King with such a vision for his realm, and it was this very moment when Aremys decided he would give his all towards helping these people. If somehow he could influence the attainment of a working peace between the two prideful monarchs of Morgravia and the north, then he would. Not for Cailech so much, but for Myrt and Byl, for Myrt's sister – perhaps he could atone for the sins of his own folk, for their stupidity all those years ago. For Maegryn and young Jos and, yes, even for Lothryn, wherever he was.

Like Wyl, Aremys wanted to believe that Lothryn was still alive. And if he was, he intended to find him. He was convinced it was the horse and its magic that would lead him to this man it seemed everyone had loved – even the King.

'Everyone except Rashlyn,' Myrt cautioned, when they were sitting in his small house a short time later and Aremys brought the subject back to Lothryn.

'Rashlyn didn't like him?'

'More to the point,' Myrt said, busying himself with a pot of tea at the hearth, 'Lothryn despised Rashlyn and the barshi knew it.'

'Why?'

'Cups are over there,' Myrt said, nodding towards a dresser. 'Lothryn objected to the influence Rashlyn has with the King. He admitted to me not long before he disappeared that it had got to the point where he felt something had to be done about it.'

Aremys almost made the terrible error of mentioning the feast and Cailech's threat to turn his people into cannibals by forcing them to eat the Morgravians. He stopped himself just in time and covered his near blunder by turning his back on the Mountain man to reach for the cups.

He brought them back to the small wooden table. 'What made him say that?'

Myrt poured boiling water over the leaves. 'Let that brew, shall we,' he said amiably. 'Well, there were many reasons. Cailech had been making erratic decisions, out of character for him – there was one particularly disturbing incident involving some Morgravian prisoners. He wanted to make an example of them as punishment to their people for killing some of ours. They weren't even the culprits, for Haldor's sake, they were just a raggle-taggle group of farmers who were sent into the Razors with one old soldier as a leader.'

Aremys held his breath. Myrt was almost certainly referring to Wyl's friend, Gueryn le Gant. He kept his voice casual. 'And?'

'The King's method of making an example of them was terrifying to say the least. I don't want to go into the details, but it never sat right with me, or any of us for that matter. Don't get me wrong, Cailech can kill with the best of them – as you know from the repercussions of the episode at Grenadyn – but he's not a cruel man by nature.'

Aremys nodded: he remembered the events on his island home only too well. He had held a crush for Lily Koreldy for several years, but she was older than he and no doubt had never even noticed the lumbering boy who turned a beetroot colour if ever he was in her presence. 'That was a terrible business.'

'Yes, but Cailech spared Romen Koreldy, even gave

him a home and looked after him for a while. They actually became quite good friends by the end of it, despite the trauma that sat between them.'

'I'm surprised Koreldy could forgive him.'

'Don't be fooled: Koreldy never forgave Cailech and the King knew it, which was why he warned him when he left that if he ever set foot in the Razor Kingdom again, he would lose his life.'

'So Koreldy was like me, eh? A very well-treated prisoner.'

Myrt turned the pot three times and grinned at Aremys's perplexed expression. 'Tradition,' he explained. 'Yes, Koreldy was dealt with in much the same way as we're treating you, except he was never entrusted with a mission for the good of our people.'

'Did you ever see Koreldy again?' Aremys asked. Myrt poured the tea, not answering. 'You know he was working for Celimus, don't you?' Aremys pressed. 'But actually he was working against him.'

That won the Mountain man's attention. 'What do you mean?'

'Koreldy hated Celimus, with good reason. The Morgravian King double-crossed him in an agreement they had. I know Koreldy stuck to the mercenaries' code of honour: he did his job and kept his counsel, but Celimus tried several times to have him killed for what he learned in doing that job.'

Myrt's eyes narrowed. 'You're talking about the death of the King of Briavel now, aren't you?' he guessed, and was glad to see he was right when Aremys nodded. 'What do you know about that?'

'Plenty. What are you prepared to swap for it?'

'What?' Myrt said, astonished. 'Swap information?'

'Yes,' Aremys said, reaching for his cup. 'Listen, Myrt, you know things and so do I. I would give my knowledge happily, but getting information from you is like trying to get milk from an ekon. Dangerous at best and fucking hard to boot!'

Myrt exploded into a rare laugh at Aremys's comical explanation.

'All right,' he said, still laughing. 'All right, Grenadyne, you win. I haven't laughed like that in a while.'

Aremys arched an eyebrow. 'I can tell,' he said. 'Your turn, Myrt. The Morgravian soldier you mentioned – is he still alive?'

'Yes,' Myrt said, serious now. He sipped from his steaming cup. 'Your turn. Whose side are you on?'

'Cailech's. I will negotiate for him and I will help to win this peace he pushes for. Understand this: I hate Celimus and will do everything in my power to undermine him. I am not an enemy to the Mountain Kingdom.'

Myrt said nothing but Aremys saw something blaze in the man's eyes. Aremys sensed it was relief.

'All right, next question for you,' the mercenary continued. 'Is the Morgravian soldier called Gueryn le Gant?'

Myrt baulked at that. 'How do you know that? How do you know him?'

A little fib would help here, Aremys decided. He could not tell the truth because no one would believe it. 'I know le Gant's niece. She's been distraught since he disappeared and I said I'd keep my ears and eyes open for any news on my travels north. Thank you for confirming it.'

'He's in our dungeon.'

It was Aremys's turn to flinch. 'I have to see him, Myrt.'

'Not until you answer my questions. Koreldy – where is he, do you know?'

'Probably scattered to the four winds by now.'

'Dead?' Myrt could not hide his astonishment.

Aremys nodded. 'Killed by one of the King's hired assassins. A woman,' he said.

'The King must be told.'

'Why? Did he want to kill him by his own hand?'

'He was certain that Koreldy, after his recent escape, would return to rescue le Gant.'

'What will the King do when he learns of Koreldy's death?'

'Kill the Morgravian soldier.'

'Then he cannot know of Koreldy's demise,' Aremys said urgently.

Myrt scowled. 'Says who? I've told you, I'll do nothing that smacks of betrayal of Cailech. Now answer me this if you want any more information or help: why are you so interested in Lothryn? It makes me suspicious of you.'

Aremys shook his head. 'Don't be. Elspyth of Yentro is known to me – you could say we are friends, although we've not known each other long. I met her soon after she escaped from here and she was hoping to return to the mountains to discover Lothryn's fate. You know they were lovers, she and Lothryn?'

Myrt grimaced. 'I guessed as much. There would be no other reason for Loth to betray us as he did, and without sharing his decision with me.'

Aremys was glad the Mountain man had not blinked at the coincidence that he claimed to know two separate women who just happened to know Gueryn and Lothryn. He could slap himself for such a clumsy contrivance but the big man was not paying sufficient attention. Aremys took his chance. 'Myrt,' he said gently, 'I know that you loved Lothryn too, perhaps more than in just a brotherly fashion—'

The Mountain man reacted as if burned. He stood up, pushing his chair away, eyes blazing with sudden hatred. 'Fuck you, Aremys.'

Aremys kept silent and did not so much as flinch when Myrt threw his cup and its contents into a corner and then kicked at his chair, smashing one of its legs. The big man turned to glare at the Grenadyne, daring him to make a move so he could punch him as well. But Aremys did not move.

'I don't want to fight you,' he said. 'I want to find him for you.'

Despite the warning, he was prepared for a fight; a black eye perhaps, maybe broken fingers. So he was ill-prepared for tears, and when they came he hated himself to his very core for shattering the barriers which had kept Myrt strong. Now the man's pain was being unleashed and Aremys was at a loss as to how to deal with it. He sat there a moment bewildered, then did the only thing one person can do for another who is hurting. He put his arms around the Mountain man's big shoulders and held him.

Eventually he spoke: 'He's alive, Myrt, I know it. From all that you've told me I don't believe Cailech would have killed him. And that's why his reply to you was so cryptic. Lothryn lives and our only clue is Galapek. Help me and we'll find him together.'

The tears were brief; dried away almost as soon as they had dared to arrive. Wrath replaced them. 'I can't!' the man roared.

'You can. We're all he's got. If you love Lothryn — as I know you do — then fight for him. Let's at least find out if he's alive and what state he's in.'

Myrt stomped around the small cottage, a new battle going on within him now. Aremys had noticed that the dwelling showed the touches of a woman — a jar of fresh hill flowers on the humble sideboard, dishes neatly stacked, floors swept and surfaces dusted. It was as neat as a pin. He wondered where the sister was and asked Myrt.

'Due back shortly,' he answered, distracted. 'Listen to me, Aremys. I'll help you because of Lothryn, not because I'm threatened by what you've learned about me. If you ever repeat what has occurred here or been mentioned between us, I'll kill you. I might be in love with a man but it doesn't stop me being capable of killing one. I want you to understand that.'

'Your secret is safe with me. Whether you prefer men or women is of no consequence to me. I've trusted you with my life — I shall go on doing so. I'm only sorry that you have to be so unhappy.'

'Don't trouble yourself. I've lived with it all my life,' the Mountain man said gruffly. 'More to the point, what can we do? We leave in a few hours and I don't think Cailech plans for you to return here.' Myrt's anger had dissipated to be replaced with despondency.

'Well, that does change things. It might be that you must track Lothryn down without me.' Aremys looked towards the ceiling, racking his thoughts for the best step.

'Can you take me to see the horse again? I think it was trying to communicate something to me on our ride.'

'You are jesting, aren't you?' When Aremys returned his gaze evenly Myrt scoffed. 'You expect me to believe the horse tried to tell you something?'

'Don't laugh at me, Myrt. I've explained about the magic. No, I'm not saying it talked,' he lied, 'but if there is something to learn, this is my last chance. I also want to see le Gant.'

'No.'

'Yes! He is not loyal to Celimus. He's like Koreldy and all the others that bastard has coerced and tricked, double-crossed and had killed. What do you think a soldier of that calibre was doing blundering about in the Razors anyway? Did you really think he wanted to be here with a gang of farmers who wouldn't know a sword from a threshing fork?' Myrt bit his lip. 'Come on, man. This was set up by the Morgravian King. He wanted Cailech to kill Gueryn but I have to see him to find out why.'

'Do you think it might help in your mission?'

'Of course, why else would I want to see him?' Aremys lied again, hating himself for deceiving this good man. 'Keep the secret of Koreldy, I beg you – just a little longer. The King will learn of his death anyway once he enters Morgravia, or, if you insist, I'll tell him myself.'

'I do insist,' Myrt said, staring hard at Aremys.

'All right. Just keep it quiet for now until I can learn some more.'

Myrt nodded. 'Where to now?'

'The dungeon,' Aremys replied grimly. 'Then Galapek.'

CHAPTER 6

Gueryn felt forgotten. It had been days since Myrt and his friend had walked with him and he had begun to think he would never smell sweet air again. Food and fresh water was being delivered daily, however, so he knew he had not dropped entirely from the Mountain People's consciousness. The gaoler, Haz, offered no news or even conversation and Gueryn had given up trying. In truth it was his own fault. Haz had made the effort to talk in the early days, but since allowing Gueryn to starve himself and feeling the King's wrath as a result, he had ignored the prisoner, doing only the bare necessities.

Rashlyn had looked in on him twice since Gueryn had been returned to the dungeon and was satisfied that his health was being maintained. The Morgravian had kept an icy silence with the softly spoken healer on each occasion.

Having decided that he was fighting a losing battle in trying to kill himself, and realising he could do more good by regaining his health and learning as much as he could about the Razor King and his intentions, Gueryn had tried to keep himself fit. Once he felt strong enough he had begun doing push-ups; now he was up to three hundred daily. As a result his upper body was muscled again. And he walked. His cell was relatively narrow but quite long and he had used this length to pace relentlessly up and down. He lost count of the times he met each wall at either end because he had given up keeping track after a thousand. And to keep his mind as agile as his body, he had taken stock of everything he knew and had begun to speculate using that information.

The hated Rashlyn knew something about Lothryn, that much was clear. And he was smug about it. This suggested to Gueryn that perhaps the brave Mountain man might not have perished as they had all assumed. Gueryn also knew the King was keeping him alive so that Koreldy would return to save him, but had no idea why Cailech should believe there was any attachment between them. Gueryn had never met Koreldy until that time in the fortress. The odd thing, of course, was that until Gueryn's sewn-up eyes had been released of their stitching he had believed that Koreldy was Wyl Thirsk! He had gone over it time and again in his mind, realising that he had just wanted to believe it was Wyl. Nevertheless, something deep down told him there was more to this than what his eyes had confirmed. Even when he saw the unfamiliar face, his heart had still believed Wyl was somehow present. And how could Koreldy know the family battle cry? Or speak to him in the way Wyl would? Nothing added up, and the King's belief that Koreldy would return to rescue him further muddied the waters of his thoughts.

Gueryn was sitting in the corner of his cell, once again

remembering the murder of Elspyth, for which he could never forgive himself, when he heard the key turning in the lock.

'You're early, Haz,' he mumbled. He had no real knowledge of time, but his body and its regular functions gave him reasonable clues. And right now his body was not yet hungry.

A huge man stepped into the cell, a man he had never seen before. 'Gueryn le Gant?'

Gueryn nodded, searching for a pithy rejoinder – any attack on his keepers felt good. 'Who else did you expect?'

The man grinned which confused him and turned to nod something to another person outside. Gueryn was sure he heard Myrt's voice saying that he would keep watch.

'What's going on?' he asked, alarm bells suddenly klaxoning in his mind.

'I have very little time, so you must listen as I explain something quickly. And you're going to have to trust me.'

'Why would I trust you?'

'I'm a Grenadyne, not one of the Razor people. And there's a single word I can say which I believe will make you trust me.'

'Oh yes? What's that, Grenadyne?'

'Thirsk,' Aremys replied abruptly. 'Now hear me out. No interruptions. I am friend, not foe.'

The name Thirsk was like a slap in the face to Gueryn. The big man had his full attention.

'My name is Aremys Farrow. I am a mercenary and was employed by your King to hunt down and kill Ylena Thirsk.'

'What?' roared Gueryn, pushing himself to his feet.

'I said don't interrupt, soldier,' Aremys warned. 'I found Ylena, but instead of killing her, I took her to safety into the north of Briavel, which was where we parted company. I hope she has made it south to Queen Valentyna. I won't go into how I got to be here but, rest assured, although I might look like a free man I'm as much a captive as you are. Cailech plans to use me to negotiate a parley with King Celimus. If I'm successful I might win my freedom, in which case I'll go looking for Ylena again and offer her my protection. There is another woman – someone you know – who holds strong affection for a man called Lothryn. I understand that Lothryn betrayed the Mountain People in helping you, Koreldy and this woman, Elspyth, to escape. Now that I've found you, as I promised Ylena I would,' he lied, 'I'm determined to find Lothryn as well. My instincts tell me the King has kept him alive in order to make the punishment – whatever it is – of aiding your attempted escape the sweeter. You should know that Koreldy is dead.' Gueryn closed his eyes as he heard this. 'And that somehow I am going to get you out of here.'

Aremys stopped. It was obvious he was sharing too much information; the prisoner looked too shocked to respond.

Then the Morgravian began to laugh. It was clearly not the reaction the big mercenary had expected, for his expression was all confusion.

'A word of thanks might be more appropriate,' Aremys suggested.

'Thank you for coming, Grenadyne. Thank you for what you're trying to do, but I'm as good as dead, man. If Koreldy is no longer alive, that's my death warrant,' Gueryn said, painful resignation in his tired voice.

'No one knows about Koreldy but myself and Myrt,' Aremys assured.

'Myrt is a good man, but he is a loyal Mountain warrior. The King will already know.'

'The King does not know. He doesn't even know we're here now. Myrt is outside keeping watch. He is protecting you.'

'Why?' Gueryn demanded.

'It doesn't matter why.'

'It does to me because it doesn't make sense.'

'Let's just say I have something on him which encourages him to help me.'

Gueryn shrugged tiredly. 'It doesn't matter anyway. Everyone I have ever cared about is dead except Ylena, and it sounds to me like Celimus will kill her too.'

'No chance.'

'If you've met Ylena, as you claim you have, then you'll know she is a pretty, indulged and fragile creature. She will not outwit Celimus — not without her brother's protection or mine.'

'She has the protection of a Queen . . . and mine.'

'Oh that's right, the protection of a new, inexperienced Queen under siege by now from King Celimus, I imagine, and a Grenadyne mercenary who is a captive of King Cailech. Forgive me if I don't hold my breath.'

'I don't know why I bothered,' Aremys muttered, clearly stung by le Gant's ingratitude and ungracious manner.

'Neither do I. Save yourself if you can. I watched Cailech kill Elspyth with his own hands and enjoy it. He will do the same to me, and to you if he so chooses.'

Aremys frowned. 'Elspyth isn't dead.'

'Yes, she is, mercenary. I'm sorry to upset you further. See this on my boots – that is her blood. Her life became forfeit when I refused to capitulate to Cailech's interrogation. I might as well have stuck the knife in her myself,' he finished bitterly.

Aremys moved for the first time since entering the cell. He crouched by Gueryn and dared even to take the soldier's hand. He felt as though he should be holding his breath. 'When did this happen?'

Gueryn shook his head. 'I've lost track of time here. It was weeks ago, I'm sure.'

'Gueryn, look at me. I saw Elspyth so few days ago I could count them on both hands and probably have a finger to spare. She, Ylena and I were all together in Felrawthy.'

'You lie! Why are you lying to me, you bastard?'

It was Aremys's turn to shake his head, but with compassion. 'I'm not. We drank tea together, for Shar's sake! Elspyth is alive and determined to return here to discover Lothryn's fate. She was on her way to Briavel the last time I saw her. She'll be there right now, I'd wager.'

A barrage of emotions raged openly across Gueryn's face as he considered what he was hearing. Aremys watched him take a deep breath. 'Farrow, I saw Elspyth of Yentro die horribly. Now one of us has been taken for a sap. I know your time is short, but I want you to tell me everything you know.'

So Aremys did, as quickly as he could, while leaving out everything relating to Wyl's magical metamorphosis. The gruff old soldier would never trust him if he began to talk that sort of nonsense. Besides, he had given his word to Wyl. He would not break that promise.

When Aremys had finished his story, Gueryn struggled to his feet and began to pace, deeply shocked by what he had heard. 'The Duke of Felrawthy is dead?' he said, so disbelieving that he repeated it. 'Dead? Jeryb?'

Aremys nodded. 'I only discovered this piece of savagery myself a day ago from Myrt, when the news filtered into the Razors. It seems Celimus is making Cailech's people the scapegoats, but it was his men, his killing rampage – I presume punishment, for the family's harbouring of Ylena. And no doubt it quashed any thoughts of an uprising from the northern duchy.'

It did make horrible sense. 'All of them?' Gueryn asked.

'So I'm told. Crys was seeing Elspyth to the border so I'm not sure about him, but the Mountain People said the whole family perished.'

'This is monstrous. That poor girl. Her husband, Alyd . . .' Gueryn closed his eyes in despair, then his courage rallied and he opened them again. This time they were flinty. 'And now you're going to negotiate a parley between these two Kings?'

'To buy my freedom, yes. What about Elspyth? Do you believe me?'

'How can I disbelieve what I saw with my own eyes?'

'Because Rashlyn was present, that's why.'

'So?'

'You do know he's a man of dark magic?'

'I've been on the receiving end of it,' Gueryn replied, remembering the hideous sensation of being suspended in mid-air.

'Isn't that enough evidence?'

The Morgravian turned on the big Grenadyne, eyed him quizzically. 'What do you mean?'

'Gueryn, he fooled you. Whether it was Cailech's idea – or, most likely, Rashlyn's – they duped you into thinking you were watching Elspyth die.'

'Don't be stupid!' Gueryn roared. 'It was her, I tell you.'

Aremys bit his lip in thought. He had not realised just how powerful Rashlyn was. 'Yes, to all intents and purposes it probably was Elspyth. Have you ever heard of a glamour?'

'No. What is it – some kind of magic?'

'I'm guessing that's what it was. We northerners are more accepting of magic than you folks in the south and growing up we tend to hear about spells and sorcery of days gone by. My grandfather once told me about a powerful enchantment that can make one person look like someone else. Only the most gifted can wield a glamour.'

Gueryn wondered how many more shocks his heart could take in one day. He stared at Aremys in stunned silence.

'Elspyth was alive and well when I left her,' the mercenary went on. 'I hugged her goodbye. I bet you didn't touch her?'

Gueryn shook his head numbly. 'I could only watch her die.'

'It was another woman, le Gant. They used some poor woman and placed a glamour on her. You said they were trying to get information from you. What was so important that they would murder a woman in front of you?'

'Cailech wanted to know about my connection to Koreldy. I had none, but it appears Koreldy had some connection to me.' He barked a harsh laugh. 'They stitched together my eyelids as part of my torture and I was blind when I met Koreldy. But do you know something, Farrow, I thought he was Wyl Thirsk.' Gueryn began to weep, all his pent-up emotion spilling over. 'I failed the boy. I failed the Thirsks.'

'No, you didn't,' Aremys countered helplessly, feeling the depth of Gueryn's emotion. 'There's so much I'd like to tell you but there's no time,' he whispered, only barely managing to stop himself from spilling everything about Wyl. 'Look, I have to go. You're safest here until I can work out how we're going to rescue you. You must hang on. Give away nothing of what we've shared.'

He reached out and grabbed the man's hand, putting it against his own heart. It was the highest form of commitment one soldier could make to another. It meant: I will give my life for you.

Gueryn was astounded by the action. There were only two men he had ever given such a signal to. Both were named Thirsk; father and son. Both dead now.

'Wait!' he said, suddenly remembering. 'Lothryn – you think he's alive?'

'I do.'

'That horse has something to do with it, the horse called Galapek,' Gueryn murmured, almost to himself, as if disgusted that he had not yet worked out an answer.

'What?' Aremys yelled, and almost raised Gueryn's feet from the floor as he lifted him to standing. This was no mean feat for Gueryn was a tall man, nevertheless the bear-like mercenary stood a head taller again and looked as if he would gobble up the other in his fury to learn more.

Gueryn shook his head. 'I don't really know what I'm saying. I just have a feeling that the horse Galapek,

Cailech's new stallion, has something to do with Lothryn.'

'What exactly do you know?' Aremys looked like he might throttle the information from him.

Gueryn frowned. He had no idea why the Grenadyne was so excited. 'Rashlyn knows the truth of what's happened to Lothryn. I overheard him jesting smugly to Myrt and Byl that Lothryn was closer than they knew. And he went on to make some joke about the meaning of the word "Galapek".'

Aremys looked at a loss. 'I don't know the word. Sounds like the old language,' he mused.

'It is. And I do understand it. Galapek means "traitor". Cailech has named his new stallion Traitor, which is just about the worst name you could call a horse.'

Aremys looked stunned. Then he spun on his heels and called over his shoulder, 'Say nothing of this! I'll be back, le Gant.'

The huge man all but ran from the cell, slamming the door behind him. Gueryn heard the lock turn and guessed where the Grenadyne's mind was heading. He himself had nothing but his sorrowful thoughts for company now.

'Well?' Myrt asked, startled by Aremys bursting from the cell.

'Let's get out of here first,' Aremys said, his head swirling with fantastical thoughts, every nerve tingling with terror. It could not be true, could it?

Fortunately Haz was not in attendance at the gaol. Myrt thanked the young, completely uninterested guard, who was obviously posted in the dungeon as some sort of punishment judging by his scowl. He merely nodded when Myrt reminded the lad that Gueryn was to be walked daily.

Outside, Myrt grabbed Aremys's arm. 'You got something, didn't you?'

'Do you know what the name Galapek means, Myrt?' he said, voice hard and low. When Myrt shook his head, Aremys closed his eyes with a mix of anger and despair. What a cruel fate. 'It's the ancient language of the north,' he said. 'Cailech's schoolchildren would probably be able to tell you. It means traitor.'

Myrt looked perplexed. 'All right, a curious name for a horse and even stranger connotations, but what's that got to do with Lothryn?'

'You fool. You poor sad fool,' Aremys said, unable to help himself. 'The horse is Lothryn,' and his voice almost broke on those words. 'Rashlyn has somehow worked his vile magic on Lothryn to turn him into a stallion, and now your oh-so-proud King can keep his former friend as his servant until he's no good for anything but the knacker's yard.'

If horror had a face, it belonged to Myrt that moment. He opened his mouth to speak but no words came. No sound at all, in fact. Aremys had once seen a man suffer what was called a heart-tremor; it had come quickly and gone as fast, leaving one side of the man's face paralysed. That was how Myrt looked now: paralysed. His facial muscles were slack and all colour had drained from his cheeks, his eyes were like dull black buttons.

Finally he found some lucidity. 'Cailech broke him. We all watched it. He did it in a special corral he'd had built. It took days. Days of painful, heart-wrenching breaking of this horse's spirit until it bowed its head before him.'

Myrt was weeping as he spoke. Aremys could feel tears stinging his eyes too; he could not remember the last time he had cried over anything or anyone. His sister perhaps, when he had seen her tiny corpse laid out, the vicious gores of the forest boar covered by a beautiful silken dress. He tore himself away from the memory.

'He said he would break him using trust,' Myrt finished. 'It was Lothryn all along. Lothryn who fought for days until he was too weak to resist his King any more.'

Aremys shook his head in wonder. 'And that's why the horse made me feel so sick. The Thicket's magic sensed the sheer power and evil of the sorcery that had been wielded to turn a man into a horse.'

Myrt's red-rimmed eyes stared at him. 'Aremys, don't lie to me now. You said something earlier that I scoffed at – that the horse communicated something to you. Did it really say something?'

Aremys nodded miserably. 'I'm sure it whispered a name. Elspyth.'

The Mountain warrior walked away to deal with his pain alone.

CHAPTER 7

It was the first time since childhood that Celimus had set foot in his father's beloved war chamber. Magnus had always enjoyed the room, even in times of peace. Its windows faced east, towards the traditional enemy, and when Celimus had paid one of his few visits here he had believed its views went on for ever. He recalled now how his father had laughed a little indulgently when Celimus had voiced that notion. It was a rare moment of shared enjoyment for father and son. It had passed all too quickly, Celimus forgotten the moment a messenger had arrived with a missive for General Thirsk, who always seemed to be at his King's side. Celimus was briskly told to find his tutor or similar — no one appeared to care where he went, as long as he left. He had understood with a sour realisation that he had no place amongst these men. He was nine and ready to watch and learn about kingship, but Magnus did not care enough to teach him. That much was obvious and he had never returned to the chamber until this day.

It was here that men had smoked and argued with one

another, plotted and schemed against Briavel. In this place many a war had been invented, but also peace had been designed. It was a room of ancient waxed timbers and leather smoothed from years of use, where, if you concentrated, you could still smell a hint of the sweet tobacco King Magnus had favoured. A once magnificent, now faded tapestry depicting a famous battle scene from centuries previous hung across one wall and a hand-twisted rug, threadbare in places, lay across the wooden floor, whose dusty boards had recently enjoyed a polish.

King Celimus held no sentiment for this chamber so loved by his father. He hated it in fact, equating it with the reason he and his mother had never enjoyed the love of Magnus, who preferred the company of his flame-haired General and other warmongers who clustered around him in his prime — or so Celimus preferred to see it. But this war room of his father's was where detailed maps of Morgravia, Briavel and other realms were stored. And he needed those maps now. He also needed to give the impression that he was preparing to declare war on his neighbour, and this was the place from which to do that.

In not appointing a General after Wyl Thirsk's death, Celimus had effectively claimed full leadership of the Morgravian Legion. This had shocked many of the noble families, who had assumed that Jeryb Donal, with his brood of sons, was the most likely successor. But Donal had refused when such ideas had been mooted. His focus, he had assured all, was firmly on the border between Morgravia and the Razors. There was no better defence than Felrawthy and he had no intention of moving to Pearlis. Celimus had made it equally clear that he did not require a General as such. He preferred to work through the captains with himself as head of the Legion. It was a new era for the realm in more ways than one as Morgravia sloughed off its past and looked towards a modern dynasty led by the arrogant son of its most beloved King.

To most Morgravians' despair, Celimus had recently given the directive to mobilise the first few divisions of the Legion. People had prayed that war between Morgravia and Briavel was for the history books now. The coming marriage had promised so much for the two realms' prosperous future together. Still, who would argue with this King? He was a law unto himself.

It was Celimus's intention that his men should depart for the Briavellian border today.

'That should give our Queen something to think about,' he said to Jessom who was standing nearby, pouring his sovereign a cup of wine.

The war room had been freshly cleaned, waxed and aired for Celimus. Someone had even placed a bowl of fruit and a vase of exquisite tannika buds in one corner. Celimus did not particularly care for either but he liked the splash of colour in this dull and dreary place. His mother, he recalled, had adored the famed buds which only flowered for a few short weeks in spring. It afforded him an ironic amusement that his mother's influence now held sway in Magnus's once firmly private, men-only chamber. If he had any of her perfume, he would dab it over every surface so that Adana's scent permeated to every corner and overwhelmed any lingering essence of Magnus. He smiled grimly at the thought.

'What are their orders, sire?' the Chancellor replied, handing the goblet to the King.

'Merely a show of strength at this stage. They await

further orders,' Celimus said distractedly, looking towards the flushed, dusty messenger being led into the war room by one of his aides. 'Yes?'

The aide bowed, as did the messenger. 'Sire,' the aide said, 'a courier from the north.'

Celimus did not mask his irritation at being disturbed. 'I take it this is urgent?'

'I'm assured it is, your highness, and to be given to you directly,' the aide qualified. He would never have dared interrupt the King and his Chancellor unless it was important, but of course he did not mention this fact. *Say as little as possible* seemed to be the new creed amongst the palace servants when faced with their King.

The courier bowed again, overwhelmed to be in the presence of the King. It was clear that since arriving at the gates of Stoneheart he had not even paused for a cup of water to quench his thirst.

Celimus leaned against the huge table where he remembered his father poring over maps and looked at the newcomer expectantly. With his arms folded and legs crossed at the ankle, his pose suggested this was all most inconvenient and he offered no words to allay the messenger's obvious nervousness.

The man realised his moment had come. He licked his dry lips and began his report. 'Your highness, I was despatched from the midlands checkpoint, having taken a message from another messenger who had been sent by your Captain at our northern base between Deakyn and Felrawthy.' He paused to take a breath, not noticing the flicker of irritation across the King's face at the preamble.

The Chancellor did. 'Get to the point, man, if it's urgent,' Jessom warned, hoping to stop Celimus erupting.

The Chancellor had sensed his King's brittle mood that morning and experience suggested it would not do to test its flexibility right now.

'I apologise, sire,' the man stammered. 'The message I am asked to deliver direct to you is that King Cailech of the Razors seeks a parley.'

A stunned silence filled the war room, then evaporated as exclamations ensued from both King and Chancellor.

'A parley with Cailech!' Celimus blustered over the top of his Chancellor's expostulations. 'Preposterous! Whatever for?'

The courier reddened. He had no further information other than the message he had been instructed to give. 'My King, I am not privy to any background to this missive, other than to report that it was originally delivered to the Legion by a man called Aremys Farrow.'

He bowed, his task concluded. Any other recipient might have considered that the man had delivered his message succinctly and ably, thanked him and sent him for refreshment. Celimus ignored him, instead glancing angrily towards the Chancellor. Before anything further could be said, Jessom dismissed both courier and aide. Whatever was to be discussed now was not for their hearing. He stilled the King's coming explosion with a guarded look and both waited impatiently for the two men to leave.

'Farrow!' Celimus yelled. 'Working with Cailech?'

Jessom deliberately kept his expression clear of all emotion although he too was startled by the news. 'We don't have all the details yet, your highness. We cannot know what has occurred here.'

'What secrets has he passed on?' Celimus raged.

Jessom shook his head. 'He knows nothing, sire. Besides, he will not share details of his paid missions with Cailech. Mercenaries of his calibre never let one hand know what the other is doing.'

'Precisely my point, you fool,' Celimus said, not caring at the insult to his loyal counsel. 'How do we know that he hasn't been working for Cailech all along?'

Experience had taught Jessom to ignore such offence. 'To what end, sire? What benefit has he gained? What secrets could he have learned during his few hours at Stoneheart anyway? Both he and Leyen were watched on my instructions. Leyen went to the baths and then spent the afternoon with Lady Bench. No one else visited the Bench house during her time there. Farrow was far more conservative. He did not leave his chamber, even washing there. Until supper with you, he did not emerge, and during your meeting the only matter of note discussed was Ylena Thirsk — and presumably she means nothing to the Mountain King. Farrow returned to his room and was gone within two hours. With respect, my King, I think we are jumping to conclusions which have no foundation.'

'Then what is Farrow up to?' Celimus roared, only mildly placated. 'What is Cailech up to?'

'Well, let's think it through,' Jessom said in a soft voice aimed to calm his sovereign's unnecessary rage. 'An ambush, possibly?'

'Hardly,' Celimus countered. 'By all accounts Cailech is not stupid. He's not going to risk himself on the vague chance he could hurt me. No, there is another reason.'

'I have to wonder what he thinks the Razor Kingdom and Morgravia have in common, sire,' Jessom said airily, about to expound further when the King cut him off.

'A mutual distrust of Briavel perhaps,' Celimus replied, his mind now working its agile way around various scenarios. 'Let's presume Aremys has no loyalty to either party — that he is working purely for personal gain. Perhaps he was captured by Cailech while he was on business for us, although that is unlikely; or, as you suggest, there could be other reasons why he found himself in the company of Cailech. Let's give him the benefit of the doubt, shall we, for now?'

'All right, your majesty,' Jessom agreed, as if the more rational approach was all Celimus's idea. 'So?'

'So, I agree to meet with Aremys Farrow on Morgravian soil. I am intrigued as to what Cailech has in mind with this parley.'

'What do you propose, sire?'

'I shall see him somewhere that can be properly guarded. It will take too long for him to be brought to Stoneheart.' The King began to think aloud. 'Perhaps halfway — Rittylworth?'

'Felrawthy, my King,' Jessom said in a tone of rich satisfaction. 'What better spot?'

'Indeed,' Celimus agreed, warming instantly to the notion of personally taking over the rich estate. Who cares if Crys Donal is alive in Briavel, he thought. He is a traitor now. Felrawthy belonged to the Crown. 'Make immediate arrangements. Send a message for Aremys Farrow to be brought to Tenterdyn. We shall meet him there.'

'At once, your highness. And Briavel?'

'Can wait for now. Let Valentyna stew. Perhaps the sight of our men will soften her resolve. She would be a fool to go into battle.'

'You would still marry her, sire?'

Celimus looked at his Chancellor as though he was conversing with a dullard. 'I don't *want* war, Jessom. I want her to capitulate, having fully grasped my strength. I don't want her as my equal — which is tragically how she sees herself — but I do want her as my Queen. I *want* an heir from her. I want Briavel, man. And then I shall have the Mountain Kingdom too. I want it all!' he bellowed, storming from the war room, his energies charged.

Aremys found the company of the Legionnaires easy and comfortable. With the Razors behind him, he was relieved to be back in Morgravia — and suddenly the chance of finding Wyl again felt possible. He still felt touched by Myrt's sorrow, Gueryn's imprisonment and the shock of what had become of Lothryn, but there was nothing he could do about any of that right now. He had a job to carry out for the Mountain King and his freedom to win.

He liked Cailech, in spite of all he had discovered. The man had a deep intelligence and quick mind, and Aremys was impressed that the King — whom he sensed was capable of arrogance and too much pride — was not too proud or arrogant to appreciate the benefit of a parley with the southern King. That Cailech despised Celimus was obvious, but he also had the capacity for pragmatism. He had admitted to Aremys that if he could stomach a meeting with Celimus and form some sort of loose bond, then the long-term benefits were immense.

They had talked over a sumptuous supper before Aremys and his escort left. Myrt had been quiet, but then Myrt was always quiet. Only Aremys seemed overly sensitive to his silence; the King was focused on the coming meeting with his southern counterpart.

'Can he be trusted?' Cailech had mused aloud.

'I doubt it. Can you?' Aremys had posed, which had made the King bellow with amusement.

'You'll do well, Aremys. Go and set up this parley for me.'

'And in return, Cailech,' Aremys had risked, 'what is my reward?'

'I allow you to live,' the King had answered. The gregarious mood did not fool Aremys. He knew only too well that the King still held deep suspicions about him, but no mention had been made of Rashlyn, other than to assure the two men that the barshi was well.

Aremys had not replied to the King's flippant comment, instead had held his ground, refusing to flinch under the King's scrutiny.

'All right, mercenary. I understand your need for an exchange of some kind,' Cailech relented. He smiled. 'What would please you that I could provide?'

Aremys had decided to risk it. 'I would have Galapek.'

The King's reaction was dramatic despite his efforts to shield it. The eyes narrowed and Aremys saw the man's jaw tighten. He had hit an artery it seemed.

'What is your interest in my horse?' Cailech had said, his tone bordering on anger.

'Only that I wish he were mine, sire,' Aremys lied. 'He is the most beautiful stallion I have ever encountered and that's saying something coming from a Grenadyne.'

'He is still new for me. I am fond of him.'

'I see,' Aremys observed, keeping his voice light so no offence could be given. It was time to pull back. 'King Cailech, I will attempt to set up this parley for you in good faith. I need nothing from you in payment – not even your fine stallion. All I ask is that you grant my freedom once you have had the opportunity to work out a peace agreement with Celimus.'

Cailech had instantly offered his hand, palm up this time. Aremys knew this was a rare show of friendship from a man who no doubt considered he had no equal, and once again he was struck by how quickly this King's mood could change.

'I will gladly seal hands on that, Aremys,' the King had said. 'I like your confidence that Celimus and I will find common ground.'

Aremys placed his own hand on top of the King's. 'You alone will make it happen, my lord. I have complete faith in you.'

Cailech had smiled and this time there was no guile; just open warmth. 'I hope you will choose to stay amongst us, Grenadyne. But I grant you your independence as soon as this deal is done.'

Aremys had opted for a light-hearted response. 'I *must* be free, your highness. My memory tells me I have a woman to find,' and had winked, much to the King's delighted amusement.

And so Aremys Farrow of Grenadyn had been provided with an escort, a fine horse and a message to deliver to Celimus, which he had duly done, emerging out of the Razors with his hands held high, insisting that Myrt and his other two companions do the same.

Aremys had deliberately asked Myrt to lead him as close to Felrawthy as they could get, having learned from Wyl that these Legionnaires were the least likely to shoot arrows first and ask questions later. They had entered Morgravia via a pass known as Haldor's Tooth, which had led them into the duchy of Felrawthy, to a village mainly inhabited by soldiers about ten miles from Brynt proper. Captain Bukanan's men were well drilled to take prisoners for interview. Aremys believed he could thank Jeryb Donal for this mercy.

He had nodded gently at Myrt to allow the Mountain men's hands to be bound. His too had been tied, and whilst the men of the Razors were led into a small dwelling, Aremys had been taken before Bukanan, who had listened to his story with an intense interest.

'A parley, you say?' the ruddy-faced Captain had repeated.

'Yes, sir. That's the message I bring,' Aremys had confirmed, his hands still tied.

'You understand how odd this is?'

'I do, sir. It's why I was chosen to deliver the message. I am known to the King and he will trust me.'

Bukanan had studied him closely and finally replied: 'You will remain in our care until we hear back from Pearlis.'

'I understand,' Aremys had said, smiling at the nicely couched words which really meant they were prisoners of Morgravia. 'You must understand, however, that these men of the mountains are not to be harmed in any way and are to be released the moment you receive word from King Celimus.'

'Who makes these conditions?' the Captain had enquired politely, although Aremys heard the edge in the tone.

'Cailech of the Mountain People. He insists his men are not to be compromised by King Celimus.'

'And he's in a position to make such demands?' the

Captain had asked, somewhat surprised at the audaciousness of the Mountain King.

'Captain Bukanan, I am merely the go-between for two powerful men. If my attempt to bring them together works, then it means you and I can continue our lives in peace. I think Morgravia wants peace, and what I want is to return to my life as a free man. Let us make this happen, you and I. If Cailech's men are harmed or kept beyond a time frame he considers fair, he will call off the parley and you may well be fighting a war on two fronts – with the King of the Mountains and the Queen of Briavel – which would be a shame, don't you agree?'

Bukanan most certainly did agree when it was put like that. His wife had just given birth to a son after two daughters and the Captain had every intention of remaining alive to raise the son he loved with such ferocity. 'We'll accept these terms, Farrow. Although you will have little to bargain with once Cailech is on Morgravian soil – for you may be sure Celimus will not agree to go into the Razors.'

'Leave that with me,' Aremys said cryptically.

The Captain shrugged. 'As you wish. We will despatch our rider this instant. Make yourself comfortable amongst us. It will take a few days.'

CHAPTER 8

Liryk had personally escorted the woman who called herself Ylena Thirsk to a small reception room. She was dishevelled and communicated little more than basic responses, insisting that her business was with the Queen, who was expecting her. Liryk had no idea whether this was truly Ylena Thirsk or an impostor and he therefore had her thoroughly searched for even the smallest of weapons. The woman gave no protest and, in fact, carried nothing with her except the riding clothes she stood in. It was all quite baffling really, but then every one of the recent Morgravian visitors had brought colourful stories – why should this one be any different Liryk reasoned with a soft sigh.

The woman certainly did not resemble the famed Thirsks. Apart from the golden hair – an obvious difference – she was beautiful, not a quality the Thirsk men had been known for. He noticed that she carried herself erect and proud – clearly of noble status – and her defiant gaze when he tried to question her at the guardhouse had told him she was not in any way intimidated by him or his men. Finally he had agreed to send a runner to the Queen.

'It is up to her majesty whether she will see you,' he had cautioned.

'Rest assured, your Queen will see me,' the woman had replied and had followed the soldier in silence to the chamber. The commander had no idea of what this sudden visit would mean to the Queen or to Briavel's future; he recognised, however, that it was fraught with danger for the marriage plans which balanced so precariously now on the mood of the Morgravian King. The nobles had called for Ylena Thirsk and it seemed Shar had answered Valentyna's dearest prayers.

'Lady Thirsk, my men tell me they found you in the woodland bordering the palace?'

'Yes, this is true,' Wyl replied. 'I was lost, Commander Liryk, and grateful for their guidance. I have already explained that my horse was lamed in Beeching,' he lied, still a little shocked from his arrival via magic into the Werryl woods. Rasmus had not been toying with him when he had offered to 'send' him to his destination. 'I left it there,' he added, realising too late this was a mistake as the commander could easily check up on his story.

'And you walked from Beeching? Could you not buy another horse?'

'To tell the truth, I did not have sufficient funds in my purse for that purchase, sir. It wasn't so far.'

'Most noblewomen would find five miles a difficult journey on foot.'

'You forget I am a Thirsk,' Wyl parried. 'Even our women are tough,' he added, working hard to keep vexation from his tone.

Before Liryk could reply the doors of the chamber burst

open and Queen Valentyna strode in, her complexion slightly flushed from her hurried passage through the palace.

Wyl had been anticipating her arrival with a hammering heart, which might account for his undue arrogance with the commander, and he felt it lurch now at the sight of her again. He hurriedly dropped a low bow, glad that he had the excuse of riding breeches to avoid the more feminine curtsey. 'Your highness,' he murmured, his feminine voice catching in his throat. He could smell her soft scent of lavender. All he wanted to do was hold her, kiss her. He could do neither.

'Please, Ylena,' Valentyna said, equally nervous but for different reasons, 'be at ease.'

Wyl looked at the woman he loved whose hand was extended towards him. He could not help himself: he took the Queen's hand in his own elegant, recently washed one and kissed it – an unusual action for a woman. He looked up and saw her frown slightly. Was it from consternation or had she recognised something in his eyes? He knew he was clutching at straws with such a notion. Surely all she saw before her was a ragged noblewoman.

'Thank you, your majesty, for permitting me an audience,' he offered. It was all he would trust himself to say at the moment, and he was relieved to be rescued by the arrival of a servant with a tray of refreshments.

'Truly the pleasure is mine, Ylena,' the Queen said, bafflement still evident in her expression. 'Let us move to the balcony, shall we? It's a lovely morning.' Valentyna led the way. 'Liryk, you're most welcome to stay,' she added, which of course was his cue to depart.

'I shall take my leave, your highness,' he said, and saw

his Queen's face relax at his decision. 'I will leave a man outside the door should you need me again,' he added, glancing towards Ylena Thirsk. His couched message was unmistakable. The Queen nodded at him, smiled her thanks at the servant and offered to pour her guest a glass of sweet wine. Liryk was already forgotten. He departed unhappily, his mood evident in his sour expression.

If Wyl's own sense of awkwardness was anything to judge by, then Valentyna also needed help easing into the conversation. He decided he should lead it as he was the one with all the secrets.

'You have been expecting me, haven't you, your highness?' he said, taking the cup of wine.

'Well, yes,' Valentyna began, then shook her head slightly. 'It's an odd thing, Ylena — may I call you that?'

I'd prefer you to call me Wyl, he thought. 'Of course, your majesty. Please go on.'

'Your letter said to wait for you and to trust you would come. My nobles insisted that without you they would not believe any of the recent claims against the Morgravian King so I prayed for you to come. And, curiously — please don't think me silly—'

'I would never do that,' Wyl confessed, leaning forward and taking her hand. It felt so natural to do so and yet, he realised, it would strike the Queen as odd for her guest to be so instantly familiar.

Valentyna did not appear to be discomforted by his forwardness. 'Even dishevelled you're really so beautiful — not at all like Wyl,' she exclaimed, and then burst into wonderful laughter and Wyl was once again reminded of how it felt when the sun broke through clouds to shine down with all its warmth. He never wanted that smile —

just for him — to leave her face. He laughed too. How could it be that this woman could say words which would normally offend and yet seem like playful affection coming from her?

'Wyl was not handsome, your highness . . . and he knew it,' he admitted.

'Ah,' the Queen interrupted, 'but Wyl, even though I knew him so briefly, was probably one of the most beautiful people on the inside that I will ever have the good fortune to meet.'

Wyl felt himself glowing at the words. 'I think if my brother could eavesdrop on this conversation, your highness, he would be more thrilled than you could ever know.'

'Blushing from head to toe, no doubt,' the Queen added and laughed again. 'Oh, I am cruel but Wyl struck me as too easy to tease,' she said, before adding more sombrely, 'He was so generous to my father and me. I can't quite shake the guilt of his death knowing that he could have saved himself.'

'It's probably not right of me to speak so openly, your highness, but Wyl was in love with you. I don't mean just a little either.'

It was Valentyna's turn to feel a hot blush stealing up her throat. 'How can you know this?'

'Romen told me,' Wyl answered and watched the Queen blink at the mention of her lover's name. It was wrong of him to do this but he felt a little out of control in her presence. It was a dangerous sensation, as though anything were possible. He reined in his spiralling emotions.

'How well did you know Romen?' the Queen asked tentatively.

'We were together for several days, travelling across country to Rittylworth and its monastery. I got to know him well during that time, as people do when they eat together, sleep together, and share thoughts that two strangers might not otherwise.'

'Romen spent time here too. Did you know that he made a promise to your brother?'

'To protect us both. Yes, he told me.'

'I – I would be honest with you,' Valentyna struggled. 'I was in love with Romen – I am still.'

Ylena could not know this and so Wyl framed an expression of gentle surprise on her face. He nodded, wanting to make it as easy as possible for Valentyna. 'I can understand that, your highness. Romen was very tender towards me and I know he was a good man despite his occupation. I can see what a fine match the pair of you would make.'

Valentyna's eyes shone at the compliment. 'Truly?'

Wyl nodded, hating himself and yet loving that he could lift her spirits so.

'No one else would agree with you, Ylena,' the Queen admitted drily. 'Romen might have been noble but my realm has its collective heart set on a union between two royal households. But forgive me bleating on like this. I'm aware of your shocking losses, Ylena, and feel ill at heart for you over them.'

Wyl lowered his head but Valentyna reached over and clasped Ylena's hand. Her touch sent a tremor of joy through him.

'I have also heard about your courageous exploits since and I know your brother would be so proud of you.'

'How have you heard this, your highness?'

'Through Crys Donal.'

Wyl moved free of her touch, surprised at such news. 'Crys is here?'

The Queen nodded. 'I'm sorry, perhaps I should have mentioned it earlier. There's so much to tell and his presence signifies tragic news from Briavel's north.'

Wyl sat back, his pulse racing not with love now but with fear. What had occurred? 'Please, tell me,' he said.

'The Donal family were murdered.'

Wyl stood abruptly, staggering slightly and gripping the balcony rail. He forced himself to breathe deeply. 'You have proof?' His voice came out as a groan.

Valentyna's reply was soft. 'Yes. Their deaths were confirmed by a witness.' She paused to allow him to collect himself before she continued. 'Crys was escorting Elspyth to the Briavellian border, which is how he escaped being killed too.' Valentyna's voice was trembling thinking on it again. 'It was Pil – the novice. You know whom I speak of?'

Wyl nodded without turning to look at her. He could not bring himself to explain that Ylena and Pil had travelled together. It was no longer relevant after this shattering news.

'It was Pil who found Elspyth and Crys and alerted them to the tragedy, and Elspyth insisted the new Duke of Felrawthy accompany her to Werryl.'

Wyl could not make his throat work to respond. It felt closed and as dry as tinderbush.

'My apologies, Ylena, I should have started from the beginning,' Valentyna said. 'It has been a shock for us all.'

'Was it Celimus?' Wyl croaked.

'Apparently so. The men wore his colours, according to Pil and Lady Donal.'

He swung around. 'Lady Donal lives?'

Valentyna shook her head sadly. 'I'm sorry, no. She died of her wounds, but the brave woman got herself as far as Brackstead, bringing the—' and she stopped abruptly, realising what she had been about to say would only upset Ylena more.

'Bringing what?' Wyl insisted.

Valentyna stood, offered her hand and ended up gently embracing her guest. She spoke softly. 'Ylena . . . let me start again and tell you everything I know.'

Wyl nodded glumly.

'Let's walk. I'll find it easier to revisit this painful story if I'm moving.' She found a thin smile but it was not returned by her guest. 'Come, let us stroll in the gardens if you're not too tired?'

'I'm not,' Wyl said, glad for any time he could share with this woman, although the shock of the news had numbed him. 'Where is Crys now?'

'I'll send for him so you can meet after our walk.'

'And Elspyth – she's here too I presume?'

At this the Queen paused and searched for the right words but found nothing of comfort. Instead she told it to Ylena in a straightforward fashion. 'She disappeared during the night. You missed her by hours, Ylena.'

Wyl could no longer be shocked. He raised weary eyes to meet the searching blue gaze of the tall woman before him. 'She's gone after Lothryn then,' he said, resigned.

'You know of him?'

He nodded. 'What a mess,' he murmured. 'What a shocking mess my life is.'

Valentyna did not understand the depth of his comment but she nodded gently and took her guest's thin arm. 'Come, the gardens will revive you even though what I have to tell you might not.'

'Your majesty, perhaps it would be best to keep my presence here as quiet as possible for the time being.'

'Oh? But the nobles asked me to deliver you, they—'

'I know, but they probably didn't think you ever could or would. They aren't going to change their minds, your highness, no matter how much I explain to them. They want this marriage to go ahead come what may – as do all Morgravians.'

It hurt him to see the pain etched in her face as they departed the chamber.

The two women, strikingly different in appearance, strolled quietly through the peaceful herb gardens. The dark of Valentyna's hair contrasted perfectly with the gold of Ylena's. Both were in riding clothes and Valentyna was quietly delighted that the noblewoman walking alongside her had not so much as blinked at her appearance. It struck her as odd, because most women she met were surprised that she preferred this masculine garb, and Ylena seemed the kind of fragile beauty who would be horrified to appear in anything but a perfectly tailored outfit. And yet here she was, entirely unself-conscious in dusty trews, her hair tied back, her face smudged and fingernails hastily but not successfully cleaned. It did not seem to match up with the woman she had imagined. Fynch had given her such a detailed description of Wyl's beautiful sister, how elegant and sophisticated she was, that it hardly seemed this could be the same person walking beside her. Then, Valentyna reminded herself of all that Ylena had been through in recent weeks, and that she was of Thirsk stock. The bloodline had to prevail, she reasoned. In fact, Ylena reminded her more and more of the Wyl she had known so briefly.

She had spared the young woman none of the details and told her everything she knew of what had happened in Morgravia as it had been related to her by others, also fleshing out the sorry tale with all that she had personally gleaned.

'Where is Alyd's head now?' Ylena asked. Valentyna was surprised at the forthrightness of the question and by the young woman's control. She had expected an outburst of grief but Ylena had shed not a single tear.

'Ylena, I know this is very difficult for you,' the Queen began, trying to step gently around the tender subject of Alyd Donal's remains. 'I will do whatever you wish.'

'Bury him here,' Wyl said without hesitation. 'Tenterdyn is soiled with enough blood of its own now. Let him lie alongside his mother.'

Valentyna nodded. 'Crys felt similarly with Aleda. He wanted her to belong here for the time being.' They had made several revolutions of the herb garden now. 'Are you tired?'

'I must be, but I couldn't sleep anyway,' Wyl replied, shaking his head. 'All of this news is shattering but there are plans to make. Tell me about Celimus, your highness.'

Bemused by her enthusiasm to share her anxieties with this woman, who could do little to help her, Valentyna told Ylena everything she knew.

'I can't believe Krell would do such a thing,' Wyl

said, alarmed at how rapidly the situation in Briavel had deteriorated.

'If you had known him, you would understand how very accurate your comment is,' Valentyna agreed. 'It was foolish beyond belief and so out of character for him to do something so rash. Celimus now knows everything.'

'Not everything, my Queen,' Wyl cautioned and Valentyna could hardly believe the thrill the fighting words sent through her. 'He has no idea where I am. We must keep it that way.'

'But it will soon get out. If I have spies in Morgravia, Briavel is surely riddled with his watchers.'

'True. It was a mistake for me to announce my real name,' Wyl admitted. 'But it was the only name that was going to get me through the palace gates. I need some time to think, your highness. Perhaps I might take that rest now, if you will permit it?'

'Of course. I'm glad you're here, Ylena,' Valentyna said, surprising herself with such naked truth. 'You may not look like your brother but your personalities are devastatingly similar. He made me feel safe as you do, curiously enough.'

Ylena's face shone with Wyl's pleasure. 'I am your servant, your highness. As my brother once pledged his allegiance to Briavel, so I do too.'

'I accept it with gratitude, Ylena, but what we two women can do against that treacherous King to the west, I have no idea. I marry him shortly, do you know that?'

Wyl did not react as he wished to. 'Perhaps you must, your highness, but not without a plan,' he said reassuringly. 'Gather all the latest information you can — everything your people can report.'

The Queen wondered at what point in their conversation Ylena had assumed such authority, but she nodded her agreement. 'My intention was to ask Crys Donal to leave Briavel,' she added.

'Yes, he cannot remain here. It will only inflame the situation now that Celimus knows he has survived. Besides, Crys may be far more help to our cause in Morgravia.'

'What do you mean?'

'I'm not sure yet, your majesty. May we talk again in a few hours?'

'Surely,' the Queen said and then, unable to help herself, added, 'It's uncanny . . .'

'What is, your majesty?'

'Either I'm going mad or Shar himself is conspiring to confuse me.' She gave Wyl a long, searching gaze and he watched, discomforted, as her eyes misted. 'It sounds so foolish, but not only do you echo your brother, you remind me keenly of Romen Koreldy in the way you talk to me. He and I plotted together not so long ago on how to keep Celimus and his marriage proposal at bay. I feel as if I am reliving that moment.' A tear escaped and ran down her cheek. 'Oh, forgive me, Ylena. I know I'm making no sense.'

'Don't be sorry,' Wyl said, reaching into a pocket and handing the Queen a handkerchief.

Valentyna gave a small, harsh laugh. 'No, you don't understand. Our mutual friend, Elspyth, asked me just a couple of days ago to keep an open mind on people who might pass through my life.'

'No, I don't understand,' Wyl admitted, trying to lighten the moment with a grin.

Valentyna dabbed at her cheeks with the handkerchief. Something tweaked at her mind but she paid it little attention. 'I hate feeling this weak. A mention, a reminder of Romen, anything which resonates of him, can undo me.'

'Then use his memory to make you strong. If he was able to make you feel safe, call upon that feeling to give you courage rather than allow it to undo you,' Wyl urged.

Valentyna was glad she had not admitted anything about the chaffinch and its song. She felt sure this brave young woman, who had lost so much herself, would definitely believe that the Queen of Briavel was losing her wits under the pressure if she shared that story.

'What were you going to say about people passing through your life?' Wyl asked.

'Oh, nothing really,' the Queen sighed, handing back the beautiful square of linen. Once more she felt a tug at her thoughts but again was distracted from it, pulling at a stalk of lavender and crushing the flower between her hands.

Wyl had to look away; it was a painful reminder of happier times, when Valentyna had crushed a head of lavender and held up her palms to Romen for him to inhale the scent. She did not offer her hands now, but then she did not know that the same person – in spirit – was standing before her.

'Elspyth is determined that I should lock Romen away and open up my heart to others who might love me,' she continued, shyly now.

Wyl heard alarms klaxoning in his head. 'And what else did the wise woman, Elspyth, advise, your highness?'

Valentyna smiled at his gentle sarcasm, not knowing

how terrifying this conversation was for her guest. 'It was an odd moment – she was most intense about her words. We were in this very place actually, and she begged me that should someone ever remind me strongly of Romen to take notice of it.'

Wyl felt his stomach twist with relief. Elspyth had obviously danced around the topic. She had learned the lesson of a loose mouth in the harshest way at Tenterdyn – and his sister had died because of it. Elspyth would not make the same mistake again, although it had not stopped her alluding to his secret.

He needed to get away before the conversation became even more dangerous.

'I am proud indeed that I remind you of someone you loved so much, your majesty,' he said and bowed to kiss the Queen's hand to take his leave. As he did, he inhaled the scent of lavender as he had not so long ago in the guise of Roman Koreldy and felt the rush of adoration and desire throughout his body.

Wyl fled from the herb garden with its painfully sweet memories and was fortunate to bump into young Stewyt, the page who had looked after his needs when he was last in the palace, as Romen. He schooled his expression to show no recognition.

'Excuse me,' he said, touching the youngster on the shoulder.

'My lady?' the lad said, bowing.

He had grown in the short time Wyl had been away. 'What is your name?'

'Stewyt, my lady. May I help you?'

'I hope so. I'm a guest here and—'

'Yes, the household staff has been informed, Lady Ylena, and I have been appointed to wait on you, if that pleases?'

The boy had struck Wyl as sharp on their first meeting and it seemed that intuition had not been misguided. The page had been very sure of himself then and it had occurred to Wyl that Stewyt was probably a spy for Chancellor Krell.

'It does please me,' he replied now. 'I was wondering where my chamber is?'

'Let me take you there, my lady. Please follow me.'

They engaged in small talk on the journey through the formal reception rooms of the palace, making their way up the beautiful marble staircase and then another flight – less ornate this time – towards the guest rooms. Stewyt was a competent guide, pointing out items of interest as they entered the western wing of the palace – a place Wyl had not been previously.

'We have arranged a suite for you, my lady. I hope you find the accommodation comfortable. Please let me know if there's anything I can fetch for you.'

'Thank you,' Wyl said, impressed by the lad's composure. He stepped past Stewyt into a freshly aired sitting room.

'The door over there leads into your sleeping chamber, my lady, and that other door is a dressing room where you might take your ablutions. Shall I send up a bath?'

'Please.'

'Would you like a maid to help with your toilet?'

'Er, no, thank you, Stewyt. I would prefer to be alone right now.' Wyl knew he should order some fresh clothes but this new existence was hard enough. The riding clothes made him feel comfortable.

Stewyt nodded. 'As you wish, my lady,' and he bowed formally to take his leave.

It seemed to Wyl he would never escape the fragrance of lavender. A fresh bunch had been placed in a jar by the window and a light breeze carried the scent through the room. The stalks were mingled with mint of all things. So typically Valentyna, he sighed. She probably ordered the arrangement herself.

He looked out from the window across Werryl Bridge. It was a magnificent sight from this high perspective. A procession of people crossed to and fro, in and out of Werryl city, and he noticed they all paid quiet homage to the newly erected statue of King Valor, who had taken his place amongst the other, more ancient royals who stood guard, made welcome and bade farewell all who travelled the bridge. The people's love for Valor was clear in the way they paused to nod at his likeness or touch the statue's foot. It was poignant to watch and Wyl wished a similar tradition was followed in Morgravia to honour its revered dead. Then he stifled a nervous laugh at the mental picture which sprang to mind of the folk of Pearlis spitting on the statue of Celimus.

I must not falter now, he berated himself, fighting the urge that he was unravelling at being so close to Valentyna yet trapped as Ylena. He decided he should lie down, even if rest eluded him. Wyl was asleep in moments.

Fynch came to him in his dreams.

I cannot stay long. I am travelling with Knave into the Razors.

Fynch! Is it really you?

Wyl, sending to you is hard for me so don't talk, just listen. I know what troubles you. Offer to go to Pearlis on Valentyna's behalf. Buy her more time.

Celimus will have me killed.

But you are already dead, Wyl. Farewell. I hope we shall speak again.

Fynch? Fynch!

Wyl woke trembling and disturbed.

CHAPTER 9

Fynch sat down hard on the small mound outside the cottage which had been built by Elysius. 'My head throbs.'

Knave prowled nearby. *It will. Each time you use the magic, the pain will become a little worse.*

'I had to.'

Knave did not comment; instead he offered some advice. *Take some sharvan leaves from the pot in the cottage. Elysius used it to alleviate the pain.*

Fynch nodded and forced himself to stand up despite the lingering ache. 'Do we leave immediately?'

As soon as you feel strong enough.

'I wish we didn't have to leave this place. I feel safe here.'

I do understand, Fynch.

'Why did he come, do you think?'

Knave knew to whom the boy referred. *To thank you.*

'Something odd happened.'

Knave remained silent although the quiet was filled with unspoken questions.

Fynch touched the dog on its large head as he moved

towards the cottage. 'Maybe I imagined it but I felt connected to the King somehow.'

We all do.

'No, it was more than that. I felt like I belonged to him,' Fynch said softly, slightly embarrassed, 'even though I know my creature is Roark, the unicorn.'

The dog offered no explanation and Fynch sensed his friend was confused when he replied: *It cannot be a bad thing to feel connected to the King of the Beasts.*

Fynch understood he would get no more insight from Knave. He knew the Warrior King had also sensed something between them. He had seen recognition flare in the creature's dark eyes. But the King had gone now and there was no point in teasing at that problem.

There was a journey to make, a man to kill and another to save.

Wyl did not feel rested in the slightest and Fynch's words had disturbed him so that he could not face putting his head back on the pillow. Soon enough, a gaggle of people arrived to deliver the bath, hot water, fresh clothes and a tray of welcome food and wine.

He took his time luxuriating in the steaming water and staring at the trio of gowns Valentyna had sent for him to choose from. He hated the sight of them; despised the fact that he would have to climb into a dress and curtsey before the woman he loved. And what was more, something terrifying was occurring within Ylena's body. At first he could not imagine what the creeping hurt was which had begun low and deep, almost at his groin. Sharp needles of pain had stabbed regularly at him since he had woken. The heat of the bath had soothed them but not

taken them away, and then a fresh ache across his back
had begun. When the dull throb of a headache gathered
he knew he was ill, but it was only as he was considering
how to explain the discomfort in order to obtain the right
herbal concoction to speed its passing that he understood
what this was all about. It was Ylena's monthly bleed. A
new wave of sickness passed over him. How much more
humiliation could he take? Did he truly have to contend
with this? Yes he did, he told himself, for no one else
could save him.

He took his mind back to easier times, when life was
bright and happy for Ylena. He recalled how she would
withdraw each month for one day at least and rest, but
he had hardly been privy to much more information than,
'Your sister is indisposed. She leaves a message that you
should visit tomorrow when she will be feeling better.'
He smirked bitterly in the warm waters. The first day is
always the worst she had told him when he had dared to
ask more than was polite. So he had to deal with this pain
for one day – and then what? How long would the bleed
last? He knew there was something about linens and
regular changing but that was a woman's world. *His* world
now . . . and he hated it. He dipped deeper into the
warmth.

Fynch's words haunted him. His friend was right: what
did it matter if Ylena died at the hands of Celimus, or
anyone else? Her death would buy Valentyna time. Wyl
Thirsk would go on living anyway, he thought grimly.
Perhaps he could persuade Celimus to do the ugly deed
and end it once and for all, and then he remembered
Elysius's warning that if he attempted to contrive his own
death the repercussions would be savage. He could not

risk another person he loved suffering and he felt sure the penalty would be levelled on someone else rather than himself.

He dropped Ylena's head to her hands in deep frustration but in truth his mind was made up. Fynch's advice was wise. Wyl could represent Valentyna to Celimus. The King of Morgravia would hardly turn down the opportunity to welcome Ylena back to Stoneheart — and no doubt directly into her former cell in the dungeon . . . or worse. He cared not. The sooner he was rid of Ylena's body, the better. He felt sick at heart that he would lose her again, but he would be glad to no longer walk in her skin.

Wyl pondered a plan as he washed Ylena's hair and readied her to present herself to Queen Valentyna. A small glow of luck saw a maid arrive to clear his tray. He begged a favour and it was taken care of in minutes. She brought him strips of linen, and a strange brown liquid that smelled awful and tasted worse to swallow.

The young maid smiled at him as he thanked her. 'The pain will go quickly, my lady. I'll have some more linens delivered.'

The Duke of Felrawthy crossed the room and swept Ylena Thirsk into his arms. 'Wyl,' he whispered into his prisoner's ear, 'thank Shar you're safe.'

Wyl felt self-conscious at the show of affection, yet knew it would appear perfectly normal to the Queen who stood regally nearby, delighting in the reunion of her Morgravian guests. She looked dazzling tonight in a dark brown gown of the simplest design. Figure-hugging with no frills or flounces, ruches or tucks, it flattered her tall, slim frame, the deep colour accentuating the brightness of her eyes against her creamy complexion and the dark hair she had twisted up behind her head with a tortoiseshell comb.

When he was placed back on the floor Wyl took the Duke's hand in his own and placed both their fists against his own heart. It was the gesture of a Legionnaire, and in Morgravian society would have looked not only odd but vulgar when performed by a woman. Fortunately, Valentyna had no understanding of the gesture, although Wyl knew Crys would know instantly its intent. For Wyl, it was the only way he could show his true self and convey the depth of his feeling for what had occurred.

'I'm shattered by the news of your family,' he said softly.

Crys momentarily lost his tight grip on the sorrow he kept locked away and Wyl saw it emerge now to march slowly, painfully, across the handsome duke's features.

'I can't—' Crys began haltingly.

'I know,' Wyl said, fighting down the lump that was closing his own throat. 'I understand.' And Crys knew that Wyl, of all people, did, for here stood someone who had lost everything but his own soul. 'Stay strong, Crys. Their lives will not have passed in vain.'

All Crys could do at this point was to gather up his hurts quickly and hide them again. Either that or break down completely. He nodded as he turned away.

It was Valentyna who rescued them both. 'Ylena, Crys, come, I've had a table set up by the fire. Let us break some bread together.'

Had the Queen deliberately chosen to entertain them in the same chamber where Wyl had first met her father, with its secret doorway and the huge tapestry covering the privy? He could not guess but it felt strangely comforting to be here again – as though he had come full circle. Nothing much had changed in the room, save a few Valentyna-esque flourishes, as he liked to think of them. A jar of blooms, some fresh lavender and herbs scattered on the floor to be crushed underfoot and release their scent, a thick rug and a charcoal-sketched likeness of Valor done by his daughter which hung unobtrusively in a corner. It was not a great work of art but she had somehow – amongst her scrawl of lines – captured the spirit of the man. It was a lovely piece and no doubt drawn with raw emotion. The final brightening touch was a tiny puppy, gambolling about near the warmth of the hearth, teasing at a bone.

Valentyna saw Wyl's amusement at the little fellow as they seated themselves and shrugged. 'I miss Knave.' Then she whispered, 'I hear you have the curse. Have you taken some raspberry leaf tea?'

Wyl nodded, no idea whether he had taken such tea or not, and startled by her candidness. Women obviously discussed these maladies openly between themselves.

Her smile was all sympathy. 'The first day is always the worst.'

Wyl wondered if his face was flushed red with the embarrassment he was feeling and was glad when Crys claimed his attention, drawing him away from the Queen's conspiratorial gaze.

'You've heard that Elspyth has gone?' Crys enquired of Wyl; the young duke was fully composed again.

Wyl felt proud of him. Morgravia could recover with young men like this to lead it into the future. If only he could rid the realm of its present monarch, there was hope. 'Yes, into the clutches of Cailech, I suspect.'

'What can we do?' Crys wondered, more to himself than to the others.

'I shall have to go after her.'

'What?' Valentyna cried and Wyl could understand how strange his comment must have sounded. 'What can a tiny creature like you do against Cailech and his Mountain men?'

'Oh,' Wyl said, finding a lazy grin which he was certain Romen would be proud of, 'you'd be surprised, your majesty.'

'But you've never been there before. You have no idea about this man!' Valentyna spluttered, the noblewoman's arrogance reminding her of someone she had once loved.

'True,' Wyl lied, and hoped the subject would rest for now or he was in for a long and tricky evening. 'But Elspyth made her own choice,' he continued, 'and we have time on our side. Presumably she is on foot?'

The Queen nodded. 'She took nothing, not even the horse she rode in on.'

'She'll be a while getting into the Razors then. In the meantime, there's a realm at stake.'

Valentyna found a sad smile for her new friend. 'I was measured for my wedding gown this afternoon.'

'As you should be,' Wyl said, hating the way any mention of the marriage made him feel. 'You must be seen to be progressing with your plans for the wedding, your highness. Let the spies report that you are preparing as any imminent bride would be.'

Valentyna put down her goblet, her expression one of disgust. 'And in the interim allow him to intimidate my people by setting up his arrogant Legionnaires in camps along our border?' She briefed her guests on everything she had gleaned from recent reports.

Wyl considered this information, sipping quietly from

his own wine, as a poultry course was laid before them. Valentyna's fare was simple but delicious, as was her choice in most things. He stared now at the roasted chicken before him, the heady scents of lemon and rosemary, even a hint of garlic, wafting up to tantalise him.

'The Legion's movements are purely that,' he said, looking up from his plate and sounding nothing like a pampered young noblewoman.

'Pardon me?' the Queen enquired, a fork speared with meat balanced halfway to her mouth.

'You think it's a ruse?' Crys chimed in.

Wyl shook his head. 'No ruse. Celimus would not hesitate to send in his men if pushed, but he has a good soldier's brain. And he's a King now with designs on broadening his empire, not losing his subjects. No, I think this is what you might call stage one. I would do precisely the same in his shoes.'

'Which is what?' Valentyna asked, stunned by Ylena's likeness in this moment to Liryk or indeed her own father. She imagined the girl's brother, Wyl Thirsk, must have sounded just like this when discussing battle strategy, and he no doubt had echoed his own father's approach.

'Parade the might of the Legion, remind Briavel of the power that lies across the border. He knows you are aware that war with Morgravia would be insanity and that you will not permit it.'

'Won't I?' she said, suddenly gloomy. She sounded as if she would rather fight. Ylena's presence, fragile though it appeared, seemed to have given her a new rush of hope.

'No, your majesty,' Wyl answered. Ylena's voice was high-pitched and very feminine, but the tone he managed to hit left no room for argument. 'You will send him a declaration of your affections instead. A reinforcement, if you will, of your commitment to the marriage and peace for the region.'

A hard blue gaze riveted Wyl to where he sat. He swallowed to loosen his throat which felt suddenly tight. Oh, how he would love to take her in his arms and kiss her, declare his love, tell her everything, and to hell with whether she might believe him or not. A roll of pain across his belly reminded him that the Queen was looking at a woman across the table and certainly did not harbour the same sentiments. What was more, her expression demanded an explanation of his statement.

He was about to continue when they were interrupted by a knock at the door. Valentyna called for one of her aides to enter and Wyl saw the irritation flicker across her face. He knew how much she would be missing Krell's competent presence in her life, realising how much he had screened from her and dealt with himself.

The man bowed. 'Your highness, Commander Liryk said you would want to have this information immediately.' He handed her a document.

'Thank you,' the Queen said, standing as she took the paperwork and nodding to dismiss the messenger. She moved to the fire to read it. 'Excuse me,' she murmured to her guests.

Both watched as her expression grew more serious as she read, then darkened like a gathering storm. She let out a harsh sound: half laughter, half despair. Wyl pushed his chair back and, despising the swish of his gown and girlish click of his heels, was at her side.

'Your highness, what is it?' He could see her pale before him.

Crys too was on his feet. 'Your majesty?'

The Queen shook her head, eyes closed, jaws firmly clamped together as she gathered herself. She opened her eyes and they were filled with tears. 'Our spies report that King Celimus of Morgravia is on his way north to Felrawthy where he will meet for a parley with the Mountain King.'

'Cailech and Celimus?' Wyl murmured in disbelief.

She nodded. 'It's a reliable source too.'

'What on earth would they have in common?' Crys said into the tense silence.

'Briavel!' Valentyna banged her fist against the mantelpiece and let out a sound of deep anguish. 'They mean to destroy us.'

'Wait, Valentyna!' Wyl cried, forgetting himself and all protocol. 'Let me think.' He began to pace.

Anyone who had known Fergys Thirsk, and perhaps his son, would be aware this was a family trait. It had always amused Magnus to see his General pacing as he formulated battle or peace plans, and if Ylena or Alyd were alive, they would be able to confirm that Wyl was hewn from the same block. Neither of the two people watching Ylena pacing now had known Fergys or Wyl Thirsk that well, but Valentyna had known Romen and she had watched him perform this very action when thinking and plotting. It struck her so resoundingly, she felt her breath catch in her throat. Even more disconcerting was the fact that Ylena was pulling at her ear as she paced. This was a habit Valentyna had teased Romen Koreldy about on several occasions during their short time together. There it was again, the tugging at the right ear, relentless slow pacing, face lost in thought. *Shar*! She was going mad. She looked away and reached for her wine, swallowed it in a single draught. The liquor helped steady her but did nothing to alleviate the shock of the news or the bewildering sense of Romen's presence.

Suddenly she was reminded of Fynch's strange suggestion that Wyl Thirsk and Romen Koreldy were of one mind. The boy had stopped just short of saying they were one person. How could it be that Wyl's sister now seemed to reflect similar traits? And then Elspyth's words blew through her mind:

I believe that some people are reincarnated. Perhaps you should listen more carefully to your friend Fynch. It is to this which he refers, I am sure. And you must promise me that should another person look at you and perhaps touch you emotionally as Romen did, reminding you uncannily of the man you loved, that you will permit it.

Permit them to love me, you mean? Valentyna remembered saying in amusement, almost teasing.

But Elspyth had nodded seriously and added, *Perhaps even a woman.*

Valentyna looked back at Ylena. *Perhaps even a woman* echoed through her mind and she gasped, turning away to hide the sound and the frightened look on her face. What was happening here? Why was Shar doing this to her? Something else nagged at the edges of her mind; something urging her to recall it, as though it was a valuable piece to a jigsaw which needed to be put in place. But it remained on the fringe, hovering and niggling, and her anxiety over this latest action of the Morgravian King won the battle and banished it for the time being. She had to focus on Celimus and his intentions, not her spiralling emotions and deranged thoughts that Ylena was somehow embodying Romen and that birds could speak to her, for Shar's sake! *Fool!* she screamed at herself inwardly.

Crys urged Wyl to speak his thoughts.

Wyl swung around, the swish of his gown annoying him again. How he wished he could at least be Faryl, tall and strong and in masculine clothes. 'I know Celimus,' he said, just pulling himself back from blurting, *I know Cailech too.* 'And I have travelled with someone who knows Cailech,' he lied.

'And?' Valentyna prompted, pushing away her own confusing thoughts.

Wyl raised Ylena's delicate hands in a gesture that said, hear me out. 'Celimus despises Cailech. He is quietly obsessed with the Mountain King, your highness, and nothing would prompt him to organise a parley with a sovereign whose realm, I'm sure, he entertains visions of destroying.'

'At least Celimus is consistent in his ambitions,' Valentyna commented bitterly. 'Go on.'

'Everything I've heard suggests that Cailech hates Morgravia's new King just as energetically – has more reason, in fact.' Wyl's mind was racing. 'So in truth, I can't see either of them making such a move of their own volition. Something has prompted it.'

'As the Queen suggests then – joining forces against Briavel,' Crys argued.

Wyl shook his head, felt Ylena's hair bob from side to side and grimaced to himself. 'No. Celimus doesn't need the Mountain King to overwhelm Briavel. The Legion could crush the Briavellian Guard resoundingly. If he was of a mind to do so, he could take Briavel by force and then combine the armies to take on Cailech. That's the more logical scenario — no offence intended, your highness.'

'None taken,' she replied, frowning. There was no doubting it: she felt as if she was being briefed by a soldier; certainly someone who understood military strategy. 'Why the parley then?'

'Does the letter say any more?'

Valentyna scanned it quickly again. 'No, just the name of the man who brought the original message out of the Razors and delivered it to Celimus's people.'

'Who was it?' Wyl said. Probably someone reliable such as Myrt, he reckoned.

Valentyna squinted at the page. 'Dreadful writing,' she murmured. 'I think it says his name is Farrow. Yes, Aremys Farrow.'

She was startled by her guests' reactions.

CHAPTER 10

Using fresh horses at intervals, King Celimus had swept through the gates of Tenterdyn in swift time. He was impressed by the sprawling estate of Felrawthy's duke and delighted to see that the manor itself was exceptionally well appointed. For a provincial home, the Donal family had not lived without their creature comforts he noticed. Freshly bathed and changed now, and having taken owner-ship of Jeryb's magnificent study with its view over the heather-laden moors, Celimus nodded at his Chancellor who had accompanied him. 'Bring him before me.'

Jessom entered the small antechamber where Aremys Farrow had been asked to wait. 'I trust there are no tricks up your sleeve, my friend,' he cautioned the mercenary.

Aremys eyed the hook-nosed Chancellor. 'Just earning my living, Jessom,' he replied. 'Lead on.'

The man turned and showed Aremys into the main chamber.

'Farrow,' Celimus said from the window where he had been admiring the vista.

'Your highness,' Aremys said, dropping a low bow.

'You are quite a surprise.'

'That is not my intention, sire,' the mercenary replied, straightening.

'Will you tell me how it comes about that you are working for my enemy?'

'Your highness, I am a man available for hire by anyone with coin to pay. I am always loyal to my employer, as your Chancellor would know. You must not fear that I have shared any secrets with Cailech, just as he need not fear I will share any of his with you. The two jobs are not connected,' Aremys said smoothly.

'So you admit he has secrets?' Celimus said, moving in his fluid, elegant manner to sit on the corner of Jeryb's old desk.

'We all have secrets, your majesty,' Aremys said carefully. 'It does not mean they necessarily impact on one another.'

'Farrow, I would know how you came to be in the Razors when you were on paid business for the Crown of Morgravia,' Celimus replied testily, tiring of the banter.

Aremys was prepared for this question. 'Your majesty, I was following the trail of Ylena Thirsk as instructed.'

'Did you meet up with Leyen?' the King interrupted.

'No, sire. But I believe she may have discovered that our prey had visited this very house.'

'Is that so?' Celimus said, olive eyes narrowing.

Aremys moved into the critical area of his fabricated story. He would have to be convincing. 'I have no idea what happened to Leyen. I presume she must have given up her pursuit for some reason, because I haven't found any trace of her since Tenterdyn. Perhaps she had other tasks to do?' he prompted carefully, and pretended not to see the glance between Chancellor and King.

'I gathered Ylena Thirsk had already left Tenterdyn before Leyen's arrival,' Aremys continued, 'and found myself giving chase to the eldest son of Felrawthy and the Thirsk woman, who seemed to be heading north to the very rim of the Razors before veering east.'

Celimus nodded. 'Into Briavel.'

Aremys hesitated, a question in his expression. Perhaps the King knew something he did not.

'We have heard reports that Crys Donal is at Briavel's palace. Perhaps Ylena is with him.'

Aremys wondered how in Shar's name the heir to Felrawthy had found himself in Werryl, although having learned with horror of the slaughter of Jeryb's clan the very night of his own departure from Tenterdyn, he should not be surprised at anything now. 'Not necessarily, your highness,' he said into the lengthening silence.

'What do you mean?' Celimus queried.

'Your spies have not reported a sighting of Ylena Thirsk, have they?'

'Not yet, no.'

'Hmmm,' Aremys said, quietly theatrical, as though thinking something complex through.

'Farrow, you still haven't explained how you come to be with Cailech's people,' Jessom prompted.

Aremys understood now why Faryl had disliked Jessom so intently. He felt his own hackles rise at the interruption by the softly spoken, painfully thin man who seemed to inhabit the shadows, watching everything.

'I was getting to that, Chancellor. I overnighted in a border village, preparing to cross into Briavel the next morning to see if I could pick up the trail of Ylena Thirsk. There was no inn, just a shorrock house, and perhaps I had one too many, I don't know. I suspect my shot was spiked with something in order to make it easier for thieves to set upon me later. It seems I wandered away from the main village in a stupor, and I do remember stumbling onto a track which I presumed would lead me into the Razors proper. I was very cold, I recall, and desperate to lie down. I remember men following me from the village, which was what drove me towards the mountains. But I'm afraid I remember very little else, sire.'

The King shook his head. 'So what occurred next, Farrow?'

'I've pieced together that the thieves did attack me but were fended off by some men from the Razors, obviously using the track to enter Morgravia. They dealt with the villagers swiftly, by which time I was unconscious and they decided to take me with them.'

'Why?' Celimus demanded.

'I don't know, sire. Perhaps they knew I would die in the cold if they didn't. They could see I was drugged and had been set upon by bandits. They felt obliged.' He shrugged.

'Obliged!' Celimus roared. 'To help a Morgravian?'

Aremys was determined not to be intimidated. He kept his voice low. 'They are not all murderers and thieves, your highness. The people of the Razors have scruples, families, a desire for peace—'

'Ah, you sympathise with the Mountain Horde, Farrow?' the King interrupted, a definite barb in his tone.

'My King, I am a Grenadyne so my soul is of the north. I like the notion that realms may prosper in peace rather than conquering each other through war.'

'Is that what this is all about then?'

'Yes, your highness.'

'Cailech is holding out the olive branch to Morgravia?' Disbelief was thick in the King's voice.

Aremys nodded slowly. 'You would like him, your majesty, if you'd agree to meet with him.'

'This is rich beyond words, Farrow. When did the leap from drugged captive to King's counsel take place, might I ask?'

'King Cailech naturally wished to meet the stranger who had been picked up lurking on the fringe of the Razors. He learned that I was from the north, working as a mercenary in the south, and on business for the Crown of Morgravia. He does not know the details of my task for you, your highness, and did not ask. I would not have shared them anyway. When the King interviewed me our conversation led us towards discussing the future of the Mountain People. When he said it was his greatest desire to create peace in the region, I asked him what was stopping him from discussing same with the King of Morgravia. I mentioned that you were preparing for your wedding, sire, and that the two great realms of Morgravia and Briavel would soon be joined in peace. It fired his imagination I think. He asked me to set up this meeting.'

'That's it?' Jessom posed. 'You are merely a go-between?'

Aremys did not look at the Chancellor but addressed Celimus. 'Yes, sire, that is precisely what I am. Because I had been employed directly by you, Cailech thought it would be easier for me to seek an audience and set up this parley. He believed you were more likely to trust me than him.'

'I don't trust anyone, Farrow, least of all mercenaries who have no loyalties.'

Aremys said nothing but he did not shrink under the hard gaze of the King either. He understood that Celimus was used to staring down others. *He must practise it in his mirror*, Wyl had once commented caustically. Aremys remembered that now and had to stop himself from smiling.

'King Celimus, I sell my services, not my soul,' he finally replied, determined to stand his ground. 'Cailech certainly does not own me — no one does. I am here to respectfully suggest that you, the reigning sovereign of a powerful kingdom, might consider it worthwhile to listen to what your northern neighbour has to say. Far more can be achieved around the dinner table, sire, than on the battlefield, I'd wager.'

'So now you're a philosopher and peacemaker, Farrow? I could have you killed for your insolence.'

'Yes, you could, sire,' Aremys said in a tone that made it clear he knew worse had happened to innocents around this man. 'But I ask your forgiveness if I have given the impression of presumptuousness. What you need to understand is that my own life is at stake, sire.'

That seemed to win the King's attention. He gestured for Jessom to pour some wine. 'Carry on,' he told Aremys.

Aremys felt relieved that he too was offered a cup of wine. Perhaps his life would be spared.

'Thank you,' he said before continuing. 'I give the impression of being a free man, sire, but I am in fact Cailech's prisoner. I have bought my freedom with the promise that I would attempt to set up this meeting. No money will exchange hands.'

Celimus held his cup towards Aremys in an ironic toast. 'You play with your life freely, mercenary.'

'It is mine to give, although I'm not sure I had any choice, your majesty.'

'And did you think I'd just say yes?'

'I could only hope so, sire.'

'In order to save your life?' Celimus mocked.

'No, my lord. To save Morgravia from war. I presume you'd like your marriage to be conducted in peace.'

Celimus arched a perfectly shaped eyebrow. 'So the Mountain upstart believes he can wage war on Morgravia — is that right?'

Aremys was tired of this but knew he was treading a fine line. From what he had heard of Celimus, the man walked his own knife edge of madness and would just as easily snuff out a person's life as swat at a fly. He needed to be careful. 'No, your majesty. I think he believes he can achieve peace between his realm and yours.'

Celimus smiled slyly and walked around Jeryb's desk to sit down. As he did so, Aremys had time to notice a child's engraving in the wood of the desk. The letters carved clumsily into the timber said 'Alyd' and he was reminded of how that young man had been treated by this very King — his life taken on a whim, and in front of his new wife and his closest childhood friend. That same friend who was now considered friend by Aremys. The mercenary felt a charge of anger when he considered that the two great families of Morgravia — the Donals of the north and the famous Thirsks to the south — had been all but wiped out on the command of the cruel man before him.

He watched Celimus lean back in Jeryb's handsome chair and sip from Jeryb's cup what was presumably a refreshment from Jeryb's cellar. His anger settled in his gut. He joined Wyl in hating Celimus more than any man, alive or dead, and determined to bring about his demise.

'Farrow,' the King began in a voice filled with tedium, as though explaining something obvious to someone stupid, 'you know full well that I will not risk myself by going into the Razors to meet with your cowardly captor, a man who sends one of my own people – if I dare call you that – to do his dealings for him.'

'I realise this, your highness.'

'So I must presume that he is prepared to risk coming here alone, for I will not brook his men setting foot on Morgravian soil.'

'They would set up camp at the border,' Aremys replied, as though he and Cailech had already anticipated as much from Celimus. He felt relieved that the Captain had not reported that Aremys had been escorted into Morgravia by men of the mountains. Aremys inwardly saluted Bukanan's foresight at not risking anything which might turn this situation ugly. Presumably the man knew how vicious his King could be and that an opportunity to make an example of Cailech's men would prove irresistible.

'I see. So that means Cailech is perfectly comfortable about coming to meet me, in Morgravia, with no protection other than the sword of a Grenadyne mercenary who is in my employ and presently under my guard?' Celimus's tone was filled with ironic amusement.

'I am not his protector, sire. I am purely his emissary.'

'Excellent. The situation is even more precarious then, for Cailech is all alone and on Morgravian soil. What is to stop me from simply killing him?'

'Your desire for peace, sire,' Aremys offered as reasonably as he could. 'The men of the Razors can be damnably elusive and they do not forgive, my lord. I am guessing that they would wage systematic attacks on your borders until their last man fell . . . the last woman, even.'

'That does not scare me, Farrow,' the King replied, lazily twirling his goblet. 'Frankly, I'd prefer his head on a spike at Stoneheart rather than holding talks in my court.'

'Of course he does have some insurance, sire.'

Celimus laughed, genuine enjoyment spicing the mirth. 'Of course he does! Now what could Cailech possibly offer me that I don't have and could possibly want?'

Aremys felt a tremor of fear pass through him. He was about to weave his most audacious lie yet, the only trump card he could produce from up his sleeve, and to a King who would have his throat slit from ear to ear this very second if he even suspected the ruse. 'I believe there is only one major item on your wishlist right now, sire.'

'I didn't know you possessed such magical insight into my desires, Farrow. Perhaps I should have you tortured and burned as a warlock?'

'No enchantments, sire,' Aremys replied calmly. 'Simple logic tells me what you covet at present.'

'And that is?' Celimus said, a sarcastic sneer on his face.

'Ylena Thirsk, your highness.'

The sneer vanished instantly, as did the casual posture. The King sat forward, suddenly alert. 'You have her?'

'I will deliver her, your majesty, on the promise that both Cailech's life and mine are ensured your complete protection. We will come to Morgravia for the parley and you will allow him an escort of his own men. Chancellor Jessom, and your two best captains, including Bukanan whom I gather is currently indispensable in the north, will stay at the border with the Mountain warriors. When the parley is complete, we will be escorted safely to the border of the Razors and permitted to depart into the mountains. With this promise in writing and announced publicly to your people, then I will arrange for Ylena Thirsk to be delivered to you.'

Celimus ignored everything Aremys had just listed. 'Do you have her, Grenadyne?' the King bellowed.

'I do, sire,' Aremys lied, furiously controlling his features to show an expression without guile. 'Although I am not at liberty to tell you how that comes to pass or where she is.' He smiled. 'I do not require payment for her capture, sire. I would not consider that fair,' he added, and chanced a soft grin.

The idea to use Ylena as bargaining power had only occurred to Aremys when he stood before Captain Bukanan and had somewhat arrogantly claimed that he had something in store which would keep Cailech's life safe. He had no clue as to where Wyl was at present or how he might reach him, but he reckoned Celimus would go along with the notion that Aremys was holding Ylena, not just because he was a mercenary paid to track her down, but because the King wanted her. Celimus's own greed and cruel desire to visit more torture on this last remaining member of the Thirsk dynasty far outweighed any doubt of Aremys's honesty — at least, that was what Aremys was counting on. How he would deliver on his promise or, more to the point, wriggle out of it was a whole new problem, but for now he was bargaining for his life and Wyl was all he had. If he could win Celimus's nod with the lie then he would also win his freedom from Cailech. He reassured himself that he had no intention of betraying Wyl; he was simply using Ylena's name as the lure to buy some time and his own safety.

Celimus leapt to his feet, as if readying himself to issue a command to his aides to have his guest's head chopped off or something equally terrifying. His eyes were dark and stormy with wrath. Aremys wondered whether he had misjudged Celimus. But he had not. The impending storm cleared as swiftly as it had gathered and the King began to laugh as he applauded Aremys.

'Bravo, Farrow. Bravo indeed. I shall guarantee your life and that of King Cailech for the duration of his stay on Morgravian soil. Is that good enough?'

'With all the other provisos in place, sire.'

'Yes, I agree. When?'

'When it suits you, your majesty. You are the host.'

'Where, Jessom?' Celimus said, looking immediately to the man he could trust to pull something special together.

'Here, of course, sire. Tenterdyn offers easy access to and from the border plus the ambience of a provincial palace. I would suggest a feast and entertainment, your highness. Show Cailech that you are a magnanimous host and prepared to extend the hand of fellowship whilst you hear what he has to say.'

'Good. See to it all, Jessom.' Celimus turned back to Aremys. 'And Ylena?'

'I will start making preparations, sire,' Aremys said, feeling very nervous now.

'Waste not a minute, Farrow. Return to your captor and pass on your news. I intend that the Thirsk woman be delivered as soon as our talks are done.'

Aremys bowed and departed, eager to be out of the King's sight.

CHAPTER 11

'So how did this Aremys fellow end up in the Razors if
he was with you in Briavel?' the Queen asked, having
discovered why both her guests had reacted so dramatic-
ally to the mention of the man's name.

'I have no idea,' Wyl replied, feeling both relief and
delight that Aremys was alive. 'We lost each other in the
north.'

'How do you lose someone?' Valentyna said, sipping
her wine.

It was not a serious question and Wyl opted not to
answer it. 'Long story,' he murmured. 'I have an idea,' he
added hurriedly when it seemed the Queen might want
to hear the long story. Fynch's suggestion would work
now, with this latest news about Aremys.

'Another plan?' Valentyna repeated, fractionally
sarcastic. She folded her arms.

'Yes. But you won't care for it much.'

'What's this about?' Crys queried.

'We have to buy some time with Celimus,' Wyl
explained, and Crys nodded. 'So we buy it with me.'

'He'll kill you!' Valentyna exclaimed.

'No, he won't,' Wyl said, not believing it himself.

'He razed Rittylworth Monastery and its village, killing dozens, before turning on Tenterdyn and slaughtering my family,' Crys said, his voice cold. 'He did this all to hunt you down. Don't tell me he won't kill you the moment he sees you.' Then he added, quietly, 'You know what will happen!' He was stilled from saying anything further by a dark glare from Ylena.

'What will happen?' Valentyna asked, sensing a new tension.

Wyl shook his head, ignoring the Queen's question. 'He won't kill me because of Cailech,' he said. 'I'll make sure to time my arrival when the King of the Mountains is present. If they're planning some sort of treaty, Celimus won't be so stupid as to demand the death of a noble before his newly formed partnership, will he?'

'Won't he?' Valentyna said, an appalled expression accompanying her query. 'You're gambling an awful lot on his sense of courtesy.'

Wyl was relieved she had been diverted and sent a surreptitious glare towards Crys warning him to be very careful and not blurt the truth.

'I know Celimus,' Wyl replied, 'I grew up around him. If he has one outstanding quality it is his charm. No, I don't think he will harm me whilst he needs to maintain outwardly calm relations.'

'And what about afterwards, when Cailech's gone? Why will he care then?' she demanded.

'Because I shall be gone too. Aremys is there – he will help me escape.'

'No,' Valentyna said from the fireplace, her voice raised.

'I can't let you do it. It's ridiculous and of no substance. I won't permit it.'

Wyl took a silent breath. He would not enjoy this next statement. 'I am not yours to command, your highness.'

The words hit her as effectively as if he had punched her with his own fist. She struggled to control her expression as intense pain battled with her defences. 'My apologies, Ylena. I think I misunderstood our talk earlier,' the Queen replied, her tone as tepid as the congealed gravy around the chicken they had all forgotten to eat.

'No, your highness. There is no misunderstanding. I *am* your servant. That will never change. But I will make my own decision on how to serve you.'

'You will be going to your death, Ylena!' the Queen snapped.

'I don't believe so, but I choose that path come what may.'

'Not on my behalf! I will not have your blood as well as your brother's on my hands.'

'I'm sure you tried to order Wyl around too, your highness, but it seems you lost that argument as well. I am just as stubborn when it comes to protecting those I love.' The bit about love had slipped out. Wyl felt his face colour afresh at the error.

Valentyna missed the slip. 'Ylena, you are barely into your womanhood,' she all but yelled.

'And it is my womanhood which demands I leave your table, your highness. Please forgive me,' Wyl said, suddenly feeling a most unpleasant release to the build-up of pain which had accompanied him all day. Still, it was a welcome excuse to get away from the Queen's commands.

Crys looked baffled but the Queen, still angry, could

only nod. She understood precisely Ylena's predicament. 'By all means.'

Wyl fled towards his chamber, clean linens and a fresh brew of raspberry leaf tea. He *hated* being a woman. And he especially hated the disdain shown to women by others of the same sex. How dare Valentyna consider Ylena unworthy! *Well, that's not really fair*, he told himself as he ran up the last flight of stairs. Not unworthy, but certainly inadequate. He thought of Faryl and wished Valentyna had had the opportunity to meet her. Then the Queen would have seen a woman hold her own with a man.

He spent the next few minutes with an expression of disgust on his face as he sipped at the raspberry leaf tea and replaced the linens. He felt quite worn out by the end of it all and, in a fit of pique, changed into his favoured trews and shirt, although he had to admit a skirt was easier to wear in his current condition.

Shar, please deliver me from this, he prayed as he drank the bitter tea. *Let me be a man again*.

A knock at the door interrupted his plea to his god. He was not surprised to see that it was Valentyna, but he was embarrassed.

'May I come in?' she asked.

'Of course, your highness,' Wyl said, clearing his throat. 'I'm sorry, I—'

'No, it's quite all right and it is I who should apologise. Forgive my interruption,' Valentyna began. 'Oh good, I see you've brewed more leaf. How are you?'

'Oh, you know, first night,' Wyl admitted like an old hand.

'Had you hoped you were pregnant?' the Queen startled him by asking in her most gentle tone.

'No, your highness. I knew I wasn't,' Wyl lied, unable to think of anything more enlightening.

'I'm sorry. I shouldn't have asked. I just thought that, newly married, you and Alyd had probably . . . well, you know . . .'

'Yes,' Wyl interjected, disturbed at where the conversation was headed. He had never felt more of an impostor. 'No baby, though.'

Valentyna looked sad enough to cry. 'You know, Ylena, there are moments when I wish more than anything that I had joined with Romen and that his seed had quickened my womb.'

Wyl had to look away. This was too painful. He busied himself with tidying his discarded clothing.

Valentyna rallied a smile and changed the subject. 'I see you've changed out of the gown. Not to your liking?'

'It's lovely, your highness. I just got so used to these comfy clothes whilst travelling. I like them.'

Valentyna nodded knowingly. 'So do I. Men have it good. I often wish I was a man, don't you, Ylena?'

'I do, your highness. I'm wishing it right now, in fact.' Wyl had never spoken a truth with more passion.

She took his intensity in a different light. 'Ah yes, I can understand why. You presumably get a lot of pain. I must admit that I escape the cramps. Shar is merciful with me.'

'Do you look forward to children of your own?' Wyl asked, desperate to move away from the subject of women's ailments and yet not doing so very successfully.

'I do. I've decided it's the one good thing which might come out of this hateful marriage. Celimus won't have my love but he can have my body. He will give me something far more precious than he takes.'

Wyl grimaced as the fresh ache from his side joined with the pain of the picture in his mind of Celimus in bed with Valentyna, siring a child upon her.

Valentyna filled the difficult pause. 'I came here to apologise for my heavy-handed tactics earlier. Even as a little princess I bossed everyone around,' she said, trying to lighten the mood swirling about them. 'I know I cannot permit or deny you anything, Ylena. I just don't want you to forfeit your life in order to save me from Celimus.'

'I don't think I can save you from the marriage, but I can give you more time to get used to the idea,' Wyl said, the resignation in his comment agonising in its truthfulness.

'But you can't guarantee that you will escape.'

'There are no guarantees in life, your highness. I have lost too much in too short a time to care any more.'

'But I don't want to lose you as well,' the Queen said, her tone just short of begging.

'You won't.'

'What exactly is your plan?' Valentyna said. 'No, wait, let's have some warmed milk sent up and we might lace it with some liquor to help you sleep and forget your pains.'

Wyl nodded. Valentyna looked outside and called to Stewyt who had been positioned for the night outside the door and sent him on his errand.

'So, now tell me everything,' she said, curling up next to Ylena on the deep sofa near the fire.

She was unbearably close but Wyl would have sooner slashed his own throat than ask her to sit apart from him. If this was all he could have, it would have to be enough.

'I shall go to Felrawthy, present myself before King Celimus – ensuring that King Cailech is in attendance – and beg Morgravia's indulgence.'

'But what is your aim? I can't see the point if I have to marry him anyway.'

'Well, amongst other things, to get the Legionnaires redeployed from Briavel's border. Their presence is making your people very nervous and rightly so.'

'But you said it was only a ploy.'

'I am assuming that, your highness. I can't truly speak for Celimus's unpredictable whims. I would rather make sure of it by seeing the physical movement of the Legion.'

'And you think he'll do it?' the Queen asked, amazed.

'Yes. I'll tell him that you are nervous, that you feel inhibited and threatened – which is, of course, his intention – but I'll play you as the innocent. I'll assure him that your personal preparations are well advanced and I'll give him a token of your loyalty to him and the truth of your claims.'

'And what's that?'

'Me.'

'So he can kill you!' Valentyna exclaimed, exasperated again.

'He won't do that in front of Cailech, your highness. But he will be appeased. He will realise that for you to relinquish me, you have been duly intimidated. The plan is perfect in its simplicity. My presence will confirm not only how committed you are to peace and the marriage, but also that you appear scared of him. So scared that you have gladly turned over his enemy who had run to you for protection.'

'And how does that save you, Ylena?'

'It doesn't, but please, your majesty, let me worry about saving myself. I have a few tricks of my own.'

'Oh, you're so frustrating!' Valentyna replied. 'You sound like Wyl and Romen rolled into one.' Then she stopped, shocked at what she had said without thinking.

'Do I? How odd,' Wyl replied.

They stared at each other, the candlelight and flames from the fire combining in a soft glow across their beautiful faces. They were so close, Wyl realised. Too near. Close enough to kiss. A madness came over him and smothered his judgement. It was the move of a lunatic and he knew it, but still he leaned across the few inches separating his mouth from the Queen's and placed Ylena's lips to Valentyna's.

The Queen reacted as if burned by a spitting coal from the fireplace. She leapt to her feet, wiping frantically at her mouth. 'Ylena!' she spluttered, shock and anger combined on her face. It was hideous for Wyl to watch.

'I'm sorry,' was all he could say. 'I beg your forgiveness, your highness.'

The Queen appeared uncertain whether to flee or to slap the woman before her. Then she gathered her wits. 'No,' she said, holding up a hand. 'I must have been giving off all the wrong signals. Forgive me, Ylena, I should not have come to your chamber tonight. All this talk of babies and changing into men . . .' She laughed awkwardly and then that awful expression of disgust crossed her face again.

Wyl stood, feeling sorry for both of them. 'The apology is all mine, Valentyna. I really don't know what came over me. I've been through a lot these few weeks and the emotions have got me all confused,' he offered. It sounded lame even to his own ears but he pressed on, desperate to fill the vile and difficult silence that would surely prevail if he did not keep talking and backing her towards the door. 'It's been a very long two days for me, without much sleep, and I shall put it down to the raspberry leaf tea clouding my judgement, your highness.'

'Yes,' Valentyna stammered, none of her mortification dissipating. 'I've heard it can make one hallucinate.'

'You don't even look the tiniest bit like Alyd,' Wyl said, hating himself for the weak jest at the expense of his beloved sister and friend.

There was a knock at the door and the Queen started, her hands wringing each other. 'That will be the milk,' she said and Wyl heard the slightly hysterical note in her voice. He lowered his head, ashamed of himself as never before. 'I'll leave you, Ylena,' Valentyna managed with some grace.

'No, I shall leave you, your highness,' Wyl said cryptically, and bent to kiss her hand. He could feel her fingers pulling away with revulsion at the touch of his lips and could have wept at his own lack of control and stupidity of moments earlier. He would never forgive himself and she certainly would not.

The Queen, flushed and agitated, pulled open the door and pushed past the same serving maid who had helped Wyl earlier.

'Thank you,' he said wearily to the girl as she placed the milk on a small side table. 'Can you ask the page to bring me some parchment and then to deliver some letters, please?'

There was nothing to pack, and nothing other than his memories to keep him here a minute longer. He lifted the letters from the desk and blew out the flickering candle, leaving behind the debris of his hurried toil — sealing wax, broken nibs, ink blotches, as well as various letters begun and screwed up on the floor where he had tossed them in frustration. He bent now to pick them up and threw them into the embers of the fire he had not bothered to tend. The paper sputtered and curled before catching and burning quickly in a brief eruption of flames. He watched until his difficult, awkward words of explanation to the woman he loved were nothing but blackened flakes — just like the fragile relationship he had clung to and now ruined.

He cast a glance at the letter in his hand. After several attempts he had finally settled on being Wyl and the words were brief and to the point. There was nothing of Romen's charm, Faryl's cunning or Ylena's courtesies, merely a simple apology for his unforgivable behaviour and a reiteration that he was making for Felrawthy. No honeyed farewell, no promise of return, no attempt at reconciling their awkward parting. He would be gone from her life once and for all. Wyl had taken care to wish her well for her upcoming marriage and had encouraged her to be brave and stoic in what she faced. To never forget who she was and to remember her promise to bring forth a babe who would rule both realms with care and affection. Wyl knew he was writing the truth of his thoughts. He could not save her this trial or the destiny of an unhappy life with Celimus, but he could let her know that he had listened to her soft words and wished her the joy of loving a child. He suspected that part of the letter might make her cry, but for the rest he knew she would read it with only relief and gratitude that he had gone.

'So be it,' he muttered to himself as he strode across the room to the door.

Stewyt was sitting outside. He was not caught napping and did not even appear tired. No need to rub the sleep from those alert eyes, Wyl thought.

'Thank you, Stewyt, for waiting up,' he said.

'A pleasure, my lady. I am here to serve,' the page said, sounding mature way beyond his years. 'May I take those for you?'

'Please,' Wyl said.

'I will personally deliver them immediately, my lady.'

'No, Stewyt, I would prefer if you would arrange their delivery in the early hours of the morning. I don't wish either recipient disturbed this night and there is nothing of such import that it cannot wait until tomorrow.'

Stewyt nodded, then he hesitated, and Wyl saw him take in the change of clothes from gown to breeches. 'Is there anything else I can do for you tonight, my lady? Perhaps I could send up some refreshment, have the fire stoked?'

Wyl cut him off with a gently raised hand. 'Nothing, thank you,' he said, forcing a smile. He had no intention of letting the curious page know of his movements. 'I am very tired and sleep calls.'

'I shall see you're not disturbed again then, my lady. Good night and sleep well.' Stewyt gave a solemn bow and moved swiftly off into the shadows of the corridor to organise the despatch of the letters in a few hours.

Wyl waited for what felt an interminable time, but he needed to be sure the inquisitive page did not see his departure. Eventually, he tiptoed from his chamber and made his way quietly down the various flights of stairs.

At one landing he noticed a portrait of Valentyna he did not recall having seen before. In the low light of the sconces, the tall figure seemed to be pulling away from the wall, advancing on him. Her expression struck him as accusatory, the faint smile mocking him. If only she knew the truth, he thought, and regretted bitterly that he could not share it with her. He extended his hand towards the painting, wished he could reach high enough to touch her on the lips but only succeeded in touching her chest. It would do.

'Farewell, my love,' he whispered and then he was sprinting down the final flight of stairs and running towards a doorway he remembered from his time there as Romen. It took him through the scullery, where he saw one sleeping attendant who should have been stirring the porridge that simmered continually through the night. The young girl looked exhausted; her lips were parted and a light snore punctuated the silence as she slumped on the table. Wyl smiled. Oh, for a simple life with only a dressing-down from cook in the morning to worry about.

He slipped out of the door into one of the many vegetable gardens, disturbing two cats gnawing on a struggling rat. One took off, the dying creature still in its jaws. The other shrieked at its loss of the night's feast. Wyl ignored them, looked around to get his bearings, and made for the stables and his journey north.

CHAPTER 12

Valentyna broke her fast early and privately on the balcony of her bedchamber. She had moved rooms not so long ago. At first, after learning of his murder, she had wanted to cling to the memory of Romen and remember every word, every smile, every touch they had shared together, so briefly, in her bedroom. These days, however, with an impending marriage she feared and the only man whom she had ever loved, save her father, now dead, she had decided she must bury those memories and put aside anything that prompted their return. Hence the move into the new quarters. Her new room had been her mother's and it was fitting, Valentyna realised, that she should move into this chamber now with its soft colours and beautiful tapestries and rugs. It was from her mother that she had inherited her taste for simple, fine things. As did her mother before her, Valentyna far preferred a single exquisite rose to a roomful of garish, expensive ornaments. This chamber and its accompanying suite of rooms used natural light and space to achieve what Valentyna now realised was a place of calm. And calm was what she needed right now. She was still deeply upset from the previous night's events and, although not hungry after her fitful sleep and fretful awakening, she had adhered to her father's long-held advice that bad news and bad moods are best coped with on a full belly. Nevertheless, she had ordered only the lightest of meals, consisting of a small sugared roll, a single lightly boiled egg, a sliced pear and a pot of dark, strong tea.

She had left the letter from Ylena unopened by the side of her tray until she had picked over the fruit and egg, neither of which she tasted, and had downed her first cup of tea. Valentyna suspected the letter would contain an outpouring of beautifully crafted yet cringing apologies and hated the thought of reading them, let alone facing the woman who had so misread her affections. She was sure her face still burned from the combined horror and embarrassment of Ylena's error, although Valentyna was uncertain whether this intense discomfort was for herself or on behalf of Wyl's sister. Both probably, she thought glumly.

She poured a second cup of tea, this time with a slice of lemon instead of sweetening honey, and waited until she had sipped from its steaming contents before breaking the seal on the letter. It was a sharp surprise to discover that it was not even close to what she had imagined. A brief and succinct apology for what Ylena called her unforgivable behaviour was followed by an equally concise confirmation that she was already on her way to Felrawthy. She specifically asked not to be followed, and added that no one would be able to track her anyway. Valentyna, angry that Ylena had slipped away in the night, could not guess at what that comment meant, for her soldiers would be easily able to track down a noblewoman on horseback. Ylena urged the Queen to write immediately to Celimus with news that she was sending Wyl Thirsk's sister as a token of her loyalty to the King of Morgravia.

The second half of the single sheet was softer in its intentions if not in its words, and reminded Valentyna of things her father might say. Unlike her father, though, the words felt as though they were written by someone not used to being openly affectionate and yet who cared deeply for her wellbeing. Frankly, Valentyna thought, drumming her fingers on her seat, Ylena just did not know her well enough to write with such tender, albeit awkward familiarity.

Tears stung her eyes and she snatched them away. She had not intended to cry but weep she did, hating herself for these last days of such hysterical behaviour. From Wyl's description of his sister all that time ago, she had expected Ylena Thirsk to be a gentle, fragile sort of character. Despite hearing how she had overcome such enormous trauma, Valentyna had still been stunned by the confident and direct woman who had presented herself at the court of Briavel.

She put down the letter, picked up her cup and let the steam from the tea warm her face which felt chill from sitting outside on this still brisk spring morning. It struck Valentyna that Ylena had behaved in a fairly masculine fashion throughout her short time at Werryl. This had occurred to her well before the kiss, even before the supper; it had begun to resonate in Valentyna's perceptive mind as early as their stroll together in the gardens. Ylena showed all the poise and upbringing of a noblewoman but she appeared to think like a man, even acted like a man at times. Valentyna prided herself on being an adept judge of character, but Ylena's disposition was not easy to explain yet niggly enough to notice – at least so it seemed to the Queen. At first she had thought she was imagining it, but during supper Ylena had taken over the conversation and led the discussion on Celimus and Cailech as though they were sitting in a war room. She had heard her father conversing with his soldiers for too many years not to recognise the similarity of the situation, but most young noblewomen would feel uncomfortable talking of such matters let alone taking charge of them.

That aside, she wondered about Ylena's uncanny habit of pacing while she was thinking? That had rocked Valentyna only marginally less than the wretched kiss. The likeness to Romen was too painful to bear. Valentyna remembered how she had had to look away and how shallow her breathing had become watching Ylena. And then the worst part – that terrible incident in Ylena's chamber. Valentyna blamed herself for its occurrence. Ylena had lost so much – both parents, her brother, her new husband, the family friend, Gueryn le Gant, whom she was so close to. Then she had learned of the tragedy at Felrawthy. The emotions had all boiled over, presumably, and she had sought affection from someone who seemed to be offering it. Valentyna made an involuntary sound of disgust remembering the kiss. And yet the explanation sounded too neat and tidy, as though she were contriving every excuse to explain the curiosity that was Ylena Thirsk.

Far more likely, the practical voice in Valentyna's head suggested, the girl had a liking for women. But even that did not make sense, the Queen silently argued. A woman who wanted to lie with other women surely did not have a male childhood sweetheart, or marry that person as soon as they were both old enough. When Wyl Thirsk told herself and Valor about the death of Alyd that night at supper, he had also described the great love between Alyd and his Ylena.

She closed her eyes with frustration. And then the nagging thought, which had called from the edges of her mind almost since Ylena's arrival, filtered to the surface of her consciousness and set a new and chilling problem before her. Ylena's handkerchief – the one she had handed Valentyna when she had wept in the garden. It struck her now with the force of a blow. It was the same linen that she herself had given to Romen! How could Ylena possibly own it?

This revelation caught the Queen so off guard she put the cup down, stood and leaned against the balcony railing. Was she imagining things? No! It was her own handkerchief. She had even mentioned it to Elspyth at Aleda's funeral. Elspyth had been weeping for Aleda and Valentyna had put an arm around her petite companion and handed her a beautiful square of embroidered linen. She closed her eyes to remember the words she had shared with her friend: *I gave Romen an identical kerchief*, she had whispered. *You keep this. Now both my best friends own one*.

She repeated the words in her mind as she gazed down onto Werryl Bridge and its endless stream of activity. It was definitely the same handkerchief. The squares had been embroidered by her mother and were treasured by Valentyna, so the recipients of these items were held in equally high esteem . . . but Romen had died in a brothel in Briavel! Ylena's only contact with Romen had been between Pearlis and Rittylworth, she calculated. Then they had parted and, according to her information, had not seen each other again before he died. Valentyna had given Romen the handkerchief long after he had left Morgravia and the Razors, and he had lived the rest of the numbered days of his life in Briavel.

A new thought struck the Queen. Perhaps that hateful woman, Hildyth, had stolen it from him. But why take a square of meaningless linen? And even if she did steal it from Romen at the Forbidden Fruit, how could Ylena now have it in her possession?

Wyl, Romen, Ylena and Hildyth – what did they have in common? Why was she even linking them in her mind? Wyl and Ylena were related, that one was obvious. Romen and Wyl had fought together in vain to save her father and had certainly saved her. Romen had rescued Ylena, keeping a promise to her dead brother Wyl. And Hildyth? Hildyth was connected only to the man Valentyna had loved, through death – a blade in the heart.

But no. There was another link, was there not? She shook her head in a futile attempt at denial but it whispered through her raging thoughts. A shining, clear notion which travelled brightly through the maelstrom of her mind and landed as sharply and painfully as an arrow. A notion which had been voiced by two separate people she trusted: Fynch subtly, and Elspyth more insistently.

Fynch had claimed that he believed Wyl and Romen were of one mind. As she thought of this she was immediately reminded of Knave and the talk of magic that swirled about the dog. Valentyna recalled Fynch's confusion when Wyl's cantankerous dog had taken so easily to

Romen, and how Romen had called out the dog's name in Stoneheart having never met Knave before. Even more baffling for Fynch was how playfully Knave had greeted the stranger. The Queen remembered Fynch describing Wyl's eyes changing colour at the witch-burning – more talk of magic which she had ignored. And then along came Elspyth with similar murmurings. She had urged Valentyna to accept the notion of reincarnation, all but confirming that she too believed Wyl somehow resonated within Romen, and that the Queen's beloved might well be spiritually present in a new person – a woman even. Wyl . . . Romen . . . Ylena.

Valentyna startled herself by being sick, turning just in time to avoid soiling her clothes. She crumpled to the floor of the balcony, upending the crockery on the tray, and gave way to deep, dry sobs. Nothing made sense any more.

She remained curled on the balcony until the cold and the smell of herself brought her back to the present and the one stark reality she could not escape. Marriage to Celimus. Today was the all-important fitting for her gown. She must attend to her toilet, tolerate the seamstresses' chatter and annoying pins and requests, before she would be free to call a hasty meeting with Crys. The time between now and when the King of Morgravia would legally bed her could be counted on her fingers.

Valentyna collected her shattered wits, put all thoughts of reincarnation and magic to the back of her mind, and steeled herself for her regal duties in the coming days.

Forging a peace was all she would permit herself to focus upon.

She had a war to dissuade and a wedding to prepare

for. She would do as Ylena Thirsk had suggested and write a letter of appeasement to King Celimus using Ylena as her barter. She might as well, now that Ylena had made her sacrifice.

Crys had risen later than Valentyna but read his letter before he dressed. Wyl suggested two options for him to consider. The first was that he try and catch up with Elspyth, whom Wyl felt was on a foolhardy mission but added that he did not believe she was in any immediate danger. Both he and Crys felt protective towards Elspyth and it was only right that, with so few allies, they all look out for one another. Failing this, he suggested Crys should put on a disguise and infiltrate Pearlis, particularly the Legion. He was to spread the word of Celimus's betrayal of Jeryb and his family. Wyl listed a few names of reliable men whom Crys should single out to receive this information. He was to tell them about the treatment of Ylena and Alyd as well. *Take the head of your brother*, he urged, *give them proof*. Crys was to be patient, though, not do anything rash and to encourage a similar conservativeness by any angry Legionnaires. Wyl asked him to lie low amongst the Legion until Wyl somehow got word to him. He reinforced that Crys was not to even hint at the truth should the Queen ask questions about Ylena. His secret was to be maintained. He signed off, wishing Crys luck and that they would meet again soon. He added a note to Crys to remember the password for he could not promise he would return as Ylena.

Crys smiled grimly at the postscript. Any stranger could walk up to him in the future and claim to be Wyl. How frightening it must be for him, Crys thought, and turned his mind to departure. Frankly, he would be glad to be on the move again and doing something constructive towards the downfall of Celimus. Wyl was right. There were far cleverer, bloodless ways to avenge his family's slaughter than trying to murder the King, which had been his first inclination.

He would leave today — this morning, in fact — and was sure the Queen would quietly sigh with relief.

Valentyna gritted her teeth and got through the gown-fitting. As she had expected, the seamstress and her assistants tittered around her for almost an hour. Sadly they did not poke her with a single pin, which might at least have given her an excuse to vent some of the frustration she was feeling. Somehow she found a fake smile when they stood beaming at the vision in the palest of cream gowns before them.

She had demanded simplicity. And simplicity she had been given, but Madam Eltor had surpassed herself on this occasion. She was used to Valentyna's likes and dislikes, having designed gowns for the new Queen since she was old enough to attend formal engagements. She did not need to be told what Valentyna would look for in a wedding gown, but she knew that in this one she had presented something that somehow embraced the Queen of Briavel's personality. It had long, clean lines in a fabric which fell so beautifully into its natural folds that it took even the designer's breath away when she saw it hanging on the perfect body.

'You're a woman now,' she had whispered to Valentyna whose eyebrows had raised slightly when she saw the neckline that plunged in a sharp V-shape from the furthest width of her shoulders. It revealed not only the shapely top of her arms but displayed the flawless creamy expanse of her chest, just meeting at its tip before any cleavage might show.

'You will have to be sewn in, of course, my dear,' Madam Eltor warned through the pins in her mouth. Having known the Queen since childhood, the dressmaker had long ago been excused from the necessity to constantly show deference by using Valentyna's titles. 'It's the only way we'll get this perfect fit across your bust.'

Valentyna nodded distractedly. 'Finished now?'

'No,' came the reply. 'Be still, child,' and the Queen of Briavel could not hide the ghost of a grin at the reprimand which Madam Eltor had been giving for so many years now they had both lost count.

The gown's only adornment was a tiny row of pearls sewn along the neckline and around the cuffs, which ended three-quarters of the way down Valentyna's long arms.

'I'll wager all of Morgravia and Briavel will be wearing this new length and slim sleeve by summer's close, your highness,' one of the assistants commented eagerly.

Valentyna and Madam Eltor shared a glance in the mirror. They had been setting new fashion trends in Briavel for years even though Valentyna had no interest in dazzling people with her wardrobe.

'Would you like to see it with the veil?' Madam Eltor enquired, already knowing the answer.

'Not today, Margyt,' Valentyna begged. 'Next time, I promise. Right now I have some urgent things to attend to and a realm to run.' She gave the older woman a beseeching grin.

The seamstress nodded as if in long-suffering pain.

'Next time then,' she said kindly, adding firmly: 'Which, your highness, will be in four days. Be warned.'

Valentyna groaned. 'Thank you, everyone,' she said, wriggling hastily out of the dress.

'Flowers?' Madam Eltor asked.

The Queen sighed. 'It is in hand. Your colleague, Madam Jen, has chosen open creamy-white roses and fairy's breath for the posy and a wreath of white buds for my head,' she answered. 'I'd prefer lavender.'

'It wouldn't work,' Madam Eltor commented, quite used to Valentyna's contrariness. 'The white buds will echo the pearls and enhance the Stone of Briavel, which I presume you'll wear?'

Valentyna nodded. She had to admit the gown suited her with its sleek look and sharp lines. She was not one for the rounded, softer look which many of the court women preferred. The Queen liked the way her dress-maker had echoed her slightly masculine edge in the sharp plunge of the gown's neckline, and the lack of affectation and adornment made her feel she could almost get away with wearing her riding boots beneath it. This made her smile inwardly. In spite of herself, her liking for the dress made the Queen wonder, if her people graciously accepted her tomboyishness without reading all manner of sinister connotations into it, why could she not accept Ylena Thirsk's more masculine way? Because it doesn't add up, she argued.

'I beg your pardon, dear?' Madam Eltor said, the wedding gown held reverently across her outstretched arms, ready to be placed into clean muslin for the journey back to her chambers in Werryl.

'Nothing,' Valentyna murmured, embarrassed that she

must have spoken her last thought aloud. 'Thank you, Margyt. I'll see you soon.' She saw the seamstress and her chittering assistants to the door and called for a page.

'Find me Stewyt, please, Ross, and also summon the Duke of Felrawthy to a meeting in my solar. I will see him in an hour.'

The boy bowed and ran off on his errands. Valentyna hurriedly tied back her hair. She wished she could wear it just like this at her wedding – tied back and plaited. She pulled at the wisps she had not quite managed to incorporate into the main plait, then made a sound of disgust at their waywardness and left them alone. A soft knock heralded the page.

'Stewyt, thank you for coming so quickly.'

'Your majesty,' he said, bowing low. 'How may I help?'

Stewyt often unnerved her with his mature manner. Talking to him often felt like speaking to Krell or someone of similar age and ilk. She realised Stewyt would make a fine chancellor in years to come; he encompassed all the right qualities, from discretion to intense curiosity about everyone and everything. He was a superb listener and rarely needed anything repeated. As she was thinking these things about the youngster she realised he was staring at her, his expression deliberately open and patient.

She cleared her throat and her thoughts. 'I wanted to talk to you about Lady Ylena.'

'Yes, your highness. You received her note, I presume?'

'I did, thank you. But you didn't deliver it. I was given it with my breakfast tray.'

'That's right, your majesty. Lady Ylena did not want you disturbed last night. She told me the contents of the letters were of no immediate import and I was to ensure both were delivered this morning.'

'Both letters?'

'The other was for the Duke of Felrawthy,' Stewyt qualified. 'Is there something wrong, your majesty?'

'No, not at all. I've been informed that Lady Ylena left the palace during the night. Did she seem upset when you saw her?'

Stewyt frowned. 'No, your highness. She was very alert, as I recall, although perhaps somewhat intense if I might hazard that thought.'

Valentyna nodded, impressed as always by his composure. 'Go on.'

'Forgive me, your majesty, but I took the liberty of watching Lady Ylena.'

'Oh?'

'Yes, I felt her manner was a trifle odd. She went to some trouble to impress upon me how tired she was and in need of sleep, yet throughout our conversation she struck me as being very much awake and caught up by a sense of urgency.'

'And you were right, of course,' Valentyna prompted.

'Yes,' the lad said, not meaning to sound smug. 'I set off on my errand as requested but doubled back, just to see if my instincts were right. Chancellor Krell taught me to follow my instincts, your highness,' he added. 'I watched Lady Ylena hurry out of her chamber.'

'She did mention in her letter to me that she intended departing last night,' Valentyna replied, determined this lad should not think Ylena was up to any mischief. She could not have gossip of that kind doing the rounds and providing any future ammunition. 'You recall, Stewyt, I asked you to keep her presence between ourselves, which is why I handpicked you as her page and Florrie as her maidservant.'

He nodded solemnly. 'I have told no one of her presence, your highness.'

'Did anything else occur which you think is worth mentioning?'

'Well . . .' The page sounded uncomfortable.

'Yes?'

'She . . .' He stopped, and started again. 'On her way past your portrait on the first landing, your highness, she paused . . . rather deliberately.'

'And?' Valentyna queried, not understanding the boy's hesitation.

'She touched it, your majesty. Touched your . . . er, your breast, your highness.'

Valentyna felt a new thrill of alarm. 'Did she say anything?'

'She murmured a farewell to you, your highness. In all truth, I would say that she was trying to reach your face but wasn't tall enough.'

'I see. Thank you, Stewyt.' The Queen dismissed the page, following him out of her chamber and heading to her solar to meet with Crys Donal.

He was waiting for her. 'Good morning, your majesty,' he said and bowed.

'Crys, you look readied for travel,' she said, noting the cloak, as she walked towards him and surprised him with a brief kiss. She felt as if he was all that was left of her allies.

He blushed. 'Yes, your highness, I've decided to leave. I think it's only right, what with your troubles with the

Legion and so on. I know I'm a thorn in your side and I agree with Ylena that I can probably be more use back in Morgravia being a thorn in the King's side.' He grinned but it looked hollow.

'You've spoken with Ylena about this?' the Queen asked, surprised.

'No. She sent me a letter which I received this morning. She suggested I should infiltrate the Legion and start spreading news of the slaughter at Tenterdyn and anything else which might help turn the army against their King, your majesty.'

'Is that her plan?'

Crys shook his head. 'I don't know what her plan is, your highness.'

Valentyna sat down in her favourite window seat with her back to her guest so he did not have to look her in the eye. 'Crys, since when did the Duke of Felrawthy — any Duke of Morgravia for that matter — take orders from a young noblewoman of little rank?'

There was a difficult pause, as she had anticipated, and then an equally awkward laugh. 'Your majesty, Ylena Thirsk is no ordinary noblewoman. The surname alone tells you the stock she comes from.'

He was going to say more but she cut him off. 'The fact that she is the daughter of the famous Fergys Thirsk and sister to the seemingly revered Wyl Thirsk does not necessarily make her a military strategist though, does it? I would have thought a woman like Ylena would have a head filled with how to embroider beautifully, fine table manners and how to make polite conversation with strangers whilst making an elegant tour of a room.'

'Just like you, your highness,' Crys said, immediately

regretting his gentle sarcasm as Valentyna turned to fix him with a stare.

'Forgive me, your majesty, I meant no insult. I admire you tremendously for the dazzling way you balance being a beautiful woman and the ruler of a realm. It's not easy, your highness, and anyone with half a brain can see that such skill requires both a feminine and masculine side.'

Valentyna dug deep and found a smile to show no offence had been taken — it was obvious that Crys was genuine in his praise, although just as obvious that he was protecting Ylena or at the very least working hard to keep something secret for her. 'I don't know, Crys, I just got the impression that Ylena would be this gentle, totally pampered young woman.'

'Which she was, I'm sure, your highness. But plenty has happened to change that, and they do say blood will out.'

'They do indeed,' Valentyna said cryptically. 'If you'll forgive me digging into a painful subject — her relationship with Alyd, did you know much about it?'

'Only that they were madly in love. His letters were filled with his adoration of both Thirsks. They were his family during his time in the south. What's troubling you, your highness?'

She struggled. Could she tell him? She needed to share it with someone and Crys was as reliable as any of her own counsel. 'You don't think she had leanings towards women, do you?'

The duke looked shocked. 'Ylena? No! Whatever gave you that idea?'

Valentyna made a face. 'Oh, just something that happened last night between us. I don't really want to talk about it.'

'Except we are,' he said, grinning, understanding dawning about what must have occurred. He felt so sorry for Wyl, and that would explain why he had fled in the night. 'No, Ylena used to write to us as well, your highness, and this was a girl who was intensely in love with Alyd. It was all she could do to talk about anything other than him, their marriage and children. They were planning a large brood.'

'So they wanted babies immediately?'

'Oh yes, even Alyd said they would begin a family as soon as they could.' He laughed. 'They even married before we expected — couldn't wait for us.'

Valentyna shook her head, baffled, recalling Ylena's confusion when she had mentioned pregnancy. It was as if the young woman did not know what she was talking about.

'Well, she's not pregnant, I can vouch for that. It's why she left the table so suddenly — her monthly flux had arrived.'

It was probably nervousness at this precarious conversation but Crys could no longer stifle a laugh at the thought of Wyl dealing with women's ailments.

'I can't imagine what's so amusing, Crys,' Valentyna said in a vaguely injured tone.

'There is nothing funny, your highness. I think I must be losing my own wits,' he said, clearly uncomfortable.

Valentyna was sure he knew more than he was telling her but could not fathom what it was that he might be hiding. 'Is there anything else you know which could help me, Crys? Please, I feel like I'm navigating through a quagmire.'

He gave her a look of tender sympathy. 'Your highness,

Ylena is true to you. After all that Celimus has perpetrated on her own family and the family she married into, her loyalties have changed. We all love Morgravia but we would rather fight on the side of Briavel as long as King Celimus sits on Morgravia's throne.' He surprised her by going down on one knee. 'You can trust me and you can trust Ylena. She is fearlessly casting herself into the lion's den you could say. Whether Celimus has her killed or not, it doesn't matter – we will never see Ylena again, that much I can assure you.' The last was said bitterly.

Valentyna reached to touch his bowed head, moved by what he had said. 'Oh, Crys, I don't want her death on my hands.'

'She has nothing else to give but her life. Your highness, Ylena doesn't want to live any more – can't you see that? That is why she can give it up so recklessly and for someone she loves.'

He felt he had gone too far by mentioning the word love, and Valentyna's anguished response confirmed it.

'I don't want her love, Crys!' The Queen was shocked by the pain that moved across the duke's open expression at her words.

'Then accept her sacrifice graciously and use it for your own ends, as she asks.'

'I don't even understand her intentions by going to Felrawthy,' Valentyna replied bitterly.

Crys stood. 'I imagine she means to disrupt those talks in the north,' he said. 'And somehow bargain for the deployment of the Legion back to Pearlis so your people can breathe easily again and get on with celebrating a royal wedding.' He took her hand. 'I don't think you can escape that, your majesty, but you can demand equality.

You can influence how this new era for Morgravia and Briavel will be felt by people. Believe me, if we can find a way to overthrow Celimus we will, but you must proceed with this marriage and do whatever you can if we fail.'

She had heard it before from others and given herself the same sound advice. It was time she got on with living it now. 'You're right. No doubt we shall see one another in Pearlis.'

'I might not go straight to the Morgravian capital, your highness,' Crys said, as if the decision had only just arrived in his mind.

'Not Felrawthy?' she asked, fear in her tone.

'No, that will have to wait, your highness. The time to seize back my family estate is not yet ripe. I've actually been thinking about Elspyth.'

Relief softened Valentyna's expression. 'You're going after her?'

'I think I should. She's a resilient woman and knows her mind, but she's still only a girl alone in a strange realm with no weapons or protection—'

'Heading off into the Razor Kingdom to rescue a prisoner of its King,' the Queen finished, shaking her head. 'I'm glad, Crys. Thank you.'

The duke shrugged. 'Elspyth was good to me when I needed to be reminded who I was and what needed to be done. If not for her insistence I would have gone tearing back to Tenterdyn and doubtless achieved nothing.'

'And lost your own life, and Felrawthy would have lost its duke.'

'Yes,' he admitted. 'She saved me from my own stupidity and anger.'

'Well, you still have every right to be angry, to want

vengeance, Crys, and because of Elspyth's advice you might yet get it.'

He sensed the sorrow behind her encouraging words. 'I'm sorry that you don't have the same opportunity, your highness.'

She forced a small smile. 'Oh, I'll find my own way.'

Crys knew as well as she did that her comment was bravado, but he returned her smile with a squeeze of her hand.

'How will you follow her?' Valentyna asked, changing the subject.

'I'll start with Liryk, I suppose. I suspect your commander is rather gratified that Elspyth is out of your life, your highness' – he grinned as she nodded conspiratorially – 'but he might help by asking his guards if they saw her leave.'

'What good will that do?'

'Well, I imagine Elspyth was in a hurry to leave Werryl and be long gone by the time we returned. That being the case, I believe she might have hitched a ride with someone.' He shrugged. 'It might help me follow her, that's all.'

The Queen nodded. 'Be safe, Crys. We shall meet again soon, I hope.'

He kissed her hand with feeling, and then the last of her allies left the Briavellian monarch to her loneliness and bleak thoughts.

CHAPTER 13

After leaving Werryl, Wyl made straight for a hide of Faryl's in Crowyll and dug up a pouch of money. He was pleased he could still remember some of the locations of her stashed coin, and although he did not care for using blood money, in this instance he was in dire need of it to save more blood being spilled.

He galloped his horse as far and hard as the beast would permit, then travelled on through the night more slowly and spent most of the coin on a new horse the following morning. Although he had not slept he was determined to press on and the replacement animal was fresh and happy to be given its head. His plan was to follow the border as closely as he could, entering Morgravia only when he believed he was far enough north to cross directly into Felrawthy. He could not risk stumbling upon any Legionnaires and being recognised.

At around midday the next day it was his good fortune to ride into the village of Derryn at a time when he not only had to rest his horse but needed food and sleep himself, and, most importantly, a chance to bathe. The pain had gone and he felt as well as could be expected considering his fatigue but it seemed that the bleeding would continue for a few days yet. How inconvenient and messy it all was.

Given the choice, Wyl decided he never wanted to be a woman again. The grooming, the curtseying, the requirement to be elegant and gracious at all times – these were merely a few of its annoying aspects. He pitied Valentyna, and yet he admired her too. Somehow she managed to balance the demands of being a woman with a strength of her own. She wasn't 'frilly', for want of a better word. Ylena had been frilly, but then that was all that had been expected of her since the day of her birth. A daughter born into a wealthy noble family, particularly one as distinguished as the Thirsks, had one main task: to marry well. To achieve this she was educated in every possible pastime which could enhance her opportunities, from how to run an effective household to the art of embroidery. King Magnus had employed a small army of women to teach Ylena such niceties from her arrival at Pearlis at a tender age. And his sister had proved herself to be an adept student.

Fresh sorrow overcame Wyl as he pondered yet again how little Ylena had deserved what had befallen her. She had no enemies, was always ready with a kind word for everyone and her smile could banish even the gloomiest of moods. She really was a beauty in every sense of the word. That her mind had been empty of the thoughts and ambitions which drove Valentyna was not Ylena's fault. She was merely following form, whereas Valentyna was one of a kind. Yet Ylena's life had unravelled over a matter of weeks and what should have been the happiest time of her life had plunged her into tragedy. Wyl felt a familiar nausea grip him and knew he must stop grieving like this over his sister. Ylena was dead and no amount of soul-searching or tears would restore her.

Wyl knew his exhaustion and the monthly flux was contributing to his morbid feelings and was convinced that a decent meal and some rest would help to lift his spirits. As he walked the horse through the main street he found there was no inn but discovered by asking a young woman passing by that a widow by the name of Mona Dey ran a guest house in the village. After stabling the horse, paying for its care and making sure he could retrieve it with ease whenever he wanted, Wyl headed for the widow's place.

He paid Mona in advance, much to her delight, and was shown to a small, neat room at the back of her large dwelling. He learned from the chatty widow that her husband had been a wealthy trader who was miserly to say the least and had had a wandering eye for other women, especially whores. She had mouthed the final word silently. According to Mona, her husband had died between the legs of a buxom twenty-year-old, a blade driven into his back up to the hilt. She told the chilling tale with a sly relish and it brought back hideous memories for Wyl.

'A pocketful of silver – that's all the slut got for her trouble,' Mona said smugly. 'I got the rest.' And she beamed. From then on her life had looked up and she had lived it to the full, deliberately spending her dead husband's money with abandon in revenge for his mean-ness, until there was virtually nothing left. 'I held back just enough to keep me off the streets,' she told Wyl, with no trace of bitterness, 'and now I take paying guests and live a quiet life.'

'I can't imagine it gets much quieter than Derryn,' Wyl commented, surprised at the widow's candidness.

'You're right there, my lady,' Mona cried, and laughed as if he had cracked some great jest.

As open as Mona Dey was about her own background, Wyl appreciated that she showed not the slightest interest in his. Either she was entirely self-centred or she was very canny, knowing that most strangers preferred not to discuss their business. It was strange, he thought, that innkeepers and their ilk had a reputation for being an inquisitive group of people. Wyl thanked the widow and paid her some extra coin for her discretion, for she had not even enquired why Ylena was travelling alone.

The evening meal, Mona told her guest, was served at sunset and no later. Wyl grimaced and politely asked whether there was any possibility of a tray in his room now. He explained how tired he was and that his flux had fair drained him of all energy. A look of deep sympathy had come his way – definitely a special sorrow only women could share, he realised – and no doubt the generous coin rattling in her skirt pocket had encouraged Mona Dey to look kindly on the young noblewoman.

'I'll see what I can rustle up for you, dear,' she said. 'Oh my, I used to suffer it something awful at your age. And my Garth, he had no sympathy at all, still claiming his marital rights.' Wyl really did not want to hear all of this, but apparently Mona Dey was starved of fresh listeners in Derryn so he adopted the right expression and paid attention. 'And pain! Shar save me, I thought I was fit to die,' she continued. 'My mother had no sympathy. She said I should get used to it for it would be the curse for most of my life – my mother was a bitter woman, you see. My father died on her young and left her with a brood of children and no money. Her bleed was bad too and left her in poor shape one week of each moon and it meant she couldn't work during some of those days and we went hungry.'

The widow looked set to carry on discussing her mother's moon cycles but Wyl feigned a swoon which stopped the monologue and had Mona rushing for cold flannels and smelling salts. When he seemed recovered, the widow suggested the young lady take a soak. There was a room in the house already set up for bathing. 'I have some herbs which will ease that pain, dear,' she offered kindly.

Wyl was grateful to her and said as much, winning a wide smile from the widow. 'And I'll fetch you some raspberry leaf,' she added. 'Chew straight on it, my lady. Tastes like hell but far more effective for your condition than a weak brew.'

Wyl stammered his thanks and allowed her to guide him to the bathing room which had a drain in one corner and a huge old tub which would more than swallow up Ylena's exhausted body. He would have been happy to wash in cold water but Mona wouldn't hear of it. 'Heat is what you need, dear, for the ache.'

Wyl did not want to start explaining that the ache was done; he just wanted peace and privacy now. So he let her fuss and organise for steaming jugs to be brought up by a small army of lads she paid to run to the smithy's where a huge cauldron of water was kept on the fire permanently. The joy of finally closing the door on Mona's chatter and climbing into the tub was second only to kissing Valentyna for the first time, when Wyl had been Romen and adored by her.

Afterwards, he ate a meal of cold roast meat, potatoes simmered with cream and some cheese, before slipping between the well-worn but fresh sheets on Mona's guest bed and drifting almost instantly into sleep.

When he awoke he was disoriented. It was black outside and as quiet as a tomb. Mona had kindly left a candle in his room and it had burned down to a sputtering nub. He had been asleep for at least twelve hours he estimated. Careful to make no sound which would disturb the household he relieved himself into the chamber pot and hurriedly dressed in his dusty but comfortable riding clothes. Wyl did not like to sneak away without thanking Mona, but with no means to scrawl a note, the only way he could show his appreciation for her care was money, which he left on the re-made bed. He thought it unlikely she would think further on the young woman who had passed through her house, but if she did, she would remember Ylena kindly for her generosity.

He could not risk making his way through the house so, thanking his lucky stars that he was on the first level, he climbed out of the window and dropped silently to the ground, rolling as he had been taught when he was a lad. He must have startled a badger or some other night creature on the fringe of the small wood that skirted the town for he heard the animal blundering disgruntedly back into the trees. He remained still, listening for any other sounds, but it seemed there was no one about. Nevertheless, he took the precaution of making his way to the stable via the backs of dwellings. As he had anticipated there was a sleeping stableboy in one corner who could barely rouse himself from his slumber at the young woman's oddly timed arrival. When he did, he recognised the noblewoman, pointed towards a stall and mumbled something incoherent. Wyl was just glad to find his horse, saddle her and be off as quickly and quietly as he could.

He ignored the fresh hunger pangs that gnawed at his belly and was out onto the open road again, Derryn behind him, within moments of leaving the stable. One more day's riding, he guessed, and he would be able to cut into Morgravia and enter Felrawthy – back into the lair of Celimus and, perhaps, a chance to get himself killed and enter a new, more suitable body.

Cailech sat in a secret cave on Haldor's Tooth, pondering the situation that was about to unfold. The Grenadyne's suggestion to forge an alliance with Morgravia had touched the very core of everything the Mountain King believed in. He was privately miffed such an obvious idea had not occurred to him in the past, for treating with Magnus and his General, Thirsk, would surely have been an easier process. He wondered why it was that he could see it all so clearly now and yet his own instincts had not offered the idea. Perhaps it was the fact that ever since Rashlyn's arrival in the Razors he had derided any suggestion of forging links with Morgravia, but Cailech was not usually a man to be influenced by others. He tried to recall why he had put aside those early notions of living as neigh-bours alongside the bordering realm, but could find no sensible reason. He smirked at the notion that Rashlyn had somehow washed them from his mind. A ridiculous thought, considering the barshi's loyalty to him.

Nevertheless, when Aremys returned to the cave and reported on how the meeting with Celimus had gone, Cailech felt a surge of anxiety. Was he walking into his own death? Why did it feel as though he was seeing life so much clearer out here on the mountainside?

'You are sure there is no trap?' he asked Aremys.

'No, sire. But I have made our way as safe as I can under the circumstances. Celimus is organising for the hostages to be delivered as required, and I have taken out some additional insurance.'

The mercenary explained that his bargaining tool was Ylena Thirsk, daughter and sister of Morgravia's two previous generals. The name carried weight with Cailech, and he had no qualms about using a Morgravian noblewoman to barter for their safety. There was just one question. 'Well, where is she?'

Aremys startled the King by laughing and shrugging. 'I have no idea, sire. But that is a worry for another day. You will be back on your own soil before I have to consider what to do.'

Cailech smiled to himself. He liked the way the large Grenadyne thought. Farrow had impressed him from their first meeting and, even though the mercenary clearly knew more than he was telling and had an uncanny interest in Galapek, Cailech privately considered the man a friend. He had never said as much but they both knew it; there was mutual respect and admiration there. Perhaps it was simply that, with his clear thinking and dry humour, Aremys reminded him of Lothryn. He missed Lothryn so deeply it actually pained him to dwell upon it.

It had been the most agonising of discoveries that his closest friend and confidant had betrayed him. How could Loth have chosen the Morgravians over his own people, over his own King? Cailech had ranted as much to Myrt, who had kept a dull silence throughout but whose lack of words said much. Cailech quietly admired the man for his loyalty to his friend. Loth could have learned much from Myrt about brotherhood, honour and trust. Cailech's pride would not permit him to show any mercy to his childhood friend, no matter how in love with the woman of Yentro he might have been or the fact that he had aided the Morgravians' escape without harming any of the Razors' warriors. It made no difference why Lothryn had made his choice, it mattered only that he had made it, and it was the wrong one.

When news came that they were bringing Lothryn back alive, Cailech had wanted to slay him on the frosted stones of the fortress's threshold. He could not bear to see his lifelong companion – now a traitor – step even one foot across it. But then Rashlyn had arrived to interfere with the King's thoughts and persuade him to exact a higher penance.

Somehow the King had been persuaded down the path of magic. Burning with a feverish anger he had listened with fascinated horror to Rashlyn's suggestion that there was a far more subtle option than an easy death by the sword. The barshi's repetition of the words 'traitor' and 'treachery' had fired the King's anguish into a white heat of vengeance. He had agreed to Rashlyn's plan, believing that by owning Loth, by breaking his spirit and forcing his subservience with Rashlyn's dark magic, he would somehow win his respect. His former friend and comrade would suffer the humiliation of knowing that he would for ever carry the King on his back, ever subservient to Cailech, never forgetting who ruled whom.

It was only now that Cailech could see how distorted and poisonous such a notion was. If he could reverse the magic he would do so, especially now that Aremys seemed to have such a dogged interest in the stallion. The truth was, his victory over Loth felt hollow. Painful, in fact. As with the threat to make cannibals of his own people, it had shown him to be base; led by anger rather than his clever mind. How had he permitted Rashlyn to guide his hand towards inflicting such horrors? He shook his head.

'A silver for your thoughts, sire,' Aremys said, approaching Cailech where he sat on a rock ledge with a clear view into Felrawthy. He brought with him a clay flask of wine and poured a cup for the King and one for himself. Myrt and the rest of the Mountain warriors were sharpening blades and checking the supplies of weapons, which everyone prayed would not be required.

'I was just thinking of Lothryn and how much you remind me of him.'

'I shall take that as a compliment, sire. I have heard people speak highly of your second, despite his final actions.'

'As they should,' Cailech said, unable to hide the sorrow that had him in its grip.

'No one can tell me what happened to him, sire. I presume you executed him?'

Aremys heard the hesitation. 'Yes, he is dead,' the King replied flatly.

'Doesn't stop you missing him though, I see.'

Cailech nodded. 'I miss him every day. We grew up together, we understood each other, we protected one another. That was what made his betrayal so shocking. We loved one another, Farrow. We were brothers in all but blood.'

'With such love between you, could you not find a way

to spare him?' Aremys prompted, hoping to lead the King into revealing more about Galapek.

'Only the barest thread separates the most passionate of opposites, Grenadyne.'

'What do you mean, sire?'

'I mean that because I loved Loth so much, it made me capable of intense hatred for what he did to our friendship.'

'I understand.' Aremys knew he would not get the admission he had hoped for.

Instead, the silence stretched between them, before Cailech roused himself from his private thoughts and addressed the question which was no doubt troubling his men too.

'Is this a wise undertaking, Farrow?'

'Many would consider it foolhardy, given the Morgravian sovereign's reputation,' Aremys replied. 'However, I do believe that once he meets you, you more than anyone have the ability to convince him that the alliance is preferable to these regular skirmishes which could so easily escalate to war.'

Cailech nodded, reassured by the Grenadyne's faith. 'And his marriage?'

'Is still planned to go ahead shortly, which is why timing is of the essence. With Briavel's army at his beck and call, who knows what delusions might suddenly cross this fanciful King's mind?'

'I am told that the Legion has been deployed to the Briavellian border. Hardly a loving wedding gift.'

'Scare tactics,' Aremys guessed. 'There is no benefit to Celimus starting a fresh war with Briavel when he can conquer the realm through a marriage union.'

'Intimidating the bride is a grand way to start an historic treaty between the two realms,' Cailech replied.

'It seems Celimus knows no other way. From what I can gather, he has been a bully for all of his young life. Why should he change now he is King?'

'Mmm – my thoughts exactly,' Cailech mused.

The silence that followed felt cryptic to Aremys, but he could not put his finger on why or what the King might have meant by his comment. 'Nothing will go wrong, sire. Just don't tarry. Say what you have to say and plan to use emissaries to do the rest. The main thing is that both Kings meet and like what they see in each other.'

Cailech nodded. 'When are we expected?'

'Tomorrow. He is planning a feast in your honour. I suggest that only Myrt, Byl and I accompany you, sire.'

Cailech's green gaze narrowed. 'A lean force.'

'It shows trust.'

'Even if I don't trust him.'

'Exactly.'

The Mountain King laughed again. 'I hope you do not find my blood on your hands, Grenadyne – or you will have hundreds of my warriors baying for yours.'

Cailech raised his glass to Aremys, who followed suit. 'To unions, sire.'

'And friendship, Farrow. Thank you for your help.'

'Does that mean I am a free man now?'

Cailech drained his cup. 'It does, but I hope you will return to the fortress with us.'

'If we are all still alive after this adventure, your highness, I would be honoured to.'

*   *   *

Celimus was riding on the moors that surrounded Tenterdyn and surveying what he now considered Crown land.

'It is beautiful, your majesty,' Jessom said from his own horse, echoing the King's thoughts.

'I was thinking I would make Tenterdyn my summer palace and Argorn could become the royal winter retreat,' Celimus replied with a smug smile, looking towards the majestic Razors which reared up as a hazy purple in the distance.

'Crys Donal and Ylena Thirsk might have something to say about that, your highness,' the Chancellor cautioned, careful to hit a tone which did not suggest either reprimand or contradiction.

'Not from the grave they won't,' his King snapped testily.

The notion had crept up on the Chancellor so quietly, he had not realised it existed until this moment, but now it dawned on him that he had tired of the King's waspish manner and complete disregard for those who strived to accommodate his whims and pander to his needs. Not a single servant was seen in any higher light than a peasant begging for coin in the gutter. In the case of Jessom, this commitment to Celimus stretched to killing for no extra reward, certainly no thanks. Jessom was no fragile soul who shirked the meting out of death; no, a kingdom could not be strong, he believed, if squeamish or too compassionate. Any successful King needed people around him who were prepared to perform tasks which involved skull-duggery and cunning at times. However, in the case of Celimus, the settling-in period of brutality was, Jessom considered, prolonged. In truth, the bloodshed seemed to be escalating.

Celimus was young and brash, and his eagerness to stamp his own mark on his kingdom – and indeed beyond – was understandable. But since Jessom had first arrived in Celimus's life he had hoped he might mould this brilliantly sharp young man into one who could be relied on to be subtle. Jessom had put all of his own life experience and extensive range of talents at the King's disposal with the aim that Celimus might learn from him.

Maris Jessom was the seventh son of a rich man, a moneylender who was involved in a number of ventures from bridge-building to breweries. But even with such wealth, a son so far down the family's hierarchy was never going to favour too highly in the shareholding. His eldest three brothers were carving up the empire between them and everyone else, including his three sisters, had to find their own way. In the case of his sisters, they had used their status to marry well. But Maris, thin and hook-nosed, had long ago accepted that he would never be a handsome man and so had decided from an early age to use his only real asset – his incredible intelligence – to get on in life. If the combined wits of his siblings were distilled into one, they still would not hold a candle to the speed, agility and vision of their youngest brother. Although Maris kept this weapon a secret, it was obvious to him that his father should have chosen his seventh son to run his financial empire; it seemed that he alone had inherited the shrewdness, perceptiveness and, yes, cunning, which had helped his father to become one of the wealthiest men in all of Tallinor. But Jessom senior had never taken much notice of his gangly youngest son and as soon as Maris was old enough he had been encouraged to leave the family home to seek his own fortune.

His mother, who loved him well, had given him a heavy pouch of gold. 'Use it wisely, Maris,' she had said, her eyes beginning to tear as she hugged her youngest farewell.

And he had, roaming the towns and villages of Tallinor from north to south and east to west as a travelling money-lender: an innovative and supremely lucrative scheme, and convenient for borrowers. Money coming to them, in other words. Perhaps people thought he would never collect on his lendings, even having watched the thin man with the dark knowing eyes enter their loan into a black leather-bound ledger. But collect he did. Borrowers learned the hard way that Maris Jessom did not extend his loans. Pay up or lose everything was his creed. He had the law on his side too, because he never called in his loans early or was so greedy as to make the terms so cumbersome that they might be considered avaricious. The young Jessom was also ruthless, a characteristic which contributed to his rapid success.

It was not long before he had to travel with a body-guard, and then two, for fear of being set upon by the new breed of bandits who seemed to think it was perfectly reasonable to steal from the rich as they could afford to lose the money. This made Jessom's anger, which was normally slow to stoke, boil up and he was soon travel-ling with a small company of his own paid mercenaries who killed bandits for a hobby and kept all the spoils.

Jessom enjoyed two decades of this lifestyle, during which time he built a network of contacts and knowledge from all over the region, before deciding to settle down in Tal, not far from his original family home. Here he planned to establish his own permanent moneylending empire, using mercenaries to do the dirtier work of collection around the realm. By this time both of his parents had died and his poorer siblings were scattered. The remaining brothers, who had inherited their father's business, had not fared so well in their endeavours and became aggressive towards their wealthy younger sibling.

It was around this time that King Sorryn of Tallinor declared moneylenders – whose number seemed to have tripled in Jessom's lifetime – to be 'a pus-filled carbuncle on society which needed to be lanced' and systematically set about dismantling their terrible grip on the poor. Jessom saw the crackdown coming and fled Tallinor well in advance of the Purge, as it came to be known.

He fled to Morgravia; a wealthy man still but homeless as well as landless and without the ties of family. Disillusioned, Maris Jessom decided on a change of career. He felt too old to find the energy to establish a new empire and so he watched and waited for whatever the stars had in store for him. Garnering information, observing trends and identifying needs was Jessom's talent. He saw an opportunity within the Morgravian royal family long before it occurred to anyone else that a King might need more than his General to be his closest counsel.

The position of Chancellor did not even exist during Magnus's reign, for he was a King who preferred the companionship and advice of his military strategist in all matters. But friendship did not necessarily provide good counsel to Jessom's mind and it was obvious that the new King would need better guidance than what was on offer at the time of his father's death. Even for a newcomer it did not take much to understand that Magnus and Celimus shared no feelings and Jessom saw that the son had learned little from the father other than how to hate.

Maris Jessom fancied himself a kingmaker; he had a network of messengers, mercenaries, informers and spies who could help shape a kingdom, plus he had years of experience in finance as well as a shrewd understanding of human nature.

He watched Celimus for long enough before he became King to know the young man was problem-riddled and it would take years of smoothing and guidance to educate him on how to run an effective realm. Jessom saw the charm too, though; he sensed that Celimus could easily turn that talent towards his kingdom and use the energy he squandered in despising people into making them loyal to him. Jessom had to admit that the proposal of marriage to Valentyna of Briavel was a masterstroke, but the killing of her father, Valor, had been plain stupidity. It was the act of an arrogant man, too inexperienced to realise that a suggestion of his power was more than enough. Jessom believed King Valor would have supported a union between Celimus and his daughter, which made his death pointless.

The murder of Thirsk had been another senseless move, although Jessom realised that there was a history there which affected the King's judgement and prevented him from being objective. Jessom had watched Thirsk too, long enough to realise the young General was loyal to Morgravia. All Celimus had needed to do was to lean on that loyalty – and the execution of the youngest Donal, the razing of Rittylworth, the slaughter at Tenterdyn plus various other deaths, including young helpless Jom, need never have occurred.

Murder was dangerous. It had a nasty habit of coming back to haunt the perpetrator and Jessom could not help but think that there were too many corpses at the King's feet — with the Chancellor's involvement — for either of them to escape the outcry that was surely coming. All it would take was one voice of dissent. One voice that counted — be that Ylena Thirsk or Crys Donal or even Aleda Donal wherever the hell she was. A few rumblings from Lord Bench could set off a catastrophic series of questions for the King to answer . . . and Jessom knew who would shoulder the blame. It would not be Celimus.

And yet, if only he would listen to Jessom, Celimus could still be a strong, powerful King ruling prosperous realms. Not one or two, but three — the very empire the King dreamed of. All was not lost yet. Perhaps they could use Ylena Thirsk to their advantage — there was always a way — rather than just murdering her.

He realised he was shaking his head and that Celimus, wearing a quizzical expression, had turned his horse to face his Chancellor.

'Your majesty, may I speak candidly?'

'Of course.'

'Well, sire, with the alliance you may well forge with the Mountain King, and what could only be described as the fairytale union with Briavel which is about to occur, you will have achieved what most sovereigns do not dare dream of, let alone attempt.'

'And your point is?'

'My point is, your majesty, that you are now in the enviable position of essentially controlling the three realms without resistance, without bloodshed, without the other two sovereigns realising how powerful you actually are.'

'Why is this a good thing, Jessom?'

'Your highness, there is a saying which holds good in

almost every facet of life: never allow one hand to know what the other is doing.'

'Don't give me riddles, you fool. Speak plainly.'

Jessom drew a deep breath to stop his disdain from showing. 'Once married, Valentyna is beholden to you as wife so she will be unable to rally against you, which effectively leaves the Mountain King in the cold should he suddenly decide the alliance is not working for him. I suspect he is much too canny for that, so he will maintain the peace and enjoy the benefits of trade and free movement as well as increased prosperity. My lord, it is obvious to me that, handled with care, you will have the empire you have always dreamed of.' The words: *Is that plain enough for you, fool?* leapt to mind, but he resisted speaking them aloud.

'Did you think, Jessom,' Celimus replied, 'that I could not work this out for myself? Is it your belief that I need you to spell out every scenario for me because I am too dimwitted to see beyond what is in front of my nose?' The tone was sarcastic and dangerous.

'Not at all, sire,' Jessom replied, equally calmly but also with courtesy. 'I just think that killing Ylena Thirsk or Crys Donal might be . . . well, shall we say "hasty" for want of a better word.'

'So you would have me leave two dangerous mouths on the loose?'

'All I suggest, sire, is that you wait. You will have Ylena Thirsk in captivity shortly. Don't do anything too soon. Think on the various situations which will inevitably present themselves. I imagine that Ylena Thirsk is feeling extraordinarily isolated these days. She has no parents, she has lost her guardian and her beloved brother is dead. Her new husband and his family – her only allies – are fodder for the worms. Apart from Crys Donal she has no one to turn to. She is a beautiful, vulnerable young woman who no doubt craves the security of being pampered again within her own private chambers with servants to wait on her, fancy gowns on her body and money at her disposal – everything back as it was. Think about it, sire, you could be her saviour. You could put all this behind you and lavish your care and riches on the lonely girl – until she becomes your supporter.'

Celimus listened this time without the smirk on his face. 'She always was a spoilt little thing. I used to think she'd jump at shadows.'

'This is what I mean, sire. She may boast the name of Thirsk but she is merely a girl. Her world has crumbled and been destroyed. What she needs now is resurrection from the rubble. If you provide that, it doesn't matter what excuses or tall stories you weave to excuse your behaviour of the past; she will believe them all because what she wants is her life back again and a sense of safety. Marry her off well – to your gain. I would go so far as to suggest you find her a high-ranking warrior from Cailech's brood. She will be no more trouble to you then.'

The King's horse was restless. 'I will think on what you have said, Jessom,' Celimus replied. 'What time is the Mountain King due?'

'Midday, your highness. We had better make for the house.'

'My summer palace,' Celimus corrected and smiled.

Jessom saw no warmth in the smile; if he was honest with himself, he would have to admit that he had never seen any genuine warmth in Celimus. Why it should bother him now was a surprise. This mood of dissatisfaction had taken him so unexpectedly that he recognised it as dangerous. He, like the King, had some thinking to do; nevertheless, he was relieved that Celimus had agreed not to kill Ylena Thirsk immediately, which had surely been his original intention. This was a small win. Now the Chancellor prayed to his adopted god of Shar that King Celimus and King Cailech would take to one another. Surely that was not too much to ask in the name of peace?

The King galloped on ahead but Jessom rode back to Tenterdyn more sedately, silent and distracted by his thoughts.

CHAPTER 14

Valentyna crafted her letter to Celimus the same afternoon of Crys Donal's departure. She wrote with great
caution, outlining that she was releasing the woman,
Ylena Thirsk, into his care. The words suggested her
expectation that he would look after Ylena even though
she was being given into the captivity of the Morgravian
Crown. The Queen expressed her desire that any known
enemy of Morgravia could not be considered a friend of
Briavel and that, as helpless as Ylena painted her situation, Valentyna did not wish to go against the express
wishes of her husband-to-be. She felt sick writing the lies
but pressed on, detailing her progress with her own
arrangements for the wedding, not describing her gown
but telling him a little of how well it looked. She discussed
the party that would accompany her into Morgravia, which
was not inconsequential, and then lightly touched on her
desire to return to Briavel soon after the ceremony so that
a second celebration could be held for her people.
Valentyna, much to her distaste, felt she should ooze some
special compliments here about how much the Briavellians

were looking forward to seeing their Queen with her new King.

By the end of it she felt revolted by the smooth way in which she had lied to protect her own life as well as how easily she was giving Ylena's precious life away. As terrible thoughts filled her mind about how Celimus might choose to kill Wyl Thirsk's sister – and kill her he would, she knew this – the guilt of knowing how generously Wyl had sacrificed himself for Briavel's heir and how she was repaying that with disdain for his family nearly overwhelmed her. Valentyna's fingers twitched with the desire to rip up the parchment with its treacherous contents.

But it was the memory of Ylena's hard words that she was not the Queen's to command, and that returning to Celimus was her own choice, that stayed her hand. It was Ylena's decision to give up her life and Valentyna realised she would probably aggrieve the young woman more if she did not carry out her wishes. Her life was forfeit anyway, Valentyna told herself. One way or another, Celimus would hunt Ylena down and complete his annihilation of the Thirsk line – this much she knew was truth. Ylena wanted to make her life count for something. It was as though she felt her sacrifice for Briavel – Morgravia's traditional enemy – matched that of Wyl's and would give some point to all the deaths that surrounded this tragic family. Buying Valentyna more time in tricking Celimus and almost having the last, albeit pointless, laugh was the only way Ylena could fight back and avenge all the pain.

'Too sad,' Valentyna murmured at her desk. 'Your life is given too cheaply, Ylena, for the gain is so little. I cannot escape marrying him.'

She had the letter despatched immediately, for fear of changing her mind, going so far as to take the parchment to the stables herself and place it into the courier's hand.

'How long?' she asked. Briavel also used a relay network for messengers and she felt sure, once across the border, the Morgravian couriers would respect the urgency of this missive.

'Two days if we all ride hard, your majesty,' the young man said.

'Then use as many couriers as you can for maximum speed. It is extremely important that King Celimus sees this message as quickly as possible.'

'I shall personally ride like the wind, your highness,' he said, and with a bow from the saddle he was gone, clattering over Werryl Bridge and heading north-west as fast as his horse would go.

Valentyna turned away, feeling hollow and more lonely than she ever had in her life. Growing up as an only child had taught her to be self-sufficient and imaginative but nothing could have prepared her for this complete loss of family, friends, and allies. And still, she realised, she could not begin to reach the depth of loss that Ylena must surely be experiencing. No wonder Wyl's sister was throwing her life away with such abandon. It might also explain why she was indulging in curious affections. The Queen had not been able to shake the memory of Ylena's kiss; it seemed to haunt her every moment. There had been such tenderness in it . . . no, it was more than that. It was filled with love. Valentyna had only been kissed once before in such a manner and that was by Romen. Although this was a different mouth, different face, a different everything, there was such aching familiarity to the passion behind that affection. But the memory of that physical love made Valentyna angry too. Angry enough to want to fight: not Ylena, but the person who had perpetrated all the pain. On her way back into the palace, in a state of absolute resentment at the way life was turning out, she sent a runner to find Commander Liryk.

He arrived slightly out of breath at her study door. 'My Queen, you wished to see me?'

Valentyna was struck by how old Liryk seemed all of a sudden. She had taken his and Krell's presence around her for granted, as if they would always be in her life, but this man was surely well into his seventh decade. The notion of him not being around one day bit hard into her thoughts, reminding her that she may lose yet another of her supporters soon. It hardened her resolve.

'Yes, Commander, thank you for coming so quickly. In the absence of a Chancellor I would like you to summon the nobles for me.'

'Of course, your highness,' Liryk said, frowning despite his courteous manner. 'All of them?'

'Yes. It is urgent. How swiftly are you able to gather them for a meeting?'

He paused and she wondered whether he was considering her question or her state of mind. He obviously anticipated that she was about to do something dramatic. 'Three days, your majesty, if I get the couriers sent immediately.'

'Do it please, Liryk. I'd appreciate it if you would give this your utmost priority.'

'Of course, your highness.' She waited, and of course the gentle objection came. 'It is unusual. Perhaps I could give them some inkling of what you wish to discuss so urgently?'

She smiled. She had expected this. 'State security, tell them,' she answered and turned away, not unkindly but certainly sufficiently firmly to let Liryk know he was dismissed. 'Thank you, Liryk,' she added, just in case he thought to try and dissuade her.

Valentyna heard the soft sigh, the protest of his knee as he bowed and then the sound of the door closing. She shut her eyes, thankful it had not turned into a discussion where she felt obliged to explain her every action. It was done. Now she had to consider carefully what she was going to say to these men that could possibly change their minds about this forthcoming union of Briavel with Morgravia.

At around the same time that the somewhat bewildered nobles of Briavel were answering their young sovereign's summons to gather in the Great Hall of Werryl, Wyl had allowed himself to be picked up by Morgravian soldiers and was relieved to see that they were genuine Legionnaires and not mercenaries. It was a young company but although he recognised none of them, they certainly recognised his name. An awkward silence spread through the group of men as Wyl finished his introduction.

'You are General Wyl Thirsk's sister?' the startled leader qualified.

'I am,' Wyl replied, his spirits soaring. He knew it was unlikely he could change the outcome of what was going to happen, but hearing his own name uttered with such reverence restored his confidence that he could at least do his best to interrupt Celimus's plans. And perhaps he might live to fight another day in another body.

He wondered whether Valentyna had taken his advice

to write to Celimus and claim she was sending Ylena to him. Their parting had been so awkward and painful, he supposed the Queen was just glad to be rid of Ylena Thirsk.

The young officer could not help himself. 'But what are you doing here? We heard you had disappeared.'

Wyl was certainly not going to start explaining any more than he wanted to give away. 'What is your name?' he asked.

'Harken,' the young man replied. 'Er, Captain Harken, I hope, by year's end.'

'Well, Harken, firstly please remember whom you address. I am the daughter of General Fergys Thirsk, Duke of Argorn, and the sister of General Wyl Thirsk. Please treat me in the fashion you should any noble.'

Harken flushed with embarrassment at the stinging rebuke. Blotches of red appeared on his cheeks and ears. 'I . . . I apologise, Lady Thirsk.'

When he saw his reprimand had worked Wyl deliberately looked behind him as if suddenly fearful. He might as well continue with his planned charade and hope that the Queen of Briavel would at least make his next death count for something. 'Thank you, Harken. Have they gone?'

'Who, my lady?' the man asked, desperate to please. He looked over her shoulder and his companions followed suit, suddenly nervous.

'The Briavellian guardsmen who brought me to this crossing point.' Swords were drawn instantly, the ring of steel loud in the silence of the morning. 'Fret not, gentlemen,' Wyl assured, 'they have no quarrel with you. The guard accompanied me here – my keepers, if you will.'

Wyl held his breath, hoping his detached manner and

confident explanation would trick them into believing he had been brought to this point under armed escort.

'Why have they brought you here, my lady?' Harken sensibly asked.

'I am a gift,' Wyl said, taking some grim amusement from the irony of his words. 'For your King.'

The aspiring Captain looked appropriately baffled as well as rattled. 'I don't understand.'

'You are not meant to, but your sovereign will and you will raise his ire if I am not taken to him immediately. I have no intention of trying to escape,' Wyl added, glancing towards the rope which had appeared in one anxious pair of hands. 'All you're required to do is escort me into Tenterdyn, gentlemen. Restraint is not necessary.'

'Put that away,' Harken snapped at a lad not much younger than he was. 'You do know who this is, don't you?' he added, more angry with himself, Wyl suspected, than the youngster. 'Lady Thirsk! She is to be treated with respect.'

'Thank you, Harken. I'm sure my brother would be proud of you.'

'I never met him, my lady. He passed away the same week as I entered the Legion, but your family's name means everything to me. I grew up with it around me and all I ever wanted to do was join the Legion and be commanded by General Thirsk.'

'Are you Laud Harken's son?'

'Yes, my lady. I am surprised you know of him.'

Wyl realised it was probably an error for him to admit as much, but then the discovery that this lad was the son of one of the Legion's finest soldiers was a surprise. 'My brother spoke well of Laud Harken. How is he?'

'Dead, my lady. He fell in the north recently.'

'How?'

Harken shrugged, embarrassed by the sorrowful tremor in his voice. 'I was told it was a Mountain warrior's arrow, but, my lady, he disagreed with the Rittylworth scandal and no doubt said too much, too loudly.'

Murmurings erupted within the group. This was verging on treasonous talk, but it told Wyl how the name of Thirsk still resonated loudly within the Legion. It provoked an honesty which might not be so forthcoming with other strangers. He was counting on this very fact to enable Crys to stir up trouble in Pearlis.

'I understand, Harken, and I am deeply sorry for your loss. Now you must take me to Tenterdyn.'

The company remained on patrol whilst the young Captain-to-be provided the escort alone. This pleased Wyl for it gave him a chance to learn as much as he could from the gullible youngster. They travelled in silence for a while before Wyl decided it was time to ease out information.

'I imagine the missive from Briavel has arrived by now?'

Harken frowned. 'I'm sorry, my lady, I wouldn't know.'

Wyl felt disappointment slice him. Perhaps Harken would be no help after all. 'Apparently there was a courier coming from Queen Valentyna about my arrival.'

Harken shook his head. 'We can find out. I will make some enquiries as soon as we arrive.'

'Who is your General now?' Wyl asked. He could see Tenterdyn sprawling in the distance. They would be there soon.

'The King is our General, my lady.'

Wyl felt sickened. So Celimus had finally got his wish and taken over the Legion.

'I see. And I hear he is expecting a parley with the Mountain King?'

'Yes. It occurs today, so I have been briefed. King Cailech arrives by midday and there is a feast in his honour.'

'You sound excited, Harken.'

'I am, my lady. If our King marries Queen Valentyna and this parley achieves a truce between Morgravia and the Razor Kingdom, there will be peace at long last.'

Wyl made Ylena smile. 'I thought most young men of your age dreamed of going to war?'

'I am engaged to be married, my lady. I dream of Alys more than I do of killing for my realm.' He returned her smile with a shy one of his own.

'Good for you. It is a worthy dream. So you trust your King to achieve these two coups?'

Harken smiled ruefully. 'If anyone can, King Celimus can.' Wyl suspected that Harken, young as he was, would not be drawn into saying anything openly traitorous, although his tone suggested he felt it.

'Peace for the region would be a rare achievement.'

'Is the Queen as beautiful as everyone says she is?' Harken gushed suddenly.

Wyl nodded. 'More exquisite than you can possibly imagine.'

'I was told you were a beauty, my lady,' Harken began, then pulled himself back. He looked stricken. 'Forgive me, my lady, I meant no offence.'

'None taken. I imagine I look a real fright, dressed like a man and having ridden for days,' Wyl admitted. 'It is not easy to feel pretty in this situation.'

'I'm sorry, Lady Ylena, that was tactless of me. Do you

mind me asking why you are presenting yourself to the King? There was a rumour that . . .' he struggled to say more.

'That he tried to kill me?' Wyl finished. The young man nodded. 'It is true, Harken. Your King is not a good man, I'm sorry to say, and I think you know it. You suspect your father's death was not as cut and dried as it was painted to be, and you are most likely right. If Laud stood up to the King's treachery at Rittylworth, then he would have paid in the most dramatic way. I am truly sorry for your family.'

Harken's eyes were wide, the first hints of fear creeping across his innocent face. They were just a few yards from entering the compound of Tenterdyn now. Wyl spoke quickly. 'Listen to me. I am here to frighten the King. Trust me that I am not here to prevent peace. Hopefully the King's marriage to the Queen of Briavel will herald the beginning of the great union of our two realms and perhaps he might forge a peace with King Cailech, but Celimus is not a man ever to be trusted. Remember that, Harken. Remember these words, spoken by someone who loves Morgravia and its people . . . and is especially loyal to the Legion.'

The young man clearly heard the desperation in his companion's voice. 'I don't want to take you in there, my lady,' he said, further stricken. Both of them saw the gate-keeper stepping out.

'You must. But you must also do what your heart tells you.'

'I don't understand,' Harken urged.

'You will. You are Legion, used to taking orders, but one of the defining characteristics of an officer of the

Legion is that he will never do anything to hurt another Morgravian unless that person is a betrayer of the realm. Keep that in your heart. Do not allow this King to lead you and your men and the rest of the soldiers down the path of darkness. Be true to the Legion first.'

'Ho, who comes?' The gatekeeper's voice ripped through the tension of their whispered conversation.

'Tell the truth,' Wyl encouraged. 'You cannot save me.'

Harken spared an anguished glance towards the woman beside him. Wyl felt sorry for the youngster who, despite knowing so little, was torn; he had sensed he was involved in something deeply wrong by escorting Ylena Thirsk into the den of the dragon King.

'Come on, boy, we haven't got all day!' the soldier urged, irritated. 'Who do you bring here?'

Wyl cleared his throat. 'I am the Lady Ylena Thirsk, sir. I wish to speak to King Celimus.'

The gatekeeper laughed. 'Yes, and I'm the Lady Twinkle and plan to marry him. What is this?' he roared at Harken.

'Watch your manners!' Harken commanded, and the soldier glanced towards the badge on the youngster's uniform. This was an officer in the making and Wyl quietly smirked at the older man's error.

'This *is* the Lady Ylena Thirsk,' Harken said, firm of voice now. 'She has already been searched but you may do so again if you are required.'

The gatekeeper, far less chirpy now, signalled to another guard who asked Wyl to alight from his horse, which he did. He was searched and Harken's papers were checked for authenticity, which, Wyl guessed, was all part of the King's fear that he could be assassinated at any time. They were permitted to enter the gate by the now slightly sheepish keeper. Another, more senior soldier arrived to ask questions and his eyebrows arched immediately at the name of the woman standing before him.

'Call the Chancellor,' he said to his offsider. Then to Wyl, politely: 'We wait, my lady.'

He turned to the Legionnaire. 'Thank you, Harken. We will take it from here. You may return to your men.'

Wyl offered his hand to the young man. 'Thank you for your escort,' he said, although he hoped his gaze communicated far more. 'Again, I am sorry to hear about your father,' he added.

Harken looked distracted and anxious. 'Sir, has a missive arrived from Briavel? It involves Lady Thirsk.'

The man shook his head. 'Nothing has arrived from Briavel and I am the first point of contact for all deliveries.'

'Perhaps I should wait—' the young man began.

'No, Harken. You have a company of men without their leader. Return to your post,' the senior man said, this time firmly enough that it brooked no further argument. Wyl knew this older man, had little time for him. He had a tendency to bully the younger men. As General, he had planned to tease him out from his senior position but life's problems had got in the way and now, as sure as water runs downhill, men like this one had found their way into Celimus's inner sanctum.

Harken bowed. When he straightened, Wyl alone saw the anger and concern in those eyes before the youngster saluted and departed the compound.

'Ah, here we are,' the older soldier muttered and Wyl turned to see Chancellor Jessom emerging from the main house, a look of pleasure on his face. He swiftly adjusted it to a thin smile but Wyl saw the satisfaction all the same. Surely astonishment, or at the very least irritation, was more fitting to greet someone they had hoped was dead by now? Not pleasure.

Jessom's stride was confident and he covered the ground between the main dwelling and the gatehouse surprisingly swiftly. 'Ylena Thirsk. Almost perfect timing.'

Wyl was confused. He kept his expression deliberately blank as his mind raced to understand this new development. He allowed Jessom to go on talking. 'Our King was wondering when you would be delivered. This will be a special birthday present for him and no doubt he will reward Aremys royally for the gift of your life into his hands.'

They were expecting Ylena's arrival? How could this be if nothing from Valentyna had arrived – and what did he mean about Aremys?

Wyl decided he had to make time for himself to discover more. 'I'm sorry. Do I know you?'

Jessom's smile thinned even further. 'My apologies, we have never been introduced. I am Jessom, Chancellor and King's Counsel of Morgravia.'

'Since when did King Celimus take advice from anyone?' Wyl replied as acidly as he could, watching the crease across Jessom's face, which passed for his smile, fade entirely.

'Thank you, Bern. I will take the Lady Ylena from here,' Jessom said to the officer nearby. The man nodded and left their company, happy to pass on responsibility, but not before both Jessom and Wyl saw his raised eyebrows at Ylena's cutting comment. Wyl unhappily allowed Jessom to guide him away from the gates but he noted that it was not towards the main house. They had other plans for Lady Thirsk.

Jessom's voice was biting when it came. 'You are in a perilous situation, Ylena Thirsk. I suggest you not make it worse on yourself,' he advised.

Wyl made Ylena's beautiful face smirk. 'How much worse could it possibly get, Jessom? The snake that sits upon the Morgravian throne is hardly going to show mercy. I do not fear him.'

'Nevertheless, I recommend you don't openly insult King Celimus. It could go very badly for you.'

'You don't understand, Chancellor. I am not afraid of dying. I am not afraid of Celimus and his savage tortures. Any opportunity I get, sir, I will openly insult him and the bitch-Queen who spawned him.'

Jessom was normally a man in control of his emotions but he drew back in surprise at the fighting words of this young woman. 'When Aremys said he could deliver you, Ylena, I'm not sure our King understood how heroic you have become. It seems your struggles to survive have toughened you. This can only mean he will enjoy hurting you all the more. I am not a cruel man and I certainly do not condone hurting women. Let me suggest again that you make this easier on yourself.'

Wyl was happy he had managed to sting the man into losing his composure, even slightly. But more important to him was the second mention of his friend. *Aremys said he could deliver me?* Wyl thought. *What is going on?*

'I am glad I have impressed you, Chancellor, but frankly, it is not my intention. I will not plead for the King's mercy. He can do with me as he wishes.'

'Then I wonder, what is your intention? What can you possibly gain through your defiance?'

'All will be explained, I am sure,' Wyl answered

cryptically. Valetyna's letter had definitely not arrived then.

The Chancellor's face betrayed his bafflement. Wyl understood this was a man used to having information about everyone and everything as best as he could achieve. No wonder he looked so confused.

'The King will see you in good time,' Jessom said, more businesslike now. 'But for the meantime, you will remain in here.' They had arrived at an outbuilding: a storage hut built in the shade of a huge oak and where Aleda had kept her cool pantry. 'I'm afraid you have timed your arrival a little prematurely, Ylena. King Cailech is due any minute.'

Wyl made a sound of disdain.

Jessom pointed to a bucket of water. 'May I suggest you clean yourself up. I can have a gown found for you, if it pleases.'

'It does not please. I will see the King exactly as I stand before you, Chancellor. And by the way, your new status as servant to the King—' Wyl emphasised the word 'servant', saw that it struck home and cheered inwardly – 'does not permit you to address a noble by anything but the correct title, sir. You will refer to me as Lady Ylena Thirsk or Lady Ylena Donal – take your pick – but you will accord me the small measure of respect I am due, prisoner or not.'

The Chancellor was taken aback by the attack but composed himself smoothly and was quick to retaliate. 'Morgravia has forgotten you, young lady, and your family's name is being dragged through the mire at every opportunity. Climb off your pedestal, Ylena. I am not intimidated by your noble line. I'm wondering how long they will respect you when your head is rotting on a spike outside Pearlis. In fact, I'll do you a kindness – I'll hunt down Alyd Donal's head for you so you can both rot together. Romantic eh?' he said, uncharacteristically cruel as he finished tying her ankle to a huge timber post in the hut. 'Now clean yourself up, woman, and make ready to meet your sovereign.'

For the first time in his life Wyl spat at someone. It was the only fierce comeback he could think of to show his hate for this servile creature of the King's. He half-hoped Jessom would kill him in a blood rush of anger. He could do serious damage walking around in the Chancellor's body.

But Jessom was not a man of violence; he was far more subtle in how he could inflict pain. Instead he made a clicking sound of reproach, as a parent might to a naughty child. 'And you want to be treated like a lady?' He laughed; the sound was harsh and filled with equal hate. 'I have been spat on all my life, Ylena,' he said, wiping her spittle from his robe, 'and I have always beaten my enemies.'

He turned at the sound of the bell from the gatehouse. It was the signal that King Cailech's party had arrived.

'Farewell, Ylena. We shall summon you in due course.'

CHAPTER 15

Fynch and Knave stood at the foot of the Razors, about to step onto a tiny, unguarded track which would guide their ascent into the mountains. They had seen no soldiers and their journey from the Wild had been uneventful, and enjoyable for Fynch who had needed time to think. Knave was not a companion who made conversation – he replied to questions, and prompted them if he considered it important, otherwise he was silent. Fynch loved the sheer size and bulk of Knave which made him feel safe and not a bit lonely.

'Why are we walking? Surely the Thicket could send us?' Fynch wondered.

You can send us, Knave said, a rare tone of amusement in his voice. *Too dangerous, though. We cannot take the chance of Rashlyn sensing a powerful spelling. The sending of Aremys might have registered with him, but he would not have known what it was and we can only hope he dismissed it. However, since then we have had the transfer of Wyl to Briavel, the death of Elysius, the arrival of the Dragon King and you coming into your power. So many surges of magic are not so easily dismissed.*

Fynch nodded seriously as he considered all of this power swirling about in such a short time span. 'Do you think he knows Elysius has died?'

I suspect he might have felt something. More importantly, I am wary that he would have felt the transference of power.

'How would he sense it? Would it be like a pain?'

The dog led them onto the narrow track. Neither of them looked behind, even though they were now officially leaving Briavel.

Possibly. More likely he would feel it as you might a seizure. Not pain so much, but loss of physical control and perhaps consciousness. It would bewilder more than hurt.

'But would he know what it was?' Fynch persisted as he pushed aside the branches of overhanging trees.

Who knows, Fynch? It would shock him to learn that his brother has been alive all this time, if indeed he did work out that the disturbance was Elysius dying, but I can't imagine he could begin to consider that his sibling's magic had been passed on.

'You are guessing this, though.'

Of course. But remember, your sensitivity towards magic and your ability to embrace it and use it is known only to those of the Thicket. Rashlyn may be a sorcerer but he is not sensitive to the natural world. Elysius was the opposite: he was at one with Shar's creation, whereas his brother is an abomination within it.

The track rose sharply ahead of them and they began to climb in silence, Fynch concentrating on the challenging, slightly slippery surface of decaying leaves. After what felt like an age they reached a plateau of rock, the trees below them now. It was cold in the open and a breeze had whipped up. Fynch shivered through his breathlessness. He did not like the cold; he felt it before most others did because of his thinly-fleshed body and was glad of the thick fleece jacket Knave had found in Elysius's home and had insisted he carry.

We must be wary, now that we have no cover for a while, Knave cautioned.

Fynch squatted on his haunches to take some deep breaths and rest for a few moments. He put on the jacket, relishing its instant warmth, then took a sip from his waterskin.

'Are you hungry, Knave?' he asked, wondering if the dog should be allowed to hunt.

I don't need food, Fynch. I only ate when with Wyl to keep a pretence of normality.

'No food at all?' Fynch was incredulous.

None. I am of the Thicket.

'You are real though, aren't you, Knave?' There was a plaintiveness in the boy's voice.

Real enough, fret not.

Fynch sighed and confessed, 'I rarely feel hungry either. I eat because I know I should, never because I want to.'

That is because of who you are, what you belong to. The powers you have.

'How can that be? I didn't possess magic until the day Elysius died.'

Fynch, you have always had the capacity to wield a certain magic. You just didn't know it until now.

Fynch shook his head, too distracted and surprised by Knave's assured claim to argue the matter. He took another draught of water to calm himself. 'How long will it take us to get to the fortress?' he finally asked, wiping his mouth with his sleeve, imagining his sister scolding him for such an act. He would give anything to be admonished by her once more but he doubted he would see any of his family again.

Yes, the fortress. I've been thinking about that, the dog replied. *It occurs to me that if we do our resting by afternoon, we might cover more ground at night.*

'Using magic, you mean?'

The dog did not answer immediately. Instead, he sniffed the air and Fynch kept the silence, knowing Knave was pondering the most difficult of decisions.

Yes, the dog said at last. *I am hoping that if Rashlyn follows a normal pattern, he may not sense small bursts of power as he sleeps. In truth I don't believe he will know what it is even if he does feel it, but I have been reluctant to take any chances.*

'But you've changed your mind now?'

Knave's voice was gentle. *I think I overlooked how slight you are, Fynch. I don't believe we will be able to cover as much ground as I had hoped. It is a long way from Briavel's side of the Razors to Cailech's fortress on their western rim – I realise now it would take us too long. We shall have to take the risk.* He said the last few words with regret.

'But keep the distances small,' Fynch added with trepidation.

The dog's dark eyes regarded him sorrowfully. *I am sorry to ask it of you. You will need to chew on the sharvan leaves regularly now.*

'Don't be sorry, it's my burden,' Fynch replied, wishing he felt more brave than he sounded. He attempted a brighter tone. 'This is how we travelled before, isn't it . . . from Baelup to the Thicket?'

Except then I had to rely on the Thicket and Elysius bringing us to them. This time we travel with all the power we need.

'Are you sure?' Fynch had no idea how he was supposed to effect such a magic. He had thought after the transfer from Elysius he might feel a reservoir of power gurgling within, a well of magic at his beck and call. But there was no sense of this. He could detect no change within himself. He mentioned this to his friend.

Knave considered the question. Again Fynch waited patiently. The dog sighed. *It is different for me. I am of the Thicket, therefore I rely on it to feed me its magic when it needs to use me, and I feel an energy buzzing within. Anyone touched by the Thicket would feel it, I'm sure. I imagine Wyl might sense it echoing within him somehow and Aremys too. They have both been touched by the magic of the Thicket.*

'Then why not me?'

I think, Fynch, because you are more than us, the dog said gravely.

'More than you?' the boy repeated, not understanding.

Knave tried again. *I belong to the Thicket. Wyl, Aremys – and others no doubt – have been touched by it; not empowered by it but affected somehow. But Elysius, and now you, are connected to it in ways I can't explain. We have no magic without the Thicket to feed it. You both do.*

'Oh,' Fynch replied, still feeling baffled.

But I think, my friend, there is far more to you.

'What do you mean?' Fynch frowned.

Knave gave a low growl of frustration, as if he could not put into words what he was trying to say. *It's as if you and the Thicket are one. Where Elysius was passing through – for want of a better way of describing it – you belong to the Thicket and it to you. Elysius only added to a power which had already been awakened within you. And the King of the Creatures never visited Elysius. I have never seen him before – most of us haven't.*

The gravity of Knave's explanation hit Fynch like a blow. The words and their intent terrified him. There was a finality to what Knave was suggesting; it was as if the Thicket had a hold on him he would never escape. He did not want to think about it any further. Neither was he ready to consider the implication of the Dragon King's visit, that knowing in his eyes. It was all too bewildering and frightening.

'So what is your plan again?' he said, deliberately forcing the fear away by changing the topic.

Knave must have sensed Fynch's terror for he switched smoothly from their previous discussion. *We travel on foot by day, then sleep from late afternoon for as long as you wish. We cannot travel by sending until the early hours of the morning, by which time I am counting on Rashlyn being asleep.*

'But what if he's not?'

If a dog could shrug Knave would have done so at that moment. *If he can sense your magic, there's not much we can do about that. We will keep the sendings short so he never feels it quite long enough to tease at it. He cannot see you, Fynch. Not even with his own magic.*

'But he might feel me coming, is that what you mean?'

Perhaps; I don't know. But he won't know who or what it is, I believe.

'All right,' Fynch said, fatalism sweeping over him. If he was honest with himself, he had always felt that way. He had never been a child to dream of the future or to make plans. He had taken each day as it presented itself and enjoyed all that life gave him during those days. He was a sunny child and his mother had said often enough that he was destined for something special, but he had never understood, just smiled into her faraway stare and loved her despite her oddities. He thought of his mother now. She had often disappeared for days but she would always return. When she did, she would be withdrawn, a little moody – sometimes angry, but with herself not her children. One evening, returning late from his toil at Stoneheart, Fynch had overheard his parents arguing. His father had called his mother a slut. Fynch did not know what that word meant, but the vehemence behind it had shocked him. His mother had laughed in her tinkling manner and given some retort which had enraged his father further. A year or so later Fynch had learned the meaning of the insult and asked his sister about it. She had looked embarrassed and even pained by his query, but was a truthful person like her brother so had explained to him that their mother was a free spirit. 'A sort of madness overcomes her,' he remembered his sister saying.

'And what happens?' Fynch had asked, not really comprehending.

'Well, it takes her away from us,' his sister had replied gently and ruffled his hair. 'Sometimes she needs space and freedom.'

Fynch was a child who needed clarity in all things and so he persisted. 'What does she do when she goes away?'

He recalled now how his kind sister had sighed. 'She allows men to take her, Fynch. It means nothing. Dad says it is a madness and best we leave it at that.'

The little boy had finally understood. He knew his mother was fey – she saw things in her dreams and heard voices whispering to her. Most of the folk around their way thought she was bordering on insane but in truth he could not imagine his mother any other way. He loved her just as she was, with all her curious ways, and although deeply troubled to hear of this new side of her life, he said no more about it. But he thought on it, wondering which men had taken their pleasures with his mother. She was pretty, there was no doubting it, with her petite frame and elfin looks. And when she let her golden hair down, and bathed and put on a fresh dress, she still took his father's breath away. He loved her so, which made her inclinations all the more hurtful. His father would drink himself into a stupor each time she disappeared, no doubt hoping the liquor would take away the grief.

Soon after learning his mother's secret, Fynch had become troubled by thoughts that perhaps he was not sired by his father. Fynch did not resemble any of his siblings closely – they were all dark and solid like his father, whilst he was fair, golden in fact, possessing those same elfin qualities as his mother. Since learning of her 'moments', as he called them, he had worked hard at convincing himself that he was simply his mother all over again, yet the thought still troubled him. He had never shared this anxiety with anyone. Well, not any person. The Dragon King had seen it in him though – Fynch was sure of it. The dragon's eyes had flared as they penetrated the boy's soul – had the dragon seen the truth of Fynch's secret fear?

As he climbed further into the Razors, Fynch thought about what the King of the Creatures had asked of him. Perhaps, in his heart, he had always known that his life would be brief and so had given his energy to enjoying the moment he lived in. So be it. He was not scared of dying any more but he would make his death count. As much as the Dragon King saw destroying Rashlyn as his priority, Fynch knew that his own loyalty lay with Wyl and did not care to share this secret with anyone – not even Knave. Somehow he had to help Wyl defeat Celimus. It was why he had risked more headaches in sending Wyl to Werryl. And, against Knave's counsel, he had sent Valentyna the chaffinch to whistle a tune he hoped would prompt her to wait for Ylena. He had even risked more pain to send dream thoughts to Wyl, urging him to face Celimus and to die again, if necessary.

Fynch was utterly committed to the cause of ridding Morgravia of its present King and somehow protecting Valentyna and Wyl. Deep down he believed Valentyna would have to marry Celimus – there was not enough to prevent it if she was to ensure peace for her realm. He worried whether she could survive their marriage for he knew the cruelty of Celimus. But far worse was his deeply held notion that Wyl would fail in his bid to become Celimus. When he tried to interpret this chilling thought, the only explanation he could come up with for his fear was that Wyl hated Celimus so much he could never live with himself in that guise. Living as Celimus would be his last life too – Elysius had said as much. But it struck Fynch that if Wyl could not achieve the end of the Quickening by becoming Celimus, it could mean an infinite lifetime of changing bodies. Or perhaps the opposite, he reasoned. Perhaps Wyl would die in the body of some lonely guard, an arrow through his back. Fynch grasped – perhaps more than Wyl did – that in any of his guises Wyl could be killed through an accident or natural causes. The Quickening, as Fynch understood it, only worked if the killer was connected to Wyl via a weapon or touch, which was why Myrren could not use the magic to save herself. She had died at the stake; the flames had taken her life.

Knave interrupted his thoughts. *We had best keep moving. We are too exposed here.*

Fynch stood, adjusted the sack across his shoulder and, after buttoning his fleece, followed the dog.

What were you thinking about? Knave asked.

Fynch was surprised. The dog rarely asked questions on such a conversational level. 'Myrren,' he replied.

Oh?

'I asked Elysius why she could not save herself with the Quickening and he explained that Myrren knew she would not die by the hand of a person; she understood that the flames would consume her. Thus the Quickening could not save her and so she took revenge instead. If only she hadn't,' he finished, more bitterly than he had intended.

It wouldn't have changed Wyl's fate, Knave said softly. *Celimus would still have sent him on the journey of treachery into Briavel. Wyl would have died by Romen's sword; Ylena would have wasted away in the dungeon no doubt; and Gueryn would have died in the Razors.*

Fynch nodded wearily. 'Yes, you're right.'

I don't approve of what Myrren and Elysius did, Fynch, but Wyl's life was forfeit from the moment Celimus took the throne. It might be worth you looking upon the Quickening as a gift rather than a curse.

Fynch rubbed Knave's great head to acknowledge the kindness in the dog's voice. No one could approve of the Quickening but perhaps some good might yet come of it. He thought about the ekon which could so easily have killed Wyl in the Razors. If the beast had succeeded, that would have been the end for Wyl, for Elysius had told him the magic worked only between humans. They had a lot to thank Lothryn for, if he still lived. The fate of a kingdom had possibly shifted on the strength of that one man's bravery.

Fynch did not know he had voiced this thought aloud in his mind and thereby made it accessible to Knave. It was only when the dog responded that he realised he needed to learn how to control the magic more thoroughly.

Fynch, do you not realise yet that the destiny of all three realms rests with you? the dog said. *It is your actions — not Lothryn's or Cailech's, not those of Celimus or Valentyna, not even what Wyl might achieve — which will save the Land. You will decide its destiny. And you will change it for the best. We creatures of the Thicket believe in you. It is why you are called Faith.*

Tears rolled helplessly down the small boy's face. I am the sacrifice, he thought hauling himself up to another small ledge. So be it.

CHAPTER 16

Rashlyn awoke from his stupor, angry to feel hands at his brow, wiping away the sweat of his ragings. He swung at the person tending him, hitting her in the face and drawing blood at her mouth. 'Begone, woman!' he roared, searching his wits to identify his location. He was in a strange chamber; it was dark outside.

'Wait!' he called to the woman who had turned her back on him.

She looked at him then, a line of red trailing from the corner of her lip to beneath her chin. Rashlyn could see the hate in her eyes – but he was used to it.

'Where am I?' he demanded. 'Why am I not in my own chambers!'

'The King said we were to watch over you here until you fully recovered,' she replied sullenly, touching her mouth and bringing away bloodstained fingers. 'He said you would not like anyone in your rooms.'

He ignored her injury. 'How long have I been here?'

'Two days.'

That shocked him. 'Where is the King?'

'Gone.' She spoke the word as a threat. 'He left with the Grenadyne the same night of your seizure.'

She called to someone and a man entered the chamber. He took one look at the woman and glanced darkly towards Rashlyn.

'I suspect I am no longer welcome,' Rashlyn said to the man, hoping to unnerve him.

'You have never been welcome, barshi,' the Mountain man replied, not at all intimidated. 'We permitted you in our house only because our King asked it. My wife has taken good care of you.'

'And I regret my odd form of thanks, Rollo,' Rashlyn answered, recognising the pair now. She was a midwife, a capable nurse, and the husband, Rollo, was a senior and trusted warrior of Cailech's. It would not be wise to insult them further.

'My apology, Kaylan,' he said, getting slowly to his feet. The dizziness was still there. 'I must have been dreaming. I am sorry for your wound.'

'Leave, scum,' Rollo growled.

Rashlyn was not surprised. Without Cailech around, the people of the mountains did not maintain the deference they attempted towards him in the King's presence.

'Be careful, Rollo. I understand your daughter is with child. We wouldn't want anything untoward to occur to the infant now, would we?' Rashlyn said conversationally, as he pushed past the couple.

The man roared, lunging towards the barshi, but his wife held him back. 'Don't, Rollo. Who knows what he is capable of,' she said, terrified now, her bleeding lip forgotten, her pride tattered as her pleading eyes beseeched Rashlyn to leave their family be.

That's better, Rashlyn thought, smirking at the cowed Rollo, enjoying the fear in Kaylan's tone. One day he would make them all pay for their disdain. He left the stuffy dwelling and gulped deeply the fresh air of the mountain night. He limped across to the nearby well to drink two long refreshing cups from the spring. It revived him sufficiently that he could make his way, without staggering, to his lonely chambers.

Once inside, he bolted the doors, double-checking the locks. Only then did he begin to relax; only then in the safety of his isolation did he permit the fright at losing two days of his life to be released. What had happened? He was aware that his periods of darkness, when he spiralled into his other self, were extending, but had no idea they could stretch to two whole days. So far the longest he had felt himself lost to such madness was half a day at most, and that had frightened him enough. But two days! Usually during these black periods, as he called them, he functioned reasonably well but it was as though he was someone else. Rashlyn did not dislike that other self; at such times he was confident, flamboyant, certainly creative. His mind was at its sharpest and great innovations often came to him. He felt invincible in this state. No drug he knew of could induce such a constant euphoric sense of power — a herald of the power he would one day wield over Nature.

Without knowing it, Rashlyn had come to the same conclusion as his brother. He believed that Nature was the reflection of Shar, and if he, Rashlyn, could exert control over Nature's beasts, for example, then surely he would achieve godlike status himself? If Elysius could do it, he could also! But when he was able to think clearly, he understood that the euphoric moods were dangerous too. During these times he was unpredictable, capable of anything. He would willingly sacrifice a limb to be able to harness that state of mind whilst still holding sovereignty over himself, but the surge of power forced him to relinquish control. It was a madness, he accepted this. It had been creeping up on him for years. His brother had seen it in him first and his father not long after. Curse their souls!

And yet this time, it did not feel quite the same. His body was still trembling from the seizure, as Kaylan had described it. Normally he would emerge out of the darkness, realise he had lost himself and discover what had occurred in his 'absence' – there was no better way to describe it. But this occasion was different. It sounded as though he had simply collapsed. Cailech must have seen him in this state to have ordered his care. Who else had seen him, apart from the King and the two who had cared for him? Where had he been when the seizure overcame him? What could he remember as his last conscious thought?

Rashlyn was famished but ignored the growling plea of his belly. Using a spell to summon a flame, he lit a fire and brought some water to boil. He added verrun bark and a handful of arkad petals and tried not to think on anything but the brewing and cooling of the infusion into a hand bowl. As soon as he tasted the first bitter sip of the brew, he felt the sky of his mind brightening as if dawn was breaking through night.

He sat himself at the window, inhaled deeply of the numbing air which helped to freshen his thoughts, and continued sipping. The tea began to work: the blurriness cleared and he was able to move backwards through the past few days.

It came to him. He had been riding with the Grenadyne and Myrt. His suspicions about the stranger had not lessened for knowing him; Rashlyn was convinced there was a mystery attached to this fellow. If he could make physical contact with the man, he was sure he could find out more. It had unnerved Rashlyn to hear from the King that Farrow had reacted strongly when he had stroked the neck of Galapek. Clearly he had felt the magic in the stallion, which could only mean the mercenary owned power himself or had been touched by it somehow. Cailech had wanted to dismiss it but Rashlyn was not convinced such a reaction could be passed off as coincidence. And so the King had agreed to force Farrow into riding Galapek with the proviso that Rashlyn accompany him to observe him.

The barshi recalled now how the mercenary had not reacted in the manner described by the King on his first encounter with the enchanted horse. Either the Grenadyne had wrestled his emotions back under his control, or they had been mistaken and the man's claim of being fatigued from his adventure in the mountains was true. And yet Rashlyn was sure Farrow was hiding something. The stranger seemed too confident, too aware that this ride on Galapek was some sort of test. He had parried Rashlyn's questions smoothly and outmanoeuvred him just when Rashlyn had got close enough to touch him. How had that happened, he wondered, and then remembered the strange dizzying sensation. He had been reaching to hand the Grenadyne a small bottle of medicine, supposedly to relieve the recurring headaches the man was experiencing, but his true intention was to touch Farrow's hand. But something had touched him instead.

He closed his eyes and took himself back to the shrieking of the horse which had echoed his own wish to scream at the immense pressure throughout his body. It had felt as though he was being pulled in a number of directions. There was no pain but the experience was frightening, then came intense nausea . . . then darkness. The woman, Kaylan, had called it a seizure so presumably he had thrashed about in his unconscious state.

'It was not my madness that caused this,' he murmured. 'So what did?'

'Magic,' he answered himself and laughed briefly, as though in the grip of a fresh insanity. 'Powerful magic,' he whispered, remembering it more clearly now.

Galapek had felt it too and had screamed. The barshi wondered if the horse was experiencing a similar weakness now also. But there was more in the wake of this strange event . . . there was also a sense of dread. He had no idea why but the ominous notion that something was coming towards him was strong indeed. For the first time in his life, Rashlyn felt very fearful.

Elspyth had decided to slip away from Werryl Palace when everyone's attention was diverted towards Brackstead and reaching Lady Donal before she died. She felt badly for leaving without a farewell to Crys, but also to the Queen. Valentyna had welcomed them warmly when they were in need; had sheltered and protected them without hesitation. Elspyth's secret departure would surely be considered a slight and this bothered the woman of Yentro. But Elspyth wanted no fuss, no teary farewells and definitely no one trying to talk her out of it — which the Queen most certainly would attempt. It seemed right to go quietly, taking nothing, not even the horse she had ridden into Briavel.

What she regretted most was the seemingly sly departure, which might be construed the wrong way, and not leaving a note for Wyl. She owed him that much. Why could she not have taken a few extra minutes and scribbled a second note for the Lady Ylena Thirsk? Elspyth was sure Wyl would come, and she could have given him an assurance she would not do anything rash, along with a promise of her return. But her head was filled with Lothryn and seizing her chance to leave without creating a commotion. She knew Krell and Liryk would be glad to see the back of her; their surreptitious glances and grimaces had left her in no doubt of their displeasure at her presence. She knew what it was too: they did not appreciate her speaking her mind about Celimus and why Valentyna should not marry him. There were moments Elspyth had felt either one of them would gladly silence her with something more painful than their stares.

So, as soon as she saw the royal party depart across Werryl Bridge, she grabbed her small sack of goods and fled via a small, barely known courtyard gate which Valentyna had admitted making good use of as a child. She stepped out of the palace grounds and kept walking, through the town of Werryl rather than across its beautiful bridge. The main township was walled and Elspyth intended to make her escape by blending in easily with the traffic that drifted into and out of Werryl daily through its most northern gate. She felt confident she would find someone who would permit her to travel with them into

Crowyll, and perhaps from there she could buy a nag and use four legs instead of two to get to Banktown in the far north, before turning west and crossing the border into Felrawthy. That was her plan but she was flexible. Frankly, she would take any ride she could get.

It was the brewery driver's child who spotted her first. The cart rolled level with Elspyth as the big old horse's ponderous tread caught up with the slow-moving crowd passing through the gate. The guards did not seem to be paying close attention to those leaving the town so Elspyth felt confident that she was unlikely to be stopped or questioned. It wasn't as if anyone would be looking out for her at this early stage of her journey. Nevertheless, her previous adventures had taught her to take precautions. She needed an innocent cover – just like this family here, she thought, eyeing the little girl who smiled tentatively.

'Where are you going?' the child asked in the way of all curious children, uninhibited by what might or might not be considered polite.

Elspyth smiled brightly. 'I'm going north,' she replied.

'And what will you do when you get there?' the child said.

'Well, I'm going home actually,' Elspyth lied and cast a gentle rescue-me expression towards the driver who shrugged his apology for the youngster's inquisition.

'Do you have a family?'

'No,' Elspyth said, surprised at the question from a child. 'I have no one in my life who worries about me, but north is where I come from and where I feel comfortable.'

'The north of Briavel?'

'The north of Morgravia,' she said theatrically.

'And where's that?'

Elspyth laughed. 'A long way away. I come from a town called Yentro.'

'And you have to walk all that long way?' the little girl exclaimed, not that she knew where Yentro was.

'Hush, Jen. Let the lady be,' the man said, embarrassed. 'I'm sorry, miss,' he added, looking at Elspyth shyly. 'She gets bored easily on these trips and we've hardly begun.'

'It's all right, really,' she replied, making a swift decision. This was her ride. She looked towards the girl again. 'I once knew a pretty lady called Jen and she had beautiful red hair like yours.' It was a lie but Elpsyth needed any leverage she could create and quickly. She knew Shar would forgive her. Her cause was a noble one.

Jen's eyes grew wide with pleasure. 'Am I pretty?'

'I think you are. I'm sure your father does too.'

'Would you like to ride next to me?' Jen asked.

She wanted to hug the child. It was the invitation she had hoped for, and travelling with a family was the safest and least conspicuous ride she could possibly hitch.

Elspyth looked deliberately towards the man. 'Oh, I don't think your father would . . .'

He reacted precisely as she had intended. 'You're most welcome to ride with us, miss,' he offered kindly. 'We're going as far as Coneham if that helps?'

'Oh, I'm sure it will,' she smiled. 'Where is it exactly?'

'Hop up. It's north of Brackstead.'

Jen shifted closer to her father and made room for Elspyth. 'Thank you,' she said, with relief. 'Will we be stopping in Brackstead?' she added as innocently as she could. She did not like the idea of running into Valentyna and Crys.

'No. We don't stay in inns or the like, miss,' the driver

said. 'We just curl up in the back. We carry everything with us.'

Elspyth smiled. It was perfect. 'Thank you, and I'm sure I can help to keep your Jen amused on our journey.'

'My name is Ericson,' the man said, an expression of gratitude sweeping across his tired face. Elspyth felt a tiny pang of guilt at how adroitly she had manipulated this kind fellow.

The cart rumbled through the northern gate, Jen chattering incessantly about anything that came into her head and Elspyth doing her best to agree where necessary and answer if required. She pulled her blue cloak tighter around herself for the morning was chill. As they passed the soldiers at the gate, she had tried not to catch anyone's eye. But Elspyth had never quite grasped how attractive she was and her dark hair and pert features could not help but win attention.

'Shar guide you,' the guard said to her. It was a common blessing used by Morgravians and Briavellians alike to bid others a good journey but it was the wink that came with it that made her grin. 'Don't stay away too long now,' the guard added, encouraged by her smile. 'I won't sleep until I see your pretty face again.'

Elspyth made a gesture of admonishment, as if to say it was improper of him to talk like that in front of her family, but the cart had already rolled on and the young man missed her mock annoyance. She lifted her hand in farewell instead.

It had been a long time since Elspyth had felt as light-hearted as she did at that moment. Perhaps it was knowing that she was finally doing something positive towards finding her love. I'm coming, Lothryn, she silently cast.

She hoped Shar would take pity on her that soon her beloved might hear her words.

As Elspyth was privately celebrating her escape, Gueryn was arguing with Rashlyn, now recovered, who had decided to visit the prisoner.

'Who would it hurt?' Gueryn demanded.

'No one, but I don't understand your request,' the barshi said.

'Because I am rotting away here.'

'Why is that my problem?'

'Because you're meant to take care of me,' Gueryn said, his tone as acid as he could make it. 'Either you make it possible or, I promise you, Rashlyn, I'll find a way to kill myself, even if it means banging my head against this wall until I knock my senses clean out!'

Gueryn knew he sounded desperate; he could hear as much in his tone, and it was highly unlikely he could fashion any genuinely expedient method to assist his own death. Still, the threat was there and the barshi looked thoughtful. Gueryn decided to press his luck. 'The King insisted I be looked after. I refuse to sit here day after day in your stinking dungeon.'

'Isn't that what prisoners do?'

The man's light voice irritated Gueryn further. 'Let me work, damn it! I'll provide an honest day's toil for the chance to breathe fresh air and work my muscles. You can keep me chained if you must.'

'Oh, I will,' Rashlyn murmured.

Gueryn felt himself losing his temper; the only thing that stopped him reaching for the barshi's throat was the memory of the magic Rashlyn had once used on him and the threat that he would make it hurt the next time.

He tried again, a little more humility in his tone. 'The King agreed to allow me daily walks so I can remain as healthy as possible considering my situation. I am prepared to work for it, for Shar's sake.'

'Where?'

That took Gueryn by surprise. He stopped his pacing and turned on the healer. 'Where what?'

'Where would you work?'

Had he won? Now he had to negotiate more carefully than a mouse stealing past a sleeping cat. He forced himself to keep the exasperation in his voice, as if the chance to escape the loneliness and despair of the dungeon was all that mattered. No one, especially Rashlyn, must guess his true intent. 'Where? Anywhere! The kitchens, the vineyards, the stables . . .' He ran an unsteady hand through his tangled greying hair to give an air of distraction.

'Your preference?'

'Does it matter?' he retaliated, wondering whether Rashlyn was testing him. 'I'm good with horses; I'm not afraid to work in an open field; and if you want me scrubbing pans, I'll happily do that. Why don't you choose?'

'The kitchens would not want you, Morgravian,' Rashlyn mused. 'And I don't want you around knives or any potential weapons.' He scratched at his wild beard and something fell out of it. Dishevelled as Gueryn himself looked and as dirty as he felt, Rashlyn's grubbiness revolted him.

'Then let me work in the stables,' he said. 'I'll muck out, rub down, water, exercise the animals – whatever the stablemaster wants.'

Rashlyn stared at him. The eyes were tiny and dark; no evidence of warmth flickered in that cold gaze. 'I shall speak to Maegryn,' he said, after a long pause. 'Remember my lesson, soldier. With the King gone, you have no protection to count on, other than what my rule deems.'

'I had no idea you hailed from royal blood,' Gueryn risked.

'Be very careful, le Gant,' the dark man warned, his lips twisted in a cruel sneer beneath the filthy beard.

Gueryn emerged into a sharply bright spring morning, his eyes stinging from the sunlight but his body rejoicing in its gently warm caress and the chance to breathe air the opposite of the stale mustiness of his cell. He had won.

He stood between two guards, neither of whom he knew, and watched a man approach. Rashlyn was nowhere to be seen.

'I am Maegryn, the stablemaster,' the man said, coming to a halt.

Gueryn nodded. 'Thank you for allowing me to work in the stables. I'll not let you down.'

Maegryn made a low sound of disdain. 'You wouldn't want to, soldier. Come with me.'

Gueryn followed as fast as the rope binding his ankles would allow.

'You're not going to make him wear that all day, are you?' Maegryn complained to the guards.

'Rashlyn's orders,' one said, shrugging.

'And who is he to be giving orders?' Maegryn said, adding under his breath, 'Haldor spare me.'

Gueryn took a chance. 'He told me he is the King's voice when his highness is not here,' he said to Maegryn, who was now slicing through the rope with a blade.

The stablemaster stood, his deep-set eyes giving away little of the man inside. 'And I'm the fucking King of the Stable so Rashlyn had better look out when he gives orders in my domain.'

The guards laughed.

Gueryn bowed. 'Your highness,' he said, and knew he had made a fragile conquest when Maegryn grinned in response. 'Thank you,' Gueryn added, looking towards his unshackled feet.

'Don't get too excited, soldier. Jos here will be hanging around to keep an eye on you.'

Gueryn eyed the huge, lumbering lad beside him. 'Nice to meet you, Jos.'

The big guard nodded, a sloping grin pulling at his deformed mouth. 'Don't give me any trouble now,' he warned, the words slightly mangled.

'You have my promise,' Gueryn assured, looking towards Maegryn too.

'But is it worth anything?' the stablemaster teased.

'As an officer of the Legion, most certainly.'

'I wish your King showed similar manners.'

'My King is a ruthless, lying, cowardly murderer. I shall kill my King if I ever get the chance.'

Maegryn gave a low whistle. 'Well, I hope our King watches his back then.'

'What do you mean?'

'I gather our people are about to make a peace alliance with your people, soldier.'

'What?' Gueryn's eyes narrowed; surely this was a jest?

'If our Cailech has his way, then the Razor Kingdom and Morgravia are soon to be allies,' Maegryn clarified.

Gueryn was shocked. 'Celimus cannot be trusted.'

Maegryn shrugged. 'So long as you can, le Gant. I'm only King of the Stables remember? What happens for the greater good of our realm is not something I have any control over. Now, I think you need exercise as much as my horses do – follow me.'

Jos stayed with Gueryn all afternoon and the Morgravian noted that the lad followed his orders dutifully, taking his responsibility of watching over his prisoner seriously. The deformity was a pity – it gave the impression that Jos was a dullard when he was anything but. It also gave the other guards reason to tease him, as Gueryn learned from the lad's shy admission. He found the youngster pleasant, courteous and charming. He laughed at Gueryn's small jests and even made a few of his own. No, the youngster was no dullard, just an unfortunate victim of the gods to be born so afflicted. Gueryn made a promise to himself to make a special effort with Jos. Confidence was all the lad needed. The harelip would fade to invisible if Jos's personality was allowed to shine through.

Gueryn had to admit he was enjoying himself after so many weeks of despair. He had walked, rubbed down and watered six horses now and was pleased with himself, despite the twinge from aching muscles and tired limbs. He had not counted on being as weak as he felt.

'A good afternoon's work, soldier,' Maegryn said, offering a linen rag. 'That's good honest sweat there.'

'Call me Gueryn,' the soldier said. When the man nodded, he added, 'Can I come again?'

'Tomorrow's fine. I'll be glad to see you. Perhaps Jos can bring you this time.'

'What about Rashlyn? Will you speak with him?'

'The man's insane. No one follows his rules. We won't say anything – he probably won't even come looking.'

Gueryn's relief showed. 'Until tomorrow, then.'

He nodded at Jos to let the guard know he was ready to be returned to the dungeon, and gave him a grin. He was building tenuous friendships here. He was a big step closer to Galapek too and that made the aches all the more satisfying. Tomorrow he might see the horse which the stranger, Aremys, had claimed was Lothryn. It still seemed too incredible to contemplate, but Gueryn could not forget the touch of Rashlyn's evil magic on his own body or the murder of a woman made to look like Elspyth. He needed to see the horse for himself.

Until tomorrow then, he said privately as he fell in step with Jos.

CHAPTER 17

Crys admired the way the Briavellian commander, despite his busy duties, offered his help. If Liryk minded, he did not show it.

'Forgive me for dragging you away from important affairs, Commander Liryk,' Crys said. 'I'm just a little worried about Elspyth, as is your Queen.'

'And rightly so, Duke,' Liryk said sharply. 'She is a young woman abroad alone. No matter how I tighten the net around bandits and cut-throats, they still exist and she makes the softest of targets.'

'Too true. Where should we start?'

'Let's find out who was on duty first during our absence in Brackstead.'

'How many gates are there?'

'Five main ones, but as you rightly point out she was leaving as anonymously as possible so I imagine she would have used the busiest outlets, which would be Werryl Bridge or the northern gate.'

It took them an hour to find and question the relevant men, drawing a blank until one young man was hurried back from a meal. He wiped his mouth in haste, concern on his face that he was in trouble. His superior introduced him. 'This is Peet. He was one of three guards on the northern gate for the morning watch.'

Liryk and Crys had already questioned the other two from the morning and all from the afternoon rotation. Crys was sure this man would offer no further insight and had resigned himself to a fruitless search following a trail that was already stone cold.

'Sir,' Peet said to his commander and nervously nodded at Crys. 'My lord.'

Liryk cleared his throat. 'Relax, man, you're not in any trouble here. We're seeking your help.'

'Oh?' the guard replied, none of the anxiety leaving his tone or expression.

'We're hoping you might remember a young woman who left Werryl yesterday. We think she might have departed via the northern gate and we're pretty certain it would have been on your watch, the early morning guard.'

Peet nodded, relieved, looking between both men. 'I'll try, sir. Can you describe her?'

Liryk looked at Crys who obliged. 'Well, she's petite. She has dark hair and is comely. Very pretty in fact.' He grinned at the young man. 'She stands about yay high to me,' he measured a point halfway between his elbow and shoulder, 'and I'm guessing now but I think she might have been wearing a soft brown skirt, pinkish sort of blouse, black boots. I really can't be sure, but they were the clothes she was wearing when we both came into Werryl.' He knew Elspyth had not taken any of the items Valentyna had given her to wear.

Peet's expression became forlorn and he sounded embarrassed. 'Hundreds of people pass through that gate each day, my lord. That description could be any of a dozen women from yesterday.' He held his hands out in a gesture of helplessness. 'So many people, you don't really scrutinise anyone unless you've been ordered to.'

Crys nodded, understanding. 'I know, it was a long shot.'

Liryk sighed. 'I'm sorry, my lord.' He was genuine in his commiseration; he did not like the antagonism the woman of Yentro had stirred up but he certainly was not happy at her going off alone into the mountains. He thought Crys had been far too flippant about her disappearance when it had been first discovered; obviously the duke had had a change of heart but a little too late, he thought privately. 'Thank you, Peet, you can return to your meal,' he told the guard.

'Oh,' Crys said suddenly, 'she did have a cloak with her. The morning was cold so presumably she had that on. It's blue, if that helps?'

Peet, who had been turning away, swung around. 'Blue cloak?'

Crys nodded. 'Does it jog anything?' he asked, noticing the man's keen attention.

'Why, yes, my lord, it does. I do remember a woman in a blue cloak. Her hair was dark, I think, she had it covered with the hood so I can't be sure.'

Liryk stepped forward. 'Well, tell us, man. Hurry now.'

Peet frowned. 'It was just some innocent cheek, sir. Guarding the gate can be tedious and she was very pretty, after all.'

Liryk sighed. 'Get on with it, Peet. What was said?'

The soldier bit his lip in thought. 'I wished her Shar's speed, my lord,' he said, looking towards Crys who seemed the most eager to hear. 'I added something along the lines that she should hurry back to Werryl because I wouldn't be able to sleep until I saw her pretty face again.' He shrugged. 'It was harmless really – I was just passing the time of day with a lovely girl.'

Crys smiled. 'That's all right, Peet. Was she alone?'

'No, as I recall she was with a family. I thought it was hers.'

'Come on now, son. What do you remember?' prompted Liryk. 'Bring the scene back. Remember all those exercises we've been doing and how to recall a moment in detail?'

'Yes, sir, I do,' Peet said. 'I can remember it well now. She was travelling with a little girl and a man who was driving the cart they were in. They – the woman and the girl – were laughing. It was a cart with one horse.'

'Did she say anything?' Crys asked.

'No. She just waved. Seemed happy.'

'The man – what do you remember about him?' Liryk added.

'Not much, sir. He said he was going to Coneham. His cart had brewery barrels on it. Only two of them, which strikes me as a little odd now but didn't at the time.'

'Why is that odd?' Crys asked.

Liryk turned to him. 'Because our brewery is situated north-east of the city. There would be no need to pass through Werryl itself, let alone the northern gate, for deliveries to Coneham. It does sound suspicious.' Liryk addressed the officer. 'Find out whatever you can on this fellow – if there's any information among the men. Get

Peet here to give as detailed a description of him as possible. Anything at all he remembers, record.'

'Is the lady in trouble, sir?'

'No, lad. But we need to find her and your information can help us track her down.'

Peet nodded and took his leave, following his superior officer.

'Not much to go on, I'm afraid,' Liryk admitted to Crys.

'It's something, though. I'll wait around a little longer – someone might think of something jogged by Peet's information.'

'Let's give it another hour.'

'And then I'm heading for Coneham, come what may,' Crys promised.

The cart slowed to a stop and Elspyth was roused from the snooze she had fallen into. She presumed they were breaking for something to eat and felt embarrassed that she had no food to share with her hosts. She did, however, have some coin which Crys had insisted she keep during their journey to Werryl. 'You may need it if we get separated,' he had cautioned and she was grateful now for his generosity. At least she could offer to pay for her keep whilst travelling with Ericson and his little girl.

Elspyth noted a hut not far away. She knew they had taken a route off the main road because Ericson had said it was a shorter route with less traffic, and she had not complained, just glad to be moving north and faster than her own feet could carry her.

'How long have I been dozing?' she said, stretching. She didn't recall climbing into the back of the cart, or feeling tired, but clearly she must have done both for that was where she found herself now.

'Oh, hours,' Jen answered in a singsong voice. 'The tea always makes the women drowsy.'

Elspyth had no idea what the youngster was talking about. They had shared some tea at the roadside not far out of Werryl. She had thought it odd, because they had only just left the city, but Jen insisted she was thirsty and hungry and Ericson had said tea and a hunk of cheese would satisfy his daughter who rarely ate breakfast. Elspyth had been happy to go along with it and had enjoyed the curious-tasting brew. 'Where are we?' she wondered aloud, imagining they might be a couple of hours north of the city.

'Just outside Sharptyn,' Ericson replied, jumping down from the cart. Jen followed.

Elspyth was taken aback. 'Sharptyn! No, wait,' she said, frowning, 'that can't be right.' Her mind raced across her imaginary map of Briavel. Sharptyn was to the west, almost into Morgravia, and many hours from Werryl. She shook her head free of the befuddlement of sleep. Perhaps she was mistaken in her mapping. 'Are you sure?'

He grinned and there was something unpleasant in it. 'Oh yes, very.'

'But Sharptyn is far west. You said you were heading north,' she said, a pang of fear tingling through her body.

His nasty smile remained. 'Did I? Well, we're here now, Elspyth.'

Ericson no longer looked tired or kind. He looked predatory and smug. 'Jen?' She looked towards the child, bewildered and frightened.

Again the singsong voice. 'Sorry, Elspyth. So, so sorry,'

Jen chanted, not even looking at the woman. 'Ericson chose you. I didn't want to. I liked you.'

'Ericson!' Elspyth shrieked as men appeared out of the hut. 'What's this all about?'

'It's not personal,' he said, acknowledging the new arrivals with a nod. 'Just business. Get her, lads,' he added.

Elspyth had no time to think; she lifted her skirt and ran. She forced her legs to move as fast as she had ever run in her life, and she screamed, unleashing every ounce of her strength and spirit. Even escaping from Cailech's fortress had not been as terrifying as this. She had fellow escapees then. Right now she was alone and she could hear the shouts and taunts of the men chasing her. They were laughing at her. She knew deep down she probably could not escape, could not outrun them, but she had to try.

She thought of Lothryn and how her pathetic attempt to rescue him had achieved nothing more than getting herself trapped, and probably killed. He would never know that she had tried to reach him. She screamed one last time as she sensed a man about to launch himself at her. He crashed out of the bushes, hitting her hard sideways and crushing the breath out of her. The others arrived panting, some laughing still. And then Ericson forced her to swallow more of the tea she had drunk earlier. It all made sense now: she had been drugged. Elspyth tried to spit out the liquid, shaking her head from side to side, deliberately gagging. Ericson hit her, which shocked her into opening her mouth to yell but succeeded only in giving her attacker the chance to pour the drug down her throat more effectively.

The men let her go, no longer interested, it seemed — for the time being anyway — now that she had swallowed the drug. She just had time to count six of them, including Ericson, before the sky began to reel and the trees felt as though they might fall in on her. She sensed something reaching towards her, something powerful trying to connect with her – or so she imagined – but it was too late. Elspyth lost consciousness again. There would be no more screaming now.

Fynch had felt Elspyth's fear as she fled from the men, sensed it when she fell. He had never met this woman of Yentro and yet somehow her terror and helplessness assaulted him. He reached towards her and could see her now; prone, presumably unconscious, with men standing around her.

Knave looked back to where Fynch stood rigid on the small ledge. The wind was whipping around them and Knave wondered whether he and the boy should be harnessed together somehow. Fynch was so slight, Knave feared that if a stiff, rogue gust came racing over them, Fynch could be blown off the ledge and down to his death.

Bewildered by the boy's closed eyes and fixed stance the dog returned to him. *Fynch! What happens now?* he asked. When Fynch did not respond, he nudged the boy, suddenly disturbed that he could not lock onto whatever was troubling his companion.

Fynch staggered and finally opened his eyes. 'It's Wyl's friend, Elspyth. She's in trouble,' he said, holding his head.

Knave knew it hurt to use the magic. Elysius had been very careful about the power. His channelling to Myrren had near enough killed him, for she had needed his company and strength for a sustained period. But Fynch was so small and inexperienced and seemed to be opening himself fully to the magic, not because he craved the power but because he did not yet know how to shield himself from it. He had obviously latched onto this woman's plea for help but this was not his problem. He had a task to fulfil.

We must press on, Fynch, Knave began.

'No. She's hurt, in trouble. Elspyth is the woman who escaped with Wyl from the Razors. She helped him. I cannot forsake her,' Fynch murmured through his pain.

Chew some sharvan, Knave suggested, determined not to show his annoyance at this new setback.

Fynch poked into his sack and retrieved a handful of the dried leaves which he had taken from the stock belonging to Elysius. He sat down and quietly chewed as suggested.

How do you know this? Knave asked.

'I have seen her,' the boy answered.

I'm not sure I understand. Is Elspyth empowered? How can she reach you otherwise?

Fynch shook his aching head. 'I don't think so. Wyl did not mention her having any sentient ability. I'm not sure, to tell the truth, whether she even knew I was there.'

What do you mean?

'She did not call to me as such. It was her fear I felt and then I heard her screams. I followed her trace.' Fynch looked at Knave with large, serious eyes that were full of pain and the dog felt grief for the small boy who had to face so much. 'I think it's the Thicket.'

Sending you her message, you mean?

Fynch nodded once, carefully. With the pain slowly clearing he did not want to reawaken it. 'You said something earlier about Wyl being touched by the Thicket and therefore sensitive to magic even though he cannot wield it?'

I remember.

'Well, Elspyth is the niece of the Widow Ilyk – the seer whom Elysius knew and used once. Do you recall that?'

Yes.

'So perhaps Elspyth, though not empowered herself, has a vague awareness of magic's touch. Wyl mentioned that she once dreamed of Lothryn calling to her.'

And?

Fynch shrugged. His head felt better, the dizziness gone and just a reminder of the pain lurking. He spat out the pulp of the sharvan. 'I'm guessing that she cast out her fears without realising she could, and it just so happened that the Thicket was listening. The Thicket has connected us all, you might say.'

It was plausible, Knave thought. *So what are you thinking now, Faith Fynch?*

'I have to find out more about what's happening to her.'

We cannot be diverted from our journey, Knave warned gravely, hoping to impress on Fynch once again that nothing else mattered but what the Dragon King asked of them: to destroy Rashlyn and rid the world of his evil.

'I know. I'm going to send a spy,' Fynch said, and chanced a grin at his black friend.

Then use a fast one. We must get on.

Fynch looked out across the hazy landscape. He knew what he was searching for and sure enough he found the kestrel, high on the wing and hovering, staring down towards the ground.

'Over there!' he said, pointing.

I see it.

Again Fynch closed his eyes and drew on his Elysian magic – as he liked to call it – to summon the bird of prey.

Knave saw the bird tilt its wing and knew that was the moment Fynch had connected with it. The kestrel swooped and banked high again, turning in their direction, and then dived towards them fast and no doubt curious. When it arrived it perched itself on Fynch's outstretched arm and even permitted the boy to stroke it in thanks for answering the summoning. Knave was impressed. He had been told that Elysius had achieved something similar once before, but not as easily; according to the creatures of the Thicket he had cajoled and beseeched them to help him. But the answer to Fynch's call was immediate. The kestrel obviously felt compelled to respond.

Knave would not normally be privy to what passed between the boy and the bird, but Fynch generously opened his mind so the dog could listen in on what was being communicated.

I need you to find someone for me, Fynch asked.

Who? the bird replied, seemingly undisturbed by the discussion. Knave wondered if the kestrel knew who Fynch was.

It is a woman – this is what she looks like, and Knave shared the picture that Fynch gave to the kestrel.

Where?

Two miles east of Sharptyn. Another picture was given: this time it was an aerial map of Briavel. Knave was spellbound; was the Thicket supplying Fynch with this practical information?

And when I find her?

Let me know what you see. I will send help.

With your powers can you not look for yourself? the bird asked cheekily.

I could, my friend, but I lose strength and a portion of my life each time I draw on my powers. You can save me some of this loss if you will make that journey for me and be my eyes.

I shall do what you ask if you will give me your name and tell me who you are.

Gladly. My name is Fynch. I am from Morgravia and was a cleaner at the castle of Stoneheart.

Oh, but you are much more than that, surely, the kestrel said, scorn lacing its voice at the boy's humility. *I must know the truth before I make this journey.*

All that I have said is true, Fynch replied evenly.

But there is a secret, the bird encouraged. Its inquisitiveness was infectious and Knave felt as though he too was holding his breath. Fynch said nothing. The silence hung between the three of them, heavy with knowledge that one of them was reluctant to share.

You must tell me, the kestrel urged. *I am like you, Fynch – I need facts . . . and I need the truth.*

How the bird could know this was anyone's guess, but Knave had learned long ago not to question magic for each answer merely led to a new question. So he ignored his queries and listened.

I am Fynch, the boy replied, his voice suddenly strong, filled with a power Knave had never heard before. *And I am the King of the Creatures.*

Fynch passed out at the last word, the link broken. The kestrel lifted from the boy's arm just in time to avoid falling with him and launched itself into the air and away from the mountains. Knave was too stunned at Fynch's words to say anything. He gazed after the bird until it was no more than a tiny speck on the horizon. Then, as it disappeared from his far-reaching sight, he roused himself from his disquiet and lay down beside Fynch to keep his friend warm until he regained consciousness.

CHAPTER 18

Cailech was flanked by only two of his own men as he slowed his horse at the gates of the Tenterdyn Estate of Felrawthy. On one side of him rode his loyal warrior, Myrt, and on the other a man he now called friend: Aremys Farrow.

Farrow was an enigma. There were secrets buried in this man – Cailech was sure of it – and yet Aremys struck him as forthright and honest. But the way the Grenadyne had reacted to Galapek haunted the King. It was obvious that Farrow suspected something about the beast. Rashlyn's attempt to flush out the truth had failed miserably, ending in the barshi's collapse and neither of them closer to their goal. In fact, it had been even more bewildering to learn that Galapek had been disturbed too, and Farrow had calmly brought the barshi and horse back to the fortress. If he was working against them, surely the mercenary would have left both to perish, or stolen the horse and allowed Rashlyn to die?

None of it made sense to Cailech and so, despite his misgivings, he had decided to trust Farrow. Cailech considered himself an accurate judge of character and his instincts about people had rarely let him down. Lothryn was his only error, but it had taken almost forty years of friendship to discover his mistake. His mouth twisted at the thought of Lothryn's betrayal.

'Sire?' Aremys said, noting the expression on Cailech's face.

'I'm all right,' he replied, 'just wishing Lothryn was here.' He expected Myrt to agree and was surprised by the grim silence at his right. He did not miss the sly glance his warrior gave the Grenadyne either. What did that look mean?

'You don't need him for this, my lord,' Aremys assured. 'Only you can achieve what we're setting out to do today.'

'He had a way of making me feel calm.'

His companions remained silent. What was there to say? Aremys believed Cailech had no right to feel sorry for himself after what had been perpetrated on Lothryn, but he was not in a position to comment so he kept his own counsel and watched the guard approaching.

'Are you ready, sire?' Myrt asked.

'As I'll ever be,' Cailech replied and glanced towards his new friend who nodded encouragement.

'Lothryn would be proud of you for this,' Aremys said.

'He would too, Farrow. This is something he would applaud.'

'Then you honour him by it.'

Cailech smiled. There was gratitude in his expression and something unreadable in his eyes — sorrow perhaps? Aremys hoped so.

The guard arrived and the mercenary addressed him. 'I am Aremys Farrow. You're expecting our party, I gather?'

The guard nodded. 'We are. Wait here, please.' He whistled to the gatehouse and gave a hand signal.

'You might care to bow in the presence of a King,' Aremys suggested to the guard whilst they waited for the gates to open.

He was relieved to see the man looked abashed; had worried for a moment that due respect was not going to be accorded to Cailech and that the Mountain King, as unpredictable as he was, might react and bring the whole plan crashing down around them.

'Forgive me, sire,' the man stammered and bowed low. Cailech and his companions exchanged satisfied glances.

An officer met them. 'Welcome, your highness,' he said with appropriate reverence. Then he looked towards Aremys and nodded. 'Farrow,' he acknowledged.

Aremys gave his reins to the men who had arrived to take care of the horses. 'Captain Bukanan, sir. Good to see you again. This is Myrt, Second Warrior of the Mountain People.'

Celimus was watching as the King of the Mountains arrived at the gate, exchanged a look with Farrow and then jumped gracefully from his magnificent stallion. The Morgravian sovereign was surprised. For some reason he had a picture in his mind that the Razor King would be dark, stocky, bearded even, with hooded eyes and a secretive countenance. He had not expected this golden-haired warrior, tall, clean-shaven and artless of dress. He had expected his enemy to be bedecked in finery to proclaim his royal status, but he was wrong again. The man wore no jewellery that Celimus could see, and his clothes were simple and yet frustratingly elegant. Celimus would have liked to own the cloak which hung so magnificently across the broad shoulders and seemed to shimmer in the daylight. This King was understated in his presentation and yet he oozed confidence. It was unsettling for Celimus who had anticipated looking down upon his counterpart for many reasons, not all physical. The man had him mystified. His modest attire combined with his imposing presence suddenly made Celimus feel like the misfit — a strutting peacock in his bright courtly clothes. He pulled angrily at the circlet around his head.

'I don't think I need this,' he muttered to Jessom who, as ever, was nearby.

'I'll take it, sire,' the man replied, nothing in his tone to suggest that he was inwardly smirking at how one glimpse of the Mountain King had provoked such insecurity.

To Celimus, Cailech looked like a warrior out on a ride to survey his lands; not someone who had come to a formal parley with a neighbouring sovereign — and an enemy no less. Was it arrogant to arrive so underdressed? And yet Celimus envied the man his casual approach. His gaze narrowed as he watched Captain Bukanan share a few words with the new arrivals. He would have to be careful with the upstart from the Razors; he was altogether disconcerting.

'It is time, sire,' Jessom said.

Celimus remained silent, distracted by his thoughts. He turned from the window and strode past the Chancellor towards the main steps of Tenterdyn, where he had intended to arrange himself so the Mountain King might come cringing towards him. But there was absolutely nothing in Cailech's demeanour to suggest he was here cap in hand, begging for an audience. If anything, he seemed utterly assured. It was the opposite of what the Morgravian had expected, and baffling.

Celimus forced away his puzzlement, replacing it with a beautifully contrived bright expression, as he emerged to meet his fellow sovereign.

So far so good, Aremys thought as he looked towards the movement at the front of the large house, which not so long ago had been filled with the Donal family. Then he felt a sudden flurry of fear when he saw the King, flanked by his Chancellor and various other military people, emerge from the huge main doors.

'Your majesty, King Celimus is here to greet you. May I accompany you?' Captain Bukanan offered.

Aremys thanked Shar that Celimus was playing this out to strict protocol. It was a heartening sign that the King of Morgravia was treating his sworn enemy with courtesy and equality, even though Jessom had no doubt been a guiding hand.

'Thank you, Captain,' Cailech said. He threw a final glance towards Aremys, who noted the glint in the King's eye and read it as a combination of pleasure and mischief. He truly admired this man who walked so boldly into his enemy's camp, unarmed and with nothing to offer but promises.

Aremys closed the gap between himself and Myrt to fall in step behind the King. He admired the superb cloak that the King had donned for this most formal of occasions. It was a pewter colour, made from the softest of wool, spun repeatedly until it shone, from the coats of the shaggy polders – a cross between a goat and a sheep.

These rare animals were found only in the mountains and he had noted how well Cailech's people cared for the two large flocks they had gathered. The animals' long hair was impervious to moisture and felt like silk to touch. The women of the Razors had done their King proud with this beautiful garment, which kept the natural silvery grey of the polder for its background while crimson and black dyed yarn had been woven into an eye-catching, intricate pattern along its entire length. Aremys marvelled at how the clever design made an already tall man look even larger. Cailech was certainly a match for Celimus in height and looks, although the Razor King was older and generally more rugged in comparison with the vain southern monarch.

The dance of Kings had begun.

'King Cailech, welcome to Tenterdyn, our summer retreat,' Celimus said, his tone full of largesse. He noted a twisted expression flicker across Farrow's face and wondered what it meant. He returned his attention to his guest, irritated further by the man's surprisingly deep voice. It made him feel as though he was a boy greeting his father and his stomach clenched.

'King Celimus, it is a true honour to meet you.' To the Morgravian's astonishment – and indeed that of all who were privy to this historic meeting – Cailech bowed his head and shoulders towards his southern foe. 'Thank you for this parley.'

For once in his life Celimus was lost for words. He had not expected Cailech to look as he did, and he certainly had not anticipated such graciousness to go with the startlingly good looks. The man was paying him homage, but in such a noble manner that it felt anything but subservient.

Everyone waited for Celimus's response. Finally it came. 'I am intrigued, King Cailech,' he said, reaching for the right words, annoyed by his higher-pitched tone even though so many people had praised his smooth, velvet voice, 'by this opportunity for Morgravia. Come, we are here to talk.' It was not as eloquent as Celimus knew he could be, but these were unusual circumstances.

Captain Bukanan, already briefed on the format for the day, returned to where Myrt stood. 'I believe I must accompany you, is that correct?'

Myrt nodded. 'We will return on horseback to a spot of my King's choosing and await word of his safe return. There are others coming with us, of course.' He stopped himself using the word 'hostages'.

It made little difference: Bukanan knew he was a hostage. The Captain nodded his understanding and took his leave from his King, as did Myrt from Cailech. The necessary paperwork was handed to Myrt by Jessom, after Aremys had read it through to check all was in order according to his earlier specifications.

Inside, the party was led by their regal host to a huge chamber which Aremys had not seen on his previous visit to Tenterdyn. At each end of the large space was a glorious stone fireplace and a long table stood in its centre. Tapestries softened the walls, as did huge windows with bench seats and elegant shutters, each one crafted with the Donal sigil. Aremys realised that the room's simplicity deliberately allowed the dazzling scenery of the distant Razors to do all the work of beautifying the chamber and impressing visitors.

'I thought you would be comfortable seeing your home from here,' Celimus said, his charm more evident now that he had taken a minute or so to gather his thoughts.

Cailech smiled in return. 'Having never witnessed its beauty from this vantage point, I thank you for such a treat.'

The response pleased Celimus. He indicated the thin man at his side. 'I took the liberty, King Cailech, of retaining only my Chancellor, Maris Jessom . . .'

'Your majesty,' Jessom said on cue, bowing his head to the Mountain King.

'. . . to match your Aremys Farrow. I believed this would be more comfortable than too many other ears.'

'I am grateful for the consideration, your highness.'

'Well, now,' Celimus continued. 'Please, be seated and let us offer you some southern refreshment.'

Jessom nodded towards a waiting servant and trays with drinks and wafers were immediately walked into the hall. Celimus gestured for Cailech to be seated at his right, so the Mountain King could see the Razors through the magnificent picture windows. Aremys was offered a seat at his left.

'I will bear witness alongside the Chancellor,' Aremys said, as deferentially as he could manage, and moved to stand beside Jessom.

'As you wish, Grenadyne,' Celimus said, unfazed.

'Smart move, Farrow,' the Chancellor murmured under his breath. 'You would fare well in court.'

'I don't belong here, Jessom, and you know it,' Aremys shot back, relieved to be out of the gaze of King Celimus who was watching a servant pour a goblet of wine for Cailech.

'Shall we dispense with our regal titles, Cailech?' Celimus said brightly as he raised his goblet.

'I thought you'd never suggest it,' the Mountain King replied, grinning and raising his own cup.

'To us then,' Celimus said with a flourish, tapping his goblet against his guest's and noticing the glint of humour in Cailech's light green eyes.

'To Morgravia and the land of the Razors!' Cailech responded, and both men drained their goblets.

'Again!' Celimus called to the servant. His cheeks were suddenly flushed with the gravity of this historic moment.

'Would your father be proud of this parley?' Cailech asked as their goblets were refilled.

The Morgravian was not ready for such a disconcerting question. 'My father?' he repeated, angry at himself for doing so.

Cailech nodded and again Celimus saw amusement sparkling in the man's eyes although his facial expression gave nothing away.

'Er . . . I'm sure he would.'

'I think he would be shocked,' Cailech said.

'Why do you say that?'

'I believe he did not see such a vision of peace as you have, Celimus.'

Aremys silently congratulated the King of the Mountains. Suddenly the parley had become Celimus's idea: it was the Morgravian's vision for harmony that was bringing together two enemy nations.

Celimus searched for any guile behind the words but saw nothing except openness on Cailech's rugged face. Again he was not ready for the man; such praise from the enemy was something to be savoured. 'I would like to think that I can bring together our realms, Cailech,' he began, warming to this vision of peace he apparently was chasing, 'as well as Briavel.'

'Indeed. In the space of just a few days, you could achieve such an amazing feat. Your jongleurs will craft songs about it, bards will write plays in homage and I have no doubt your artists will record the events so that future generations will understand this momentous time in Morgravia's history.'

Aremys felt Jessom shoot a warning glance his way. Cailech's praise was honeyed but it should be diluted before it became too much like treacle. So far Celimus was lapping it up, Aremys noticed, and he was fully convinced that the Morgravian King would personally commission the songs, plays and artworks should they not eventuate unprompted. Wyl had told him that the man was vain, but he also recalled Wyl's warning that Celimus was clever; that behind his charm and looks was a stunningly sharp mind. Yes, Aremys thought, Cailech would have to be a bit wary.

The servant had been dismissed now. It was just the four of them.

'And tell me how you fit into all of this, Cailech,' Celimus said, leaning back in his chair.

'Quite simply, I wish us to stop being enemies. I see no reason for it other than our own stubbornness and I am offering you the hand of friendship and alliance from hereon if you wish to take it. My people will respect your boundaries utterly. There will be no further threat of raids, no incursion into your lands without your permission.'

Celimus nodded. 'And what will your people gain from that?'

'Freedom of movement without harassment or threat

of injury. We wish to have permission to trade freely with the people of Morgravia and Briavel. I would also suggest you sanction a delegation of your people to visit the Razor Kingdom to gain a greater understanding of our people, our culture and our living standards. Perhaps you will allow a similar delegation from the Razors into Morgravia? I firmly believe that the more we can appreciate each other's culture, the more peace will be achievable.'

'Interesting. I am not averse to anything you have suggested, Cailech. There would have to be a governing body made up of delegates from both realms to supervise the . . .' Celimus searched for the right word '. . . the melding of our Kingdoms.'

'Of course. My thoughts entirely. But I don't believe we could ever live as one, King Celimus,' Cailech cautioned, addressing his counterpart with highest courtesy now. 'Our ways are too different to yours. By the same breath, there are many areas in which we are similar. I want the same things for my people as you want for yours. I want our young to be educated and literate; I want free trade so marketing and commerce can flourish between our realms; I want my people to eat and sleep well, secure in the knowledge that their own are safe no matter which borders they are moving across.'

Aremys could have applauded Cailech for building his case eloquently. He doubted whether Celimus could find anything at fault in what Cailech was presenting and it seemed the Morgravian King was paying attention rather than just paying him lip service. He listened as Cailech continued.

'Nevertheless, my people do not want to be Morgravian and I know you have no intention of taking your people into the Razors. Let us agree that we are different but we will tolerate each other's differences. We will learn to admire those differences which make us the people of the Razors and your people the sophisticated Morgravians.'

'Bravo,' Jessom whispered to Aremys under the guise of softly clearing his throat.

Before Celimus could respond there was a knock at the door. The King looked towards his Chancellor, irritated. 'See to it, Jessom,' he said unnecessarily, for Jessom was already making for the door.

The other three remained silent as the Chancellor listened to the hurriedly spoken message. He turned. 'My King, apologies for the interruption. There is an urgent missive from Queen Valentyna. Apparently you have insisted that anything from Briavel is to be delivered to you immediately.'

Celimus nodded. 'Forgive me,' he said to Cailech.

'Never keep a woman waiting, Celimus – least of all a bride and a Queen at that,' Cailech responded with mischief.

Celimus laughed. 'Bring the messenger in,' he ordered.

The man was permitted to enter. He bowed and then moved towards Celimus. 'Your highness, this was sent in haste.'

Celimus waved his hand at him, saying nothing, having already broken the wax seal. He scanned the letter. Jessom shooed the messenger out of the door. It seemed he, along with everyone else in the room, was holding his breath. Aremys had not realised how much tension had been created through Cailech's proposition; it was only now he saw that he had been hanging on Cailech's every word, waiting for Celimus to agree once and for all to a formal union. This messenger could not have come at a worse time.

'Nothing wrong?' Cailech queried, his voice casual, although he glanced towards Aremys for guidance. Aremys shook his head, glad that no one noticed the exchange.

'Farrow,' Celimus said, taking Aremys by such surprise he almost jumped.

'Yes, sire?'

'The delivery of Ylena Thirsk . . .'

Suddenly the King's tone sounded cunning and his body language was sly. Aremys heard alarm bells ringing somewhere in his head.

'Yes?'

'It is in hand, as agreed?'

Aremys hoped he was not reddening. His collar certainly felt a tad tight and he forced himself not to visibly swallow. 'It is, sire.'

'Interesting,' Celimus said, standing. 'Listen to this,' and he read Valentyna's letter aloud.

When it ended, Aremys was convinced he could hear his own heart pounding, the silence in the room was so profound. He made himself look directly at the King and from somewhere – he would never know where – he found his best lie ever and delivered it with such aplomb he too almost believed it to be truth. 'That's right, sire,' he confirmed. 'I sent a message to the Queen to release Ylena.'

Celimus frowned. '*You* did!'

Aremys nodded, determined not to look at Cailech whom he felt sure would be grinning, slyly enjoying his friend's discomfort, although this was no laughing matter.

Cailech could never know what a fine line Aremys was walking right now with the most dangerous of men.

'You know Queen Valentyna personally?'

'Not personally, sire.'

'Well, how exactly do you know her then?'

'I'm sorry, sire, I can't divulge my sources. You understand that, I'm sure.'

Jessom could see that his King's ire was stoking frighteningly fast but there could be no scene right now with Cailech so intrigued and quietly watching this new event unfold. Jessom felt abashed that he too had been caught out by this missive. He had presumed Ylena had been brought to Tenterdyn via whatever means the mercenary had at his disposal. The fact that Queen Valentyna had become involved was something of a shock.

'Your majesty,' Jessom interrupted as gently as he could, 'Ylena Thirsk is already here.'

'Here?' Celimus repeated, a storm gathering in the olive eyes. Jessom knew the signs all too well.

'Yes, your majesty, she arrived just minutes before your guests. Circumstances prevented me from bringing her before you.'

The King gave his Chancellor such a murderous look that even Aremys, who could not care less about the conniving servant, felt his blood run cold on his behalf. But Aremys also realised the King had been diverted: his wrath was directed at Jessom now, rather than himself, and he pressed that advantage.

'As we know, sire, Ylena went to Briavel. I have contacts there and, before I was attacked in Timpkenny, I sent word to follow her and keep her under observation.'

'Why, by the hairs of Shar's arse, would you do that,

Farrow, when I wanted her in Morgravia! Why not have her captured, man?'

Cailech laughed openly at the curse. 'I shall have to remember that one, Celimus.'

The King of Morgravia caught his famous temper, the laughter reminding him that he was being watched carefully by another sovereign.

Aremys, wearing the most innocent expression he could muster, began to embellish the lie, his mind already racing towards how he might get to Wyl before anyone else to ensure their stories coincided. If Wyl told a different tale, they were both as good as dead. 'I figured that the noblewoman would be dangerous wherever I held her in Morgravia, your highness. And as I didn't have her in my own hands, I thought it best just to have her watched. I knew I could get to her whenever I needed to so long as I knew where she was based. I also felt she was a captive of her own fears, sire. If she felt safe in Briavel, she would not leave the realm and I would not have to give further chase.'

'But when did you plan to carry out your mission for me?' Celimus asked, following the Grenadyne's line of thought.

Good question, Aremys acknowledged silently. He was making this up as he went along and again Wyl's warning about Celimus's sharp mind nudged him. 'Immediately, sire. I was in the north, and Ylena Thirsk was presumably well south by then, which meant I didn't have to hurry and run unnecessary risks of being discovered. I knew my people would pick up her trail and keep watch until I was ready to make my move. I didn't expect to be carried into the Razors, sire. That was a surprise.' He glanced at Cailech whose mouth was, as he had expected, twisted into a wry grin. 'And a good thing too that I had people on task in Briavel.'

'So then what?' Celimus persisted, as if determined to prolong Aremys's agony. The mercenary began to wonder if this was just public humiliation before the death squad came to fetch him.

'My people are tactically placed, sire. It was simply a matter of getting word to them from the Razors.'

Celimus switched his attention to his royal guest. 'You were aware of this word being sent, presumably, Cailech? If Aremys is your prisoner, as he tells me, surely you didn't give him such freedom as to pass messages out of your realm to enemy states?' It was phrased as a question but no one could miss the challenge in the Morgravian's words.

To his credit Cailech did not so much as hesitate. Aremys had told him about his plan to use Ylena Thirsk as bait; he would have to trust his new friend for he had little idea of what game was now being put into play. 'I permitted him a message, yes. It was to Briavel, to a dignitary in the Queen's court. You must remember, Celimus, that you and I were enemies until just moments ago. I would have done anything to undermine you. Allowing this man to send a message into Briavel did not disturb me. Had I known, at the time, he was working on your behalf, however, I might not have been so generous.'

Satisfied, Celimus returned a steely gaze to Aremys who felt like kissing the Mountain King. Perhaps he still would, he thought, relief coursing through his body.

'Anyway, Celimus, has this not achieved the outcome you wished for?' Cailech's question surprised everyone.

'Pardon me?' was all the King of Morgravia managed.

The Mountain King waved a hand in mock disgust. 'It's just that we seem to be wasting time over petty details. You wanted this woman, you have her. Aremys has delivered as he said he would. Why is there a case to argue?'

Cailech was right. Jessom communicated as much in the gaze with which he impaled his King. Why was Celimus so intent on making this conversation public? He was the one making a fool of himself. Unless Jessom was very wrong, Farrow seemed to be telling the truth.

There was no accounting for the moods of Celimus or the shifts in his thinking. His whole body seemed to relax after Cailech had posed his question, and Aremys could not help but compare the two kings for their capriciousness. They made a good match.

'Why indeed, my friend?' Celimus echoed. 'You are right,' he added, nodding slightly at his guest and then returning his attention to the mercenary. 'Thank you, Aremys, for delivering Ylena into my hands. To be honest, I hadn't thought you would trust me sufficiently to hand over the bait you dangled in front of my nose *before* you and your new employer left my realm for the safety of the Razors. After all, it was your insurance.' His last few words were not lost on anyone in the chamber.

Aremys took the moment to bow and cover his intense relief at Cailech's support. After straightening, and the chance to gather his thoughts, he said, 'Your majesty, as I have explained before, I am a mercenary and always for hire. You have shown me nothing but generosity and I would have been foolhardy not to trust such a powerful monarch.' He nodded at the King. 'I would like to be able to work for you often, sire. Ylena Thirsk is nothing to me. My communication to your Queen simply suggested that the person to whom she offered sanctuary was your open enemy, and that she would be wise not to risk her new King's wrath by sheltering her.'

'And it worked, by Shar!' Celimus said. 'You are a cunning man, Aremys Farrow.'

As are you, you snake, Aremys thought; instead he replied, 'I am simply a man for hire, my lord. I take opportunities where and when they present themselves. Do you still wish me to kill her, sire?'

'I think I can manage that myself if and when needed,' Celimus said, a cruel smile flitting over his mouth. Cailech frowned but held his tongue. 'So where is she?' the King continued, looking at Jessom.

'In one of the outhouses, sire. I said you would summon her at your pleasure.'

'And how is she?'

'Surprisingly feisty,' Jessom commented.

'The Thirsk girl has found some spine, has she? I shall enjoy seeing this. So will you, Cailech. Do you know of the Thirsks?'

'Only by reputation,' he said. 'This is the daughter of General Fergys Thirsk, I presume?'

'Mmm, yes, the sister of Wyl Thirsk – finally back in my care.' Celimus laughed. 'Have her presented to me during this afternoon's feasting, Jessom. I should like Cailech to see how we deal with treachery in Morgravia.'

Aremys felt as though the blood had stopped running through his veins. He needed to warn Wyl. The thought that his friend would probably die again in a few hours disturbed the Grenadyne so much that he could not breathe. He loosened his collar.

'May I see her?' he said, shocked that he had spoken without thinking it through.

'Why?' Celimus looked at him sideways.

Aremys thought quickly. 'She knew I was following her, sire. I just want to remind her that I always catch my prey.'

Celimus clapped. 'You have a nasty streak, Grenadyne. By all means. Jessom will go with you. Get her ready for us,' he said to his Chancellor.

He turned to Cailech. 'Let us get some air. How about a ride — just us? That horse of yours looks splendid. I should like to try him for myself.'

The Mountain King, smiled. 'Delighted. Am I to assume that we are done here? Formalities concluded?' He sensed a trap.

'Well, my friend,' Celimus replied, and Cailech noted this was the second time the southern King had addressed him this way, 'I am about to be married to the most beautiful woman of our age. Aremys here has just kept his word and delivered to me the last of the Thirsks whom I shall see die before my eyes shortly. I can't think of anything I feel less like right now than the threat of war between our realms — which is what I presume is the alternative to an alliance?'

Cailech watched his counterpart carefully as he spoke. He noticed also that Celimus was deliberately parading over him. This man had no intention of honouring a union. What he wanted was sovereignty over Briavel and the Razor Kingdom. The marriage achieved the first, and the pretence at friendship would achieve the second. The green gazes of two powerful men met and each understood the other very clearly.

'It would mean war, yes,' Cailech finally answered,

realising what a sham this whole event had been. His thought that he could charm this man or appeal to his good sense amused him suddenly. He had been carried away by the vision of the Grenadyne, but both of them had misunderstood the main point: Celimus did not want friendship or even harmony. All the King of Morgravia wanted was absolute authority over his neighbours. He would rule the whole continent – that was his dream. Neither Cailech nor Aremys had factored in the southerner's avarice or his self-delusion of might. They had gone into this like excited boys, stupidly believing that Celimus would also be seeking peace, trade, community. How innocent and how ignorant he had been. And now he was trapped. Would Celimus allow them to leave here alive? Perhaps he cared not for the lives of those held ransom, and although Aremys had bargained for safety using Ylena Thirsk as bait, it seemed Aremys had delivered early. Why? What had he to gain from that? Why had he trusted the madman who ruled Morgravia?

'That must be avoided then,' Celimus commented. Cailech had to remember what he was referring to. *Ah yes, war.* It was time to unleash his final trick then, all that stood between him and certain death at the end of this man's sword – or more likely, that of one of the King's henchmen. It was unlikely Celimus would dirty his hands with Mountain blood.

'King Celimus,' Cailech said, standing now to look at his enemy eye to eye. 'My emissary here, Aremys, may be far too trusting, but I am not. Until now I could not be sure that you would see things in a similar way to me. I had to take the precaution that your desires might differ from mine.'

Aremys felt as though the temperature in the hall had dropped to freezing point. The gently crackling fires at either end of the room had no effect on the cold which had descended. He had to admire Celimus when the southern King barely twitched at the couched threat that now lay between the two monarchs. What had Cailech kept up his sleeve?

Celimus asked the question which burned at the silent lips of Aremys and Jessom. 'Ah, further insurance I gather. Tell me, King Cailech, so that I understand clearly, why is it that, although you don't trust me you also don't fear me, even though you are on my land, in my house, under my guards' watchful eyes?'

'Please don't take it personally, Celimus, it's just the simple caution of a King who knows how easy it is to give trust too quickly.'

Celimus nodded indulgently as if to say he truly understood.

'There are two thousand Razor warriors currently gathered in the foothills,' Cailech said.

'Two thousand!' The number clearly took the Morgravian's breath away.

Cailech grinned good-naturedly. 'And another two thousand camped a little bit higher.'

Aremys closed his eyes. He had definitely underestimated Cailech – as had Celimus.

'And what are their instructions?'

'To hit Tenterdyn with full might if my second, Myrt, does not give the all clear by nightfall.'

'Nightfall? You hadn't factored in much time for the feast, my friend.'

'I wasn't sure I'd make it to dinnertime.'

'Bravo, Cailech. You are a man after my own heart. You will make your rendezvous with your men.'

'Alive?'

'Alive,' and Celimus laughed, genuinely now.

Aremys felt as though a fist which had been gripping his insides had suddenly relaxed.

'I hope you and Farrow will at least agree to dine with me,' the King went on.

Cailech nodded, green eyes ablaze with triumph. 'And our union?'

'Begins today,' Celimus lied. 'My men will be instructed that people of the Razors are no longer targets. I will put together a delegation, to be led by Jessom here, and I suggest you do the same. They can nut out how we shall run this union. Let us clasp hands, before our two witnesses, to signify the formal alliance of our two realms.'

The King of Morgravia held out his hand and King Cailech of the Razors gripped it firmly. 'To peace,' he said, no longer believing it could happen as long as this King sat upon the southern throne.

'To peace,' Celimus echoed, privately laughing.

CHAPTER 19

Wyl heard the approaching footsteps but had anticipated soldiers arriving, not the two men who entered the hut.

'Look, Ylena,' Jessom said, a note of triumph in his voice, 'I've brought you a visitor.'

Aremys spoke before Wyl could answer; it was his only chance for a warning. 'I thought it would be polite of me to introduce myself, Lady Ylena, as I was the one pursuing you on behalf of King Celimus. It was I who encouraged your protector to hand you back to Morgravia.'

He watched the surprise leave Ylena's face and felt safe in the knowledge that Jessom would not interpret the truth. There was a momentary hesitation before she replied, but so slight he was sure he alone was sensitive to it.

'Congratulations, sir,' Wyl said. 'Do come closer and allow me to spit on you and the trade you ply.'

Bravo, Wyl, Aremys thought, *thank you for saving my life. Now how am I going to save yours?*

'You high and mighty Legion wives and daughters are all the same – don't think your men are any different. I've heard what happened at Rittylworth—'

Aremys was interrupted by the arrival of a Legionnaire at the doorway.

'Chancellor Jessom, the King wishes to speak to you before he leaves on his ride.'

'I'll be just a minute, Farrow,' Jessom said. 'Try not to make the wildcat too angry — her claws are sharp,' and he smiled thinly as he left the hut.

'What are you doing here?' Wyl whispered.

'Listen to me, Wyl!' Aremys urged in an equally terrified whisper. 'They are going to kill you.'

'And that's supposed to frighten me?'

The big man frowned. It had not occurred to him that this was not a catastrophe. 'I . . . I suppose not.'

'That's why I'm here — I *want* him to kill me.'

Aremys shook his head. 'This is all too much for me,' he groaned. He stole a look over his shoulder to the court-yard where Jessom was conversing with his sovereign. 'Look, I used you as bargaining power. I told Celimus I could deliver you to him — it was my insurance to get Cailech and myself out of here alive.'

'I gathered as much,' Wyl said, just a touch of sarcasm in his tone.

'I had no idea you would deliver yourself. It was just a ruse — to buy us time.'

'Well, I'm here now. What intrigues me is how you and Cailech come to be here together.'

'It was the Thicket. It separated us.'

Understanding dawned on Ylena's face. 'I thought as much. Any plan in mind?'

'None,' Aremys said and looked at Ylena's lovely face with despair.

'I'll think of something. When do you leave?'

'Tonight,' Aremys replied, then heard Jessom's footsteps approaching. He gestured to Wyl, who quickly switched Ylena's expression to one of rage.

'Get out!' he screamed.

Jessom entered to hear her shriek. 'Oh dear, I did warn you, Farrow.'

'Don't worry, I'm going. What are you going to do to her?'

The Chancellor looked thoughtful for a moment. 'Well, the King wants her dead, as you know.' It was a callous comment designed to frighten Ylena.

'Good, I can't wait,' Wyl said.

Jessom was unable to hide his astonishment at Ylena's fearlessness. 'I was going to say that I was hoping to persuade him otherwise, but the young lady seems determined to die.' Jessom shook his head in wonder. 'I imagine King Celimus will make an example of her.'

'That's risky, isn't it?' Aremys queried.

The Chancellor sighed. 'He will want to impress his regal companion.'

'He won't – not in this manner,' Aremys said, desperate to prevent Wyl's death, no matter how much his friend wanted it.

'We shall see. Come, Farrow, I trust you have gloated sufficiently. Farewell, Ylena. Prepare yourself to meet your King.'

'He is no King of mine, Jessom!' Wyl called out after the two men. A memory of kneeling before King Magnus filled his mind, and he recalled how he had pledged his life for Celimus. 'And gladly will I give it,' he muttered now. He hoped Shar would hear and let Magnus know.

*   *   *

Cailech allowed Celimus to ride the exquisite white stallion which had been bred in the Razors. The Morgravian King's silence as they guided their horses towards the back of Tenterdyn where the lush plains stretched towards the mountains attested to his enjoyment of the beautiful beast.

'He is extraordinary,' Celimus finally said, when they halted beneath a small stand of trees.

'He is yours.'

'I could not—'

'No, really. Let me gift him to you to seal our historic union. It is appropriate. I reared this horse from a newborn colt. He has a twin brother, identical. His mother is one of my most treasured brood mares and his sire is a tough old rogue with perfect bloodlines. He suits you as much as he does me. Now we shall both have white stallions of the same family. Fitting, don't you think?'

Celimus gave Cailech one of his dazzling smiles. This gift pleased him more than anything the Mountain King had brought with him; it meant more than the alliance itself. 'Thank you. I will think of you whenever I ride him.'

'His name is Wildfire, like the falling star trails we see on a clear night in the Razors.'

'And what can I give you in return?'

Cailech shrugged. 'Oh, I'll think of something,' he said, and both men laughed.

'Whatever you want, it is yours.'

'Be careful. That promise sounds wide-reaching. I might choose your bride-to-be.'

Celimus gave a wolfish grin. 'Whatever you want that is here in Felrawthy, then.'

'Our fathers would be proud of this alliance, Celimus,' Cailech said, his voice suddenly wistful.

'Not mine. I never made him proud.'

'What you have done today, and what you have achieved between Morgravia and Briavel, should make him sit up in his tomb and applaud.'

Celimus liked the notion. He laughed, enjoying his companion despite not wanting to, despite deliberately planning to betray him. He liked Cailech. They were similar. Not in looks of course but in . . . what was it? He reached for that intangible something that he had recognised in Cailech. Texture; that was it. They had a similar texture. Both kings, both ambitious. Celimus believed the Mountain King was as ruthless as he himself was. The likeness pleased him; made him feel confident in a deeper sense, rather than relying entirely on ego. Cailech's personality, though less flamboyant, was just as large and domineering as Celimus's own. His father had seen these facets of his son as flaws, and yet here they were reflected in another man whom his father had considered powerful, talented, intrepid. Celimus shook his head.

'My father hated me, Cailech. We hated each other, in truth. He killed my mother – I'm sure of it – and if he could have been granted a single wish, no doubt he would have seen me dead too.'

Cailech wanted to suggest that this was a paranoid perspective, but wisely reconsidered. The youngster was opening up; it would be imprudent to antagonise him now. Surely this was not part of the planned script for the meeting?

'You will carve your own way for your own realm, my

friend. Forget him. He is dust. Not forgotten, I grant you – you will always feel his shadow falling over you – but remember, that is all it is. A shade, no substance. He cannot hurt you now or command you. You rule Morgravia and you have vision. Your people are fortunate.'

Celimus's chest swelled with pride to hear his fellow sovereign speak of him with such respect, but it deflated as he pondered the last few words. 'No, they don't see it that way. They fear me.'

Cailech reached down to stroke the mane of the borrowed horse he was riding. 'Is that such a bad thing?'

'Your people are in awe of you. My people are just frightened of me.'

'You have the power to change that, Celimus. And within weeks, not just your people, but the citizens of Briavel and even my people, will see what you have achieved: peace throughout the whole region. What an extraordinary time this is and you are the one who has brought it about. I am proud to be a part of it.'

Celimus searched the Mountain King's face for guile, suspecting this man was simply oiling him up, but he saw nothing but the hard green gaze of a man determined to forge peace. He saw the truth in his neighbour's eyes and in that moment he made a decision which went against everything that made Celimus who he was. He dared himself to take the challenge. Charged by this man's encouragement and pride he decided to maintain the alliance. He would not betray Cailech as planned; he would keep his promise and spare lives. He would ensure that the union worked, even though it meant compromising his grand plans of imperialism. In one of the rarest moments of his life, Celimus smiled and meant it. 'Let it be so then,' he said, his voice almost catching with the emotion he felt.

Cailech saw it and realised that he had just saved hundreds of lives and ensured a new peace for his kingdom. He felt invigorated by what had been achieved by a simple conversation on horseback. 'Remind me to gift you a horse more often,' he said, his eyebrow arching.

Celimus threw back his head and laughed boyishly. 'I'll race you across the fields and show you how fine this beautiful stallion really is.'

Wildfire sprang forward and Cailech followed. But inside he felt a twinge of regret, for the Morgravian's words had reminded him of Galapek and his growing sorrow at what had been worked upon the poor beast.

Gueryn was permitted to walk without being shackled this time. Even his hands were free to swing at his side as he luxuriated in the warmth on his back from another beautiful morning.

'How are you today, Jos?'

'Just fine,' came the mangled reply but Gueryn understood.

'Only one of you today?'

The big man nodded. 'We trust you,' he said and gave his crooked grin.

'I won't run away if you have more important duties to attend to,' Gueryn assured.

The response was garbled but he worked out that Gueryn was Jos's most important duty. 'I can't let the King down by losing you.'

'All right, I do understand. But you have my word,' Gueryn offered. His intent with this conversation was to build a friendship and some trust. He had no idea whether he would ever get an opportunity at escape but his chances were increased if he could lull his captors into believing he would never make such an attempt. Descending the Razors was no easy prospect, and vivid memories of an arrow thumping into his body served only to discourage him more, but it was spring and there would never be an easier time with the King and Myrt away.

'Morning,' Maegryn called, stepping back from a horse whose hooves he was inspecting.

'And what a fine one it is,' Gueryn replied.

'Did you ache from your work?'

'Yes, but it felt good.'

'A treat for you. A ride, with Jos here and another guard.'

'Oh? How come?'

'Three of our stallions need a proper exercise.'

Gueryn could see his own pleasure reflected in the grin from the stablemaster. 'A ride.' He said it as though the words were brand new on his tongue.

'I'd come myself but one of the King's brood mares is in labour and I have to be around for the delivery. She's struggling a bit so I can't risk not being close.'

'Can we help?' Gueryn asked reflexively. He had been around horses since he was a child and had been involved in enough births to be useful.

'I appreciate it but I'm hoping the little one will be born before you lot return. And the mother's best with fewer fussing around her.' Gueryn showed his understanding with a slight nod. 'Jos, you'll be on Charger — he's out sunning himself over there in the paddock. He's a fiery character but let him loose. He needs a good run.

Rollo will be accompanying you. He's on Dray, the older stallion.'

'And me, Maegryn?' Gueryn asked.

'Well now, Morgravian, I thought I'd allow you to ride something very special. You might have to prove your worth as a horseman today because you'll be calling on all your skills.'

Gueryn grinned. 'Do your worst, Maegryn. I'd ride a donkey right now just for the chance to be back in a saddle again.'

'This is no donkey, le Gant. This is the King's most prized horse and he's a flighty one. That's him you hear right now making all that noise.'

Gueryn frowned. 'He does sound agitated. What do you call him?'

'Galapek.'

The joy of learning he would soon be on horseback, however briefly, had temporarily sapped Gueryn of his wits. It had not occurred to him that one of the mounts could be the very horse he was trying to track down.

'Galapek,' he repeated, taking a moment to gather himself and ensure no recognition showed in his expression. 'That's a sorrowful name indeed for a fine stallion.'

'Oh? I've been told it's from the old language. How could you know old Northernish?' Maegryn asked, intrigued.

'My ancestors on my maternal side were from a place even more north than here. The old language stayed alive in our family. I learned some of it as a child.'

'So what does it mean? We've all been dying to know,' Jos chimed in, his excitement torturing the sounds of the words.

Gueryn looked towards Maegryn, baffled. He had missed what Jos was trying to say.

'I think he said that none of us know what Galapek means.'

'It means traitor,' Gueryn answered, surprised. So none of these men had an inkling about the stallion, not even the irony of the King's choice of name.

'Traitor?' Maegryn repeated. 'What sort of a name is that for a horse?'

Gueryn shrugged. 'Perhaps your King has a sense of humour.'

'Stupid name, if you ask me. This is an extraordinary beast, le Gant. You Morgravians would never have clapped eyes on anything as remarkable. He's the most beautiful stallion I've ever seen.'

'Grenadyne?'

Maegryn's eyes seemed to sink into his skull even further, if that was possible. 'He was a present. I have no idea who sired him.'

Gueryn sensed the withdrawal. He had worked too hard to lose this precious friendship, however fragile it was. 'Well, let's see this splendid beast. You've made me feel envious already.'

'Here he comes now,' Maegryn replied, forthcoming again. 'Admit it, le Gant. He's the finest horse you've ever seen.'

Gueryn felt his breath catch in his throat. The horse was massive through the chest. He came towards them, proud and majestic in gait. He shook his head and his long mane flicked in a shiny wave of fluid movement whilst his black coat all but sparkled in the bright morning. He was beautiful, there was no denying it, but

Gueryn saw the ugliness in the horse's eyes. They were wide, as if in permanent fear, and his flesh appeared to twitch incessantly.

'Ah, here's your other companion,' Maegryn said. 'Rollo is one of the King's most trusted men, le Gant. No tricks, eh? He's also one of our best archers and won't flinch to sink an arrow back into that shoulder of yours.'

Rollo did not smile. No jest was being made here.

Gueryn recalled with vivid intensity how the arrow had ripped through skin and nerves, muscle and bone. He was in no hurry to feel that sensation again, yet knew he would risk it if the opportunity for escape presented itself. 'Have no fear,' he assured, lying easily.

Maegryn gave some final instructions regarding the horses and Gueryn submitted to having his hands loosely strung together.

'You can still handle the horse with ease. Just a precaution, you understand?' Rollo said.

Gueryn pulled a face which suggested it was of no consequence to him and then made use of Maegryn's offered leg-up to hoist himself into the saddle. The other men followed suit and, after a nod from Rollo, the party eased itself away from the stable compound.

'Give them a slow drink at the lake,' Maegryn called after them. 'We haven't watered them since this morning.'

Gueryn smiled. He had been captive so long he had forgotten how much he loved life, wanted to cling to it, but right now life felt marvellous.

CHAPTER 20

They had travelled a short distance that night using magic. Knave had wanted to do a test, mainly to see how much pain it created for Fynch. The boy had performed the magical transportation and then slept restlessly, sometimes crying out, presumably in pain. Now awake, he squatted pale and quiet, chewing sharvan leaves.

Knave wanted to ask Fynch what he had meant the previous day when he answered the kestrel's question so audaciously, but he did not dare. When Fynch had finally roused from the curious stupor he had fallen into after the bird's departure, he had been withdrawn and Knave had sensed it was no time for talk. Movement was best and so he had suggested they walk for a time and then sleep until the early hours, which they had done. When the time came, Knave had marvelled at the speed with which Fynch had conjured the spell to create what could only be described as a bridge to the Thicket. When the Thicket responded, Knave felt a pulse like a thick plume of air punched into his side. The next moment he landed, breathless, alongside Fynch on a safe ledge deeper into the Razors and closer to their prey.

'All right, Knave?' Fynch had whispered.

Yes, he had replied and that was the end of the conversation. Fynch had settled immediately and slept. Once again, the dog had lain down beside his companion and kept the youngster's body warm with his own.

Now it was time to move again. *Are we waiting for something?* Knave risked.

'For Kestrel. I feel him.'

How is the pain?

'Not unbearable,' Fynch answered. 'Thank you,' he added and Knave knew he meant it. Then: 'Kestrel speaks,' and Fynch opened his mind to share the communication with Knave. *Where are you?* he asked the bird across the leagues that divided them.

Just outside Sharptyn. I have found her.

Good, he replied calmly, as though talking with a bird was something he did most days. *What can you see?*

She seems to be a prisoner — she walks with shackled hands and feet. There are others, all women. Men guard them. And there's a child — a small girl belonging to one of the men, I think. The girl talks to your friend.

Is Elspyth injured?

Pretty name. There was a pause. *Not injured but she looks frightened.*

What are they doing now? Fynch pressed his temples and Knave knew the pain was back.

I can't really tell. I would guess that they are stretching their limbs because they came out of a shed a short while ago.

Fynch. You must stop, Knave urged.

Fynch nodded. *Kestrel, I am so grateful to you. Can I trouble you to remain there a while longer?*

No trouble.

Thank you. I'll talk again shortly. Fynch closed the link.

You cannot keep doing this, the dog cautioned.

'We must save her.' Fynch's tone was stubborn.

How?

'You must go to Valentyna and get her help.' The dog chose silence to show his exasperation. 'Please, Knave.'

We have a task to complete.

'And I will finish it as promised. But I also promised that I would help Wyl's cause. I will not forgive myself if Elspyth perishes.'

We are helpless.

'Not helpless. Just distant. I can fix that.'

No, Fynch.

'Yes. If you won't go, I will.'

A difficult silence lengthened between them as the huge dog regarded the trembling yet implacable boy. Knave knew the suffocating pain Elysius had suffered, even though the sorcerer had used his magic infrequently and with utmost care. Knave could not imagine the burden Fynch was bearing right now.

You'll send me?

'And bring you back when you've delivered her a note.'

That will still take days.

'Not if I send you the entire distance.'

Fynch! It will kill you.

'Trust me. I am stronger than you think.'

The dog felt helpless. He had no doubt his companion would send himself back to Werryl if Knave did not comply. *And you will promise to continue on alone?* he asked.

Fynch covered his face, pushing his fingers against his eyes. His answer was mumbled and weak. 'Yes, of course.'

Rashlyn will sense the magic, Knave warned.

'I don't care. Elspyth could die.'

So could you.

'I am already sacrificed.'

Oh, Fynch.

'I'm sorry. I don't mean to sound cruel but you must do this for me. I will prepare a note. Valentyna can send help.'

Can you write? the dog asked, grasping at any excuse which might prevent this madness.

'I know some letters . . . enough to convey the urgency.'

Knave looked at him gravely. *There is a cave over there. You must rest a while before you travel on.*

'I think you're right,' Fynch admitted. He dug into his sack for a scrap of parchment he had had the foresight to throw in, but although he had brought a quill he had forgotten ink in his rush. 'I'll use blood,' he said matter of factly and, without hesitating, dragged a small knife across his palm.

He scrawled five words only, spelt incorrectly but clear enough he was sure: Elspyth, Sharptyn south, huts, danger. He had to dip the quill frequently into the pool of blood in his palm. Knave could not watch, disgusted with this turn of events but also feeling helpless.

'For Valentyna only, you understand?'

I understand. Knave allowed Fynch to tie the parchment around his neck with some trailing grass vines. It was fragile but would make the journey.

'Ready?'

Do it! the dog instructed, unable to conceal his disdain any longer.

'I'll wait to hear,' Fynch said, hugging the dog briefly.

Without wasting another word he sent Knave tumbling through a magical tunnel arcing from the Razors to Werryl.

Used to this mode of transport by now, Knave landed softly on all fours, checked that the parchment was still in place and then took his bearings. He was in the woodlands just beyond Werryl city, where the Queen liked to ride. Sighing to himself, he set off at a lope towards the palace and, no doubt, a stunned Valentyna.

Back in the Razors, Fynch retched pitifully with the pain, but there was nothing to be expelled. He curled up, exhausted, in the cold but dry cave and, chewing on his decreasing supply of sharvan leaves, drifted towards sleep – the only place where respite from his aching head was to be found.

It was late afternoon of Elspyth's second day as a prisoner. The first day had passed in a blur, caused by the drug and the shock of her situation. Elspyth was still too stunned to take in all that had happened to her, but it had sunk in by now that she was amongst women only; there were no male prisoners. The men were their captors. Released from the huts, she found the courage to speak to one of her fellow prisoners.

'What are we doing here?'

'Finally found your voice then. Don't worry, we're all the same when we first arrive.'

'What is this place?'

'We're prisoners. They trick us, trap us and keep us here.'

'What for?'

'Who are you? You're not Briavellian, are you?'

'My name is Elspyth. I'm from Yentro, northern Morgravia.'

The woman raised her eyebrows. 'You're a long way from home, Elspyth, and you'll certainly wish you'd never been duped by Ericson. I'm Alda, from south-eastern Briavel.'

'He's trapped us, you say?'

Alda nodded. 'For his sport.'

Elspyth gaped at her companion, unable to decipher what in Shar's name she could mean by that comment. 'Sport?' she repeated.

'Well, it's for all of them really. He just gets paid a lot for finding us.'

'Alda,' Elspyth said, her voice shaking now. 'You'll have to explain because I don't understand any of this.'

A bird screeched in the tall trees. Both women glanced up but neither could see the kestrel perched there.

'We fight and they bet on us. After three wins, we're sold on apparently. I've got one more win to go to get out of here.'

Elspyth had not thought life could get more complicated, but it just had. 'Sold?'

'There's a good slave trade out of Morgravia's south. Didn't you know?' the woman asked, clearly surprised.

'I had no idea.'

'Oh, yes. A very good trade. Ships from the Exotic Isles slip into and out of a tiny bay called Cheem, east of Ramon, west of Argorn. They pick up slaves regularly.' She shrugged at the disbelief on the newcomer's face. 'At least it's an escape from this – but you have to survive three bouts, of course.'

It was too much for Elspyth to take in. 'What sort of fighting is it? Bare hands?'

Now the woman laughed harshly and Elspyth heard a hint of despair. 'Blades, you fool. This is to the death. You will be fighting for your life tonight, my girl, and the right to be shipped off as a slave. Forget your former self – it doesn't exist any more.' Then she became wistful, the bravado shattering. 'Perhaps one day I'll see my family again, track down my son, but right now I have to make it through one more fight.'

Elspyth grabbed her companion's arm. 'Alda, I don't know how to fight.'

'None of us know, girl! It's pure animal instinct that has kept me alive. I suggest you find some or your blood will be splashed across the main hut's dust tonight.'

Elspyth could not help the tears. This was all too much of a shock.

Alda pushed Elspyth's hands from her sleeve. 'Expect nothing from me, or anyone else for that matter. No one has friends here. We don't know who we'll have to kill next to survive. Two days ago I killed someone I liked. I don't want to know you or feel sorry for you, because you might be the woman I have to kill tonight. They do it for entertainment – they bet on us and then they sell us on. Ericson dreamed it all up apparently. Did he use the young girl to lure you?'

Elspyth nodded blindly through her tears.

'No good blaming yourself. I fell the same way, accepting a seemingly kind offer of a lift, trying to get back from Werryl to my family more quickly than I could on foot. They're experts at picking the perfect mark.'

'What were you doing in Werryl?' Elspyth asked, desperate to prolong any conversation that might take her mind off what was hurtling towards her. She heard the shriek of the bird again but ignored it, finding herself on her knees in the dust, clinging to the skirts of this woman who had no intention of further confidences.

'It doesn't matter. I don't want to share anything more with you. Don't think we're friends: I can't help you — won't help you. You'd best prepare yourself. It's either kill or be killed. Get that straight now.'

Alda ripped herself away and hurried to the other side of the compound. No one saw the tears she shed there over her own cruelty. What sort of monster had these men turned her into?

Wyl too was preparing for death, except he wanted to embrace it. Dying again would be his salvation in this instance and he wondered who he would become. In truth he did not care; all he knew was that he could not bear to be Ylena for much longer. Instead he clung to Fynch's quiet belief that random acts could change the course of Myrren's gift. He desperately wanted to believe in anything that might spare him living as Celimus. As much as he loved the idea of marrying Valentyna, the notion of walking in the body of the present King of Morgravia was repulsive. Every time he saw the vision of Celimus's face before him he had to draw on all his strength to force it away.

In the end, to distract himself from his downward-spiralling thoughts, he washed Ylena's face and combed her hair. Wyl tied it back once again, not prepared to allow the soft waves of golden tresses to pool around her narrow shoulders. He also refused to change out of his riding trews. There would be no curtseying today. He did, however, dust his garments as best he could, having decided that Ylena should not die looking ragged and filthy. Wyl knew appearance and presentation were high on his sister's list of priorities and it was the least he could do for her considering that he was contriving to bring about her death – a second time.

He looked in the small tarnished mirror that Jessom had provided and acknowledged how the glass suited Ylena: both she and the mirror were damaged and no longer much good to anyone. Nevertheless, not even its rusted surface could hide the ethereal radiance that shone from Ylena's visage. She was gaunt now, but somehow that only added to her ghostly beauty; it reminded Wyl of their mother, when he had seen her laid out following her death.

The wasting fever had shrunk his mother's willowy figure to a skeletal state, and she died gasping for one more lungful of air, but in her death repose Helyna of Ramon remained breathtakingly lovely. Ylena would be the same, Wyl promised himself, as he stared out through eyes that looked even larger than usual because she was so thin and so full of sorrow.

Wyl threw the mirror down, shattering it across the flagstones, glad that it would never reflect that sad, haunting face again.

He turned at the sound of footsteps. It was Harken, together with the older officer from earlier in the day.

'I thought you had gone,' Wyl said, gathering his unravelling emotions.

'Our company was called back this afternoon to guard the arrival of the Mountain King.'

'You have been summoned,' the older soldier cut across them both. 'The lad here seemed determined to see you again.'

'And how kind of you to let him,' Wyl said, bitterness lacing his tone. 'It is a pity you don't feel the same loyalties to General Thirsk that I would expect from a soldier of the Legion.'

'He's dead, or hadn't you noticed?' the man answered with a cruel grin. 'Thirsk is no good to us now. We're stuck with the nasty royal brat and the only way any of us will survive is to follow his orders.'

Wyl mustered as much contempt as he could on Ylena's face. 'You snivelling coward! The Legion could overthrow him in a blink if it would only find its spine. What has happened to all of you?'

The man did not bother to reply, simply held out the manacles to be put around Ylena's wrists. Wyl obliged; there was no point in wasting energy on a man like this. He turned his attention to the dumbstruck Harken.

'I'm so sorry,' the young man finally stammered. 'I just had to see you again.'

'And I'm happy you did. There is nothing you can do for me, but I urge you to rally your men against the Crown.'

He expected the old soldier to strike him for saying something so treacherous, but the man simply laughed. 'Don't be daft, lad. These are the ravings of a condemned woman. Follow orders – that's the Legion's way, isn't it? And you have yours.'

'Harken, look at me!' Wyl commanded. 'Do this, if nothing else. Throw your support behind Celimus's bride. When he marries Valentyna of Briavel, she will be your Queen. Help her. Don't let him crush her as he has all of you. Make your men pledge their allegiance – she is your only hope against his brutality.'

Harken, stunned, could only nod. His companion gave Ylena a shove. 'Come on, lass. Let me follow my orders. I've got just another winter to get through and then I'll be out of the Legion and off mending fishing nets in the north-west. After that I don't care what the young bloods do. Right now we have instructions to bring you to his majesty and that's what we're going to do.'

Wyl rubbed at Ylena's burdened wrists. 'Let us go then,' he said.

Elspyth stood with about sixteen other women in what was akin to a cattle pen, which Ericson and his cohorts had built inside the main stone building. She had been forced to strip herself of clothes and given a grubby length of linen to cover whatever she could. One end of the cloth was stained with blood and, with her terror of dying and her crushing despair at failing Lothryn, it was all Elspyth could do not to scream at the testimony of another's injury, perhaps her death.

The men had been drinking for most of the afternoon. They were well and truly intoxicated now, eager for the naked women, for fighting, for killing. The volume of noise in the building rose noticeably as the audience became more excited, especially when the women were herded into their pen, clutching at the useless fabric which barely concealed their modesty.

The smell of liquor, combined with sweat, vomit and the unmistakable scent of congealed blood, made some of the jumpier women gag. Others began to wail. They knew what was coming and that, in the next hour or so, they could be taking their last breath. Elspyth could cope with the stench but her rising fear would surely undo her. She had learned that the men had not found 'fresh meat' for a week or more, and one kind soul had told her she would be a definite on tonight's menu. There were no more tears to cry and there was no one coming to save her. If she was to survive this, Shar help her, it would be because she managed to kill three of her fellow captives.

Elspyth looked around the pen and wondered who she might be partnered with tonight. She noticed all of the women were in relatively good health; no one older than around thirty-five summers or so it would seem. She smiled grimly to herself. Of course they wouldn't choose anyone much older – the naked bodies would not offer the same spectacle.

'I've heard they sometimes rape the winner,' a woman nearby murmured, no doubt awaiting her first bout, her eyes panic-stricken.

'They're not here just to look, you fool,' her neighbour warned.

Elspyth gritted her teeth and turned away, her glance catching that of Alda on the opposite side of the pen. The other woman looked calm yet menacing, as if violence lay just beneath that expressionless exterior. Madness and the threat of death whirled around them all, but Alda's attention was riveted on Elspyth alone. It was unnerving. When Elspyth saw torches being lit around the central area and a man approaching to get the first fight under way, her emotions frayed. She would not show her fear to the men, but inwardly she screamed her pain towards Lothryn, knowing he too was helpless but needing to say farewell.

She reached Fynch instead.

*   *   *

The boy woke, consumed by Elspyth's anguish. *Lothryn, I love you, I'm so sorry! Shar, help me!* Her scream came through a gossamer-thin link that threatened to tear away at any second. But this time Fynch was quick enough.

We're coming. You must hold on, and then the link was ripped away, her terrified voice a memory. But her fear was contagious and it remained like a bad smell, festering around him. Fynch shivered. The pain was back in his head; he was not sure it had ever left or whether he would ever be free of it again. He wanted to chew on more sharvan but resisted, knowing he was turning to the leaves too quickly. Knave had counselled him to fight the pain, not let it control him.

He focused on Knave now and sent his message. *Where are you?*

At the palace gates. I believe I've just enraged a number of Briavellians with some ferocious barking.

Fynch smiled despite himself. *Thank you for going, Knave.*

How are you?

I'm all right. I've just woken. Elspyth reached me again. She sounds in desperate trouble.

The note is intact. Here they come now. I hope they remember me.

No one could forget you.

We'll speak again soon. Chew some leaves — you'll need them after this.

Fynch did not reply. He broke the bond and cast a silent prayer to Shar to guide the message into Valentyna's hands. She alone had the power to act to save Elspyth.

*   *   *

Knave barked again, for good measure, as the guard limped towards the gate. 'Shar's mercy, look at the size of that thing,' he muttered to his younger companion. 'I'll send an arrow into its heart if it doesn't quieten down.'

'Wait! That's that black dog of the boy's, isn't it?'

'Which boy?'

'You know – that Fynch lad. One of the Queen's favourites.'

'Shar spare us, so it is. I must be going mad not to recognise it.' The older guard made a sound of disapproval, knowing he had been caught napping when he was supposed to be guarding the western gate.

'Do we let it in?'

'Search me. You take a message to the Captain.'

'Looks like it's got a note tied around its neck,' the young soldier said, nodding towards the dog as he left.

'You'd better hurry,' his companion called after him.

Several minutes passed, with Knave stalking the breadth of the gate impatiently and the older guard watching, a little mesmerised. Knave was convinced the man was still half asleep. He barked, just to make sure he had the fellow's attention, and the old boy nearly leapt out of his skin.

'Bastard animal,' he murmured, then turned to see his superior approaching. 'Captain Orlyd, sir,' he said, giving a stiff nod.

'Barnes,' the Captain acknowledged. 'Ah, the dog. Yes, I believe that's the same one. Commander Liryk says it's to be given entry.'

'Righto, sir. You're sure it's not dangerous?'

'It's a dog, Barnes. Haven't you seen it playing around these very grounds with the young lad, Fynch?'

'Er, once or twice, sir.'

'Then you'll know it's harmless. Move, man. Let's see what the note is about.'

When the gate was raised, Knave padded in and obediently sat in order that Fynch's note could be taken from his neck. Fynch had taken the precaution of scrawling a 'V' on the outside, as he had seen on some of Valentyna's personal items.

'This is for the Queen,' Orlyd said as he patted Knave's large head. 'Good fellow. You'd better come with me.' He shook his head as Knave stood to follow him. 'Smart too, eh?'

Man and dog took the quickest route towards the royal apartments, where the Captain knew Liryk had been having a meeting with the Queen and the duke from Morgravia. Several high-ranked servants queried the presence of a dog in this part of the palace but as soon as they realised it was Knave, Orlyd was permitted to pass.

He gave a message to a man acting as the Queen's secretary and wondered again at how sorely missed old Chancellor Krell was. If Krell had been at his desk, Orlyd would probably have been taken directly into the Queen's chamber. The former Chancellor had an uncanny knack of knowing when something was important enough to warrant such attention. Orlyd was sure this was one of those occasions.

Liryk emerged with a quizzical expression. 'I trust this is urgent, Captain?'

'I believe it is, sir.' He held out the note.

'Shar strike me. It's Knave,' Liryk said as he took the note. He bent to greet the dog and at that moment Valentyna appeared at the doorway, looking for one of her servants. She squealed with delight at seeing Fynch's dog and their reunion was filled with licks and joyful sounds.

'Is that a note?' the Queen asked, still grinning from Knave's particular form of salutation.

'It appears so, your highness,' Liryk replied, handing it to her.

'It will be from Fynch, of course. I've been dying to hear news of him. I presume he is nearby if Knave is with us,' she said, unravelling the parchment from its leafy twine. It took only seconds for her to read it. 'Shar save us!'

Liryk, who was in the process of dismissing his Captain, turned back in alarm. 'Your highness?'

'It's Elspyth. She's in trouble.'

'How does the boy know?'

'I have no idea. But I'm glad Crys was lingering over his farewells. He wouldn't have gone yet, would he?'

'At the stables still, I imagine. Captain Orlyd, please prevent the Duke of Felrawthy from leaving until the Queen has spoken with him.'

'Right, sir.'

'I'll be straight behind you,' Valentyna called after him. She looked towards Liryk. 'She's in Sharptyn. You know what this is, don't you?'

He nodded, his expression grim. 'It ties up with a few other disappearances we can't explain.'

'I'm sure of it,' she said, eyes blazing. 'And now we have the location of where these scoundrels are holding the women. Come, Liryk, Knave. We'll send the guard with Crys.'

The old man broke his usual sense of protocol by grabbing the Queen's arm. 'I trust the duke is not to be put in charge of my men, your highness? We have been chasing clues regarding these disappearances for many months now.'

Valentyna realised that in her excitement she had over-looked something important. She reminded herself to learn from it. Her impulsiveness could make her careless – her father had told her this many times, even though he was usually referring to her horse-riding. 'No, Liryk,' she said, covering his hand with her own. 'You are in charge.' Her voice was gentle. 'I will send Crys because Elspyth is his friend and she trusts him. It will give him a reason to leave us too, whereas I think he has been feeling obliged to leave because his presence might cause us trouble.' Liryk nodded. 'It also means I send one less man of our own.'

'Thank you, your highness.'

Valentyna had not moved yet. 'Commander Liryk, I cannot do all that is ahead without you. I hope you understand how much I rely on your counsel and support. I don't see myself as an island.'

It was an odd comment and yet a timely one for the old soldier, long in need of some assurance from his sovereign. He found a smile. It felt like his first in a long time.

'I am obliged, your highness,' he answered in a thick voice. 'I sometimes feel us old fellows are no longer much use to you.'

She frowned. 'You have been part of my growing up, which makes you all the more important to me now. I hope you understand I will never do anything which is not solely in the interest of Briavel.' Valentyna knew the statement referred to virtually everything that had happened since she had taken on the monarchy – from her relationship with Koreldy to trusting the Morgravians and dismissing Krell.

'I don't doubt you, your highness. But you are under more pressure than most royals would face in their first year of rule. Let us get this girl rescued before it's too late.'

'I know you don't like her, Liryk,' Valentyna added, determined – whilst they were talking so candidly – to take this opportunity to discuss Elspyth. It was time to exert her authority as the ultimate decision-maker for this realm. Until now it was as if she had been serving some sort of apprenticeship, with Krell and Liryk guiding her, smiling benignly at choices they considered wise or grimacing when she followed her instincts and went against what they thought was right. Elspyth came into the latter category.

'It's not personal, your majesty,' Liryk began. He searched her face, as if the words he looked for were written across her forehead. She stared back at him intently, giving nothing away. 'It's just that Chancellor Krell and I felt she was a dangerous influence here.'

'A dangerous influence on me, you mean?'

He sighed. 'We felt she was driving you to say and think things which might put the realm at risk.'

'Never, sir. Never!'

'I'm sorry, your majesty.'

'You're entitled to an opinion; indeed, I would be troubled if you didn't have one.' She raised an eyebrow. 'But I am also entitled to like whomever I choose without sanction from the people around me.' Valentyna saw her words bite; she had meant them to do just that, having long ago tired of Krell's and Liryk's exasperated glances between each other. 'Yes, we made our friendship quickly – women often can if they take to each other immediately – but Elspyth seems to know things we don't. This marriage with Celimus is not as cut and dried as you think. My instincts are screaming at me that it is wrong, that it is a bad decision for Briavel, and yet I can't convince anyone of it. The nobles want the marriage so much they can taste it! The rest of Briavel wants it so they can get on with their lives in peace. I seem to be the only one who doesn't want it and yet the Legion is breathing down our necks on the border, seemingly preparing to invade. I have no choice in this, Commander Liryk,' she said, deliberately lowering her voice to just above a hard whisper. 'I have to marry Celimus because there seems to be no other option, and yet people like Crys Donal, Elspyth and Ylena Thirsk – all Morgravians – truly believe it is the worst decision I could make.'

Liryk clearly felt it was his turn to be forthright. 'Your majesty, with all due respect, if you don't continue with your preparations for the wedding, we will go beyond the point where a marriage can save any of us. The King of Morgravia is threatening war. It is a war we cannot win, your highness, not even if we whipped up a frenzy of patriotism. The sheer weight of his army will crush us, your majesty, and I would have to lead our boys into that fray knowing we would all be slaughtered.' His voice wavered as emotion swelled through his words. 'This is not King Magnus, your majesty. This is not a man of compassion. Celimus will brutally slay every Briavellian man and his son, and his son's son, if necessary, if we choose to go to war against him. What we are seeing now is only the threat. He is making sure we understand that the only thing to prevent this war is you, your highness. You and the gift of marriage. If you love Briavel and you love its people—'

Valentyna stepped back, aghast that he could think otherwise. Liryk continued, ignoring her shock. 'If you love Briavel and its people,' he repeated, more gently this time, 'you will hurry up and marry the King of Morgravia.'

He bowed, not reacting to the telltale glisten in the Queen's eyes. 'I shall prepare to leave for Sharptyn, your highness, and I shall bring back the woman of Yentro for you. I give you my word that I will achieve this for you or die trying.'

Valentyna said nothing. She watched Liryk's broad back go down the corridor and she felt hollow.

CHAPTER 21

Elspyth watched through her tears as the body of the woman who had been wailing earlier gushed its lifeblood steadily into the sawdust. Her killer, an older woman, stood bowed above, no doubt in shock and bleeding from several wounds. The victor had struck a lucky blow at the top of the wailing woman's thigh which had hit a major artery in her groin. Death had followed not long afterwards. The men did not even give the woman the grace of a peaceful death; instead they cheered hysterically whilst the winners gleefully collected on their bets. The women in the pen watched in silent horror as another soul was collected by Shar's Gatherers. Most did not even know her name. As Alda had cautioned Elspyth, there was no point in getting to know each other because it made the killing harder. The corpse was dragged away by the hair and would be burned later with the rest of the dead, their bodies piled up from the evening's entertainment. The victor, still staring at nothing with glazed eyes, was led roughly out of the arena.

'It's her first kill,' a voice said close by.

Elspyth had no idea that Alda had sidled up beside her during the fight. 'And the dead woman?'

'She was on her third fight. If she'd won tonight, she'd be on her way to the boat. Stupid fool — she could have easily won too. Still, one less for me to kill.'

Elspyth looked up at the taller woman. She felt sorrow that a mother had become so hardened. And yet it was because of her child that this woman planned to win at all costs. It did not matter: Elspyth already hated Alda. 'Get away from me.'

The Briavellian made a sound of disgust. 'I hope you're next!' she said, nodding her head towards the man approaching. 'Time you found out what it's like out there.'

Elspyth ignored her, her gaze fixed on the obese fellow waddling towards them with his hated parchment of names. She had given a false one but it would not change anything.

'Next up, ladies, is Olivya,' he said in a jovial voice, but they were all too fearful to pay much attention to his manner. 'Where is Olivya?'

No one moved. Terrified gazes met more resolute ones — those succumbing to a sense of fate.

'Come on, now. Small, pretty, dark. Ah, there you are, my dear. Cast off that sheet now,' he said to Elspyth. 'It's your turn.'

Elspyth had forgotten she had called herself Olivya. Her legs felt too weak even to hold her body up, let alone carry her across the pen and into the arena. She began to weep. Elspyth did not want to have to kill someone, but that was her only choice if she was ever to escape and find Lothryn.

'Come on, lass. Haven't got all night,' the man urged, scowling now.

Alda pushed Elspyth forward viciously. 'Who's she fighting?'

'Ginny. Where are you, Ginny?'

'Let me fight her instead.'

'You're not down to fight tonight, Alda,' the fat man replied. 'We're going to make you lose some sleep over your third.' He smiled without kindness, sweat running down his oily face.

'I'll make it a real spectacle,' Alda said desperately.

Elspyth felt her breath had been trapped inside her. What was Alda thinking? She could see the blood lust in her face. She knew the Briavellian would enjoy killing her – perhaps because she was Morgravian, or perhaps because she was pretty and Alda was anything but. More likely, she reasoned through her terror, it was simply that Elspyth looked like she would be easy to beat. Perhaps Alda sensed a straightforward kill and a short cut to the boat and away from this place.

The notion of being considered a pushover dragged Elspyth from her stupor. She sucked in air with a huge angry gasp and suddenly the noise, the smell, the woman's blood still wet and gleaming on the floor, and now, the fat man and Alda bargaining over her death, galvanised her. Elspyth felt the fear leave her in a tingling, angry rush. It pushed upwards through her throat and exploded in a cry of fury, and something she had never felt before oozed from every fibre of her being. It was rage. It did not burn within like a fire. Instead it bubbled through her as a white-cold flame, torching her thoughts, sparking her emotions, scorching her with its devouring wrath. Fear, which had left a puddle of urine around her feet only minutes earlier when she had seen a woman die, fled.

Elspyth was consumed with hatred and a blood lust of her own. She stepped away from her own mess, cast aside the flimsy linen and addressed the fat man in a voice that was animalistic and predatory. 'Let me fight Alda!'

The fat man looked at her. This was new. Normally the women fought each other under protest, all but helping each other into the ring, apologising for having to hurt one another, then weeping over each death. But these two women were eager to kill one another; with those sort of emotions, the spectacle was sure to be especially entertaining for the men.

His thick tongue flicked out to wet his rubbery lips as he considered this option. 'My, my,' he said, unpleasant smells wafting towards Elspyth as he moved closer to her. 'You must be confident.'

'Just announce it,' she answered, eager to get the fight done. If she was going to die, she'd rather do so now than spend further hours agonising over others.

Alda clapped her hands with pleasure. The Morgravian had admitted she did not know how to fight. It was going to be easy.

'All right then,' the fat man replied. 'Don't say I never give you girls what you want,' he added with an obscene chuckle. 'Off with your linen then, Alda. Both of you oil up. I'll make the announcement.'

Wyl walked between the two men, his arms held in front and tied at the wrist. He did not feel scared. This was the death he wanted; he just wished he could somehow spare Ylena's body being mistreated in the process. He spent the time during the frigidly silent walk towards the main hall contemplating what would be the kindest death

for Ylena and decided a blade into her heart was preferable — just as Faryl had killed Koreldy. That way, when
her body was cleaned, covered and laid out in Argorn, as
he fully intended it to be, no one would see the ugly
wound that had felled her. She could remain beautiful for
eternity in their minds.

But it nagged at Wyl that Celimus was unlikely to have
in mind something so straightforward as a knife being
plunged into her body. He would draw this out as if it
were a game; in the same way that he had taunted Wyl —
forcing him to witness Alyd's death and Ylena's suffering
— he would now mock Wyl's sister in front of his honoured
guests. Except Ylena was not who he thought. This Ylena
walked to her death with a light heart.

'Are you all right, my lady?' Harken whispered.

'I am fine. Remember all I have told you. If you think
well of the Thirsk family, then be assured they would have
sworn their allegiance to Valentyna the moment she
became Queen of Morgravia as well as Briavel. Do the
same, for all of us.'

Wyl sensed Harken's fear but also his pride at being
singled out. 'I will do it for you, my lady.'

'Then I am glad to have met you.'

'Be quiet,' the older soldier warned. 'We're here now.'

Dusk had fallen so quietly Wyl had not noticed. The
north seemed to have an ability to drape itself with
evening's calm without the usual cacophony of noisy birds
telling the world around them it was time to roost. But
there was still sufficient light that he had no doubt of the
identity of the man waiting at the grand doorway of
Tenterdyn to welcome him towards death.

'Good evening, Ylena,' Jessom said, all politeness. Wyl

did not reply, simply stared at him. 'As you will,' the Chancellor replied, not at all offended.

'Thank you, gentlemen,' Wyl forced out of Ylena's lips. It was meant only for the young soldier and he qualified this with a brief glance towards him. He was careful not to name Harken. Jessom was far too sharp to let the soldier leave if he thought any sort of alliance – no matter how tenuous – had been formed.

'We'll take her from here,' Jessom said to Ylena's escort. Two burly guards stepped out from behind the Chancellor and took position either side of Ylena. 'Follow me.'

Wyl was led past familiar rooms towards a part of Tenterdyn he had not seen on his former visit. He heard the murmur of voices and small explosions of laughter, which got louder as they approached a wing which he remembered had been shut off by doors. They were wide open now, the corridor lit by torches and guarded by yet more soldiers. Two kings were present; it was little wonder that the level of security was so high.

'Wait here,' Jessom commanded, touching Ylena's arm. Wyl shook off his hand and the man's thin smile arrived. 'I must let the King know his lamb has arrived.'

There was no mistaking his meaning. If Ylena's mouth had not been so dry with tension, Wyl might have tried spitting again at the Chancellor, for the amusement of soiling his robes if nothing else.

Jessom disappeared around a corner. The sounds of men eating and entertaining themselves filled the frigid silence between Wyl and his guards. The aroma of food wafted towards them and one man's belly acknowledged it with a growl. Wyl turned towards the sound and met the culprit's grumpy expression.

'Do you know that I am brought here to be killed for sport in front of your King?'

The guard shrugged, although Wyl sensed there was embarrassment hidden behind it.

'We just follow orders, my lady.' It was the man on his other side who answered.

Wyl looked at him. 'And as a Legionnaire you are comfortable with the notion of slaughtering an innocent woman – a noble no less – from a fine family who has given its life to the Legion? You are old enough to have known my father.'

The man did not respond but his eyes betrayed him. There was pity in them.

Jessom rescued him. 'Come, Ylena Thirsk. Your King awaits you.'

'I'm sorry,' the guard whispered but Wyl ignored him, striding towards Jessom and determined that Ylena would be seen to die with courage by these men who claimed loyalty to her line yet who had betrayed her.

Elspyth stood at the fringe of the rough circle mapped out by string tied to small stakes in the earth. She was naked but no longer cared, ignoring the sounds of appreciation from men enjoying the sight of a lovely body. All that mattered right now was the person on the opposite side of the ring, also naked, also breathing hard, and no doubt hoping that her cold stare would be enough to intimidate her opponent into submission without a blow being struck.

Fat Man was stirring up the excited crowd but Elspyth ignored him too. She knew where Ericson was sitting and briefly entertained the idea of flinging her knife, Koreldystyle, at his bulk. She had a vision of him flailing in shock as the blade hit him squarely in the throat. But in her heart she knew she could never throw true. The blade would probably make it only half the distance and then clatter pathetically on the ground to wild applause, leaving her ready to be slaughtered by Alda. A bell sounded and dragged her back to the insanity before her. She knew her knuckles were white as she clutched the single small blade which stood between her and death.

She heard Fat Man remind her that this fight was to the death, then his explanation that Alda was fighting for her third win and her right to be given over to slavery. The men cheered, no doubt imagining profit from her sale as well as her win. Elspyth forced herself to withdraw completely into her mind. She recalled the long night journey to Deakyn with Wyl – he walked as Koreldy then – and how he had told her that a warrior preparing for battle must draw every ounce of his conscious self into a closed section of his mind that no one could penetrate. She had smiled a little indulgently at his description then; now she understood completely what he had meant by those words. She was not sure whether she was doing it properly but the fear, although still there, was no longer impacting on her. Fury had iced it over and a numbness had taken hold. She felt nothing but frozen wrath for the woman standing before her.

The bell sounded again and Alda began moving, circling. *This is it*, Elspyth thought. *Kill or be killed.*

'To you, Lothryn, my love,' she murmured, remembering how he had given his own life in order to save others. She suddenly felt sure that Lothryn's feelings at that moment of decision – the knowledge of certain death, the grief of losing his new son, and sorrow that their love had not been spoken between them — were identical to her own. It was a tearing free of all ties, a casting loose of all fears in the pursuit of one thing: kill or be killed.

Alda lunged and Elspyth's mind went blank.

Wyl stepped into a large chamber that was warmed by a fire at either end. A few men milled around with goblets in their hands. He recognised none of them, which meant there was no one who might object to a Thirsk being treated in this way. His boots crunched on the floor and he realised he was walking over the remains of Aleda's fine cranberry-coloured glassware. To him the broken glass represented the state of this once powerful and utterly loyal family of the north: shattered, forgotten.

And then he laid eyes on the man responsible for it all. Celimus, brimming with self-importance, sat at the head of Jeryb's oak table, goblet in hand, making some toast, his cheeks slightly flushed from the wine and the general joviality. Around him was the remnants of his feasting. To his right sat Cailech; the Mountain King looked less comfortable and there was less debris about him, as though he had been more cautious in his enjoyment of the repast. Wyl knew the man well enough to recognise that the smile fixed on his face was fake. Cailech raised his glass in answer to whatever Celimus had said but did not drink; meanwhile his penetrating gaze soaked up all around him as effectively as a sponge. He was bare-armed; the muscles sculpted and tensed, as if he was ready to leap to his feet and charge, like an animal disturbed. No, Cailech was not happy here but he was pretending well enough. Next to him sat Aremys, unsmiling and rigid, no sign of wine or even food about him.

Wyl saw how the three men showed different reactions to Ylena's arrival. Celimus looked savagely delighted, his eyes darkening with pleasure at what he knew was coming. Cailech, however, looked taken aback. His roving gaze settled intently on Ylena and the contrived smile faded. Her beauty had taken him by surprise, Wyl realised. Poor Aremys looked like a chained dog; one that knew it was about to take a hiding. He paled, his already unhappy expression settling into a blank mask, as if he were steeling himself. He could hardly make eye contact with Wyl, such was his despair.

The room quietened as people noticed their presence but Jessom allowed the hush to settle fully before he spoke. 'Gentlemen, may I present Lady Ylena Thirsk, daughter of the late General Fergys Thirsk and sister to General Wyl Thirsk, may Shar bless their souls.'

Some repeated the last few words and Wyl enjoyed seeing the Morgravian King's mouth tighten. The smile turned acid and Wyl knew he would pay for the loyalty to his family with blood.

'Ylena Thirsk, how enchanting to have you back amongst your fellow Morgravians,' Celimus said, flashing a bright smile towards his honoured guest. 'Come, Cailech, you must meet the woman who escaped my punishment through the aid of a mercenary by the name of Koreldy.'

Cailech turned a cold green gaze to his fellow King. 'Koreldy?'

'You know him?'

'I will flay the skin from his bones when I find him again.'

Celimus, fired by the excellent wine from Jeryb's cellars and feeling very pleased with himself at being about to do away with the final member of the hated Thirsk dynasty, which had so clouded his own existence, threw back his head and laughed with delight. 'Then I have done you a service, my friend. Koreldy is dead.'

The Mountain King's face was set in stone, his eyes unreadable.

'Well, actually,' Celimus continued, noticing the reaction and enjoying it, 'I think we have my bride-to-be to thank for his death.'

'How so?' Cailech asked, unable to say much more it seemed.

Celimus drained his goblet of wine and slammed it down. Droplets of red launched from his mouth like blood as he shook his head. It was fitting, Wyl thought, for blood would flow tonight. 'Koreldy fled to the safety of Briavel, pretending to be a champion to my Queen.' Celimus made a gesture of nonchalance. 'She was unaware of his identity, of course, until I revealed it to her.'

'Why don't you admit it was the only way you could escape death from Koreldy's sword, you snivelling coward,' Wyl shouted.

Exclamations rang out in the hall and Celimus's eyes shone with hatred. He walked towards Ylena until he towered above her. 'The Thirsk bitch lies. She wasn't there so how could she know? Where were you, Ylena? At Rittylworth, wasn't it? Cringing in the cellar of a monastery before you fled to Felrawthy. It is fitting that your journey ends here. No one can save you now.' He sounded as cruel as Wyl could ever remember.

'Nor do I want them to, you son of a whore. Thank

goodness your father killed your mother. The only pity is that he did not do it before she birthed you—'

He got no further with his insult. The punch to Ylena's face was expertly levelled and the room went dark for Wyl. Everyone else stood in shocked silence. Jessom was the first to gather his wits and nodded towards one of the guards to pick up the woman sprawled across the flagstones, her head bleeding from where she had gashed it on the table.

Cailech glanced towards Aremys and saw his stricken expression. He didn't know what was going on here but he didn't like it one bit. There was clearly a connection between Aremys and the woman, yet, more than that, it seemed to him that this whole charade was for his benefit. But if Celimus thought his neighbour would get pleasure from watching a noblewoman humiliated and injured in this fashion, he had entirely misjudged. Cailech was the first to admit that he was no soft-hearted monarch; he had not flinched at having the Morgravian woman staked out for roasting, or killing her later to trick Gueryn, but she was a prisoner of battle. She had been caught infiltrating the Razors and Cailech firmly believed in the old saying, 'A tooth for a tooth', Celimus had killed too many Mountain people for Cailech not to make an example of the captured prisoners. But this Thirsk woman struck him as a pawn in whatever game was being played out between Celimus and the Thirsk family. And Cailech wanted no part of it. He raised an eyebrow in silent question to Aremys, who glared back at him as if to say 'Do something'.

Celimus turned back to his guests and rubbed his knuckles. 'She has a head as hard as stone – like all the

Thirsk trolls.' Nervous laughter sounded in the room. 'Get her ready!' he ordered Jessom, who escorted a prone Ylena Thirsk, held in the arms of a guard, out of a side door.

Cailech wanted to bring the evening to a rapid close. It was time to get away from here, but the sight of the golden-haired beauty and her magnificent defiance of the man everyone in Morgravia feared, compelled him to learn more. He knew Celimus was watching him and so he said smoothly, 'You were telling me about Koreldy,' as if the interruption had been of little consequence.

Celimus continued with similar aplomb, seating himself and bidding everyone do the same. 'Yes, forgive the disturbance. I revealed Koreldy's true identity to Queen Valentyna, who was mortified – as you might imagine – for the mercenary had killed her father, King Valor.'

'I see. And?'

'Well, she banished him, which made it possible for one of my assassins to deal with him. I had no intention of allowing Koreldy to roam the land after betraying me.'

Cailech could not believe his ears. 'You have proof of Koreldy's death?'

'A finger, still wearing a signet ring with a deep bloodred stone and marked with the family insignia.'

'I know the ring,' Cailech replied, feeling suddenly empty. He had been denied the pleasure of dealing with Romen Koreldy, it was true, but he had not expected the acute sense of sorrow that pervaded him. In spite of their differences, not to mention the bad blood, there had been respect between them. He felt sure Koreldy would have preferred to be felled by a Mountain warrior's sword than a Morgravian assassin's blade. 'I always thought the man had lives to spare,' he commented, trying to hide the bitterness in his tone.

'Well, he used them all up once he crossed me, my friend,' Celimus boasted and urged more wine to be poured.

Cailech had tired of being referred to as friend by the Morgravian King. He gave a subtle nod towards Aremys who understood its meaning but made no move; instead he glanced again towards the door where the woman had been taken. Cailech frowned. What was it between those two?

'That woman – what is to happen to her?' he asked, twirling his half-empty goblet.

'She will be executed in your honour, sir,' Celimus answered.

Cailech spilled some of the wine in his surprise. 'Certainly not in my honour!'

The King of Morgravia shrugged. 'Well, she is to die anyway – I'd like her to be my gift to you. You're not squeamish, are you?' It was a challenge.

Cailech did not like the sound of the gift or the suggestion of his gutlessness. 'Celimus, we have enjoyed your hospitality long enough. You will forgive me if I take my leave now.'

'I could not forgive you if you did, my friend.'

'Why is that?' Cailech asked, gritting his teeth.

'We still have some time before the appointed rendezvous and I would like you to partake of the evening's entertainment.'

'Which is?'

Celimus's voice was sly. 'Tell Jessom we are ready,' he said to a waiting servant.

It was terrifying. Elspyth had never fought in any sort of hand-to-hand combat in her life, not even as a child, enacting pretend swordfights and mock battles with other children in the pursuit of laughter and competition. Now she found herself facing a woman who seemed utterly determined to kill her. Elspyth had no tricks to draw upon, no skills which might help her to protect herself.

Alda's lips were drawn back in a tight snarl. There was no doubt in Elspyth's mind that Alda viewed herself as the predator and her opponent as the cornered, helpless prey. The hunter laughed, springing forward and feinting towards her right. The hunted fell for it and tried to dart in the opposite direction, but found that path cut off and a blade slashing towards her. Elspyth shrieked and twisted away, feeling the knife cut cruelly down her back.

The men roared; more bets were exchanged in Alda's favour. The cheering and jeering continued without respite. The audience insulted Elspyth and shouted that Shar's Gatherers were running towards her so fast, she might as well give up now.

Again Alda pounced, this time trying to slash her opponent's face – which was all the prettier, many in the audience conceded, for its pleading expression. Elspyth reacted instinctively and put both her arms up, which won her a nasty gash on the arm where bright blood bloomed instantly. It was not life-threatening but it was the arm she held her blade in and it began to go numb almost immediately. She cried out in despair.

Alda was enjoying herself. Elspyth realised the woman

was simply playing with her. She had promised the fat man a spectacle in exchange for being allowed to kill the opponent of her choice, and Alda was delivering on that hard-hearted promise. How many more slashes would she make before the killing blow came, Elspyth wondered through her tears, as Alda leapt again, missing so slightly that Elspyth heard the whoosh of the blade through the air. Alda laughed harder, whilst Elspyth's exertions made her blood flow freer. It was running down her back, she could feel it, and her front was splashed with blood from her arm wound.

The numbness made it hard to feel her hand gripping the blade. That was probably Alda's intention, she realised, impressed. Not all for show then. Her would-be killer was making strategic wounds, designed for disabling as much as exhibition. No wonder Alda was still alive and on her third fight. No doubt she would make it to the slave boat.

Or will she? a small voice questioned in Elspyth's mind. Why must she win? Why can't you find some spine and at least die attacking rather than be slaughtered mercilessly like a frightened lamb?

She felt the sadistic bite of the blade again, this time expertly delivered across one breast, rapidly followed by the wet sensation of blood spouting forth in answer to the vicious pain. Elspyth staggered, hardly daring to look down at the ruin of her body. When she did she saw only red, running freely and draining her of strength and the will to remain standing. Opposite her swaggered Alda; no cuts or injuries but covered in blood nonetheless . . . Elspyth's blood.

And then Alda did something which she had no idea

would re-awaken the primeval instincts in her opponent. Responding to the chanting of the male audience, now calling for the end to the young woman who was ragged, breathing hard and bending as if under the weight of her pain and despair, Alda licked at the blood that spattered her mouth. It drove the men into a frenzy of lust and greed.

But for Elspyth, it helped her find her rage again. Watching that theatrical gesture, as if Alda thought Elspyth was hers to consume, the injured woman felt the searing white flame of anger once more. She straightened, threw back her greasy hair and screamed. And her fury travelled and hit its mark, cutting through the shields of sorcery, streaming loudly into the consciousness of a man trapped in a horse.

It was as if, just for a moment, he saw it all.

Kill her, Elspyth, he cried. *Survive*! And then he was gone, slipping away from her mind like sand through fingers.

'Lothryn!' she shrieked but silence was all that came back. Thick, dark silence and the sinister presence of Alda stalking her.

'It's time, Olivya,' the woman called sweetly, like a mother to her child. Except the sweetness was tainted and false.

'Do it then, bitch! End it!' Elspyth screamed back over the excited clamour of the audience, who knew the blade would fall only once more.

Alda was not prepared for this. She had anticipated begging and weeping, but not aggression. Then she frowned to see Elspyth crouch as if in disabling pain and lay her blade in the sawdust.

'I have no more to give,' Elspyth whispered, 'no more.'

Her opponent became angry. 'You gave nothing! You didn't even try and defend yourself, you weak fool. Now I have my escape from here. Thank you, Olivya – your life has bought something precious,' and she quickly covered the ground between them.

'Make it swift,' Elspyth pleaded.

'I will,' the woman said, wiping blood from her mouth, hardly able to see flesh through the red liquid covering her opponent's body. 'Bare your throat!'

Elspyth turned her head slightly sideways, knowing she looked like a lamb with its neck exposed for the quick killing slash.

In her excitement, all Alda saw was a girl giving herself willingly to death. She did not notice Elspyth's hand reaching slowly for the blade by her side. Some of the men did, and began screaming for Alda to beware, but she could not hear them in the cacophony. She had eyes now only for Olivya's creamy throat and raised her blade high into the air.

Elspyth wondered if Shar's Gatherers were queuing behind Alda as the woman raised the knife. She watched the weapon reach towards the zenith of its arc . . . Now! She could not tell whether she said it aloud or just heard herself think it. Whichever it was, Elspyth moved faster than she ever had before. It was a once-only effort and it had to be accurate. Wyl had told her that when you sense the opening in someone's defences, you have to strike as fast as your body allows and put your full strength behind it – as a cat does when it leaps or pounces. Elspyth was that cat now. She felt her legs push up hard as she poured every ounce of her courage and her love for Lothryn into one savage leap. Propelling herself upwards, she thrust the blade before her and, unbelievably, saw it embed itself in the centre of Alda's throat.

Elspyth felt pain as Alda's knife, intended for her neck, missed its mark and sank itself deep into her shoulder. It hurt, more than she cared to think about, but it would not take her life . . . unlike Alda, whose spluttering surprise was cut short by a horrible gurgle.

Elspyth, trembling with shock, knelt beside Alda's slumped figure and took her hand. She did not want her to go to her god amidst hate. The woman wanted to speak — it was in her eyes, already glazing over. Was it regret that she had lost her chance for the slave boat or sorrow for her cold-blooded actions that had brought her this far? Elspyth would never know, but she felt the slightest squeeze of her hand as the dying woman struggled not to relinquish her soul to the Gatherers, even though she knew she had already lost this fight.

A hush blanketed the audience in eerie silence. Much money had been lost this evening for the underdog had won against the odds.

Alda's blood mixed with Elspyth's, forming a pool between them. 'I'm sorry,' Elspyth whispered, unable to control her tears. 'May Shar guide you to his peace.'

Alda died with a crooked smile, as if in thanks for Elspyth's blessing, and then her mouth relaxed into death and her blood ceased pumping over the kneeling victor.

The strangled silence of disbelief was broken by the angry shouts of soldiers who burst into the building. One of them was Commander Liryk, roaring orders, but it was Crys who saw Elspyth first.

The sight of the two bloodied figures in the middle of the makeshift arena horrified him, stopping him in his tracks. One woman was obviously dying, or most likely dead, but the other was sobbing.

'Elspyth,' he called into the noise which had cranked up afresh. She did not hear him. 'Elspyth!' he yelled, fury overtaking him as images of his own dead family scorched a path to the front of his mind.

She looked up, her body trembling. 'Crys?' He saw her mouth move hesitantly, as if unsure what she was seeing was true.

He was at her side in a few angry strides and scooped her into his arms, the blood that covered her body wet against him. Crys was unable to force out another word, such was his shock. All he could do was bury his face in her lank, bloodied hair and weep with her.

Kind hands finally loosened his grip on Elspyth and a blanket was thrown around her shivering body. Liryk squeezed Crys's arms. 'Steady now,' he said, and Crys was grateful for the reminder that he must hold his strength in front of the men. He nodded, communicating his thanks silently to the senior soldier. 'She's hurt,' he said, at which point Elspyth sank to her knees.

'Get her out of here,' Liryk barked to one of his men.

'No, wait!' she begged. 'Have you got the leaders?'

Liryk shook his head. 'Are you up to helping us with that?'

'Can't you see her wounds—'

Elspyth interrupted Crys. 'It's all right. Please. Ensuring their heads roll at the swipe of an axe means everything to me.'

'Good girl,' Liryk said, impressed, for he had seen the woman of Yentro's injuries and knew most men would be screaming for attention to them by now. 'Point them out.'

Crys helped Elspyth to her feet and wiped her face with a damp towel he was handed by a guard. The cool water and the cleaning away of the blood revived her slightly.

'Come,' Liryk encouraged. 'They're rounded up outside.'

'What about the women?' she asked.

Liryk gave a low whistle. 'I'm shocked by this. We had no idea of its extent.'

'You knew about it?' Elspyth could not help the accusation in her tone.

'Suspected it,' Liryk corrected. 'But we've been waiting for something or someone to give us a lead to follow.'

Elspyth made a sound of disgust but said no more, feeling the slight pressure at her shoulder which was Crys suggesting she hold her tongue. She turned to follow Liryk, but when she tried to walk unaided she fell down.

Crys picked her up gently and Elspyth felt warmed by the sad smile on his face. 'Let me support you, Elspyth, if you won't permit me to carry you,' he said and circled her waist loosely with his arm so she could lean against him as she needed to.

'Thank you,' she whispered. 'How did you find me?'

'Later,' Crys replied. 'Let's get this ugly business done.'

Outside, Elspyth pointed out the men who had led the betting and then took much pleasure in asking Crys to take her to where Ericson was trying to stand unnoticed in the mob.

'That's him,' she said. 'He calls himself Ericson. He is the leader of this rabble, the one who acquires the women for his sport.' She said the last word as if it was poison in her mouth.

Ericson was dragged from the crowd and bound and

shackled alongside seven other men who had been involved.

'Is this it?' the commander asked.

'Yes. The rest are just cruel onlookers.'

Liryk nodded, as if weary of life. 'We show each other more respect on the battlefield than they have shown these women. Right, men, hear me,' he said, addressing the soldiers. 'I want proof of the name of each man here. If he has no proof, he will be executed. Those who provide proof are to receive forty lashes each. If they survive the whipping, they can drag their sorry arses home and explain it how they will. Remember,' he said, turning back to the prisoners, 'we will have a record of your names and the towns you hail from. If you err again, at any time, your family will be stripped of their assets – homes, land, money, belongings. Is that clear?'

Elspyth saw the men blanch with fear on hearing about the physical ordeal ahead. Perhaps now they might under-stand a tiny measure of what they had put the captured women through. She had no sympathy in her heart for them. She wondered what Liryk had in store for Ericson and his band of followers. She did not have to wait long, impressed by Liryk's speed and ruthlessness in meting out punishment.

'The leaders will have their heads removed from their bodies,' he said, glaring at the cowardly Ericson who visibly staggered at the sentence.

Silence gripped everyone.

'What are you waiting for?' Liryk said calmly to one of his captains.

'I'm sorry, sir. Do you mean now?'

'I do. All of these men are to watch, as a reminder that

Briavel's Queen will not show any mercy to those who break the most sacred laws of life.'

Despite her flagging strength, Elspyth still had the energy to feel sorry for the Captain who, to his credit, gave a salute despite his sudden pallor. Liryk was certainly showing no mercy to these evil men and he soared in her estimation. She stayed conscious long enough to bear witness to Ericson's sobs as he was forced to kneel and lay his neck across a log. She looked around for his daughter, but the girl with the singsong voice was nowhere to be seen as the axe fell and her father's head rolled from his body.

'They say the head knows it has been removed from the body for several seconds afterwards,' Crys commented absently, still supporting her with his arm.

'Good,' Elspyth mumbled and slumped against his shoulder.

CHAPTER 22

Wyl was brought back into the hall of the Donals where an air of expectancy greeted him. He glanced at Aremys's stricken face and wished he could reassure his friend that death did not frighten him any more. Any escape from the sheath of Ylena's body was welcome.

At Jessom's bidding, and with an awkward silence prevailing, he was taken by the two guards to a spot at one end of the chamber where his hands were tied to a timber framework, no doubt hastily erected for his benefit. His ankles, still manacled, were unnecessarily tied to the timbers as well. *This is novel*, he thought. Celimus was obviously getting more creative. He stared defiantly at the Morgravian King.

Celimus took a swig from his goblet. 'The last of the great Thirsks, strung up for our pleasure, gentlemen. Call in the archers,' he said, then glanced towards the stony-faced Mountain King. 'Come on, Cailech, I thought you people were . . .' He paused.

'Barbaric?' Cailech offered.

Celimus smiled, sly and cunning. 'Fun-loving, I was going to say.'

Cailech did not reply. He turned to look at the intriguing woman and was met by a hard blue gaze which had fire burning behind it, fuelled by hatred and anger. He felt his breath catch, as it did each time he looked at her. He admired the defiance, her complete disregard and indeed disrespect for where she was, the company she was in and the lack of fear for what she surely knew was coming. She had the courage of the Mountain People in her soul, he thought fancifully, caught by the golden hair which had fallen loose. Ylena Thirsk looked dirty and dishevelled but she was nonetheless desirable, he admitted to himself.

He had to look away from her fierce stare. 'No trial?' he asked as two archers were brought in.

'None required,' Celimus said. 'She pays the price for the treachery of the men of her family.'

'Shar won't grant you forgiveness for this, you evil scum, Celimus. This is like the Witch Myrren all over again, isn't it?' Wyl forced out a laugh as the similarity of the situation struck him. He saw that it struck home with Celimus too and took pleasure in seeing the King flinch. 'She beat you and I'll beat you. I won't scream, I won't give you any satisfaction, you cowardly—'

'Shut her up!' Celimus ordered a soldier.

But Wyl was going to have his say, even as the embarrassed guard moved towards him. 'Your father wished many times that my brother could be King so you got rid of both of them – and the King of Briavel, Koreldy and the Donals. Watch out, Cailech, he'll be planning to kill you next. And no doubt his bride. He'll slaughter everyone until—'

Ylena's mouth was bound. No sensible words were coming out because of the linen tied across his face, but Wyl kept raging at the man who had destroyed the lives of so many good, loyal people of Morgravia. He saw Cailech shake his head; noticed the Razor King wore an expression of wonder.

'Where are you going, Aremys Farrow?' Celimus asked loudly over Ylena's accusations. 'Be quiet, Ylena, or I'll slash your mouth so it can't move properly.'

Wyl quietened. He had promised himself he would keep Ylena as unmarked as he could. There was nothing more to be achieved anyway. He joined everyone else in the chamber in looking towards the mercenary.

Aremys had hoped no one would notice him slipping away from the hall. He could not witness this. He could not save Wyl – he was one man; they would cut him down before he even reached him. They would both die, but only one of them would live again. Granted he could probably reach Celimus, but then what? He had no weapon. *Bite him to death, I suppose*, he thought sourly as he straightened from the bow he felt obliged to give before his retreat. But the Morgravian had seen him from the corner of his eye and was now expecting an answer.

'Apologies, sire. I thought I should go and check on the horses and be ready to move out after the . . . entertainment.'

'Everything will be readied for your departure, Farrow. I'd prefer you to stay. In fact I rather thought you'd like to see your prey being felled?'

'Not in this manner, sire,' Aremys risked.

Celimus did not react as Aremys thought he would. In truth, the King was enjoying everyone's discomfort.

Except for Cailech, he noted sourly, who seemed more troubled than affronted. 'Your King has remained, and as this is in his honour, I expect you to share in this gift,' he ordered.

'Of course, sire. As you wish,' Aremys said, glancing towards Ylena and privately agreeing that it was probably for the best. He would need to know which of these men in the room Wyl would become. And then a chilling thought occurred to him. Did Myrren's gift only work if Wyl was slain by hand — that is, someone connected to the weapon? His mind raced. Wyl had never mentioned it but then perhaps Wyl did not know! Koreldy was killed by Faryl, who plunged a knife into his heart with her own hand. Faryl was killed by Ylena, who held the blade which slashed the assassin's throat. If Celimus was planning to loose arrows into Ylena, no one would be connected to the weapon when it landed in her body. Ylena would surely die . . . but perhaps so would Wyl.

The sense that he had stumbled across something important so terrified Aremys that he shouted into the thick, expectant silence: 'Sire!'

'Yes, Farrow?' the King said, his temper rising.

Aremys looked at Ylena and then at Cailech; saw the Mountain King frown and knew he suspected something between him and the woman. 'King Celimus,' he began, clearing his throat nervously, 'this is a messy end, sire, particularly for a celebration. Why don't I just take her out the back and kill her for you?'

'You had your chance, Farrow. Now I will show you how to finish a job.'

'But, your majesty . . .' His words died away and he

felt a twinge of fear as Celimus turned to stare at him, no longer indulgent of the emissary of the Mountain King, no longer prepared to be generous.

'Don't push me, Grenadyne, or you'll find yourself staked out like the Lady Thirsk there.'

'I would have to object to such treatment of a protected guest,' Cailech warned icily and nodded at Aremys to continue.

'Let me finish what you asked me to do, King Celimus. I will cut her throat here and now before you.' It was his last desperate try. At least he could be sure Wyl would live on.

Celimus found himself cornered. He wanted to have some fun with Ylena's death but he could tell he had over-stepped the mark where Cailech was concerned in threat-ening Farrow. He knew from the expression on Jessom's face that the Chancellor was urging him to take the easy way out: have the mercenary finish off the woman. He was angry but this was not the time or place to make a scene.

'Well, at least her blood will not be on my hands.' He smiled. 'Go ahead, Farrow. Finish the job I paid you to do.'

Aremys risked a glance of thanks towards Cailech, convinced that without the Mountain King's timely com-ment and brittle tone, Celimus might not have relented. Cailech returned the gaze with an expression of utter bafflement.

'I will need a blade, sire,' Aremys said.

Celimus gave an order and one of the soldiers at Ylena's side pulled a mean-looking knife from his belt. 'It's sharp,' he murmured. 'Make it quick.'

Aremys nodded. Everyone wanted this ugliness done with. He took a deep breath. So this was it. He was about to die and Wyl would become him. He stood close to Ylena. 'As One,' he said and grinned sadly at the irony of the words. He saw the tears well in her eyes as she heard the Thirsk family motto.

Aremys raised the blade, knowing precisely where to strike to slash the jugular for a swift death. But Ylena began to scream and struggle, disturbing everyone but the two Kings. Wyl saw that Celimus's eyes shone with joy at this horrific scene.

'Arrow! Arrow!' Wyl shrieked in Ylena's high voice, determined to stop his good friend giving up his own life.

'What's she saying?' the Morgravian King enquired, determined to drag out the agony.

'She's simply yelling my name,' Aremys answered.

'Er, I think she's saying "arrow", sire,' one of the guards confirmed.

'Oh, perhaps she'd prefer to be killed by the archers?'

'No, sire,' Aremys said as firmly as he dared. 'This is best.'

'Wait!' the King replied. 'Let's ask her. It's the least we can do, isn't it?' He cast an appealing glance around the hall, playing the magnanimous sovereign.

Aremys glared at Wyl. 'You fool,' he said angrily, under his breath.

The guard ripped away the bindings around Ylena's mouth.

'Step aside, Farrow,' Celimus said, enjoying himself hugely again. The big man did so reluctantly, but not before glaring at Cailech who frowned again, taking in all the strange nuances on display here.

'Ylena,' Celimus said; it sounded almost tender. 'As a final act of generosity towards your family, I'm going to allow you to choose how you die. By Farrow's blade across your throat or cleanly with an arrow fired expertly?'

'By the arrow,' Wyl said fiercely, not daring to look at Aremys.

'As we suspected. Good choice, Ylena,' Celimus replied and stopped just short of rubbing his hands in glee. 'Thank you, Farrow. It seems your job is complete. Move away.'

This time Aremys looked at no one as he returned to his spot near the door. He stared at the floor. He would not watch Wyl die.

'Ylena, my dear, I did have some sport planned with the archers but as everyone here seems to want you to have a speedy end, I'll send them away and instead I will do the necessary.'

'As you wish,' Wyl replied without blinking, knowing he was spoiling Celimus's fun by being so accepting. It worked. The King's face darkened with a scowl.

'Give me a bow!' Celimus said, his tone furious. 'Let's finish this.'

'Why don't we?' Wyl said, in the most bored tone he could achieve. He could hardly believe his luck that Celimus had chosen to do the deed. He would become the Morgravian King within the next few moments and, as much as he hated the thought of being Celimus, what pleasure it would be to finally kill him. 'Hurry up, sire! I am eager to be gone from here.' He saw Cailech give a grin of astonishment at Ylena's bravado but it was the last thing she would say, for Celimus was finally taking aim. He switched his attention briefly to Aremys but his friend refused to look at him. Wyl could not understand why: Aremys knew he would live again and this time he would be King.

'Farewell, Ylena Thirsk. May Shar send you to wherever your predecessors have ended their days.' Celimus stretched the bowstring taut. 'Heart or eye? Or shall I let it be a surprise?' he asked with a cruel smile. Everyone could hear the slight strain in his voice of holding back the string so tightly.

Wyl refused to answer and instead closed his eyes. Celimus was an excellent shot. He held no qualms that the arrow would end his life as Ylena.

Cailech's astonishment was complete. This woman was extraordinary; she should not be wasted in this manner. Ylena Thirsk stirred more emotion in him than any woman had in his entire life. Cailech had been accused of being cold towards women. That was not true; he liked women well enough, he had just never met anyone who truly excited him. But Ylena Thirsk fired in him a swirl of inexplicable feelings. He wanted this woman! He had no idea from where this sudden desire had erupted, but one thing was for sure: he was not about to let her die trussed like an animal at the end of one of Celimus's arrows.

He moved as fast as a pouncing cat and pushed the Morgravian King's wrist up just as the arrow was loosed. It shot high into the air, burying itself with a resounding thump into a solid beam overhead. Everyone followed the quivering motion of the shaft, not sure whether to be horrified by Cailech's action or relieved. Wyl opened Ylena's eyes with angry disbelief with no idea of why the arrow had missed its mark. Aremys had to ball his hands into fists to stop himself clapping.

Celimus turned the darkest of stares onto his fellow King.

'I've just decided about that gift you offered me, Celimus.'

The Morgravian's expression did not change nor did he utter a word in response.

'I want her,' Cailech said, pointing towards Ylena.

'What?' Celimus roared.

'You heard me,' Cailech replied calmly. 'I shall take Ylena Thirsk from you. She will travel with us high into the Razors and will never trouble you again.'

'What possible interest could you have in her?'

'I'm sure if you think about it long enough you'll work it out,' Cailech said and winked.

Impossibly, Celimus began to laugh. Jessom slowly let out his tightly held breath. Cailech had certainly taken a risk but the Chancellor could not think of a better idea to handle this situation. He had even suggested once to Celimus that he should marry Ylena off to a Mountain warrior and be done with her. There would be little chance of her escaping the Razors, and once the royal marriage was complete, no one would care about the Thirsk name. Everyone would be deliriously happy that Morgravia and Briavel were unified. 'My lord, this is an opportunity,' he risked.

Cailech grinned. 'You see, Celimus, even your own counsel likes the idea.'

Wyl began to rage, Ylena's voice becoming hysterical as he shouted, 'Kill me, you bastard' over and over again.

'Oh, someone get her out of here,' Celimus said, more exasperated now than angry. He could not help but like Cailech's idea as he watched Ylena being dragged away screaming.

'You did promise me a gift. Anything, you said,' Cailech reminded him.

'That's true, I did,' Celimus agreed, looking at Cailech. 'There would have to be conditions, though. Koreldy tried something similar.'

'I am not Koreldy,' Cailech bristled.

'Why do you want her?'

'Why would any red-blooded man want her? Does she not affect you so?'

'No. Her mere name sickens me.'

'Well, that's history, Celimus. I don't have the same issues. She's a beauty. Let us truly bind ourselves in our treaty – I will take a Morgravian as my wife.'

'Your wife?' Celimus exclaimed, unable to hide his incredulity.

'Yes, why not?' Cailech was grinning widely now. He glanced at Aremys who could hardly keep his own smile in check.

'You jest, surely?'

'I would never jest about anything so grave as the sacrament of marriage. If you can marry a Briavellian, Celimus, why shouldn't I complete the triangle of our realms and marry a Morgravian?'

'Why not indeed, sire?' Jessom said, daring to join the conversation. 'It is a perfect union.' His eyes pleaded with his King. This was better than any of them could have dreamed. Surely Celimus could see that?

'There would be conditions,' Celimus said again, frowning as his agile mind ran through this new turn of events.

'As you said,' Cailech replied. 'Although I can put your mind at rest. Ylena Thirsk would not be permitted to leave the Razors. I make that pledge to you right now.'

'Ever?'

'Ever.'

'And as your Queen you would not permit her to make any decisions which might affect Morgravia – or our treaty will be disqualified and I will wage war on your people. Not just the Legion, Cailech, but the full might of the combined Morgravian and Briavellian armies.'

'She would be Queen in title only. I am the power in the Razors.'

'So how do we effect this?' Celimus said, looking towards his Chancellor.

Cailech took the lead. 'I will take her with me now. Your men can escort us to the border and see that she is taken safely into the Razors, from where she will never emerge. Your Chancellor here can draw up the paperwork and your delegates can talk with mine. I will sign whatever you need to effect our treaty and this new understanding regarding the Thirsk woman.'

Celimus shook his head. He could pick no ruse: Cailech seemed earnest in his desire for Ylena. 'All right, I agree. Ylena Thirsk is yours to take. She is my gift to you.'

'Thank you,' Cailech said, surprising himself by how delighted he felt. He turned to his companion. 'Come, Aremys. Ready the Thirsk woman for travel. She rides with me.'

CHAPTER 23

In the end, Wyl was given his own horse for the first part of the journey. He sat sullenly astride the bay next to Aremys, a thick and uncomfortable silence between them as the two Kings made their official farewells.

'You have no idea how angry I feel by what's happened tonight,' he finally said in a low voice to his companion.

Aremys bristled. 'This was Cailech's idea, not mine, but I'd be lying if I didn't say I'm ready to kiss the ground he walks on because of it!'

Wyl glared at his friend. 'What's that supposed to mean?'

The Grenadyne cast a glance around to check they were not being eavesdropped upon, particularly by the Chancellor. 'It occurs to me,' he muttered, a bite in his tone, 'that perhaps Myrren's gift only works when the killer is still in touch with you somehow.'

Wyl frowned. 'I don't get you,' he replied.

'Did Elysius explain how the gift works?'

Wyl shrugged. 'What's to know,' he said, bitterness underpinning his reply as he watched the sovereigns clasp hands and shoulders in the tradition of parley and peace.

Aremys sighed. He understood Wyl's angry mood; it would be ludicrous to even pretend he could imagine what it felt like to be trapped as Wyl was, or how much courage it had taken to welcome the agony of whatever form of death Celimus had wished upon Ylena Thirsk. 'I began to wonder, back in that hall, whether whoever killed you had to be connected with you through the weapon.'

That won Wyl's attention. He paused in thought. 'I've never considered that. You mean if the arrow had been shot I might be fully dead, but if you'd slit my throat I would be you?'

'Exactly,' Aremys muttered beneath his breath. 'You might truly have died and then all would be lost. That's why I acted as I did.'

Ylena's face looked newly distressed. 'So I do owe Cailech my life.'

'Possibly, is all I'm saying. I don't care to test my own theory,' Aremys admitted. 'And I'd prefer it if you didn't either.'

Wyl glanced at Aremys again and this time Ylena's expression was chastened. 'Thank you,' was all he had time to say before Cailech was striding back to their party.

'My lady,' the King of the Razors said. Wyl was unable to read the soft tone or the gentle expression on Cailech's face. All he could do was nod.

Aremys felt a new fear thrill through him. He had not had time to explain that although Cailech might have saved Wyl's life, the new situation was just as dire, with the King announcing his intention to marry Ylena. He was glad, in fact, that he had not had to give that explanation yet or deal with its consequences.

When Cailech was seated on his horse Celimus strolled up. 'Safe travels, my friend.' Cailech simply nodded. The Morgravian turned to his prisoner. 'Another lucky escape, Ylena Thirsk, but this time I fear it is your last. I won't be seeing you again.'

'Oh, you'll see me, Celimus,' Wyl promised, a determined, somewhat sly smile touching Ylena's lips. 'In a place I call hell.'

Celimus laughed. 'Good luck with her, Cailech – as I understand it, her husband ploughed the furrow only once. She'll be nice and tight for you. Remember your promise to me.'

Celimus's words shocked Wyl, but he put them aside in order to take this last opportunity to have the last word. He had never heard Ylena's voice sound as cold and threatening. 'And you remember my promise to you, Celimus. When we meet again, you will die and I will bear witness to it. Just you and I, Celimus – as it should be.'

The words sounded strangely prophetic to Chancellor Jessom. He was not sure why but the threat felt so very real on this cold night in the north, and yet how could it be, coming from a helpless captive; a young woman at that? Nevertheless, a chill passed through him as he watched Ylena Thirsk stare at the Morgravian King. Jessom was missing something here, he was sure of it, but even his sharp mind could not fathom what it might be. Ylena was too confident, too unfazed by Celimus – she had demanded her own death, for pity's sake. What person in their right mind did that? It did not make sense. He glanced at Aremys and was surprised to see the mercenary was watching him. The clue sat between Aremys and Ylena; Jessom was convinced of it. He narrowed his gaze in thought and saw the Grenadyne nod towards him as the party, escorted by Legionnaires, moved out of Tentcrdyn.

Jessom watched them depart in silence, seized by an unshakeable notion that, despite what either King promised, they had definitely not seen the last of the Thirsks.

The journey back to the border was uneventful and mostly silent. That suited Wyl; he was content to let his horse follow the party whilst he fell into deep thought about this new turn of events. Being pulled further from Celimus was confusing but then Fynch had warned him of the randomness of Myrren's gift. Perhaps this was one of those occasions. It did not mean the outcome had changed, only the timing. He fully expected to meet Celimus again – and next time, as he had promised, he would not fail. His mind turned to what the King of the Razors might have in mind for him. Why had Cailech stayed the hand of Ylena's would-be murderer? He felt a sudden gratitude to the Mountain King, for perhaps Aremys was right; so far all his deaths had involved someone killing him with a weapon they held. He noticed Cailech beckon to Aremys, who nudged his horse to draw alongside the King, but he could not hear their conversation and lost himself in his thoughts again.

'What is it between you and the Thirsk woman?' Cailech asked Aremys, direct as usual.

'Sire?'

'Don't play the innocent with me. I'm sure I deserve better.'

Aremys sighed. 'It's true, my lord. I did not want to see Ylena Thirsk murdered.'

'That much is obvious. But why?'

'Because she is innocent of all that Celimus lays at her feet.'

Cailech made a soft sound of exasperation. 'I can work that out for myself, Grenadyne. Tell me something I don't know, something which accounts for that look in your eyes that fairly begged me to step in and halt the proceedings.'

Aremys knew he would have to skirt the truth as carefully as possible. Cailech was not about to let this topic go. 'When I was picked up unconscious in the eastern part of the Razors by Myrt and his companions,' Aremys began, 'I had lost my memory, as you know.' The King nodded but said nothing. The horses slowed to a walk. They could see flaming torches being waved in welcome from a distance. It would not be long now before they were reunited with their men. 'As my memory returned I remembered the paid task I was involved with at the time of being set upon by the thieves in northern Briavel.'

'I'd like to hear the end of this before we actually reach the others, Aremys,' Cailech admonished gently.

Aremys nodded and got to the point. 'I was hired by King Celimus to track down and murder Ylena Thirsk.'

'I had guessed as much.'

Aremys was not surprised. 'Celimus has, as I understand it, my lord, designed the deaths of Wyl Thirsk, Romen Koreldy, King Valor of Briavel, perhaps even his own father, and no doubt countless others.'

'You knew about Romen?' Cailech interrupted.

'It only came back to me recently. I didn't know him, my lord, only of him.'

'Why do you think you mentioned him when you awoke from your stupor?'

Aremys was reminded again that Cailech missed very little. 'I suppose because Ylena Thirsk mentioned to me that he carried a blue sword.'

'So you did actually meet up with her?' Cailech said, his mind moving swiftly now.

'Yes, sire. I met with her at Felrawthy and had no intention of killing her as instructed. We talked of Koreldy because she was so grateful for his help in saving her life the first time. Having learned all that had befallen the Thirsks and accepting that this girl was an innocent, I followed Koreldy's lead and decided to help her. Mercenary I may be, sire; cold-blooded murderer with no good reason, I am not. It was I who took her into Briavel where I felt she would be safe. We lost each other at Timpkenny when I wandered out for some air and got set upon.' His story suddenly sounded horribly thin. He continued quickly. 'We'd already discussed her going to Werryl and throwing herself on the mercy of the Queen, so she must have followed the plan in my absence.'

'So the note to Valentyna of Briavel, which you claimed to have sent — that was a ruse?'

Aremys nodded. 'I had to lie — I was trapped. But who would have thought the Queen would give her up in the fashion she did? I had both your and my life at stake, as well as Ylena's. You'll recall when I told you about my insurance that I had no idea how to deliver the Thirsk woman.'

Cailech nodded. 'I could, of course, be forgiven for thinking that Ylena Thirsk wishes to die. Perhaps she forced the Queen's hand?'

'Perhaps and, frankly, who could blame her?' Aremys offered, not wanting to say much more, nervous that he had got this far on lies.

'And your need to rub salt in the prisoner's wounds was actually your way of warning Ylena — am I right?'

'Again, yes, sire. I needed Ylena's story to match with mine in front of Celimus, or I feared none of us would leave that hall alive.'

'The Chancellor knows nothing?'

'Nothing, my lord. He watched Ylena and myself argue. I was fortunate that a message came for him during that time in the outbuilding. We had but a few moments.'

'I see,' Cailech replied. He fell silent. They were almost at the rendezvous point — could see Captain Bukanan and the other dignitaries being brought down to be exchanged. 'One more thing, Aremys.'

'Yes, my lord?'

'Why do you care about Ylena Thirsk? What hold does she have on you?'

And here we come to it, Aremys thought, struck suddenly that he had no answer to this question. Cailech waited as the mercenary's mind raced to find something to offer the King. The carefully constructed web of lies could be torn down in a second if he said the wrong thing now.

'What is it, Aremys? Why do you hesitate?' Cailech asked, more pointedly. 'Are you hiding something I should be concerned about?'

'No, my lord. It's not that—'

'Then what!' Cailech demanded. Aremys noticed Ylena glance behind at the disturbance of a raised voice. 'You will tell me, Grenadyne, before we meet our men

. . . before I permit you to enter the Razors again, before I—'

It was Aremys's turn to interrupt. 'Because I love her!' he blurted, shocked by the vehemence in his voice and surprised by where the statement had come from. But the last thing he wanted was to be separated from Wyl again and this was the best reason he could manufacture. It was not so far from the truth: he loved the person that was Wyl and had certainly desired Faryl. He had admired Romen since he was a lad, so all in all he was not really lying even though he was not wholly telling the truth.

Cailech looked at him, astonished. For a moment neither man spoke and Aremys knew he must hold that hard gaze no matter what. To look away now would show weakness or deception. Who knew which way the wily King of the Razors would interpret it?

'You jest,' Cailech said eventually.

'I do not, sire,' Aremys said sadly.

'But—'

'Let us not speak of it any more, my lord,' Aremys said, glad for the cover of darkness to shield his embarrassment. 'I have not yet expressed my deepest thanks for what you did today for Ylena. Let me do so now.'

'By Haldor's arse, man, I didn't do it for you,' Cailech said, still rocked by the Grenadyne's admission. 'I did it for purely selfish reasons. I would be lying if I did not admit here and now that I desire her more than I have desired any woman. I meant what I said.'

Myrt arrived. He took one look at his King and knew something was awry. He nodded to his sovereign. 'Welcome back, sire.'

'Get rid of the Morgravian escort, Myrt, and make

the official exchange,' Cailech said and turned back to Aremys.

Myrt accepted the salute of the Legion's senior officer and oversaw the departure of the men. When he returned, he glanced between Aremys and the King, unsure of what to do.

'We'll be right with you, Myrt,' Cailech said. 'Take good care of the noblewoman we've brought with us.'

Myrt took the reins of Ylena's horse and led the creature into camp without another word.

'I mean to make her my wife, Aremys.'

'Without even knowing her,' the mercenary replied softly, careful not to sound judgemental.

Cailech looked towards the stars and gave Aremys the truth. 'I've never been so affected by a woman and I've barely so much as shared a word with her. She is dishevelled, dirty, angry. She is magnificent. I want her.'

'She is certainly different to any woman I've ever known,' Aremys admitted, unable to help himself. 'Be careful, sire.'

'Of what!'

'Of getting your heart broken.'

Aremys meant it sincerely. He knew Wyl would shout loud and long when he heard of the King's intentions and Aremys could only wonder at how long Ylena would keep her life once Wyl set his mind to losing it this time. Minutes probably, after hearing the word 'wife' uttered.

Cailech, however, took the mercenary's meaning a completely different way. A dawning spread across his expression. 'Oh, poor Aremys. The Lady Ylena has rejected your advances.'

'No, my lord,' Aremys corrected. 'I have never made them.'

'She doesn't know?' he asked, aghast.

The Grenadyne shook his head. 'I prefer it that way.'

'Then what do you mean about getting my heart broken?'

'Only that she loved her husband, Alyd Donal of Felrawthy. She will never love another.'

'We shall see. She has nothing else,' Cailech said, matter-of-factly. 'We have cleared this between us then?'

'My lord?'

'I can't have you mooning around the woman whilst I'm seducing her, man! I don't want us to fight over her.'

Aremys smiled for the first time in a long time. 'Good luck to you if she will have you, Cailech.'

The King of the Razors grinned and held out his hand; again, it was palm up in absolute sincerity. Aremys laid his own palm upon it. 'You constantly surprise me, Grenadyne. Now if you'd be so kind, I'll ask you to introduce me to my bride-to-be.'

Elspyth was laid out on a makeshift pallet on the ground, blankets piled over her small frame to keep out the bite of the cool spring night. A nearby torch lit her face a ghostly colour.

'Am I dying?' she asked Crys who held her hand.

He mustered the crooked grin she loved. 'No, but we've got to get those wounds closed up. Drink this,' he said, and helped her to sit up slightly. 'It's warm, sweetened tea. Good for shock, my mother always says.' He sighed. 'Said.'

'Crys, take me home.' It was a plea. She squeezed his hand. 'I know you've probably got better things to do than travel to Yentro but I just want to get back to the north.'

'To Lothryn?' he wondered, his voice gentle.

'Both. I can get well quicker at home and I will feel closer to him with the Razors in sight. I've had enough of roaming the land. The last time I slept in my own bed, ate in my own cottage, did something simple like going to the market, seems a lifetime ago. I need to see if my aunt is still alive and I need to take stock of my life. Wyl doesn't need me now.'

'Will you promise me that you won't go off into Cailech's lands if I do take you home?' Her pause was telling. 'I won't let you waste yourself, Elspyth. You know how I feel about you—'

'Don't, Crys,' she begged softly.

'I don't mean it like that,' he urged. 'I know where your heart lies. But I care too much about you to let you risk yourself, and Wyl would kill me anyway if I did.'

She found a smile for him. 'He'd be wrathful for sure. You saw him in Werryl?'

He nodded and laughed. 'Supremely cranky too. He'd got the flux and he made an inappropriate move on the Queen.'

Elspyth could not help but be amused by Crys's well-timed jest, and the theatrical arch of his eyebrow had her spluttering into painful laughter and then groaning at the way it tore at her wounds. 'Oh, I mustn't laugh at him,' she said, 'but I can't help it. I wish I'd known Wyl before Myrren's gift.'

'He was no painting,' Crys commented, determined to see her smile again. His timing, as always, was perfect and she found herself giggling once more.

They were interrupted by Liryk. 'Well, this is all very heartening.'

Crys cleared his throat. 'Anything to keep her conscious and her mind off her woes,' he admitted and winked.

Liryk nodded. 'Elspyth, I'm so sorry we let you down.' It was the second time he had apologised but he felt this time she was paying more attention. 'I promised my Queen I would find you for her.'

'Please, Commander Liryk, the fault is all mine. It was stupid of me to leave as I did and even more naive to fall for that man's cruel trap. Did you find his daughter, by the way?'

'We did. We'll take her back to Werryl and see if we can find the rest of her family.'

'Good. She was part of the scheme, I know, but she's so young. Her father used her as much as he used the women.'

'Well, he's gone to answer for his sins to Shar now. Now don't think me odd but we do need to get you stitched, my girl. Those wounds risk infection if we don't and that would be life-threatening even if the injuries aren't.'

'Do you have a physic in the company?' Crys asked.

Liryk gave a nervous smile. 'No, but as it happens a Master Rilk passed through an hour ago. One of my men recognised him and hailed him.'

Elspyth nodded. 'Is he a doctor?'

The Commander looked sheepish. 'He's a tailor.' He waited for the outburst from Crys to settle. 'Hear me out. Next to Madam Eltor, there isn't a more adept person with a needle and thread in the whole of Briavel. He crafts for the top nobility in Morgravia too — that's where he is travelling from.'

'A master tailor to sew me up?' Elspyth queried.

'He has the finest silken thread and a light touch, Elspyth. It's the best we can do. He's rather nervous but has agreed. Those wounds need to be sutured and rather than let one of my men do a hack job, I'd far rather allow a talented craftsman to work on your skin.'

Elspyth felt even more light-headed at the notion of being laid out like fabric for a tailor to work on.

Crys was frowning. 'I suppose, under the circumstances, this is the best option?'

Liryk nodded; he had already motioned to the soldier behind him to bring the tailor forward. 'This is Master Rilk,' he said, and looked at the craftsman. 'This is Duke Crys Donal and our patient, Elspyth.'

Crys shook the tailor's hand. 'She's got four major cuts.'

The little man was already perspiring, even though it was a cool night, and Crys had to wonder if he was up to such a grisly task. 'Can you stomach it, sir?' he asked.

'Oh, yes. I've done something similar but it was for my son's beloved pet.' He chanced a grin but no one returned it. 'I'm sure Miss Elspyth will have far finer skin,' Rilk assured and then his tone became brisk and businesslike. 'Can we have her gently moved to a table, please? I'll need lots of light and clean linens and hot water. I presume you have some antiseptic?' Liryk nodded. 'Good, I'll need plenty of it. Do you have any shorrock or liquor with you?'

'I'm sure we can find some,' Liryk said.

'Do it quickly, please, and get some down Miss Elspyth's throat to dull the pain. Not too much, mind, just sufficient to help her drift off a bit.'

Elspyth had already drifted, frightened yet too exhausted to keep her attention on what was about to happen.

Knave was back at Fynch's side. The boy was pale and trembling from the exertion of returning the dog to the Razors.

This is exactly what I was afraid of, Knave growled into Fynch's head.

'I'll be all right soon. I just need to sleep.'

Have you taken some sharvan?

'No. Just let me be.'

Knave looked around, quietly exasperated. Fynch had made no progress since they had parted. He had obviously become too weak to send himself anywhere after the efforts of transporting Knave.

'How was Valentyna?' the boy mumbled.

Worried about you. Liryk and his company left immediately.

'Good . . . ah wait, here is Kestrel.' It took Fynch some pain to open up his mind but he wanted Knave to share this.

Kestrel's thin voice entered their heads. *Elspyth is safe. Quite badly injured from what I can tell, but alive and talking to some of the men who arrived.*

What are they doing? Fynch asked.

Perhaps I can show you? Kestrel wondered.

Yes, let's try, the boy said, a new excitement cutting through his pain.

Knave sighed. He felt sure Fynch would die before they even left this plateau.

Fynch concentrated. His eyes were squeezed tightly shut. *That's right, Kestrel. Open your mind completely to me. I won't hurt you, I promise. I just want to see through your eyes, if I may.* There was a pause and suddenly a picture appeared in Knave's mind.

I see it, he admitted grudgingly to Fynch.

An awning of sorts had been set up. Torches burned brightly around it and some men held candles as others bent over a prone figure. Kestrel must have perched himself on a low branch nearby; his sight was keen and they could clearly see all that they needed to.

'They seem to be sewing her,' the boy said. 'There's Commander Liryk. And . . . oh, wait, is that Master Rilk?'

You're right, Knave said. *It's the tailor.*

'He's mending her,' Fynch said in wonderment. They watched Rilk snip a thread then step away and arch his back. *She's pretty, isn't she?* Fynch said absently into his companions' minds. *I'm glad we were able to help. She's going to be all right.*

Is that enough, Fynch? Kestrel asked.

Enough, Knave answered, determined now that his charge would rest.

Perhaps I'll follow the pretty lady, the bird added. *I've got nothing better to do.*

Thank you, Kestrel, Fynch replied weakly, his head pounding.

We'll speak again soon, the bird said and all connections closed.

Knave bristled. *I can feel the echoes of your pain, Fynch. You've got to stop using magic for a while.*

'We can't,' he moaned and retched helplessly into some bushes.

We have no choice. You must recover your strength before we proceed. We'll make camp here. I'm going to find you some food.

You may not feel like eating but your body is mortal, Fynch. It needs nourishment.

The boy did not reply. He had collapsed into a small, curled shape like a tiny animal and he slept.

CHAPTER 24

Valentyna looked at herself in the mirror and glumly permitted a brief, silent admission that the dress was exquisite.

'Oh, my Queen, you make the most glorious bride,' Madam Eltor said. 'The fit is perfect.' She looked at the breathtaking woman before her and sighed. 'A smile would help.'

'I'm sorry, Margyt.'

'I have to ask you to try on the veil now, my dear,' the woman continued.

Its cream gauze and seed pearls completed the beautiful vision.

'Thank you, it's lovely,' was all the Queen could force out.

'You know, Valentyna, perhaps it's not my place to speak, but we would all like to think that you enter this union with some joy.'

The Queen and the seamstress had known each other too long for lies. 'I'm sorry that I cannot,' Valentyna said. 'I do this for Briavel, Margyt, because I know it brings us peace and, I hope, new prosperity but I cannot love him. There is no joy.'

'Because of another?' the woman risked.

Valentyna shook her head gently. 'No. Simply because I don't love him. We can't help our feelings, can we?'

'No, child. This is true. My husband and I could never claim to have loved one another as I know other couples do.'

'But you have a good partnership,' Valentyna said.

'More than that, to be honest. We are the closest of friends. But yes, a great partnership too — as you will enjoy with King Celimus. You will make it so. You will give us heirs and make us proud.'

A smile ghosted across Valentyna's mouth. 'That is my fervent wish.'

Margyt Eltor patted her Queen's hand. 'Let me snip those threads now and release you.'

'Are all the preparations in hand?'

'Yes, your majesty,' Madam Eltor said, back to her formal role. 'I shall be taking two dressers and a couple of other girls for errands and any other needs we might have. The various gowns we spoke of are also ready.'

'And the new riding clothes?'

'Completed. You didn't want new boots too, did you?' the seamstress asked, frowning, her mind already racing towards how quickly the cobbler might work.

'No, I like my comfy old ones,' Valentyna replied.

'As I understand it from our earlier discussion, your highness, we depart for Morgravia in ten days?'

'Yes. The wedding was supposed to be at the close of spring but I see no point in holding off and will send a message today to King Celimus. It should please him. I'll have one of my assistants confirm everything with you shortly. We'll take it slowly with a view to four days' journeying. I can visit some of the towns and villages along the way to pay my respects to our people.'

'I imagine the party will be quite large,' Margyt commented as she sliced through the threads that had effectively stitched the Queen into her wedding gown.

'I suppose so,' Valentyna said, not really caring. 'Perhaps Commander Liryk will split it into smaller groups and send them by different routes.'

'Yes, that would be sensible,' the seamstress agreed. Then: 'Are you giving the King a ring, your highness?'

The Queen nodded. 'Studded with jewels in the colours of Briavel.'

'Lovely,' Margyt said, as she helped her sovereign to lift the gown over her head.

'Why are you alone this time?' Valentyna's voice was muffled from beneath the garment.

'Because I don't want my girls twittering that our Queen goes to her marriage as if to a funeral,' Madam Eltor admonished. 'I sensed from our last fitting that you were not getting any pleasure from the preparations. I thought privacy was best, your highness.'

'Thank you again, Margyt. Your sensitivity always makes you my favourite,' Valentyna said, finding a playful tone.

The seamstress responded, glad of it. 'Oh? I hear Master Rilk gets plenty of your business, your highness,' she said archly.

'He wanted the wedding gown,' Valentyna replied, pulling on her clothes.

'The cheek of the man!'

The Queen laughed. Madam Eltor and Master Rilk had

been married for as long as she could remember. And between them they crafted everything Valentyna wore.

'I will take my leave, your highness. There's still plenty for me and my girls to do.'

'You're a treasure. I promise to be smiling next time we see each other.'

'Make sure of it, child. You will be preparing to take holy vows in the grand Pearlis Cathedral next time I stitch you into this gown.'

Madam Eltor's words remained with Valentyna long after she had departed, reminding the Queen that there was no way off the path she was now on. Her meeting with the nobles had gone badly. Having called them together to broach, once again, the subject of the marriage being a sham, Valentyna had been met with cheers and rounds of congratulations that the Legion had begun to withdraw from the border. Word had begun to filter down from the north as troops dropped away.

She had listened to the deep voice of Lord Vaughan, quietly praising her actions in returning Ylena Thirsk to King Celimus, and when Valentyna had displayed astonishment that he could know such a thing, Lord Vaughan had simply nodded and admitted that there were spies everywhere.

'Watching me, do you mean, sir?'

'Observing all that happens in the capital, your majesty,' he had corrected with his habitual sombre expression.

The nobles were a network of their own, she realised for the first time, and there were few secrets, if any, she could protect. It was a useless exercise gathering them like this and hoping for their support. Now she knew for sure that they were counting the days to the marriage ceremony, many intending to take their families to bear witness to the event in Pearlis. Ylena Thirsk's arrival had made not a scrap of difference; in fact, they were delighted she had been returned to Morgravia, back into the clutches of its hateful King.

Valentyna had not even bothered to air her carefully planned speech. Instead, she smiled as required, accepted their praise and hid her despair behind the mask she knew she would now wear permanently at either court.

Nothing and no one was going to save her from Celimus. She wasted no further time in sitting down at her desk and crafting, with her own hand, a message to her groom to set a final date for their wedding ceremony.

Wyl recognised Myrt and several of the Mountain warriors, all of whom treated the stranger, Ylena, courteously. He was not sure what to think of this new situation. It felt dangerous – all his senses told him so – but at the same time it was reassuring to be back with Aremys.

Someone handed him a bowl of broth. 'My lady.' It was Myrt, Wyl realised, when he lifted Ylena's chin to glance at the owner of the soft voice. 'The King tells us you have been treated inhospitably in Morgravia.'

'He speaks true,' Wyl admitted.

'I'm sorry there is still a long journey ahead but he hopes you will eat something before we leave.'

'We leave tonight?'

'Yes, my lady. We wish to be deep into the Razors by midnight.'

'So you travel comfortably in the dark?' Wyl wondered.

'We need no light but the moon,' Myrt said, with a polite nod, then left.

The broth was surprisingly good. Hearty and rich with the flavour of meat. Wyl finished the bowl, glad for the warming nourishment. Aremys entered the cave holding a candle. He looked distracted and hesitant; Wyl figured it could not be easy for the mercenary to find time alone with the Mountain King's new captive.

'We're breaking camp now, leaving immediately. How are you?'

'Fed,' Wyl said. 'Myrt brought me food.'

'Does he know you recognise him?' Aremys asked, alarmed.

'No, I've been careful about it.'

'Good. He's sharp.'

'How much aren't you telling me about this turn of events?'

'There is more, but first let me tell you the story I've given to the King about you and I.' Wyl nodded and Aremys briefed him. Someone called into the cave that the King was preparing to leave in a few minutes. Aremys asked the man if scouts had checked that Celimus had sent no tracking party. The man confirmed that they had and there were no spies trailing them.

'So, are you going to tell me the rest?' Wyl asked. 'We don't seem to have much time.'

Aremys scratched his head. It was best to give it to Wyl straight, he decided. 'Cailech's taken a fancy to you.'

'Oh, Shar save me!' Wyl groaned. This was alarming news. 'You're serious, aren't you,' he said, and it was no question.

'It gets worse,' the big man continued.

'How can it?' Wyl asked, letting Ylena's head drop between her knees.

'During your absence from the hall, Cailech declared to Celimus that he would make you his wife.' Wyl looked up sharply. His horror was reflected in the Grenadyne's despondent expression. 'It took everyone by surprise. There was nothing I could do.'

'I understand, Aremys,' Wyl admitted, bile rising. 'You were helpless back there. But we're not helpless now,' he declared, standing to Ylena's full height which barely reached halfway up the mercenary's chest.

'Please, Wyl,' Aremys said, checking they were not being listened to. 'Go along with this for the time being.'

'Go deeper into the Razors, back to that fortress?' Wyl hissed. 'Are you mad? I've escaped it once. I don't think I'll be able to do it again.'

There was nothing for it but to tell Wyl all that he knew. 'I've found Gueryn,' Aremys said firmly, knowing it would stop Wyl's tirade.

It did. Ylena grabbed his shirtfront angrily. 'You're sure it's him?'

Aremys nodded. 'We spoke briefly. I said I'd come back for him. He's in the dungeon and, considering his situation, looks quite good for it, but now that Cailech knows Romen Koreldy is dead I fear for his life. And then there's Rashlyn, the most unpredictable factor in all of this. Apparently he's used magic on Gueryn a few times now.'

'What do you mean?'

'Too long in the telling now. Suffice to say it's been used for good in healing the arrow wound, but for bad too and it's rattled your old mentor.'

Wyl paced, pulling at his ear, thoughts racing as to what would be the best course of action. He did not want to go with Cailech – the Mountain King's intentions for him were just too revolting to contemplate. But Gueryn's needs called strongly. He could not desert his dearest, oldest friend, not after the sad way they had parted.

Aremys sensed Wyl needed a final push and gave it. 'I've also found Lothryn.'

Ylena's eyes blazed in the soft light. 'He's alive? I knew it!'

'But not how you remember him, Wyl,' Aremys cautioned.

'How so?' Wyl asked. His frightening dream at Felrawthy, of the man's voice screaming at him from behind a barn door, returned to haunt him.

Before Aremys could reply, Cailech appeared at the mouth of the cave. 'I hope I'm not interrupting anything?'

'I can't imagine it would matter if you were,' Wyl replied, flustered by his friend's various revelations and the discomfort of seeing his captor – his husband-to-be – smiling so disarmingly at him.

'No, I suppose it wouldn't,' Cailech admitted, his smile broadening. 'I hope my men have treated you deferentially, my lady?'

'Thank you, sire,' Wyl replied, remembering Ylena's manners. He glared towards Aremys though.

Cailech did not miss the glance between them. 'Ah, I suppose Aremys has explained why you're here.'

'He has, King Cailech.' Wyl was at a loss for what else to say. He understood his friend's reasons for wanting him to return to the fortress, but this was a perilous situation for him now.

'Don't be frightened, my lady. In the south you know us as barbarians but we may surprise you.'

'Romen Koreldy spoke highly of you, my lord. He told

me much about the ways of the Mountain People and I have an appreciation for your sophistication,' Wyl said, believing it best to flag now that he knew something of the culture. Any misjudgements he made in seeming too familiar with the Razor Kingdom, he might now be able to hide behind Romen's teachings.

'Did he now?'

'He liked you,' Wyl offered.

'I hope you will too, Ylena. Come now, we must journey.'

There was nothing for Wyl to do but follow the King's guiding hand. 'You will ride with me, my lady,' Cailech added, and it was fortunate indeed that neither the King nor Aremys saw the look of despair that swept across Ylena Thirsk's face at this news.

Wyl gritted his teeth and allowed strong hands to help him up onto the saddle, but much worse was the sensation of the King climbing up behind him. Cailech's arms passed around Ylena's tiny waist and took the reins from her.

'Allow me,' he said graciously.

Wyl grimaced towards Aremys who looked away in embarrassment.

'Comfortable, Ylena?' the King enquired.

'May I not ride a horse of my own, sire?' he risked.

He sensed the King's wry grin behind him. 'It is good for my men to see me take ownership of you, my lady. It is critical they understand how highly I regard you. Life in Morgravia is no longer possible, Ylena, you surely agree?'

'I do, my lord,' came the grudging reply.

'And it seems your life is now worthless in Briavel too, where a Queen must bow to the whims of her powerful neighbour and soon-to-be husband. So the only realm where your life can be protected – and, might I add, revered, my lady – is the Razor Kingdom. My men are surprised by your presence, I'll not lie,' Cailech said, his mouth so close to Ylena's ear, Wyl felt sickened. 'But in seeing us together like this, they will now offer you the highest respect, my lady, as befitting a noblewoman and my future wife.'

Gueryn was still smiling from the thrill of riding Galapek. Not even the sound of the door hammering closed on his tomb again – as he had come to think of it – or the sound of the key turning in the lock could tarnish the day's experience.

He, Jos and Rollo had taken the horses around the lake and beyond for several hours, returning late in the afternoon. Gueryn had felt exhilarated. It was true he had not had a chance to confirm his suspicions about Galapek, but the joy of being in the open and on a horse again was exquisite. He had wept towards the close of the ride, when they neared the stables again, embarrassing himself.

Jos had given him a consoling pat on the shoulder. 'I'm sorry you are our prisoner, Gueryn,' the young man had offered.

'I too am sorry,' Gueryn had replied, 'but thank you for this wonderful escape, however brief it has been.'

'What do you think of our fine stallion?' Maegryn had asked on their return.

'That I wish he was mine,' Gueryn had answered truthfully.

The stablemaster had laughed. 'Everyone does. But he belongs to our King.'

'Can I rub him down?'

'Most certainly,' Maegryn said, but sadly for Gueryn, who had hoped to be left alone with the horse, the head of the stables had remained.

Despite Maegryn's presence Gueryn had managed to whisper once to the horse, begging the animal to give him a sign that he was Lothryn but nothing had occurred. And yet he could not doubt the sincerity of the stranger, Aremys. As the incredible words had tumbled from the big man's mouth, horror lacing each one, Gueryn had nevertheless believed. His brief but terrible experiences with Rashlyn confirmed that the mercenary had hit on the truth.

Being Morgravian, Gueryn had always been scornful of magic; frightened of it too. Along with most Morgravians, he had accepted the persecution that not so long ago had been visited on anyone perceived as a witch or warlock. But now, after hearing Aremys's story and feeling the effects of Rashlyn's power for himself, Gueryn was forced to accept that magic was at the heart of the mystery surrounding the horse Galapek, and indeed Wyl himself.

Myrren of Baelup came to mind and, inevitably, Wyl's attempts to protect her from further suffering. The memory surfaced fresh and clear now. At the moment of the witch's death Wyl's eyes had changed colour, reflecting the exact strange hues of Myrren's eyes. The very reason for her persecution was mirrored in Gueryn's own beloved Wyl Thirsk. And he was not the only person who had seen it. The tiny gong boy, Fynch, had shared the experience. They had not both imagined the presence of some magic.

Gueryn's good mood evaporated as the sour thoughts

overtook his mind. If he could accept that Wyl had somehow been touched by the magic of the witch, then surely it was possible that Lothryn could be so remarkably changed by sorcery, especially when wielded by one so deeply wicked and heartless as Rashlyn. But what about Wyl? How had Myrren's magic affected him?

He was still wrestling with the question, haunted by the memory of how Romen had tricked him into believing he was Wyl, when the key turned again in the lock. Gueryn was startled. He moved back into the shadows, away from the nub of candle and its light which was now permitted him as a small kindness.

He instantly recognised the figure that appeared in the doorway and his stomach clenched in fear.

'Le Gant,' Rashlyn said, in his light, irritating voice. 'You can't hide from me in this dungeon.'

'Have you come to share my ration of water, Rashlyn, or perhaps some conversation?' Gueryn asked, forcing himself to fight back his fear.

The small man laughed. 'After tonight's proceedings, I imagine conversation will be the furthest thing from your mind. Take him,' he commanded to two men, who now pushed through the doorway. Gueryn recognised neither. His heart lurched with new terror.

'There will be a reckoning with your King over this, Rashlyn,' he warned in desperation, all bravado gone now. If he was to die at this man's hand, who would back up Aremys's claim?

'But it was the King who gave me permission, le Gant. He agreed that I could use you for my own . . . um . . . interests, shall we say. Come now. I'm sure we'll both find it interesting.'

Gueryn did the only thing left to him. He struggled with the guards and bellowed his protestations as loudly as his lungs could manage, in the faint hope that someone might hear and bear testimony to his disappearance at the hands of the barshi.

CHAPTER 25

Fynch lay still enough to be dead, curled on the floor of the small cave they had come to call home these past few days. Knave had worried throughout the first day at the boy's weakness, but Fynch had grown stronger through long healing sleeps and the dog had to assume that this was the way of the magic. No doubt Elysius had done the same. He regretted they had not asked the manwitch for more information about the sickness.

Kestrel had communicated that Elspyth was also healing through long rest periods after her surgery with Master Rilk. Knowing that Elspyth lived and would recover from her injuries had helped Fynch to let go of Wyl's friend and become more focused on the trial ahead and his own health.

Knave understood that the boy had no idea of what they were up against. Not even he could imagine it, to tell the truth, but he had heard the gravity in Elysius's voice when speaking of his brother and had seen how much the manwitch had fretted at the thought of passing the magic to such a youngster and essentially presenting him to whatever Rashlyn might do to him. But all of that had paled in comparison to the arrival of the Dragon King. His presence alone had impressed upon Knave the dire task they faced. For the King of the Creatures to come to them from his abode high in the mountains of the Wild, where no man or possibly no other animal had ventured, made it clear that Fynch's trial was more important than any of them could know.

The dog was still to ask Fynch about his claim to be the King of the Creatures. They had shared few words since that moment when Fynch had answered Kestrel's question so audaciously. But Knave was patient. Fynch's survival and his health was all that mattered right now.

The youngster stirred, his eyelids fluttering as consciousness arrived. Then his eyes opened and he regarded the dog. 'You make me feel so safe, Knave,' Fynch admitted.

Knave only wished he could protect the boy from all that was coming towards them. But this was no time to scare him. They needed to be strong together. *I'm never far, remember?* the dog replied.

Fynch sat up and stretched. 'I feel better than I have in days.'

You must eat, Knave said, unable to hide the elation in his voice.

'You sound like my sister.'

Well, perhaps it's because we both love you.

Fynch reached out to hug the dog. 'I'll eat for both of you then.'

He was able to start a fire with the smallest trickle of magic and Knave quietly marvelled at how quickly his friend had accepted and embraced his new powers. Fynch himself did not talk about or even comment on the wondrous nature of the new skills he possessed. Knave understood that the lad treated this gift as he treated everything in his life – with serious care. The dog knew Fynch would never be playful with the magic or test its boundaries; he would no more send messages to animals unnecessarily than he would try out his own ability to fly or even become invisible . . . if he could. Fynch simply accepted his lot, as presumably he always had.

The boy refused the rabbit which Knave had killed for him. 'I can't, it repulses me for some reason.'

You don't like rabbit?

The boy frowned. 'I don't think I like meat any more. How strange. I'll find some berries.'

There were some cirron berries growing nearby and Fynch made a meal of them with a knuckle of bread.

'I feel well enough to travel now,' he said in between tiny mouthfuls.

It is time we made a move, the dog agreed. He was about to say that they should travel as far as they could during the morning, and that Fynch should sleep in the afternoon before sending them ten leagues east or thereabouts, when Fynch cut across his thoughts.

'I'm going to risk Rashlyn today.'

This caught Knave off guard. *What do you mean?*

'Well, I'm tired of all this patience. I'm tired of feeling sick and wearied by the magic. If it's going to be this harmful to me, then let's not waste more time. Let's really use it.'

What are you talking about, Fynch?

'I'm talking about sending us all the way. I did it for you to Werryl, and I know I can do it now for the two of us. I can get us right to the door of the fortress if we feel that bold.' Then he grinned shyly. 'Perhaps I should send us somewhere a little safer.'

No! Knave replied. *Too risky, too dangerous for your health, too—*

'Hush, Knave. I know my limitations.'

I'm not sure you do, Knave said, more testily than he had ever spoken to the boy.

Fynch knew it was fear taking hold in the dog. 'Trust me. I think I can blur the magic.'

I do not understand. Exasperation gave way to weariness in the dog's tone.

Fynch shrugged. 'Hard to explain, but whilst I was sleeping I think I dreamed an idea or perhaps . . .' He hesitated.

Perhaps what?

'Perhaps the Dragon King spoke with me,' he finished, embarrassed.

Knave was surprised but he pressed on. *And?*

'I believe I can try and muddy the magic going out, so to speak. Whether Rashlyn senses it or not, I might be able to confuse him sufficiently that he can't lock onto us or what we are.'

That's a big gamble.

'Yes, but time is not on our side. I'm getting bad feelings about things.'

Things?

The boy pulled a face. 'Just a sense; again, hard to explain. I thought it was my fear for Elspyth but it's more than that. It's Wyl, it's Valentyna. There's something very bad happening in the Razors; something not right.'

Unnatural, you mean?

'That's it. That's exactly what I mean. There's a taint

of evil on the wind or in my mind. I can't tell. But it's talking to me in my dreams.

What do you see?

'I can't really see them, only sense them. Two men. Both in pain. One I believe I might know but can't be sure . . . I mean, how could I?'

And Rashlyn's behind it?

Fynch nodded glumly. 'I think he's the source of what's bad. I could send a creature to find out more . . . perhaps Kestrel even. But it's more time-wasting. We should go ourselves.'

Perhaps that's why the Dragon King spoke to you.

'Yes, it's what I believe. So will you trust me?' Fynch said, picking up his small sack and pulling it around his body.

Now?

The boy grinned again, not so hesitantly this time. 'I've already opened the bridge to the Thicket. It awaits us.'

Knave suddenly felt the thrum of magic from the Thicket. He took a deep breath. *I'm ready.*

Fynch put his arms around the dog and Knave sensed the pressure of the air thickening around them. He knew what came next and braced himself for it. The next thing they were rolling, but on this occasion Fynch had mastered his sending skills and had used a pillow of air to cushion their landing. Knave was on all fours in a blink and by the side of the little boy who was vomiting violently into the undergrowth.

Take your time, he whispered helplessly, wondering what kind of toll the magic would take this time, so soon after Fynch's last use of it.

Fynch grasped for his sack and the sharvan leaves. He

forced a handful into his mouth, which tasted sour from the recent meal he had lost.

Knave could only feel guilt that he had agreed to this madness when he had just managed to get his charge to eat something. *Sip lots of water*, he advised. *I'm going to scout around.*

Fynch said nothing, chewing intently to get the painkilling juices flowing down his aching throat. Using the magic might have been a good idea, but it was a bad one in terms of his health. He felt as though he could die.

Knave saw that the boy's eyes were bloodshot and, for the first time, a thin rivulet of blood ran from his nose. The dog felt uncharacteristically angry with everyone: himself, Elysius for passing on the magic, his King for entrusting this lovely child with such a huge task, even Fynch for accepting the challenge of sending them so far. He could not begin to count the cost this would take on the boy's health. He stalked away, his mood as dark as the fur that covered his body, and blended into the cover of the foliage. When he returned, his companion lay on the ground; he looked dead. Alarmed and forgetting what he had hurried back to tell, the dog nuzzled the boy, his fear almost making him whine.

'Knave?' Fynch croaked, his complexion ghostly as he raised his head.

I'm here, the dog replied, his relief evident. *There are people coming and horses, quite a reasonable number of them, but we're well hidden so we just need to remain still.*

'It's Wyl,' Fynch said groggily.

The dog was confused. Wyl was in Briavel, with Valentyna. *How do you know?*

'When I sent us, I tried something new.' He coughed

and blood splattered from his mouth. 'I'm sorry,' he said, his tone flat.

No! I am, Knave said, his anger at last finding its way into his tone. *This is not right, Fynch. You're going to die if you don't stop using this magic.*

Fynch looked at his friend with a sad expression. 'I'm going to die soon anyway, Knave. Be at peace over this. I accepted my end gladly. I have met Roark and I have paid homage to the Dragon King, and I have been privileged to know you. I am prepared,' he said gravely.

The dog was lost for words, so Fynch continued, wiping his bloodied mouth on his sleeve. 'I cast out as we travelled, trying to lock onto Rashlyn and using the magic of the Thicket to shield us. I found Wyl instead. I think the Thicket did this deliberately.'

Why?

'Probably because Wyl is not meant to be in the Razors. He should be in Briavel with Valentyna. It's warning me. It knows Wyl and I are linked souls.'

Did it tell you what to do?

'No, unfortunately. That's up to us, Knave. I think we should just follow at a distance and take stock of the situation. He's surely not here by choice.'

Are you up to following them?

'I'll manage,' Fynch said.

Knave had to look away, unable to bear the pain in the boy's face. *They'll be a few minutes yet*, he said. *Just lie down until then.*

For once Fynch obeyed.

Crys made a sound of exasperation. 'It's too soon.'

'I don't want to spend another second in this blood-soaked place,' Elspyth said, grimacing as she pulled her cloak on.

'Please, Elspyth. At least let me take you to Sharptyn.'

'No, Crys. I want to leave the region. I nearly died here and I'm not talking about from my wounds. Before you arrived . . .' Her voice quavered but she steadied it. 'Before you brought the Briavellian Guard, which I still haven't thanked you for.'

He waved her embarrassment aside. 'Master Rilk said—'

'Master Rilk is a tailor!' Elspyth cut across his words. 'I'm grateful to him, grateful to you all, but I'm leaving now.'

'Where will you go? Surely not into the Razors?' he beseeched. His hurt expression added new injury to her aching heart.

'No. I'm not fit enough for that. I shall go home first.' She looked around her. 'This place almost looks . . .' she searched for the right word '. . . clean again.'

Crys risked reaching forward and buttoning her cloak for her. 'Liryk and his men have done a good job.'

Elspyth smiled at his gesture but wished he would not show his affection for her quite so openly. 'They have. When does the Guard move out?'

'Today, I believe.'

'Then my timing is perfect. And you? Where will you go?' she asked. Where could he go that was not hostile?

Pain fleeted across Crys's open face but he wrestled his expression back under his control. 'Not Briavel. I'm a hindrance there and Valentyna will be making preparations for her journey to Morgravia now.'

'Poor soul. She intends to go through with it then?'

'She has no choice. I don't believe it can be avoided, Elspyth. And with Wyl taking himself off to die again at the hands of Celimus . . .' He trailed off.

'She could just say no,' Elspyth blazed, then grimaced at the sour look her words won from her friend. 'No, I know. That would mean war. Do you think the next time we meet Wyl, he'll be the King of Morgravia?'

Crys gave an involuntary bark of a laugh. 'Oh, I don't know,' he said, a helpless tone in his voice. 'Wyl's so stoic. Where did he find the courage to march into Celimus's den, knowing he goes towards a horrible death?'

Elspyth sighed. 'I think we're all capable of being heroic when it comes to those we love, Crys,' she said sadly, and knew he understood by his equally sorrowful nod.

'Well, a happy ending for Wyl and Valentyna perhaps?' he tried brightly.

'But not for us, eh?' she responded in kind.

'It could be if only you'd let it,' he said then wished he had not. 'I'm sorry, Elspyth.'

She accepted his apology readily. 'Come with me,' she said, knowing how badly the Duke of Felrawthy needed the anchor of friendship, and she herself did not feel like hitching any more rides with strangers for a while.

'Really?' Crys said. He could hardly believe he had heard right.

A smile lit Elspyth's face. 'Why not, but there are terms.'

'Of course. No kissing or any attempt at seduction,' he said, grinning. 'No suggestion that Lothryn is a wasted cause or that you're too small, too fragile, too womanish to save him.'

She laughed openly now. 'I like that you use your wit to hide your emotions, Crys,' she said, meaning it with affection.

'It's all I have now. I feel so bruised and battered, I need to hide. Thank you for allowing me to accompany you. I won't let you down, Elspyth.' They both knew what he meant by that comment.

'I appreciate that,' she said. 'Did Wyl have any ideas before he left?'

'Well, yes, he did suggest I could stir up some trouble within the Legion.'

'In what way?'

'Reinforce the name of Thirsk, remind the men that the Donals were true, insist that Celimus is a destroyer of realms.' He ran his hands through his hair. 'And a slayer of souls.'

She touched his arm. It was all the solace she could offer right now. 'Shall we go via Pearlis perhaps?'

'Could you stand to? I mean, it's not as direct as you probably want.'

Elspyth paused to consider his question. 'No, but I'm not really well enough to be any good to anyone, and a couple of extra days will not make much of a difference to my journey.'

'Perfect. Can you ride?'

'Let's take Ericson's cart. He's not going to be needing it,' she said, feeling ghoulish at her pragmatism. 'You have a horse, don't you?' He nodded. 'Then we're set. Let's go and do some damage to our King.'

Crys felt the thrill of danger course through him. He loved this woman's spirit. He wanted to kiss Elspyth, to tell her that his fondness for her was not diminishing and that it was unlikely he could keep all of his promises, but he would not break his word. He owed her that much.

Rashlyn stepped back to admire the fruits of his toil. He was drenched in sweat; it beaded in his tangled beard and soaked the already soiled shirt he had worn for days. He chuckled. 'Better, definitely better,' he muttered, and swallowed a cup of the rejuvenating brew he had made before he began his ugly work.

He knew from past experience that crafting this sort of magic was exhausting, but now he believed it actually drained the life from him. A measure of his essence had been used to create the spell – that was his sacrifice, the price he had to pay to get better at this manipulating magic. And better he had certainly become. The dog stood on all fours before him, trembling so badly Rashlyn was sure it would collapse soon. It snarled, despite its obvious suffering.

'I suspect that was none too pleasant for you,' he said to the creature. 'In fact, I imagine it was nothing short of excruciating. I'm surprised you lived through it . . . and rather pleased you did.'

Again the dog growled weakly, baring its teeth, pulling helplessly at the restraining chain that held it to a ring in the wall.

'How does it feel to be a dirty dog, le Gant? A filthy Morgravian dog?'

The dog leapt forward and managed to make the sorcerer flinch. But the chain dragged it back viciously and it fell over. It lay on the ground panting hard, eyes glazed, its energy spent.

'Oh, don't die on me now, le Gant. I do so want to

show the King my handiwork. I'm going to give you to him so he can feed you the crumbs from his table, or perhaps break your ribs with his boot if that takes his fancy. I suggest you change your attitude, Morgravian dog. You are nothing now. You never were,' he finished.

The dog snapped once, but so weakly that Rashlyn did not even hear its jaws come together. He was lost in admiration at his skill. The dog could hear and could react. The horse Galapek seemed nothing more than a void, but le Gant the dog showed spirit. Very good.

He was so close to full control now. He could hardly wait to present his latest creation to Cailech. Together they would rule not only the men of the land but its creatures and birds as well. Imagine Cailech going to war with the south with bears, wolves, wild cats, even a troop of ekons under his command – it was more exciting than Rashlyn had ever dared to dream.

The barshi left the semi-conscious dog to lie in its own mess, slamming the door shut on yet another tomb. The dog, hurting deeply and wondering how it could bring about its own death, whined softly as it passed into unconsciousness and a dream of running alongside a majestic black stallion.

CHAPTER 26

Wyl sank into a glum silence as their party neared the higher ground and the inevitability of the fortress. The terrain was familiar and once again he felt a weak but nevertheless sickening pull of Romen's fears as what little was left of him recognised where they were.

Cailech had been generous enough to leave Ylena to herself during the journey. At night she was permitted to sit alone in a tent made from animal skins which the warriors rigged up for her rest. Fresh water was always found for her ablutions and Cailech had even promised a dip in a hot spring where he insisted she would have privacy. He had been formal and courteous in all conversation and their only physical contact had been during the hours on horseback. Wyl realised that Cailech must be enjoying the feel of Ylena's slim body pressed against his chest and although Wyl made a huge effort to sit as far forward as he could, ultimately by day's end the journey would wear him down sufficiently that, without meaning to, he would be leaning against the King's broad, hard body. There were occasions when Cailech wanted to show something to Ylena and then he would win her attention by gently touching her arm or speaking quietly close to her ear as he pointed out a soaring eagle or a particularly jagged series of peaks, so distinctive to the Razors. And each time Wyl would withdraw just a bit further within to what was purely him.

This was the third morning and they had broken camp a couple of hours ago. Aremys dropped back to ride alongside Cailech in the middle of the party where his warriors insisted their King ride for safety. This deep into the Razors Cailech had no fears of ambush but he respected their desire to protect their sovereign. Wyl had been surprised to find that Aremys had essentially ignored him these past two days, preferring to keep company with Myrt and a fellow called Byl. He guessed that the mercenary was anxious and embarrassed by the situation Wyl found himself locked into.

'I imagine they're restless to be home now,' Cailech commented, nodding towards the men Aremys had just been talking with.

'They are. I don't think any of you Mountain People feel comfortable outside of the fortress and its compounds.'

Cailech grinned. 'This is a good thing.' He inhaled the sharp mountain air. 'Can you smell that, Ylena?'

'Yes.'

'Those are tiny white flowers called thawdrops which burst through at the first hint of spring and flourish towards mid-spring when their perfume becomes intense, as it is now. The fragrance is being blown here from the valley where you'll see the flowers soon. It's quite a sight. I shall pick you some.'

Wyl remembered the valley – it had been bare last time

he passed this way. It meant they were just miles from the fortress now. His stomach clenched at the thought.

'Your friend is very quiet, Aremys,' the King said, amused, as if Ylena was not there; not encircled by his arms, not the prisoner of his words or his promise to marry her.

Aremys shrugged, not daring to look Wyl's way. 'I hardly know her, my lord, to appreciate what her personality is like,' he said carefully.

'You have us baffled, Ylena, you see?' Cailech said and Wyl could feel the King's face touching the back of Ylena's head as he leaned forward. 'Are you not happy to have escaped Celimus again? Can you not share your pleasure with us?'

'I wanted to die, sire. You denied me my revenge.'

'How so?'

'I wanted the blood of both Thirsk heirs on his hands, your majesty. I wanted it mingling with that of the blood of the holy men of Rittylworth and the loyal souls of Felrawthy whom he had slaughtered.'

'And Koreldy's,' Cailech said quietly.

'Yes, Romen's too. And King Valor.'

'Do you think he will kill his bride?' Cailech suddenly asked, wonder in his tone.

Wyl flinched. 'He is capable of it.'

The King nodded. 'Is that his plan though, do you think?'

'No,' Wyl admitted. 'He wants heirs. Perhaps three, one to sit in each realm,' he added craftily.

It did not rattle Cailech as intended. 'I have an heir, Ylena,' he replied. 'His name is Aydrech, and I am hopeful you will give me more sons.'

Wyl felt a fresh wave of nausea, all his own, mingle with Romen's. He fought back, unwisely. 'I hear that Aydrech is not truly your own though, sire.'

Cailech's right hand left the reins and raised itself in the air. The men behind obediently slowed and stopped their horses, as did Cailech. Aremys looked uncertain, glancing between King and guest.

'What did you say?' Cailech said, his voice hard.

It was too late to retract it; besides, Wyl felt he had nothing to lose. He hated his life as Ylena and the threat of being touched by this man was coming closer by the minute. Death was surely stalking him whichever way he looked at it, because nothing in Shar's name could convince Wyl that sleeping with Cailech was worth any cause.

'You heard what I said, your highness, and your very reaction proves its truth.'

Myrt had dropped back. 'My King, is everything all right?'

'Move all the men forward, Myrt. I have a private discussion to finish.'

The big warrior nodded and shot a surreptitious glance towards Aremys who also felt the dangerous tingle in the air but had no idea what was going on. The other horsemen moved by, averting their eyes, and Aremys made to follow.

'Wait, Aremys,' the King commanded, leaping down from his horse with agile grace. He walked around to where he could look his bride-to-be directly in the eye. Wyl knew that stare well. 'Now, Ylena. Finish what you have to say or I shall slit your throat here and now.'

'I have said it, my lord, so go ahead and do your worst,' Wyl replied. 'Celimus wants your kingdom. He wishes to destroy it and you. He dreams of empire, your majesty, can you not see that? If he has a brood of children with Valentyna, he will ensure each takes a throne for maximum control.'

'He may try, Ylena,' Cailech said, gentle condescension in his voice, 'but he will not succeed.'

Wyl shrugged Ylena's narrow shoulders. He could not care less about either of these ambitious Kings. There was only one sovereign now whose life he would protect and, sadly, she was the one most likely to lose it.

'It is not your prediction, however, that intrigues me, my lady. It is your accusation,' Cailech continued.

Wyl remained silent. Aremys shifted uncomfortably on his horse.

'What do you know about my son?' Cailech said, and his tone was now edged with a fire that had not been directed at Ylena previously.

'Only what I said, sire.'

'And how do you come by such information?'

Wyl considered his options in those few moments of highly charged tension. He was tempted to say that he had learned it from a dream, but then visions of Ylena being hailed as some sort of witch and handed over to Rashlyn's care came to mind. He decided that no one could hurt Romen any more, so he could be the scapegoat.

'It was Koreldy.'

The King looked shocked. 'How could he know?'

Aremys wanted to know as well, although he feared Wyl's answer and feared even more this nest of vipers which Wyl had seemingly deliberately uncovered.

'Did anyone mention to you the love between Romen

Koreldy and Queen Valentyna, my lord?' Wyl asked, and enjoyed watching the surprise flit across Cailech's face and then immediately be masked.

'You jest, of course.'

'I have no reason to, your majesty. You heard Celimus tell you that Romen was at Werryl Palace, acting as champion to Queen Valentyna.'

Cailech nodded. 'She fell for his charms,' he said, and smiled at an old memory of Romen's flirtatious manner.

'She fell in love, your highness,' Wyl corrected. 'He was not charming her . . . he was wooing her.'

'It sounds like Koreldy,' Cailech said, somewhat disparagingly. 'So what?'

'So he told her things – things he would normally keep to himself. A man truly enraptured by love reveals far more than he would to a woman he simply lusts after.'

'He told her about my son,' the King finished.

'He told her about a man called Lothryn whose wife bore a new son, sire.'

'Aydrech is of my flesh, Ylena . . . or perhaps the Queen did not hear the whole story.'

'She knew of it, my lord, and mentioned as much. Lothryn explained to Koreldy about the boy. I gather it shocked Romen, as it does me, to learn that you would take another man's wife purely to produce an heir.'

At this the King found his lazy grin again, which infuriated Wyl. 'As I am doing with you. You were married to Alyd Donal. I'm sure he won't mind if I bed you, although I am sorry that you see me in such a harsh light. I am genuinely intrigued by you, Ylena. You have kindled a fire in me I have not felt burn so bright.'

'And I'm supposed to be flattered by that?' Wyl asked

incredulously. 'What about how I feel?' he hissed. 'You are treating me with the same contempt that Celimus treats Valentyna.'

Cailech did not react to Ylena's stinging words but changed topic adroitly, frustrating Wyl who had hoped to enrage the King sufficiently to end Ylena's life here and now. But Cailech was too wise to fall for the baiting. 'You sound as if you admire the Queen, Ylena.'

Wyl shook Ylena's head at the deft way Cailech could defuse tension. He glanced at Aremys, who looked as anxious as he had in the hall at Felrawthy. 'I do, more than any other woman I've ever met, sire.'

Cailech made a sound of disgust. 'This is the same woman who sold you out to Celimus, knowing full well he was hunting you down and was determined to kill you.'

Wyl's anger flared. 'And if you believe that, your highness, you are even more ignorant than the southerners believe you to be.'

It happened fast. Wyl felt Ylena's body being wrenched from the saddle. Cailech's strength was immense and her body in his hand was like a rag doll. She hung on the end of the Mountain King's fist, the tips of her boots only just touching the unforgiving rock they stood on. Aremys was off his horse in a blink, unsure of what to do.

Cailech dragged Ylena even closer. 'Don't you dare use that high-handed Morgravian tone with me, Lady Ylena. Remember, you breathe only because I allow it.'

'Then disallow it, sire,' Wyl taunted. 'Kill me now as you threatened. I don't wish to marry you. I would sooner die. Why can't you understand that I went to Celimus to lose my life?'

The light green gaze narrowed and studied her hard. 'You went to Celimus? Willingly?'

Wyl nodded as best he could in that grip.

The King let go of Ylena and Wyl explained. 'Valentyna was as determined not to release me from her protection as I was to leave it. She could not help me, sire. But I could help her. Presenting myself to Celimus, as if I had been relinquished by his bride-to-be, meant I could probably get the Legion called off. It only needed some small spark to ignite a fire which could turn into war and Celimus is so unpredictable that I could not be sure he wouldn't welcome it. So I made the sacrifice.'

'Why? Why do you owe her anything?'

Wyl had no ready answer to this most pertinent question. 'Because Wyl died trying to save her, to save her father. My brother must have had good reason to swap his allegiance to Briavel, sire. Can you imagine a Thirsk doing that without cause?'

Cailech said nothing, continued to stare at Ylena. Wyl looked towards Aremys whose expression begged him to win back Cailech's trust. 'I decided to give what little I had to General Wyl Thirsk's cause, my lord: Queen Valentyna. I have no reason to live. She has every reason to. Don't be misled, my King, Valentyna alone is what stands between Celimus and the Razor Kingdom.'

'How so?'

'I think she can influence him. If she handles this right, Valentyna might just guide him from the path of war.'

'I don't know her but I agree,' Cailech admitted. 'Something occurred back there at Felrawthy. I can't be sure but my instincts usually serve me true. I believe Celimus might hold to the promise we made to each other.'

'And you, my lord?'

'I have no reason to start a war, my lady, or I would not have wasted my own time or breath in meeting with Celimus.'

'I would be lying if I said I was not impressed.'

'Perhaps we can build on that then?'

Wyl looked sharply at Cailech. 'What do you mean?'

'I mean, Ylena, that I understand your reluctance to be here and your fear of the Mountain Kingdom, its people and particularly its sovereign. But perhaps my determination to forge a lasting peace with the south is a place from which we can build this new relationship. Your life is forfeit anywhere outside of the Razors – you do understand that, don't you?'

Ylena nodded.

'Good. Then take my protection. It is mine to bestow on whom I please. I will not rush you, my lady, but I will make you my wife. I have given my word to our neighbour. It is on that understanding that he released you.'

Cailech watched her take a breath to interrupt and went on: 'I know you wished for death. I could see it in your eyes. But I will not permit such beauty to be wasted, nor such a feisty spirit. You are the last of the great Thirsk family, Ylena, surely you wish to see its name flourish again?'

Wyl was ill-prepared for Cailech to touch on the very topic that was closest to his heart; one that provoked such a storm of emotion and pain for him. He felt Ylena's eyes water and turned away. It was in that moment of despair that he caught sight of a dark shadow which disappeared almost the instant he saw it. Knave! It was definitely the dog. Which meant Fynch was here too. Why?

New fears and confusion erupted. He was cold and he was tired. Ylena's fragile body needed rest and it was obvious he could not provoke Cailech into a swift killing. Despite his private anxieties, he could not help but feel his spirits lift at the thought that his friends were close. How they could be here was a mystery but it meant help. He would have to go along with Cailech's plan for now and rethink his options once inside the fortress.

And so he gave Cailech a response which he knew would please the King. 'I wish that more than anything in the world, sire. I just could not see how the Thirsk name could survive.'

'Through me, Ylena,' Cailech said gently, greatly relieved by her answer and beguiled by her sorrowful beauty. 'I give you this pledge: any child of ours will bear the name of Thirsk. This will infuriate Celimus, of course, which is really rather satisfying,' he said, winking at Aremys. 'Does this please you, my lady? I would allow you to call him Fergys or even Wyl to honour your dead.'

'It pleases me, sire,' Wyl replied, taken aback by Cailech's generosity.

'Then come, my lady. Let me take you to your new home and allow me to show you off to your new people. I will make you a Queen, Ylena.'

Wyl sighed and dredged up a wan smile for Ylena's face. 'You honour me, sire,' he said. His mind was racing for a way to escape the Razors again and quickly – or, at the very least, to die trying.

Fynch could barely raise his head when Knave returned.

It is Wyl, as you warned. I think he is with King Cailech, the dog said.

The news roused Fynch, although he could not sit up, could only open his eyes. 'How do you know it's the Mountain King?'

I heard them talking and I saw the men defer to him. Ylena shares his horse and his cloak is far grander than any of the other men who travel with him.

'How in Shar's name could this have occurred?'

No point in us speculating. They had an altercation. From what I can gather, Wyl was at Briavel but somehow convinced Valentyna to hand him over to Celimus.

'Celimus! Where is he?'

I couldn't tell from their conversation. But I do know Wyl tried to get himself killed.

'He cannot invite death!' Fynch exclaimed and coughed. Knave saw blood on the boy's hand when he took it away from his mouth. 'Elysius mentioned it to us, remember . . . after Wyl stormed out of the cottage in the Wild?'

I do. He risks much — the King got angry but it didn't go any further.

'We've got to see him, Knave,' Fynch bleated, feeling helpless.

You don't seem so well. Knave deliberately kept his voice toneless.

'I'll be all right,' Fynch replied, lying. It did not fool Knave.

Stand up then. Let's be on our way. The dog loped off.

Fynch tried and failed. Tried again. Knave reappeared, looming over him. 'I'm so sorry,' the boy whispered.

The dog hardly heard the apology, his mind searching for the best course of action. *You can't stay here, Fynch. It's too open. The warrior scouts could pick you up.*

'I can drag myself to somewhere perhaps?' the boy offered, feeling ashamed that he had let Knave down.

Use what strength you have and climb onto me.

It was obvious that Fynch understood the depth of his sickness or Knave knew he would have objected. Instead the boy used his reserves of will and somehow got himself draped across the large animal's back.

I'm sorry, Knave.

Don't send! Save yourself. Now let me get you somewhere safe and dry.

Knave moved silently and slowly, picking his way, careful not to dislodge the child lying across him. He hardly felt the weight. The boy fell asleep and the dog was relieved. At least with sleep there was no pain. A new thought came to him, so strong that he stopped walking. The Thicket! It could send them both to a safe spot, surely? It had done so before when they were travelling. He called to the magical place; disappointment knifed through him when it replied and he learned that he was no longer connected to it in the same way. He could feel its magic but only through Fynch's link. The Thicket had turned its focus to the boy. Knave was considered part of Fynch now and no longer had the powers of the Thicket at call. He wished he could tell it that Fynch was dying, but then he grasped that the Thicket probably knew and had made its own decision.

He pressed on towards a ridge and sent a plea to whoever might be listening that there would be some protection here from the elements, and that it would not be the final resting place of Fynch the gong boy.

Kestrel had tried to reach Fynch but could not raise a response. He had followed the pretty woman and her companion as far as the outskirts of the big southern city known as Pearlis. It was obvious they were headed into its centre and that was where he would lose them, he figured, and wanted to let Fynch know. He sighed as he watched the two people blend into the constant flow of people either making for or leaving the main city gates; time for him to leave. Kestrel dipped his wing to the right and made a new course. It was warmer here and he would not have minded a few days of hunting with the sun warming his outstretched wings. Spring was already turning its face to welcome summer in the south, but north was where Kestrel was headed – to cooler climes and an intriguing young lad who compelled Kestrel to obey him and dared to call himself King of the Creatures.

Elspyth had no idea that a bird of prey had just bade her a silent farewell. She was not feeling at all well and, for all her bravado, thanked Shar's blessing that he had seen fit to send her an angel in the disguise of Crys Donal. To tell the truth, without Crys she wondered how she would even have left Briavel. Sheer will was one thing but having the physical strength to carry out one's will was a different matter entirely. Her injuries reminded her constantly of her ordeal and the pain sapped her energy. She would never have made it into Morgravia if she had carried out her threat to head off alone. Yentro seemed wishful thinking, and the Razors and Lothryn a plain impossibility now.

Self-pity was corrosive and pointless. She pushed away the melancholy that threatened to overwhelm her and permitted Crys to use his body to shield her against the sudden crush of people. They had travelled in the cart until they neared the city and then left it at the roadside for some fortunate finder. Crys's horse carried them both from there, but progress was slow because of the stream of people flocking into and out of Pearlis. Still, it was not nearly as crowded as Elspyth's last journey into the city, when she arrived with her aged aunt for the tournament. That felt like a lifetime ago and yet she would have fingers to spare if she counted back in moons. Was it really such a short period since she had first clapped eyes on Romen Koreldy in Yentro, before she had learned that he was no longer the dashing mercenary but General Wyl Thirsk of Morgravia?

She thought about Wyl as Ylena; felt a pang of sorrow for his suffering and wondered where he was now. Was Ylena already dead and Wyl walking as someone new? Time alone would tell. Time and a password which would reassure them he still lived.

'A regal for your thoughts?' Crys murmured from behind.

'That you're clutching me too close,' Elspyth replied.

He squeezed her harder. 'My only legitimate chance,' he said.

'Is it always this busy?'

'Yes, so I gather. Still, it was a good idea of yours to ditch the cart and expensive clothes.'

'How does it feel to be an ordinary citizen?'

'Better. The Donal name is cursed for the time being.'

'We'd better think of a name for you.'

'I can be your brother, how's that?'

'I approve. I've always wanted a brother.'

'And what would you call a brother if you had one and could choose?'

'Jonothon.'

'That's who I am for the time being then. I'll hop down and lead you in on the horse. Hopefully we'll slip by unnoticed.'

'There's no register at Pearlis,' Elspyth offered.

'Nevertheless, some bright spark might recognise me. Alyd and I are . . . were incredibly alike in appearance.'

'Good idea to tie your hair back like that then.'

'Thank you, sister. Here we go. Don't look anyone in the eye but don't avert your gaze too obviously.'

'Let's just talk. You're making me nervous with your instructions.'

'So how old would cousin Jemma be now?' Crys replied, without skipping a beat.

They were passing through the main gate now and Elspyth risked a laugh towards Crys. 'Oh, I think she'd be marriageable age. I hear she's very pretty.'

'I don't like flaxen-haired women. I like dark-haired beauties as you well know,' Crys continued conversationally. He nodded at a guard, who ignored him, and then he laughed. 'I am not marrying her even if it does mean you can come and live in the city.'

'We're through,' Elspyth said, touching his shoulder with relief.

'Well done.'

'Now where?'

'Lord and Lady Bench are old friends of our family. I think they're the best starting point and they will be able to get some medicines for your pain. You look pale.'

'Are you sure we'll be welcome?'

Crys grinned his reassurance. 'Trust me.'

'Famous last words,' she groaned but felt safe for his

confidence. She could tell that the wound on her shoulder had reopened and was glad her cloak was dark enough not to give away their secret. 'Let's hurry.'

It took longer than Crys had anticipated to wend their way into the quieter, more affluent neighbourhood where Lord and Lady Bench kept their family home. In the end, he stabled their horse and hailed a carriage to take them the final half mile or so.

'This is better, Elspyth. If for any reason their house is being watched . . .'

'Why would it be?' she said, collapsing into the seat.

Crys gave the driver instructions. 'I don't know,' he said patiently. 'But we should know from his track record that Celimus is too smart to allow one of the most powerful people left in this kingdom to go about his business without some form of observation.'

Elspyth did not want to talk any more. It was all she could do just to hold herself together now. The pain had stepped up to a most determined throb, she could feel heat at the shoulder wound and her head was pounding.

'Infection,' Crys muttered when she told him. 'You need a physic. The Benches will see to it.'

'Let's hope they're home.'

Fortunately the Bench mansion was encircled by a huge privet hedge and the driver was able to take them into the sweeping driveway and unload them unseen, not that he was aware of any clandestine behaviour from the couple he was depositing. Crys paid him some extra coin nevertheless; it might buy silence for a while. Then he all but carried Elspyth to the door, which was swiftly opened by a dour-faced servant.

'Is the family at home?' Crys enquired.

'That depends, sir,' the man said, looking the shabby couple up and down. 'Who is calling?'

'If Lord Bench is in residence please inform him that . . .' Crys hesitated; perhaps this fellow could not be trusted. It paid to be cautious. 'Tell him it is an old family friend from Brightstone.' Crys remembered that the Bench family had a seaside property in the far north-west, and also recalled a nickname his father had for his long-time friend. He had called him 'Booty', for apparently there was no item that Eryd Bench could not appropriate if he set his mind to it.

'I will need a name, sir,' the servant said. He had an irritating manner of condescension, closing his eyes as he contrived a fake smile.

Crys took a breath. 'Just say it's Booty. Now hurry, man, this woman needs medical attention.' Elspyth was feeling like dead weight in his arms, although she was conscious and gave him a brave grin as the manservant disappeared.

'Booty?' she asked.

'It will work, I promise. The main thing is that he is home.'

They stood awkwardly in a hush for a minute then suddenly there was a lot of noise. A plump, powdered woman came bustling through some double doors closely followed by a tall, silver-haired gentleman, presumably Eryd Bench.

'Shar's wrath,' the woman exclaimed. 'Is that woman sick?'

'She is, my lady, and urgently requires attention.'

Before Crys had finished speaking, the older woman, obviously Lady Bench, had turned to the manservant.

'Arnyld, why are you still standing there? Fetch help, man, and send a runner for my physician at once! Tell Physic Dredge to waste no time.' She turned back to Crys. 'Put her over here, son,' she said gently, pointing to a long low bench seat.

'I'm bleeding, Lady Bench,' Elspyth began, 'I'll ruin—'

'Hush, child,' Helyn admonished. 'Do as you are told.'

Crys obeyed. He bowed and took his chance whilst there were no servants visible, turning to Lord Bench. He was met by a grim-faced stare.

'I wondered who had the audacity to use old Jeryb's nickname for me to gain entry,' Eryd Bench said in his melodious voice. 'Introduce yourself truly now, before I call a Legionnaire.'

'Lord and Lady Bench, my apologies for arriving in this manner; but circumstances demand it. I am Crys Donal, Duke of Felrawthy.'

The couple standing before him were obviously too shocked to respond. They looked thunderstruck and Lady Bench reached for her husband who helped her to sit down next to Elspyth. Crys felt instantly guilty and looking at their blanched expressions he was relieved to know the physic was on his way.

CHAPTER 27

Knave whined softly, his great head on his paws, his body encircling the sleeping boy whose breathing sounded dangerously shallow. Something was happening to Fynch but his close companion could not reach him. All he could do was watch, wait and pray to the Dragon King that this was not Fynch's time.

Fynch was dreaming but it was not like any dream he had ever experienced previously. He felt himself flying, with the wind whipping through his hair and whistling past his ears. He thought he might be dreaming he was a bird. But the view around him looked too real, the wind felt too real, and so was the voice that suddenly spoke.

Not long now.

It was the Dragon King and Fynch realised he was riding him, feeling each powerful beat of his wings as they worked in tandem to drive the creature faster through the air.

My King, Fynch sent, his voice unashamedly filled with awe. *Where do we go?*

*To a private place, my son. Somewhere safe. Where you will
be free from your pain and where no one can hear us.*

Am I truly with you?

Your body is with Knave, Fynch. Your spirit is here.

How can I do this?

It is my way of honouring you.

Honouring me?

We ask so much of you.

Whatever you ask, sire, I give it gladly.

Brave boy. You are more than worthy.

Of what, my lord?

Of Kingship, Fynch.

Fynch did not understand.

You will, the King said gently into his mind.

What, sire?

Understand. It is why I have brought you here.

Wyl felt a sense of despair as they entered the gates of
the fortress. Cailech was immediately surrounded by well-
wishers welcoming back their King, and stealing interested glances towards the golden-haired beauty he had
left on the horse. It was Myrt who arrived at Ylena's side
to help her dismount.

'May I show you to your rooms, my lady?' he asked,
taking her hand to help her from the horse, much to Wyl's
discomfort. 'The King has requested you attend supper
with him later.'

Wyl worked hard not to show how he felt about such
an invitation. It reminded him of being trapped in Leyen
and having to meet Celimus. 'Thank you, er . . . ?'

'Myrt.' Aremys had arrived and now offered the formal
introduction. 'He is a friend, Ylena. You can trust him.'

Wyl nodded towards Myrt who gave one of his rare smiles. Aremys had already explained that Myrt knew about Aremys's suspicion of Lothryn's fate, but he could not come clean about Ylena and so the etiquette of Aremys being polite but distant to Wyl's sister had to be observed.

'I will see you later perhaps?' Aremys said to Wyl, and then to Myrt, 'Shall we meet at the stables?'

The big warrior nodded. 'Come, my lady,' he said, and Wyl had no option but to be guided away, deeper into the fortress of the Mountain King.

They had landed but Fynch remained curled on the Dragon King's vast back. The creature's darkly vibrant colours seemed to pulse bright one moment and soft the next, illuminating its scales. Fynch felt warm and safe for the first time since leaving the Wild, yet he knew he was not really here. He was back on a freezing ledge near the home of the Mountain King and he was dying, with Knave's body curled around him.

He twisted to lie on his back, loving the deep connection between himself and the Dragon King. The magnificent beast remained silent whilst his guest acclimatised himself to the breathtaking scene below. They were on the highest peak of the Razors, but not in the north-east where Fynch's body lay.

Are we in the Wild, my lord?

Yes, Fynch.

The boy sighed. *If I died now amongst this beauty, my King, I would die happy.*

The King did not reply.

I am dying, aren't I, sire?

This time the creature did answer. *You have pushed yourself too hard. The magic you have called upon is so potent it is poisoning you.*

Elysius managed to live with it, Fynch said.

This is true, son. But Elysius did not draw upon the magic of the Thicket, nor was he required to use magic for years on end. He preserved himself by prudent use.

I am sorry I have been so careless with it.

The Dragon King twisted his sinuous neck and his massive head came close. A monstrously large eye, which seemed to Fynch to be all-knowing, regarded the tiny figure that lay on its back. *You need make no apology to me, Faith Fynch.*

It moved Fynch to hear these solemn words and tears ran down his face. *I am not afraid to give my life, my lord – I hope you know this. But I am so afraid of failing you that I am impatient to reach Rashlyn.*

The Dragon King gave a murmured growl of agreement. *I know, child. You will not fail us.*

But I am not sure I can recover in time, my King. I will likely end my life where Knave and I lie.

That is why I have brought you here, Fynch, the King said, his voice so deep the boy could feel it rumbling the length of his own body, and yet it was so gentle in its tone. *I shall restore you. But, as always with magic, there is a price.*

I will pay it, Fynch said bravely. *I wish only for my strength back to do your bidding.*

I accept your sacrifice, and in return you deserve an explanation. I have seen something in you, Fynch, which you must know.

I felt it too, my lord, he admitted. *I sensed you recognising a part of me I barely know myself.*

Can you not guess, child?

Fynch considered the King's question and closed his eyes. Yes, he could guess, but he wanted to take this moment to be sure it was something he truly wanted to know. Fynch assumed that the price he must pay for the temporary restoration of his health was death. This did not deter or frighten him. He had already accepted as much, and if it had to be sooner rather than later, then he would not fuss. Life could never be the same anyway. He made his decision.

It is connected with my mother, I feel.

Go on.

Fynch felt a breeze break through the protective wings of the huge beast and brush against his cheeks. More tears were falling but he ignored them. He was not crying because he was sad or frightened; he was weeping because this was the most emotional moment of his life. The Dragon King was about to confirm a fact that was integral to Fynch's being. The boy understood that the knowledge was something he had always known but had held buried within, never even allowing it to surface as a tease to lure him to learn more. It was a secret but, even without clues, he had sensed it. It was something far more devastating than the magic which he had recently learned he possessed and that which he had been given. This secret had far-reaching repercussions and could affect the course of a realm were it revealed. But the secret had been kept until now.

I believe I am not of my named father's flesh.

A tremble passed through the Dragon King. *You are correct, my son. So who fathered you?*

Fynch did not want to speak the name. He didn't know

why he was so sure it was the truth; all he knew was that in the moment the Dragon King saw it, he had glimpsed it within himself too. It had surprised the King of the Creatures, but for some strange reason it had not surprised Fynch; it had empowered him. It was one of the reasons he could face death now with no grief other than the loss of his siblings and Wyl.

Fynch looked out again over the majesty of the Razors, its hidden valleys emerging from beneath the snows as spring staked its claim.

I didn't know it would thaw this high up.

We are in the Wild, my son. Everything is possible.

Fynch nodded. The Dragon King was giving him plenty of opportunity to consider his decision, but now it was time. *My mother was fey. At each new moon she would experience a sort of madness, or so I was told. When I was old enough to understand it, I gathered that the madness took the form of lust.* He hesitated.

Go on, Fynch.

She would tempt other men. She had no control over it.

And?

I was conceived during one of those moon times.

Yes, you were. Who is your father, Fynch?

My father is . . . He almost dared not speak the name but knew he must. *My father is Magnus, King of Morgravia.*

Indeed. You are part of the dragon throne line and thus a part of me.

Was Magnus aware of who I was during our conversations at Stoneheart?

He felt a strong connection to you, Fynch, as you did with him. But no, he never knew you were of his flesh.

At the great creature's final word Fynch felt a rush

of warmth and love seep into his body. He did not know whether it was at the news of who his true father was or whether it was the dragon himself – but he was certain of some sort of new and intense link between it and himself. Whatever the reason, Fynch experienced a new and powerful sense of belonging to both Kings.

CHAPTER 28

Elspyth was propped in a chair, determined not to miss out on the conversation with Lord and Lady Bench. Helyn's physic had called, had commented that the wounds were neatly sutured and it was only the one at the shoulder which had begun an infection. Fortunately it had been caught in time and the physic promised to send over a course of a special brew that would clear up the problem within days. Rest and quiet were also integral to the healing. Helyn had not hesitated in confirming that Elspyth would remain with them until she was fit and well.

'I cannot impose on you for so long, my lady,' Elspyth said.

'Child, you'll be going nowhere until the fever is gone and the infection has cleared. Be assured of this,' Helyn had cautioned and Elspyth understood there would be no arguing with this powerful woman.

Now they sat comfortably in a drawing room hung with family portraits and softened with lush furnishings and drapings. Crys and Elspyth had related the worst part of their tale. A small porcelain brazier burned gently in the corner. Elspyth thought it similar to those the Mountain People favoured and said so.

'As a matter of fact it is from Grenadyn,' Eryd replied, 'but I am impressed that you have seen one in the Razor Kingdom and intrigued as to how a young woman – a Morgravian – has lived to tell the tale.'

Elspyth blushed. 'It is a long story, sir, and after the one we've just told you, I can't imagine you would want more of the same,' she said, hoping to deflect his attention from how she had come to be so far north.

'Indeed,' he said, eyeing her gravely but not pursuing it for now. After the story of the murder of the Donals, the Benches were already in a state of shock. 'Crys, I regret having to tax you further on this subject but are you quite sure that the Crown was behind the slaughter at Tenterdyn?'

Crys nodded. 'My mother died in my arms and her last wish was for revenge. Her haunted eyes spoke of the horrors she had witnessed – the killing of my father and brothers and then the burning of their bodies. The massacre at Rittylworth was also definitely the work of Celimus – Ylena Thirsk confirmed it and Elspyth happened along quite soon after the raiders had left. She took the message from Brother Jakub to my father.'

Helyn handed Crys a goblet of wine. 'None for you, I'm afraid, Elspyth. Sorry, please go on,' she said, with a soft smile to the young duke.

Crys hoped the tremble in his voice would disappear with the help of the liquor. 'As I explained, we have been at Queen Valentyna's court. She offered her protection without question. I hadn't expected the diversion of tracking down Elspyth,' he said, 'or I would have been here much earlier.'

'What can we do though?' Lord Bench wondered aloud. 'I feel so helpless.'

'Wy—' Crys stopped himself in time. 'Ylena suggested that I come to Pearlis and try to stir up some trouble for the King.'

'Ylena Thirsk did? Where is that girl now?' Lord Bench demanded. 'To tell the truth, I thought she must have gone home to Argorn after Wyl's death. Now we know about her husband's murder, all the more reason for her to flee Stoneheart.'

'No, sir. Ylena was thrown into Stoneheart's dungeons and it was a mercenary called Romen Koreldy who rescued her.' Crys quickly outlined how Koreldy fitted into the tale, manipulating the truth by telling them how he made a promise to the dying Wyl to find his sister. 'Then, after escaping Rittylworth, Ylena fled to Felrawthy. She carried proof of my brother's murder there with her – which is why Celimus sent his assassin to find her. Leyen, of course, never—' He stopped abruptly as both his hosts flinched with obvious alarm. 'Is something wrong?'

'Leyen?' Lady Bench said, her expression aghast. 'Is that the name you used?'

Crys nodded, glancing towards Elspyth for guidance. They were getting in deeper and everything pointed towards Wyl Thirsk. How would they keep him a secret?

'Can you describe this woman?'

There was little point in lying and Crys was not one to tell untruths to such fine people as the Benches, who had been close family friends since before he was born. He gave a quick summary of Leyen's appearance.

'But that's her!' Helyn exclaimed, her expression all confusion. 'I know this woman. She came to our house, for Shar's sake. I have been protecting her from Celimus since I first met her and he began asking questions about her. She told me she was a messenger — a go-between for the King and Queen Valentyna!' she said, exasperated.

'She is an assassin, you say?' Eryd said sombrely, looking towards his wife to be calm.

'Well . . .' Crys hesitated. He had made a mistake. He should have said Aremys Farrow, but how was he to know that the Bench family would know Faryl or Leyen or whatever her name was!

'Out with it, young man,' Eryd urged. Duke or not, Lord Bench saw Crys as a young pup still. It was inconceivable to Lord Bench, even after days of trying to accept it, that Jeryb Donal was dead. The old rogue was stronger than several oxen; he had been destined to outlive them all. Friendship aside, it upset Eryd deeply to think that Morgravia had lost not just such a fine man but also its finest remaining strategist and soldier. Celimus would pay for that loss.

Crys looked helplessly towards Elspyth. She knew he wanted to tell the truth, yet he would not break his promise to Wyl. Crys was trapped by duty whichever way he turned: to his parents, to the realm, to these fine people, to a friend. She had broken her promise to Wyl once before, though, and although there had been traumatic consequences, breaking that promise again was still easier for her than it would be for Crys to betray his oath to Wyl.

'My lord, my lady,' she interrupted, and both turned towards her, sensing something pivotal had just occurred. 'I have a story to tell, which you will not want to believe;

no doubt won't be able to believe once you have heard it.
But I am telling you the truth, for I have borne witness
to it with my own eyes.'

'As have I,' Crys joined in, a mixture of terror and relief
flooding his body as he saw that Elspyth had made the
decision for him. He hated breaking oath with Wyl but
he hated lying to Lord Eryd Bench even more, particularly as the old man reminded him so much of his own
father. And the truth was, they needed allies. Someone
had to help share the burden of Wyl's woes. It had sounded
fair enough at Tenterdyn to keep this terrible secret, but
someone in power had to know of Myrren's gift. Others
must be convinced and rally to Wyl's cause. All of this
churned in Crys Donal's mind as he justified to himself
what he and Elspyth were about to do.

Eryd glanced between them. 'This sounds dire,' he said.
He had thought he had heard their worst but it seemed
far more terrible information was yet to be revealed.

'Why do I suddenly feel I don't want to hear what you're
about to tell us?' Helyn Bench added, surprising herself
that in this instance she could resist a tantalising tale.

'You might regret our sharing of this with you, Lord
and Lady Bench. But once told, you must promise us you
will aid us and act on it.'

'My dear,' Helyn said, truly wishing now she had joined
her daughter, Georgyana, for a day of shopping, 'you make
it all sound so sinister. What is this about?'

'It is the story of Wyl Thirsk, and I shall tell you everything I know, even though he will never forgive me for
sharing it.'

Elspyth began.

*   *   *

As Elspyth was explaining the truth behind Wyl Thirsk's death to a stunned couple in Pearlis, in the Razors Wyl was explaining to the women attending Ylena that he preferred not to wear either of the two dresses that had been brought to his chamber.

Cailech had organised for Ylena to be accommodated in a suite of rooms. Once again, Wyl was arrested by the simple beauty of the Mountain People's creativity. A fresco of vines and their fruit trailed the circumference of each room's ceiling and the whitewashed walls were hung with paintings on wood of the stark Razor landscape. A thick rug on the floor and an equally colourful bedspread added yet more brightness to the natural light flooding in through the huge windows favoured by the King throughout the fortress; he liked to bring the mountainscape he loved inside.

Last time Wyl was in this stronghold, in winter, as Koreldy, braziers had warmed each room. Only the endless hallways and cavernous spaces connecting the chambers were left unheated, and those were freezing he recalled. But it was well into spring now and the hardy Mountain People had done away with the heating.

Ylena's body trembled from the cold as he tried again to politely decline the garments. 'Thank you, but I prefer not to,' he said.

'Both gowns are woven from the coat of polders, my lady,' the woman assured. Her tone suggested this was equivalent to being spun from gold.

Wyl was none the wiser for the explanation but was courteous enough to touch the dress and smile. 'It is very beautiful,' he agreed.

'Please, my lady, we will get into trouble if you do not wear one of these dresses.'

'Oh, surely not.'

They nodded. 'Our King told us to dress your hair as well. He has had fresh thawdrops brought up from the valley.'

Wyl looked towards where the women glanced. He had not noticed the vase holding the tiny white flowers Cailech had spoken of and promised to pick for Ylena. He felt more trapped than ever. It struck him that this situation had a horrid sense of inevitability. He wished he could reach Aremys. Perhaps he should just make a run for it and hope someone would bring him down and, if he was lucky, kill him. It would likely be a man and then at least he could inhabit the body of a male again, but if he was felled by an arrow or a knife thrown at him, then he may not live to see Valentyna again or avenge Ylena or any of the other people he loved who had been murdered.

Valentyna. His heart ached as he remembered the disturbed and disgusted expression she wore the last time they were together. If only he could be a man again he would somehow make it up to her . . . even if only to apologise on Ylena's behalf for her stupidity.

The women were staring at him and the silence had stretched embarrassingly long.

For you then, Valentyna, so I can see you just once more, he decided and nodded to the waiting women. 'Which one suits me best do you think?'

The two women beamed. One reached out and touched Ylena's hair. 'You are so beautiful, you would do either of them justice.' Then she took Ylena's hand. 'We have longed for the day when our King would take a woman for his own,' she said shyly.

Wyl was touched in spite of the horror he felt. 'Do you not mind that I am Morgravian?'

She shrugged and looked towards her companion who made a similar gesture. 'That you have captured his heart is enough. You will be his Queen . . . our Queen. That lifts our spirits. And, my lady, rumours abound that our two kingdoms have signed a peace treaty. This makes your marriage to our King even more special. How could we not accept the woman our King loves?'

'Loves?' Wyl repeated, aghast. 'He doesn't even know me.'

'The King is a great judge of character,' one said, stubbornly. 'He has chosen you, my lady. We do not question his choice, and in truth there is no one suitable within our own kingdom. Whoever he chose to marry, it would have caused jealousy between the factions. You have no allegiance to any Mountain family. This way he offends no one and at the same time bonds our realms closer.'

'He's told you we are to be married?' Wyl asked, further alarmed.

They nodded. 'Oh, yes,' the other woman said. 'The news is spreading like fire around the fortress.'

'And has he said when?' Wyl held his breath.

They hesitated, sensing her trepidation. 'The day after tomorrow, my lady,' the older one said finally. 'A gown is being stitched from pure white polder – our most rare colour. Animals are being slaughtered today for the feast and people are already gathering to catch a glimpse of you.'

They saw the noblewoman's hands fly to her face and press against each cheek in horror. Her look of desperation frightened them.

'He will be gentle with you, my lady,' the older one assured, imagining the angelic beauty was fearing for her wedding night.

'Oh, stop, please,' Wyl said, determined now to find a way to flee or bring about his own death. Then he remembered the warning from Elysius and realised that this was why, despite all of his taunts, neither Celimus nor Cailech had killed Ylena. It was not possible for him to invite his own death, and clearly Myrren's gift had been resisting it or protecting him. But randomness was still possible, as young Fynch had assured. That was what he needed now to save him. A random act — be it madness, violence or anger. Whatever occurred, he had to be rid of Ylena's guise within the next few hours.

'You're sure of this?' Myrt hissed in a whisper.

Aremys nodded, trying to look nonchalant as he lifted the latch on the side door leading into Galapek's stable. He forced himself not to glance over his shoulder which would immediately look suspicious. 'Where's Maegryn?'

'He's always around somewhere. You'd better have a story at the ready if we're caught.'

'Perhaps you should wait outside,' Aremys suggested. 'I can't risk you getting into trouble with Cailech. Once committed there's no going back,' he warned.

Myrt shook his head. 'I have to see the horse and its reaction for myself.'

The set of his friend's mouth assured Aremys there would be no further discussion. He nodded and stepped into the darkness. His eyes took a few moments to adjust to the minimal light that filtered through the stable's timber boards. A snort told him Galapek was in the shadows to his right. He immediately began a stream of soft words to the creature.

Myrt closed the door and remained silent behind Aremys. He realised he was holding his breath, in dread of confirmation that his friend was truly trapped inside this beautiful beast. He watched Aremys raise his hand and place it on the animal's majestic face and, as man and beast touched, he felt a surge of emotion. Was this really Lothryn?

'Lothryn,' Aremys murmured, 'if you're there, give us a sign. I've brought Myrt.' He nodded at Myrt to step forward. 'Say something,' he whispered.

Myrt moved from behind the Grenadyne and cleared his throat. 'If that's you, my friend, prove it.'

'I can feel the magic shivering through his body,' Aremys said. 'He's fighting it, that's why his flesh is trembling.' He turned back to Galapek. 'Come on, Lothryn, do it for Elspyth. She's alive. She's coming for you. And Wyl's here too!' he added, hoping it might help. The horse reared up onto its hind legs and squealed. Aremys fell to the floor, pain filling his head as a voice, equally pain-filled, growled into his mind, *Turn me loose!*

'It's him!' Myrt whispered as he tried to calm the horse, which was kicking and pounding at the wall. 'Quick! He could hurt you.'

'He won't hurt me,' the Grenadyne said, disgusted with himself for falling. His head throbbed but his satisfaction was intense, as was his awe for this sickening magic. 'It is him, Myrt. He spoke to me. He wants to be turned loose.'

The warrior turned an anxious gaze towards him. 'What do we do?'

Aremys frowned, as much with frustration as helplessness. 'Well, we can't just let him go. We have to think this through. There's Gueryn to consider too.'

'Forgive me if I don't lose any sleep over a Morgravian soldier,' Myrt said. 'I care only about Lothryn.'

'Understood. Listen—' He got no further. A shaft of sunlight made them both swing around towards the side door where Maegryn had just entered.

'Myrt? What are you doing here? And that's the Grenadyne with you, isn't it?' the stablemaster said.

Myrt was not so adept at lying as Aremys and his hesitation, as well as the guilty glance towards his companion, was telling. 'I . . . that is, we . . .'

'We got back today,' Aremys continued for his faltering friend. 'I was hoping we could go for a ride.'

Maegryn looked quizzically at them. 'But you've been riding for days.'

'This is true,' Aremys said, mentally kicking himself and giving an embarrassed grin. 'A lot has happened these past few days, Maegryn. I felt like being as alone as I am permitted to be. Can't think of a better place than in Galapek's saddle.'

'Surely you weren't thinking of taking the King's horse without his or my permission?'

'Of course not,' Myrt said, regaining his composure. 'We were just passing and thought we'd look in on the animal. Aremys is fond of him – brought him a red apple because he knows he hates green ones.'

The stablemaster was not to be put off so easily. 'I heard Galapek. What was all the noise about?'

Both men shrugged and Aremys knew they looked more guilty for that single concerted gesture than any of their stammered responses or awkward pauses. The stablemaster had already made it clear to Aremys in a previous discussion that he would not be drawn on information relating to the King's horse, and the Grenadyne mercenary could tell from the guarded look in the stablemaster's eyes that Maegryn was suspicious of their intentions.

'Where are you going?' Aremys said when the man turned away. He knew very well where Maegryn was headed but he was desperately stalling for time.

'The King . . . if he'll see me. I'm sorry but I have my orders.'

'Who from?' Myrt demanded, thinking much the same as Aremys now: they were in serious trouble and needed time to think through their next move.

'Rashlyn.'

'Since when do you take orders from him?' Myrt spat.

'Since le Gant went missing,' the stablemaster replied. 'The barshi insisted that anyone acting suspiciously around the King's horse would meet the same fate.'

Aremys felt a chill move through him. 'What do you mean "fate"?'

Maegryn shrugged, not picking up the fact that Aremys should not know of the Morgravian prisoner. 'According to the barshi, le Gant has been dealt with.'

'Dealt with!' Myrt repeated. 'I thought only the King made decisions about our prisoners?'

'Listen, Myrt,' Maegryn began, his anger stoking fast now, 'I hate Rashlyn. You of all people should know that. But I won't interfere in the King's business — you should know that too. Lothryn, Haldor rest his soul, learned the hard way about crossing the King. I don't intend to be given into the keeping of Rashlyn because I've invoked the ire of King Cailech. I can't help you.'

'Is that what's happened?' Aremys pressed. 'Rashlyn took le Gant?'

Maegryn looked down. 'I don't know what's happened. I suspect Rashlyn took him from the dungeon, yes.'

'What are we coming to, Maegryn, when we are too scared to speak out,' Myrt commented. He did not mean it as an accusation; it was more a sad-sounding reflection on his own shortcomings.

'Lothryn stood up to the King and Lothryn paid the price!' Maegryn yelled. 'I don't have his courage.'

'True. And where is Lothryn do you think?' Myrt asked, advancing on the stablemaster.

'Be careful, Myrt,' Aremys murmured, his senses highly tuned over the years to when a man was feeling a blood rage.

'I . . . I don't know. Dead, I suppose,' Maegryn answered, stepping back. 'Don't threaten me, Myrt.'

'An honourable death, do you think?'

Maegryn nodded slowly, unsure of where this interrogation was headed.

'He's not dead. He's alive!' Myrt boomed, close to Maegryn's face. 'Rashlyn told us as much. It's just taken me a while to work it out.'

Maegryn's expression was shocked now. 'Alive? Where?'

'Here, Maegryn. Right beneath your nose,' Myrt said, a cruel tone to his voice that Aremys had never heard before. Myrt was too upset. This was dangerous.

The stablemaster frowned, stepped back again, closer to the door. 'What are you talking about?'

'I'm talking about magic, Maegryn. I'm talking about Rashlyn and his sinister ways.'

'I don't understand,' the man muttered, licking his lips nervously. He looked deeply scared now, as if he too sensed that the situation had turned nasty.

'You'd be right to feel petrified,' Myrt went on, noting the man's fear. 'Lothryn is in your care.'

Maegryn's eyes widened, the nonsense of Myrt's words giving him courage. 'You're talking in riddles, man. What's he saying, Grenadyne?'

Aremys was not convinced this was the right path. Sharing what they knew with Maegryn, who was as loyal to Cailech as any of his warriors and did not share Myrt's single-minded dedication to Lothryn, was fraught with danger. 'Maegryn,' he started, his mind racing as to how best explain such a terrifying concept and calm what had become a somewhat explosive situation. 'It's going to be hard for you to believe us—'

'Galapek *is* Lothryn, you fool!' Myrt interrupted, spitting his fury and advancing on the cringing stablemaster. 'Rashlyn, with the King's permission, used his dark magic to change him into Galapek. That's why you don't know where the horse came from, and why the King is so careful about who rides him or asks questions about him. And that's also why you've been sworn to secrecy. You've always known there was something odd about the whole situation surrounding the horse. Admit it, damn you!'

'Lothryn?' Maegryn repeated, shaking his head in confusion. He looked at the huge horse and saw the anger in its eyes then returned his anxious gaze to Myrt. 'No,' was all he said, his head moving slowly from side to side in denial.

'You know it's true, Maegryn. You've had doubts of your own from the start. Right from the beginning when Cailech said he would break this horse's spirit and earn its loyalty with trust. What do you think that whole charade was about, eh? I don't blame you, because I was taken in by it too. If not for Aremys, none of us would be any the wiser. The King was humiliating Loth, destroying his closest friend, his truest follower, and then rebuilding him in the form of a beast. A mute beast which would have to carry the King on his back for the rest of his life and thus pay homage like any slave or lowlife. An honourable death was too good for our best warrior, Maegryn. The King wanted to make him pay; he wanted revenge and humiliation for Loth's betrayal.'

Maegryn retaliated, reacting to the pain of realisation that he was hearing the truth even though he could not bring himself to believe it. 'Lothryn chose the Morgravian woman over his own King, his own people!' he cried, desperate to make Myrt understand that he would never be a part of something as dark as he was describing.

'And he deserved to become this, did he?' Myrt boomed. 'An animal! He still lives, Maegryn. That's the worst of it. He knows. He's trapped inside that body, in agonising pain.'

The stablemaster shook his head again, as though he himself was in pain. 'No. This isn't true. Can you prove it?' he demanded, looking between the two men. 'Show me how this is Lothryn. How can you know?'

Aremys answered in a tone of such resignation, Myrt knew they had lost the opportunity of convincing Maegryn. 'I can feel the taint of the filthy magic.'

'That's it, Grenadyne — your word? And what . . . you

are gifted with sentient power?' He looked at his fellow Mountain man. 'Have you gone mad, Myrt? You would trust this foreigner over your own King?'

'It's the truth, Maegryn.'

The stablemaster gave a harsh laugh, feeling a small measure of control return. 'The truth?' he scorned. 'Says who? Another prisoner? For that's what he is. I have no gripe with you, Farrow, but don't ask me to take your word over that of my King.'

Aremys said nothing. What was there to say?

'You don't know anything of substance, Myrt,' Maegryn continued. 'You're just believing the Grenadyne. Have you heard Lothryn speak? Has the horse communicated anything to you?'

Myrt shook his head, anger trembling through his body. 'He spoke only to Aremys.'

'To Aremys!' Maegryn repeated, still more scorn in his tone. 'No proof, nothing but this man's say-so, and you're prepared to believe that Lothryn has been turned into a horse. Does that not sound ridiculous to you?'

Myrt nodded. 'It does, but not when you say that same sentence with Rashlyn attached to it. The barshi is evil and you know it. His influence on the King is curious, to say the least. Lothryn felt it and said as much to me. I don't think our King ordered this. I think Rashlyn did. I believe, as Lothryn did, that the barshi is able to sway the King against his own wishes.'

'Rashlyn uses magic against the King?' Maegryn clarified, aghast.

'Yes. That's what I now believe. I think he can persuade Cailech to agree to things he would not choose himself.'

Maegryn put his hands up in a warding gesture. 'That's

enough, Myrt. I don't want to hear any more. You speak treachery against our sovereign and it is my sworn duty as one of his men to make this betrayal public. I'm sorry, Myrt.'

The stablemaster had just opened the door slightly when he felt the breath cut off from his lungs as huge, powerful hands closed around his throat. He let go of the door's iron ring, gasping. Fear pounded through his ears and the blood pumped desperately through squeezed veins and arteries. As if from faraway he heard the Grenadyne yell to Myrt to stop. He found enough strength to twist around to see through his bulging eyes the rage in the bigger man's face but he could not loosen the warrior's grip to beg for his life. 'I'm sorry too,' were the last words he heard before Myrt intensified the pressure and crushed his victim's neck. Maegryn slumped in his killer's arms, dead.

Aremys was shocked that this terrible event had unfolded so fast and angry with himself for not preventing it. But the deed was done. Instead of accusations he offered help. 'Where can we hide the body?' he said matter-of-factly. Myrt was in a state of shock, his rage gone the moment Maegryn had died beneath his fingers. He did not reply, crouching instead by the corpse. 'Come on, man! It's done with. You can't bring him back. We have to hide him.'

'I'm a dead man. We Mountain folk are strict about killing our own kind.'

'We're probably both dead men anyway. It will all unfold quickly now, Myrt. There's a lot happening outside of this that you don't know about.'

'Like what?' The big man scowled at him.

'Trust me, neither of us needs to involve ourselves,'

Aremys said carefully, wishing he had not spoken. 'Come on, help me. We have to hide him and buy some hours.'

'For what?' Myrt said, all sense of hope vanished.

'Everything is going to unravel, my friend. The King is getting married to a woman who does not want him and whom he does not know well enough,' he said, arching an eyebrow. 'Strange stuff is going to happen – believe me. Time is our enemy now. I know you don't want to, but you have to choose between Lothryn or your King and you have to do it now! This is what I wanted to avoid, why I asked you to remain outside.'

Myrt nodded sorrowfully. 'I have already made my choice, Grenadyne. I chose Lothryn.'

Aremys continued, more gently this time, 'All right then. We now know we are in the presence of your friend and we must find a way to release him.'

'Can we?' Myrt asked, his spirits lifting.

'By death if necessary,' Aremys answered gravely. 'We need to find out more from Rashlyn.'

'He has Cailech's protection,' Myrt warned.

'Not whilst the King is enamoured by Ylena Thirsk he doesn't. We must get to Rashlyn now whilst the King is preoccupied . . . and perhaps he will lead us to Gueryn.'

'I told you, I don't care about him.'

'But I do. And so will Ylena Thirsk when she finds out her guardian is a prisoner here.'

Myrt looked at him, startled. 'Her guardian? Does the King know?'

Aremys shook his head. 'I shouldn't think so but I'm going to tell him. I'll seek an audience with the King. You establish where the barshi is and keep him from Cailech at all costs.'

'And Galapek?'

'Will have to be patient a little longer,' Aremys said softly, turning to stare at the stallion in the shadows. 'Myrt, this choice you've made – you do understand you'll have to leave the Razors?'

'Escape, you mean?'

Aremys nodded. 'I won't let you go alone.'

The warrior sighed. 'This is how Lothryn must have felt when he helped the Morgravians to escape. Damned if he did and damned if he didn't. I will betray those I love whichever choice I make. I'm sorry, Aremys. I can't promise I'll leave.'

Best not to force the issue, Aremys realised. The circumstances would no doubt make all the decisions for them. 'Come on, we've got to hide this body,' he said.

Myrt nodded. 'I know where.'

CHAPTER 29

Lady Helyn Bench was begging her husband to reconsider his decision. *How the tables turn*, she thought, remembering how, such a short time ago, he had been in her dressing room pleading with her to see reason over Leyen.

She reluctantly held his jacket as the man she loved slipped his arms into the sleeves. 'I wish you wouldn't,' she began again.

He turned in her arms and hugged her. 'My mind is made up, my dear. I don't like this cloak-and-dagger stuff. I think we must air the grievances tactfully.'

'Eryd,' she said, fear combining with exasperation, 'how tactful can you be when you're about to accuse someone of murder?'

'Indeed,' he said, and pointed to a silk scarf. 'Would you help me with that, please?'

She flounced to the chair and picked up the length of silk draped across it. 'And not just anyone,' she continued. 'The King!'

'Helyn, I am not a dimwit. Perhaps you have noticed this over the years?'

'Taking witnesses won't stop him!' she cried. 'He'll just have you all killed.'

'Don't be ridiculous, woman. Kill me and then Lord Hartley? Then I suppose he'd have to kill Lord Jownes and Lord Peaforth because they would follow in our footsteps. And then who else is left to advise, to cajole, to administer this city? He needs us.'

'Then don't go. Don't do this.'

'I shall know from the way he reacts whether he is lying or not.'

'Eryd!' she replied, just short of a screech, hating the way her husband closed his eyes in despair. 'Do you believe that the Donals are not dead? Not hacked to bits, raped, burned? Or that the massacre at Rittylworth is a misunderstanding and the monks are in fact alive and well?'

'No, Helyn,' he said and the tone in his voice chilled her. She wished she had not resorted to sarcasm. He was deeply angered now; she knew it. She had overstepped the mark. The first time since twelve years ago, when she had interfered in a deal, speaking out when she should have kept her own counsel. The deal had fallen through and Eryd had blamed her. He was right to: her words had been ill-chosen and yet, for the life of her, she could not remember now what she had said to so offend. His deep voice dragged her back to her latest mistake. 'Please do not speak ill of the dead. I am painfully aware of the deaths of my friends, the Donal family, and the innocent men of Rittylworth.'

'I'm sorry, Eryd, I—'

He cut her off, too angry to hear more. 'Enough, wife. The three remaining powerful lords of Morgravia cannot disappear! Now hush your ramblings and get this scarf tied, or I shall be late.'

'What did you tell the others?' she asked, understanding there was nothing more she could do to stop her husband walking into the dragon's den.

'All that we know.'

'Not about Wyl Thirsk, surely?'

'No. That revelation I am keeping to myself until I can see this phenomenon with my own eyes.'

'Do you believe our guests though?'

He nodded, slowly, reluctantly. 'How could I not? Their tale is so shocking and mysterious, no one could make that up. Jeryb Donal's son would not lie to us, Helyn. You can see it in his face that he is as petrified of this . . . this Myrren's gift, as they call it, as he is intrigued by it. We have known Crys Donal since he was a babe in arms. He is as open a man as any, I am sure. No, there is no lie there but I can't accept it fully yet.'

'That Wyl Thirsk is his sister, you mean?'

'That he was the Koreldy assassin, that he was Leyen, whom you delighted in so much, that, yes, he has become his sister.'

'But it does make sense, doesn't it, my love?' she said. 'If he did not become this Koreldy fellow, it is odd that a Grenadyne mercenary would bother to rescue his enemy's sister from the dungeon of his benefactor.' Eryd nodded. 'Then take her to safety before going to look for that Widow Ilyk person to learn more about himself.'

'Is that the seer's name?'

'Yes, I'm embarrassed to admit she has done readings for me in the past.'

'It's all nonsense, Helyn, you know that,' Eryd grumbled.

'I thought so until now,' she replied, before hurrying on. 'Then the Grenadyne is trapped, taken into the Razors and, instead of bargaining his way out – as presumably he could with that Mountain King – he risks everything to get Gueryn le Gant and Elspyth away. Does that sound like a hardened mercenary, or like Wyl Thirsk trapped inside the body of one?'

'I agree, Helyn. It's not that I need convincing. I just—'

'So then he makes his way to Briavel to offer his protection to Queen Valentyna. Why? Well, of course, he'd saved her life once before from a potential assassination attempt and had fought to save her father's too, losing his own life in the effort. But then King Celimus comes along and it all goes wrong. Wyl gets killed by the King's own assassin, Leyen—'

'They called her Faryl too.'

'Whatever her name was. That girl, as much as I liked her – and I guess now it was simply Wyl I was liking all over again – was not used to womanly things.'

'What do you mean?'

'Well, the baths. Remember I told you?'

'You must have.'

'And you weren't listening as usual,' she admonished. 'She was so hesitant about going into the pavilion – that's where we first met. She was terribly embarrassed about showing her body, and let me tell you, Eryd, no woman who looks like that is ever coy about her body. She had no idea about the soap leaves and when I mentioned the razing of Rittylworth, her whole demeanour changed. That's because it was Wyl, fearing for his sister.'

Eryd nodded. 'I understand, Helyn. I want to believe

it, but I believe what I see with my own eyes, not hearsay.'

'I know. As you say though, it's too chilling not to be real. I believe it, I need no further convincing.'

'About what, Mother?' came a light voice. It was the Benchs' daughter, Georgyana.

'Were you listening?' her father asked, anxious that his young, fanciful daughter might have heard more than he wished.

'No. But I wouldn't tell you if I had,' she answered and pulled a face at him, but not before taking his hand and squeezing it. That father and daughter worshipped each other was obvious. Helyn sometimes wondered how they ever found room for her in their lives. 'Did you meet our guests, darling?' she asked.

'No,' Georgyana said, shaking her golden tresses which she wore long and loose.

'We have visitors downstairs,' her father said. 'I suppose you came in through the back like a servant?'

'I'm hungry,' his daughter pouted. 'I wanted to see what was cooking.'

'Well, come and meet them,' Helyn said, glad of Georgyana's noise and distraction.

'Do I have to?'

'You'll like them,' she assured.

'Who are they?'

'The Duke of Felrawthy and a lovely girl called Elspyth who is from the north.'

'Oh, another stuffy old man like father?' Georgyana said, winking towards Eryd.

'Far from it, my love,' Helyn replied. 'Crys Donal is one of the best-looking men in Morgravia, and soon to be the most eligible when word gets around of his new status.'

'Ooh! What are we waiting for, Mother?' her daughter squealed. 'Off you go, Father. Bring me back something small and sparkly.'

Eryd rolled his eyes with exasperation. 'I am hoping for an audience with the King, Georgyana.'

'Well, steal something from the palace for me then,' she said and giggled as she left the chamber.

Helyn gave her husband a searching glance. 'My love, please—'

'Don't say it,' he warned gently. 'You know I will be.'

She said nothing and left, fearful of letting herself down with tears.

Knave was amazed at Fynch's recovery. His surprise drew a grin from the boy. 'Truly, I am well,' he said, stretching. 'I'm even hungry.'

No headache?

'All gone . . . for now.'

How can this be?

Fynch owed it to Knave to tell him more. 'The King came.'

The Dragon King? Again! He was here?

The boy nodded. 'But not in the way you think. He came to me in my dreams. I flew with him, Knave. He carried me to the Wild.'

You were here all the time, Knave said quietly. *I noticed you were restless in your sleep though. I feared it was pain . . . death*, he admitted.

Again the boy smiled, gently and without smugness, but there was something in it that Knave noticed. Some knowledge perhaps.

I don't mean to pry, Fynch, but you appear miraculously well.

'I am,' Fynch said, and laughed. He stood. 'And I don't need sharvan either. He healed me.'

The King did?

'Yes. He said he would restore me so I can fulfil my task.'

Suddenly Knave could not look at him; he understood the way of things. *But nothing comes without a price, am I right? he asked, sadness in his voice.*

'Don't dwell on it,' Fynch replied softly. 'I am at peace, my friend. The King shared something with me which has made me happy. Happier than I have ever felt before.'

And this sharing was a secret?

He nodded.

I understand, Fynch. I'm glad you feel so well. I hated to watch you suffer.

'I know. You are a better friend than any I could wish for,' he said, and he hugged the large dog. 'Now,' he continued brightly. 'I must eat something and then we must go. I am strong now, Knave, and ready to face our enemy.'

Knave said nothing. He had not anticipated when he first clapped eyes on the small gong boy in Stoneheart that he would lose his heart to him in friendship. He had been given a task by the Thicket but had never guessed he might come to resent the burden placed upon his shoulders.

It was as though Fynch read his thoughts. 'If we don't destroy him, Knave, he will destroy the world we love and the Thicket. The magical creatures will die and the Dragon King will be exposed. We have no choice.'

Knave did not respond but Fynch sensed the resolve in the dog and knew he had said the right words at the right time to remind his companion of their role in life.

Eat, Knave finally said. *We have a journey to finish.*

The Duke of Felrawthy was getting on famously with the unashamedly flirtatious Georgyana Bench. From the moment they touched hands and the young woman curt-sied to the duke, Elspyth realised Crys might never stare at her in that sad-eyed, wistful way again.

She was surprised how it hurt, tried to shake it off as simply feeling clingy about the person who rescued her from death, but she knew deep down it was all about her longing for love. She did not want Crys Donal – of this she was sure, for she loved only one person – but she would be lying if she did not admit to enjoying the duke's attention.

It was embarrassing when Lady Bench dropped in on her private thoughts. 'Forgive my daughter, my dear. I had made an assumption that you and the duke were . . . well, attached.'

Elspyth reddened and smiled awkwardly. 'Not at all, Lady Bench.'

'Oh, do call me Helyn,' she interrupted, touching Elspyth's arm as they sat together, withdrawn from the pair who were chatting animatedly.

'Thank you, Helyn,' Elspyth said. 'Crys and I are great friends. I think terror and fear bring people painfully close, and we have shared much, not the least of which was learning of his family's deaths. But our relationship is not physical, I assure you.'

'You have been very strong for him, Elspyth. Don't underestimate how he might feel.'

Again Elspyth smiled, sadly this time. 'He's made that perfectly clear actually,' she said. 'But I love another, Helyn, and I really must make tracks soon to return to him. I'm glad, truly, that Crys and Georgyana are getting on so well. He needs a reason to smile and a woman who might enjoy him.'

Lady Bench lifted her eyebrows. 'I know I shouldn't speculate so soon, but it's true that they would make a marvellous match, and Eryd would be delighted to join our family with the Donals.'

'Where is Lord Bench?' Elspyth frowned, not really wanting to discuss a potential love match between Crys and Georgyana.

Helyn Bench grew serious and looked away from her laughing daughter and into the soft eyes of Elspyth. 'He's gone to the King.'

'What?' Elspyth started to rise.

'No, wait,' Lady Bench calmed. 'You need to understand.'

'Lady Bench, he is sworn to secrecy about Wyl Thirsk!'

'And that secret will be kept, my dear. Have no fear, we are not about to start broadcasting news of magic in this city.' She shook herself, as if casting off a dire thought. 'We only stopped burning suspected witches less than a decade ago, as you would know.'

'So what will Lord Bench say to Celimus?'

Helyn Bench's face darkened. 'I believe he intends to confront the King – in his wonderfully articulate and polite way – about the Donal family and no doubt Rittylworth.' She put a hand in the air to stop Elspyth's oncoming tirade, then noted the fear in Elspyth's face. It reflected her own anguish, although she hoped she was disguising it well enough.

Elspyth glanced towards Crys who was clearly entranced by the vivaciously pretty girl who had engaged him in lively conversation. She returned her gaze to Lady Bench. 'I think his action is unwise, Helyn.'

Her carefully chosen words sent a chill through her companion; they echoed her own anxiety that Celimus would not permit Eryd Bench to leave his court alive. She began to weep, no longer able to hide her worries.

'Oh, Helyn, please don't. Can we reach him?'

The older woman shook her head. 'And he is adamant anyway. He would not listen to me earlier when I begged him not to do this.'

'What is his reasoning?'

'He believes in sovereignty, Elspyth. He desperately wants our King to act like the true Crown of Morgravia, to behave with care and compassion and to listen to wise counsel from his own lords.'

'Eryd has listened to our horrific story and still believes he can change this cruel King into a compassionate ruler?' she asked, shocked.

'He believes we must follow the rules of our kingdom. Talk before action. No accusations before all information is sought and gathered. He does not intend to ruffle feathers, Elspyth. Eryd will be careful.'

'Listen to me,' Elspyth said, enunciating carefully as if talking to a dimwit. She did not mean to act so; she was frightened. Petrified, in fact. She knew Crys had noticed her fraught body language when he excused himself from Georgyana and crossed the room. 'Helyn, Eryd is in grave peril. His life is at stake. So is yours and that of your daughter. The moment he raises this topic with the King, he will flag how much we know and the

King will instantly see him for the danger he has become
. . . unintentionally.'

Helyn was weeping again. 'I feared as much.'

'Elspyth?' It was Crys. She told him briefly what had
transpired and watched him pale. 'He killed my father on
a simple suspicion and then had the rest of my family
executed just for good measure,' Crys said. 'Lady Helyn,
forgive me, but what Lord Bench has done is virtually
signing his own death warrant. We have to get you out
of here. Immediately. Elspyth, do what you can – I'll ready
transport. Pack only essentials, and warm clothes. We're
going north.'

Helyn Bench, trembling, reached towards her daughter.
She seemed as if in a trance.

Georgyana, however, began to protest. 'This is preposterous. I have engagements and—'

'Be quiet, Georgyana, and do as you're told!' Elspyth
admonished. 'We're trying to save your life.' Elspyth
seemed to be the only woman thinking clearly. Suddenly
the pain of her recent injuries was no longer important.
Fear took it away. Fear of death and failure again and the
need to flee.

Crys tried a different tack. 'Georgyana,' he said, amazed
at how his stomach flipped when she turned those huge
eyes on him, 'I could not live with myself if anything
should happen to you.' His expression pleaded with her
to follow them without further protest.

Clearly she saw something else in that expression,
something Crys thought he had disguised. 'Oh? Could
you not, Lord Donal?' she replied, and her smile said it
all.

* * *

Eryd Bench and his colleague sat in a small waiting chamber at the foot of Stoneheart's war tower. He had no idea why they had been escorted here, but Chancellor Jessom emerged just as he began to privately question the reason for this curious venue.

'Lord Bench, Lord Hartley, it's good to see you on this mild eve. Are you both well?' The visitors made all the right noises and Jessom continued. 'My apologies to have kept you waiting. The King, as you see, is working from his war room tonight – I hope you don't mind meeting with him here?'

Eryd was slightly less anxious for Jessom's warm greeting. 'Not at all. I am grateful he could see us at such short notice.' He looked towards Hartley who simply nodded in agreement. Lord Hartley had offered to come along as support when Eryd had confided his reservations about the truth of the slaughters at Felrawthy and Rittylworth.

Jessom smiled benignly. It was not an expression that came easily to him, particularly in the light of the situation. Two lords asking for an audience at sudden notice, and Lord Bench at that – it all smacked of trouble. 'Thank you, Lord Bench. As you know, his majesty has only just returned from the north. I'm sure he will be pleased to tell you more when you see him.'

'I look forward to it, Jessom,' Eryd replied. 'I heard he was at Tenterdyn?'

'That's right,' Jessom said carefully.

'And rumour has it there was a meeting of Kings at Tenterdyn.'

The Chancellor attempted another smile. 'No smoke without fire, Lord Bench. Perhaps you might enquire of the King for more information. I am a simple chancellor.'

'Nothing simple about you, Jessom,' Eryd said, deliberately softening his voice to avoid giving offence.

Jessom bowed to the two lords. 'Not long now, gentlemen.'

He returned several minutes later. 'Lord Bench, King Celimus will see you now, alone.'

Eryd looked towards Hartley who stared stonily back. 'Go ahead, Eryd. You speak for all of us,' he said cryptically.

'This is unusual. We are both here for an audience with his majesty,' Eryd tried, but the thin Chancellor shrugged.

'My apologies, Lord Bench, this is what the King requests.'

Eryd nodded. Too late now. He would just have to be especially careful with the slippery sovereign, with no one else present.

'Will you wait?' he asked Hartley, who nodded. 'Thank you, Chancellor,' he said, gesturing for Jessom to lead the way. At least with Lord Hartley in attendance, he had someone to vouch for him even if not to bear actual witness to his meeting with the King.

He followed Jessom, filled with intensifying trepidation as his wife's cautions rang in his ears. Perhaps this was not such a good idea after all. Perhaps Hartley was not the right choice. He was an unmarried man; his only son dead of the fever some years back.

Which had been precisely the King's thinking when he heard of the arrival of the two lords. 'Separate them and take Hartley down to the dungeon,' he had ordered.

'But, sire,' Jessom had said, startled, 'could we not wait and see what it is they wish to discuss with you?'

'We know what they're here about, Chancellor!' the King had said, voice rising. 'They're here because they don't believe that the noble family of Felrawthy was slaughtered by Razor warriors. They suspect this because word has got around that I was meeting with the Barbarian King. It's not hard to follow their thought patterns, Jessom.'

'No, sire. But the dungeon is a fairly radical step for someone of Lord Hartley's status.'

'So is death, Chancellor. Be careful I don't ask you to kill him for me.'

At which point Jessom had kept his thoughts to himself. Experience told him it was the same old argument which he would never win. Expecting the King of Morgravia to show restraint, respect or even the most simple of courtesies was a waste of energy. He was a power unto himself, not caring for any advice. In fact, Jessom, if he was truthful with himself, was well past the point of believing there was a prosperous future to be shaped under Celimus. His personal dreams of becoming a kingmaker had been cracked by Rittylworth's shame, shattered by Felrawthy's calamity and, he suspected, were now well on the way to dust for he did not expect to see Lord Eryd Bench live out this night. Not if Bench was here to question the King's actions and motives, no matter how elegantly couched those accusations might be.

The fragile treaty with Cailech would also be broken soon enough, Jessom suspected, and was saddened by it. King Cailech had shown tremendous courage and foresight in his actions and the Chancellor rather admired his man, Farrow, for brokering the meeting. Bringing Ylena Thirsk to Celimus had been the mercenary's trump card under intense pressure but still he had shown himself to possess a cool head within the eye of a storm. All these men could be valuable to Morgravia and yet Celimus was systematically destroying any chances of loyalty. How much longer would the nobility put up with his ways? Not long, Jessom suspected, and he was not about to be the King's scapegoat.

Their only chance, in truth, was Queen Valentyna. This marriage presented opportunities and not just in deflecting attention away from Celimus's ugly deeds since he had taken the throne. Valentyna was bringing something positive and shiny bright into the lives of Morgravians.

A dazzling Queen crowned during the pomp and ceremony of a formal wedding was their new hope. Her beauty and composure, not to mention her personal power and wealth, was the sparkle that had long been missing in Pearlis – not forgetting the promise of heirs. Valentyna was the ideal diversion from all the death and destruction. It would not go away of course, but it would be put aside for a while – perhaps long enough to lose some of its potency, by which time Valentyna of Briavel would have worked her own magic simply through her presence. With the people's hearts won, no one – not even the lords – would want to upset the balance of the two realms with hard questions. Sleeping dogs would be left to lie, as they say, Jessom thought, as he guided Lord Bench up the tower stairs. He could hear the old man puffing behind him.

His mind turned again to Valentyna, and something bright and sharp, like the first ray of sunlight that slices through the dark sky at dawn, cut through his thoughts.

Perhaps his own loyalties should be aligned with the Queen. She was intelligent and wanted peace and prosperity for her nation; this meant she was open to advice and still young enough to be malleable. Perhaps it was Valentyna he should dedicate himself to; he could be not a kingmaker but an empire-maker.

Jessom arrived at the King's chamber feeling far more light-hearted than when he began the climb. He looked behind him.

'All right, Lord Bench?'

'Yes,' the man wheezed. 'I had forgotten the tower was so tall.'

'It is deceptive,' Jessom answered, and tapped on the door.

'Come!' the King called.

Jessom swung open the heavy timber door and announced the visitor.

'Eryd,' Celimus said, beaming from behind the desk. 'I imagine you are familiar with this chamber, eh?'

The voice was so friendly that Lord Bench felt himself relax momentarily. 'Yes, my lord. Your father spent much time here briefing us in years gone.'

The smile remained fixed on the King's face, bright, dazzling and, Eryd suddenly realised, predatory. It was the first time he had seen right through to the heart of the young man. He had always considered him supremely smart and quick-witted and felt these were qualities which would serve him well as King. He had heard troubling stories from years ago, when Celimus was something of a hellraiser, but had put it down to youth and riches. Like most of the nobility, he had hoped that despite the cool relationship between Magnus and his son, Celimus would shine as King if the right people were around him. He had always intended to be a pillar of support and wise counsel for this new King.

But too many of the lords were muttering that, for all their advice, the King was making his own decisions without reference to council. He did not even show the courtesy of informing some of the most senior people of his plans. The proposed war with Briavel had come out of nowhere and had escalated so fast it had ignited a private war of its own, with many of the senior officials – like Lord Hartley – quietly declaring that permitting the King to continue in this way was too dangerous. Such treacherous talk, even privately, was seriously disturbing. Civil unrest was the last thing the realm needed after Magnus had left it so strong, but then he was a ruler who was loved and gladly followed. His son had not earned any loyalty; in fact he was driving away the very people who might encourage others to give it.

Amongst the power-brokers of Morgravia, it was obvious that only Eryd had any proof of the King's treachery at Felrawthy although many suspected that the Crown had been involved somehow in the razing of Rittylworth. However, the news of the brilliant union between Morgravia and Briavel had worked wonders in pushing aside hard questions and political reprisals. But for Celimus to then suggest war with the very realm he was making peace with seemed ludicrous. Everyone was confused, but Eryd saw it more clearly now having heard Crys Donal's story. Celimus was waging the most dangerous of games, clearly subscribing to the notion of not allowing one hand to know what the other was doing.

The business of Wyl Thirsk was too incredible to credit.

It was all hocus-pocus surely? Then again, Crys Donal had always been a level-headed, honest young man and he had no reason to lie now. Eryd had to admit that the young duke's eyewitness account of this strange phenomenon which saw the cursed soul of Wyl Thirsk inhabit someone else – his sister now, for Shar's sake – was hard to dispute.

And for all his loyalty to the Crown, Lord Bench knew he would be lying if he did not admit to his faith being truly with the powerful families of Morgravia who had kept the royal family so strong. Particular families including the Thirsks, the Donals and, yes, the Benchs. His committed friendships with men like Jeryb Donal and Fergys Thirsk meant he could not just ignore this claim of the young duke's that the true General of Morgravia, Wyl Thirsk, lived on and was working towards the downfall of the new King whom he was insisting could not be trusted.

Eryd shook the confusing thoughts away.

'Are you all right?' the King enquired and Eryd was reminded that he was standing before his sovereign.

'Yes, your majesty. My apologies. I think I was taken aback there momentarily by memories.'

'The new breed is in place now, Lord Bench,' Celimus admonished and although his manner was genial there was bite in the sparkling tone. 'I know I can count on your loyalty.'

Eryd coughed. 'Of course, your majesty.'

'Which is why,' Celimus continued, 'I am glad you came this evening. Where is your lovely family, by the way?'

Eryd glanced at the Chancellor who was handing him

a glass of wine. Jessom's expression was blank, giving no clue as to why the King would ask such a curious question.

'Er . . . at home, sire. Why?' Eryd sipped, recognising a superb southern red, fruity and earthy with hints of juniper and blackberries. Normally he would relish the opportunity to share such a fine drop but the King's carefully couched question turned the wine instantly sour on his tongue.

'Oh, no reason. I just thought it would be lovely to see your charming Georgyana again. It would have been a pleasure to have you all here,' Celimus replied evenly.

The answer arrived as smooth as silk but it was loaded and, sugary sweet as it sounded, Eryd was not fooled. He felt suddenly dry-mouthed and the ball of fear in his stomach, which just moments ago had felt small, now grew to ten times the size. Unless Eryd was mistaken, the King had just made a supremely well-disguised threat. Eryd sipped again from the glass, a bigger, more nervous gulp, but could hardly bring himself to swallow it because his throat suddenly felt as though it was closing up.

Chancellor Jessom was at his side, topping up the goblet.

'To your good health,' Celimus said and raised his cup. Lord Bench was paying scant attention. His thoughts had fled to Helyn and Georgyana.

'Tell me why you came,' Celimus said, suddenly turning to business.

Eryd was feeling light-headed. He thought it was anxiety but he noticed how warm the room had become and yet there was no fire burning. He tugged at his collar to loosen it. 'I wished to talk to you about Felrawthy, your majesty.'

He saw the King glance towards his Chancellor and the subsequent twitch of a smug smile was not lost on Eryd either. So the King had expected him. Had anticipated this meeting. They were lost.

'Oh, yes? What can I tell you, Lord Bench?'

Eryd felt worse by the moment. His vision was blurred and his thoughts were swimming. He forced himself to stay focused. 'I heard a rumour, your majesty, that you have signed a treaty with the Mountain King.' He was sure he was slurring.

'That's right, Eryd, I did. We are now peaceful neighbours. I had hoped to make this announcement at my wedding, as the icing on the cake, you could say.' Celimus laughed softly at his own jest. 'But it seems my learned lords are well ahead of my news.'

Eryd drew a shaking hand across his forehead. 'Forgive me, your majesty, I suddenly feel very unwell.'

He heard the King tsk-tsk comfortingly. 'Oh dear. Some more wine perhaps?'

'No, no, thank you,' Eryd said, holding the goblet towards Jessom who was once again at his side. The Chancellor did not take the cup though. 'I think I should go, your highness. Perhaps we could continue this talk when I am feeling better. Tomorrow?'

'Sit back, Eryd, and listen,' the King said. It was said in a friendly manner but was clearly meant as an order. He obeyed, feeling a soft ringing in his ears.

'I think you came here this evening to see if you could shed some light on the slaughter at Tenterdyn. Would I be right?'

As if no longer in control of his own body, Lord Eryd Bench nodded his head. The movement felt slow, as if a puppeteer were pulling strings to cause his actions. He could hear the King's voice but it came to him as though he was deep inside a well, echoing around his mind.

'Good. And I believe you might have heard something along the lines that I ordered the killing of the Donal family? I think I'm right in presuming it might be Crys Donal who told you?' Celimus said, still friendly and speaking softly.

Against his wishes Eryd nodded, as if compelled to give the King what he wanted.

Celimus smiled. 'Thank you, Eryd, for your honesty. I am afraid I can confirm that I did give that order, and I regret my men missed the Donal heir who, I assume, is now running around Briavel causing trouble and sending people like you these treacherous messages.' Eryd frowned. Had he heard right? 'Is this not making sense, Lord Bench?' the King asked gently. 'I suspect you are wondering now about Lord Hartley, or perhaps about those closer to your heart . . . your wife and your beautiful child? I would forgive you for not paying any further attention to me for you have good reason to be worried about your family, Lord Bench.'

Eryd tried to stand, thought he might even have made it to his feet, but he was imagining it. Just wishful thinking. He found himself paralysed.

'My apologies, sir,' Celimus continued, as nonchalantly as if he were discussing the weather. 'I took the precaution of poisoning your wine. Won't be long now. I'm right, aren't I, Jessom, in thinking that Lord Bench would be experiencing some sort of paralysis now?'

Eryd could not turn to see the disgusted expression on the Chancellor's face as he nodded. If he had, he would have known that Jessom had murdered one of the most powerful men in the realm tonight only under pain of his own death. He heard Jessom's voice though — a whisper as the Chancellor removed the goblet from his catatonic grip. 'Forgive me, Lord Bench,' he said and then was gone, stepping aside to reveal the heinously grinning face of the King of Morgravia.

'You are dying, Eryd, in case you hadn't quite grasped it. We shall say it was your heart. I will ensure a proper ceremony for your funeral, you can count on it, and all your noble friends will come and pay their respects. I'm afraid I can't promise the same for your women, although I will make you an oath that they don't suffer, how's that? Pretty Georgyana, such a shame.'

Eryd began to growl unintelligibly, the only voice left to him now. His vision had turned dark and, although he could hear, he no longer listened. The cruel words were too painful. He felt his chest constricting and his heart seemed fit to burst from the little space it had left. He tried again to move but it was useless.

His last cohesive thought was that the King had got it wrong; for all his smug satisfaction, he had no idea that Crys Donal had returned to Morgravia and was in fact already in Pearlis. Perhaps, Eryd thought, as his breathing came in shallow gasps, the young duke had already taken the Bench women and escaped, for he would surely not have liked the news of this visit to the King. Please don't let Georgyana die, he prayed as the paralysis took him and he gurgled a final heaving gasp. He died, eyes wide open, saliva dribbling down the dark robes he favoured.

'Check him,' Celimus ordered.

Jessom obliged in silence, seeking a pulse at the neck of Lord Bench. He shook his head. 'Dead.'

'Good. That is a most effective weapon, Jessom. I might ask you to use it again some time. I gather you didn't enjoy that death.' Jessom did not reply and the King did not care. 'You've already sent the men?'

'They left for the Bench household not long after the two lords arrival, sire.'

'Hartley knows too much.'

Jessom knew it was wasted breath to try to convince the King not to kill again tonight. 'I shall see to it, your majesty.'

'Arrange for him to be dealt with by men you trust, Chancellor. I want no wagging tongues.'

'May I ask, your majesty, how we are going to explain the disappearance of Lord Bench and Lord Hartley?' Jessom risked.

'That is what I pay you for, Chancellor. Don't trouble me with details. Be gone.'

Jessom turned, and so did something inside him.

CHAPTER 30

Wyl entered the same impressive chamber he had been escorted to when he was Romen Koreldy. And once again he was greeted by the Mountain King, who immediately dismissed the two warriors he was speaking with.

'Ylena,' he said, moving swiftly from the huge windows where he had been gazing out across his valley. 'You look enchanting.' He kissed her hand and moved back to the panoramic view, this time with her in tow.

Wyl closed his eyes with revulsion but permitted the courtesy. 'Thank you for the fresh clothes.'

'Can't have you looking like a man all the time,' Cailech replied, his light green eyes sparkling in the dying light. 'Are you hungry?'

'Not especially.'

'Mountain People are always ravenous,' he admitted. 'I'm afraid you'll have to be polite and pretend you're eating plenty. Just push the food around if you must, but let the kitchen know you've appreciated their efforts tonight.'

Wyl nodded. 'Of course.'

'Your hair, it's so beautiful and soft,' the King said, touching it.

Wyl stepped closer to the window, trying to avoid the King's caress. 'This is certainly a magnificent place in which you live,' he said, keeping his voice steady, mind racing as to how he was going to escape. No ideas had presented themselves, save death, and he was not permitted to force that. The Quickening was sinister enough without antagonising its magic. He thought about those still left to him whom he loved — Fynch, Elspyth, Gueryn, hopefully, and, of course, always Valentyna. He could not risk these precious lives and he was terrified Myrren's gift might strike at them if he broke its laws.

'This is your home now, Ylena. I hope you'll come to love it in the same way that my people do.'

Cailech watched the Morgravian noblewoman smile wanly at him. 'May I ask you a question, sire?'

'By all means. Come, sit, let me pour us something to enjoy whilst we talk.'

Sitting was good, Wyl decided, for there were no chairs in the room which could take the two of them. 'Thank you,' he said and walked deeper into the chamber towards the hearth.

'I had a fire lit. I presumed you might be feeling the cold.'

'Just a bit,' Wyl said and shivered for effect. It made the King grin.

Seated, Wyl broached the subject which had burned on his lips ever since meeting Cailech again. 'My lord, I have learned that someone very precious to me was sent into the Razors a little while ago with a scouting party.'

The King did not reply, simply arched an eyebrow in

query as he handed Ylena a small exquisite glass of a honey-coloured wine which looked syrupy and delicious. 'This is my personal favourite. Please enjoy.'

Wyl nodded his thanks and sipped. It was Romen's distant memory which recalled the wine – a burst of sharp fruit whilst somehow being achingly sweet – but it was Ylena's mouth that smiled with pleasure. Again the King grinned.

'He is Morgravian,' Wyl continued. 'An older man. His name is Gueryn le Gant.'

Cailech's expression remained unchanged. 'Yes, I know of him.'

'Is he alive, sire?'

'I don't know.'

Wyl's heart twisted in his chest but he had to be especially cautious here. He could not let on that he knew anything more than Ylena herself could know. 'I see. But you had him as a prisoner?'

'That is correct.'

'Could we find out if he has survived, my lord?'

'That depends.'

'On what, your majesty?' Wyl drew on all his sister's sweet manners.

The King put a finger to his lips at the sound of a knock on the door. 'Come,' he called.

A servant appeared. 'Forgive me, your majesty, Warrior Borc wondered if you could spare a moment. He said it's extremely important.'

Borc! Wyl remembered the name all too well – the man who had nearly prevented their escape from the fortress last time. He should have killed the man instead of respecting Lothryn's wishes.

The King showed his irritation at being interrupted. 'Very well, I can spare only a moment, and tell him it had better be vital news for this disruption.' The servant disappeared. 'Forgive me, Ylena,' Cailech said, 'this won't take long.'

Wyl nodded, a polite smile on his sister's face.

Borc entered nervously. Wyl stiffened as he saw the man still carried himself with a limp – the legacy of Romen's sword wielded in his own hands.

'This had better be good, Borc,' the King warned. 'I have company.'

The young warrior nodded towards the noblewoman, embarrassed, and made a low bow to his sovereign. 'Please forgive me, sire, but I bring dire news.'

'Dire?' the King repeated, not taking the younger man too seriously. 'Get on with it then, man.'

'Should I speak freely?' he asked, glancing again towards the King's guest.

'I would have said so otherwise,' Cailech replied, his tone brusque.

'Yes, your majesty.' Borc bobbed another bow. 'I . . . er, well, I was passing the stable earlier this evening, sire, and there was a terrible commotion from within. It was your stallion, my lord.'

'I see, and where was Maegryn?' the King asked.

'That's what I'm here to tell you, sire. Maegryn is dead.'

The King paused deliberately in an attempt to steady his erupting emotions. 'Killed by the horse?' he wondered aloud, mind racing as to whether Lothryn could or would do such a thing.

'No, your majesty. Killed by one of our own and the Grenadyne.'

'What?' Cailech roared now, no longer caring for control.

Wyl stood and backed away, his own mind in a swirl of confusion as to what could have happened between Aremys and Galapek to provoke such a thing.

'Farrow was there?' the King demanded.

Borc nodded. 'It was not Farrow who did the deed, sire.'

'Tell me.' Cailech's face had darkened, his eyes were narrow. A storm was only barely under control. Wyl knew the look, had seen it through Romen's eyes. Everything was warning him to flee but there was no escape. They had forgotten him in the shock and he frantically scanned the room now for a way out. But there was no side door, no entry other than the one presently blocked by Borc. Ylena was trapped.

'It was Myrt, sire.'

The room became deathly silent. Even the air seemed to thicken in that moment of dread.

Cailech's voice, when it came, was strung taut. It was a groaned whisper as the impact of a second betrayal from a trusted warrior hit hard. 'You are sure of this?'

The man nodded, eyes darting towards Ylena and anxiously back to his King. 'I was taking a tumble with a girl, sire. Forgive me. We were in the hayloft above your stallion's stable when two men came in. I recognised Myrt immediately, and of course the Grenadyne was easy to distinguish even in the low light of the stable.'

'Go on,' the King urged, his body tensed like an animal ready to pounce on prey.

Borc looked as though he regretted the whole idea of bringing this alarming news to his sovereign. *Gone is the smugness now, eh, Borc?* Wyl thought, deriving momentary pleasure from the uncertain expression on the warrior's face as he tried to explain something the King did not want to hear yet insisted on being told.

'Myrt and Farrow, they . . .' Borc looked embarrassed.

'What? What did they do?' the King demanded.

Borc took a breath. 'They talked to Galapek, sire.'

Wyl had not thought the atmosphere in the room could get more potent with foreboding or that the King could hold himself more still or more tense, but he now saw he was wrong. It was an ominous sign.

Borc tried to fill the silence. 'The Grenadyne spoke to the horse as if it could hear him, sire, and so did Myrt. They . . . well, I feel awkward about this, sire,' he said, looking to his King for help.

'Say it!'

'They called your stallion Lothryn.'

Cailech swung around, a sound of anger combined with anguish escaping his throat. He swatted at the clay flagon nearby and it shattered on the granite floor, the smell of honey and syrupy sweet wine wafting through the chamber.

'Finish it, Haldor damn you, Borc!' the King said, rounding on his warrior. It was the first time Wyl had ever witnessed Cailech lose control.

Borc swallowed. 'The horse reared when they called to him, sire, then it began to scream and kick at the walls. Farrow told Myrt that the stallion wanted to be let loose.'

'Did they do that?' Cailech demanded.

Borc shook his head. 'Maegryn interrupted their planning. He questioned what they were doing around Galapek. Myrt seemed unsure at first, sire. The Grenadyne did all the talking, said he wanted to go out for a ride or some such excuse. Maegryn said he had to report them because the barshi had given orders since the disappearance of the Morgravian prisoner that anyone acting strangely around Galapek was to be singled out.'

Wyl kept Ylena's gaze on the floor but sensed the King steal a glance towards her at the mention of Gueryn. He worked hard to give the impression that she was embarrassed to be sharing this information and especially did not react to the mention of the prisoner.

Borc was in full flight now, racing to the end of his sordid tale. 'Maegryn said he was coming to see you, sire, and that's when Myrt grabbed him. Farrow told him not to but there was blood rage there, sire, Myrt couldn't stop. He strangled Maegryn but I didn't stop to see what they did with the body, your majesty. I jumped from the small window upstairs and came straight here, although I gather the Grenadyne is also on his way to see you,' he said, looking behind him as if Aremys might already be standing there.

'And Myrt?'

'Has gone to find Rashlyn, your majesty. Farrow wants to know what has happened to the Morgravian prisoner. Maegryn mentioned that he thought the barshi had taken him for his own uses.'

Cailech twisted away in angry thought, staring out of the window. He could only barely see the great shadows of the mountains in the distance now, as darkness fell quickly in the Razors.

'Borc.'

'Sire?'

Cailech's voice was as cold as the ice that covered the

Razors' peaks in midwinter. 'Assemble the senior warriors. Tell the gatekeeper no one leaves, not even our own. Send reinforcements to the portcullis in case they use force. Have several guards posted on every gate — even those into the town. Neither Myrt nor the Grenadyne are to be permitted access in either direction. Release the dogs. Understand?' Borc nodded. 'Send Rollo to me immediately with one other of his choice — have runners sent for him if necessary. Tell Rollo everything and then find Myrt. Go now, don't fail me.' Borc bowed and departed.

The King turned slowly to face Ylena. Wyl set her face impassively and took the lead. 'I'm sorry, your majesty, that I witnessed this. I'm sure it was a private concern.'

'It was not your fault, Ylena. I should have taken more precaution.'

'That man of yours was speaking about Gueryn le Gant, wasn't he?'

The King nodded, staring so intently at Ylena that Wyl felt himself falter slightly. Perhaps it was not a good idea to question Cailech right now. But there may never be a better opportunity, and time was their enemy. 'Gueryn le Gant is my guardian,' he said. 'When our mother died, Gueryn was all we had, for my father was away at Pearlis with the King. When I was sent to Stoneheart to be raised as the ward of King Magnus, Gueryn was there too. He is family. He is all I have left.' Wyl made Ylena's soft tones beseeching.

The news took the King by surprise but he had no time to respond for there was another knock. Once again he hushed Ylena with a gesture. Both knew who it was going to be this time. The same servant appeared with an expression of apology but Cailech hardly noticed.

'Is it Aremys Farrow?' he asked before the man said anything.

'Yes, sire.'

'Send him in.'

Aremys was shown in and Wyl immediately sent him a look of warning.

'Sire, you were expecting me?' Aremys said, trying hard not to show his surprise.

'I guessed you would come around soon enough,' Cailech said, his tone casual and his body language relaxed. Behind him Wyl shook his head towards Aremys, desperately cautioning him against saying anything incriminating.

Aremys faltered. The smile he would normally give to the man he now considered a friend did not arrive. He realised that someone had reached Cailech or Wyl would not be communicating such a warning.

'Care for a cup of wine, Farrow?'

'No, sire, I came here only briefly to pass on a message. Forgive my interruption, I thought it was important.'

'Apparently there are a number of important messages to be communicated tonight,' Cailech replied.

The cryptic response was not lost on Aremys. 'I can come back later, sire.' He saw relief move across Ylena's face and then froze as Cailech also glanced towards her. The King was fast and much too smart to be duped.

'No, please, come and join us,' Cailech said, affably this time. 'I'd like to share some wine with you.'

Wyl looked at the shattered flagon and Aremys followed his glance, taking in that something dangerous had occurred here tonight. Tempers perhaps had frayed, for if it was an accident Cailech would have called for a servant to clear the mess. 'Are you well, Ylena?' he said, suddenly wondering whether Cailech had hurt Wyl.

'I am, thank you, Aremys. I was just about to tell the King about Queen Valentyna and all she mentioned to me from Romen's tales of the Razors.' Aremys nodded, frowning slightly, and Wyl took the risk. 'You know, about Romen's escape with the help of Lothryn, and how he later worried about what might have happened to the brave warrior who betrayed his King.'

Wyl had fast reflexes but Ylena's body moved slower than he was used to. He saw the King's sudden action but could not avoid the hard, stinging slap. Another blow from a different King but with the same result: Ylena's small body flew across the room. She gashed her leg on a small table and sprawled across a chair before tumbling to the granite floor. He lay still, trying to assess if anything had been broken. From the terrible pain, he suspected her slim shoulder had dislocated during the awkward fall.

Wyl heard Cailech ranting above his sister's body. 'Do you think I'm stupid, Ylena?'

Wyl had no choice; he spoke quickly to his friend. 'He knows about Maegryn,' was all he managed before he felt himself lifted easily from the floor and flung again across the chamber. He glimpsed Cailech's enraged face and heard his roar of anger. Ylena's body crunched awkwardly against the stone fireplace and this time something definitely broke. It was her leg, badly snapped with bone poking through the shin. Fresh pain klaxoned through her frail body. Wyl released a scream, part out of helplessness, part designed to keep Cailech's attention on Ylena and not Aremys. It was too late though – Cailech's men had arrived, amongst them someone Aremys clearly recognised.

'Hold him, Rollo!' the King commanded, pointing at a startled Aremys who was unsure whether to run towards Ylena or out the door. Either way he had left his decision too late and Wyl closed Ylena's eyes in despair. He moved her bleeding, broken body into a sitting position and prayed the King would not hurt her body further. He could handle the physical pain but the battering of Ylena both at Tenterdyn and now here was more than Wyl could bear emotionally. He wanted to scream that she had already suffered enough, but of course that would make no sense to anyone except the other prisoner in this room, now desperately struggling in the arms of his captors.

'Be still, Farrow!' Cailech commanded. 'There is no escape.'

Aremys obeyed. 'What is this about, your highness? I thought I was a free man.'

'You were,' Cailech said, advancing on his new victim, Ylena forgotten. 'Until Borc brought me some dark news this evening.'

Aremys wore a confused expression. 'What news, sire?'

'You snake!' Cailech spat. 'Am I that gullible, Farrow? Perhaps I am,' he said, answering his own question with a weariness in his voice. He smiled ruefully. 'I trusted you. I thought you were on our side.'

'King Cailech—' Aremys began.

'Don't, Grenadyne,' the King warned. 'Don't begin to spin any lies. Rollo, is everything secured?'

The man nodded. 'Borc and others are seeing to it, sire.'

'Myrt?'

Rollo looked uncomfortable at the mention of the

senior warrior's name. 'He is being followed to the barshi's quarters, sire, as you ordered.'

As soon as Aremys heard Myrt's name, he lowered his chin and his body slumped slightly in the grip of the men. They were all as good as dead now. He looked over at Wyl, equally helpless at the other end of the room, and felt something inside him break.

Rashlyn had been experiencing an inexplicable sense of doom for the past few hours. The Stones, which he had cast for himself, kept showing him the coming of a dragon. It made no sense. Dragons were creatures of myth, along with the winged lions, unicorns and other strange beasts worshipped through the ages – and still revered in Morgravia. The Stones had never given him such a picture before and yet they insisted, time and again. Considering he had cast the Stones only a few times in his life on his own behalf – and had always found them accurate – this was wildly unsettling, particularly as it made no sense.

He had been pondering this curiosity for many hours, wondering what it could mean for Cailech and, more to the point, himself. Now, he felt a light was dawning: perhaps the vision pointed towards the changing of a sovereign in Morgravia. It had come to him that the King of Morgravia sat upon the dragon throne; that the King's emblem – and mythical creature of the Crown of Morgravia – was always the dragon. So did the coming of the dragon shown by the Stones mean a new King for the southern realm?

That made little sense, however, for the present King was young, virile and seemingly in excellent health according to Cailech, whom the barshi had spoken to briefly on his return. They had exchanged a smattering of words with the promise to meet later that night. He was awaiting the summons now, eager to share with his King this telling from the Stones.

Perhaps they were suggesting that the marriage of Celimus to Valentyna would change the Crown somewhat, bringing a new Queen to the throne. Except the Stones were specific: they spoke only of the dragon and a new coming. Valentyna was not in any way connected to the dragon throne, nor, to his knowledge, did the Briavellians have any link to mythical creatures in the manner of Morgravia.

No, he pondered, pulling at his tangled beard, this was specifically about the Dragon King. There it was again: change. Before Cailech had left for Morgravia, the Stones had spoken of change and Rashlyn had thought they referred to something sinister. As it turned out, Cailech had returned triumphant, not only with a new truce and a peaceful neighbour but a bride as well. Rashlyn nodded to himself, congratulating the Stones on their accuracy. Change had indeed occurred for the King of the Razors. Everything had changed for the better.

But now this . . . this time it felt sinister, threatening. The Stones pointed towards the coming of the dragon, but he had done this casting purely for himself, not Cailech. This foretelling was about him. The dragon was coming for him – was that right?

Deep in his thoughts, he jumped in alarm as the door of his chamber crashed open and the huge body of Myrt filled the doorway.

'Good evening, barshi,' Myrt said. The words were polite, but the tone and the expression on the big man's face belied them.

'What are you doing here?' the small man stammered, immediately summoning a spell of protection.

'I've come for the truth about Lothryn – or should I say, Galapek?'

Rashlyn's madness was his best protection; better than any spell. The insanity that held the barshi in its grip took over now and he no longer felt intimidated. However, he was sufficiently intrigued by the big man's discovery that he held back the magic he had prepared to hurl at Myrt. 'What do you know?' he asked, his voice light and taunting.

'Where is the Morgravian prisoner?' Myrt responded.

The barshi gave a mad cackle. 'I'll be happy to show you,' he said, and pointed to the corner where a large grey dog sat, chained and quivering.

Myrt was aghast, unsure of whether to take the deranged barshi seriously, yet somehow knowing he was being shown the truth. 'Gueryn?' he asked the dog tentatively.

The dog whined. It was in pain but it pawed the floor in frustration and strained against its chain.

'Like my work, Myrt? It's so much better than Lothryn, whom I'm afraid I must have killed in the process. As you can see, le Gant is alive within the beast and fully aware of his new status.'

'You stinking—'

Myrt got no further. Pain exploded in his head and his nose and ears began to leak blood.

'Shut up!' the barshi screamed. 'Or I won't even give you a choice of what I turn you into, you stupid fool.' Myrt was moaning unintelligibly. 'I guess that hurts, eh?' Rashlyn continued. 'Well, listen to me now, big man. I'm going to take away the pain and then you are going to tell me who else knows my secret.'

Myrt shook his head vigorously and blood spattered the barshi. Rashlyn seemed not to notice; instead he stepped up the punishment and the warrior's eyes bulged as a fresh wave of pain hit. His arms became rigid and hung unnaturally in mid-air, his torso began to tremble and his breathing came in erratic, shallow grunts.

'Do just as I say, Myrt,' Rashlyn warned. His fingers moved slightly and the warrior was pushed back and held against the wall. 'Better?' he asked, dispelling the pain.

Myrt refused to co-operate even though his body was released from its agony.

'Who else knows?' Rashlyn asked, moving towards the warrior.

'Just me and, I presume, the King,' Myrt spluttered. Although the pain had lifted, the toll on his body was significant enough to make him gasp still.

'Oh, yes, the King knows. It was his choice to punish Lothryn that way, you see. I think it's beautifully subtle. And Galapek is so magnificent—'

Rashlyn suddenly stopped and cocked his head, as if listening to something. He turned slowly, fear coursing through every fibre of his being.

'What?' Myrt said.

'Ssh!' Rashlyn hissed, swivelling his body as if trying to lock onto something. 'It's coming,' he murmured.

Myrt, connected to the barshi through the madman's magic, also sensed the approach of something. He was stunned at the immensity of power which was being communicated. 'What is it?'

'The dragon,' Rashlyn whispered, suddenly letting go

his magic hold on Myrt as his own fears got the better of him.

Myrt fell to the floor, hitting his knees hard and yelling his protest. He was forgotten as the barshi began to spin around in the chamber, a look of terror on his face. Myrt took advantage of Rashlyn's confusion to drag himself across the floor to the dog, who cocked his head towards a key on the table. Myrt nodded, reached for the key and unlocked the chain that secured the dog. It barked once and stretched on unsteady, gangly legs.

Blood was running freely from his nose; Myrt only noticed it now. He tried to wipe it away but more replaced it. He was thinking he should ignore the weakness imposed by the barshi's magic and somehow make his way to the door, crawling if necessary, when the doorway was filled by a large figure.

'Hello, Borc,' he said, disdain lacing his tone. He did not like this young man, blamed him for the capture and torture of Lothryn.

The warrior looked over at Rashlyn who seemed to be in a trance, mumbling to himself. 'What have you done?' he demanded of Myrt.

'Nothing. He's off in his own world, muttering about the coming of the dragon or something. Why are you here?'

'Why are you on the floor . . . bleeding?' Borc continued angrily, dismissing the question levelled at him.

'The last time I checked,' Myrt began, working hard to ignore the weakening sensations in his body, 'I was your superior, Borc. Do I need to remind you of how to speak to a superior?'

'And the last time I checked, Myrt,' Borc sneered, 'you were busy murdering someone.'

'Ah,' Myrt replied, hiding his shock. He would not give this snivelling youngster the satisfaction he surely craved of the most senior of the warriors grovelling to him.

'I told the King,' Borc added triumphantly.

'Yes, I'm sure you have, you arse-licking fuck!'

Borc's reply was cut off by the arrival of a boy who appeared to step straight through the granite blocks of the high tower's wall. He was surrounded by a shimmering light which blinded the three men momentarily before it dissipated. He looked around at them and Myrt realised this was no vision; the boy was flesh and blood – scrawny and small but terrifyingly real.

Rashlyn's wildness intensified. 'Who are you?' he screeched.

'I am your destroyer, Rashlyn,' the boy said.

Everything happened so fast, Myrt hardly saw it unfold. Rashlyn leapt through an open window. The drop meant certain death yet Myrt glimpsed the barshi hovering in the open air before he disappeared from view.

He noticed the boy smile before he seemingly dissolved back through the wall. Borc watched it too, open-mouthed and filled with disbelief. It was his slowness to recover which gave the grey dog a chance to leap and bring the man down.

Myrt watched in horror as the dog, its limbs still trembling, struck for Borc's throat. Myrt reached for his dagger but so did Borc. The younger man was strong and despite his fear he struck at the dog with the blade, wounding it many times in its side. The creature refused to let go. It had him by the throat at last and it was experiencing the blood madness that comes over both man or beast when defending its life or those it loves.

Myrt raised himself painfully, still suffering the effects of the magic, and all but fell onto Borc and the dog. It was growling fiercely now, its huge jaws locked around the man's neck, tearing at his throat. Borc made one final valiant effort and managed to gouge at the animal's eye and sink his blade once more, this time into its chest. The dog screamed and rolled away but Myrt was not going to let Gueryn's quarry live. He would mete out death on behalf of the dog who had saved his own life. Raising his dagger he struck deep into Borc's lacerated throat and hit the artery he was looking for. The younger man stared with dismay at the plume of blood that erupted and grabbed at his neck in a sad attempt to retain the precious liquid. He even managed to drag himself to his knees before Haldor claimed him and Borc of the Mountain People fell heavily across the prone dog, dead.

CHAPTER 31

Crys Donal rode Eryd Bench's chestnut mare through the Pearlis town gates and nodded to the watchmen.

'Shar guide you,' they called to the lone rider, who raised his hand in friendly salute but said nothing in return.

Not long afterwards a black carriage, like any other public carriage that plied its trade on the streets of Pearlis, also left the gates.

'How long, Gordy?' one of the watchmen cried as the driver paid his toll, recognising him from the pool of men who entered and exited the city many times a day with paying passengers. The man shrugged and the gatekeepers caught sight of two women in the carriage whom they recognised as Lady Bench and her daughter. 'Evening, Lady Bench,' one said, showing the right courtesies.

Helyn Bench smiled back, the men never knowing how much courage that gesture took. The younger woman did not look at them at all. 'Onwards, driver,' Lady Bench called.

It was at least another fifteen minutes before a petite

figure, cloaked in blue, walked a horse out of the city gates to whistles of approval from the men. It was not dark yet so they could see her pretty features set in a pale face. Fortunately for Elspyth they could not see the dark bloodstain on her cloak or the fierce effort it required for her to first mount and then urge the horse to carry her gently beyond the reach of King Celimus. She forced a smile and said, 'See you soon, lads,' as if she was only going to be away for a few hours, then she too disappeared down the road. She knew she had two bends to make before the third one would claim her fully from the watchtower's view. It felt like a lifetime and she wondered if the men were scratching their heads and asking each other why the horse was being walked so slowly down the road.

Finally she caught sight of Crys Donal. He rushed towards her and, as much as she wanted to be composed and not show how sick she was, Elspyth all but fell from the horse as she leaned towards him. As they had before, the strong arms of the Duke of Felrawthy cushioned her and she was carried gently to a patch of soft grass. She would be lying to herself if she did not admit it felt good to be in his embrace again, even though right now his eyes held anything but mischief in them.

'Elspyth,' Georgyana said, 'I'm sorry you had to do that but—'

'Hush, Georgyana,' she replied. 'There was no other way. It would have looked too odd for you to ride out after your mother's carriage, especially alone.'

'We can only hope those guards make no connections. Two of us were strangers and easily forgotten,' Crys reassured. Elspyth noticed how his gaze softened when it fell upon the Benchs' golden-haired daughter. She felt another pang and a reminder that Crys did not belong to her and that she had pushed his gentle and usually amusing advances away too often. She was spoken for . . . but was it by a dead man, she wondered sadly.

Crys glanced towards Lady Bench, who sat on a milestone staring straight before her at nothing in particular, clearly dwelling on thoughts of her beloved Eryd. He walked over and put his arms around her. She was a friend of his mother's, around her age. He tried to imagine how Aleda must have felt watching Jeryb Donal die. Crys was sure Eryd was dead by now too, and knew the effect on Lady Bench would be no less painful for not witnessing it.

'I'm so sorry, Helyn,' he said softly.

'Are you sure it's useless, Crys? I mean—'

He cut off her teary words which were too painful to listen to again. 'We cannot risk Georgyana, Lady Bench. You must see to her safety first. I promise you I will return to Pearlis, but first I insist on ensuring you three ladies are out of danger.' He hugged her again, suspecting that her inclination was to send Georgyana on with him and take her chances back in Pearlis. 'Please, Lady Bench, Celimus showed no mercy to my parents, or my brothers, the youngest of whom had barely reached your daughter's tender years. He will have no qualms about killing you, Lord Bench, Georgyana and anyone else who looks like getting in his way.'

'In the way of what?' she said.

'Of whatever it is that he wants,' Crys said, keeping his voice calm and not withdrawing his embrace. 'He is mad, Lady Bench. He dreams of empire. The wedding is a sham. He will destroy Valentyna and Briavel one way or another — it just appears more respectable if he can do it diplomatically. Listen to me,' he said, taking the liberty of turning her face towards his earnest one. 'If he is prepared to murder my father, who was the most loyal of Morgravians, then he will respect none of his senior counsellors' lives. Please trust me.'

'So you think Eryd is already dead,' she said, her voice flat.

There was no point in giving empty placations after making them flee for their lives. 'I do.'

She did not break down into sobs as he had expected; she did not even shed another tear; instead she echoed the words of his mother. 'Avenge him,' she said, 'for all our sakes.'

'Celimus has many deaths to answer for, my lady. I intend making him accountable for each of them, rest assured.'

She squeezed his arm, unable to speak for her tumbling emotions.

'Come, we will ride in pairs now,' he continued. 'Elspyth won't be able to make it far so we will split company once I am sure we are in a safe place.'

Elspyth, breathing hard and helped by Georgyana, arrived at his side. Crys reached for her hand. 'Can you go a bit further?'

'Yes, let's go,' she said, unfairly enjoying his touch in front of Georgyana.

'You and Lady Bench ride together, Elspyth. Georgyana can come with me,' Crys said, instantly putting to rest any delusion that he was not utterly infatuated with the young noblewoman. It was fitting that he align himself

with his own kind and they would make the most handsome of couples, Elspyth thought. She scowled privately,
but convinced herself that her acid mood was from the
throb at her shoulder.

'Where are we going?' Georgyana asked, unaware of
the sour emotions of the pretty woman by her side.

'They will expect us to go north,' Crys said, 'as we all
have homes and links there.'

'So we go south?' Georgyana finished for him and he
smiled indulgently.

'Yes, my lady. South to Argorn.'

Jessom stared at the sputtering candle. Its erratic flame
held his attention in an otherwise darkened room. His
thoughts were distracted, roaming. A light perfume
wafted up from the soap leaf he had used to wash his
hands after touching Eryd Bench's body. He had killed
twice himself, and had many deaths carried out at his
order, but none had ever felt like this one. Lord Bench's
death had been as unpleasant as it was unnecessary.
Unpleasant because Jessom had been forced to administer
the poison personally and very much against his own will,
and unnecessary because it had achieved nothing but
another dirty secret to keep hidden.

He linked his newly washed fingers as he contemplated
the afternoon's proceedings. To the King, the report of
another corpse, no matter how high-ranking, was akin to
hearing that a kitten had died from the kitchen cat's latest
litter. He just kills on a whim, Jessom thought bitterly.
Bench and his fellow lord could have been so easily
diverted, sent on some special mission even, but left alive
to remain important in the fabric of Morgravia.

'Shar knows, that fabric is wearing very thin,' he muttered now.

If Lord Bench was questioning the King and his motives then this was surely the end of the road, for Eryd Bench would never have considered making his concerns public without many weeks of soul-searching. If Lord Bench, the most loyal of the senior courtiers, was wavering, then most of the others would have had their say on the King's actions long ago.

'And civil unrest is the next stage.' Jessom finished the thought aloud.

It would only take someone like Crys Donal, now the Duke of Felrawthy, to stir up sufficient emotion and the civil unrest could turn into an uprising. Jessom was not so naive as to believe that the famous Legion would not follow its instincts, which would be screaming in favour of Lord Donal after what had happened in the north. The Legion had suffered several blows recently – enough to provoke the men into turning against the King they hated.

Jessom listed them in his mind: Alyd Donal, Wyl Thirsk, Ylena Thirsk, most of the Donal family, Rittyl-worth's holy community. Even the death of King Valor of Briavel was beginning to be viewed suspiciously, particularly given that Wyl Thirsk was in Werryl on the King's business when he lost his life alongside Valor. Jessom had heard mutterings that the two deaths were not as cut and dried as they were said to be. Then there was Jorn, a popular lad around Stoneheart – his torture and death had hit hard and for what result? The Legion had not recovered from the deaths of its own men either – all in the pursuit of missing taxes. Too many had been impaled and left to die long, horrible deaths. Celimus was too cruel;

too quick to punish without consideration of the repercussions. As for all the mercenaries who had lost their lives – well, few cared, but Jessom hated killing for no good reason. Almost all could have been spared – they were on the Crown's side anyway.

He slammed his hand down on the table in frustration. And now Lord Bench was dead and Hartley was languishing in the dungeon. Jessom had finally rebelled against Celimus and refused to kill pointlessly again. He would find a way to spare Hartley yet.

Chancellor Jessom lit a fresh candle and extinguished the sputtering one with a pinch, hardly feeling its warmth on his fingertips. He was too deep in thought about his own future. He assessed his options. They were few and mostly unpalatable. He could remain with Celimus and stay loyal to his belief that the King of Morgravia was too strong to be challenged. He could raise the Legion himself by telling its officers the truth, but then what? They could unseat Celimus but there was no heir, which potentially meant some distant relative from Parrgamyn perhaps laying claim to the throne. Jessom's experience of the Parrgamyse told him that was not a wise path. Alternatively, he could argue that a new dynasty be created from within – someone like the new Duke of Felrawthy perhaps – but Jessom, kingmaker or not, could not be sure of bringing about such a change in culture. He could leave. Disappear this night and begin a new life elsewhere. But where? And if Celimus survived as King then he would have Jessom hunted down. The Chancellor could not bear to dwell on what the King would do with him when caught . . . and he was sure he would be caught, even if it took Celimus years.

That left one last option. And as he reflected on its merits, he realised it was, without question, not only the best of the alternatives but perhaps his most inspired idea ever. If it worked, he would never have to worry again. If he failed, it meant an horrific death. So he must take precautions.

He would need the help of an expert in fashioning a failsafe capsule of the juice of the Deathbloom, a plant so rare most people had never heard of it. But Jessom had and he was taking no chances with Celimus. If he was caught in this last and desperate measure, then he would not hesitate to bite down on the capsule which would deliver death so swiftly that no one would even realise what had occurred. By then, his body would be stiff in the rigor the plant's poison so effectively provoked.

He smiled thinly. 'Not that I intend ever taking that capsule,' he whispered.

Wyl stared at Aremys through Ylena's glazed vision. He must have passed out momentarily, he realised; he had slumped to one side and must appear dead. It looked as though the fight had gone out of the Grenadyne. The King was pacing before him, poking his finger into his chest, sneering at him with cutting words. The two guards either side of Aremys looked uncomfortable. Wyl fought the pain back as Gueryn had taught him and righted Ylena's frame against the hearth. No one saw his movement; everyone was intent on Cailech.

He had to move, broken leg and dislocated shoulder aside, not to mention sundry other fractures. Go down fighting – was that not the Legion's way? Wyl rallied his spirit and called upon anything left within him of his and

Ylena's predecessors to find the strength to move towards Aremys.

'So you don't deny Maegryn's death?' Cailech demanded of the mercenary, his anger back under icy control.

'No, sire. It was a mistake.'

'Mistake!'

Aremys blinked. There was no way out of this; no possible explanation – except the truth, of course – for the death of the stablemaster. He no longer cared about Cailech and the peace treaty or about the Mountain People. In truth, if he boiled it down, he cared about the man trapped in the broken woman's body in the corner, he cared about a man driven mad with pain and anguish by being transformed into a horse, and he cared about bringing about the death of a southern King.

Nothing much else mattered – not even his own life, it seemed, because it had not occurred to him to count it in his list. He stole a glance at Ylena and realised she had moved. Not dead then; brave Wyl was crawling towards him in a broken body. What could they achieve against two huge warriors and an enraged King now reaching for his blade?

'Lost for words, Farrow? Perhaps this will loosen your tongue,' Cailech said, swiping his knife across the Grenadyne's face.

Aremys saw the red splashes spatter across Rollo's face. The man blinked but said nothing. To his own credit, Aremys hardly flinched. Perhaps it had been too fast. How he found the wit he would never know, but he enjoyed it. 'Haldor be praised that your blade is kept so keen, Cailech. I didn't feel a thing.'

The King's gaze narrowed as he watched the bright

blood drench the face of the man he had called friend; the man he had thought might fill the yearning gap of friendship caused by the loss of Lothryn. But this man was now facing death *because* of Lothryn.

'Why, Aremys? You could have had it all with me,' Cailech said, a touch of sadness creeping into his tone.

'Because you are a puppet King,' Aremys replied, defiance rising in him as he accepted death. He could see the pulse at Cailech's temple beginning to throb.

'Explain yourself, Farrow.'

He shrugged, revelling in his nonchalance. It was amazing to let go of fear; he suddenly felt empowered. This was how Wyl must have felt when he was baiting Celimus into killing Ylena at Tenterdyn – except Wyl had not expected to die, he thought, and a rueful grin crept across his bloodied face.

'Answer me!' the King roared, raising the blade.

'I'm not afraid to die, Cailech, so threatening me will not help you learn what you need to. But I shall tell you anyway. You are a puppet to Rashlyn. Ask your men. Ask Rollo here what he thinks of your mad barshi and the way he controls you. Ask poor Myrt, who would crawl over the very icecaps for you but hates you now for what you have done at the barshi's whim. If only you had bothered to ask Maegryn, he would have told you the same. You are controlled by the mad sorcerer who uses magic on you, my King, and makes decisions for you.'

Aremys felt the change of atmosphere in the room immediately. The grip of his captors lessened and he saw Cailech's face move through a series of expressions from disbelief to rage.

'You lie!'

'No, Cailech. Look at your men. Ask them. You turned Lothryn into a beast. Galapek is an abomination – your abomination – but it was not your idea, was it, sire? It was Rashlyn's. And now the Morgravian prisoner has disappeared. Where is Gueryn le Gant, your majesty? Magically twisted into another abomination, that's where. Can your people trust you with this sort of misery and sorcery hanging over them?'

When Rollo spoke, it broke the spell. 'My King, is this true? Have you used magic on Lothryn?'

Cailech's hesitation was damaging.

'And now he's going to have Myrt killed, Rollo, because he knows the truth too.'

Rollo dropped his hands from Aremys and his second followed suit. 'I cannot permit this, sire,' he said, shaking his head, disbelief raging in his eyes. 'I hate the barshi. But I loved Lothryn like a brother, and Myrt is our leader even though you are our King. You would kill the two I trust most? Rashlyn is evil, sire.'

Cailech's eyes darkened in the granite face. He was the only man in the room with a weapon. 'Do you challenge me, Rollo?'

The warrior backed away. 'I don't know the truth, sire. I don't understand any of it. If Myrt killed Maegryn then I wish to hear why. I want his side of the story, not the words of Borc who would sell his own grandmother to get into your good books.'

'I order you to take this man to the dungeons,' Cailech said. His words were slowly spoken and chillingly intense as he willed the man before him to obey.

Rollo shook his head equally slowly, hardly believing

he was defying his own sovereign. 'Not until you bring
Rashlyn here . . . and Myrt.'

The room had become still with tension. Cailech stared
at Rollo and then back at Aremys. His silence was telling
as he considered his options. Finally he nodded wearily.
'Go. Bring them both here.'

Relief flooded the warrior at the King's capitulation;
inside, he was still reeling from his stand against Cailech.
He wasted no time and nodded to his second to follow
and then to Aremys, who would have liked to thank Rollo
for his courage. It was pointless though. As he stared at
Cailech and the King returned the glare, both knew the
Grenadyne would not live beyond a few moments of the
two warriors' departure.

Aremys could have said as much, and perhaps changed
the course of how things unfolded, but he had seen something out of the corner of his eye, something everyone
else had missed. It might work. He cast a prayer to Shar
and, just in case, one to Haldor as well, then left it to
the gods to decide which would answer it.

When the two Mountain men had departed, Cailech
rounded on Aremys.

'I know you don't intend to let me live long enough
even to clap eyes on Myrt again, sire,' Aremys said, playing
for time.

'How instinctive of you, Farrow. I'm glad we understand one another. You have betrayed my trust.'

'Lothryn got to be a horse. Nothing so exotic planned
for me, Cailech?'

'Nothing leaps to mind,' Cailech growled, stepping
closer.

'Or do you have to wait for the puppeteer to arrive in

order to make the decision for you? So he can cast his magic and make you dance precisely as he wishes?'

Cailech shook his head in mock disgust but Aremys could see him grinding his jaw so hard, he felt sure teeth were being shattered in the process. And then his plan was destroyed. Cailech turned nonchalantly to gaze down at the figure of Ylena Thirsk, who had painfully and silently crawled the length of the room, a trail of blood behind her.

'Ah, Ylena, good. You've arrived painfully I see and just in time to watch your rescuer die. I think Aremys was counting on you to divert me, although I have to wonder what, without a weapon, he had in mind. Perhaps he was going to bite me to death.' He laughed. 'Here, my dear, let me help you,' and he reached down almost tenderly to pick her up.

Aremys felt his gut twist. It was over then. He had been counting on Wyl to achieve some diversion. Between them they might have been able to get the blade from Cailech and hold him off until the others returned. It was a stupid idea, but desperate people conjured desperate thoughts in desperate times.

'There we are,' Cailech said, placing a grimacing Ylena into a chair just in front of Aremys. 'Now you have a good view.' He lifted her skirt to look at her leg and made a tutting sound. 'Nasty. That must really hurt. I'm constantly impressed by your courage, Ylena.' He returned a savage gaze to Aremys. 'How would you like this done, my friend? Throat? Gut? Heart?' he asked, irony lacing his voice.

'May Haldor rot your heart, Cailech!' Aremys said, helplessness washing over him. He looked once more upon Ylena. 'I'm sorry I failed you.'

'You haven't yet,' Wyl answered. 'Remember who I am. Use me!' he urged.

Cailech smiled. 'Such a brave pair. What is it between you two? I could almost feel jealous. You seem to have one another in some sort of thrall. It's not ardour or lust, for I would have sensed it. It's more than that—'

Aremys was not going to listen to it any more. 'Get on with it then and look to your back, Cailech. Celimus will never allow you or the son you foisted on Lothryn's wife to live.' He rolled the die once more. Perhaps there was a chance yet. 'I've already told Celimus about Aydrech. Security, in case you did not keep faith with me. He will come looking for both of you. The boy will not live to see a year.'

Cailech's howl at the biting threat was filled with a venom that Aremys had only previously experienced in battle. It was beyond anger or fear; it was a state in which a man cared for nothing else except the kill. Many hardened fighters spoke of the moment when nothing but blood – the enemy's blood – could cleanse them of that wrath.

Aremys saw the blade rise in tandem with the King's howl of despair and took his chance, feeling sickened as he did so. It was up to the gods now.

It was no god that came to his rescue that day but a damaged man trapped in a woman's body. Broken and bleeding Wyl allowed Ylena's slight frame to be wrenched up by Aremys with perfect timing and thrown between the blade and the place where it was meant to bury itself.

The mighty blow nearly cleaved Ylena in two, cutting flesh and sinew, cartilage and bone, finally coming to rest buried between her breasts.

Her sad, lovely eyes met Aremys's as she fell to her death at last. Her gaze was triumphant.

Cailech groaned. The sound was deep and guttural, and filled with rage. He was bent double, his body was shaking and his large hands clutched at his head as it swung angrily from side to side as if in denial. The Mountain King suddenly arched his back, fists clenched, his expression a contortion of such pain that Aremys took a step back. Cailech let out a final low and desperate growl, slumping forward before he straightened, staring at the bright blood on the hand and arm that had dealt the murderous blow. The King took a deep, shuddering breath and lifted his formerly light eyes to meet those of Farrow.

Aremys, hating to have put Wyl through more pain, noted their curious ill-matched colour and did not know whether to cry with relief or share the despair of loss. He laid his hand onto the hard, muscled arm of King Cailech and whispered, 'Welcome back, Wyl.'

Wyl Thirsk, now King Cailech of the Razors, flexed his broad shoulders and sighed. 'Let's go find our friends,' he growled in Cailech's deep voice.

CHAPTER 32

Fynch sat cross-legged, staring at the man who had brought so much hate and potential destruction into the world. Now he must die.

Rashlyn did not know Fynch could see him, but he could feel the boy, sensed his powerful presence here amongst the Razors. He looked so small and helpless; how could a child possess such potent magic?

Rashlyn had fled without thinking, but leading the boy into the small wood behind the fortress now seemed like madness. Perhaps the child would die of cold. Perhaps he might. He summoned a spell to warm himself and pondered his next move.

It was not in Fynch's nature to be violent, but he was a destroyer whether he cared for the role or not. The blood of the dragon line pounded in his veins and the Dragon King himself demanded this of him. He would not fail. He might die but he would not let them down.

Not far away from him sat Knave, silent, filled with dread and powerless. His part in this adventure was over.

He had guided Fynch to Rashlyn and now all he could do was bear witness.

It seemed to Knave that the barshi had disappeared, but still Fynch sat and waited.

How do you feel? Knave could not let go of his concern.

Well enough to face what I must.

Does your head still pain you?

Yes. There is no more sharvan, before you ask.

Where is he?

Hiding, he thinks. He is confused and frightened but he will face me soon enough.

Are you frightened?

No.

I am.

Don't be. This is what you and I were meant to do.

Who are you, Fynch? Please share it with me before . . . Knave hesitated.

Before I die? Knave did not reply and Fynch did not force it. *I am the son of King Magnus of Morgravia, half-brother of Celimus. I am of the dragon's blood.*

Is that what the King saw in you?

Fynch nodded.

What does it mean?

Nothing really, Fynch said, shaking his head gently. *Hardly anyone knows. My mother, and she's dead. The Dragon King, you, and me. Magnus perhaps, but he is cold in his tomb.*

Shouldn't you tell someone?

Fynch smiled and shrugged. *Best kept between us. I know who I am now and where I belong. It is enough. I am one with the Dragon King. It's why he took me away as I slept — he wanted me to know the truth before I faced Rashlyn. He restored me temporarily so I could fight a King's fight.*

So where is the barshi?

Over there, Fynch said, pointing to the wooded area. *He thinks he is hidden.*

Invisible?

Apparently. But I see him.

Fynch, what are you planning to do?

Nothing.

What does that mean? You won't fight him.

He must attack me.

But you'll then respond?

Wait and see. Be brave now, Knave, you've told me that often enough.

I don't want to see you die.

Hush, here he comes.

When Jos arrived at the antechamber outside King Cailech's meeting room he was greeted by a look of disdain from the servant who manned the desk. Guards were posted as normal.

'Are they sending halfwits to the King now?'

'Shut up,' Jos growled, towering over the man and glad to note the words sounded perfectly enunciated. 'Do your job and let me do mine.'

The man sneered but backed away and knocked at the door. Curiously, the King opened it himself. This dismayed the servant. He was not used to talking to his majesty in person. 'Er, sire, there is a messenger for you.'

Wyl looked over the servant's head to the bear of a lad behind him. No memory of his face registered within Cailech. 'Who are you?'

'Jos, sire. I've been sent by Rollo.'

The King looked back into the room, spoke briefly, then nodded. 'Come in.'

Jos entered to find the Grenadyne wiping blood from his face with a dampened linen and a woman, clearly dead, laid out on the floor with the King's cloak covering her face.

The King looked at him with a stony expression. 'I believe you know Aremys,' he said. Jos nodded, his eyes riveted on the dead girl. 'This is Ylena Thirsk. She was not a good choice in the end as a bride,' Cailech said.

'What did you have to tell us, Jos?' Aremys prompted, the blood finally cleaned away although the wound still seeped slightly.

The warrior turned his confused gaze on his King and bowed. 'Apologies, your majesty,' he said, remembering his manners and the message he had been sent to deliver. 'Rollo sent me. They've found Myrt, he's badly injured. Borc is dead. Rashlyn is nowhere to be seen.'

Wyl sighed. 'Where is Myrt?'

'In the barshi's tower.'

'All right. Jos, I would consider it a personal favour if you would have Ylena Thirsk's body shrouded and readied for travel on horseback. I'm returning her to Morgravia where she belongs. Please use people we trust; no one with a loose mouth — you understand?'

'Of course, your majesty.'

'Good. Then can you ready some horses for myself and Farrow.'

Jos's eyes sparked with pleasure. He was rarely involved in any tasks other than lifting, carrying and general menial duties around the fortress. 'Certainly, your majesty.'

'And, Jos, after we depart, I am leaving Myrt in charge. Rollo will be his second and I am appointing you as Rollo's deputy.'

The hulking lad looked towards Aremys and could not subdue a beaming grin. It did terrible things to his already twisted mouth — which was why he rarely smiled — but that did not matter any more. 'Thank you, your majesty,' he repeated, bowing again. 'You carry on, I'll fix everything here,' he added, hoping the King understood him.

He did. 'Good lad.'

The King and Aremys left hurriedly, with strict orders that only those whom Jos permitted were allowed to enter the King's meeting room. Jos gave a twisted smirk towards the servant who was not quick enough with his bow to miss the young man's sarcastic gesture.

'How do you feel — or is that a stupid question?' Aremys asked as they strode through corridors.

'Shaky, but I'm getting used to this strange arrival into another's body. Relieved to be a man again.'

'A King, don't forget.' Aremys watched Cailech's face break into a reluctant grin. 'You wear him well.'

Wyl took no pride in knowing he had just destroyed another life. 'I didn't think I was going to make that leap.'

'Neither did I. When I heard you scream, I just figured you'd used the wrong leg.'

Wyl could not help but laugh. Aremys had good timing for his jests. 'Cailech fought me. I wasn't sure I could win.'

'Inside do you mean?'

He nodded. 'Such anger. I don't know what he saw — presumably me, the real Wyl Thirsk, but perhaps he glimpsed Romen as well. I certainly saw him. Whereas the others capitulated in shock, he was savage in his intensity to hang onto life. But Myrren's gift was too strong.'

'It's a pity he had to die. Cailech had admirable qualities. He was a good King most of the time.'

'Without Rashlyn he would have been the greatest sovereign of his time,' Wyl agreed.

'We have another King to worry about now,' Aremys reminded.

'Poor Ylena. I so wanted to keep her whole.'

'You did her proud, Wyl. Don't dwell on it. She's at peace now and we aren't. I presume we're headed to Pearlis?'

Wyl shook Cailech's proud head. 'Werryl. I have to see Valentyna, if I can make it before she leaves for Stoneheart and Celimus.'

'You can't prevent the marriage,' Aremys warned, knowing it was a useless waste of breath.

'I know. I just have to see her. Do you know where we're going?'

'Yes. Up these stairs and then out across the courtyard towards that tower over there. And what makes you think the Queen of Briavel will take kindly to a visit from the King of the Razors?'

'Valid question. I'll think of something. Knave is here by the way; I saw him before we arrived at the fortress.'

'Does that mean the boy is here as well?' Before Wyl could answer, Aremys added beneath his breath, 'Remember to acknowledge your people, King Cailech.' He nodded towards a group of warriors approaching.

Wyl received their salutations appropriately, Cailech's essence guiding his gestures and facial expressions. He answered Aremys: 'Yes, Fynch is most likely here too, though I can't for the life of me think why.'

More people, more polite salutations, and then Firl, the lad Aremys had allowed to beat him during swordplay when he first arrived in the Razors, greeted them.

'Your highness; Farrow,' he said breathlessly and bowed.

Wyl nodded. 'How bad is he?'

'I'm not sure, sire. We can't find Rashlyn to help.'

'Have any other healers been called?' Aremys asked.

'Arrived a minute ago.'

Wyl pushed Cailech's tall body past the young man and ran up the stairs with Aremys directly behind. Rollo's men were guarding the door but automatically stepped aside at the sight of the King. Wyl entered the chamber. He had anticipated the worst but was surprised to see Myrt sitting up.

It was Aremys who spoke first. 'I hope you haven't made us run up those fucking stairs for nothing, Myrt.'

It broke the tension and Rollo and Myrt grinned whilst Cailech's face twitched in that way it did when he was amused but thoughtful. Wyl realised he still had to win Rollo's trust and clear up the business of the barshi and his effect on the King.

He immediately addressed Rollo. 'We need to speak.'

Rollo raised his hands. 'The fact that Farrow is still alive, sire, says plenty. Forgive my insubordination of earlier.'

'Already forgotten, though we will speak more about your concerns shortly,' Wyl replied. He moved towards Myrt and glanced at the dog lying on the floor, Borc's body next to it. The dog did not seem to be breathing and had puncture wounds on its body. For some reason Wyl felt dizzy and nauseous. It was not the sight of its blood, but the feeling that the animal was tainted with magic.

'Are you all right, sire?' Aremys asked, noting the King's sudden change in demeanour.

'Is that Rashlyn's dog?' Wyl said, fighting back an urge to throw up.

Myrt had already received a signal from Aremys that the King was on their side; was to be trusted. He did not understand what had changed but he trusted the Grenadyne and desperately wanted to trust his sovereign. He glanced towards Aremys now, then nodded at Rollo who moved to shut the door. 'Best to keep this between ourselves for now, sire.'

Wyl frowned. 'Speak,' he said, moving away from the animal and positioning himself where he could suck in some fresh air from the open window.

'According to the barshi, the dog is . . .' Myrt hesitated, looking embarrassed, and glanced again at Aremys. The mercenary had only just become aware of the smell of magic. He no longer had to touch the beast to know it; he could sense it. The reek was not as bad as it had been with Galapek but it was there all right. He despaired for Wyl at what was surely coming.

Wyl followed Myrt's gaze, sensed the awkwardness. 'Say it, Myrt.'

'Yes, sire. Um . . . Rashlyn was boasting that the animal is the Morgravian prisoner. He used sorcery to turn him into a dog.'

The King's face was suddenly a mask of anguish. 'He what?'

Aremys moved to his side. 'Careful now, Wyl,' he muttered. 'You mean like Lothryn?' the Grenadyne said aloud, already knowing the truth as he looked back to Myrt. The big man nodded, his eyes fearful.

Aremys decided to impress some reassurance on these men, now so apprehensive around Cailech – and with good reason, he thought. If only they knew who Cailech's puppeteer was now. 'We can speak freely,' he said to the Mountain warriors. 'The King has accepted that he's been entranced by Rashlyn on occasion and magically urged to agree to things he would normally never entertain. We've deduced that the spells only work if the barshi is near to the King, or his majesty would never be free of his hold – as he is now. He will execute the barshi when and if we find him.'

He looked directly at Rollo now. 'It is because of this sorcery that our King has been duped into allowing Lothryn to be . . . changed,' he said carefully. 'It was not his idea. He would never have agreed to something so horrific, so against our law of honourable death for our own.'

Wyl spoke up as if in a trance, stunned at the horrifying news about Gueryn. 'He will never have that effect on me again. I am free of him. Do you men believe me?'

Something in the timbre of his voice, its ferocity, and his cold, hard gaze had the right effect. Both Myrt and Rollo nodded.

'I will find Rashlyn and kill him,' he added and they believed him. He moved to crouch by the dog and stroked it tenderly, battling the revulsion the magic caused. 'Gueryn still breathes.'

'He saved my life, sire. Borc would have killed me if not for the animal's courage,' Myrt said.

Wyl stopped himself from saying all that he wanted to about Gueryn's bravery; he was ferociously fighting back the tears and took a moment to compose himself. 'I will personally deliver Rashlyn to whichever god will accept him,' he said.

'No need, sire,' Myrt said. 'You haven't heard the rest of my story.' And he described the mysterious arrival of the boy through the tower walls, bathed in light and claiming to be Rashlyn's destroyer.

Wyl closed Cailech's eyes. He could hardly believe what he was hearing. 'His name is Fynch,' he said into the heavy silence that followed Myrt's startling revelation. 'He is known to me.'

No one dared ask how or why, which was fortunate, Aremys thought, because he could not imagine how Wyl would explain it. Cailech looked haggard, he noted. It had been one shock after another for Wyl: his sister, then Gueryn, now Fynch . . . not to mention another death, another body, another person to learn about.

'And you are recovered?' Aremys asked Myrt, taking the attention off the King so Wyl could gather his thoughts and emotions.

'Rashlyn used his filthy magic on me to weaken me but the effects are wearing off. I'm ready to do your bidding, sire.'

'Good!' Wyl growled. 'Because you and Rollo are being left in charge here.'

'Where are you going, sire?'

'To Briavel,' came the reply. It provoked surprise and confusion on the men's faces but Cailech's tone suggested it would be imprudent to argue. 'Call for the animal physic,' Wyl commanded.

Rollo nodded and opened the door to the guards. 'Get Obin. Hurry!'

'Gueryn's life is to be saved, so help you all,' the King muttered. Rollo and Myrt exchanged another confused look. 'Where did Rashlyn and Fynch go?' Wyl continued.

'Sire, as I said, one floated out of the window, the other through the walls,' Myrt said, shaking his head. 'I still think I was seeing things.'

'No, you weren't,' the King replied, deadly cold. 'You were witnessing two sorcerers throwing down the gauntlet at each other in a fight which has nothing to do with us.'

It had come to Wyl now what this was about. He sensed it related to the sense of doom he had felt for Fynch when he left him in the Wild. He pieced it together as he paced the room, waiting for the animal doctor. Elysius had said they would not meet again. The sorcerer had died, Wyl guessed, and he remembered now a strange sensation of loss he had felt when he first arrived into Briavel, courtesy of the Thicket. He had dismissed it as worry at leaving Fynch and his fretting over Ylena, not to mention being magically tossed hundreds of miles across the land. But perhaps Myrren's gift had kept him linked with Elysius and when the strange little man died, Wyl had felt it. *But you didn't die without luring Fynch into your web of despair, did you?* he thought savagely, hating Elysius in that moment.

He addressed the men again, his anger at what was happening to Fynch and what had been perpetrated on Gueryn spilling into his tone. 'Everything which has occurred tonight stays between us and a young warrior called Jos, whom I've appointed as your deputy, Rollo. In my absence, Myrt makes the decisions for our people. Agreed?' The Mountain men exchanged worried glances. 'Is that clear?' he shouted.

'Yes, sire,' they said in unison, neither wanting to point out that nothing was clear about tonight. Not the King's strange behaviour; nor the incredible sight of a ghostly boy appearing through granite walls or Rashlyn jumping through an open window and hovering outside; nor talk of sorcery or men being changed into beasts. Nor why Myrt, who really did not want the task, was now leading the Mountain People.

'What about Lothryn, my lord?' Myrt risked.

'I'm going to find Rashlyn. Before I kill him, he will restore Lothryn and Gueryn le Gant.' No one wanted to ask what would happen if the magic could not be reversed.

'Aremys,' Wyl said.

'Sire?'

'Stay with the dog for me. If he dies . . .' Wyl could not finish. 'Just see him cared for. I'll meet you all at the stables in one hour.'

Fynch bowed, much to Knave's surprise. 'Rashlyn,' he said. 'I have been sent.'

The barshi had appeared as if out of nowhere. He looked rattled.

'By whom?'

'Can you not guess?' Fynch asked, echoing a King, a dragon, who had promised him so much not long ago.

'Elysius?' Rashlyn whispered in wonderment.

Fynch nodded.

'Why could he not face me himself?' the barshi demanded. He sounded deranged, his voice controlled and soft one moment, high and angry the next.

'He is dead.'

'Then I do not fear you,' Rashlyn cackled.

'You should,' Fynch said, unfazed by the madman's baiting. 'Elysius was not the only one who wishes you destroyed.'

Rashlyn sounded arrogant now. 'I know dozens just

amongst the Mountain People who would slit my throat happily, if not for the King. I have his protection.'

'Not any more, I'm afraid.'

That won the barshi's attention. 'What do you mean?'

'Cailech is dead.'

Rashlyn could not speak as he tried to absorb the terrifying news. Then, 'I don't believe you – you're just a child.'

'You should. My age makes no difference. You have no protection now; Cailech will not save you. In fact, I would imagine the King of the Mountains is stalking you this very minute for the abomination you have imposed upon two men.'

Rashlyn began to yell at Fynch and then stopped. 'You just said he's dead. How can a dead man stalk me?'

Fynch just grinned.

'Why are you here?' the barshi screeched. 'If Cailech is dead then I am lost anyway, as good as dead.'

'Not good enough. We wish to destroy you.'

'We?'

Fynch nodded. 'The Dragon King.'

The sorcerer looked at the boy, puzzled by the riddles he was giving for answers. He regarded the self-possessed child from beneath hooded lids and asked the obvious. 'Who is the Dragon King?'

'He is the King of the Creatures.'

'And who are you?'

'I am the Dragon King,' Fynch replied and opened a bridge to the Thicket.

Wyl ran on long, muscled legs which covered the hard ground easily. Before leaving the tower he had taken a deep breath and laid his hand once more on the barely breathing dog. Its eyes were glazed and blood seeped from its nostrils. Its tongue lolled on the floor from between its jaws and it was all Wyl could do not to weep as he whispered to Gueryn to hold on. The dog did not move and Wyl left, not risking another word for fear of his voice breaking.

'Let him live,' he prayed to Shar as he ran now. He felt the wood calling to him; sensed the hum of a powerful magic. It was the Thicket, he recognised its trace. And something else. Something bright and powerful and good, overlaying an ugliness which he presumed was Rashlyn.

He burst into the clearing, drawing his sword, and pulled to a sharp stop when he saw Fynch standing there, bathed in a fierce glow of golden light. Knave was nearby and instantly covered the gap between himself and the new arrival, nearly knocking the King over with his welcome.

'Hello, Wyl,' Fynch said, not turning his gaze from Rashlyn. 'I'm sure you know who this is,' he added.

'Fynch,' Wyl replied, feeling a new sense of awe as he looked at the small gong boy suddenly so infused with power, so composed . . . so brave.

'King Cailech, I——' Rashlyn began. He looked still more confused, his gaze darting between boy and man.

'I am not Cailech,' the familiar voice said, turning a hard gaze on Rashlyn. 'I am Wyl Thirsk.'

The man groaned. 'The General? You can't be. I . . . I would know it.'

'Your eyes deceive you, Rashlyn,' Wyl replied. 'You didn't know me when I came here as Romen Koreldy either. Your brother's magic has given me this power to possess others. Clever, eh?'

'No! I won't believe this,' the man said, shaking his head against what he knew to be true. It looked like Cailech but did not behave as Cailech; worse, Rashlyn could almost taste the magic emanating from his former protector.

'You know I speak the truth,' Wyl said.

'Tell me how,' the barshi begged. 'I must understand it!'

'Not until you lift the spell on Gueryn le Gant,' Wyl demanded.

The wild man's mouth split into a thin, cruel smile beneath the tangle of his beard. 'I cannot. It is irreversible.'

Wyl had to fight his urge to rush at Rashlyn and cut him down.

'Don't,' Fynch warned, reading his thoughts. 'It is what he wants.'

'And Lothryn?' Wyl asked, already knowing the answer.

'Even more of a problem. At least with your friend le Gant, I knew what I was doing. Didn't hurt him as much. But Lothryn – that was horrible, even for me. He could not have survived it anyway. You're wasting your time. The barbarian scum is dead.'

It was Cailech, not Wyl, whose anger rose now, who raised the sword and ran at the barshi. Wyl could not help but join with Cailech's lust to hack the magic man from skull to feet.

'No!' shouted Fynch and Wyl felt Cailech's body slammed high into the air. It felt as though he had hit a stone wall. 'Do not attempt to kill him. That is my job,' the little boy commanded. His tone demanded respect.

Rashlyn screeched with laughter. 'Now even your own people work against you, Thirsk. Perhaps I should kill you.'

'You cannot. My protection will repel anything you cast against him.'

Rashlyn did not believe Fynch. He moved his hands and a huge flaming ball roared towards Cailech's suspended body. Wyl held his breath. There was no way he could escape this, even if he had free movement. But the ball of flame bounced against something Wyl could not see and fell away helplessly to extinguish itself in a pool of thawing snow nearby.

'Wyl, I want you to go now,' Fynch said.

'I can't leave you.'

'You did before and you will again. We walk different paths now.'

'Will I see you again?'

'I think not.'

'Fynch—'

'Don't, please. There is nothing more to say except that I have loved you as a brother. Go now and do what you must.'

'I need Knave.'

'I know. He will go with you.'

I am not leaving you, Fynch, the deep voice growled in the boy's head.

You must. It is the only way we can save Wyl. You are his guide now.

I don't understand.

You will. Now go.

Fynch . . .

Knave, go!

'Rashlyn is running,' Wyl warned.

'He cannot escape me.'

'Why do you have to do this?' Wyl's tone was pleading.

'Because no one else can.'

'Let me go then,' Wyl said wearily and felt Cailech's body being lowered gently to the frosty ground. 'What about Gueryn and Lothryn?'

'I do not know,' Fynch said, knowing he broke Wyl's heart. 'I must deal with Rashlyn.'

And you will die, Knave crashed into Fynch's mind.

So be it.

'Do you and Knave talk?' Wyl wondered, noting the odd silences and the expression on Fynch's face.

'Yes, ever since Elysius passed his magic to me.'

'I thought as much,' Wyl said, feeling helplessly sorrowful.

'Wyl, Valentyna is to marry Celimus in a matter of days. You cannot save her that trial, you know that, don't you?' Wyl nodded. 'But I know you wish to see her and you have something to tell her.'

'I do.'

'Tell her everything. Let there be no secrets between you. She must understand who you really are.'

'I cannot!' Cailech's expression became dismayed.

'You must. Please, trust me,' Fynch urged. 'And in turn she will trust you.'

Wyl had no answer to Fynch's request. The boy had never been wrong before.

'Now please go. It is time I faced the barshi.'

'Who are you, Fynch?' Wyl asked, fearfully.

Fynch's face broke into a beatific smile. His golden hair seemed to radiate a bright glow which spread to outline his tiny frame. 'I am the Dragon King, Wyl,' he said, and vanished.

Knave threw back his huge black head and gave a chilling howl. It silenced the twittering birds that had come home to roost amongst the trees and echoed throughout the Razors.

It was the heralding of death and Wyl knew he would never see the brave boy again. Somewhere deep inside he felt a part of his heart had been cut away. No tears and no amount of time would ever heal the loss.

CHAPTER 33

Obin had taken one look at the grey dog and shaken his head. Aremys nodded, sad for Wyl. Another death he had not been able to prevent and, knowing his friend as he did, Aremys was sure Wyl would blame himself for this one too. One man; so much sorrow. Myrren and her father had plenty to answer for in Shar's plane. Aremys thanked Obin and then, wrapping the dog in a sheet he found in Rashlyn's rooms, he hefted the animal into his arms.

'I'll take you to Lothryn,' he murmured to the dog, who was still breathing in short, desperate pants. The dog whined but its eyes did not open.

When Aremys finally made it to the stable, staggering under the seemingly dead weight of the large dog, he heard Galapek whinny. The horse knew; Lothryn knew. Another man had been broken by Rashlyn's twisted magic.

Aremys lay Gueryn down in some fresh straw and lit a lamp. He explained to the horse who this was; all self-consciousness about talking to a horse had ceased. The animal reared, angry, and Aremys tried to calm him with soft words and soothing hands. As he touched the stallion he sensed the enormous and agonising effort it took for Lothryn to communicate with him. The horse begged to be set free. Aremys was torn with indecision as to what was best. Footsteps approached and the new King of the Razors stepped inside the stable and immediately flattened himself against the wall.

'Fight it, man,' Aremys said, realising Wyl was overcome by the tainted aura of magic. 'You'll get used to it, as I have.'

Wyl lost the battle momentarily, gagging and then retching into a corner. 'Oh, Shar,' he groaned. 'What has he done to them?'

Galapek whinnied again, a sound which nearly broke Wyl's heart and his spirit. He forced himself to find composure, wiping his mouth on Cailech's sleeve. He saw Gueryn lying in the straw.

'Could Obin save him?' he asked.

Aremys shook his head. No point in lying.

Wyl leaned against the wall again, closed his eyes and groaned. It was so filled with anguish, Aremys had to look away. How much more could Wyl take, he wondered, before he gave up on his fight. Or, more likely, found a way to take his own life.

A huge black dog entered the stable, startling Aremys out of his bleak thoughts. 'Shar's wrath!' He had never seen a dog so big.

'Meet Knave,' Wyl said, flat-toned.

'Ah, the famous beast,' Aremys replied. 'May I?' he asked Wyl, his hand reaching to stroke the animal.

'Knave alone decides,' Wyl said, and Aremys detected a hint of humour in the tone. Perhaps Wyl would get through this.

'Hello, Knave,' the Grenadyne said and risked touching the great head. Knave growled with pleasure as Aremys scratched his dark brow.

'Welcome to the chosen few,' Wyl said, coming back from the dark place he had been moments ago. 'Knave is particular about who he lets touch him.'

The black dog gave a deep-throated, suspicious bark and walked over to the horse first. Galapek did not flinch. Knave sniffed the creature and whined gently. He knew. Then he padded over to where another dog lay dying. This time he growled softly and began licking at the wounds of the grey dog.

'Speak to Lothryn,' Aremys suggested, wanting to divert Wyl's gaze from the touching scene in the straw. It was too painful to watch. 'Breathe through your mouth, it makes it easier.'

'That's how Fynch overcame the major hurdle of being a gong boy,' Wyl said, his mind going back to a time when he lived the simple life of a Legionnaire.

'Where is Fynch?' Aremys wondered.

The fragile shell Wyl had built around his emotions fractured again. 'Gone to his death, fighting Rashlyn.'

Aremys wished he could bite his own tongue out. 'I don't understand.'

'You don't have to. None of us do, except perhaps Knave. It is not our battle.'

The big man had no idea how to respond so he left it as yet another heart-wound for Wyl to cope with. 'Come, Lothryn can talk to us.'

Wyl stepped up to the horse. 'He's beautiful despite the repulsive magic.'

'So true. Touch him.'

Wyl did so and his eyes widened. Startled, he fought the reek of the evil magic and laid his head against the sleek forehead of his rescuer and friend. 'Lothryn,' he wept, 'it's me, Wyl.'

The magnificent horse nuzzled him, as if in thanks, and Aremys too felt the sting of tears. This was so moving and yet he knew in his heart that worse was surely to come for Wyl and those who supported him.

Wyl, the horse whispered weakly into his mind, *I knew you would come. Didn't expect you to look as you do now.*

'I'm sorry I took his life.'

Don't be. He lived it fully. Paid the price for his decisions.

'We will find a way to restore you.'

Turn me loose, I beg you. Tie the dog onto my back and let us go.

'Aremys,' Wyl gasped, 'touch him. Hear what he's planning.'

The Grenadyne laid a hand on Galapek and shared the conversation.

I must save my strength, Lothryn said, *what little is left. Please, put Gueryn on my back and turn us loose.*

'Why?' Wyl beseeched.

I don't know, in truth. It seems right. Don't leave us here like this.

'Do you know how to rid yourself of this guise?' Aremys asked, heart lurching with hope.

No. But something is compelling me to escape from here.

Wyl frowned. 'Why take Gueryn?'

Do you want him to die here . . . in a stable?

Aremys grimaced at the harsh words. 'Where will you go?'

I don't know. Give him to me. You must leave, let us do the same.

'We could lose you for ever,' Wyl pleaded.

You've lost us already. Let me try — let me see what or who this is calling to me.

Wyl nodded, resigned to the endless misery of losing those he loved. 'Let's do it,' he said to Aremys.

They fashioned a sling from the linen in which Aremys had carried Gueryn to the stable and found a sack to hold the dog. Knave finished tending to the grey's wounds.

'Odd that he would do that,' Wyl commented absently.

'An instinctive attempt to heal the wounds perhaps?' Aremys offered.

'Or simply Knave's way of showing his sorrow.'

'He can breathe easily through the sackcloth,' Aremys said.

'He won't be breathing much longer,' Wyl said, stroking the dog's face.

'Come on, Wyl. You have to be strong,' Aremys warned. 'Like Fynch.'

Fighting words. They rallied Wyl's flagging spirits. 'Yes, you're right. Fynch is off fighting a lost cause; I should at least try.' He hefted the injured dog into the sack and together he and Aremys tied the sack into the sling then onto a saddle on Galapek's back.

Aremys watched the King reach again towards the majestic face of Galapek. He knew this was intensely difficult for Wyl.

'Haldor protect you, Lothryn,' Wyl said.

Shar go with you, Wyl. We shall see each other again.

'Elspyth will kill me in an ugly fashion if not,' he said, trying to lighten the heavy moment.

Lothryn did not reply, simply waited for Wyl to make his farewell to Gueryn.

Wyl cupped the grey dog's face in his huge hands and kissed it, hoping that love and honour would somehow pour through that touch and reach the brave, dying man trapped inside.

'As One,' he whispered to the dog, and then the horse was off, moving through the great doors Aremys had pushed open.

Galapek did not look back or make any noise of farewell; he simply cantered off into the blackness of the night.

Rashlyn felt himself compelled to return to the clearing, even though every fibre of his being told him he should run. Curiosity had him in its grip and now he knew that the boy, Fynch, called himself the King of the Creatures, he wanted to know what that meant.

'Come, Rashlyn,' a voice called. It startled him, for he could see no one. Then Fynch shimmered before him. 'It is time.'

'For what?' the barshi screamed at the child.

'For you to die,' Fynch replied, a new gravity in his voice. He too had left behind everyone he loved, deliberately cutting himself away from Wyl and Knave. He could not carry out his task, could not offer himself as Sacrifice, if they were near.

Sacrifice. He understood now. It had taken some time to ponder its meaning and how he must apply it to this battle with Rashlyn. It meant more than death. It meant yielding. Fynch smiled, pleased that his neat, ordered mind had worked it out and could put it away now. He no longer had to tease at its complexity to unravel its secret.

Faith Fynch. Sacrifice.

The first wave came as Rashlyn hurled a magical avalanche of blows at Fynch, screaming with madness and anger as he loosed his powers.

Around them the creatures of the mountains quietly gathered in awe. They had instinctively known for many hours that something momentous was about to occur, but were not sure what exactly. Now they knew. Ekons, ice bears, deer, snow hares, even the birds who had been spreading the news since dusk, gathered side by side, predator and prey, forgetting their fear or hunger for the time being as they witnessed a wild man doing battle with a creature they had never seen before. They knew of it only through stories handed down through the ages. A dragon.

Rollo, Myrt and Byl saw Cailech glance at the muslin bundle tied over a horse. They could not see past the stern expression to the emotional battle going on inside. Wyl steeled himself not to look at Ylena's corpse again. It was over. Her life was spent and had been given bravely, like all Thirsks before her.

Beside Cailech's horse stood a huge dog. He explained its presence to the Mountain men. 'This is Knave. He is going to help us with what we must do, and is one of the reasons why Rashlyn no longer has any hold on me.'

'Where is Rashlyn, sire?' Myrt asked. He seemed fully recovered from the barshi's attack now.

'He is dead,' Wyl risked, hoping he was telling the truth.

'And Lothryn, your majesty?' Rollo added.

They deserved to know. 'I have released him. Aremys here can talk to him and that was what Lothryn wanted.'

Rollo gasped. All the talk of magic had been confusing enough, but now the King was saying the Grenadyne could communicate with the magically created animals? It was too much. 'What? How?'

'Myrt knows,' Wyl replied. He was not in the mood to go into further discussion tonight. 'He will explain. Right now we ride for Briavel.'

'May I ask why, sire?' Myrt said. His tone was hesitant but his manner firm.

'To make a new peace treaty, this time with a Queen who needs the support of the Mountain People.'

'Against the Morgravian Crown?' Myrt asked, quickly grasping his King's intent.

It was Aremys who replied. 'Celimus has no intention of keeping his promise to the Razor Kingdom. Our only hope of peace is with Briavel.'

'But, sire,' Rollo pleaded, 'she is marrying Celimus. Her loyalties stand with him!'

'Not necessarily,' his King replied in a tone that discouraged further argument. 'I need you to trust me. I have never led our people wrong so far. I will not do so now.'

'Shouldn't we come with you, sire?' Myrt asked, far preferring to ride headlong into danger with his King than take over royal duties.

'No. I need you here, Myrt. You and Rollo will keep everyone steady. And in case the horse returns – he will need friends, allies who know the truth.' He said no more.

It would not serve any purpose to get their hopes up that Lothryn might be restored.

Myrt asked anyway. 'Can the spells be reversed?'

'It's my keen hope they can be. According to Aremys, it is why Lothryn asked to be released.'

'Where has he gone?'

'We don't know,' Aremys replied. 'But he took the grey dog with him. We just have to hope he knows more than us, now that Rashlyn is finished.'

Myrt nodded unhappily, a glum Rollo by his side. 'Haldor keep you safe, sire.'

Cailech nodded back, appreciating the warrior's suffering and his wish to protect his King. 'It is better this way, Myrt. We two can slip into and out of Briavel far more subtly than a mass of Mountain barbarians storming Werryl Palace.'

'Get word to us the usual way,' Myrt said and cocked his head towards a small box fastened to the side of the horse that carried Ylena.

Wyl frowned, taking a moment to delve into Cailech's memories. He understood. 'I hope those pigeons are strong flyers,' he said.

'The best,' Myrt answered. 'Rollo's top birds,' and he grinned towards his companion.

'All right. Keep faith. Look after Aydrech. If anything happens, if Celimus sets a raid, the boy must be protected at all costs.'

The big man nodded. 'I will take care of him personally.'

'Good,' Wyl said, adding, 'Rotate the watches more regularly. I have no idea whether Celimus will attempt anything or not.'

'Possibly not with a wedding not far away,' Aremys commented drily.

'Nevertheless,' Wyl replied, 'the child's safety is paramount.' He leaned down and clasped each man's hand in farewell, knowing full well that neither of these loyal Mountain warriors would see their King again.

The horse arrived at the edge of the wood. Lothryn felt drawn towards the trees and as he entered their cover he felt the pulse of magic emanating from somewhere deep inside the forest. He also noted that he was feeling stronger, more himself, than at any time since the change had been inflicted on him. It was as though his own essence was a tiny flame flickering within the horse and now that flame was burning a fraction brighter. Pain continued to be his companion but, although he reminded himself he could be imagining it because the stunning arrival of Wyl in the guise of Cailech had so warmed his spirit, he believed the pain had lessened ever so slightly.

Lothryn was reassured by the connection between him and the dog. He could feel its heartbeat – weak but still there. *Hang on, Gueryn*, he passed through the link, even though he had no idea whether the trapped man heard him or could even register something as subtle as another's thoughts.

Still following the compulsion, Lothryn pushed deeper into the wood until he came to a clearing. He stood at its fringe and looked in wonderment at the sight that confronted him – a huge dragon coated in a shimmering armour of scales. Its serpent-like neck was twisted and the great head was thrown back but there was no sound. The great beast was silent as wave after wave of sickening magical power pounded its body. Lothryn saw that deathly magic as a sickly brown colour, impenetrable by light. It was Rashlyn who was dealing the blows, his face a twisted mask of hate.

Lothryn felt the impulse to rush forward and pummel the barshi with every last ounce of strength he could muster from Galapek's powerful body, and yet something stopped him. He stared at Rashlyn and knew that if hate, madness and despair could be embodied then it would look exactly like the sorcerer punishing the magnificent winged creature before him. The dragon looked to be foundering as Rashlyn muttered a stream of unintelligible words. Although the sorcerer looked exhausted he was standing and seemed to be in control of this frightening drama.

Looking around, Lothryn became aware of other creatures – dozens, no scores of them – clustered amongst the trees and dotted around the nearby foothills. He even saw ekons and flinched in fear, before realising they were as paralysed by the same awe that he was experiencing.

A dragon! Who would have thought they truly existed? Lothryn had always considered them creatures of myth.

Fight back! Lothryn begged.

He won't, replied a voice, startling him.

He twisted to see who it was. A bird on a nearby branch stretched its wings. *Who are you?* the horse asked.

I am Kestrel.

And who is that? Lothryn asked, hiding his surprise at being able to communicate with a bird.

That is the King. The King of us all. And he is sacrificing himself to save us. He was once Fynch.

I gathered Fynch was a child?

He is so much more.

But I see him as a dragon, Lothryn persisted. *There's no boy there.*

He is still a child but the dragon reflects who he truly is.

Lothryn was none the wiser for Kestrel's explanation. He looked back at the dragon, which staggered slightly. *Why doesn't he use his powers? Surely he can topple a man!*

Oh yes, he could overcome the sorcerer with ease but he refuses to kill. That is the child in our King. He made a pact with himself, I think. I sensed it when he first spoke to me. There is no violence in Fynch. He agreed to destroy Rashlyn but in his own way.

Lothryn felt his spirit lurch with grief for this brave boy, Wyl's friend, now — like all of them — somehow changed by enchantment. *So how can he beat the barshi?*

Kestrel's sorrow came into his mind like a gale. *By taking everything that is Rashlyn. He will absorb the storm of magic, consume the pain, devour the evil. Already his glow lessens. When the battle began, the King of the Creatures burned golden bright. See how the murky evil has dimmed him.*

But then he will die himself, Lothryn said, aghast.

I suspect so, Kestrel agreed, bitterness now in his voice. *But not before Rashlyn burns through his power until there is none left.*

Both creatures fell silent and kept vigil with all the other animals of the mountains, still gathering to pay homage to their King.

CHAPTER 34

Wyl and Aremys set off from the fortress in the dead of night, Knave trotting at their side. The Grenadyne chanced airing his concern to the grim-faced King at his side. 'We cannot travel the Razors successfully at night, Wyl. Surely you know that the way down is treacherous?'

'I do. We won't be going far,' came the reply, which hardly addressed the question.

'If you're intent on this mad journey into Briavel, why not leave at first light? We would easily make up the poor advantage of departing now.'

'I'm sorry, I haven't explained myself,' Wyl said, turning to look directly at his anxious friend. 'Leaving by horse was purely for appearances.'

'What?'

'I have another method of travel, much faster – though horribly unpleasant.'

'Has becoming a King gone to your head?' Aremys began to sound truculent. The night's proceedings had worn down his emotional reserves. He was tired, angry at losing Cailech, furious at failing Lothryn and Gueryn, sad for Wyl and altogether sick to the back teeth of magic. He must have murmured the last thought aloud because Wyl answered him.

'Well, just a little more magic to go. It was you who gave me the idea.'

'Me! Whatever are you talking about?'

'I'm talking about the Thicket, Aremys. We will use the Thicket to travel.'

That won the Grenadyne's attention. He felt like he had been punched in the belly and could not speak for a few moments. Finally he said, 'How?'

'Knave. It's why I insisted he come.'

'He looks none too happy about it.'

'He isn't, believe me. I've never known him be this aloof.'

'Because he had to leave behind Fynch presumably?'

'Correct. The two of them are inextricably linked.'

'But you told me he was your dog.'

Wyl sighed. 'It's complicated,' he said and smiled sadly. 'Knave loves us all and has protected all of us. Now he is having to suffer each of us dying, and me so many times over.'

Aremys did not want to talk of death again. 'So how can the dog help us?'

'He is of the Thicket. He is our connection to it.'

'And?' Aremys was still baffled.

'Remember how you suddenly found yourself between the fringe of Timpkenny and the Razors . . . ?'

Aremys frowned, and then a dawning occurred. 'Oh no, you jest, surely?'

He saw Cailech's eyes — now settled back to their pale

green – sparkle in the light of the flaming torch he carried. 'Not this time, my friend.'

Aremys began to stutter, words falling out on top of each other. 'But how do you summon it, command it, control it?'

Cailech's shoulders shrugged and a twitch of a grin at his mouth disappeared as rapidly as it arrived. 'We just have to trust the Thicket.'

'That place is no friend of mine, Wyl. It cast me out, remember? What if it hurts me this time?'

'It won't.'

'You sound so confident,' Aremys blustered, unsettled by this idea of Wyl's. He did not trust the Thicket.

'I am. The Thicket will not hurt either of us – firstly, because we travel with Knave, and secondly, because of our connection to Fynch. The boy means everything to the Thicket, I believe.'

'How do we know it can do this?'

'It threw me all the way to Briavel in seconds,' Wyl said.

Aremys gasped. 'I didn't know that.'

'There is so much you don't know,' Wyl said, his voice laced with regret. 'The fact that Fynch will die this night, doing what he has done since I first met him.'

'Which is?'

'Acting out of sacrifice, loyalty, love. He has always put others before himself. Or that Valentyna will marry Celimus, come what may.'

Aremys now felt utterly baffled. 'I thought we were going to Briavel to try to prevent it?'

He saw Cailech shrug. 'I can't read the future,' Wyl said. 'Elysius told me that she *will* marry the King of Morgravia.'

'Why do we go then?'

'Because Fynch told me that Myrren's gift is still subject to randomness.'

Aremys looked quizzically at the King of the Mountains. They were moving slowly, often raising an arm to acknowledge scouts and guides on higher ridges who were recognisable only by the flicker of their small fires. A special flame burning on top of the fortress told these guards that their King was passing, so the two men had no fear of being attacked or stopped. 'I don't understand any of this, Wyl.'

'I hardly understand it myself,' Wyl admitted. 'Fynch believes that random acts can still affect the outcome of Myrren's gift.'

'And so you will try and do something to prevent the Queen marrying Celimus, is that right?'

'In truth I don't see how I can. I think I am going there simply so that I may see her before I die again.'

Aremys reined in his horse and Wyl followed suit, knowing his statement was too provocative to be ignored. 'Why?' his friend demanded. 'Stay as Cailech – you can achieve so much. Let's turn back. You say yourself that you cannot affect the outcome of the marriage. We have friends here, loyal people. You are a King. You can live. Stop the gift now!'

'Only one thing will stop it, Aremys,' Wyl said, weariness in his tone now.

'What?' the Grenadyne asked, sensing Wyl knew more.

Wyl raised King Cailech's head and looked his friend directly in the eye. 'When I become the sovereign of Morgravia.'

'Celimus?' It came out as a choked exclamation.

Wyl nodded. He was deadly serious now and Aremys was shocked to the core. 'Is that what this is all about? Myrren's gift is to make sure that you become him?'

Cailech's face twisted into a snarl. 'It's about revenge. Myrren suffered at Celimus's hands, so she and her father worked out a way to make him suffer in return.'

'But why involve you? You did nothing but offer her pity.'

'I am nothing but a pawn in this complex game,' Wyl said softly. 'She has used me to avenge her torture which Celimus so enjoyed.'

Wyl could see the big man's horror at this news written all over his face. He recalled his own despair at the discovery of the truth of Myrren's gift. Now Aremys was reflecting a similar anguish. Perhaps it was even worse for the mercenary, Wyl thought, having always believed that watching those you love suffer was more intolerable than living through the suffering yourself.

'Wyl,' Aremys began, recovering himself. 'This is worse than I could ever have imagined, I'll agree, but can you not think of it in the more positive light,' he ventured carefully, 'that you will be King of Morgravia and your Queen will be Valentyna? Can the notion that you will be together soften the damage which has been done? You cannot bring back those you have lost but perhaps you can make their lives count by making Morgravia great again under a good King. Sire heirs with Valentyna and establish a new dynasty. Imagine it – Morgravia ruled by you, not Celimus. One more death, my friend, that's all it will take.' There was a new brightness in the Grenadyne's voice, as if suddenly he felt everything could be righted.

Wyl looked down at his new large hands with their prominent knuckles and long, blunt fingers. He had thought of the same scenario which Aremys was now so taken with many times since learning of his destiny. And every time he tried to convince himself that this terrible episode of his life could end happily, he hit a wall. The wall was called Celimus. 'Aremys,' he said softly into the chill spring night. 'I don't want to be him.'

Aremys had not considered this. 'You have no choice apparently.'

'I will not live as Celimus,' Wyl said, slowly, defiantly. 'I would sooner die.'

'But you will have everything—'

Wyl cut him off. 'I will have nothing but hate and despair. You don't understand – when I become someone new, much of who they are remains with me. I have their memories, their dreams. I have their ways and mannerisms. I have their darkness, Aremys. I will not live as the person I hate most in this world and who in turn has hated the Thirsks for two decades.'

'So what are you going to do – die again?' Aremys's tone was heavy with sarcasm as he hoped to jolt his friend from this current attitude. Wyl remained silent and continued staring at Cailech's hands.

The Grenadyne shook his head slowly with disbelief. 'Tell me you're not planning to die once you're him, Wyl?' Aremys urged, a fresh wave of fear washing across him. He realised that once Wyl became Celimus, he would no longer have Myrren's protection. He would be as vulnerable to death as anyone.

Wyl spoke in a grave tone: 'When it happens – and it will, for my destiny is to become the sovereign of

Morgravia – you will end my life once and for all.'

Aremys was rocked by Wyl's words. 'I won't,' he shouted. 'I won't do it.'

'You will! You will do it because I demand it. I will be King of Morgravia, don't forget, and I will command you.'

'Or what? Kill me?' Aremys yelled.

Wyl ignored him, kept speaking: 'We shall set it up as an accident. It doesn't have to be by your hand as such, if that revolts you too much. We can manipulate it through others, but you will help me to achieve my death. An arrow, clean and swift to the heart. I would prefer it to be you, Aremys, I know you shoot accurately. This is about friendship, love, loyalty.'

'No, Wyl. What about Valentyna?'

'I can't think about what might happen after my death. That will be beyond my control. But Valentyna will be released from her sentence of being married to Celimus, free to return to Briavel and begin her life afresh.'

'But it's not *him*. It's you.'

'Valentyna will not know that. She will look at me with disgust: she will detest my touch and speak my name with loathing. No, Aremys,' Wyl said sadly, 'I would rather be dead, truly. Elysius said I cannot contrive for others to kill me but I am counting on the fact that once I have become Celimus, as Elysius and Myrren intended, the gift will have run its course and will no longer be able to hurt me or those I care about.'

Aremys shook his head; it was too painful. They had battled against so much and come through it, but for what? Only for Wyl to die, and for good this time. 'Don't make this decision yet,' he beseeched. 'Fynch warned of the randomness — let's wait and see how it all turns out.'

Wyl recalled Fynch begging him to tell Valentyna the truth, and was reminded once again that the boy had never led him astray. Fynch had always been true. He would make his own decision on whether or not to share the truth with Valentyna when he met her again, although, if he was honest with himself, he knew he could never live sheathed within Celimus. Even if it did not revolt her — and it should, looking daily at the man who had organised the deaths of her father and Romen as well as countless others — it would certainly revolt him. 'Fair enough,' he said. 'We will not discuss it again until I become Celimus, after which I will give you one night's grace, which I shall spend with Valentyna, and the next day I will expect you to take my life. Agreed?'

Aremys was cornered. There was no way out of this bargain. 'Agreed,' he said, deeply unhappy.

'Good,' Wyl replied, feeling suddenly brighter for airing the decision he had been brooding on for so long. Now it was time to ask for the Thicket's help.

'Come, we'll try from there,' he said, pointing to a small outcrop of rocks.

'Do you know what you're doing?' Aremys asked, leading his horse in the direction of the rocks.

'Not really, but the journey will take too long by conventional means. I have to try.'

Aremys sighed audibly. 'So what do we do? Turn the horses loose or remain on them?'

Cailech shrugged broad shoulders. 'I haven't even brought anything for her,' he said, his mind elsewhere.

Aremys lifted his eyes to the heavens and asked Shar

to help them. 'Come on, Wyl, what do we do?'

Wyl collected his thoughts. 'Knave,' he said, 'please would you call on the Thicket? I need it to send us to Werryl Palace, like it did for me before.'

Knave could not explain to his friend that he no longer enjoyed the same contact with the Thicket.

There was nothing for it now, he realised: he would have to contact Fynch . . . if he was still alive. He growled at the King, knowing Wyl would understand.

Knave let his mind flood with the trace that was Fynch and cast out to him, begging him to be alive, to answer him . . . not because he needed his help but because he wanted to hear his sweet voice again.

Knave. It sounded more of a groan.

Always here, the dog answered, keeping his voice steady even though he was frightened by the pain communicated in that single syllable of Fynch's response.

Is Wyl safe?

Yes. Knave knew not to waste time on small talk. Fynch was fighting for his life. *We need to use the Thicket to travel quickly to Briavel. I'm sorry to—*

Wait. There was a silence and then Fynch was back; his voice sounded even more fractured and filled with pain than just moments earlier. *I've set up a bridge. Use it, but hurry — I can't hold it together for long.*

Fynch, what's happening?

Hurry, Knave. Please.

Knave closed his eyes in grief. It sounded as though Fynch was near to death. He linked to the Thicket, feeling guilty at drawing on Fynch's waning reserves. He could not understand it. Fynch was strong in his power. Surely he could easily overcome Rashlyn?

It was Rasmus who answered the unspoken question. *Fynch is following his destiny, Knave. You must do what he has commanded. The Thicket will allow this request.*

There are horses too, Knave replied, disguising his rising fear for Fynch.

The owl made a sound of disgust in his mind. *Wyl Thirsk never makes it easy,* the bird said testily. *We'll have to be careful how they land. Tell the two men to sit on horseback. Then we only have to control three 'parcels'.*

Just two. I plan to return to Fynch.

No. You have been commanded and you must do as he wishes. Now make ready.

Knave cut the link angrily. He was unused to feeling such emotion, but then he had never loved anyone before. He felt a keen loyalty to Wyl and would give his life for him if asked, but with Fynch it ran much deeper. It was love. Not something you turned your back on.

Thank you, Fynch, he sent, filled with sorrow.

He could barely hear the reply but he felt it. *I love you, Knave, farewell.*

If a dog could cry, Knave would have done so at that moment when he felt the loss of Fynch as the boy cut their link. Knave whined softly, then he turned to Wyl and gave a low growl.

Aremys shook his head. 'Do you understand him?'

Wyl nodded. 'Sort of. I've been around him long enough to grasp what kind of message is being communicated.'

'And that one meant?'

'We wait.' He turned to Knave. 'I know you're hurting, boy, but I need you to come with us.'

Wyl's comment was timely. Knave realised, much as he hated to admit it, that he was not of much use to

Fynch right now, whereas Wyl needed him for this trip to Briavel. He would go.

The men began to dismount but Knave barked.

Aremys frowned. 'What now?'

'Wants us to remain on horseback, I think,' Wyl said. 'Is that right, Knave?'

The dog gave a familiar growl and Wyl nodded to his friend. 'Yes. I guess we're taking the horses.'

'This will take some explaining at the other end,' Aremys said as the air around them began to thicken.

'Here we go,' Wyl cautioned. 'It's not pleasant, I warn you.'

'I think I remember it now,' was all Aremys had time to say before he felt a huge pressure on his body and all went dark.

The blinding golden light which had initially shimmered around the dragon had gradually dimmed to a soft glow and taken on a dirty bronze colour. The dragon's wings hung limply and each breath was laboured but still it stood upright and continued to absorb the magic slamming into its body.

'Die, beast,' the barshi screamed, clearly confused as to why the creature would not retaliate. 'You came here to destroy me,' he yelled. 'Yet you can't even shield against my magic.'

He blasted the dragon again with a powerful spell and saw the beautiful beast stagger for the first time, its head drooping.

Fynch! Lothryn screamed.

He can't hear you, Kestrel warned. *He won't listen anyway. He is dying, wants to die . . . has to die, I think.*

We must do something, Lothryn sent back to the bird. He marvelled at how much stronger he was feeling. His own light — if he could call it that — was burning bright.

We are. We bear witness to his sacrifice.

We let him die? We could all rush at Rashlyn together and destroy him. He can't kill all of us at once, surely? Lothryn tried.

Kestrel tutted. *He is already being destroyed.*

What do you mean?

With every spell the sorcerer weakens. He cannot feel it yet but we can see it. His magic is a filthy brown, tainted and ugly, not bright and golden like that of the Dragon King. The man has been careless — he has used most of it up.

And?

Fynch will absorb the evil magic, the pain, until there is no more left in the sorcerer. And by doing so, Fynch sacrifices himself.

A collective groan echoed around the forest and up to the mountain ridges as the animals saw the dragon slump to one side, its golden light no more than a slight wash of colour around it now.

Rashlyn was laughing maniacally. 'It is you who dies, you fool. Am I so strong? Can you not fight me? I am the King of the Creatures, not you. I will rule them all. I can change them and bend them to my will.' He shook his bony fist towards the animals who watched. 'You will all hail me as your King. Look at the dragon now. He dies. I have vanquished him and I shall take all of his power and wield it as I will.'

It was true. The King of the Creatures had rolled onto his side and was breathing so shallowly now that death was surely imminent.

If Lothryn had not been mesmerised and moved by the boy's courage, he would have closed Galapek's eyes to avoid seeing the dragon die. But he could not do that. Instead he focused on Rashlyn and, because he was helplessly linked to him through the evil man's filthy magic, he could feel the barshi summoning everything he had within. Curiously, Lothryn himself felt stronger than ever. He was truly himself again inside this horse; no longer a shrunken spirit barely clinging to existence. The pain had diminished; his flesh no longer twitched and trembled. The enchantment was waning as Rashlyn gathered all of his power to hurl at the dying dragon.

'Finish it!' the animals heard their King whisper. Fynch's words were met by a hysterical cackle from Rashlyn.

The barshi unleashed a primeval howl and launched every ounce of magic he possessed towards the dragon. The animals who had gathered to pay homage bore witness as Fynch, King of the Creatures, rolled back onto his clawed feet again in a last defiant show of strength and will. He too loosed a roar – a death roar – which every creature felt rattle through its chest, and he accepted the powerful killing spell, magically dragging it towards him . . . except when he had absorbed the spell he did not stop. He went on, sucking hard at the barshi whose twisted face of triumph turned to surprise. He was no longer giving his magic, it was being stolen from him, pulled in a great and dirty arc into his opponent.

I take it all from you, Rashlyn, were the dragon's final words.

Lothryn and Kestrel watched in awed silence as Fynch,

howling with anger, dragged the very essence of the barshi's being into himself and consumed it in golden fire. The brilliant light pulsed brightly around the dragon before extinguishing itself.

The King of the Creatures fell and appeared to be consumed by himself, reducing in size and stature until, where the mighty dragon had stood so proudly just hours earlier, the tiny shape of a boy lay curled tightly into himself on the forest floor.

Each creature present cried out in sympathy and then, as if on a given signal, all but the ekons began to move towards the child, who looked as though he was sleeping. One by one they nuzzled or sniffed the tiny body, each whining softly in thanks for the sacrifice that had been given to preserve their lives and their ways.

In Briavel, Knave threw back his head and howled; a sound to chill the souls who stood nearby. He did it again and again and Wyl knew the black dog was grieving for Fynch.

He lowered King Cailech's head in grief. 'Fynch is dead,' he said to Aremys, and the mercenary knew better than to offer hollow words of comfort.

A man staggered between the trees, his body burned and shrivelled, his hair flaming. His tangled beard was a blackened mass and patches of charred flesh ate at his face. His eyes were unseeing, scorched black, and he moaned, arms outstretched as he blindly felt his way. He was a mere husk of who he had once been. He began to scream and his empty cries echoed off the mountain peaks and returned to taunt him.

'Yes, scream, you evil bastard,' a voice said.

Lothryn looked around, wondering which of the animals had spoken aloud, but it was no animal who mocked Rashlyn. Beside the stallion stood a man; a tall, handsome older man with silver grey shot through his hair and the same silver glint in his short beard.

'Who speaks?' shrieked Rashlyn, swinging around in the direction of the voice.

'It is Gueryn le Gant.'

'The dog?' Rashlyn whispered, awed.

'The man,' Gueryn said, and it sounded like a threat. 'You have no more magic, Rashlyn. You cannot bind me and so I am freed.' He looked at the horse, sorrow knifing through him. 'I see his magic was not used in such sophistication on you, my friend. You remain entrapped.'

Having felt his spirit soar with untold joy at seeing Gueryn whole, Lothryn experienced the sickening fall of disappointment at realising that he, of course, remained as Galapek. He turned his great head towards the man but could no longer communicate with him by sending thoughts.

Gueryn lifted his finger to his lips to calm Lothryn. 'We will find a way,' he whispered to the horse, knowing the man inside could hear.

'How did this happen?' yelled Rashlyn, his voice trembling. 'You were stabbed, dead.'

'The other dog, Knave, healed me. He licked each of my wounds and sealed them with his own magic. He sensed I would be returned if you lost your power.'

'Lost my power,' the barshi echoed, as if he had not registered the change.

Gueryn advanced on the wild man. He could smell the charred flesh and took great pleasure in noticing injuries which would normally turn his gut. 'Try your magic now,' Gueryn taunted. 'If you can.'

Rashlyn screamed his despair as he discovered his loss.

Gueryn laughed. 'Fynch may not have had the desire to kill, but I do, Rashlyn,' Gueryn said. 'I do.' He closed on the staggering man who was now walking in circles, arms outstretched. But then he looked up and had a far better idea. Most of the animals had scattered since the demise of their King, but one type of creature, the most intimidating, remained. They were gradually closing in on the three that remained in the clearing, but Gueryn could see their attention was focused on the charred man rather than himself and Galapek.

'Ah, a better idea,' he said gleefully. 'A fitting one, Rashlyn.'

Spinning towards his voice, Rashlyn began to weep. 'What?'

'Do you know what ekons look like?'

The barshi fell to his knees and began to plead for mercy. Gueryn laughed, amazed at the man's audacity. 'Go to your god, Rashlyn, and I hope he burns you in eternal fire.'

Gueryn bent down to the boy, not wasting time to check for a pulse or even whether he breathed. He lifted the tiny mass of limbs and cradled the child in his arms. Fynch's head rolled against the soldier's chest. Gueryn called to Galapek and rapidly hefted himself onto the stallion's broad back, Fynch all but weightless in his arms, and bade the horse to get them out of there.

Galapek's powerful frame carried them swiftly from the grisly scene that unfolded in the clearing as two massive ekons descended on a screaming man who understood all too well, blind or not, that death had finally arrived. Only one creature remained to witness the barshi's bloody end – a kestrel perched high in a tree's branches.

CHAPTER 35

Aremys felt that coming to Werryl was a stupid idea. It was clear from what Wyl had said that Knave would prefer to be back in the Razors, and even Wyl's good sense must surely be screaming at him to get as far away from Briavel as possible. And yet here they were, taking deep breaths to recover from travel by magic and preparing to waltz up to the Queen of Briavel and present King Cailech to her, sworn enemy of the southern realms and newly agreed partner-in-crime with the treacherous Morgravian monarch.

'Do you think the Queen will start screaming like a banshee or do you imagine she'll keep her composure and offer the Mountain King high tea?' Aremys said sarcastically. 'That is, if we make it past the hail of arrows.'

'We'll send Knave,' Wyl said, smoothing back Cailech's long golden hair. 'How do I look?'

Aremys laughed, harsh and brief. 'Like the fucking King of the Razors.'

'I meant,' Wyl replied calmly, 'am I untidy?'

Aremys shook his head. 'What does it matter? Let's go, Wyl, and get this done with.'

'Trust me, my friend. She will see us.'

'And kill us,' the mercenary growled.

'Not with Knave leading us, she won't. She trusts the dog more than me.'

'Who is "me", Wyl?' Aremys asked angrily.

'Romen,' Wyl corrected. 'You're welcome to remain here,' he offered, tiring of the Grenadyne's bitterness even though he understood.

'No, it's always fun watching you die,' Aremys cut back swiftly. He regretted it instantly as he watched pain sweep across Cailech's face, the eyes darkening with barely contained sorrow. 'Forgive me, Wyl,' he groaned. 'I didn't mean that.'

'I know you didn't,' his friend said softly. 'I just have to see her once more, Aremys, before I become Celimus and am forced to see her through his cruel eyes.'

'How will it happen do you think? The Queen will turn you over to him . . . again?'

'Probably,' Wyl said, resigned to his fate. 'Come, I hope she has not already left for Pearlis.'

Valentyna was taking a late supper with Liryk. Conversation was hard won from her this night, just a day before their departure to Pearlis. She was trying, of that the commander was certain, but gradually her gaze had clouded and now she had withdrawn into her private, no doubt grim imaginings of life as Celimus's Queen.

Liryk wished he could spare her the sorrow she was

feeling, but he thought of her father and imagined how proud Valor would be of his only child and the brilliant gift she was giving Briavel. The gift of peace.

He watched her pushing food around her plate, her fork never once lifting any of it towards her mouth and the only sound in the room its clink against the porcelain. He watched sadly as she lifted her beautiful face to look at him, aware of his gaze.

'Forgive me, Liryk.'

'Nothing to forgive, your highness.'

Valentyna smiled wanly. 'My thoughts are elsewhere this eve – a bride's prerogative, I think.' She tried to widen the smile but failed. Tears welled instead. Liryk rushed to share with her his thought about her gift of peace to the realm. 'Thank you, that's really very lovely. I shall think on it as I make my wedding vows.'

'But still you keep hoping something might save you from the marriage?' he ventured.

She shrugged. 'Nothing can save me from this, Liryk.'

They both started at the sound of a knock at the door.

'Let me, your majesty,' Liryk offered and rose to answer the messenger. He returned tight-lipped and frowning.

'Important?' she asked, presuming it was for him. 'Don't fret, you're excused from my dazzling repartee this evening.' He gazed at her, wishing he did not have to tell her anything, wishing they could leave for Pearlis tonight. 'What is it? Not bad news, please . . . unless,' she laughed harshly, 'it's to tell me that Celimus had died in an accident.' She instantly apologised with her eyes, her demeanour suddenly contrite.

'Far more intriguing, your highness. Knave is on the bridge.'

She stood. 'Knave's back! Is Fynch with him?'

'No, your majesty.' Liryk's hesitant tone snapped her to attention.

'He's not alone though, is he?'

'He brings with him two men. One is Aremys Farrow.'

Valentyna's mouth dropped open. 'The man Ylena Thirsk and the Duke of Felrawthy spoke of – the one brokering the peace treaty with the Mountain King?'

Liryk nodded.

'And who accompanies him?' Valentyna asked, then frowned at Liryk's silence. 'Come on, Commander, the suspense is irritating.'

Liryk wiped away the perspiration which had coated his forehead since the wide-eyed messenger had brought the news. 'King Cailech of the Mountains, your majesty.'

The silence that met his words felt as heavy as the dread in his own heart. He watched his Queen's hand fly to her throat but, to her credit, she gave away nothing more than the initial shock. She visibly gathered her composure and turned towards the double windows, unlatched and threw them open, then stepped out onto the balcony.

He joined her in looking down upon the famous Werryl Bridge where three figures stood, surrounded by soldiers. One was familiar; as if on cue, the dog raised his great dark head now and looked directly at Valentyna. Liryk considered it uncanny but Valentyna read it differently. She felt that penetrating gaze cross the substantial distance between them and pierce her heart. She had to stop herself clutching her breast, where an old ache, barely buried, resurfaced to taunt and frighten her.

'He has brought him back to me,' she whispered to

herself as a notion, more insane than the thoughts of the
lunatics they sent for safekeeping to the Isle of Maguria,
hit her.

'Beg your pardon, your majesty?' Liryk said.

Valentyna closed her eyes momentarily then calmly
replied, 'Bring them to my study.'

'Your majesty, I don't—'

'Now, Liryk, please. Search them and remove their
weapons. I'm sure you will organise an armed guard too?'

'Yes, your highness.'

She disappeared from the balcony, leaving Liryk to look
down upon the strange trio once more.

'Now what have you sent us, Shar, to disrupt her peace?'
he muttered.

Valentyna splashed icy water on her face and took several
deep, steadying breaths as she held the drying linen to her
cheeks. She groaned. What was happening to her? Where
had that strange and maddening notion come from?

She raced through the various questions alarming her.
How could Knave know the Mountain King? Why bring
him here? How could they have come so far without
encountering the Briavellian Guard? It was impossible,
she realised. Unless they materialised out of thin air, she
thought sarcastically. Two riders and a huge dog would
not escape notice.

Knave's return inevitably reminded her of Fynch and
she recalled his last conversation with her, when he had
implied that the man she loved was not decaying in a
tomb within the palace crypt. *If I suggested this was simply
a dead body and not really the Romen Koreldy you loved, what
would you say?* he had asked, shocking her. And she had

replied that it would be cruel to say such a thing. Still he had tried, dear Fynch, to make her understand something which she could not believe, and yet now felt so deep in her heart. *Although Romen's corpse lies here before us, the man you knew – the man you loved, your highness – is not dead.*

And looking down at the trio on Werryl Bridge, she had felt as much, even though neither of the two men looked remotely like Romen. But if Fynch was right, and Romen was not dead, then what could possibly provide an explanation for such madness?

'How in Shar's name . . . unless . . .' She hesitated to even say the word, but it hovered nevertheless on the tip of her tongue. Magic.

'Magic,' she said aloud, recalling Elspyth's warning about being open to different ways of understanding. She had spoken of reincarnation and told her that love might return in the shape of another. Elspyth had been trying to convey a message; Valentyna had heard it in the urgency of her tone, her desperation to imply something important whilst not actually saying it. Elspyth had said that love might present itself as a woman even and Valentyna had laughed. Yet Ylena Thirsk had tried to give her love. Valentyna had rejected it, disgusted and upset that a woman would make such an approach to her. *But that was no ordinary woman, was it*, she thought to herself now, throwing down the linen and staring at her reflection in the mirror. *If you were truthful to yourself, you would admit there was an attraction there. You could not explain it if you were asked to, but if your life depended on it you might whisper that Ylena behaved with you as a man would . . . as a particular man would.*

She watched helpless tears roll down her face as she permitted the truth of her thoughts to be unleashed for the first time. Ylena Thirsk walked and talked like a woman but acted like a man. Like Koreldy, damn it! She even had the same curious habit of pulling at her ear and pacing when in deep thought.

Say it! she urged herself.

'Like Romen,' she whispered to the mirror. 'She kissed me like Romen did.'

But there was more — Fynch had connected Romen with Wyl Thirsk too. The boy had told her a long time ago that he believed Romen embodied General Wyl Thirsk, the red-headed, shy and courageous emissary from Morgravia who had saved her life and given his own in an attempt to save her father. Both her father and Wyl had died but somehow Romen had survived. Koreldy was a mercenary in the pay of King Celimus who had ordered the slaughter, so why did Romen then search out Ylena Thirsk, who was nothing to him? Thoughts clamoured and clashed in her head until she could no longer bear it.

She heard a gentle tap at the door and gave herself one last look in the mirror. She looked tousled and unsure of herself but had no time to care about inconsequentials when the worst and most terrifying notion of all was threatening to overwhelm her.

Fynch had told her that Knave responded to no one but those whom Wyl Thirsk loved. Wyl hardly cared for Romen Koreldy or King Cailech or indeed Aremys Farrow, another stranger. And yet the dog had effectively brought all three of these men to her. Why . . . if they weren't connected to Wyl?

Valentyna dug deep and found enough strength to call out, 'Enter.' Even so, she was not ready emotionally for the two strapping men who stepped into the room behind Commander Liryk, both towering over him. Knave pushed around their legs and bounded towards her.

Tears came to her eyes at the sight of King Cailech, and the unshakeable, inexplicable feeling that she was once again in the presence of Romen Koreldy. She pretended they were for the dog and bent to pat his head and then hugged him fiercely, whispering, 'Thank you', although she was not sure why.

The rattle of her guard's weapons as the door closed behind her visitors reminded her who she was and where she was. Valentyna straightened, ignoring her wet cheeks, and raised her eyes to meet the warm, dark eyes of Aremys Farrow and the cool yet somehow burning gaze of the Mountain King who was staring at her hungrily.

'Gentlemen, forgive me. As you can see, I am overwhelmed to see my friend Knave again,' she said, amazed that her voice sounded so steady.

'Your majesty,' King Cailech said, bowing low, 'the apology is all ours for disturbing you at this hour.'

Valentyna felt a thrill tingle through her body at the warmth in his tone. His voice was as deep as she had expected, yet also layered with humour and something else . . . affection, she thought fancifully. She curtsied, paying due respect to a King. 'I'm not sure how we should greet you, your highness. This is altogether unusual, as I'm sure you can imagine,' and she saw those light green eyes sparkle with amusement at her understatement. 'You must be Aremys Farrow,' she continued, turning to the bear of a man who stood awkwardly beside the King. She stepped forward and extended her hand. 'I have heard about you from Lady Ylena Thirsk and the Duke of Felrawthy.'

Aremys took her hand and kissed it. 'Your highness,' he said, wanting to say a dozen other things but resisting the urge.

'Come,' she said, 'are you hungry?' Both men shook their heads. 'A drink then, of my father's finest wine. I cannot imagine the tale I am about to hear about how two men of the Razors — one a King, no less — covered hundreds of leagues of my realm without a single guard spotting them.'

'Indeed,' Farrow muttered.

'Valentyna.'

Something in the way Cailech said her name made her heart leap in her breast.

'Yes, Cailech?' she responded, and they both smiled at the sudden lack of formality.

'May we speak as sovereigns . . . in private?'

She noted how Aremys Farrow glared towards the King. It was an odd reaction, unless theirs was a friendship that extended beyond that of monarch and bodyguard.

'Of course,' she offered, glancing towards Liryk who looked astounded at the suggestion.

'Your highness,' he began, determined that she not be left alone with this man.

Valentyna held a hand in the air to stop her commander, knowing precisely his concerns but somehow not at all daunted by the supposed enemy in their camp. 'Can we trust you, King Cailech?' she said.

'Far more than you can your husband-to-be, Queen Valentyna,' he responded, and Valentyna saw Liryk close his eyes with despair at the King's inflammatory words.

* * *

Aremys was fuming as Commander Liryk escorted him from the room. If he had had a knife in his hand he felt sure he would have happily plunged it into Cailech's chest himself, out of sheer frustration. Nevertheless, he could not blame his friend. Ever since a treacherous King had sent him on a mission of death, Wyl had known nothing but violence and despair, frustration and sorrow – save a few days in Briavel, as Romen, when he wooed a Queen.

And here he is doing it again, he thought, not realising he had voiced that thought.

'I beg your pardon,' Liryk said. He looked as angry as Aremys felt.

'I'm sorry, Commander, it's been a long journey,' the mercenary said. He noticed the man's eyes widen in further wrath.

'Yes, I'd like to talk to you about that, Master Farrow.'

Aremys sighed. He did not want to discuss it, had no idea how to explain their mysterious arrival. 'Actually, first I need to relieve my bowels,' he said, knowing this remark would throw off even the most persistent pursuer. 'Also, I am famished and I need to bathe and rest. Then I shall attempt to answer all of your questions, I promise. But please remember, I am only a bodyguard to my King. A foot soldier if you will. It would be best if you saved your wrath for him.'

And with that, Aremys Farrow took himself off in the direction Commander Liryk, filled with surprise at the rebuttal, pointed. Aremys just hoped Wyl had some plan to get them out of here as easily.

* * *

Valentyna, self-conscious and uncharacteristically blushing, showed the tall Mountain King towards the comfy sofas in her study. The room had once been her father's but was now very clearly her own. Wyl noticed the new Valentyna-esque touches around the room: a painting of horses being led out of a stable, flowers in vases on various surfaces and the unmistakable fragrance of lavender being crushed underfoot.

'Are you cold, sire?' she asked, then her face fell as he smirked. 'Ah yes, how silly of me, I hear your people don't feel the cold.'

He shook his head gently. 'I'm sorry. By all means, let us sit by your fire.'

She smiled. 'I'm afraid I do hate to be cold,' she admitted, 'although I must give it away soon. Each eve is milder than the next these days.'

'Which means summer is beckoning,' he reminded, and she did not miss what was left unspoken.

'Is that why you are here?'

'Yes. This is a most pleasant room.'

'Thank you. Is Farrow your friend?'

He grinned at the odd question. 'As a matter of fact he is.'

'Which would explain his fury at being asked to leave?'

He nodded. 'No doubt, although he has no right to feel that way.'

'Indeed, sire. I hear that you don't treat your friends all that well,' she baited, handing him a cup of wine.

'I can't imagine what you refer to, Valentyna.' He feigned confusion.

'I refer to Lothryn, your second in command, your closest friend. The man you murdered.'

'He is not dead,' Wyl answered simply, glad for the banter as he began to wonder why in Shar's name he had come here. How would he explain any of this to her? What could he possibly say – other than that he worshipped her – which would make her listen to him and not order the courier to be sent to Morgravia this night?

'Not dead?' she spluttered. 'But Elspyth told me—'

'Elspyth is wrong, your highness. I have left Lothryn alive in the Razors.'

Valentyna knew that there was no love lost between Cailech and Elspyth and that, given the chance, he would have her killed. But every fibre of her being screamed at her that this man was an impostor, in the same curious way Ylena Thirsk had seemed to embody someone else, and she decided to test him. 'Elspyth may never live to hear that good news, my lord.'

'What?' Cailech said, spilling wine on his hand as he leaned forward in his chair. His demeanour suggested fear for someone he cared for.

Intrigued by his reaction, she continued: 'The last I heard, she was near death and being carried to Pearlis – or so Liryk tells me.'

The King's face drained of colour momentarily. 'What happened to her?'

'Why do you care? She is a Morgravian slut to you, surely?'

She watched the King hesitate, his gaze darkening as he collected his thoughts.

'I care,' was all he said. 'Is she alive?'

'Yes,' she said. 'But that's all I know.'

Wyl put the cup down and, without realising it, began to pull at an earlobe as he thought on this news. He did not notice the sudden sick expression that crossed the Queen's face. Presumably Crys Donal was with Elspyth, he decided. He asked as much and the Queen nodded. He could not know that she did not trust her voice to speak, her eyes riveted on the habit she had seen in four people now, starting with Wyl Thirsk.

'Valentyna,' Cailech began, but the Queen was no longer interested in the strange game that was being played out between them. She stood suddenly and demanded: 'Why is it that Knave sits at your side? He belonged to Wyl Thirsk and looks kindly only on those Wyl loved. So why does he choose to accompany you?'

Wyl could no longer stand the tension between them. He put down his wine and stood also, facing the woman he so loved. He was very close and a head taller than she. To her credit, he thought, she did not flinch. Any other woman would have been screaming for the guard by now, but the defiance in Valentyna's eyes only fired his desire more and he took her hand and pulled her towards him. This time he would kiss her as a man and to hell with the consequences.

Valentyna did not fight him. She did not think she could have resisted him even if she had wanted to. It shocked her to realise that she did not much care whether she was kissing Wyl Thirsk, Romen Koreldy or even Ylena Thirsk, for Cailech, King of the Mountains, had a raw and blistering charisma that burned around him like a halo. If her heartbeat had increased for Romen then it was hammering for Cailech, and if her body had yearned for Romen's touch then she wanted to throw herself down now before the hearth and have Cailech take her like the barbarian he was purported to be. The ardour she had felt for Romen was nothing in comparison to the carnal desire she was experiencing for this golden man who was standing too close, his huge hands gripping her upper arms, their faces a hair's breadth apart, the fire of passion burning between them.

Wyl found his courage. He kissed Valentyna and instantly became lost in a sizzling rush of desire and need he had hungered after for too long.

The fire had burned so low it was only glowing embers but neither noticed the cool of the air. Their naked bodies were still entwined and to Valentyna it was as though they were one. She could not feel where her lean limbs began and his muscled limbs ended. They lay facing each other and she stroked his golden hair while he held her in an embrace she never wanted to leave and stared at her in a way that made her heart leap all over again.

'Perhaps I should have asked first?' he said.

She laughed, full-throated and tinged with a devil-may-care happiness she had never thought she could feel again. 'Particularly as it was my first time,' she said, pulling a face.

'I'll kill myself if I hurt you,' he admitted.

'That's not the sort of comment I would expect from a barbarian King.'

'We are not barbarians,' he said, dropping his hand away.

Her expression betrayed her anguish. 'Oh, Cailech, no, I didn't mean it that way. It was a jest. It's just that . . .'

'Just what?' he asked softly, returning his hand to the crook of her back and resting it in the soft dip before the rise of her buttocks.

She felt his fresh arousal and smiled to herself as she realised what power women had over men. Even a King could be made so weak. No weapon, no threat, no blood; just a woman's body was all it took to make an enemy King compliant. Celimus should have come and seen her before to discuss the problem in the north – she and her kind could have solved it in an instant, she thought. But this man is no enemy, she decided, delighting in the fact that she had just lost her virginity to him. She did not have to gift it to Celimus.

'It's just that I feel as though I know you,' she risked, daring to venture towards her wild thoughts of earlier.

'You do,' he said gently, watching her carefully.

She sat up, her breasts high yet irresistibly heavy and rounded. Wyl wanted to pinch himself to make sure that he was really here with her and she was not just returning his affections but inviting them, loving them. He too sat up and reached towards her but she took his hands and put them into her lap.

'We've known each other less than a couple of hours, Cailech, and we've spent more than half of that time making love. No preamble, no honeyed words and romantic gestures. It's impossible that I would act this way – impossible! But I felt a burning for you from the moment we met. Before, in fact. I watched you from my window as you stood on Werryl Bridge, surrounded by guards, and my heart was pounding for you then.'

'Valentyna, I—'

'No, wait. I have to say this.' She smiled, suddenly embarrassed, and pulled around her the dress which she remembered him unbuttoning not so long ago and helping her to step out of. 'There are a lot of voices crowding in my mind – a boy called Fynch, for one, whom I adore.' She noticed something dark flicker across his face at the mention of Fynch but she pressed on, determined to say what had been niggling at her for so long. 'He once said something profound to me, which I dismissed as a child's fancy. I think now I was wrong. Then Elspyth encouraged me to open my heart to someone else after I was betrayed by the man I loved, Romen Koreldy. He was not true, but I have never stopped loving him.'

Again Wyl tried to speak and again she hushed him, this time with a hand to his lips. Tears welled in her eyes at the mention of Romen. 'A noblewoman called Ylena Thirsk came to me to offer her help and then gave herself up like a sacrifice to King Celimus so that the Legion would be withdrawn from our borders. You were there at Felrawthy, Cailech, you would have met her. It was a lie that I sent her to him. It was all her own selfless idea to walk into the dragon's den.'

He nodded and she saw the grief in him. 'Where is she now?' she asked, almost too frightened to hear the truth.

'She is dead, Valentyna. She showed the courage to match her name. The Thirsks have always been true to Morgravia and yet both Wyl and Ylena pledged themselves to you. They both loved you in their own way.'

His words made her weep openly now. 'Who killed her?'

'I did,' he whispered.

She looked at him, not understanding. 'You?'

He nodded so sadly she had to believe him. 'It was an accident. I rescued her from the grip of Celimus – he had planned a horrible death for her which I won't sully your presence by describing. Suffice to say it was up to his usual cruel and humiliating standard. Aremys and I took her away from Felrawthy and into the Razors.'

'What happened there?'

'She did something very brave — may I leave it at that? I find it painful to think on.'

Valentyna heard the tremor in his voice. The description Romen had given of Cailech was of a man who was anything but tender like this. She ticked it in her mind as another factor on the side of impostor. Too many ticks were mounting on that side of the ledger and so far nothing pointed to this being the arrogant sovereign of the Mountain People. But then that description was hearsay — always second-hand. She needed to find out the truth for herself.

'I will grieve for Ylena. She was my friend.'

It was Wyl's turn to take a chance. 'She told me you parted on bad terms.'

Valentyna pushed her hair back from her face. 'We parted amicably, although there was something between us . . . Ylena tried to make love to me,' she stammered, surprising herself with her candour.

Cailech looked down at their linked hands. 'Yes, she told me her error. Wished she could take it back.'

'I wish I could have reacted differently. But Knave, Cailech — how is it that this dog favours you in the same way he favoured Wyl Thirsk, Fynch, Ylena and Romen?'

I could tell her, Wyl thought frantically, *and see what happens*. Or he could preserve the lie and not trouble her life with talk of magic. Already a plan was forming in his mind. Now he had possessed her so completely he knew he could never let her go, never allow her to be with Celimus. The most daring yet logical scenario seemed to be to call the Mountain warriors into Briavel and take their chances on war with the Legion. If Crys Donal had taken his advice, then he would be stirring up trouble within the Legion anyway, and with powerful people such as the Benches behind that push perhaps Celimus would not have so many of his Legionnaires to count on.

He made his decision. 'I have a plan, Valentyna, which may prevent you marrying King Celimus. It is fraught with danger, and no doubt spells death for some Briavellians, but I believe it is the proud path for your realm. You know Celimus has killed so many, not the least of whom was your own father,' he said, hating to see how his words brought tears, 'and so perhaps it is the way you want to go anyway. Until now I haven't been able to help you. I thought you were as trapped as I am.'

She looked at him and frowned. 'You're not making sense. Why are you trapped?'

It was time. This had not been his intention when he set out from the Razors, but then he had not expected for a moment that he would be holding a naked Valentyna in his arms and able to speak the love he had felt for her for so long. Sharing her body had changed everything. He swallowed hard, wondering at how she would react. 'I have to tell you something,' he said.

'I hear fear in your voice,' she replied. 'Why does what you are about to say scare you?'

'Because it requires an honesty I have been unable to find before with you. I was scared it would push you away.'

She shook her head. 'But you have never met me before,' she said, feeling the soft hairs lift on her arms and behind her neck. This was it. This was what she had searched her soul for. He was going to give her the answer.

'I have met you before, Valentyna. I first met you and fell in love with you in this very chamber. Your father was present and we took supper together and you laughed at me because I was too short in your opinion to be an emissary from the King of Morgravia.'

If time could stand still, if a heart could stop beating, if all breath could cease and one could still live, Valentyna would believe that was what was happening to her now. She kept silent, her eyes riveted on Cailech's.

'And when I met you again, my beloved,' the King reached for his trousers, pulling from them a handkerchief, 'you gave me this.'

Valentyna was sobbing now, deep, heartfelt sobs. She shook her head in denial. What she had wanted to hear suddenly sounded too frightening to contemplate. 'I gave that to Romen Koreldy,' she pleaded, squeezing Cailech's hands so tight her own felt numb. 'He was a Grenadyne nobleman, a mercenary.'

'He was me,' Wyl said gently, tears welling in his own eyes. 'It was me you loved, Valentyna. Romen was dead – you never knew the real man. I am Wyl Thirsk and I was trapped in Romen's body.'

Words failed her. It was as if she was listening to a language she did not understand. He continued, driving the nails of pain into her heart.

'I returned to your life as Ylena, my own sister. My brave girl tried to stand up to Romen's killer.'

'Hildyth, the whore,' Valentyna whispered.

'Her real name was Faryl. She was an assassin sent by Celimus to kill Romen, which she successfully achieved, except that it was me inside Romen's body and the magic, known as the Quickening, forced me to take over her life and she died instead.' He pulled Valentyna close and, to his surprise, she permitted it. He went on, determined to say it all. 'Ylena heard about Faryl. She took her chance at Tenterdyn as I raced to catch up with her and Elspyth, and a lucky blow killed me once again, this time compelling me to take my sister's life.'

Valentyna gave an audible sob.

'I had to see you, to try and help you,' Wyl went on. 'I came back to Werryl and tried so hard not to make a fool of myself, but still I succeeded in doing so. I have loved you, Valentyna, since that very first night. I'm sorry for humiliating you and making you feel so bad about Ylena.'

Valentyna took the linen handkerchief from his lap and dried her eyes. She told herself to find some strength. Her father would be ashamed to see her so undone, and yet it was unlikely he had ever faced anything this daunting in his long life. She sniffed and tried for a watery smile, but failed. She raised her hand to wipe away Wyl's tears too.

'I think I knew it then. Your sister showed too many masculine traits – habits I recognised as belonging to Romen. But I just couldn't make myself believe something so incredible. And so,' she continued for him, 'Ylena lost her fight again and became King Cailech, is that right, Wyl?'

To hear her speak his true name was more than he had ever dreamed. He kissed her and stroked her hair. 'That's right,' he said, 'I'm Wyl. I'm so sorry for duping you but I was just trying to protect you.'

'From myself,' she said harshly, 'because I wouldn't

accept the existence of magic.' She thought of all the occasions when Fynch had tried so hard to convince her.

'Don't blame yourself,' Wyl urged. 'I would not have believed it either if it had not happened to me. I am cursed. Cursed by the witch Myrren with a gift I never asked for.'

'But you see, Wyl, others believed you – I presume Aremys knows?' He nodded. 'You see. You have people who trust you. I hate myself because I did not.'

'You didn't know!' he said, desperate not to upset her any further.

'I saw the clues. It was all there for me. Knave did everything but speak to me,' she cried. 'But that means Romen wasn't real.' She was wavering between belief and denial again.

'Oh no, Valentyna, no! Don't cry. Romen was real. As real as I am here. I was Romen; he was me. It's me, Wyl, who loves you, who said all of those things to you as Romen.'

'You?' the Queen said, dazed. 'Wyl Thirsk. Poor redheaded Wyl.'

'That's right,' he whispered, sad to feel her draw away from him. 'It's always been me. I stopped you giving yourself to Romen that night; I planned the feast celebrations; I gave you a dove mask and told you I loved you. I wore the black mask and fought Celimus. I would have killed him too, if not for you. It broke my heart to see my betrayal reflected in your eyes.'

She stared back at him, wanting to believe but struggling to cope with such shattering news. He understood.

'Know this, Valentyna. Whatever happens now, I have loved you with all my heart. I love you now and I will love you for ever, whoever I am. There is nothing you could ever do to make me feel another way, and I shall never give my heart to another. It is yours – I am one with you.'

Valentyna sighed. What could she say in response?

He rescued her. 'May I tell you my plan?'

She hesitated, then seemed to relax. 'I don't really know how to reply to your sweet words. I . . . I loved Romen, and I cannot give you – whoever you are – up.'

Wyl nodded, afraid, yet daring to hope she might be able to love him back. Her suggestion of not being able to give him up now made his spirits soar.

'Wyl,' she began again, but was interrupted by a frantic knocking. Her soft expression turned to one of terror. 'Quick, we must dress!'

Wyl was into his few garments in moments, and was impressed at how quickly and deftly the Queen threw on her gown despite the intimidating banging on the door. 'Stall for time,' he urged, helping her to button the back.

Valentyna was about to call out some excuse for the delay when the door burst open. It was Aremys. He took in the scene in a second and a look of deep apology swept across his face, but the palpable sense of fear which entered the room with him caused all three to forget their embarrassment.

Valentyna was at his side rapidly, praying to Shar that none of her men would notice her dishevelment or guess that her gown was still undone at the back. 'We'll be fine, thank you,' she said, closing the door on the anxious guards.

'What is it?' Wyl asked, stepping to Valentyna's side and finishing off the buttons on her dress.

'Celimus,' Aremys answered. He could not hide the distress in his voice.

'What? Here?' Valentyna rushed to the window.

'I'm afraid so. Come on, Wyl, we leave now!'

'You called him Wyl,' Valentyna said, turning from the window. She had seen the riders flying Legion colours below. It was true then. Out of Wyl's affectionate embrace, the intimate moment lost, the reality felt harsh and suddenly ridiculous.

Aremys shrugged, sheepish. 'Well, your highness, I assume he has told you the truth. Is that right, Wyl?'

Wyl nodded, glancing towards the Queen with a heavy heart. It was over so soon . . . before he had even had a chance to put his plan into action.

'Wyl!' Aremys repeated. 'We go now! Sorry, your highness.'

Wyl did not move.

'Go!' Valentyna urged, catching Farrow's infectious anxiety. 'Please. The Legion is entering the palace.'

'Is Celimus here?'

'I don't know. I can't—'

Aremys interrupted, angry now. 'He's here in person, Wyl. I beg you, let's go.'

King Cailech took some time to right his clothes, then a calm smile broke across the rugged face that truly reflected the mountain region which raised him. 'This is meant to be, Aremys,' he said, his voice soft and sad. 'This is it, the culmination of Myrren's gift.'

'No!' the Grenadyne yelled, striding towards his friend. 'We can escape. If you won't think about yourself, think about Valentyna and how your presence might reflect on her.'

'What are you talking about?' Valentyna said. 'Why is this meant to be?'

Aremys caught the stern glance from Wyl and knew this was one secret which was not going to be shared. He knew when to keep his own counsel.

Liryk saved them further argument by barging in, all protocol disregarded. He was startled to see Aremys there. 'Who let you in, Farrow?'

'Sorry, Commander, I told a lie to your guards.'

'This is preposterous, your majesty. I am supposed to be taking care of your security and it seems anyone can come and go as they please.'

Wyl had not considered how Celimus might react to finding him here. Aremys was right: he had to leave, if only to protect Valentyna from any suggestion that she was consorting with the enemy behind the Morgravian King's back.

Valentyna took charge, concerned now that King Celimus might catch her in Cailech's company. 'Liryk?' The tone brooked no further delay.

The commander adopted a formal tone which old Chancellor Krell would have been proud of. 'My Queen, although this seems rather unlikely, I am here to tell you that King Celimus has just arrived in the bailey.'

Valentyna took a steadying breath. 'Thank you. King Cailech cannot be seen here and I need to . . . tidy up.'

Liryk was still flustered at finding Farrow in the room with them. If only he knew, it would have been safer for Valentyna had Farrow been there all along, Wyl thought.

'King Cailech,' Liryk said, 'I will organise an escape route and divert the Morgravian party but you will leave now. You have made your peace with Celimus – now let us make ours!' The vehemence in his voice surprised them all. 'Your majesty, please go ahead to your chambers. I will let your husband-to-be know that you are not far away,' he finished, choosing to emphasise the word 'husband' as he took in her dishevelled clothes and the heightened colour in her cheeks.

Liryk had no idea what had transpired during their conversation but he could see for himself that the rug was crumpled and the lavender stalks strewn on the floor were crushed in one spot. Their fragrance overlay another one he knew well from places like the Forbidden Fruit . . . no, he certainly did not want to take his thoughts down that path. One more day and Queen Valentyna would be on her way to Pearlis where she would marry King Celimus and finally unite the two realms. That was all Commander Liryk cared about right now and he would permit nothing to get in the way of that vision.

Valentyna felt cornered. She nodded at Liryk. 'Thank you, Commander.' Then, 'King Cailech, it has been enlightening,' she said, extending a hand. The Mountain King kissed it too long and too tenderly for Liryk's liking.

'Come, gentlemen,' the commander urged. 'Your highness, I will wait for you in the main salon.'

'Use the secret door,' she said and he nodded.

Liryk did not miss the long, meaningful glance exchanged between his Queen and the Mountain King, but felt more relieved with every step he and the two visitors took closer to the door and the passageway which would lead them out of the palace.

Cailech turned just before ducking to enter the secret stairwell. 'Valentyna, remember all that I've said. It's the truth.' And then he was gone. Gone again from her life. Leaving her to face Celimus and a desperately unwanted marriage whilst her heart's light burned fiercely for Wyl Thirsk.

CHAPTER 36

Aremys had persuaded Wyl as far as the gates, hurrying Cailech's bulky form down into the bowels of the palace. The guard accompanying them directed them to a little-used gate, which brought them out into a courtyard near the chapel.

When Aremys cursed their lack of weapons, Wyl remembered that Koreldy's blue sword was stored in a secret spot in the chapel. Against the guard's wishes they hurried in, startling Father Paryn.

A familiar voice greeted them. 'Aremys!' Turning, they saw young Pil, the monk who had escaped with Ylena from the massacre at Rittylworth.

'You know these men, child?' Father Paryn asked the novice.

'I know Farrow — we met at Felrawthy, Father. But I don't know his friend.'

'Pil,' Aremys said, his voice spilling its relief. 'This is—'

Wyl would not permit it. 'I am King Cailech of the Razors,' he said, bowing.

Father Paryn drained of all colour. To his credit, young Pil recovered quickly and bowed. 'Why are you here, your highness?'

'We're running from King Celimus,' Aremys growled, hurling an angry glance Wyl's way.

'King Celimus is here?' Father Paryn asked.

'I'm afraid so,' Wyl said calmly. 'We must not be found or it will look bad for the Queen, you understand?' Clearly neither of them did, going by their confused expressions. Wyl pushed on; confusion was good in this instance. 'Anyway, we need Romen's sword.'

'No fighting in the house of Shar, King or not,' the priest cautioned.

'There won't be, Father. We just want to take the sword and leave. I promise no blood will be spilled.'

It was too late. There were shouts outside and the guard accompanying them shrugged. 'I'm sorry, sire,' he said, 'I shall have to turn you in. I've been briefed by Commander Liryk not to risk the Queen's reputation.'

Wyl nodded. 'I understand.'

'What?' Aremys roared. 'Wait!'

'Be quiet, Aremys,' Wyl commanded and suddenly everyone paid attention to King Cailech. He turned quickly to Father Paryn and Pil. 'Hide him,' he said, indicating the Grenadyne, 'and help him escape the palace compound. I ask no more than you give him Koreldy's weapons. Queen Valentyna will thank you for it,' he said firmly, adding, 'She has sanctioned it.' It was a lie, but he no longer cared at this point.

Both holy men nodded dumbly then watched King Cailech of the Razors stride out to meet the Legionnaires and the Briavellian Guard.

'Quick!' Pil said, and, with no choice left to him, Aremys Farrow hung his head and followed the novice.

A few minutes later he heard the soldiers walk in and receive a predictable roasting from Father Paryn for bearing arms in the chapel. They tried to explain but achieved nothing but the threat of damnation in Shar's eternal fire if they did not leave at once. 'Curse you all for disturbing a man at prayer,' the priest called after them.

Pil left Aremys in a small room behind the main chapel while he went for news from Father Paryn. 'Where did they take the King?' Aremys asked when Pil returned, wondering how he might free Wyl from a company of Legionnaires and the Briavellian Guard.

'I gather he's in the gatehouse. There are soldiers everywhere. Is he really the King of the Razors?'

Aremys looked sorrowfully at Pil and nodded before adding, 'He was also Ylena Thirsk, Faryl of Coombe and Romen Koreldy.'

The boy's eyes widened. 'Wyl Thirsk!' he exclaimed in a hushed tone of wonder.

'That's right. And now the King finally has him in his clutches.'

'What are we going to do?' Pil asked, terrified.

Aremys decided that trying to rescue Wyl right now was pointless. He needed time to think it through, and Celimus would not do anything too risky on Briavellian soil just a day or so before his wedding. No, he would save Cailech for some sort of spectacle after the marriage ceremony, no doubt.

'You're going to stay here and keep our secret,' he told the novice. 'And I'm going to take Koreldy's sword and make my way to Pearlis.'

'That's where he's being taken, I gather, to Stoneheart.'

'Good work, Pil,' Aremys said, knowing the praise would help the frightened young monk.

'Is there anything else I can do?'

'Lead me out safely and then let the Queen know that I've escaped.'

'What about a horse?'

Aremys shook his head. 'Too risky and Celimus is too smart. No, I'll go on foot and hitch a ride somehow.'

'There are plenty of nobles and merchants headed for Pearlis, Master Farrow,' Pil said excitedly. 'I'm sure you can get a lift with one of them.'

The Grenadyne tried to smile but failed. 'That's what I'll do then.'

Most of the nobles making the journey to Pearlis for the royal wedding had their own men for protection but Aremys was counting on the strata of society below the nobles not having reliable security. A number of middle-class families had decided the opportunity to witness the marriage ceremony combined with a sight of the great city of Pearlis was irresistible and were also preparing for the trip.

After lying low in the northern part of Werryl for a couple of hours and carefully watching the procession of travellers, Aremys offered his services to three couples who were obviously travelling together. Aremys knew he possessed one of those inherently honest faces, which was certainly a helpful asset in his more secretive assignments. In this instance it won favour with the ladies – along with his suggestion that although Briavel was relatively safe, Morgravia was riddled with bandits who preyed on wealthy merchants.

And so Aremys found himself sitting alongside Mat, a purveyor of fine foods to the nobility, who was driving the carriage that carried the rest of the party whilst another man, Bren, brought up the rear, riding one of the two fresh horses they had brought along.

'I've never seen a sword tinged with blue like that one,' Mat commented.

'Aye,' Aremys answered, more sadly than he meant to sound. 'It belonged to a friend who gave it to me as a gift.'

Mat whistled. 'Some gift. Must have set him back a penny or two. My brother's a craftsman in weapons but I've never seen him work on anything like that.'

'I believe it was made by Master Craftsman Wevyr.'

'At Orkyld,' the man said in awe.

Aremys nodded. 'He was a good friend.'

'I guess so,' Mat agreed, some irony in the grin he cast the Grenadyne's way, then the two men settled into a comfortable silence as the carriage cleared the city and headed onto the main road which led to Morgravia.

Aremys appreciated the quiet to be alone with his grim thoughts about how he had lost Wyl in the panic of Celimus's arrival. It had been his panic alone, if the truth be told; Wyl had not so much as raised an eyebrow in distress. He remembered Wyl's chilling words: *It is meant to be*, he had said. *This is it, the culmination of Myrren's gift.*

Mat's voice brought Aremys back to the present as the carriage bumped along the road.

'Pardon?'

'I said, you're very quiet. Is everything all right?'

'Sorry, when I'm concentrating on the road I can lose myself.'

'No bandits this close to Werryl, Farrow. Relax, join us in a song,' Mat urged.

Singing was the last thing Aremys felt like doing as he imagined what Celimus had in store for King Cailech.

CHAPTER 37

Valentyna descended the staircase to the main salon, feeling as though she were now two people: the one who was gliding in a soft blue gown to welcome her betrothed, whom she despised; and the one who – in mind, certainly – was fleeing with King Cailech and Aremys Farrow.

The truth of the Mountain King's identity had still to fully sink in. It was all she could think about, her mind, moving back through time spent with Wyl when he was himself, with Romen, with Ylena. And as much as she wanted to find holes in the story – just one would do – it was complete. There were too many arguments in favour of Myrren's gift being the truth. She had never really got to know the real Wyl, but comparing Romen with Cailech yielded frightening similarities and when she threw Ylena into the mix it left her numb. Why had he never tried to tell her?

She answered her own question: she would never have believed it. Not when he was Romen; not even with the miraculous arrival of the chaffinch, which seemed to herald Ylena's visit. She had considered the finch's song as a timely coincidence, not magical, but it had been magic of some kind she now realised. Wyl had not had time to tell her about Fynch; how he was, where he was, nor enough of his idea of how she could avoid marrying Celimus. What would she not give to hear it now? She had considered every scenario possible and had not been able to find a way out. Only a few more steps now, she realised, emerging from her disquieted thoughts, and Celimus would be kissing her hand and offering sugary platitudes. What could he be doing here? Well, he could just turn around and go home. She still had one more day before she had to leave for Pearlis.

She took a deep breath and nodded at the guards outside the salon as the doors were pushed open for her entry. Valentyna had already pictured King Celimus bowing elegantly, then striding majestically forward, smiling widely with those perfect teeth. She had already planned her own contrived expression – a delicate balance of surprise and feigned pleasure that he was in Briavel. But she did not have to contrive any surprise. It came up and slapped her hard in the face when she swept into the room to be confronted by a snarling, struggling Cailech and a smugly grinning King of Morgravia.

'Valentyna, my love,' Celimus said, expansively, 'look what I found sneaking out of your palace like a rat.'

She stopped all movement and was convinced her breathing had stopped too, such was the shock. She saw Cailech shake his head, knew what he wanted her to do. Her heart broke. Again; it was happening again. Once more he was offering himself up to save her.

Everyone was waiting for her to speak.

'I've already explained,' Wyl yelled, shaking off his

captors' hands, 'that I never got to speak with the Queen.' Valentyna noticed the manacles around his arms and ankles.

'I heard you the first time, Cailech,' Celimus spat, turning back towards his bride. 'My dear, is this true?'

Don't hesitate, Valentyna, just agree, Wyl prayed.

For Briavel then, she decided, rapidly assessing the helplessness of the situation. She summoned her most regal tone and hurled it back at Celimus. 'Of course it's true,' she answered tersely. 'Who is this man?' She pointed towards Wyl – presumably Aremys had escaped, 'And how dare you hold anyone against their will in my court, King Celimus.'

That startled him. He was not prepared for her wrath, having already decided she was as guilty as the Mountain People, conspiring against him. His first instinct not to trust Cailech had been right; it was a mistake he would never make again.

'Your majesties.' It was Liryk. 'Allow me to escort the prisoner to a secure place and perhaps then you might discuss—'

'Yes, why don't you do that, Commander,' Valentyna agreed, cutting across whatever else he was going to say and so seizing control. 'This is unforgiveable, King Celimus. You called him Cailech. I still don't know who he is.'

Celimus had also regained some equanimity. 'Don't you? Let me introduce you to the treacherous King of the Razors, who just days ago was signing a peace treaty with Morgravia at Felrawthy.'

Valentyna feigned shock, which hid her despair as the man she had loved through so many lives was led away.

Cailech turned his head, spoke over his shoulder. 'I'm glad you have finally met me, your majesty.' The word 'me' was loaded with meaning only she would grasp. 'We'll meet again,' Wyl said to her alone.

'Oh, I'm sure you will,' Celimus said. 'I shall insist my wife is present for your execution.'

She saw Cailech's sad smile and did not understand it. Dismissing everyone, she swung around on Celimus the minute the door had closed. 'How dare you, sir!'

'Valentyna, please,' he cajoled. 'I came with only romantic intentions. My Chancellor suggested that it would be wonderful for both our peoples if we could be seen together. His idea was that I bring an escort to accompany you on this symbolic journey across our two realms. I know I should have sent word but it sounded like such a worthy plan I was excited and in a hurry to catch you here before you left Werryl Palace. I've had a special carriage made, my love, emblazoned with our new heraldic device which my craftsmen have been designing for months now. It flies the colours of Briavel and Morgravia, sweet Valentyna, and no, they don't clash. We have woven the crimson with the emerald and violet so beautifully, it seems we were always meant to be one,' he gushed.

Valentyna was taken aback by his enthusiasm. She could see how the idea had great merit for the people of their realms but she hated surprises being sprung on her at the best of times, let alone by the hated King of Morgravia.

She had promised herself one day. One final day to mourn the loss of her status. One night to remember with love the touch of Romen, of Cailech . . . of Wyl Thirsk. Now Celimus had taken that from her too.

'What do you plan to do with Cailech?'

'I'm not sure yet. I shall be taking him with us to Stoneheart.'

'Surely you don't mean a trial and execution?' she wondered, a new terror chilling her. He could not die again. She could not lose Cailech as she had lost Romen.

'I said I don't know. Death would be my choice.'

'Why must he die?' she demanded.

'That you need to ask such a question baffles me, Valentyna,' Celimus replied calmly but followed it with a condescending smirk.

'But you said yourself that you'd just signed a peace treaty.'

The King's famous temper began to stoke. He had done well to get this far without losing his patience. 'Which he broke by setting foot into Briavel — and that, I might add, is a whole new mystery. How the King of the Razors can infiltrate your realm and cover almost its entire length without being noticed is a puzzle.'

'It certainly is,' Valentyna replied abruptly. 'Which is why I don't agree to any decision on your part, sire. He is my prisoner on my land. I will decide his fate.'

A new note crept into Celimus's voice, one she had not heard before but one she was very sure was more true to this cruel King of Morgravia. Gone was the affected brightness, the sugary tone. 'I'm sorry, Valentyna, you will not. I've noticed how you deal with treachery — you send it off to a brothel for the night.'

If only he knew how deep his words cut. 'Leave me, Celimus,' she commanded, not trusting herself to say more.

He impaled her with a stare, which she returned with

defiance, and then he nodded. 'Fine. We shall leave tomorrow as you had planned, and Valentyna, you had better wipe that scowl off your face by then. I will marry you and I will reserve the right to execute my enemies if they are found on my soil.'

'You mean my soil, don't you, Celimus?' she hurled back, trembling from the hate that was threatening to overwhelm her and make her do something unwise.

He shook his head. 'It's mine from now on, Valentyna. Get used to the idea. We can marry and please our realms and I'll provide peace for your people. Or we can do it the hard way and I promise I will slaughter every man, woman and child of Briavel if it comes to it.'

She had not thought he could shock her but the venom with which he spoke now – in a way she had never been spoken to before – chilled her to the point where she felt the wispy hairs on her arms stand on end. This was no way to speak to a Queen and in her own palace, but she felt powerless to stop him. All she had was words for weapons. She threw them at him now.

'You are a snake, Celimus. Wyl Thirsk was right.'

'Wyl Thirsk is dead, Shar rot him, as you will be if you don't put on a happy face, come serenely to Pearlis tomorrow and take those wedding vows in a few days, as planned.'

'I think I would rather be dead.'

'It's your choice,' he snarled. 'No more wooing, Valentyna. This is your new life – as my Queen but not my equal. The only good you'll do me is to give me the sons I crave and, believe me, if you won't give them to me willingly, I will take my pleasure as I see fit.'

*　　*　　*

Wyl sat glumly in the guardhouse. Liryk could not bring himself to have the King of the Razors incarcerated in the palace dungeons. This way it felt less like he was imprisoning him and more like he was offering rustic guest accommodation. Legionnaires were posted throughout the guardhouse – one for each Briavellian soldier.

'Did Aremys get away?' Wyl asked Liryk.

The man nodded. 'You shouldn't have hesitated, sire.'

'It was wrong of me to run.'

'Your pride aside, this is all very dangerous for our Queen.'

'She handled it well. I won't make any further problems for her. Thank you for upholding our secret.'

The old soldier sighed. 'I'm not sure I understand your coming here, or your calm acceptance of what is certain death at the King's hands.'

'This is how it is meant to be,' Wyl said, resigned to his fate. 'This is Myrren's gift playing out precisely to plan.'

'Myrren's gift?'

Wyl smiled. 'Take no notice of me.'

Liryk was baffled by this man but his relief that Valentyna had not told the truth to Celimus overwhelmed his curiosity. 'How did the King know? He sent men looking for you immediately upon his arrival.'

Wyl shrugged. 'It was my horse,' he replied, grateful to Cailech's memories.

'What?'

He pulled Cailech's hair back from his face and tied it behind his head. 'I gave Celimus my white stallion as a gift at Felrawthy. He fell in love with it so I insisted he have it because I had its twin back at the fortress. Identical.'

Liryk understood now. 'He saw your horse, the twin.'

'He's probably riding its brother. How could he miss it? You won't tell him about Aremys, will you, Liryk?'

The old man shook his head. 'No, sire. I want no further grief for her majesty. No one needs to know about the mercenary, and the Briavellian Guard can be trusted to keep the secret.'

'Thank you.'

'I shall see to your comforts, sire. We leave for Pearlis tomorrow at dawn.'

Wyl nodded, no longer caring.

Valentyna escaped her anger and Celimus by taking her horse out, refusing to have him accompany her. This would be her last ride as a single woman through the woodland of Briavel and onto the moors. Next time – if there was a next time, she thought, remembering the King's threat – she would be married to Celimus. She would have the grand title of Queen of Briavel and Morgravia, but it would be an empty title.

She glanced back at the odd medley of guards following her, comprising her own men and Legionnaires. Celimus was taking no chances with her. There was nowhere to run and hide anyway, and it would be unseemly for a monarch to flee her own realm. No, Valentyna was made of sterner stuff. She would face this trial and bestow the gift of peace she had promised upon her people.

But the memory of Cailech's touch still burned in her mind and on her body, which had responded so eagerly. It had been such a rushed, frantic episode and yet she could remember each moment of it, relive it in her thoughts in a delicious slow-moving scene. No longer being a virgin was still hard for her to grasp; it had all happened so fast. She could never have planned for this to occur and yet nothing gave her greater satisfaction – nothing! – than knowing her greatest possession had been given to the man she loved, not the one who would steal it from her under false pretences.

Cailech . . . no, Wyl, she reminded herself, was such an enigma. She could claim she had known Romen and yet she knew so little about him really, other than that he had loved her, would die for her – *had* died for her. Poor Wyl, she thought, sympathising at how he had learned to cope as a woman; two women in fact. She could not imagine how he had survived the killing of his sister. Wished she could ask him, have time with him.

Well, it was up to her now, she decided. She would marry Celimus and she would give everything of herself towards preserving the life of the King of the Razors. Even if she could never see him again, it would be enough to know that he lived. Celimus would not execute Cailech because she would forbid it. She had taken the wrong approach with Celimus, she realised. All she had done was anger him, corner him into making rash statements. Her father had always said she must learn to curb her tongue. Being a good royal, he had cautioned, was about diplomacy, careful choice of words and always giving oneself time to consider. She had ignored his advice with Celimus, but then she had not had time for consideration: she had been put on the spot and it was either lie and save lives or tell the truth and cause bloodshed.

No, she had done the right thing, but she should

never have argued with Celimus later. He had obviously been shocked to find Cailech in Werryl and, like a wounded animal being baited, had struck back. She should have sensed the danger lurking there; Valentyna admonished herself for such clumsiness. If she was going to survive in the court of Celimus, she would have to play him more intelligently than she had today. She must fuel his vanity, make him feel omnipotent, make herself irresistible. Valentyna slowed her horse to a walk, in no rush to be back in the palace, and remembered how powerful she had felt on realising what a woman can do to a man. For all his strength and stamina, his status and bearing, Cailech was so vulnerable. He was only a man, she smiled, and faced with naked desire and a compliant partner, he became putty. Could she achieve the same with Celimus?

She recalled that Chancellor Krell had intimated that, if she approached the marriage smartly, she could use her feminine wiles to get what she wanted. Her revulsion for Celimus aside, if she could play the role of affectionate Queen, impress his people and thus please him, she might be able to enjoy small wins of importance to her.

Her first priority was Wyl. She understood that there was no changing his status as prisoner; Celimus would want to make an example of him. So be it. But she would put all her efforts into ensuring that was the extent of the punishment. They had lied once already. No doubt Wyl could dream up some clever reason as to why he had come to Briavel. Surely there must be a feasible explanation. Her mind raced towards what this could be, and was pleased to come up with the idea of a secret festival that Cailech wanted to organise with Celimus's Queen in homage to the magnificent King of Morgravia for forging peace between all three realms.

The idea gained purchase in her mind. She would need to get word to Wyl.

CHAPTER 38

The journey across Briavel and into Morgravia passed
uneventfully. In any other situation, Valentyna would have
truly enjoyed the trip and the chance to mix with her
people, for they came out in their hundreds to wave the
royal procession through their towns and villages. And
what a procession it made: the Briavellian Guard was in
full formal dress in emerald and violet, whilst the
Legionnaires looked dashing in their crimson and black.
Trailing the rear came a cavalcade of nobles, dignitaries,
servants and attendants, not to mention Madam Eltor's
personal retinue in charge of the Queen's wardrobe, as
well as cooks, pastrymakers and bakers – all the people
required to provide a joint wedding feast that blended
Morgravia's culinary specialties with Briavel's fine foods.

And in the midst of the brightly coloured entourage
rode a smiling King and Queen, graciously accepting the
crowd's blessings for their happiness.

'You can almost believe it,' Valentyna commented and
aimed a shy smile towards the King.

He did not look at her but she heard the softer tone

in his voice. Perhaps it was hard work being vicious all the time, she thought. 'Why not? They love you. And they love me for marrying you and for bringing peace to the region.'

'It is a good thing, Celimus.'

'Do you mean that?'

She caught a posy thrown by a young lad and blew him a kiss which won a roar of approval from the happy mob. 'I regret my behaviour of yesterday, and indeed throughout our courtship.'

Now he finally turned away from the mass of happy faces and looked at her. 'And?'

'I wish us to start again, here and now. Neither of us have parents to guide our choices, no family to lean upon.' She sighed. 'We are trying to achieve something extraordinary: two young monarchs, new to their thrones, forging peace and prosperity. I did a lot of soul-searching last night, Celimus, and realised that what you have worked so hard to bring about will become a landmark era in the history books.'

It was clear he could hardly believe what he was hearing. 'But last—'

'Yesterday was different. You frightened me and I was rattled to think that King Cailech had infiltrated Briavel without my knowledge. Did he tell you why?'

'No. I thought I'd find out courtesy of Stoneheart's clever men of the dungeons,' he offered unkindly.

Valentyna did not react. Celimus, like any bully, was always looking for ways to hurt others. He had not changed from the little prince who had smashed a princess's clay doll simply because he could. Yes, Celimus was still the angry child. Instead she planted the first seed of her lie.

'Cailech told Liryk that he wanted to meet with me to talk about a surprise festival he wanted to throw in your honour.'

Celimus had not expected this. 'My honour!'

'Yes. He wanted to hail you as the region's peacemaker who is bringing long life and prosperity to the three realms.' She held her breath through the pause that followed, forcing herself to wave to the crowd, smiling incessantly through her fear.

'That might change things,' he said softly.

Instead of leaping on his words and giving away her excitement, Valentyna shrugged. 'Yes, well, it is of no matter to me but perhaps you can find out more in due course. It would be a pity to lose a friend in the Razors now that you have worked so hard to establish the truce.'

'Indeed,' he said drily, but obviously the notion that Cailech was not in Briavel for sinister reasons had been successfully planted. She would need to water it subtly throughout the journey, Valentyna realised.

'To get back to what I was saying earlier, my lord, you can rely on me to be faithful and dutiful. Let us make this marriage the success everyone wants so badly.'

He laughed derisively. 'I know you don't love me, Valentyna.'

'As you don't me, sire,' she countered with care. 'But that doesn't mean we cannot be a successful royal couple. Respect, affection, co-operation – surely these are all qualities we can work towards?'

'Surely. But I don't understand.'

'What puzzles you, sire?'

'The change in heart. One minute a spitting cat, the next a kitten.'

'I dreamed last night of my parents, Celimus. They

came to me,' she lied, trying not to recall her true dream of Cailech's passionate embrace, his ardent yet gentle deflowering of her maidenhood, his kisses so tender and deep. His declarations of love – she felt herself going hot in all the wrong places.

'Yes?' the King prompted.

'And . . . and they urged me that this was a match made by Shar for the good of the realms. They told me that Shar's angels, if we let them, will guide us to hold our marriage fast and be good to one another. That we will have sons – strong boys – four of them,' she said, feeling nauseated now at her own creative invention. 'Are you superstitious, Celimus?'

'Not really,' he lied, although she knew he was. 'Why?'

'This morning I found a white rose on the bush my father planted for my mother at her death.'

Celimus looked at her quizzically although she could tell he was intrigued. 'What is the significance?'

'Ah, perhaps it is only in Briavel we believe this. Legend has it that if a white rose bush produces a single bloom, which opens before any other buds show themselves, any dream recalled from the previous night is destined to come true.'

'No matter whether it is good or bad?' he asked.

'Apparently. We all believe it. That is why I went looking for the rose, because my dream was so profound, so vivid. I could see our sons, Celimus – dark, strapping boys, like their father.'

He grinned. 'That's very interesting, Valentyna. I'm pleased that you feel so positive suddenly.'

'I intend to be a good wife to you, sire. I will make you proud and happy.'

Celimus looked into her clear blue gaze and saw no guile. He reached across the distance between their two horses, his white, hers black, and took her hand. The crowd gasped, then cheered uproariously when King Celimus bent to lay his lips against the back of the hand of his Queen.

Valentyna felt nothing but revulsion. She was relieved she had chosen to wear gloves this day.

King Cailech was travelling amongst a different cavalcade but towards the same destination. Tied, gagged and thrown in a covered wagon, he was driven hard. There were no stoppages for food or rest. Fresh horses took over at various points until, just by the smell of the air, he knew he was approaching the city of Pearlis. Wyl had lost track of time and thought. His mind felt like a skein of tangled wool and it was easier to give up on the business of separating all the threads of thought than to fight it and keep thinking of ways of escape.

He imagined how Stoneheart would be looming up ahead of them now – proud, dark, defiant. Its famed gargoyles would see them first, he thought, recalling a fanciful notion which had struck him the very first day he arrived at the Morgravian palace. He'd been just a young lad then, Gueryn by his side, some of his father's retainers riding with them to add weight to the arrival of the new General of the Morgravian Legion. How much older he felt now. Not just because of the body he was in or those he had travelled through, but old in his mind, weighted with despair and a savage sense of loss.

Those early months at Stoneheart had been happier times, especially when Alyd arrived, even though it had felt so bleak to be forced away from Argorn. Barely thirteen and still capable of being lost in daydreams, Wyl had looked up at the daunting stone monolith that first day and had spotted the gargoyles. Three of them. He had given them names and fancied that they were the King's private lookouts who could spy friend or foe long before the Legion's scouts could.

'Can you see me now, Bauz?' he whispered to the leader of the gargoyles, the one with a beak. 'It's me, Wyl Thirsk, returning.'

'Stoneheart ahead!' he heard a soldier cry and smiled to himself. Death was upon him. Myrren's gift was reaching its climax and the Quickening would come to an end.

He hoped Aremys had managed to make his own way to Pearlis and that his friend would keep his solemn promise to end the life of King Celimus soon after the change occurred. He thought briefly on Fynch's caution of randomness, and took solace from it. It was randomness that had given him Valentyna by the fireside not so long ago. Nothing could ever take away that time of exhilaration, that delicious loss of thought and control, that intense passion which had sealed his love for her.

Valentyna was his. They were one, coupled in love and desire; it had been like an exquisite pain when they reached that final dizzying, breathtaking pleasure in one another. He would take that sort of pain over and over if he could, but if he could only have it the once, that was enough too. He had known her in a way no other had. Her maidenhood had been given gladly, lovingly, to him and he had taken it with a trembling, feverish joy. Celimus might marry Valentyna but the Queen of Briavel belonged to the King of the Razors . . . to Wyl Thirsk.

If he was permitted only one experience of Fynch's randomness, then he would not swap his lying with Valentyna for anything – not even in exchange for his life. He could die happily now, for he was loved – and loved as Wyl Thirsk. She had uttered his name.

His thoughts were interrupted by soldiers unfastening the hood of the cart. He cast a final thought towards Knave, wished he had had a chance to say goodbye to the faithful dog, then did not struggle as rough hands dragged him from the cart and led him to a place in the depths of Stoneheart. A place from which few people returned.

For the first time in his life Knave had neither mission nor magic to call upon. He was still driven though, urged by a force more complex than anything he had known before. It went by the name of sorrow.

He had felt it as a drawing of something personal and intimate from his being. The sensation had occurred a few hours ago, just before dawn. He had hidden himself in the palace compound, close enough to watch the guardhouse for any movement of Wyl. He had made sure that the Grenadyne had got out safely from Werryl and had seen him organise transport with some Briavellian folk on their way to the wedding festival in Morgravia. Then he had returned to the palace and kept Valentyna company on her ride, watching her fall so deep in thought that her horse ended up strolling so slowly it probably could have stopped and grazed without her realising it.

He had watched Celimus prowl around the gatehouse, giving orders to his Legionnaires, making sure they remained alert and that nobody visited the prisoner without his express permission – not even the Queen. The palace had finally settled down for the night, although a constant quiet movement of servants prepared for the departure the next day.

Knave had wandered away to the woodland where he had spent favourite times with Fynch. He found the spot where they had slept the night, where he had heralded the death of Romen Koreldy with a piercing howl into the dark. He lay there, his head on his huge paws, as the hours crawled by and he mourned the loss of the boy he had come to love, the boy who had given his life to destroy the enemy of all that was good and natural in the world.

Knave threw back his huge head and howled in grief. It seemed the Thicket had heard him, for once again he felt himself connected to its magic.

Knave? came a voice.

Rasmus, he groaned, his throat swelling from the pain of his emotion.

We promised Faith Fynch we would aid Wyl Thirsk, the bird said.

Knave waited, his head hung low. He did not want any more instructions.

Go to Argorn, Rasmus finally said. *Find Felrawthy's Duke and return him to Pearlis where he will meet Farrow.*

And then?

They will know what to do. Go now. The Thicket will send you.

Knave closed the connection, too numb to care what happened now that Fynch was gone. Very soon he was hurtling through the dark towards the region of Morgravia which had produced Wyl Thirsk.

CHAPTER 39

Wyl sat on the cold floor of one of Stoneheart's dungeons, his head resting on his knees. Moments earlier he had turned to prayer, beseeching Shar to watch over and protect Valentyna, to heal Elspyth, to restore Lothryn and to welcome Ylena and Alyd, Fynch and Gueryn into everlasting life. As the list of souls lengthened he stopped, overcome by distress. How many lives had been lost or destroyed because of Celimus? Wyl's anguish deepened as he accepted that he was helpless now. There was nothing he could do from the dungeon except wait for Myrren's gift to mete out its final crushing blow and hope that Aremys would keep his promise.

And so he sat in silence, wishing the guards would come for him and speed his death. A strange tingling sensation coursed through his body and then a blue shimmering light forced him to look up. He recognised the feeling – it was connected to the magic of the Thicket.

'Fynch,' he whispered as the shimmering coalesced to reveal a vision of his young friend.

Hello, Wyl, the boy said into his mind.

Are you alive?
Not in the way you mean.
Then you died during the battle with Rashlyn?
Wyl, Fynch interrupted gently, *my time with you is short.*
What is it that I must do?
Just trust me.
To do what?
To forge a Bridge of Souls.

Wyl felt comforted by Fynch's visit. It had been inspiring, calming even, to witness the ghostly vision of his friend and to hear Fynch speak so surely. He had insisted that Wyl should trust him, and Wyl did – but that was all Fynch had told him, other than to promise that the Bridge of Souls would save his life. All Wyl had to do was call Fynch's name. But, in truth, Wyl did not believe there was any escape from this dungeon or from his fate to be the sovereign of Morgravia. He had accepted this. Wyl appreciated Fynch's attempt to soothe him but he was thinking only of death now – real death. There would be no coming back from the end of Aremys's sword.

Wyl looked around the cell, touched the cold black stone that encased him. Not so long ago Stoneheart had been his home. A place that embraced him with the love of Magnus and the security of his title as General. He recalled how the castle had been a playground for two boys – one red-headed, one golden-haired; both dead now. There had been such laughter in the short time they had known one another. He recalled a promise by a lake to always fight side by side, but it was not to be. Stoneheart was no longer friendly. Now the castle was the lair of his foe and its cold walls would witness his death twice over in the coming hours.

Wyl's gaze roamed absently in the dim light which filtered through from an outside cresset. It fell upon an inscription scratched into one of the bottom stones. *Avenge me, Wyl*, it said. His heart pained. He had come full circle. This was surely the work of Myrren, who had suffered in this very cell all those years ago. Her touching plea still had the ability to move him.

He hated Celimus for being the cause of so much suffering. As if on some silent signal, he heard the click of boots on flagstones. There was only one person with that arrogant stride. He turned away, did not want to see King Celimus gloating over his rival King's downfall.

Liryk had got a message through to Wyl from Valentyna explaining that she had found a way to explain Cailech's presence in Briavel. Liryk had watched Cailech shake his head at the idea, but had not had the heart to relay the Mountain King's attitude to the Queen. Wyl had no intention of making excuses.

He soon discovered this was also the reason for the King's visit late into the night.

'Tell me, Mountain King, was there a good reason for you visiting Briavel without an invitation?' He gave a soft, deprecating laugh as he flicked some mote of dust from his jacket. 'You see, the Queen seems to think you had very fine intentions of joining forces with her to plan some special festivities on my account.' He shook his head with mock embarrassment. 'How very jolly.'

'I would not plan any festival around you, Celimus, other than your funeral,' Wyl enjoyed saying.

The King laughed in obvious delight. He clapped his

hands, loving Cailech's defiance because it meant he could execute him with a clear conscience – not that conscience was something that ever troubled Celimus. 'You obviously want to die, my friend. Valentyna was surely throwing you a lifeline here.'

'Thank her for her generosity,' Wyl said. 'And I'll wait to see you in Shar's eternal fire. We shall settle our score there, Celimus . . . if not sooner.'

Celimus had looked at him quizzically, not understanding his final words, but Wyl did not elaborate. Intent on having the last laugh, the King gave his dazzling smile. 'Is there anything I can do for you in the meantime?' he asked.

'Yes. Do it yourself.'

'Pardon?'

'You heard me. Kill me yourself.'

Celimus made a sound of disapproval. 'I might miss and merely injure you – oh dear, that could be messy and painful.'

'I'll risk it. Let me feel the touch of your blade.'

Celimus smiled and nodded. 'Perhaps. We shall see what mood I'm in tomorrow. Sleep well, your highness,' he said and left, chuckling.

Wyl felt even more hollow than before. Not once but thrice he had betrayed her. First as Romen, later as Ylena and now as Cailech. She would never be able to forgive him. He sat in the darkness, which matched his thoughts, disturbed first by the scuffling of rats and then by the sound of yet another arrival. It was certainly a night for visitors.

Once again, there was no need for introductions. 'King Cailech, I regret to find you here, sire,' Chancellor Jessom said. 'Is there anything I can get you?'

'Other than the key, you mean?' Wyl murmured, refusing to turn and make eye contact with the King's servant. He would make him speak to his back.

'A rug perhaps, sire?'

'You forget, I am of the Razors, Chancellor. We don't feel the cold.'

'A candle then. Let me at least light this grim space for you, my lord.'

'Do what you wish. It matters not to me.'

'I meant what I said, King Cailech, I regret to see you incarcerated here. When the rider gave me the news of who was being brought here, I thought the man had been duped, charmed by a hedgewitch.'

'Be careful talking of witches in here, Jessom. Or you may find yourself on this side of the bars.'

The Chancellor cleared his throat. To be fair, even though Wyl was not in the mood to be anything of the sort, there was an abashed tone in Jessom's voice. Perhaps he was genuine in his surprise and regret at the arrival of the new guest in the dungeon.

Wyl heard the rasp of a clay plate being pushed through the bars and shadows leapt across the walls as a soft light eased the darkness.

'There, that's better, surely,' Jessom said.

'What is it, Chancellor, are you looking for absolution?'

'What do you mean?'

'All the deaths – so much blood on your hands.'

'I don't understand you, sire.'

'Why not? I am speaking the same language you do.'

'But what could you know of me?' Jessom replied. 'We are all but strangers.'

Wyl admonished himself to be careful. It was true: Cailech would hardly know the Chancellor, other than by name and sight from Tenterdyn. However, the truth was, he was not of a mind to be careful any more. He wished Celimus would hurry up and bring about the final death in Myrren's ghastly plan. He ignored Jessom's question and posed his own instead. 'Where is your King?'

'Asleep, I hope. He has a big day tomorrow.'

'So the wedding goes ahead as planned?'

'Of course, sire. Why would you think otherwise? I'm afraid the city will shortly degenerate into mass celebrations and no doubt drunkenness. It is but an hour to dawn.'

'The Morgravians want the marriage as badly as the Briavellians,' Wyl commented, more to himself than for the Chancellor's hearing.

'Of course. It is a brilliant union.'

'Not for Valentyna, Jessom.'

'Why do you say that, sire?'

'Because he will destroy her.'

'He wants her very much.'

The words fired a new anger in Wyl and he swung around to face the Chancellor now. 'He wants what she brings him, Jessom. He wants to own the glittering jewel of Briavel, and everything else that Briavel can give him. He doesn't care about Valentyna. He wants her body and the sons she can provide, the peace and prosperity she brings. The people love her, and because of her they will love him, for surely they hate him right now.'

Jessom cleared his throat. 'You seem to have a very deep understanding of the south, King Cailech.'

Wyl grunted. 'It is my business to know these things.

Mark my words, Jessom, if he destroys her — and he will — the people will rise up against him. Already I suspect there are mutterings within the Legion. The right whisper in the right ear and the army will move against the Crown. You know it is powerful enough.'

Wyl realised that the Chancellor was actually paying attention to what he was saying. The man had not come here to bait him. If he could sway this powerful person, he might be able to help Valentyna from beyond the grave. Fynch had told him that Jessom would provide the key but Wyl had not understood and Fynch had not explained further. He could hardly imagine the potency of the magic it had taken for Fynch to transport his ghostly image all the way to Pearlis.

Jessom interrupted his thoughts. 'The King has placed his own people in senior positions in the Legion. They would not move against him,' he said.

If Jessom was truthful, he would admit that Celimus had played his last vicious act. Imprisoning and executing the King of the Razors with whom only days ago he had signed a peace treaty, much to the delight of his people, was sheer madness. But Jessom's first attempt at arguing against killing the Mountain King had failed and a second might have dire consequences. Jessom knew the arrogant Morgravian King saw the killing of Cailech as ridding himself of the final obstacle to becoming Emperor Celimus. Jessom could imagine precisely the machinations of his King's mind. And he did not agree. Not at all. It was a mistake.

'When someone like Eryd Bench knows the truth of what's been going on, his voice alone will be enough to motivate the Legionnaires,' Wyl assured.

Jessom could not guess at how King Cailech could know of Eryd Bench, but that did not matter now. The death and destruction had to stop. Morgravia and Briavel had a chance to achieve something never before seen in their history. Unification and peace was at hand. Jessom wanted to be the powerful Chancellor behind the most powerful Crown and to get on with the business of making Morgravia – through its peace with its neighbours – the wealthiest realm. But Jessom feared Celimus was not the monarch who would lead them to greatness. Whenever the King took a dislike to someone or felt in any way threatened, he turned to killing. There was no future in this. Such a sovereign would ultimately destroy the whole region.

'Lord Bench is dead, sire, I'm sorry to say.'

Jessom was astonished to see Cailech react as if punched. His head rocked back, his eyes closed in agony, and he threw his body towards the bars, gripping them with white knuckles. 'Dead?'

Jessom had sensibly stepped back. He imagined those huge hands closing around his throat and snapping his neck with the greatest of ease – and who could blame him? Cailech had nothing to lose.

'I'm afraid so, King Cailech,' Jessom confirmed.

'How?' Wyl rasped.

'How else?' Jessom replied, revealing more of his private feelings than he had intended. Still, this King was a dead man so what did it matter. 'Let's just say our King took umbrage at Eryd Bench's gentle enquiries about certain events in the north.'

Wyl groaned. His hands fell away from the bars and he slumped against the wall, slowly sliding his tall body to the ground. 'His women – Lady Bench, Georgyana?'

'How can you know them?'

'Are they safe?' Wyl yelled, no longer caring how he might be confusing the Chancellor.

Stung by the Mountain King's venom, Jessom answered truthfully. 'They escaped. A servant told our men that two guests had arrived, a man and woman. The woman was injured; dark-haired, small, apparently attractive. The man was probably Crys Donal of Felrawthy.' He surprised himself by offering so much information. There was something compelling about King Cailech. He seemed entirely different to the arrogant, sharp-witted man he had met in the north.

'Elspyth,' Wyl whispered to himself. 'No sign of where they are?'

Jessom shook his head. 'May I ask why this interests you, sire?'

'No. But I will tell you this, Chancellor Jessom: your days as a powerful adviser to the Crown are numbered. Mark my words, you will be dead at the hands of your King in a matter of days . . . perhaps hours. You will be lucky to see out the next few days, this I promise you.' Wyl enjoyed the sudden insecurity that coursed across the angular planes of the Chancellor's pale face.

'He needs me,' Jessom said.

'No he doesn't, Chancellor. I can sense your disgust at his actions. If I can, he already has.' And Jessom heard the ring of truth in the Mountain King's warning.

'He doesn't know that Lord Hartley still lives,' Jessom muttered to himself, his agile mind racing towards where he might have made an error.

'Lord Hartley?'

The Chancellor looked up, his thoughts clearly elsewhere. 'Yes, Eryd Bench's close friend and confidant. Celimus ordered his death but I let Hartley go – he's in hiding now. I can call upon his help to rally the other nobles and reveal to them the truth of our King.'

'Not before the King kills you,' Wyl said as cruelly as he could. 'But I have an idea, Jessom.'

Could it work? He would give it one last try. Fynch was right – they could use Jessom.

'It's too late for me, Jessom – and for you, I fear,' he said, 'unless . . .'

The man's mortified expression was quickly replaced by wrath. He was no coward then. It was not death he feared, Wyl realised. It was loss of power, wealth and position. 'Unless what, sire?' Jessom asked. He was composed now, his tone curious.

'Unless you put your considerable knowledge and influence behind Queen Valentyna. Protect her, befriend her, put your faith in her. Someone else will deal with Celimus, trust me on this. He will not live to see old age. He may not even live to see out the spring,' he added cryptically. 'But the Queen can live to a ripe age if she is given the right defences. She can win over the Legion, she can woo the nobles. Through her, Morgravia can achieve peace with Briavel and retain the truce with the Razors.'

'The Mountain People will make war on Morgravia and Briavel if you are executed.' No more diplomatic language, Jessom decided; King Cailech knew he could not escape his fate. There was a bargain being made here. He was not sure he understood it, or why Cailech cared about the peace in the region or supported Valentyna's cause, but Jessom was a pragmatist and as smart as he was cunning.

He agreed that Valentyna was the key to the region's future. He had felt for some time now that if there was a way to rid themselves of Celimus, the three realms had a chance. Cailech was right: Valentyna was the future, especially if she were to quickly become pregnant to Celimus. Then nothing but the Queen and the heir – the true Crown of the newly unified realms – mattered.

'You echo my thoughts so closely, King Cailech, it is uncanny.'

'Come closer, Jessom. I have something to tell you and I do not wish to be overheard.'

'I cannot save your life, King Cailech,' Jessom warned, preferring to be candid at this point, in case the Mountain King had ideas of escape.

'I understand,' Wyl said and extended Cailech's blunt fingers through the bars.

Jessom smiled thinly. He was curious to hear the bargain this imprisoned, doomed King could offer. The Chancellor stepped closer but drew his blade to show the man of the mountains that he was not naive. He would shake hands but he would be cautious too.

'No need for that, Jessom. I have no intention of anything but sealing our bargain.'

Palm met palm and Cailech's fingers closed around Jessom's hand. The King was smiling and there was something unnerving in that predatory expression. The Chancellor baulked, tried to release himself from Cailech's grip, but it was too late. A shimmering blue light flowed around their hands. A seal.

CHAPTER 40

Valentyna stood forlornly in a grand chamber at Stoneheart, her own heart feeling as cold as the dark stone surrounding her. Madam Eltor had permitted only her most senior and trusted assistant to help her dress the Queen. Valentyna sensed rather than saw the surreptitious glances between the two older women as they took in her grief-stricken expression.

'Come now, my Queen,' her seamstress tried once more. 'Please don't stain your face with tears.'

'There are no more tears left within me,' Valentyna replied.

'This is your wedding day, your highness. The happiest day ever for the people of Briavel and Morgravia,' the assistant risked.

'Not for me though,' she replied, not caring that it provoked a raising of the assistant's eyebrow and a stern gaze from her superior.

The women had worked fast and fluidly. Valentyna was already stitched into her gown, although Madam Eltor had tut-tutted, warning. 'You've lost weight, my girl. This was perfect last week.'

Valentyna just shook her head. 'Let's get it over with.'

'That will be all, Maud,' Madam Eltor said, dismissing her assistant. 'I hope I don't need to remind you that what is discussed in our presence always remains private.'

Maud curtsied and left hurriedly, the news no doubt already spilling out of her that the Queen went to her wedding as full of grief as when she had attended her father's funeral. 'Valentyna!' the seamstress snapped. 'Stop this!'

'I don't love him,' she said, balling her fists and closing her eyes, trying to get a grip on her spiralling emotions.

'We don't care!' Madam Eltor replied, deciding that harshness was the only solution now. 'He brings our peace. I regret that you are the currency we buy it with, your highness, but it is too late now.'

Valentyna was stung. 'Yes. Of course, you're right. Forgive me.'

The seamstress wished she could take back the brutal words, but Valentyna's whole attitude to this marriage was wrong. There was no way out so she needed to straighten her shoulders, lift her head high and act like the Queen she was.

'Be stout of heart, Valentyna. You are Briavel's jewel. The brightest jewel now in Morgravia's crown − do not forget this. Imagine how proud you would make your father today.'

'Yes, by marrying the man who murdered him,' Valentyna muttered.

Her companion gave a gasp of shock and Valentyna realised that hurting Madam Eltor achieved nothing. The truth of Valor's demise did not change the fact of his death or her decision to marry Celimus. She hated the way she veered between courage and weakness: one moment she felt sure she could make the marriage work, would bear his children, would make Briavel safe and prosperous. The next, she plunged into gloom, remembering a passionate hour or so in the arms of King Cailech. How could she wipe that from her thoughts? How could she lie with Celimus this evening and not feel anything but revulsion?

Because you must, she told herself in a small, urgent voice. *Because Briavel's future rests upon it.*

'I'm all right,' she reassured her seamstress. 'My nerves are jangling. I'll be fine once we leave for the cathedral, I promise. Put the veil on.'

Madam Eltor did not believe her but she obediently followed her Queen's instructions. She draped the exquisite veil over Valentyna's head and face, primped it a little, then stepped back to admire her work. 'You are breathtaking, your majesty. The Morgravians will fall in love with you instantly.'

Valentyna found a small smile for her lifetime friend. 'I'm ready,' she said.

Celimus had ordered a glistening white carriage to convey his bride to the cathedral. It sported the new device linking Morgravia and Briavel: the intertwined initials of the King and Queen painted in their national colours. Four stunning white horses, imported from Grenadyne, pulled the carriage. Accompanying the Queen were members of the Briavellian Guard, beautifully outfitted in emerald and violet. A proud Commander Liryk waited, as did all the crowd, for their first glimpse of the Queen.

As if Shar himself had ordained it, the sun appeared from behind a cloud and bathed the main square of

Stoneheart in a dazzling golden light. People screamed their delight as the Queen appeared on the steps of Stoneheart's main entrance in that same moment.

Trumpets sounded above the din and, without a male family member to do the honours, it was left to Commander Liryk to walk stiff and proud up those stairs to escort her. He bowed low before her, as did all gathered.

Valentyna was moved. A lump formed in her throat and she recalled the similar tumultuous welcome she had been given on her arrival into Pearlis. It had been a deafening, exhausting couple of hours making their way through the cheering city. Everyone had seemed to be holding squares of linen in the colours crimson, black, emerald and violet. They were waving them hysterically now, creating a sea of moving colour that mingled the two realms more effectively than any other device could.

She curtsied low and long to the people. The gracious acknowledgement drove them into even wilder applause. Liryk smiled into her eyes hidden behind the veil. 'You are already their Queen,' he said, his breath catching.

Valentyna thought she might cry again. 'I hope my father is watching,' she managed to say.

He took her hand and squeezed it. 'He will be cheering alongside your beautiful mother, both of them so proud.'

'Thank you, Liryk, for all you have done for me. I'm sorry I have been difficult in recent times.'

'Your highness,' he said with genuine reverence, 'I am your servant.'

Valentyna was warmed by the sentiment of her commander and the pride his words evoked within her. She could do this. She would win their hearts and become

Morgravia's Queen and somehow . . . somehow, she would work out how to exist alongside Celimus without fracturing the peace their two realms considered so very precious.

'Come, Liryk. Lead me to my husband.'

Wyl could hear delirious cheering as he was led out of the dungeons into a courtyard he had never seen before. The people of Morgravia were clearly delighted at the prospect of a new Queen.

'Has the Queen left the palace?' he asked one of the senior soldiers, a man he recognised.

'I think so,' the man answered, embarrassed by his task. This was a King, after all, and they had been led to believe a peace agreement had been made with the Mountain Dwellers.

'And where do you take me now?'

The man hesitated and checked the manacles were secure on their prisoner. 'We have orders to move you, King Cailech.'

'That doesn't answer my question, soldier,' Wyl insisted. 'I asked where.'

To his credit, the soldier looked directly into the hard eyes of the Mountain King. 'To the block, sire.'

Wyl sighed. 'I see.' Celimus was wasting no time in executing his northern rival. He wondered if the cruel sovereign would force Valentyna to witness the death. As much as he wanted to believe otherwise, he knew in his heart that Celimus would revel in the notion of making her watch. And she would have no choice. Executions were something royalty had to face whether they had a stomach for it or not. Perhaps days ago the victim might not have mattered to Valentyna. But now she would not be watching a stranger die; she would be watching the head of the man she loved be severed and lifted in triumph above his slumped corpse. He hated to think about how this would hurt her very soul, and did not want to ponder how she would respond to his transference into Celimus. He did not have to dwell on that, however, for he had no intention of remaining so. No matter how much anyone argued that it was Wyl Thirsk inside, he could not, would not, live as King Celimus.

Wyl heard the crowd cheer again and wondered how the Queen of Briavel must look today. Serene, he decided; she would rise above her sorrow and do her realm justice. Her gown would be simple with little if any adornment, as was her way. He imagined she would wear her raven hair loose, and smiled sadly to think how the bridal veil would be a welcome sheath between her and the reality of her situation, a barrier between herself and Celimus. But not for long. Once their vows were exchanged, the King would claim a kiss to seal the holy pact made before Shar. Celimus would then raise that veil and tear away Valentyna's last protection. She would feel suddenly naked but she would find a smile to cover her despair and, in spite of her sadness, be the most beautiful bride for Celimus.

Wyl could not help but recall how he had fallen in love with Valentyna at first sight. Dusty and dressed in riding breeches, she had smudges on her cheeks and her hair was falling about her face; she had reeked of horse and leather. Yet it had been his pleasure to kiss her hand and his heart's desire to ask for it in marriage himself, rather than petition her father on behalf of another. A smile had broken across her face like new sunlight; he had bathed in its warmth and his heart became instantly hers.

But that was over now. The struggle to save her from Celimus was done with. Above the roar of the crowd he could hear the cathedral bells pealing, heralding the impending marriage. Soon she would be the Morgravian Queen, married to his enemy, and he himself would be past caring about.

Wyl felt sickened. He stumbled slightly and the soldier walking by his side instinctively threw out a steadying hand. 'I'm not used to being in chains,' Wyl lamented. The man nodded, clearly awkward about his role.

And so I move between Kings today, Wyl thought; it was his greatest sorrow in this sad life of his. He had let his father down. He had not lived out the great Thirsk tradition and fought to the death on a battlefield; instead he succumbed to death enmeshed in a battle of magic he could not win. He was nothing more than an unwilling puppet, chosen because of his connection to Celimus.

'Wait.' Wyl stopped as a new notion occurred to him. 'The King will be present, I take it?'

'Yes, sire.'

Relief flooded him. 'Good. I want him to share my death,' he said, and surprised the Legionnaires around him by smiling fiercely.

Wyl realised he had been brought to the rarely used courtyard through which he had escaped with Ylena a lifetime ago – or so it seemed. It was sparsely guarded but he was not going anywhere anyway. This was it. He wanted Myrren's gift to be done with him. It struck him as odd that Celimus had not organised to display the

Mountain King to the people of Pearlis and proclaim his treachery. But perhaps the notion of a public execution hard on the heels of the first royal wedding in decades was too vulgar even for Celimus's sick mind.

Aremys arrived only hours before the wedding procession, exhausted and dirty but relieved that he had made it into Pearlis in time. To those at the front of the sea of people, it was despicable that this huge bear of a man, who had got to the cathedral long after they had, used his strength to bullock his way to the front. One man risked hurling his displeasure at the bear who simply turned and scowled at him through dark, hooded eyes. 'Shut up!' was his reply and all within earshot did just that.

Valentyna caught her breath at the first sight of the famed Cathedral of Pearlis. Its grandeur had a powerful impact. Bells were pealing and heralds trumpeted her arrival into its grounds. She tried to imagine what Celimus was feeling inside the cathedral. Satisfaction, she decided. He had won. It seemed he always did where she was concerned.

Meanwhile, inside the hushed cathedral, King Celimus took the nod from Jessom that the Queen's carriage was pulling into the compound. He stood and conferred with the man, who looked more thin and vulture-like than he had ever seen him. Celimus had heard the whispered jokes about his Chancellor's likeness to a carrion bird. It was actually a very good description, particularly today, he thought, wondering what was passing through Jessom's sharp and slippery mind. He did not trust him as much as he once had. There was defiance lurking behind that well-guarded facade. The King was not fooled: Jessom would switch allegiance in a blink if he thought the cards were going to fall the wrong way. And Celimus had begun to believe that his Chancellor might be considering his future quite carefully.

Jessom's fierce disagreement with the King's latest idea regarding King Cailech's execution had further fuelled Celimus's mistrust. Where did the Chancellor's interest lie that he would advise so strongly against taking the Mountain King's life?

'Is everything ready?' he whispered now.

'Her majesty arrives, sire, yes,' Jessom confirmed.

'Not her, you fool. Cailech!'

Jessom nodded in that slow, reptilian manner of his. 'As you ordered, sire.'

'Good. Now get out of my way, you're blocking the view of my latest conquest. This is a good day, Jessom. A very good day. Two monarchs brought to their knees before me.'

He laughed quietly, straightening the front of his black jacket. He knew he was resplendent in a dashing outfit of crimson and noir with flashes of gold and a cape of the blackest yarn lined with the fiery red of Morgravia. He was looking forward to claiming Valentyna's maidenhood tonight and did not plan on being gentle about it either. A husband must impress on his wife that he was in charge. He would dominate her with his strength and his prowess as a lover.

Aremys watched with a heavy heart as Queen Valentyna alighted from the carriage, aided by Commander Liryk. He had mixed feelings for the Briavellian who had helped him escape whilst at the same time aiding in the capture and imprisonment of King Cailech.

The Grenadyne presumed Wyl was already cooling his heels in Stoneheart's dungeons. During the frenzied dash from Werryl to Pearlis, he had been comforted by a sort of peace he found in his fatalistic capacity to accept events and worry only about aspects he could personally influence. His focus had been on getting to the capital and finding a way to help Wyl rather than dwelling on what had already occurred.

The promise he had made to Wyl burned brightly in his mind now. Would he be able to do it? Could he murder his closest friend in the land? He had watched this man's strange journey through three lives and had come to love him in the same way that King Cailech had once described his feelings for Lothryn: brotherhood, friendship, loyalty. Aremys felt all of this for Wyl, coupled with an intense sorrow for his suffering, but he was not sure whether he could find the courage to kill the man he loved as his brother, even out of kindness.

Aremys had worked hard to understand the depth of Wyl's pain and how he could never live as Celimus. But he could not grasp how anyone could choose death over life. If only Wyl could see how good his new life could be as King of Morgravia, living alongside the very woman he had loved for so long. Surely that was worth wearing the skin of the enemy?

Not for Wyl, it seemed. He was true to himself and he demanded death.

Aremys pulled himself out of his dark thoughts and watched Valentyna approach. She looked more beautiful than he could ever have imagined, gliding alongside

Commander Liryk, smiling softly to the crowd and carrying herself proud and erect. As she passed, and the cheering around him increased to its highest volume, he roared her name, not really expecting her to hear. Amazingly, she did, swinging around towards his voice.

When she saw him she faltered. 'Aremys,' she mouthed as she passed and he lifted a hand in greeting. They were both thinking the same thing: *Wyl*. When she cast a last glance over her shoulder, looking at him through her veil, he nodded his encouragement as if to say: You can do this. Be strong.

And then she was gone in a fanfare of trumpets, through the massive double doors of the cathedral, which swallowed her into its dark depths and an uncertain future.

Crys Donal had seen the bride too, but had not been able to make eye contact with her – not that she would have recognised him easily if he had. His yellow hair was now a deep brown and he sported a beard and moustache, also darkened. Gone were the fine clothes, replaced with the uniform of a Legionnaire. He blended into the crowd perfectly and, as neither King Celimus nor those he kept close knew Crys Donal by sight, he felt relatively secure.

He used his height and newly assumed status to shoulder his way through the crowd towards the cathedral. As a Legionnaire it was acceptable for him to be seen crossing the unmarked line that separated onlookers from the participants, particularly when an officer hailed him.

'Soldier, are you on duty?'

'No, sir,' Crys answered crisply. 'Just part of the cheering crowd.'

'Well, you're back on as of now. Get down to the cathedral's entrance and move that mob back. The happy couple won't be able to get out of the church if we don't create space for the carriage to come through.'

'Understood, sir. Right away.'

'Good lad,' the officer said and moved on.

Crys was able to jog down the street in front of yet another sparkling new carriage designed for this special day. Black with crimson flourishes, it bore the King's personal device and its gold dragons glinted in the sunlight whilst bunting in emerald and violet flickered in the spring breeze.

Other soldiers had been sent in as well so Crys simply joined them in pushing back the happy mob.

'If you tread on my foot again, I'll rip that beard off your chin, sonny,' one big fellow said.

'Hello, Aremys,' Crys murmured and won the shocked gasp he had expected. 'It's Crys, or perhaps I should say carving knife? I'm not sure any more.'

Aremys grinned in spite of his bleak mood. 'What are you blathering about, Donal?' he said quietly. 'Good to see you.'

Crys looked around to see that no one was watching them. Not only could no one hear, but no one cared. The mood was festive and fun-filled. All the people wanted was their new Queen and they chanted her name ceaselessly.

'The King won't care for that much,' Aremys commented.

'He'll have to get used to it. It's her they've turned out in their thousands to see.'

'Crys, I heard about your family. Shar, I'm so sorry, lad. I wish—'

'I know,' Crys said softly. 'Everyone does.'

Aremys nodded. 'Where's Elspyth?' he asked to change the subject, then wished he had not when he saw how the youngster's face darkened.

'Come with me,' Crys said. 'They'll be an age yet and we need to talk.'

He dragged Aremys out of the crowd and away from the main entry of the cathedral. They found a slightly quieter spot around the back. Crys told him everything but saved the worst until last. 'A new infection has her in its grip. She seemed all right for a while and I assumed she would recover after the physic in Pearlis pronounced her wounds in good shape, but the trip to Argorn was so hard for her. By the time we got there, she was feverish again and high-coloured.'

'Why did you leave her?'

'Knave arrived — you know, that strange dog of Wyl's?' Aremys nodded. 'Out of the blue, just walks into Argorn Manor.'

'And?'

'Elspyth rallied slightly at seeing him; she obviously understood better than I that he had come for us. Don't ask me how he knew where we were.'

'You don't want to know,' Aremys said. 'It goes hand in hand with the Quickening and magic.' He grimaced at the news of pretty Elspyth's sickness. 'Is she under good care?'

'Yes, I suppose so. She had to stay in Argorn, of course, no chance of more travel. Another physic has seen her, but you know, Aremys, it's a bit like she's given up on herself, as though she doesn't want to fight any more. It was so nasty what she went through.' He shrugged awkwardly. 'I just think she's accepting death.'

'Go back there then. Make her fight!'

Crys shook his head. 'No, I'm no good for her. It's tricky – there are two other women there. Lady Bench and her daughter, Georgyana. The daughter is . . . well, she's lovely, and . . .'

'And what?' Aremys quizzed.

'Shar, you can be as dense as you look sometimes, Farrow. I like her and she likes me. I think that makes it worse for Elspyth because she's so in love with Lothryn, as you know, and it must hurt her to see us falling for one another.'

'It can't kill her, surely?' the big man growled.

'No, but that infection might, especially when she denies herself food, fights the medication, can't sleep – won't even try. She talks about leaving to find Lothryn, weeps that he's in pain, that he's been changed somehow.' Crys ran his hands through his dark hair. 'But she was lucid when Knave arrived. She seemed to know that he wanted us to go with him. I'm ashamed to say we had to tie her to the bed to stop her from trying to accompany us.'

'She's no good to anyone here,' Aremys said gravely.

'I'm not sure any of us are any good here. She wept when I left, said we'd never see each other again. It's left me hollow, I can tell you.'

'You're sure the women are safe there?'

'No one knows they're there, and Argorn has sealed its collective mouth you could say, having heard our story. What about your story – what's happened since we parted? Where is Wyl? More to the point, *who* is Wyl?'

'Would you believe me if I told you he is currently King Cailech?'

It was Crys's turn for disbelief. Aremys told him the whole story.

'So he's here right now? That's why Knave came for us.'

'In the dungeon. I have no idea what's planned for him, though.'

The Duke of Felrawthy turned ashen. 'I think I do,' he said. 'Hurry, we must get to the dungeon. But first we need to disguise you as a Legionnaire.'

CHAPTER 41

The newlyweds emerged onto Stoneheart's largest balcony, known as the wedding balcony because so many Morgravian Kings had stepped out there with their new Queens to present them to the people.

Valentyna's heart was pounding yet she felt numb. It was done. The ceremony within the cathedral had dragged but she had spoken clearly when asked to take her vows, had even found a smile for the despised man beside her as she uttered the words which bound her to him for life.

Their exit fom the cathedral into the sunshine had provoked a rapturous noise she had not imagined was possible. As the royal couple walked to their new carriage, its dominant colours not lost on Valentyna, she had been showered with rose petals from blooms especially culti-vated beneath glass. Their pastel colours joined the fresh whites of spring flowers. Underfoot, just before her, she had noticed a spray of lavender land; it was so out of keeping with the roses and so dear to her heart that Valentyna had turned towards the man who threw it. The

Legionnaire had grinned, and she had suddenly recognised the Duke of Felrawthy despite his disguise.

'Thank you,' she mouthed, but much as she wanted to bend and pick up the purple heads of her favourite flower, she had not wished to draw the King's attention to it. He was far too sharp not to wonder who had thought to throw lavender to the new Queen. She had stepped on it instead, crushing the heads and releasing their fragrance to enjoy briefly before Celimus had helped her into the carriage.

The noise had been deafening as they had made their slow way back towards the castle. Valentyna had searched for Aremys or Crys but had not seen either again. Inside the carriage the time seemed right, so she had reached inside the small cream velvet pouch she carried.

'This, my lord, is for you,' she had said in the sweetest voice she could muster, knowing she had to preserve this fragile bond they had formed.

Celimus had looked puzzled as he took the small, exquisitely lacquered box. She knew he was captivated by the way his mouth opened as he saw the gift inside.

'It is a lovely ring, Valentyna,' he had whispered and kissed her, much to the people's joy. 'Will you put it on me?'

She did so. 'I'm glad you like it.'

'I will wear it always. I have something for you too,' he replied. 'It's being readied for you now.'

'Oh?'

'A special surprise,' he had promised and turned away to wave to the crowd.

And now she found herself waving from the wedding balcony to the sea of people below who had crowded into the main square before the castle.

'They are so proud of you, my lord,' she leaned close to say above the din. She hated her obsequiousness.

'And they love you. I knew they would. You are very good for me,' he replied. She knew he did not mean it as a romantic compliment. Celimus meant it literally: Valentyna made him look better; she was good for his image.

There was truly no hope for them, she thought. She envisaged herself struggling for a lifetime to be a sugary-sweet doormat just to keep the peace between them. She could not do it. Just maintaining the delicate truce, forged by her careful words on their journey into Morgravia, was destroying her soul. She hated him. And tonight she was expected to respond passionately between the sheets with him. As she gazed across the ocean of smiling faces, Valentyna felt she would rather die than have Celimus touch her intimately.

It seemed he had the same scene on his mind. 'Tonight,' he began, 'when all the formalities are done with and we are finally in bed, I mean to teach you something.'

Valentyna tried but failed to sound seductive or indeed even interested. 'That sounds rather intriguing, my lord. What can you mean?'

'I mean to teach you that I am not someone to be trifled with.'

Valentyna felt her body chill. He meant to hurt her. 'I don't understand, my lord.' She tried for levity in her voice.

'I will teach you how the King of Morgravia expects his Queen to behave.'

'Have I disappointed you during the marriage proceedings?' she asked, all other sounds now fading to the background as she focused on his voice alone.

'You lied to me, barefaced and at a particularly poignant moment. I am hurt by this.'

She could not imagine Celimus being emotionally hurt by anything, least of all words. 'You will have to explain this to me, Celimus,' Valentyna said, more firmly now, her mind racing as to which particular lie he might be referring to.

'Cailech denied your story to me in person last night. Of course I had hoped it was true, hoped I was the one who had jumped to the wrong conclusion.'

Something in Valentyna died. She felt as though the tiny candle which had burned inside her, had supported her through the wedding, had been snuffed out. Her love for Wyl Thirsk and the secret they shared was that tiny flame but he had blown it out by refusing her gift of life. 'I . . .' She struggled to form a response.

'Now,' Celimus began brightly, waving to the people and encouraging her to do the same, 'I forgive you this misdemeanour. You have behaved perfectly since our arrival at Pearlis. I believe that you did not invite Cailech to Werryl, nor did you know of his arrival there or his intention to stir up war using Briavel as an ally. My belief is that you lied to save further bloodshed; you hoped to preserve the peace between the three realms. And I am delighted by the wedding gift you have given me. So I forgive you. But you will learn an important lesson tonight.'

Valentyna began to say something but he hushed her with his hateful hand against her mouth, which he replaced quickly with his own lips, much to the crowd's delight and her disgust.

'Hush, my love, take your medicine and be pleased it's

not harsher. I appreciate that you are a virgin, though I cannot promise to be as gentle as I might have been a few days ago. So wave farewell to your people now and let me cheer you with my own special wedding gift as promised.'

'I—'

'Hush. I shall wait whilst you change. I want you to wear crimson, the colour of Morgravia.'

Aremys followed Crys blindly as they made their way to the Legionnaires' barracks. Stoneheart was like a town in itself – a maze of streets and openings, corridors and court-yards. When they finally reached their destination, the barracks were virtually deserted. Everyone was either on duty at the wedding or joining in the celebrations. Crys was able to sneak into the provisions office and take the biggest-sized uniform he could find.

'I have no idea if this will fit,' he said, returning to the small outbuilding where he had left Aremys, 'but it's genuine Legionnaire so it should do the trick and get you past security. Everyone's so preoccupied anyway – they'll see the crimson and black and no questions will be asked. Let's face it, it's likely none of the guards on duty around Cailech are going to be proper Legionnaires anyway – they're probably all mercenary impostors.'

'I hope you're right,' Aremys grumbled. 'I'm sensing we have to get into the dungeon, right?' Crys nodded grimly. 'Don't you think it will be heavily guarded, no strangers permitted?'

'We're not strangers. We're guards.'

Aremys did not have the heart to argue. 'Lead on,' he said.

At the dungeon Crys discovered that the royal prisoner had been moved.

'We've been sent along to make up extra numbers. King's orders, apparently,' Crys said to the officer there, trying his best to sound as uninterested as possible. 'Who is the prisoner, anyway?'

The man ignored him. 'Who sent you?'

Fortunately Crys knew the senior officers and captains of the Legion. 'Captain Berryn.' He was one of the more aggressive captains and Crys was sure the name would have the right effect.

The man's tone changed in an instant. 'All right, how many of you?'

'There's two of us but I don't know how many others he is sending. We were told to report to you here,' he lied, almost feeling sorry for the confused officer before him.

'Why can't they send a runner and inform us of what they want? I'll tell you, it was different in the days when the Thirsks ran this outfit.'

Crys shrugged, pretending he was too young to know.

'Get your companion and follow me. I'm on my way there now. And listen, sonny, this is no sideshow, all right? Today we execute a King and you will behave with due respect. Is that clear?'

'Yes, sir,' Crys said, straightening himself, glad to know the act had worked. 'I'll fetch Farrow, sir.'

Crys and Aremys remained silent as they walked a few steps behind the officer. The man was so preoccupied with what was ahead that he ignored them totally anyway.

They arrived at the courtyard, at almost the same time as the King and new Queen entered, but both had eyes only for the prisoner.

'Cover up, you know the drill,' the officer said, handing them black hoods from a small sack he carried. He left immediately to confer with one of the captains on the other side of the courtyard.

Crys explained the hood to Aremys in a low whisper. 'An old custom dating back to the first persecution of witches and sorcerers. It was held that empowered people had to see a person to cast a spell against them. So the mask was introduced to ensure that anyone present at an execution was impervious to their magic. The tradition died out over the centuries but soldiers are still required to cover their faces at executions.'

'Suits me,' said Aremys. 'At least we won't risk being recognised by the King or Jessom.' Nonetheless, he wished there was some way he could let Wyl know they were near.

Valentyna stood in the crimson gown which Celimus had ordered made for her and then demanded she wear. She did not notice the trio of Legionnaires arrive in the courtyard. Anger, fear and the hideous injustice of the position she found herself in quickly gave way to a desolation of emotion when her gaze followed the path to where the King's finger pointed. Chained to a post like an animal, but still looking proud, was King Cailech: tall and golden, fury burning in his eyes and a defiant set to his jaw. Now she felt weak – overcome by a combination of terror and an overwhelming rush of love.

Wyl's light green gaze left her and fell on Celimus. A smirk crossed Cailech's face and he raised a fist and turned the clenched fingers towards his Morgravian counterpart. A northerner would know that this was the sign that the tribes of the Razors gave to indicate a declaration of war.

Crys looked helplessly at his companion for enlightenment.

'He's baiting the King,' Aremys muttered.

'Why? Surely there's enough bad feeling?' Crys whispered.

'Wyl is trying to ensure that the King will personally kill him, although I'm not sure the Quickening obeys such laws.'

Dawning spread on the duke's face beneath his hood. 'He will be our King, then?'

Aremys nodded as they watched Wyl being unchained from the post. But not for long, he thought in private anguish.

Valentyna felt as though she could no longer breathe. Tears were streaming down her face.

'I didn't know you cared for him that much, my love,' Celimus cooed.

'Why must he die?'

'Because he can't be trusted. He will always be a danger to us.'

'But killing him will merely enrage the Mountain People and encourage them to wage their own war against both our realms.'

'You have no realm now, beloved.'

'What?'

'Briavel is now part of Morgravia.'

'That is not my understanding, Celimus.'

He tutted in a condescending way. 'Valentyna, please grow up. I now rule both our realms — that's my job. Your job is to swiftly become pregnant with my sons and be a smiling, loving wife to me. You will no longer worry about realms, politics, war, strategy — I shall take care of all that. I am not the slightest bit intimidated by either Briavel or the Razor Kingdom.'

Valentyna could not stand to be beside him for another moment. With a final glance towards Cailech's granite expression, she feigned weariness and asked to be excused.

'Soon enough,' Celimus said. 'But first let me deliver my gift to you.'

'What do you mean?' she asked, fresh anxiety washing over her.

'You must bear witness, my love. I am executing King Cailech in your honour. He will never trouble you again.'

'I refuse—'

'You refuse me *nothing*, wife! Remember, you belong to Morgravia now, and its King.'

CHAPTER 42

Wyl was led up onto a hastily built wooden stage. Despite that touch of theatre, it was a lonely setting for a King's end. The only witnesses were the two royals, a few guards, the Chancellor and, of course, the masked executioner, who had just arrived.

Wyl was not afraid. The truth was, he could not wait to die again, and feel the Quickening release him from Myrren's gift and her curse over his life. He would not have to live long as Celimus. Just long enough to be with Valentyna again, to hold her once more.

And if it all went sadly awry, he would still live – this time as a burly man of enormous strength and stature. Wyl had taken the precaution of discovering the executioner's name: Art Featherstone. He wondered briefly how in the guise of the executioner, he would ever contrive to get close enough to Celimus for Myrren's gift to come into play again, but gave up the line of thought. Whoever could have thought Wyl would become Romen, or that Faryl would claim Romen's life, or that Ylena – he faltered on hearing her name in his thoughts – would kill Faryl and become her brother's host? And now here he was, the King of the Razors, about to become the King of Morgravia . . . or the burly executioner.

But he had laid the seed. Surely Celimus would find the temptation irresistible to personally separate King Cailech's head from his body? It would be another triumph for the Crown.

A huge Legionnaire came up with a cup of water. 'Orders,' the man said to the executioner, who nodded, uncaring.

Wyl's spirits lifted at the sound of the man's voice. 'Aremys,' he whispered as the Grenadyne gave him the cup.

'I beg you, don't make me keep the promise,' Aremys muttered beneath his breath.

'You will keep it if you care anything for me,' Wyl said.

Aremys stared into the green eyes and then nodded sadly. 'As One,' he said and left.

A single trumpet sounded and Wyl noticed for the first time that Valentyna was dressed in a crimson gown. The colour of Morgravia. The colour of blood. She was solemn-faced and looked intensely frightened. He wished he could spare her this; had hoped against hope that Celimus would come without her.

Valentyna would not look at anyone – not even at Wyl. He could not blame her. It must have felt like a shocking betrayal to hear that he had denied her fabricated story as to why the Mountain King was in Briavel. He understood, but it did not make it any easier to see her ignoring him. Was it just two days ago they had been making love at Werryl? He would cling to that. As the executioner's sword fell he would remember what it felt like to lie naked with Valentyna and love her as she loved him.

Celimus guided his wife to a pair of throne-like seats hurriedly erected in the courtyard. He kissed her hand, winning a sickly grimace from the Queen. Her expression did not seem to matter to Celimus who was now announcing why the King of the Mountains was to die.

Wyl looked towards Jessom as the King spoke and remembered the strange blue light entwining their hands in the dungeon, binding them to each other. He wondered if Fynch was right: whether the Chancellor might somehow provide that random element that could outwit Myrren's gift. Death was moments away – it was pointless wondering any more. Wyl turned his attention back to Celimus's speech and heard that he was to be sacrificed as a wedding gift to Valentyna. At this he withdrew into himself to wait for his death.

Valentyna had withdrawn too. There surely was nothing to live for any more. Soon she would have to witness the man she loved die, his head savagely removed from his neck with, hopefully, one swing of a cruel sword. It was too much for her heart to bear.

And after all of that, all that was left to her was Celimus – a despicable man who had made his intentions very clear. Her notion that she might be able to dupe him into believing she was true had been naive. Celimus was too sharp to fall for that, but he would still expect her to treat him as she had promised, even if she was pretending every minute of every day.

And he would continue to hurt her – first taking Wyl

from her, then Briavel, no doubt ultimately taking away every son she bore. Her life would be utterly controlled by the mad King. Bile rose to her throat as she imagined what he was going to do to her this night. Rape, she was sure, would be the very least of it.

Celimus had finished explaining his reasons for executing the treacherous Mountain King and the sudden silence dragged her out of her thoughts. She looked at Cailech whose shirt was being cut away to reveal his broad torso, sculpted with muscle. She remembered that body well, riding above her in an urgent rhythm, each thrust taking her to a higher level of pleasure. She wanted Cailech to be her lover, to be the man who would stand proudly beside her, as she had wanted Romen. And both the men she loved were really Wyl Thirsk. It was Wyl who loved her so deeply, so truly. But it seemed she could have none of them.

Chancellor Jessom, looking appropriately sombre in black robes, gravely pronounced the Crown's sentence on the accused. 'Have you anything to say, Cailech, King of the Mountains?' he asked finally.

Wyl spoke clearly. 'Legionnaires, remember who you are. Remember your oath to protect and serve Morgravians above all others. Above all others,' he stressed, 'even above your King—'

'Enough!' roared Celimus, enraged.

At the King's signal the beefy executioner backhanded the prisoner who stumbled but did not fall despite his ankles being manacled.

Wyl knew the guards were probably not Legionnaires – Celimus would not risk them witnessing such an unlawful execution. Nevertheless, he hoped the insult had been sufficient to provoke Celimus into swinging the death sword himself.

'Get on with it!' the King ordered the executioner. 'My wife and I wish to continue our wedding festivities.'

'I challenge you, King Celimus, to mete out the punishment personally,' Wyl roared. 'You accuse me of treachery, so deal with me yourself – or are you too squeamish to risk my blood on your fine garments?'

His challenge was greeted with stunned silence. Finally, Celimus said, 'I have never been scared to spill your blood, Cailech.'

'Then prove it!' Wyl shouted.

Valentyna could not bear it. Wyl had already severed the lifeline she had thrown to him and now he wanted to make sure that Celimus chopped his head off. What was wrong with him? Why bait Celimus? Surely he would prefer the accurate swing of an executioner over the perhaps deliberately clumsy hacking by a man he had publicly scorned? Wyl had gone mad. He was not only making it worse for her but so much worse for himself. He would die painfully and then Celimus would—

Valentyna caught her breath audibly as the realisation hit hard. And then Celimus would become Wyl!

Oh Shar! He was doing it deliberately so that Celimus would die and Wyl would take over his body and become the King, and her husband. Wyl would live on because of Myrren's gift! Now her breath came hard and fast and her pulse began to race. Death would have been so welcome just moments ago and now she wanted to live! And she wanted Wyl to live too.

Valentyna stood. 'Do it for me, Celimus!' she cried, her cheeks flushed, her heart pounding.

The King swung around in surprise. 'You want me to kill him?'

'Yes,' she demanded. 'He has driven a wedge between us with his underhand dealings. I hate him. I hate his treachery. Kill him, Celimus. Do it with your own hand so that we are truly free of his curse on our lives. That would be my ultimate wedding gift, sire,' she said, and curtsied low ensuring her husband saw the swell of her breasts.

Celimus grinned ferociously. He looked like a wolf closing on its prey as he peeled off his cloak, the crimson lining reminding everyone of the blood he would shortly spill.

Valentyna could hardly believe it. Her spirits were soaring with the hammering of her heart. She would have Wyl. She would have Romen. She would have Cailech. He would be Celimus, but the real Celimus would be dead. Thank you, Myrren, she whispered to a dead witch. Thank you, Shar, she cast to her god.

'Come, stand closer, my love,' Celimus called to her. 'You must share in this, my wedding gift to you.'

Cailech was forced to his knees to meet his death. Valentyna, no longer afraid, glided confidently towards the husband she despised, her eyes locked on the man who would soon be her one love. She leaned forwards and kissed Celimus, making it as tender as she could without gagging. She wanted him to know how much this meant to her.

Wyl was thrown back to Fynch's vision: how could they have guessed Cailech was the prisoner? He felt sickened by the sight and closed his eyes. He knew Valentyna had guessed what was going to happen; had seen it reflected in the blaze of her eyes and the hungry expression she suddenly wore. But he did not believe she could live alongside him once he was in the body of the Morgravian King. Celimus had damaged them both so much. Hurry, Shar damn you, he thought, opening his eyes and silently urging the King to execute him. He lowered his head to the block and bared his thick neck.

But Celimus hesitated. He too had noted the change in his wife's demeanour. The kiss was a surprise, especially after his threat on the balcony barely an hour ago. He thought about her behaviour since: one moment despairing, the next filled with a fervour he did not know she possessed. She looked rejuvenated, excited . . . she looked hungry. What could possibly have had that effect? Surely not the mention of blood. Even the little he knew of her would confirm she was far from bloodthirsty – this was the woman who was marrying a man she did not love simply to prevent bloodshed. No, it was not that, yet her whole manner had changed at the suggestion that he kill Cailech himself, galvanising her into this lustful creature. Her eyes blazed with a passion he had not seen since that night in Briavel when they had danced together. And even then he had felt sure the fervour was not for him.

Celimus's sharp mind worked across every possible scenario but came up wanting. He could find no logical explanation for this odd change of heart. Valentyna had lied to save this man's life, had wept at the thought of him dying just moments earlier; yet now she was begging for his execution at the King's own hand. His instincts screamed that there was duplicity here although he could not pinpoint it. And so Celimus made a decision. He would get to the truth. He would test her.

'No!' he roared. 'The King of Morgravia will not tarnish his wedding day with blood on his hands.'

'But, my lord,' Valentyna cried, 'this is for me. I want his head.'

'And you shall have it, I promise.' Celimus turned back to the executioner. 'Do your job: behead the treacherous sovereign on behalf of Morgravia and Briavel,' he ordered.

Celimus took Valentyna's hand and led her back to their thrones. She felt breathless with panic. The King had thwarted them. If Myrren's gift continued, then Wyl would become the bald-headed executioner and she might wait years before he found his way back to Stoneheart to challenge Celimus again. What a terrible irony, she thought despairingly. Only weeks ago she had scorned Fynch for believing in magic, and now here she was pinning everything on the hope that if only Celimus would kill his enemy then Wyl would live again. If that hope failed, Valentyna knew in her heart that she would not lie with Celimus tonight . . . or any night. She would take her own life if need be.

She shook her mind clear as the executioner lined up for his single killing blow. The least she could do for Wyl was bear witness to his brave death. She watched the big man raise his sword slowly, carefully, smoothly. It reached the apex of his swing and was just a second from falling with its severing blow when she heard herself yell, 'Wait!' The man teetered and then stopped, looking angrily towards King Celimus for guidance.

'What is it, Valentyna?' Celimus asked smoothly. Perhaps now the truth of her strange behaviour would reveal itself.

'Let me do it, sire,' she begged, for his hearing only. It was the only way out for her.

For the first time since knowing him, Valentyna saw hesitancy and alarm in his face. 'You would kill this man?'

'For you, Celimus. It is the only way I can resolve the difficulties between us.'

'Through his death?' he queried, wondering if she had gone mad.

'Yes,' she whispered. 'He will release us. You will know I am true to you if I do this.'

Celimus shook his head, baffled. Valentyna had obviously had a trying few days, granted, but this behaviour was unhinged. Nevertheless, the shock of her suggestion titillated his sadistic streak. He rather liked the idea of her executing Cailech. Such an act would haunt her for ever, but that offered further opportunity for exploitation: she would be even more easily controlled when the demons paid regular visits to remind her of this ugly spectacle. It would also, of course, show her to be a strong person, either terrifying or inspiring the few onlookers — either way suited him. She was offering herself up to him in the most intriguing fashion.

He studied her and she stared back at him hungrily. There was no doubting that she meant this.

'It is not a pleasant thing you request, Valentyna. You will have to live with this memory all of your life.'

'You have no idea how important that notion is to me, sire.'

He shook his head as if washing his hands of her. 'As you wish.'

He turned to the executioner. 'Bind the prisoner's mouth,' he ordered, knowing Cailech was likely to make a loud fuss when he learned of this new and exciting turn of events. The idea of his Queen killing a man made Celimus feel like rutting. His mind slithered towards the bedchamber this evening. An heir would be made tonight, he was sure of it. He would have his first son before next spring.

Wyl looked around, confused. He had no idea what was going on between the whispering royal couple or why his mouth had suddenly been bound. He had fully expected to be the executioner by now, trudging home with his day's pay to a wife and brood of children. But here he was, still alive, still praying for deliverance.

He watched Celimus stand once again, hoping against hope that the King had had a change of heart and would deliver the killing blow. But it was Valentyna who walked towards him. Valentyna who had chosen to kill him.

'No!' he shouted from beneath the bindings but it came out as a strangled cry. His eyes were wide with horror at her decision.

Valentyna glided towards him in her blood-red gown and Wyl was suddenly reminded of his dream at Tenterdyn. This was it. No dream, but a premonition. She bent towards him, tears streaming down her face. 'Forgive me,' she whispered and he roared his anguish, not caring that it appeared he was about to die cringing like a coward.

The executioner pushed Cailech's head down onto the block again. 'Don't make it harder for her,' he growled. 'She'll never survive it if she misses.'

Wyl knew the man spoke the truth and he stopped struggling. He did not want to become Valentyna. He did not want her to sacrifice herself for him. He could hear her shallow, terrified breathing behind him. The courtyard was so silent he was sure he could hear her heartbeat too. It was too much for his own bleeding heart. Wyl closed his eyes and begged for a miracle that might thwart Myrren and her cursed gift.

Fynch! he called in his mind.

Valentyna lifted the sword. She took a moment to pray for her own soul then screamed her despair as she poured all her sorrow, her pain, her anguish into the downward sweep that severed King Cailech's head from his body.

She sank slowly to her knees in his blood, her heart aching, tears streaming, and waited for the change to come over her body. She had no idea what to expect or how the magic worked. All she knew was that she would accept him gladly. This would be the ultimate sacrifice, the final demonstration of her love.

Behind her, Celimus's dark olive eyes sparked with the fire of lust for this woman and the joy of knowing his final enemy was slain. He would be Emperor now and perhaps Valentyna had shown herself worthy of the title of Empress.

Nearby, Chancellor Jessom's body sagged and he hung his head as he struggled slightly to breathe. He would need to gather his composure quickly.

The King of the Razors's body was slumped forward over the block. The executioner bent to pick up the head which had rolled to his feet. For the umpteenth time he wondered whether the brain remained alive just long enough to know its head had been removed from its body. At the King's nod, Art Featherstone placed the head of the Mountain sovereign in a leather sack. He would take care of the body once the royal party had departed.

Valentyna felt nothing. Not even a single tear. There was only numbness. Was she now Wyl? Had her soul left her body? It was too confusing amongst the pain of the day. Her hands were slick with his blood, that was all she could focus on through her wet eyes.

'Come, Valentyna,' said the voice she hated more than any in the world and then she felt the King of Morgravia's touch. She turned away from the headless body to look upon Celimus and knew in that instant that something had gone terribly wrong. It had all been a lie. The Quickening was not real. Cailech was dead and the story about Wyl Thirsk had been some sort of cruel ruse. She was alive and her husband awaited her.

'Jessom,' the King said.

The Chancellor looked up and cleared his throat. 'Sire?'

'Help Queen Valentyna to her chambers. I will see you both there shortly.'

'Yes, your majesty,' the Chancellor said and offered his arm to the Queen. Her pale skin was spattered with the blood of a King. 'You, guard,' he called to Aremys and beckoned. Aremys moved silently towards the Chancellor; he could not risk being recognised. 'You look a burly enough fellow. Help the executioner to remove the body immediately and lock it away. Bring the key to me. No one is to be permitted entry. Is that clear?' Aremys nodded.

Then Jessom looked directly at Crys. 'And you, take an inventory of all present, including guards and the herald. I want the names brought to me immediately in the Queen's chambers. Is that understood?'

Crys looked puzzled beneath his hood, but nodded, avoiding speech for the same reason as Aremys had.

Jessom felt as stunned as the Queen at how events had turned out. Still gathering his own wits, he hurried her from the scene of death and, using back corridors which only he seemed to know about, he led the silent, shivering bride to her suite of rooms.

CHAPTER 43

Chancellor Jessom was surprisingly tender with her but Valentyna was too lost in her own darkness to notice. He wet a linen and wiped her face and hands clean of the blood, and tried gently to get her to talk. There were important things she must understand before the King arrived. 'What can I do to help you, my Queen?' he whispered, wondering how to revive her from this stricken state before he began to explain his new situation.

Valentyna was in utter turmoil. What had gone wrong? She was still herself . . . and Wyl – he was gone. Cailech was dead. She had killed him but Wyl had not possessed her as she had believed he would. She groaned involuntarily. It was a sound of such anguish that she saw fear pass across the hook-nosed Chancellor's face. Why was he showing her such concern when she hated him too? Everyone had lied to her. Fynch had almost duped her into believing in magic, along with Elspyth, but it was Cailech who had won her full trust. He had made her truly believe the strange tale of Wyl Thirsk . . . but why?

'Your majesty?' Jessom whispered, trying to bring her back to the present.

'Kill me,' she whispered. 'Before I have to spend a night with him.'

'I cannot do that, your highness.'

'Then I shall kill myself,' she said, colour flushing her ghastly, almost yellow complexion.

She saw him flinch. 'Please don't, your majesty. I would never forgive myself. Listen to me: I made a promise to King Cailech yesterday that I would offer you my protection. Rest assured, my word is true when given. I am now your servant, your highness.' He broke with protocol by taking her hand and placing it on his heart. She tried to pull it back, repulsed, but he held it firmly in place. 'You must trust me,' he begged her. There was so much to tell her. 'King Cailech—'

She cut across his words. 'Why do you offer your allegiance to me? You are the King's man.'

'Just trust me, please,' he repeated. He took her dull silence as agreement. 'The King is on his way here, your majesty. I have important information to share with you, but let me organise some refreshment so it arrives before Celimus does. I will be only moments.'

Valentyna did not move, knowing he would not leave her alone long enough to end her life. He had said he would be only moments. It briefly occurred to her that the Chancellor was treating her far more kindly than she would have expected. Perhaps the Mountain King had indeed managed to persuade him to watch over her. Jessom could not protect her, however, from Celimus's attention tonight. She was surely alone now. She had stupidly clung to a notion of magic being able to save her this final despair, but it was not to be. She had behaved madly and had killed a man in her delirium – and not just any man. She felt bile rise again, thought she might be sick, but beat the sensation back with the hollow comfort that at least Cailech had been killed by someone who loved him. It was clear now that the whole tale of Myrren's gift was some sort of elaborate, cruel hoax. It mattered not – by tonight she planned to be dead herself.

Jessom returned. He was breathing hard, as if he had been running. 'Ah, here we are now, your highness. Please drink this.'

'What is it?'

'The King's favourite wine. It has a rich and full flavour. It suits only the heaviest of foods because it tends to over-power other tastes, but then the King does not take a midday meal and thus favours the heaviness.'

Valentyna wondered why the Chancellor was giving her such an in-depth description of the wine. Perhaps he thought she needed educating on Celimus's preferences.

The door suddenly opened and there stood the King of Morgravia himself. His cheeks were flushed and he looked triumphant. 'You were magnificent, Valentyna,' he said and laughed. 'Do you still have his blood on you, you savage Briavellian?'

'I washed it away, your highness,' Jessom said softly. He was ignored by both King and Queen.

Valentyna stood and curtsied. 'I don't know what came over me, sire.'

'I do,' Celimus said, taking the proffered goblet of wine from Jessom without even looking at his Chancellor. 'It was a wonderful demonstration of patriotism. I am proud of you.'

Valentyna remained silent, noting that Jessom had a cunning ability to slide away into the shadows almost unseen. She wondered why Celimus had not dismissed the Chancellor, but then Celimus was too filled with his own bloodlust to take much notice of others around him.

'To us,' he said, raising his glass.

'To us,' Valentyna echoed. She thought of her father's small dagger which she had packed and brought with her to Morgravia. It had been for the sake of sentimentality that she had wrapped it so carefully in muslin and laid it amongst her things. Shortly it would serve a different purpose, bringing welcome death when it opened the arteries at her wrists. Thinking about her father, her plan suddenly felt right. She would somehow get through this afternoon and then she would find time to slip away by herself and finish it once and for all.

Celimus drained his glass. It was swiftly taken away and refilled by Jessom, then returned as surreptitiously.

'Are you feeling up to the feast, my love?' the King asked.

'I will change, I think,' Valentyna replied drily, looking at her stained gown.

The King sniggered at the jest. 'Of course, go ahead. The nobles can wait. I'll hang onto the gown for posterity, though; Cailech's dried blood will make an amusing keepsake.'

'More wine, sire?' Jessom said, stepping forward.

Valentyna watched Celimus drain his second glass of wine and knew that by tonight he would be intoxicated and even more determined to keep his promise. Jessom filled the glass for a third time and Valentyna grimaced, wishing the Chancellor would stop plying the King with so much liquor.

'I won't be long,' she said, backing into her dressing chamber as she saw the King stagger slightly.

'Are you all right, sire?' Jessom asked.

'Shar, but I feel odd,' Celimus said.

'Well, I imagine that's the poison I put in your glass, sire,' Jessom offered matter-of-factly.

Valentyna's mouth fell open. 'Poison?' she echoed. Her gaze moved from the King's suddenly haggard expression to the victorious face of his Chancellor.

'Yes, your majesties,' Jessom replied. 'Valentyna, you don't love the King, I most certainly don't love the King, the nobles despise him and Morgravia will hardly miss him – I decided we were all better off without him.'

Celimus tried to move towards his Chancellor, but failed.

'Ah yes, I think the paralysis must be setting in now, and because you drank two . . .' Jessom gave a soft chortle as he checked the glass decanter in his hand '. . . almost three glasses and a hefty dose of the poison, it will work fast. So let's talk swiftly. But first I shall wait a moment to be sure you are in fact dying, sire. Do you mind?'

Celimus made to speak, but nothing of sense came from his lips. He spilled the tiny amount left in his glass down his front, the glass itself rolling off his lap and hitting the edge of the chair before falling to the floor and shattering.

'No matter, sire, we can clean that up along with your corpse. This is a wonderfully lethal potion Jessom discovered just recently. It kills cleanly, without a giveaway smell and no telltale signs left behind on the body. I'm afraid it's not a very pleasant death for the victim – no doubt quite similar to the one Eryd Bench would have experienced,' Jessom went on. 'A hideously agonising end, which is less than you deserve, sire, if I might say so.'

Valentyna was slowly shaking her head in disbelief: Celimus tried to scream but all he managed was to bare his teeth.

'Not long now, sire, I promise. Your highness,' Jessom turned to a stunned Valentyna, 'if you have anything to say to him, say it now. We have about ten minutes at most before his heart stops.'

She had never been more unnerved. 'You have really poisoned him?'

The Chancellor nodded. 'I had to run back to Jessom's rooms to get the vial, which is why I was so out of breath, your majesty.'

She frowned. 'Why do you speak of Jessom as though he is elsewhere?'

'Oops. How forgetful of me,' the Chancellor replied, clearly enjoying himself. He gave a sly grin which Valentyna did not understand. 'Look at me, Celimus,' Jessom demanded, his voice no longer playful as he moved to stand directly in front of the King. 'Watch carefully.'

Chancellor Jessom closed his eyes; Valentyna could swear she heard him softly call the name Fynch. A blue shimmering light appeared around his body, burning him, dissolving him it seemed. Then her hand moved to her mouth to stifle the scream of disbelief, for beneath the shimmering another man was emerging. As Jessom disappeared into the blue furnace, it was Cailech who lifted his proud head, Cailech's eyes that opened to look into hers, Cailech's beloved face that looked at her with such love.

Valentyna felt herself begin to tremble and she wept,

unable to comprehend what was happening. Could this be true?

Thank you, Fynch, Wyl whispered across the miles. And deep in the heart of the Thicket a boy smiled.

'It is I, Valentyna,' Wyl said gently.

She shook her head, hardly daring to trust him. 'I killed you.'

'You killed Jessom.'

'How?' Her voice was a groan through her tears.

'Fynch made it possible for me to swap places with Jessom temporarily, and for the Chancellor to inhabit Cailech's body – not that he had much say. Fynch called it the Bridge of Souls.'

'Magic?' she whispered.

'That's right, my love, a clever glamour and a trans-ference between bodies. Fynch came to me in the dungeon and asked me to trust him. I was not of a mind to grasp what he was offering; I only believed it when I realised Cailech was screaming and yet it was not me making that sound. I was suddenly standing behind everyone, watching the scene through Jessom's eyes. Fynch gave his last reserves for us, Valentyna. He worked out that if Myrren and her father could weave such a curse, he could reweave it to truly become a gift.'

'A gift of life?'

Wyl nodded. 'In the truest sense. I don't plan on changing again. I hope you like me well enough as Cailech.'

Valentyna put her head in her hands, overwhelmed by emotion. Wyl took her in his arms and kissed her bent head. Then looked across to Celimus; the King's eyes were disbelieving and glassy, and he dribbled through lips pulled back in a rictus of anger.

'I think we have just enough time left for me to tell you a story, Celimus,' Wyl said coldly. He settled Valentyna in a chair and held her hand, but stared directly at the dying King as he spoke briefly and succinctly, starting in the dungeon of Stoneheart where a young woman called Myrren was being tortured and a boy called Wyl Thirsk offered her pity and was thus given a gift.

Valentyna felt awed at hearing the story in its entirety. Somehow it was fitting that its full telling should take place before the man who had been the source of it all. Myrren was truly avenged now.

'And Jessom?' Valentyna asked when Wyl was finished. She needed to understand how the Chancellor's fate had become so closely linked with her future happiness.

'Jessom was a parasite, Valentyna. He might not have made the cruel decisions himself but he saw that they were carried out. The blood of too many people was on his hands. It was fitting he should suffer for his sins. I suspect he was ready to swap allegiances but instead the Bridge of Souls saw to it that he swapped bodies. Fynch turned the Quickening back on itself.'

'He mocked Myrren's gift, you mean?'

Cailech's face broke into a smile, the first in a long time. 'Yes, that's exactly what he did. He made a mockery of it.'

'So you knelt there and let me kill you,' she said, aghast.

'It wasn't easy. You must know I was happy to die, and I had hoped to die by Celimus's hand,' he said, glancing at the King. 'Fynch warned me once of the power of random acts to affect the Quickening, but I could never have foreseen that you might make such a sacrifice. Fynch could see these things and he took appropriate precautions.'

'He knew I would kill you?'

Cailech's head shook sadly. 'None of us did. Not even you, I imagine. Fynch just seems to see the whole picture. I think he accepted that an unpremeditated action might change the pattern of fate, and he put his Bridge of Souls in place so that I might be saved come what may.'

'That child is too clever by half.'

Wyl fixed her with his green gaze, knowing he could not hide the truth from her. 'I believe Fynch is dead, Valentyna.'

Her throat swelled with new grief. 'No!'

'He used what little was left of his spirit to help us. It is a long story, my love; one I shall share with you later. First I must finish my task here.'

Celimus groaned. His fingers had shaped themselves into claws and Wyl had no doubt that the King would have given anything for a few more seconds of fluid movement. 'It's over, Celimus,' he said, feeling very little satisfaction at seeing the once-proud body arch in its death paralysis. 'Let Shar's Gatherers take you now, and may our god alone have the generosity to show you mercy.'

Celimus found one last spurt of energy to gurgle his fury and suddenly Wyl felt a new sensation. It was a sharp pain, like a blade of ice, cutting through Cailech's body and forcing a cry from him.

'What is it?' Valentyna said, grabbing his arm. Wyl barely felt her touch or heard her, his vision dimmed and he could no longer see the chamber around him. But he knew where he was. He was with Celimus.

You! Celimus whispered.

And Wyl understood: this was Myrren's parting gift. She was showing Celimus the truth. It was her final vengeance.

I'm glad you can see me at last, Celimus. It was no longer Cailech before the King, but a short, red-headed man. Wyl Thirsk, General of the Morgravian Legion.

The Legion and the nobles will not permit it, Celimus screamed into the mind of his nemesis.

You forget, they do not see me; they see only a crowned monarch whom you yourself have forged a truce with. Very few know I was captured and incarcerated, and even fewer know of my death.

Celimus hung on his last hope. *You will not take my throne. Morgravia will never accept a Mountain King.*

I don't have to, it's already gone. You gave it to Valentyna the moment you married her, Celimus. She is the ruler of both realms now. But I will become sovereign of Morgravia too, when I marry her. I have to, you see, to fulfil Myrren's gift and rid myself fully of the Quickening. It demands that I be sovereign.

The King of Morgravia screamed his despair into his rival's mind as he sighted Shar's Gatherers approaching.

CHAPTER 44

There was a knock at the door. 'Chancellor Jessom?' a voice called.

'It's Aremys,' Wyl said, closing the eyes of the dead King. He had hoped to have a few minutes alone with the Queen, but the Grenadyne had obviously done his duty quickly. He strode to the door and pulled it open. Instantly the colour in the two familiar faces before him vanished. They were seeing the ghost of a man they had watched die just moments before.

'What in Shar's name—' Aremys began.

'Hush, come in quickly,' Wyl said. He felt sorry for their shock but there was no time to spare for niceties. 'Shut the door behind you. Hello, Crys. Oh, I think I should say "carving knife".' He grinned.

The newcomers entered the chamber tentatively and, at the same moment, spotted a familiar figure slumped in a chair.

'Celimus is dead?' Crys whispered, his gaze moving to Valentyna and then returning with fresh fear to Cailech.

Wyl nodded.

'Wait!' Aremys demanded. 'What's going on? *Cailech is* dead! I watched it happen. I waited for the Quickening but saw no evidence of it. I feared you had died for good.'

'As you see, I'm very much alive,' Wyl replied, taking a grim pleasure in his friend's shock. 'It was Fynch. He worked out a way to channel his own magic to save me without disturbing Myrren's gift.'

'How?' the two men asked at once, awe in their voices. Then Crys nudged Aremys and both bowed to their Queen. 'Your majesty,' they said, embarrassed at their lack of etiquette.

Valentyna smiled and shook her head. 'I am too unsettled to even notice any lapses in protocol.'

'Tell us,' Aremys said, turning back to Wyl. 'What exactly did Fynch contrive?'

'He swapped my spirit with Jessom's.'

'So Jessom was executed?' Aremys said, his wonder obvious.

'Fynch called it a Bridge of Souls,' Wyl answered. 'He came to me in the dungeon, although it was not truly him. Just a sending,' he said wistfully. 'He begged me to trust him and mentioned the Bridge of Souls, but he did not explain it and I didn't ask him to elaborate. My mood was grim and, much as I treasured seeing him once more, I didn't think anything could change the course I was on.'

'I thought you'd become the Queen,' Crys finally said, his relief evident. 'No disrespect, your majesty,' he added to Valentyna.

And then suddenly Aremys had King Cailech in a bear-like hug. Wyl reached out a long arm to encompass Crys into the embrace. Valentyna had to look away, the rush of emotion she felt at witnessing their relief echoing her own. She wished she could join them, but sensed this was a special moment between the three men. There would be time ahead for her and Wyl to share their feelings.

Finally the men pulled apart and the newcomers had to see for themselves the cooling corpse of King Celimus.

'What happened?' Aremys asked, delight obvious in his voice.

'Jessom poisoned him – I mean, I did. And when the King was as good as dead, I was released from the glamour and could reveal the truth to him.'

Aremys scratched his head, unsure of what to say or do. He followed his gut instinct and knelt before the two royals. 'Your majesties, my sword is yours to command. Although do not ask me to use it on you now, Wyl.'

The King laid a hand on his bowed head. 'I won't, Aremys, my great friend. Only we four know of what has truly occurred today. No one else need ever find out.'

'So you will remain as Cailech, is that it?' Aremys asked carefully as he stood. He realised now why Jessom – or rather, Wyl – had given such curious orders to himself and Crys. 'But Myrren's gift demands that you become sovereign of Morgravia, surely?'

Valentyna spoke now. 'We shall marry as soon as it is feasible, but it must be with the nobles' permission. Most would have accepted that my marriage to Celimus was strategic, so why not a second union in the name of peace?'

Crys Donal nodded. 'That's true. And there are rumblings amongst the true Legionnaires about a civil uprising backed by key nobles. It doesn't seem to be idle gossip any longer. But how will you explain the King's death?'

Wyl began to pace the room. Shocked and overwrought

as she was, Valentyna could not help but smile to see Cailech's large hand tug at his earlobe in a gesture unique to Wyl Thirsk.

'Jessom poisoned the King and then fled,' Wyl said. 'The only other person in the chamber was Valentyna, but she had retired to her dressing room to change into her gown for the wedding banquet. She saw the Chancellor pour the wine for the King before she left the room – and we still have the wine in the decanter to prove that it was poisoned. When Valentyna returned, ready to attend her wedding feast, she found the King in his death throes and raised the alarm. You and I, Aremys, had come to pay our respects to the newly married couple, and so were on hand to hear the Queen's cries. We hunted down the Chancellor and despatched him quickly and without honour, as befitting a traitor. That will also explain his corpse's headless state, should news of it get out.'

Wyl paused and looked at his friend. 'Is this all right with you?'

'My pleasure to be responsible for his death,' the big man replied. 'I'll ensure the body is disposed of carefully too.'

'What about the executioner?' Valentyna asked. 'He will know that it was Cailech I executed, not Jessom. And there were a few other guards in the courtyard too.'

'Apparently they were all mercenaries, your majesty,' Crys offered, 'not true Legionnaires, and I have a list here of their names, as Jessom – I mean, Wyl – ordered. We can easily track them down and either pay them to keep their silence, or use other means. Same for the executioner.'

'No, the executioner need not die. He is a good man,' said Wyl, remembering how Featherstone had asked him not to make Valentyna's task any harder. 'When you find him, bring him to me. I shall explain.' He offered no further explanation and no one pushed him for one.

'What reason do we hazard for Jessom's betrayal of the King?' Crys asked.

Wyl tugged at his ear again. 'I can say I had a discussion with Jessom the night before the wedding and shared with him my understanding that Celimus intended to lay the blame for so many deaths firmly at the Chancellor's feet. The King would have needed to explain the deaths to the nobles somehow, and that would be an ideal solution. And so they can assume that Jessom killed Celimus out of revenge. Let's be honest, few of the nobles are going to grieve at the news of the King's death.'

'They'll probably have to grit their teeth to prevent themselves from cheering, if truth be known,' Aremys commented.

'Then we have the perfect opportunity at the wedding feast to explain our position,' Wyl continued. 'We should be as honest as we can. Celimus is dead – we cannot escape this.'

'I shall throw Felrawthy's support behind Valentyna as the new sovereign of Morgravia,' Crys Donal offered. 'Hopefully others will follow the Donal lead.'

'That's generous of you, Crys,' Valentyna said, 'but I worry about Morgravia accepting me. Surely there is another family they would argue is more suitable?'

'They might,' Crys said, 'but that family is my own; we are distantly related to the Crown. I would not accept, however. Believe me, it's the last thing I wish for. I belong in the north, and you, Valentyna, already have one crown on your head. In marrying Celimus you accepted the second.' He shrugged as if to say she no longer had much choice in the matter.

'He's right,' Wyl said. 'And I think they will accept you if the right voices are behind you. We must speak with Lord Hartley too – he is a powerful voice and will probably be the most pleased amongst the lords to hear of Celimus's death, as he only just escaped being killed himself. We can thank Jessom for that mercy.'

'You can't be seen here, Crys,' Wyl went on. 'The nobles have been told that Cailech slaughtered your family so it's unthinkable you would even be in the same room as him. In fact you should go and change into your formal wear, get your hair colour back to normal and join the nobles to hear what is said at the wedding feast.'

Crys nodded. 'So I know nothing of this, right?'

'Correct,' Wyl said. 'But we shall be revealing the fact of Celimus's death at the banquet so you can have your say then.'

Valentyna said aloud what they were all thinking. 'I know this is all a lie but Celimus and Jessom deserve no better.'

Aremys had one last question. 'What about the Quickening?'

Wyl smiled and turned to Valentyna. 'I believe the magic will be satisfied if I become sovereign of Morgravia through marriage, instead of through Celimus,' he said. 'That is, if Queen Valentyna will have me?'

Crys and Aremys had gone off to fulfil their various roles in getting Morgravia to accept the death of their King and the reign of their new Queen. Wyl and Valentyna were finally alone.

Wyl took Valentyna's hand, ready to pour out all that was in his heart, when there came a knock at the door. He smiled sadly and nodded at her to answer it. 'We have a lifetime ahead now, my love,' he said, and kissed her fingers.

The Queen took a moment to compose herself, then called out, 'Who is it?'

'It's Renton, your majesty.'

My page, Valentyna mouthed to Wyl. She went to the door and opened it a crack, to hide the interior of the chamber from curious eyes. 'Yes?' she said.

'The nobles are gathered in the banquet hall, your highness. They await their King and Queen.'

CHAPTER 45

A tall man clutching a child walked into a sunlit clearing, emerging from the tangled mass of the curiosity known as the Thicket. He was followed by a magnificent black horse.

Gueryn looked at the boy in his arms, pale and lifeless, and wanted to cry. To him, the death of young Fynch was the embodiment of all his sorrows. The passing of this courageous child echoed the bravery of so many who had died since that terrible day when Wyl Thirsk's eyes had first changed colour. Gueryn had no idea what they were doing in this strange place that reeked of magic, but he had been drawn here, with Fynch and Galapek, as if he no longer controlled the direction he moved in. He had braved the sinister darkness of the yews to emerge into this clearing. What must he do next?

His wonderings were answered, somewhat disturbingly, by an oversized owl who pierced him with a grave yellow gaze and said into his mind, *Put him on the ground, please. The Thicket wishes to feel him.*

Gueryn obeyed. He had seen so much that was strange, not even a huge talking bird could shock him now.

We of the Thicket are pleased to see you restored, Gueryn le Gant.

Gueryn bowed to the bird. 'It was Knave, I believe, who saved my life.'

He is here, you can thank him yourself, Rasmus said and turned his head to where a massive black dog bounded out from the shadow of the yews.

'Knave!' Gueryn called, kneeling to greet the dog. 'I owe you my life,' he whispered to his saviour, hugging him close.

The dog barked and then, as he looked at the child on the ground, began to whine sadly, sniffing every inch of the boy's body.

'Can you help Lothryn?' Gueryn asked, the plea evident in his voice.

A great evil has been wrought upon this beast, Rasmus replied. *I cannot undo it.*

Gueryn laid his hand on Galapek's strong neck. Had this journey been for nothing then? As he mourned the tragic fate of the Mountain man, the sun-drenched patch where they stood was suddenly darkened by a great shadow. Gueryn looked up and was astounded to see something huge descending upon them. He could not guess what it was.

The King comes, Rasmus said reverently.

Now Gueryn could make out the shape looming above them. 'A dragon?' he whispered, overcome by awe.

The massive creature landed, shaking the ground. Its scales shimmered with dark, seemingly ever-changing colours.

Gueryn was on his knees in a second, in veneration. He lifted his head a fraction and dared to stare, goggle-eyed, at the fantastic creature before him.

Welcome, Gueryn le Gant, it said. *We owe you our thanks for returning Faith Fynch to us.*

'Can you help him, sire?' Gueryn pleaded, unsure of how to address the magical creature the bird had called King.

Not in the way you would like, the dragon's deep voice answered gently. *But yes, although Fynch's life amongst your kind is over, he will live on in a new form.*

The dragon turned its attention to the trembling horse. *Come to me, poor Galapek.*

The stallion came to stand before the King of the Creatures and effected a gracious bow of sorts. The scene brought tears to Gueryn's eyes. He instinctively stepped back from the horse and the dragon as he sensed — that was the only word for it — the thrum of a powerful magic gathering. The clearing exploded into a dazzling golden light which burned for several moments. Although he tried to peer through it, its intensity prevented Gueryn from seeing anything. It blazed like a huge fire; he could feel its warmth and hear its crackle as it flamed around them, then suddenly disappeared. The rays of sunlight remaining seemed dull by comparison.

Standing where Galapek had been was a huge man. His body was shaking and his head was thrown back, mouth open in silent prayer.

'Lothryn!' Gueryn called, tears flowing freely now, running down his face into his straggly beard. He ran towards the Mountain man and grabbed him just as he toppled, taking them both heavily to the ground.

Let him recover for a few moments, the dragon advised. *He is weak now and will remain so for some time.*

Gueryn nodded. 'When I was bringing Fynch here, I

thought I heard the boy call Wyl's name. It was the only word he uttered. Did I imagine it?'

Fynch did not die at Rashlyn's hands, as you suspected. He died because he chose to relinquish his spirit and his power. If he had kept both, things might have turned out differently.

'What do you mean, your majesty?' Gueryn asked, hoping he used the right title.

Fynch was a sacrifice, the Dragon King said and Gueryn heard genuine sorrow in the creature's tone. *We demanded so much and he accepted all that we asked of him, giving his life freely. His one request was that he could use his power to aid your Wyl Thirsk. He asked for nothing for himself. Rashlyn did not kill the boy. Fynch was far stronger than even we had anticipated.*

'But I thought—'

You heard true; Fynch did call Thirsk's name. He needed to send himself a long way to reach Wyl, and he was so weakened by the fight with Rashlyn that he had to make a decision. He could not maintain life in his body and also send himself to Wyl. It was a risk he was prepared to take.

'He chose Wyl?' Gueryn could not contain his emotion. Perhaps all was not over for his precious boy.

Fynch made the ultimate sacrifice for his friend. He gave his life.

Gueryn bowed his head. He grieved for the child yet he so badly wanted to know that Wyl lived. 'And Wyl Thirsk?' he asked, frightened to hear the reply.

Wyl Thirsk lives, le Gant, as the Mountain King. And Celimus is dead.

It was all such a shock, but – apart from Wyl being alive – this was the best news he had received. 'I don't know what to say,' Gueryn admitted. He could tell that the dragon, along with the strange creatures he now noticed gathering around the fringe of the clearing, were hurting at the loss of Fynch. Even the Thicket itself seemed to be pulsating with a sense of sorrow.

We shall provide horses to take you and Lothryn from here, was all the dragon replied.

Lothryn spoke as a man for the first time in as long as he could remember. It hurt, just as it hurt to breathe, even to think. 'Elspyth?' was all he could manage. The dragon turned to regard him with huge black eyes which seemed to absorb light instead of reflecting it. *She clings to life, Mountain man. Go to Argorn in Morgravia, and hurry.*

Both men paid homage once again to the King of the Creatures. But there was still one thing left to ask.

Gueryn cleared his throat and looked at the tiny bundle on the ground beside him. 'The boy? Should I take him back to his family or . . .'

We are Fynch's family now, the dragon replied gently. *He is one with me and my flesh.*

'I don't understand, sire,' Gueryn said as he helped Lothryn to his feet.

Fynch was no ordinary gong boy. He was sired by Magnus, King of Morgravia.

Gueryn paled. 'Did Magnus know?' he asked, astonished he could sound so composed.

No.

'What are you telling us, your majesty?'

That Fynch is the true Dragon King. As you know, the Kings of Morgravia have always been bonded exclusively to the dragon. No one else but they are permitted to claim union with me.

Gueryn shook his head with wonder. 'This is a revelation, your majesty. You mean Fynch was a Prince of Morgravia?'

Now Celimus is dead, he becomes a King.

'There must be something you can do, great one,' Gueryn said, looking around wildly. 'This place is enchanted. Surely Fynch can be saved?'

There is something I can do, Gueryn, the dragon said patiently. *Watch*. The two men looked on incredulously as the creature of legend tenderly lifted the tiny boy in its huge claws. A blaze of golden light surrounded Fynch the instant the dragon touched him, and the gold in turn was fringed by a riot of dark iridescent colours that echoed the creature's ever-changing hues.

We are one – dragon and king unified. The dragon's voice boomed deep in their minds as he wrapped his vast wings about the tiny body, cocooning it. Then he threw back his head and roared. It was a sound of triumph and his scales all became gold, dazzling and sparkling in the drench of sunlight. He opened his wings to their full span and both men inhaled sharply. Fynch's body was gone.

And then a new voice spoke to them. *Thank you, Gueryn, Lothryn. Courageous Knave, I shall never forget you*. It was Fynch.

Knave leapt up and let loose with a howl that even the men could tell was one of victory. They clung to one another, tears and laughter mingling as they shared in the creatures' triumph that Fynch lived on. He *was* the Dragon King.

Farewell, Fynch called. *This will be our secret. I trust you will honour it.*

The dragon beat its powerful wings and the resulting air movement drove the two men backwards. They held onto one another as the great beast lifted effortlessly into the sky, disappearing towards the east, into the Wild.

Rasmus broke the awed silence. *It is time for you to leave us*, he said, looking to where two horses emerged from the yews. *They are yours now.*

Gueryn nodded, still tongue-tied from all the emotions surging through him: sorrow and joy, elation and awe. It had all happened so fast.

Elspyth is in Argorn as you have been told, Lothryn, Rasmus continued matter-of-factly. *Wyl is in Stoneheart, Gueryn. We shall not meet again, although Knave has agreed to accompany you. Brace yourselves, the Thicket is sending you . . .*

They arrived moments later beneath the cover of a small stand of trees. The air was sweet-smelling and Gueryn instantly recognised their surroundings as the region of Argorn. He knew precisely where they were too: in a small copse barely an eighth of a mile from the Thirsk family estate.

He looked at his companion. 'How do you feel?'

'I'm not sure. Weak enough to lie down here and never get up again, yet so energised by the thought that Elspyth is close that I could run all the way to her.'

'Then do that, my friend. And when you reach her, hold her tight and never let go. Bring her to Stoneheart as soon as she is well. She may be in a position to bear witness to some events, and I'm sure you will have things to work out for your people in the Razors.'

Lothryn smiled. It felt strange to be happy, to know pleasure again. 'Thank you, Gueryn. May our realms never be enemies again.'

'Between you and Wyl, I'm sure you'll see to it.'

'I shall raise Aydrech as a proud ally.'

'Hurry to the capital,' Gueryn reminded him. 'I'll let Wyl know you are coming.'

The two men embraced and then parted to follow separate paths. The Mountain man rode towards the grand manor where he knew an ailing woman waited for him. The Morgravian, with a huge black dog coursing beside him, galloped off towards Pearlis.

EPILOGUE

Cailech's long arms reached around Valentyna and hugged her close. They were standing on the small balcony of Magnus's old war tower. It was the only place Wyl could think of where they might be truly alone for a short while.

'Do you have to go north so soon?' she asked.

There was amusement in his voice. 'You already have the nobles twirled around your little finger, Valentyna. Truly, you'll handle yourself brilliantly and I'll be back before you know it. The meeting with the nobles went much better than we could have dreamed.'

She shook her head with wonder. 'Thanks to Lord Hartley coming out of hiding and revealing just how treacherous Celimus was, even to his own nobility.'

'We shall be married by summer's end, how's that?'

Valentyna nodded glumly, knowing it would simply not be appropriate any sooner.

Wyl continued, 'I know you understand that I want to be with Crys when he returns to Felrawthy. We shall grieve together at Tenterdyn and our prayers will cleanse it.'

The Queen sounded uncharacteristically sulky when

she replied. 'Crys is so smitten with Georgyana Bench, I'm sure he'll hardly notice your presence.' She saw his expression turn serious and was instantly contrite. 'I'm sorry, I'm just so scared of losing you again.'

'I know,' he said gently and kissed her head. He loved being taller than her. This was the end of the curse on his life: he would remain Cailech now until he took his very last breath. Considering some of the guises he had lived in, he was happy to settle for this one, especially as he knew Valentyna found the King of the Razors irresistible. 'You won't lose me again, I promise you.'

'How long will you be gone? It was Aremys who told me you'd be going to the Razors. Were you too scared to share that news with me yourself?'

Wyl laughed. 'Yes, as a matter of fact. I may be Wyl to you, but I have to make an effort to be Cailech to everyone else. I must return to the Razors and do the right thing by his people.'

'You're going to appoint Lothryn to rule in your stead, I gather?'

He nodded. 'It's fitting. The people will understand that now I am planning to marry the southern Queen, I will spend a lot of my time here. But an absent King is not good for their needs so Lothryn will administer the realm – and far better than I can, I'm sure.'

'There's a child, though, is that right?'

'Yes. Cailech fathered the boy, but on Lothryn's wife. Loth has always thought of Aydrech as his own and now he can rightfully raise him as his son.'

'Will he be King?'

'Yes, bastard children are recognised as heirs in the Razors.'

Valentyna nodded. 'It must feel good to put everything back into balance again,' she admitted. 'I'm so happy for Elspyth too. She's glowing. Did you ever think things could work out so right after everything felt so hideously wrong?'

Wyl turned her to him and kissed her softly, his lips lingering on hers so she could enjoy the tenderness and passion behind his affection. 'I never thought I would win you. That time at Briavel was enough, if that was all I could have. Shar has blessed me.'

Valentyna pulled him closer still and whispered into his ear, his golden hair tickling her face. 'Shar has blessed you with more than you think.'

He pulled away and looked at her quizzically.

'Shar, but you can be thick for a King, Wyl Thirsk!'

'What am I missing?' he begged, laughing at her insult.

'Marry me fast, my lord, for I am pregnant. It seems we shall have the first royal heir to both thrones by the close of next winter.'

She watched the light green eyes of the northern King – soon to be a southern King too – fill with tears. She carried on talking, knowing he was lost for words. 'If he's a boy we shall call him Wyl, and I'd better start remembering to call you Cailech all the time – do you mind?'

Finally Wyl found his voice. 'And if we have a princess?'

'Ylena, of course. What else but a name that signifies such courage and represents so much love in both our lives?'

'Valentyna . . .' Whatever else Wyl was going to say was choked by a soft sob of joy. He hugged her tight and showered her hair and her face with his kisses. 'If I died right here and now I couldn't be happ—'

'Don't! We're both going to live until we're so old we will need servants to help us on and off the privy because of our creaky bones.'

They laughed amongst their shared tears. 'That's right,' he said. 'We shall grow old and creaky together.'

'Make Aremys bring you home to me quickly. I can only believe you are safe whilst I can see you, hold you,' she said fervently. Wyl understood. He would have to be very careful with Cailech's body until they were married and he was finally King of Morgravia.

Valentyna sighed, looking out across the landscape. 'It's beautiful here. I miss my woodlands but this is certainly a wonderful view. I feel like I can see all the way to Briavel.'

'That was the point. This war tower was built so it offered a view in all directions, but especially towards Briavel.'

'Well, we shall give this tower a new purpose. I shall dream something up by your return, King Cailech.'

He grinned, and as he did so a shadow fell across them. 'What's that?' he said, shading his eyes against the sharp sunlight as he looked up.

'I can't imagine,' Valentyna said, squinting into the sky. 'An eagle?'

'Not in these parts, and it's too big anyway.'

Knave, who had been slumped drowsily close by, leapt to his feet and began to bark.

'What is it, Knave?' Wyl asked. He was rewarded with an answer from a voice he had never thought to hear again. *Hello, Wyl.*

Fynch! he sent back. *Oh, Shar – is it really you?*

Tell Valentyna. She can't hear us – she's not linked through the Thicket. And fret not, I've made myself invisible to all but you three.

'What is it?' Valentyna asked, baffled.

'My love, you won't believe it.' Wyl did not think he could grin any wider or feel any happier than he did at this moment. 'It's Fynch! He's alive.'

'Where?' Valentyna asked, amazed.

'Up there,' he said, pointing. *What are you?* he sent.

A dragon! He heard the boy laugh in his head and the sound was one of pure joy.

<u>MEDALON</u>

The Demon Child Trilogy: Book One

Jennifer Fallon

A breathtaking fantasy adventure is about to unfold.
Enter the extraordinary world of Medalon . . .

According to legend, the last king of the ancient
Harshini race sired a half-human child. Now the
demon child must be found – and it must be killed.

It is a time of upheaval among the ruling elite of
Medalon. Intrigue is rife and treachery is the only
means of political advancement. It is a time when lies
conceal more lies and the truth has been long
abandoned. It is a time when only the
most ruthless survive.

It is into this world that a forgotten magic is about to
be unleashed. And it is two siblings, R'shiel and
Tarja, whose story will become one with the legends
of the land.

The first volume in a stunning new epic fantasy
trilogy, MEDALON is Jennifer Fallon's debut novel.

THE MAGICIANS' GUILD

The Black Magician Trilogy: Book One

Trudi Canavan

Each year the magicians of Imardin gather to purge
the city streets of vagrants, urchins and miscreants.
Masters of the disciplines of magic, they know that no
one can oppose them. But their protective shield is not
as impenetrable as they believe.

For as the mob are herded from the city, a young
street girl, furious at the authorities' treatment of her
family and friends, hurls a stone at the shield, putting
all her rage behind it. To the amazement of all who
bear witness, the stone passes unhindered through the
barrier and renders a magician unconscious.

It is an inconceivable act, and the guild's worst fear has
been realised – an untrained magician is loose on the
streets. She must be found, and quickly, before her
uncontrolled powers unleash forces that will destroy
both her, and the city that is her home.

THE MAGICIANS' GUILD is the first volume in a
stunning new fantasy trilogy, that ripples with magic,
action and high adventure.